K88

and
Tell of Time

and
Tell of
Time

LAURA KREY

HOUGHTON MIFFLIN COMPANY · BOSTON

The Riverside Press Cambridge

FIRST IMPRESSION, JUNE 1938
SECOND IMPRESSION, AUGUST 1938 (PRIOR TO PUBLICATION)
THIRD IMPRESSION, AUGUST 1938
FOURTH IMPRESSION, SEPTEMBER 1938
FIFTH IMPRESSION, OCTOBER 1938
SIXTH IMPRESSION, NOVEMBER 1938

The Riverside Press
CAMBRIDGE · MASSACHUSETTS
PRINTED IN THE U.S.A.

to

Susan Mary

IN GRATITUₗE

Contents

Foreword to the Reader

The men who rode across Kentucky with clanking spurs a century ago are dead now; and the men who brought their slaves, and their wives, and their children out of Georgia and Carolina and Louisiana into Texas are all dead, too. But thirty-five years ago some of them were still living, sitting quietly under the warm sun, ready to talk and to die.

One of my own family, for instance, could describe every turn of the road from Carolina to Texas. All that the wise and the learned have ever read in musty documents about the opening of the Southwest, he knew firsthand. For in 1830, when he was barely seventeen, he set out with his black boy, Lot, to explore the world that lay beyond the mountains in North Georgia and Tennessee. Soon, he put his horse on a flatboat and floated down to join an older cousin already in the Delta where (everyone said) cotton grew as tall as young trees in soil twelve feet deep. Two years later he traveled on to New Orleans to look with his own eyes upon the spot where a kinsman had stood off the British. From there he took ship to Galveston, and arrived by chance on his twenty-first birthday, with his saddle-bags and his servant Lot, at his great-uncle's home on the Brazos.

Once having reached the shining Gulf, he planted yellow roses and wistaria beside his front door and never again in his life wished to move on. To the end of his days, he counted himself a citizen of the 'Republic,' and he drew a warm content from its rich soil, its deep, slow bayous, and its prairies wide and white under the Texas moon. When he was old and blind he would ask me: 'Are the bluebonnets and rain-lilies up? Is the crepe-myrtle out? Tell me, is the bayou rising? Let me feel the ground to see if it is time to plant.' But that was long, long after he had settled for good and all beside the yellow Brazos.

There (as the Goliad Declaration of Independence recites) 'he tempted the forest's unbroken silence, braved the prowling Indian, opened and subdued the earth.' Then, in 1836, when his patience was worn thin, he appealed, with his friends and neighbors, to the 'opinion of a candid world,' and, leaving his cotton unplanted, rode off across the muddy prairie to Groce's Bayou and San Jacinto. That battle over, he sent to New Orleans for more slaves and great iron kettles, and to Kentucky for prancing horses to enter in county trots and tournaments, their curving necks decorated with rosettes and ribbons. He set out sugar cane and dropped cotton-seed into deep, rich loam as black as ink; he married one wife, and then another; he fought through the Confederate War; and he returned to endure Reconstruction and the state police until, at last, he could endure no more. He saw barb-wire fences put up where none had ever been before, and toward the end of his life he watched Texas soldiers marching off to avenge the Maine ('in strange uniforms' he said). In 1900, he laid himself down to die, full of years and urgent memories.

Night after night, on his long front gallery, as the dark came on and the hoot-owls flew out of his chinaberry tree, he would tell me what he remembered. He had a thin and vigilant face, wrinkled and worn, a high-bridged nose and a firm, yet tender,

mouth. He always sat in a chair made out of hickory splints
and rested his absurdly small feet on a footstool carved out of a
cypress stump. Uncle Lot would drop down on the steps close
by, his black hands clasped around his knotted stick, and his
head sunk upon his breast; but he could be depended upon to
wake up and remember whatever his master might forget.
Sometimes, if the night was warm, the old negro would mix us
a cool drink, or he would fan us with a big palmetto fan, his
strokes slow and even. In the dusk his little, beady eyes would
shine alive and eager; and you could tell by watching him when
he thought his turn had come to finish the inch or two of amber
liquid that was always left in the glass for him to enjoy.

As the evening breeze from the Gulf stirred in and out the
cypresses down by the river, the soft night would suddenly
close in upon us, and the two old men would begin to remember
their past. Like that I learned history — as simply as that; and
even yet it seems strange to me to read it, cold and dead, shut
up in books.

THE AUTHOR

Part I

Virginia and Georgia:
1775—1865

All-changing Time now darkens what was bright,
Now ushers out of darkness into light.

HORACE, *Epistle to Numicius*
Translated by Francis Howes

And tell of Time, what gifts for thee he bears,
What griefs and wonders in the winding years

   .   .   .   .

Life is such a little thing.
Lo, their present is departed
And the dreams to which they cling.

From *The Bacchae* of Euripides

Now when none remembers . . .
Let us pause here amid the half-picked cotton and ask ourselves,
*   dismayed . . .*
If Sherman were careless with Fate as well as fire.
. . . Notwithstanding the banks . . . and the bag factories . . .
*   capital resources . . . and vacuum cleaners.*

From *Bentonville* by JAMES GILMER WHARTON
in *The North American Review*, Winter, 1938

Chapter 1

SPRING came late, the year the war closed. It was the end of April before the earth began to give off the sweet, wet fragrance that marks the turning of the Southern sun. In the mountains the young leaves still lay folded like gray and crimson butterflies against the bark that half enclosed them; but in the valleys the bloom, so long delayed, burst forth, and warm mists, heavy with the fragrance of oleander and jessamine, floated inland from the sea.

All April and May the Confederate soldiers drifted slowly homeward along red rutted roads, past peach orchards gleaming like copper under the pale blue sky, past rounded hills and yellow willows, past damp, dripping woods and thickets, where, a month late, the doves had begun their soft, monotonous chanting.

At first, they moved along the quiet roads content merely to be alive — to sleep to wake, to watch white clouds drifting in the wind. But soon most of them began to feel the sharp surprise which so often overtakes people who have survived grief and loss, only to find the world indifferent to their suffering. They paused, then, for long moments, astonished to see crows still flying low over fields as peaceful as they had been before the war — before Gettysburg and Chickamauga and the slow, desperate retreat from Atlanta into Tennessee. Staring across the black rail fences and the old, dim furrows in front of them, they would remark, time after time, in puzzled tones, that nothing seemed changed, nothing at all.

Many of the men stooped as they walked, and, without thinking, picked up handfuls of earth, sifting the damp soil slowly and expertly through their rough fingers. And whenever they sat down to rest, their hands would begin to grope, by old habit, through wet, packed leaves to the solid earth, so comfortable in its permanency. Slowly the sensations of warmth and moisture began to penetrate their minds. Then, as if surprised that they were still alive, that the ground still bore fruit, one after another of them would exclaim, 'Why, there's time to plant!'

Thus their thoughts shifted at last, almost without their knowing it, from hunger and pain and endless marching to seed-time and harvest, to the seasons, and to the earth's wide turning. For the first time, then, in many months, they began to think of the future — of corn springing up out of brown-red furrows, of cotton loaded with pink blossoms and then weighted down with white bolls, of waving yellow oats and creeping green watermelon and sweet potato vines. They did not try to plan ahead, nor did they often reflect on all that had passed; but, suddenly conscious of warm, damp soil pressing against their hardened feet, they began again to speak carelessly of tomorrow, of planting and of old, familiar things — of cool water from a deep Louisiana well, of a spring house on a Virginia hillside, of a sloping Georgia meadow, or a curving Texas creek. Then, drawing in their breaths sharply, they pushed ahead in long, quickened strides.

All April, Virginia was full of tired, hungry men wandering down from the sweet-scented mountains and up from the swamps and the sea, all hurrying somewhere, all meeting and jostling against one another in the narrow passes and on the long, red highways. Highways that curved and twisted and bent around panoramic views beautiful enough to make any but a blind man pause.

There were boys on these roads who had grown up in the low country, who never in their lives had watched blue mountains rising up out of sweet spring mists, a blur along the pale horizon. Yet, on their way out of Virginia, they did not cast even a single glance upward. There were other soldiers — boys from beyond the Mississippi — who had never read a date on a tombstone earlier than 1800; but, as they passed old churchyards full of graves and sunken slabs, they did not so much as check their steps. And the Valley boys had seen all they ever wanted to see of the flat woods back of Richmond, and of the yellow muddy James. Recalling the high peak at Afton, where a man could look clean across the state, they thought it was no wonder so many Tidewater families had been moving up the Shenandoah, this past hundred years. Every soldier, no matter where he came from, was thinking, not of the landscape so richly spread out around him, but of one thing only: To get home as fast as he could, wherever that might be.

The Texans were nearly all making for Danville — Texans from the Rio Grande used to fighting Indians and Mexicans; Texans from the piney woods of East Texas, with their long, flat drawl; Texans from North Texas, where, the South Texas people claimed, a man was born half Yankee to begin with; Texans from the deep bottom-lands of the Trinity and the Brazos, where the big plantations were, boys whose slow voices were not very different from those of the upper South. All Texans, however, who swore to one another, as they hastened down the twisting roads, that they wouldn't give an acre of their level state for whole counties of Tennessee and Virginia mountains.

They had had two complaints, anyway, ever since they had crossed their own border: The Virginians seemed to think they were running this war, and nearly everywhere you went, outside o' Texas, you got kinks in your legs, climbing a hill. They were glad enough to settle down awhile, the last year of the fighting, outside of Richmond, which was nice flat country, they nearly all wrote home in relief.

Of course, now, if you'd been with the Terry Rangers, you could have spurred your horse up and down the highest mountains; but the first call had been for volunteer infantry companies, and, overnight almost, every cotillion and hunting club along the Gulf had begun to drill — Left, Right, Left, Right. Lord! A soldier's feet got mighty tender!

It was a long time, now, though, since Cavin Darcy of the Fourth Texas had given a thought to his feet. He had worn his boots till they gave out, then pulled on a regular pair of rough army brogans, and, at last, had hunted around for anything he could find to put under his soles. Anything, that is, his negro Jake could find — Jake, the tall angular darky, about his own age and size, who was stepping along behind him at a quick, but reluctant, pace.

'Lawd! Mas' Cavin,' Jake complained, 'you runnin' 'long heah lak you's still in de ahmy.'

'I reckon maybe we oughta've taken the boat out o' Yorktown,' the white boy conceded, turning his lively blue eyes back toward his servant, 'but I didn't hear about it till too late. All I heard about,' he grinned, 'was the flatcars they say we can hop at Danville.' Then, pausing, he waited, in complete good humor, for Jake to catch step with him. 'You better lift up yo' feet, if you want any supper,' he suggested mildly, stooping to rub his own shins as he spoke. 'Seems like I remember hearing Pa tell about somebody with wings on his ankles, way back yonder. Wish they'd start sprouting on us.'

'Dey hurts,' cried Jake, rolling anguished eyes imploringly toward his master. 'Let's set down a minute.'

'If you set down,' Cavin warned him, 'they'll hurt you a damn sight worse when you go to get up. Danville's not far, now,' he promised, flinging out a crumb of comfort.

'Ain't it?' asked Jake, momentarily hopeful. But his face fell almost instantly. 'You been sayin' dat evey hour tow-day,' he remarked in a resigned voice.

On they walked, giving no thought to the country through which they were passing. The black boy was following his master, and his master was hunting for Danville and the flat-cars everybody said were drawn up there to take you part way home. They'd take you on to Greensboro, North Carolina, too, the Texas soldiers were whispering, if you felt like joining the Terry Rangers and Joe Johnston there, on the Haw River, where they had gathered, so the rumor went, to drive out Sherman and save the lower South.

There wasn't any use in mentioning that possibility, though, to Jake, not yet anyhow, Cavin thought. As for himself, he was free to do as he pleased, because if his colonel had started looking around for him while they were stacking their guns at Appomattox, he must have been right puzzled. The idea amused him a good deal.

Well, he'd been missing all right, quite a time, counting the two weeks he had been laid up with a fever in Mrs. Prentice's nice house, just outside of Chatham. One morning, Jake had told him, he began waving his arms and talking mighty foolish, refusing to get up and keep going. They'd been sleeping, that chilly, rainy night, in an old broken-down barn; and, when he woke up acting that way, Jake got worried and hurried out to find somebody to tell him what to do.

'Fus' house I come to,' Jake reported later, 'de lady shut de do' tight in my face an' say, "Shoo! Go 'way! Niggers done made us too much trouble already."

'Den I see a big old red house off down de road,' he went on. 'I runned aroun' to de back do', an' took off my hat nice, an' rap one, two, t'ree times. Putty soon, a lady come to de winder an' look out — a lady wid gray hair and spectacles, and a shawl tight 'round her shoulders.

' "Who you, boy?" she ast me, peart as a wink.

' "A Confedrit soldier, ma'am," I said, "an' I politely begs yo' good help."

'Lawd!' said Jake to Cavin, telling him about that morning. 'She laugh fit to kill. "You been raised right, boy," she say.

' "Whut you want?" she ast me, again, when she ketch her bref. An' den,' Jake reported, 'she hurry down an' look at you, an' her face turn whiter'n chalk. Den, quick as a wink, she sen' me back to tell her cook to come a-runnin' wid a mattress. An' den, us took tuhns nussin' you,' he concluded, telescoping the next two weeks.

'I don't know how to thank you,' said Cavin, preparing to leave, when his fever had left him, and his strength had partly returned.

His hostess took his thin young face between her hands. 'You don't need to, son,' she told him. 'You've already done more for me than I could ever do for you. Are you sure you're well enough to start out?' she asked him anxiously.

'Yes'm,' he replied, a little awkwardly, for he hated farewells. 'I better be getting along.'

'Yes,' she answered, and he had been afraid she was going to cry. 'I suppose you had. Well, tell your father I've enjoyed having you, and let me know when you get home.'

'I will,' he promised, and, yielding to a sudden impulse, reached up and kissed her cheek. To his surprise, she kissed him in return, then hurried back into her house, and shut her thick, heavy door, with the beautiful sidelights shining against its dark, polished wood.

And now here he was, way at the very end of April, only down as far as Danville, when he ought to have been fighting with the Rangers in North Carolina by this time. It would be plenty nice, he meditated — O Lord! wouldn't it? — to feel a horse's legs moving under you again, instead of your own.

They stumbled into Danville about good dark, equally foot-sore, the tall, thin, white boy, with light yellow hair and darting, blue eyes, and the very black negro boy with pleading, brown eyes and restless hands.

'Whar's dem cars now?' mumbled Jake. 'Whar's dat 'ar deepo? Whut's us gwine-a do fur supper?'

'I reckon,' said Cavin, momentarily at a loss, 'there'll be some kind of a place for soldiers to eat at. We better look around,' he ended vaguely.

They turned down the main street paved with red brick and — 'Lawd God!' groaned Jake. 'Dar's anudder hill.' The street sloped undeniably upward, with a huge spreading tree at the center, where it divided, and with pleasant houses, set far back inside walls and fences, flanking it on either side.

'Jake,' said Cavin, starting resolutely up the hill, 'I bet you a dollar and a half some general or other in the Revolutionary army surrendered under that tree.' Pausing halfway to the top, he waited for his negro to catch up. He was laughing, what for Jake could not imagine. 'I just got to thinking,' he explained, 'when this war's over, the Virginians are going to be kept pretty busy marking trees. Just the same,' he announced in a clear, firm voice, 'it's given me a notion to go home and put up a sign where Santa Anna surrendered, down there by Lynchburg.'

'Mas' Santy — who?' asked Jake. 'Oh, yeah!' he said, slow recognition creeping into his reply. 'I'se heared about him. You means de one in *our* wah, de one yo' Cousin Willyum always talkin' 'bout back home.'

'That's the one,' said Cavin briefly, gesturing toward the divided street. 'Which way you reckon's the best bet?' He started, then, as a light touch fell on his arm.

A gentleman in a black frock coat was standing beside him, holding his hat in one hand and a little girl by the other.

'Can I be of any service, sir?' he asked as courteously as if Cavin were a general. 'Most of the soldiers have already passed through, by now. Were you looking for someone?'

Cavin stepped back and smiled a disarmingly boyish smile. 'I was looking for ——' He hesitated, ashamed to confess his need, like a beggar. 'I was on my way to North Carolina ——'

'Hadn't you heard that Johnston has surrendered, and the government — there is no government,' said the man gravely.

'No, sir,' said Cavin, too appalled to say more. 'No, sir, I've been sick,' he explained.

The little girl pulled on her grandfather's hand. 'It's time for supper,' she protested.

The word was too much for Jake. 'Supper!' he groaned, in an anguished bass. 'Lawd Jesus! Supper!'

The man talking to Cavin gave him a keen look. 'What is your regiment, sir?'

'The Fourth Texas,' replied Cavin, holding up his head with a broad smile and gesturing, by a scarcely perceptible movement of his wrist, toward Jake. 'I hope you'll excuse my servant.'

'I am Ransome Porter,' the gentleman returned, nodding in the direction of a red-brick house, with a wide white portico, a little way down the street. 'We must have met in the Wilderness, somewhere.' He glanced at Cavin sharply again. 'Will you do me the honor to accompany me home for supper? It is only across the street, over there.'

'Thank you,' said Cavin, and looked down at his clothes. 'I am hardly —— ' Then he broke out into a full, hearty laugh. 'I won't deny it, sir — my boy and I are half-starved.'

After supper, they got out a map and tried to figure out what route President Davis was following southward. There was a rumor, Major Porter told Cavin, that he had decided to make for Texas, whither he had already dispatched General Hood.

'But who knows?' asked the Major sadly. 'Nobody knows what will happen. All we are sure of is, we are at the enemy's mercy.' He bent his sombre eyes on Cavin. 'We can expect anything, anything at all.'

Cavin leaned forward and his glance kindled. 'I believe we could stand 'em off forever in Texas!' he declared. 'Now, if we could only retreat —— ' He began to expand his idea, running his finger along the crackling map laid out on the polished table.

Major Porter, however, shook his head. 'It is hopeless, my boy, or General Lee would never have surrendered.'

Cavin's eyes, hurrying along a diagonal line to the southwest, paused. 'Why, there,' he exclaimed in surprise, putting his finger precisely on a spot, 'is Camp Mountain, where I used to go in the summers with my mother to visit our cousins, the Lyttleton family.'

'Where?' asked Major Porter, interestedly bending his head. 'There — close to Atlanta? Pleasant country,' he observed. 'I once visited a distant cousin there, myself— Major Connor. Poor man, he is dead now,' he broke off, his face falling again into sad heaviness.

'Connor!' Cavin repeated. The name stirred echoes in his brain. 'They had a house — Orchard Hill. Why, they're our cousins, too.' His bright eyes shone. 'Cousin Ella always kept her safe full of fried peach pies.'

'The same!' returned the Major, delivering himself of an opinion which never ceases to surprise anyone. 'The world is very small!' Rising, he made a courteous bow. 'I am doubly glad to have met up with a kinsman, if you will permit me to call myself such. I can only regret,' he added, his voice falling, 'that I can do no more for you. How will you get home? Perhaps you will take a boat?' he suggested.

'No, sir,' said Cavin, coming to a sudden decision. 'I believe I'll stop by and look up my cousins.'

'But that's across two states — all out of your way, isn't it?' Major Porter objected, repeating his first advice. 'You could take a boat —— '

'Two of these little states!' Cavin reminded his host, scornfully. 'You could set 'em both down in a corner of Texas!'

The Major smiled and threw up his hand.

'*Every* Texan talks the same way!'

'I hope, sir,' said Cavin, when he started off, the next morning, 'that you'll be coming out our way.'

Major Porter wrung his hand.

'I'd like to, my boy, but if I don't —— ' He paused and shook his hand again. 'Pass it on, pass it on, that's all any of us can ever do in this world.'

There were soldiers hurrying home from North Carolina also — remnants of the scattered army of Tennessee, tired troops from the Departments of Georgia, South Carolina, and Florida. Alabamians were among them, too, and Texans, and other soldiers from across the Mississippi, and the oddly assorted forces that Stephen D. Lee had been able to gather together at Augusta — pickles, the Texas soldiers called the Augusta troops, mixed pickles. Now, in late April, the Carolina roads were as crowded as, three weeks earlier, the Virginia pikes had been, for Johnston's soldiers, not Lee's, were now moving homeward, pausing only to hunt for food that was even harder to come upon in Carolina and Georgia than in Virginia. For Sherman's fine rations, they said, would choke an honest man.

Shelby Lyttleton was twenty years old the day he rode away from Bentonville, whither, only a few weeks before, he had hurried with Stewart's Georgia corps to join General Joseph E. Johnston — hurried in vain. For, after a few indecisive skirmishes, Johnston had laid down his arms.

Shelby never liked to recall the weeks he spent in Carolina. All the way from Mississippi there, he and all the other soldiers had been expecting heavy fighting. Then, to their surprise, after a few half-hearted skirmishes, they had had to stand by inactive while negotiations were being carried on between Sherman and Johnston and the Confederate cabinet assembled at Greensboro. The men were restless and irritable, uncertain what to expect. They had not marched across country to look at the scenery, many of them said. There was even talk in the camps of joining Wade Hampton and retreating across the Mississippi, to make a final stand. If that failed, the soldiers said, they could break up into guerilla bands and hold out forever.

On the twenty-fifth of April — a fine, bright morning — Johnston addressed them, urging them to be patient, but Hood's soldiers looked at him critically, their hearts sinking into their boots. This little man, with his crisp side-whiskers, his level, emotionless voice, and his tight, severe expression, might know all the West Point rules, but, by God, he was nobody you could follow in rain or sleet, in victory or defeat. They knew that as soon as they saw him. There was nothing about him that made a man want to cry and whoop all at the same time, and then go out single-handed and capture a hundred Yankees. The soldiers remembered all too well how little disposed this general had ever been to capturing Yankees — to fighting them either, for that matter. At Seven Pines, didn't Jeff Davis have to ride out on the field himself? At Atlanta, didn't he have to throw in another general who liked better the smell of powder?

Shelby watched the men's faces while Johnston was speaking and knew what they were thinking, knew that their hearts, like his, had dropped into their boots.

'I bet you anything he's aimin' on turnin' us all over to Sherman,' one tall, loose-jointed Texan — one of Hood's scattered troops — morosely predicted. 'You see if he don't. Jeff Davis'd do better to hand over this here army to Wade Hampton and the Rangers.' His eyes roved disgustedly over the group around him. 'Bedford Forrest now, there was a general! If we picked up his men and Morgan's and Mosby's, the Rangers could stand off hell on the Texas border.'

He sat back on his haunches the better to consider the very idea that Jefferson Davis himself was just then pondering over. 'They say Hood's already started down that way.' Then, rolling his large blue eyes, he delivered himself ecstatically of his final opinion. 'My God-a-mighty!' he exclaimed, 'when we got thu whuppin' 'em, we could go right on down and take over Mexico, like Jeff Davis started out to do, at Buena Vista!' Plainly enamored of his visions, he rose to his full height. 'My pa was right there with him, in the Mississippi Rifles. Why,' he demanded of the air, 'ain't there nobody in this army with sense enough to see it?' Receiving no answer, he glared at the man next to him and subsided, muttering.

'Naw, Old Joe ain't gonna *really* surrender,' a Georgia soldier hotly replied. 'He's got somep'n up his sleeve. A dog wouldn't surrender to Sherman.'

'I don't know,' the first soldier persisted with a sceptical frown. 'Johnston looks to me kinda like a Yankee, anyhow. Just compare him with your General Stewart, for instance, or with General Lee, or Hood, or our colonel. There's something——' He shook his head, puzzled. 'Something about him that's not like us. They say,' he commented shrewdly, 'that Johnston cain't ever forget about that air high monkety-monk uniform he took off to join our army.' Throwing his head back, the soldier laughed in bitter amusement.

Two mornings later there was a stir, a commotion in camp that presaged definite news of some kind. Shelby hurried to find out what it might be. Pushing through a cluster of silent men, he saw a brief notice staring him in the face. His large dark eyes ran over it, but his mind refused to take in its meaning. Standing stock-still in front of the bulletin, he read its first words over and over again.

April 27, 1865. General Orders No. 18.

By the terms of a military convention made on the 26th instant by Major-General W. T. Sherman and General J. E. Johnston, the officers and men of this army are to bind themselves not to take up arms against the United States.

The blood drained out from under his skin leaving it a pale grayish cast, and he gazed bleakly at his companions, who were as speechless as he. The breeze blew a lock of his reddish hair over his forehead, but he was conscious of nothing except the words before him, and those he could not — did not want to — believe. Never had he seriously contemplated the possibility of a Southern general actually surrendering to Sherman, who had bluntly reminded Hood that in war there was no use talking about either God or humanity.

Although Shelby knew as well as anyone how many Southern soldiers this last year had sneaked off at night to hide in the mountains, yet their going had scarcely disturbed him.

'Let them go!' he had thought in disgust. 'Let them go! We are better off without the cowards.' Not in any nightmare had he ever dreamed of laying down his own arms and begging Sherman for the food his army had stolen out of Southern smokehouses.

A surging anger suddenly roared up in his ears. The generals had betrayed them all, he thought bitterly — him and all the other soldiers who had known right along that a man had better be dead than taking orders from anybody on this earth. Especially from people who seemed to think it was actually a sin for a white man to have a lazy black boy around to polish his boots and saddle his horse. Stewart's corps had marched into Carolina to drive Sherman back where he belonged, not to surrender to him.

'Yes,' Shelby thought, arriving at a conclusion which, though he did not know it, he shared with his President, 'the generals have given up this war, not the foot soldiers, not the cavalry on their poor starving horses.'

'Now we'll have to do what they tell us,' he thought desperately. 'That's what that notice means.'

Not even Hood had stayed with his troops — Hood with his broad, fine forehead, his sad, deep eyes, and a head lifted as proudly as Lee's itself. John B. Hood, whom his Texas and Georgia troops would have followed into a lake of fire and brimstone, whom indeed they had followed, daring the impossible, out of Atlanta, in the fall of 1864, back into Tennessee, up the bloody Franklin pike to Nashville and Knoxville. And then — alas! — down again, like a slow death march, with the cavalry protecting their retreat, to Mississippi, where they had gathered, shivering and hungry, around their campfires wondering where the brave Hood, the dashing Hood, would next venture to lead them. But Hood, alas! would venture no more; for day and night the dead walked with him.

Now in Carolina, Shelby recalled that cold January morning in Tupelo, Mississippi, when he had first learned Hood's intent to resign his command. Was it possible that the General would desert his troops — his troops that had trusted him and followed him until half of them were dead? He could not believe it, just as he could not now make himself believe that Johnston had surrendered to Sherman, just as he had refused to accept the news from Appomattox until, on his march across Georgia to Carolina, he had met Lee's hungry soldiers returning from Virginia.

Five days later — five interminable days — after the officers had signed all their papers, he flung himself on his horse and started off, as the crow flies, from Bentonville toward Columbia, Augusta, Atlanta, and Cedar Ledge, his home on Camp Mountain.

Each place aroused a fresh torment within him. Augusta! There only a month ago Stewart's corps had joined Stephen D. Lee's forces, marching on to help Joe Johnston drive Sherman out of Carolina. Only a month ago! Columbia! He skirted its ruins. Atlanta! It, too, he gave a wide berth. The very name turned his heart sick.

For Shelby's father, Beauford Lyttleton, had lost his life at

Atlanta, supporting Stewart's flying, hopeless charge on Peachtree Creek. That evening, when the battle had turned, his son and his servant, Jed, went out to look for him, and, after a long search, came upon his body lying in the muddy, trampled angle where the creek flowed redly into the Chattahoochee. There in the half-dark, surrounded by troops retreating to their rifle pits, Shelby stooped to lift Beauford's head in his arms, and in that moment his youth dropped from him like a garment never to be used again — his youth and his bright, confident expectations.

Late that night, after they had brought Beauford back to Atlanta, and, on a friend's verandah, had straightened his limbs and crossed his hands upon his breast, Jed raised himself upright and turned his worn face to Shelby.

'Yo' pa ain't gwine-a res' in his grave away from Cedar Ledge,' he said, shaking his head sorrowfully.

They were standing close together under the wan light of breaking dawn. Off to the north and east, the sky was lighted by fitful cannonading, but neither Shelby nor Jed was conscious of the firing.

'Us has gotta carry him home, somehow, you an' me,' Uncle Jed persisted. His sunken old eyes searched Shelby's with anxious intensity.

'Uncle Jed,' Shelby replied slowly, 'our troops still hold Green's ferry over the Chattahoochee, by Nickajack Creek. The Yankees are on the other side of town, toward Jonesboro. Do you think we could cross the river and follow the creek till we strike the hill road where we used to hunt? That road comes out in our field, doesn't it, just back of the graveyard? We could take two horses.' His young voice shook and fell, then ceased. After a moment, he concluded, half-questioningly. 'We could work at night.'

Uncle Jed drew a long, tremulous sigh.

'The Lawd Himself must 'a' tol' you whut's best to do, Mas'
Shelby,' the old man said simply.   'Us better be startin'.'
Straightening his shoulders, he raised his cropped gray head in
a gesture curiously like one of Beauford's own decisive movements.   'I'll be gettin' de hosses, whilst you goes atter our
passes,' he told Shelby.

There was a chance, a bare chance, for a furlough, Shelby
decided.   Stewart's corps had been ordered inside the rifle pits
for thirty-six hours' rest whilst Hardee went into battle south
of Atlanta.   A day and a half— that would give him just time
to get home and back, he calculated.   General Stewart might
even remember the very tree on Camp Mountain under which
Beauford, his close friend, had always expected to lie.

With a flush of warm emotion, Shelby recalled the General's
face — his high and beautiful forehead, his gentle, thoughtful
eyes, with deep, humorous wrinkles around their corners, and
his firm, steady mouth.   He was a man like Jeb Stuart, like
General Hood, like Beauford himself, Shelby thought — a man
who had only to hold up his sword for his troops to follow him
anywhere.   Yes, he felt certain that, if it was possible to do so,
General Stewart would grant him leave.

He left Jed and made his way back through the crowded
streets to a tent where he knew the generals had assembled to
try to untangle the confusion occasioned by Hood's unexpected
elevation to command.   How he was to see them and put his
request he did not know.   But he was certain there was no use
wasting time appealing to under-officers.

He paused uncertainly, at a tall guard's challenge.   Then his
face lighted up in sharp relief.

'Sam!' he exclaimed, raising startled eyes toward a cousin's
freckled cheeks — a cousin with whom he had hunted all over

Camp Mountain. He dropped his voice and outlined his plan. 'You know the road,' he ended, 'the one back of our home field.'

'Yes,' Sam agreed thoughtfully, 'it's possible.' He stood meditating, and beckoned to a tall, dignified negro, with a head of white, tight-curled hair, who was standing just outside Hood's tent, inside which General Stewart was closeted.

'Uncle Henry,' Sam asked significantly, 'when you goin' to take the generals in some coffee?'

'Well, suh,' Henry replied, understanding at once the tone in which he was addressed, 'dey'd prob'ly lak a pot right about now.' Then he recognized Shelby. 'I'se mighty sorry, suh, to hear about yo' pa,' he said gently.

Sam held out his hand for the brief note which Shelby had been rapidly writing on a slip of paper torn out of the back of the Testament Beauford had carried in his pocket. Henry's black fingers closed over it, and Shelby sat down to wait. In half an hour the negro was back, with the identical note in his hand. On its reverse side was scrawled, in a hurried hand, the furlough Shelby had asked for, a furlough signed by Stewart and countersigned by Hood himself.

As Shelby turned away, there were, for the first time that night, long white streaks upon his dusty cheeks.

It took Jed and Shelby all day to reach Camp Mountain. It was dusk when at last they walked in total silence down its rocky slope across the oatfield to where the gravestones loomed white and tall under the circling cedars. They had scarcely spoken all day; now they remained still silent while they unstrapped from between the two horses the long board on which Beauford lay and put it gently down on Nathaniel's high bricked grave — Nathaniel, Beauford's grandfather, the first Lyttleton to lie in Georgia soil.

'I must tell Mother,' said Shelby, speaking at last in a voice that sounded strange even in his own ears. This was the part of his task he dreaded the most.

He knew that Susanna had refused to take refuge in Florida when it was clear that Sherman proposed to cut a clean path through Georgia. 'This is my home; here I shall stay,' his mother had written him, and he had had no doubt that she would hold to her resolve. Susanna, he knew, was not easily turned from any intention.

He, therefore, expected to find her and his sisters at home, as he walked up the narrow path that led from the cemetery to the summer kitchen. He had no fear that she would be unable to bear up under the blow he had to give her. Once, he remembered, in his boyhood, she had sent him back out into Long Creek Meadow when, one night, he had come in from it, panting with fright. 'A Lyttleton afraid of the dark!' she had exclaimed, opening her blue eyes wide, and had instantly sent him out again. He knew that she would demand of herself now what she had then demanded of him. But he wished that he might spare her, and knew that he could not.

Already he was at the back door. He went in quietly, through the latticed verandah into the dining-room, out into the front hall, on into the parlor, and then up the wide stair. Laying out his hand to grasp its polished rail, his fingers fell on air. The rail was gone, he suddenly realized; and then the deep silence struck through his senses to arouse his mind, numb with fatigue and grief.

He was aware then, for the first time, that the dark house was bare and empty, swept clean, like a house after a funeral. His ears listened in vain for the tick of the tall clock in the hall — the one in which he remembered his great-aunt Sarah had hid herself one day when she was a very tiny child and had not been found till morning.

'How strange to be thinking of Aunt Sarah now!' he said, watching his thoughts go round, with the curious detachment that mercifully overtakes those who would otherwise be unable to bear the first onrush of some sudden grief.

His mind recorded dully the fact that his mother and sisters were not where he expected them to be. 'I'll have to find them,' he told himself, repeating his purpose aloud, like a chorus, over and over. 'I'll have to find them. I'll have to find them. I'll have to find them.' The words, however, seemed to have no meaning, to arouse no feeling in him, only to register some dim purpose that he would have to perform sometime in some dimmer future.

Leaving the house, he went back down the path to the spot where Jed was sitting under the cedars, keeping guard over Beauford's still body.

'There's nobody at home, Uncle Jed,' he said. For a long time they stood motionless, looking at one another in puzzled, anxious silence. On hearing the news Jed raised his two hands high, as if to ward off a blow. Then, dropping them heavily, he sighed, and turned, without speaking, toward the shadows behind him.

It was full dark when they had finished. Shelby stood beside the new earth and began to repeat what he could recall of the burial service. To his surprise the words came flooding into his mind automatically, as if they had always been lying there ready for his use.

'Shelby,' Beauford had once said, opening his prayer book over a slave's grave, 'some day you will have to read this service over me.' The quiet tones of his father's voice that day came back to him now to steady him.

He recalled, with a clearness that racked him, every line of Beauford's face — his nose, with its finely cut nostrils, his smiling dark eyes, his carefully clipped beard that ran from ear to ear concealing a firm, yet tolerant, mouth. He recalled, too, as clearly as if Beauford stood alive in front of him, his carriage, the assured lift of his long head, the swing of his square shoulders.

'Lord, let me know mine end,' Shelby heard his young voice repeating, but it was his father's voice, not his own, that rang in his ears. 'World without end,' he said, at last, his low words dying away in the silence. 'Amen,' Jed responded.

The moon was now floating round and golden in a clear sky, and casting on every tree and leaf that diffused radiance so typical of the Southern night. Shelby and Jed turned to walk up the path that led through the cedars out to the kitchen garden. As they turned, the negro touched Shelby's arm, halting his step.

'Whut's dat?' he exclaimed, scarcely breathing.

There, to the left of them, a plain wooden cross stood out stark and white, for the bright moon, now well above the horizon, cast a glow even under the shrouding trees. For a moment Shelby stood motionless, confused. Then he knelt close to make out what was written on the gleaming wood.

'Susanna, wife of Beauford,' he read, repeating the words in a slow, dull monotone, like a lesson half learned.

'Uncle Jed' — began Shelby, pausing uncertainly, dreading to express what, as yet, his mind refused to acknowledge. Suddenly he remembered how Susanna had looked the last time he was home, more than a year ago. All his life he had believed her to be the most beautiful person on earth, with her serious blue eyes, her brown hair coiled round her head, and her smiling, sweet mouth.

Jed leaned over and laid his rough hand on Shelby's bent shoulders. 'It mus' be so, suh. Dat mus' mean yo' Ma,' he agreed, his old face shaken. 'De Lawd is sho' rainin' down sorrow an' trouble upon us, dis night.'

He waited a moment for Shelby to speak, and then stepped away, back under the shadows. When he could tell, by the stars, that midnight was well past, he got up from the ground where he had been sitting, his head against a tree, and moved over to his master. 'Mas' Shelby, suh,' he said gently, 'Mas' Shelby, yo' knows us has to git back.'

Atlanta had fallen and Hood had moved back into the mountains before Shelby heard from his sisters, Margaret and Lucina. Susanna's life, they wrote, had flickered out as quietly as a candle that has used up all its wax. They were staying with their Cousin Ella at Orchard Hill, for they could not live alone on Cedar Ledge, where their mother's death pressed too fresh and close upon them, anyway, to be borne.

'By now,' thought Shelby, 'they must have discovered Father's grave.' He wrote them, but he had no way of knowing whether they ever received his letter.

Then there had followed the long bitter season of defeat in Tennessee.

The troops hoped desperately that, if they could hold out until spring, the Western Confederacy might rally around them. But it was a vain hope — and Johnston knew it. Even the President, sitting with his cabinet at Greensboro, could not argue him down.

'Three times and more outnumbered,' Johnston repeated stubbornly over and over again; and at last he signed his name exactly where Sherman told him to.

As Shelby rode homeward, his thoughts roamed around only one set purpose — to reach Cedar Ledge. Beyond that single hope he did not venture. It was as though some homing instinct moved him, like that which drives dying ponies across the South American pampas to the particular spot where they were born, or forces salmon, on their last trip upstream, to their death.

In one respect, he was more fortunate than most of the soldiers making their slow way back from Carolina and Virginia to Georgia that spring. He had a good horse to ride — a horse with an arching neck and well-turned fetlocks. In his last skirmish in Carolina he had come upon the big bay animal standing in quivering terror in the heavy brush where Shelby, too, had taken refuge. This was the horse that he rode home to Georgia, in a saddle marked U.S.A., a horse that he promptly named Eagle in memory of the sorrel he had ridden away from home at the beginning of the war.

When he reached the hills that flank Augusta, he began to avoid the crowded road, and to cut freely across passes that he remembered from hunting trips.

Hurrying past Atlanta, up the slope toward Camp Mountain, he wondered by what good fortune Cedar Ledge had been spared. It was thirty years or more before he was to learn from a chance meeting with a Union soldier that the officer sent to burn the place had, instead, marked it for his own when the war should be over. He did not, however, survive to enjoy his prize; and the Northern troops, pushing southward, did not again pass that way. Therefore, Shelby was not, like so many of his friends, homeless.

He came upon the main road, as he had thought he would, just where the spring freshet leading down the mountain had been deflected under a bridge. The bridge, he saw at once, was gone, but this did not surprise him. He had had to ford almost every stream in Georgia. Now he knew that, around the next bend, the curving avenue up to his home led off from the main road, and, running on a long slant upward, ended at the summit, in a circled carriage drive.

Eagle caught the excitement that tightened his rider's muscles, and of his own accord broke into a gallop. Shelby did not look about him; he did not even notice that there was no longer an entrance gate blocking the drive. Nor did he observe, as he rode along, that the great cedars which Nathaniel, is great-grandfather, had set out no longer edged the way. All that he saw was the white house in front of him, glowing in the warm light of late afternoon. For a long time after his horse stopped, he did not move, and when, finally, he summoned the courage to dismount, his legs carried him only as far as the single low step that ran the length of the verandah.

Sitting there, his eyes roved again and again over the sloping garden stretch, over the gray rocks that skirted the Ledge, over every bush and twig. He did not know, until the next morning, that what he was looking at was nothing that actually lay in front of him, but the picture that he had carried so long in his mind. Sometimes, in the years that he had been away, he had closed his eyes and tried to recall every blossom in the garden, every path that led out to the fields and to the stables, every turn of the lattice that shut out the sun at the end of the verandah. Now, mercifully, he saw, not desolation and ruin, but the bright and perfect memories of his childhood.

When it grew dark, he thought of Eagle. Stumbling with weariness, he unsaddled him, and automatically started down the path to the water trough. He remembered just how it looked, full of clear water and long floating fronds of green moss. He knew with what delight Eagle would dip his sensitive nose into it, drawing the cool drink through his teeth with long whistling breaths. But when he reached the place where the trough had always stood, there was nothing to see except bare ground. No matter, he thought, still drugged with weariness. There will be grass in the field and water in the creek.

When he returned to the steps, he unstrapped his blanket from his saddle, and rolled himself up in it. He did not once think of going inside; some dim caution warned him that, if he did, the sudden peace that possessed him would disappear. Clutching it to him, like an anodyne, he fell asleep before it passed.

Night closed over him, and the tireless moon floated overhead, covering him with its radiance, as it had covered sorrowful Greek captives at Syracuse, dreaming of white coasts they would never see again; as it had covered Incan captives chanting incantations to the goddess who, they believed, dwelt in the bright, round sphere above them. But Shelby, as his eyes closed, remembered only that, as a boy, on hot nights he had often slept on a pallet, where he now lay, watching the dark trees under the flooding moonlight.

Chapter 2

THE house where Shelby slept was not the first house that had been built on the ridge that commanded a view, in fair weather, almost as wide as that from Monticello. Alongside it, lower down the gray slope, was a log cabin which Nathaniel, the first Lyttleton to live on Cedar Ledge, had built for his bride.

The cabin stretched low on the ground, with lines that suggested the use of better materials than rough logs, and it had been set exactly where its occupants could catch the best view across the open valley as the sun went down. Its wide red chimneys had been modelled upon a more pleasing design than a frontier brickmason would have been likely to think of; and the trellis-work around the porch, though contrived of rough, unpeeled branches joined together by wooden pegs, followed a symmetrical pattern commonly seen in the coast cities of the South. The fact that in 1865 the porch neither sagged nor cracked was enough to show with what care Nathaniel had raised his first house in Georgia.

Until the Revolution, Nathaniel had always thought of himself first as an Englishman, and then as a Virginian. It had never occurred to him to do otherwise. He had been tutored on his father's plantation for Oxford, and most of the supplies his family required were left, in large boxes and barrels, on a

wharf against which, all his life, he had watched ships from
England dock. His father's clothes, and, as he grew up, his
own, were made in London; and the wallpaper on their walls,
even the ivy in their garden, had come from across the sea.
Both Nathaniel and his father, Andrew, regarded themselves
as English citizens, as much so as any men alive. They did
not suspect, any more than the fortunate and the powerful in
this world usually do, that the growing discontent around them
might, in time, overtake and overwhelm them also. When,
on summer evenings, they lay in hammocks on their wide lawn
and looked down the long green slope to the James, they
wondered how best to put a stop to all the nonsense being
talked in the colonies by hotheads.

'Ah, well! it will pass,' Andrew would remark comfortably,
as old Cato would appear bearing the thin slices of currant
cake and the spiced cordial that Nathaniel's mother, Cecilia,
before her death, had warned her servant never to forget to
serve at bedtime.

Nathaniel was not so certain as his father that matters would
blow over. He had sat longer and more frequently than
Andrew in the inn at Williamsburg, discussing public affairs
with men who had come down from the mountains, with small
farmers who had once been bond servants, and who, though
they now owned a slave or two, knew how sweet the taste of
freedom was. Some of his own young friends even were becoming excited, welcoming, as young men always have, any test
of their convictions.

Andrew was spared a decision that would have been harder
for him to make than for Nathaniel, for he died three months
before he would have been asked to decide between Virginia
and his King. In the end, Nathaniel could not bring himself
to repudiate his friends; but he would have been sorry to know

that his grandson, Beauford, and Beauford's son, Shelby, would be called upon to make a similar choice.

Having decided, Nathaniel cast in his lot with the most fervent supporters of Independence — his lot and his fortune. He therefore found it hard to bear that, on his return at the close of the war, his associates were as little inclined to forget his long earlier indecision as to appreciate his subsequent resolution. Had Nathaniel been an older man, he might simply have sighed, recognizing that ingratitude is perhaps the commonest trait of man.

He was, however, far from being old when the war closed. He was, in fact, only twenty-six; and at that age one's feelings are easily outraged, one's pique keen and, one supposes, lasting. Then one does not know, as Saint Jerome once wrote from the desert, that 'all things pass and change but death' — even the most righteous and well-nourished indignation. Certainly Nathaniel had no idea when he decided to leave Virginia that, in his old age, on his Georgia hilltop, he would look back on the hot anger of his youth and marvel at it. Then, at twenty-six, he only knew he would be happier in the wilderness than in Virginia — in the wilderness that he had so often heard described over card games in the Williamsburg Inn.

Nathaniel was moved to undertake his long quest by two sets of impulses. He was filled with the sudden disgust for society that so often overtakes soldiers and priests who have looked too long into the abysses of human nature. Saint Francis, who preferred the company of birds to that of men, would have understood how he felt; or Marcus Aurelius, who once sat on a hilltop observing his shining legions, and wrote, as he watched them, that life was vanity and effort vain. But beneath Nathaniel's impulse to renounce the world flowed

another more compelling, if less conscious, resolve — to see it.
To see the great new world beyond the mountains, to go wherever his fancy led him. And of the two impulses, the last was
the more compelling, as it is to every young man.

Whatever the reason, he sold his land and his negroes
to a rising young farmer who had found the war profitable,
and, in 1782, after storing his furniture and the portraits off
his dining-room walls, gathered his cloak around him, and
shook the dust of Virginia, he thought, forever from his feet.
Flipping a coin, he decided whether to ride out of Williamsburg
to the north or to the south. 'South,' he said negligently,
turning the silver.

It took him two years — while a slow peace was being nego-
tiated at Paris — to find a wife and a home. At first, he
travelled through North Carolina, making his slow and lonely
way over a route he had followed once before in a coach with
Andrew. 'I will know where I want to live,' he said to himself,
'when I see it.' Avoiding the coast cities because, in his own
mind, they offered no better salve for his spiritual wounds than
Williamsburg had afforded, he took his time journeying southward. For a year or more he lived in an abandoned cabin on
the Savannah River, hunting and fishing in company with
two other soldiers as footloose as he.

Then, suddenly, his desultory existence palled upon him,
and he began to realize that if he wanted a wife, he would have
to leave the wilderness he had learned to love to find her.

In 1784, the second year of his pilgrimage, he rode into
Savannah. Shedding his woodsman's clothes, he took himself
to a tailor; he practised his steps until he could dance again;
and he polished his conversation. His friends in Williamsburg
would have recognized him, but not the hunters and traders
he had camped with in the mountains.

He was twenty-eight now, old enough to know what kind of wife he wanted and handsome enough to win any girl's heart. Or so Martha Shelby thought the first time she laid eyes on him seated in her mother's drawing-room in Savannah, one soft April evening. She came in from the garden with her white dress floating around her and paused in the doorway, her slight figure tense, her smiling blue eyes suddenly arrested. Nathaniel looked at her, and could not stop looking. Behind her, he was vaguely conscious of a garden, its brick wall overgrown with a vine from which fell a cascade of purple bloom, its walks edged with bright flowers like those Martha carried in her arms. Still gazing at her, he rose slowly to his feet, leaving a sentence half-uttered, floating in the air.

Mrs. Shelby turned from the tea-table and saw her daughter in the doorway. 'Come in, darling,' she said, looking at Martha in proud affection, 'come in and talk to your cousin.'

For a moment Martha did not move. Her swift glance took in the ruddy bronze of Nathaniel's hair, his lithe, strong figure, the curve of his hard, tanned cheek, and then her eyes met his, returning their smile. Stepping lightly inside the door, she paused again, with her gaze fixed on his head of curling hair.

'Martha,' her mother said, 'this is your cousin Nathaniel Lyttleton, from Virginia. You will want to find him a pretty girl to take to the dance tonight. You remember hearing me talk about my favorite cousin, when I was a girl — Cecilia Beauford?' Her eyes roved a moment until they picked out a tiny miniature on a table near-by. 'There is her portrait, when she was just your age. Nathaniel is her son. You two must be good friends.'

'Never friends,' Martha's racing heart pounded. 'Never cousins! Only lovers!'

She was right. Nathaniel knew how it would be as quickly as she. Within a month, they were married.

Then Nathaniel set about in earnest finding the spot where he wanted to live. He talked the matter over with Martha. He did not think he was made for towns, he told her; he would like to see what it looked like up in the mountains, or across the divide. The two years he had spent arriving in Savannah lingered in his mind; he could not forget the shadows of the clouds on the mountains, the still, blue smoke drifting over long trails, the new land that was his for the taking, back in away from the coast. He felt an urge that he could not subdue to see what kind of existence he could establish around his own efforts in the country north of Savannah.

'Indians?' he thought, once, and answered himself, 'There were Indians at Jamestown!'

The desire would not down — the desire that had led Andrew to try his fortunes in Virginia, and which, over the next century, was to urge Nathaniel into Georgia and his children across the Gulf to Texas, where there was another new world waiting for them to shape and form.

A sculptor can always see in a piece of unmolded clay a more perfect figure than he can ever hope to shape. Just so, Nathaniel's intent lay out before him clearer than he would ever see it when once he was actively engaged in bringing it to fruition. In the end, he could not persuade himself to stay in Savannah, in a life already fitted around him.

When Martha's mother heard of Nathaniel's intention, she took Martha aside. 'Why do you want to do such a foolish thing?' she asked.

'I don't,' her daughter replied, 'but I'll never tell Nathaniel so.'

She never did, not even when a tall Cherokee, one day, leaned over her son's cradle to compare his own papoose's bronze cheeks with her child's pallid ones.

There in upper Georgia William, Martha's only child, was

born. When they saw there were to be no more children, they thought of adopting a boy, to keep William company, and a girl to please themselves. But the years went by, as they hesitated; and in the end they were to rejoice that they had saved Cedar Ledge for William's son, Beauford.

As a young man, William went down to Savannah to study law, and had there found himself a wife. Two years after their marriage, soon after their son Beauford was born, the young couple succumbed to the malignant diphtheria then raging throughout Georgia — the diphtheria that they called abscessed throat and treated, in vain, with hot tar and vinegar.

Martha used to ask herself, in the next few years, what they would have done without the child, Beauford, to comfort them. After a while, though, as they grew older, both she and Nathaniel gradually accepted him in William's empty place. Beauford, strange to say, had tastes more like Martha's and Nathaniel's than their own son had ever had. For even as a child, William had never liked the foothills or the quiet existence that pleased Martha and Nathaniel. He was always eager to set off for Savannah, where at last he stayed by preference, returning only for brief vacation periods. He died before his parents ever came to realize that he had as little affection for the land they had been developing as for the kind of life they had chosen.

Beauford, however, by some curious prevision of nature, was the very child of Martha's and Nathaniel's own hopes and dreams. He loved the shadows moving dark and mysterious upon the whitewashed walls, where he lived; he loved lying for hours, with his head upon his arm, gazing out through the clear air across the valley where Nathaniel's slaves were busy at work, across the shining creek that watered all their labors.

He enjoyed thinking, as he rode his pony alongside Nathaniel, that the ground under him was his own; that, as far as his eyes could see, Nathaniel's land extended; and that beyond that lay miles and miles of other quiet forests and sunny valleys. He himself was never to venture out across them, as his children were to do, but it gave him the same sense of expansive delight to think that they lay there, open for all, that, long ago, Nathaniel had felt when first he set out from Virginia.

Beauford liked to follow his grandfather around their fields and to plan with him at night the next day's work on the place. Nathaniel, as he grew older, would often say to Uncle Isaac, the negro headman, when he came up with the overseer to receive instructions: 'Take your young master along. He will know what to do.' Thus, little by little, while Nathaniel was yet alive, Beauford began to assume full direction of the place.

At times, as Beauford grew up, Martha and Nathaniel debated whether they ought not to insist on his going down to Savannah and studying, as William had done. They were not far enough removed from the world to have forgotten that a different way of living from the one they had chosen was to be had in the country; and they were clear-sighted enough to realize that their own enjoyment of their existence in the mountains was based on a full knowledge of what lay outside them. They steeled their courage, then, and, when Beauford was eighteen, sent him, as they had sent William, down to Martha's people in Savannah for further schooling than his tutor could supply on the Ledge.

Within two years, Beauford was back, bringing with him a large collection of books and his bride, Susanna Hartwell, whom he had met at a ball at his cousin's house one night, and had promptly married, the next week. As soon as he saw Susanna's proudly lifted little head, and looked into her steady blue eyes, he knew what he wanted. He wanted to marry her and live on Cedar Ledge and never let her out of his sight again.

'What could I ever do that would bring me as much happiness as all this?' he asked Nathaniel triumphantly, as they stood on the verandah, the first morning after his return with his bride. Throwing his arms wide toward the land that lay moist and ready for planting beneath them, he faced his grandfather, waiting for a reply.

'Nothing,' Nathaniel answered. And again more emphatically he said, 'Nothing,' ashamed to confess how much Beauford's choice pleased him.

For a while Martha and Nathaniel shared their cabin with Beauford and his bride, while Nathaniel took Beauford over the place, explaining his ideas to him.

Nathaniel felt as if he were about to start on some long journey and that, while there was time before he left, he ought to acquaint Beauford with all that he wanted him to know, all that he himself had learned in his long life.

'It's like this, Beauford,' he said. 'Don't you see? No man can be free who has to depend on anybody's favor.' He smiled at his grandson. 'Do you remember Cicero tells you that? No,' he added hastily, 'I suppose you don't. I didn't notice it either, when I was learning cases and tenses to please my tutor.'

He paused awhile, his mind going back over the years. He found it hard to think of himself as a boy studying Latin, harder yet to believe that he was the same hotheaded young man who, nearly fifty years ago, had galloped out of Virginia, to marry Martha and settle at last on top of a mountain in Georgia. It was easier to imagine that his waning life had taken new hold in Beauford than it was to see himself now as old and feeble and worn. He drew his horse over by his grandson, and, as he did so, he felt a sudden peace rise up in his tired frame.

'A man can die,' he thought, 'if he knows his work is going on.' The idea comforted him strangely.

'This is good land,' Nathaniel went on, 'and there are enough slaves to keep it in good shape. I have always tried to treat them fairly and to teach them our religion. I hope you will do the same.' He paused again, trying to imagine a time when Beauford, not he, would be making plans for this place and the people on it. Finding it quite impossible to do so, with a shrug he returned to his subject.

Beauford had no doubt that he would know how to manage well enough without so much advice, but he was fond of his grandfather and let him talk on, undisturbed. He did not suspect that every word Nathaniel said would rise again, in due time, to the surface of his and his children's minds.

'I have always thought it very poor judgment,' Nathaniel went on, 'either to buy anything I can raise, or to raise only what I can sell.'

Beauford continued to listen dully, but politely, his thoughts on the sweet curve of Susanna's face, and Nathaniel continued patiently to plant his ideas in his grandson's mind.

'There's another thing,' he warned Beauford, 'that you want to be careful about. Don't let our people stay idle, any time. It's the ruination of 'em, if you do.' He observed Beauford carefully, to see if he was paying attention to the instruction he was receiving. 'Set the women to sewing and making quilts and the men to turning wheels out of the carpenter shop. And don't forget to see that the children learn how to say their prayers and feed the chickens. Aunt Lottie, now,' he suggested, turning in his saddle to peer earnestly into Beauford's face, 'Aunt Lottie is as good a nurse as there is anywhere. I always

have her show the smartest girls how to take care of the sick.'
He sighed. 'Ah, well! You'll know what to do. There's no
use my trying to think of everything.' He looked a long time
at his grandson, without speaking. 'I'm glad you're back,'
he said, at last.

Up at the house, Martha, too, spent hours telling Susanna
in what spots certain plants would grow best, warning her
(which Susanna already knew) that Beauford's naturally gentle
disposition would turn vicious, if suddenly opposed; explaining
to her which of the cooks was the best choice for making fruit
cake and sausages.

The last year of Nathaniel's life, he and Martha decided on a
sudden plan. When they had thought of it, they wondered why
it had not sooner occurred to them. 'Beauford,' they agreed,
'ought to have a house of his own.'

Nathaniel looked all around the cabin which they had so
long occupied. He did not want to move, nor, he thought,
did Martha. The cabin was warm and comfortable in winter;
cool and open to every breeze in the summer. In the dark, he
could lay his hands on anything he wanted. Bit by bit, Martha
had brought up from Savannah the furniture that she needed,
and Nathaniel had had shipped down from Virginia the pieces
he had stored there, more out of sentiment than forethought,
when he had suddenly ridden away in disgust to North Carolina.
At first, it was strange to him to see Cecilia's and Andrew's
portraits, which had once hung against a panelled wall in
Virginia, now leaning against bare logs; and Martha, too, found
it odd to see her own walnut bureau, which once had stood
between silk curtains in her Savannah bedroom, now pushed
flat against a wall, where the windows were curtained, not in
silk, but in muslin and calico. Gradually, however, house and

furniture had fitted together; and now neither Nathaniel nor she wanted to move.

They could see, however, that their idea of building a new house pleased Beauford and Susanna, and Susanna's father, too.

When old Stephen Hartwell heard about the plan, he came up the mountain to see his daughter. His eldest child, Mary, had married early and had gone to live with her husband, Philip Darcy, in Florida; and his son, Justin, next in age to Mary, had joined his uncle's law practice in Charlottesville. Already, Susanna's father, whose wife had died shortly after Mary's wedding, could foresee a lonely old age.

When he arrived on the Ledge, he spoke soberly to his youngest daughter. 'You'd better have the money now I had planned on leaving you, Susanna,' he said, and eyed her carefully with the sensitive forethought of the old, to see how she would receive his next remark. 'Add an extra wing for me to live in, later on, and I'll stand half of what it costs to build the house you are planning.'

She bent over and kissed him. 'That makes it perfect,' she cried, and her father settled back, happy that the Lord had given him a child like Susanna.

Nathaniel lived only to see the frame of the new house go up. One day he leaned over to show a bricklayer how to hollow out the thick white mortar between the red bricks that were to form the base of the lower front verandah. He never raised his head again, but slipped to the ground as quietly as if he were preparing for his afternoon's nap.

He was seventy-seven years old the day he died, and Martha was well over seventy-two. She found it hard to believe, after his death, that Nathaniel now lay out with William and his wife, in the corner of the garden which she and Nathaniel had set aside in their youth for themselves and their children. Then the possibility of their needing it had seemed to them too remote to think seriously about. Now Martha rocked all day on her verandah, brooding; and one night, shortly after the new house was completed, she closed her sad, dim eyes forever — the same eyes that, fifty years before, had sparkled and danced at the sight of a handsome young man, with ruddy hair, sitting beside her mother's tea-table.

In planning their house, Susanna and Beauford drew only on their taste and desires. They might have gone down to Savannah and consulted architects trained in England and on the Continent; but they did not think of doing so. They both knew what kind of house they wanted to build — a house which, though they did not know it, would one day rise again, like a ghost of itself, on the slow, yellow Brazos.

They built it low and long, of broad white clapboards chiselled into oblong blocks, with shadowy upper and lower verandahs opening out onto the rose garden that edged the cliff, and with two broad red chimneys at each end. A wide central hall passed through it opening onto a back verandah identical with the twin latticed ones in front — a hall closed at each end by doorways copied from Susanna's home in Savannah.

Above each door a fluted fan delicately carved in wood tempted Uncle Abner, the head carpenter, to an unexpected flight of his own fancy. Seized one day by a strange excitement that he could not account for, he carved on the broad base beneath each fan an irregular row of small, deeply graven stars and a thin, floating crescent. Standing back, he gazed thoughtfully upon them, and a new idea occurred to him. Hurrying to the storeroom, he returned with several brushes and pots in his hand. Cautiously he applied a thin coat of gilt to one star;

then, recklessly, with fast, hurried strokes, to all. Led on by a growing sense of achievement — the most delightful known to man — he painted the surface under the stars and the fluted fan above them a deep, soft, misty blue. 'Like the sky at night,' he told Susanna, when she questioned him.

Then he went to find his mistress, and with a shaking brown finger, pointed silently to what he had done.

She stood a moment studying his work, and then called Beauford in a voice almost as excited as Uncle Abner's.

'It's lovely!' she declared. 'Don't you think so, Beauford?' Then she hesitated. 'I've never seen a doorway like it, though.' She turned uncertainly to him. 'There are usually leaves — or buds — or water-lilies ——'

Beauford stood back examining the doorway. Never so quick as Susanna to decide on a new course, it always took him longer to arrive at a conclusion.

'No,' he answered thoughtfully, 'I never have, either, but does it matter?' A moment longer he stood studying the fan, while Uncle Abner fidgeted restlessly about. Then he turned decisively to Susanna. 'The bricks in the chimneys go well with that blue,' he agreed, his gaze moving slowly back and forth across the length of the verandah. 'The blinds had better be the same color, I suppose.' Suddenly, he swung around on Uncle Abner. 'Why don't you see what you can do with the verandah ceiling, Uncle Abner? Just a few, I should think,' he suggested. 'You know — the way the sky looks just before good dark?'

Uncle Abner drew a long, happy sigh. The only critics he knew or cared anything about had accepted his work — accepted it and praised it and asked for more.

When the house was nearly finished, Susanna went down to Savannah to order wallpaper and brocaded curtains from

London and to buy huge crystal chandeliers for the hall and parlor — chandeliers to hold the numerous candles they needed for light. She bought rugs, too, to lay over her white, sanded floors, and spent a week studying gardens on which to model her own.

On her return, she set out at each end of the garden the rosebushes she had brought back with her and fenced them off from the woods by a tall white trellis covered with sweet climbing vines. She started a white garden, too, full of white hyacinths and violets and tuberoses and snowdrops and the delicate cape-jasmines that so often frosted in northern Georgia. And, since she liked to sit on the verandah at night with perfume floating around her, she planted next to the house, in the warm chimney corners, a bed of aromatic sweet herbs — thyme and mint and sweet basil, and the lemon verbenas and the rose geraniums whose fragrant leaves always flavored the cakes at Cedar Ledge.

At the rear of her house, which looked directly out onto the woods, Susanna decided to follow Martha's example and use only the bushes and plants native to the low mountain on which they lived — a mountain in name only as compared with the higher ranges north of them. She was surprised to find how many of these wild things there were, and how they improved under cultivation and care. Gradually, she built up a back garden that pleased her as much as her roses, and gradually she brought her new garden and Martha's older one into harmonious and ordered relation.

In this house on Cedar Ledge, surrounded by this garden, Susanna and Beauford lived during the years that nullification was being debated up and down the country, during the panic of the late thirties, and during the Mexican War. Beauford

might have taken more seriously the call of the South Carolinians to resist a discriminatory tariff had not Andrew Jackson
chosen to yield when the Georgians insisted on their right to
deal as they pleased with the Indians inside their own borders.
Then Beauford was inclined to consider Calhoun something
of a firebrand, needlessly worked up over the tariff, and Henry
Clay, with his fondness for moderation, a man of good common
sense. It was twenty years before Beauford was to see the matter as Calhoun saw it in 1833. As for all the furor about the an-
nexation of Texas, and the Mexican War, these events scarcely
disturbed the even current of Beauford's existence on his
Georgia hilltop. If slavery was going to break up the Union,
he thought reasonably, maybe it was just as well not to press for
its extension. It was ten years more before he was to see clearly
that the North would never be satisfied with that measure of
compromise — a compromise which, in fact, most of his friends
were less willing to grant than he.

About these matters, Susanna, surrounded by her growing
family, thought scarcely at all. True, there were times, during
those years, when Beauford went around looking worried,
talking about panics and the United States Bank, and whatever
was the country coming to, but Susanna let him do the worrying.
She could not imagine having no money, none at all; and, when
you came down to it, you could get along for months on a
plantation without spending a dollar. As for Mexico, she
thought idly, it must be nearly as far away as China. True,
Mr. Lamar and Mr. Troup and a good many other Georgians
had picked up and gone to Texas, which was right next door
to Mexico, they said; but Susanna could not think they had
showed very good judgment, and, in her own mind, considered
them lost to their friends.

Her own life flowed on, undisturbed by all this argument

about tariffs and state's rights and slavery. Her father came, as he had planned, to spend the last years of his life with her. There also at intervals Justin came down from Charlottesville with his wife and boys; and Susanna's sister, Mary Darcy, several times brought her family up from Florida to the mountains for the summer. Twice Susanna returned her visits, when the winter winds of Georgia made Florida seem a pleasant refuge.

Here on Cedar Ledge Susanna's three children were born — Margaret, her first child, in 1838, the sixth year of her marriage, when she had begun to fear that they would remain childless. She soon found, however, like Catherine de' Medici, that a slow beginning made a late ending. During the next ten years, she bore two more children, Shelby in 1845, and Lucina, her last child, two years later.

Susanna threw herself with passionate interest into the rearing of her children. She loved them all ardently and she poured into their training the patience and care she had used in designing her house and gardens. She knew, though, that the girls would marry and leave Cedar Ledge. 'But Shelby,' she told herself contentedly, 'will keep on living here, all his life, long after we are gone.' Her heart, therefore, turned oftenest toward him, of all her children.

As she grew older, she began to understand why Martha had spent so many hours talking to her when she, Susanna, was a bride. 'I'd like to tell Shelby's wife,' she thought, 'how to protect the tender roses on frosty nights, and how to flavor the Christmas eggnog. "Rum *and* whiskey, darling," ' she heard herself saying. ' "Rum and old whiskey, and the *very lightest* grating of nutmeg. A little heavy cream, if you like, but very little, very little indeed, my dear." '

She realized, too, that young girls seldom know how to make

the most out of marriage. You could ruin a good husband by the slightest wrong twist of your hand, just the way you could so easily spoil the taste of a julep by thoughtlessly pouring in too much Bourbon. 'Now,' she thought longingly, 'if I could just explain to Shelby's wife ——' Her mind went racing on into the future. There were so many things she ought to explain to Shelby's wife.

The war crept up on Susanna unawares. All along she had thought the men would settle their quarrels, certainly they would. It was impossible to believe that sane people up North could be willing to throw the whole country into war over poor old colored people like Aunt Lottie and Uncle Peter and Uncle Abner, for instance, who would all be as miserable away from Cedar Ledge as she or Beauford. Any sensible person would know that. Of course some masters did occasionally whip their slaves. Didn't people have to punish their own children sometimes? But a man who abused his slaves pretty soon learned what his neighbors thought about him. As for free negroes, she knew Aunt Lottie despised them as the very scum of the earth, and wouldn't even let one in her yard. Susanna would shrug her shoulders and tell herself men were always getting wrought up over politics. For at least a year, now, Beauford's face had been getting longer and longer, whenever he heard Lincoln's name. 'The man is possessed,' he had told her one day — 'possessed. There'll be war if he's elected.' She hadn't listened very carefully.

Not until she stood watching Beauford and Shelby riding off down the drive in their new uniforms did she clearly realize that Cedar Ledge, and all it stood for, was actually in danger.

'Why do they hate us?' she kept asking herself then over and over. 'Why do they hate us, up North?' Try as she would, she could find no reasonable answer to her question.

Then, as the slow months crept on, she ceased to ask why, and night and day tortured herself, picturing Shelby and Beauford wounded, missing, dead. Never once did it ever occur to her that in her family she herself would be the war's first victim; that, on Shelby's return, he would sleep, his first night home, on the hard verandah floor, while she and Beauford both lay outside in beds far darker, and colder than their son's.

Chapter 3

WHEN Shelby opened his eyes, in the cool of early morning, he could not, at first, bring his scattered thoughts together. He lay on the verandah relaxed and tranquil, remembering in half-conscious amusement, that his nurse — a tall, yellow woman — had often warned him never to get up in a hurry for fear that his fugitive soul might not have time to creep back into his body through his ears, forsaking its nightly flight. Time and again the old woman had cautioned him against arising in too much haste, lest demons should enter into him, and his soul have to seek out another habitation. He had no desire to get up as he lay there in the soft early morning, looking out into the forest that Nathaniel first saw so long before.

People who have suffered grief always dread to wake; and, having waked, if for the moment they are at peace, they hesitate to stir. So it was with Shelby. He knew that his slightest move would shatter the content that enfolded him, and, like a swimmer floating on his back in the midst of rising waves, he lay there on the quiet verandah taking his rest, before he would have to swim out into the storm.

Then, without warning, a swift impression he never forgot swept over his senses, and all his days seemed to rise up plain and clear before him. His feelings, in contrast with those of the dying, stretched not backward, but forward; and, in one momentary flash of understanding, he realized how meaningless are sections of time, how strangely merged in one are past, present, and future. There poured over him then, as he lay there half asleep on the verandah, that strong sense of timeless, mysterious beauty which sustains poets and saints, which once, long ago, overwhelmed Saint Paul as he journeyed to Damascus.

Shelby did not know how rare and fleeting are these quick, passing glimpses of a deeper reality than experience usually affords. Nor did he suspect that they are granted oftenest to the old who, at last, are able to read some meaning into the scattered events of their lives, or to the young, on whose spirit some quick happiness has acted like a solvent, dissolving barriers of time, catching them up in a transient delight so urgent that every question seems answered, every desire granted. But as he lay there, stretched out on the hard, cold floor, the whole earth seemed to him beautiful and mysterious; and, in a sudden, flooding consciousness, he was aware that his spirit was part of all time and all creation and fashioned strong enough to endure what it must.

He might have remained there longer, wrapped up in his blanket, if he had not felt Eagle's nose against his hair.

'Now, how did he get in the garden?' he thought, his mind coming to sudden focus, and he rose on his elbow to see that field and garden were now one; that the garden paths were overgrown with grass and weeds, not neatly laid with white sand and raked crosswise in the ladder-like design that Nathaniel and Beauford had always insisted upon.

Throwing off his cover, he stood up, stretched his stiff legs and arms, and stepped to the side of the house, where he could look off in all directions.

Sending a running glance over the valley he saw that the orchard had been cut to the ground, every pear and peach tree gone. Close at hand, the rose garden was a mass of thistles, the white garden filled with weeds and brown, matted grass. There were no outbuildings left, either, no cabins, no smoke-house, no corn-crib, no tool-shed, no blacksmith shop, no stalls to shelter Eagle in bad weather. And the house itself stood like some gaunt skeleton, its white bones picked and bare, with the blinds gone from the windows and the trellises torn off the galleries.

Hastily Shelby turned toward the graveyard which lay on the outer curve of the ledge, surveying the valley through which the creek still flowed serenely on, indifferent either to clamorous armies or the fall of states.

As a child, he had often stretched himself out in this plot, watching the clouds move in and out the twisted branches above him, or watching the red ball that was the sun sink below the horizon, into China he had been told. Here in this cemetery he and his sisters had played, never once thinking of those who lay around them as strangers, frightfully shrouded in cold death. Instead, they understood that in their own young veins flowed the strengths and weaknesses of these, their ancestors; and they thought of the dead, as they did of the living, all as part and parcel of the life that flowed around them.

Sinking down now upon the familiar bench that stood in the corner where the trees lifted to reveal the fields beyond, he remained there, looking out across the fields until the sun was high in the sky. Then he rose, and made his way back to the house, and entered it at last.

It was empty, completely empty; and the doors, where there were any doors, were flung back crookedly against the walls. The long, gilded mirrors which had hung in the parlor were missing, as were the crystal chandeliers. Glancing up, he saw two gaping holes in the ceiling and understood what had happened.

Running his hand by chance over the window-ledge, he withdrew it expecting it to be covered with dust, but, to his surprise, his fingers were clean. It came to him, then, that the paths in the cemetery, too, had been raked and swept, while all the others were overgrown with grass and weeds.

'The girls!' he thought, with a start of surprise. 'They must have been over.' Suddenly he was eager to see them.

Stepping out into the open air, he was conscious of being weak and sick from hunger. His mind roamed over the various possibilities. What was there to eat? What was he to live on? He began to shake with a laughter that was more racking than tears as he remembered how often, on long marches, he had pictured to himself the hot sausage and good, light battercakes he would have for his first breakfast at home. Now the well was stopped up by rubbish and he had not even a cool drink. His tongue clove to his mouth in thirst.

'There will be something at Orchard Hill,' he consoled himself. Lifting the heavy saddle on Eagle with a difficulty that surprised him, he started off down the circling road.

Where the creek crossed the road, he let Eagle drink, and, guided by old habit, got down to refill his canteen. As he pulled it out of his saddlebags, he brought with it, by accident, the small piece of cracked mirror by which he had accomplished his toilet for over three years. Looking in it, he saw a thin, brown face covered with a soft, untrimmed beard.

'They'll never recognize me,' he said to himself in sombre amusement, and ran his hand over his hair, trying to smooth it down. He did not know that his eyes were more changed than any of his features; for he had left with the eyes of a boy in his head and had come back with laughter blotted out of them.

Pressing on, he saw, as he turned off the main road, the charred foundations of the house that once had closed the avenue to Orchard Hill.

Beyond the blackened brick, in the field, was a small house set in cleared ground — a house with tall green pines surrounding it, and a trumpet vine over its front door. There, in the overseer's old cabin, he surmised he would find his sisters and his cousin.

Seeing smoke curling up across the low eaves, he dismounted and walked around to the back yard, where a woman was bending over an iron pot, stirring and lifting clothes. For a moment, until she turned, he did not know whether she was black or white. Then, having no hat to lift, he raised his hand, out of old habit, to his head and smiled.

'Good evening,' he said pleasantly. 'Could you tell me if Mrs. Connor is living here now?'

'Yes,' the woman answered, in the expressionless voice one uses toward strangers. 'If you want to see her ——' She motioned toward the field, and then stopped short, halted by some familiar quality in the tones of the voice she had been listening to. Pushing back her ruffled sunbonnet, she looked more closely.

'Shelby!' she cried, 'I almost didn't know you!' Throwing her arms around his neck, she kissed him again and again.

'Nor I you,' he returned, embracing her warmly. Then, pointing to the wash-boiler, he glanced at her spotted gray dress, her wet hands, and asked, as if he could not trust his eyes, '*What* are you doing?'

She threw him a half-humorous glance. 'I get them white,' she replied. 'Did you know you can make soap out of lye water and drippings?'

Suddenly she remembered all the other soldiers who had been stopping by wanting food. 'Shelby!' she exclaimed contritely. 'You must be starved. We've one cow and a few hams left,' she added, with a flush of triumph. 'Come in! I'll find you something,' she promised, preceding him up the narrow steps, into the kitchen.

As she talked, she began slicing meat, and dipping thick milk from a crock into the wide, tall goblets that Shelby remembered the servants had always used for clabber. He recalled seeing them add young onions and black pepper to the sour milk, into which they would then crumble corn bread. As a child, he had thought the food as good as manna, and had often climbed on Uncle Jed's lap to beg a share of it for himself. Now he began, without thinking, to prepare the mixture for himself.

Laying a slice of smoking ham in front of Shelby, Margaret sat down beside him.

But Shelby did not take up his fork. 'Tell me what happened,' he demanded in a cold, dead voice. 'I mean, when Sherman came through.'

As he sat listening, his gaze expressed both horror and relief, for he had imagined even worse than he was now hearing.

'I dream of it, yet, night after night,' said Margaret, shivering as she spoke. 'The soldiers — the smoke — the swearing —' She broke off and faced her brother with dilated pupils and a face drained of color. 'We had no idea what they would do!'

Drawing a long breath, he asked, slowly, 'How did Mother stand it?'

Margaret lifted her head and a warm glow spread over her features. 'You might have thought she was a queen.'

Shelby looked hard at his plate. 'Yes, I know,' he said,

under his breath. Then, raising tired eyes, he asked, still in the same dry, expressionless tone, 'When did you find out about Father?'

'We had a telegram,' she answered, 'but we knew before that. Next morning, I think, we went over.'

He nodded slowly, obviously forcing himself past thoughts neither of them could bear to put into words.

Getting up, with a sudden resolute movement, she tested with her finger the water heating on the stove.

'There's enough for a bath,' she told her brother in a brisker tone than she had yet used. 'The tub is hanging on the wall, outside the door. I'll find you some clothes.'

Shelby brought the round zinc tub in, and began to fill it, recalling, as he did so, the mornings when he had wakened to see Uncle Jed coming in to light the fire and pour hot water into the long painted tin tub which Beauford and his son used for bathing. Andrew had brought one like it into Virginia from England — a tub with water-lilies and river sprites painted on its green outer surface.

When he had dried himself, he found outside the kitchen door a fine white shirt and a pair of trousers that he recognized as Beauford's, and a pile of fresh underclothes, sweet from sun and air. There was something vaguely familiar about the heavy underwear. What was it? He searched his memory, and in a moment it came to him: the slaves who worked the fields at Cedar Ledge had worn garments like these.

'Ah, well!' he said to himself, grimacing, 'I'm clean and' — with sudden exuberant gratitude he completed the sentence — 'alive.'

Stepping outside, he saw three women hurrying homeward across the fields, their figures etched, stark and clear, against the brilliant skyline, like the goddesses on the Greek friezes pictured in Beauford's old mythology books.

Lucina caught sight of her brother first and ran far ahead, throwing herself impetuously into his arms. She was eighteen, sobered by war, but untouched by it in the depths of her spirit.

'I knew you'd come back!' she cried, her dark eyes lighting up. 'I always knew it!'

Mrs. Connor and Margaret were just behind him now. His cousin kissed him affectionately and raised a calm face to his, but her expression was sad and weary. Shelby remembered, as he looked at her, that she had lost both her son and husband in the last year's fighting around Richmond. He had seen veterans, just out of one battle and facing another, who, like her, were keyed up to persevere, but not to hope.

Taking him by both arms, she gave him a little shake. 'There aren't any peaches left, my dear; but I can offer you a dried persimmon pie, even if meal does make mighty poor crust.'

Shelby put his arm through hers, and they walked back slowly to the house, where Uncle Jed was waiting for them, his battered hat twisted between his black hands.

'Thank de good Lawd,' the old man said. 'He's kep' you safe. I been lookin' fur you, since de day you sont me home,' he exclaimed with feeling.

'Uncle Jed!' Shelby cried, grasping Jed's gnarled old hands and shaking them fervently. 'You know I'm glad to see you! I'll take you back to Cedar Ledge with me tonight!'

'You're going to stay right here till morning,' Mrs. Connor told him.

Uncle Jed moved the kitchen table out into the yard, and began setting it. Looking at the heavy tumblers critically, he shined them with extreme care, and dropped the two-pronged, black-handled knives and forks disdainfully into place. 'Whut kin' o' table is dis for white folks to set down to?' he complained to Aunt Lottie, as he did every night.

After supper, Shelby sat watching the star that hung high and bright over Cedar Ledge. So it had hung there, he mused, before Nathaniel broke the first trail up Camp Mountain, and so it would continue to hang long after he was dust, and his present sorrows forgotten. The idea comforted him, consoled him, why he did not know.

He fell to studying his sisters, where they sat below him on the steps, their arms around each other. Margaret had a light and a lilt to her hair that came to her straight from Nathaniel's, but her eyes were gray, flecked with brown — a compromise between her double inheritance. Her nose had always distressed her. When she was little, she had tried pinching it together with a clothespin to shorten it, but in the end she had been forced to accept its length as her inheritance from the Shelby family. After her cousin, young Justin Hartwell, was killed in the Wilderness, however, she had ceased caring much whether her nose was long or short. Her skin was not pale white, like a cape-jasmine, but ivory-colored, with a rich creamy cast, like the bud of a magnolia; and there were now a few freckles on her smooth cheeks. Lately, though, she had been too tired to notice them at night.

If you had asked Margaret whom she loved most on earth, she would have said at once, now that Justin was dead, 'Why, Lucina, of course.' She was going on ten, when Lucina was born — Lucina, the baby adored and spoiled from the beginning. There are rare natures that seem to be sweetened by such adulation, and Lucina's was one of them. Only her parents' death had, as yet, quenched the natural joyousness of her spirit; but it had been almost a year now since that unhappy time, and her first sharp grief had passed.

She was as short as Margaret was tall. The top of her head came just to her sister's chin. Beauford's brown eyes looked out of her vivid face, unchanged, but her hair, parted in the middle and drawn behind her round ears, was straight, black, and shining, darker than any that Susanna or Beauford could remember in either of their families. Susanna had sometimes looked at her youngest daughter and asked Beauford whether perhaps Pocahontas had not been among his Virginia ancestors. Lucina had a mouth too large for the thin and delicate nose above it, and her skin was always too full of warm color to please her. She would have given all she owned to have had a complexion like Margaret's.

Tonight she was watching the road, unconscious of her brother's scrutiny. For a week, now, John Martin had been riding over from Sunny Fields this time of evening on the only animal he owned — Samson, a tattered old gray mule that had helped to pull the heavy guns along the muddy, boggy roads from Richmond to Petersburg.

John had grown fond of the rawboned animal, who would steadily strain and tug away at his loads, even when all the other mules were down, floundering in the mud. He would turn and stare ludicrously at them, and then would twist his long head back toward his driver, as if to comment on the strange failure of his team-mates. Then, alone, he would begin stubbornly to pull, his massive muscles bulging, his long, thin flanks heaving and quivering. Watching him, John thought: 'That's the kind of mule I'll need when I get home, to haul my plantation out of the mud and weeds.' He named him Samson, and, after Appomattox, rode him back to Georgia.

It would have been hard for John to have gotten home on his own feet; for the rest of his life he would walk on a wooden stump below his left knee. He had gotten used to his limping step by now, however, and thought of it as seldom as Lucina did.

Before the dusk had deepened into night, she caught sight of his shaggy mule picking his way down the rough trail to the overseer's house. Dismounting, he tied Samson to a low overreaching limb and loosened the girth on his saddle. Then he opened the gate and started up the path, which was marked off by rows of brown bottles half sunk into the earth. His tall, thin form suggested that he was a boy, too quickly grown. But his face, like Shelby's, was sober and more mature than his figure. His eyes were blue and distant, set deep in their sockets, under brows as dark as his hair. He smiled at Lucina, as she walked down the path to meet him and handed her a cracked cup covered with mosquito netting.

'Mother sent it to you,' he said, his gaze lingering on her upturned face. 'She made some yesterday, for her chapped hands.'

Lucina raised the perfumed mutton tallow appreciatively under her nose. 'Oh, thank you!' she cried. 'There's nothing I need more.'

'I wish I could give you anything on this earth you want,' John began impulsively, when he caught sight of Shelby, whom at first he did not recognize. Then, forgetful of his limping gait, he hurried up the steps.

'We've been watching for you every day!' he exclaimed. 'I've been back myself only a week — that is, what there is left of me.' He motioned to his foot in casual good temper. 'I hope you had better luck — yes, I see you did. How do you like sleeping in a bed?'

Shelby smiled and held out his hand. 'I haven't tried it yet, but it doesn't look like we are going to have much time to sleep, anyway.'

John laughed. 'Do you remember old Uncle Si on our place? He could turn over a whole field while I'm getting started. Have you ever done any plowing?' he asked, amused at his own question. 'Well, you've got something to learn. I've been at it most of the week, but I haven't got the hang of it yet. Sometimes I wish more of our negroes would come back,' he observed, his voice falling to a worried note, 'and sometimes I wonder what on earth I'd do with them if they did. I've heard rumors that the Yankees are going to set them up in business on our land.' Looking sceptically at Shelby, he inquired, 'Do you reckon they'll do it? Did you get any wind of that plan?'

Shelby shook his head. 'Nobody knows. Anything can happen. How many of us are back, anyway, in this county?'

The girls sat still, listening, glad enough to share their anxieties. John and Shelby talked on and on, comparing their experiences, trying to plan what they had better do. It was late before John rose to go, without having addressed to Lucina a single one of the pretty speeches that, before the war, he would have had on his glib tongue's end. In his pocket was a little book he had intended to read to her, but it was too late, now.

He got to his feet, explaining, 'I have to be up soon in the morning. We're planting black-eyed peas.' His glance sought Lucina's. 'Could I come over again tomorrow night? There's a book I thought we'd read ——' He broke off, turning his face toward Shelby. 'Do you remember the cave in the hill pasture where we used to play Indian? Well, that's where Mother hid all Father's library. I understand,' he went on, more as a question than a statement, 'that they didn't touch Cedar Ledge?'

'Wait till you see it!' Shelby warned him.

John sighed. 'Yes, I know,' he said, 'what they didn't burn, they ruined.'

Riding homeward, he admitted to himself that plowing was worse than marching. At twenty, he was a cripple with a mother to support: his home was partly destroyed, his country fallen. Still, he whistled softly as he jogged along the road bordered by plants wet with silvery dew, their leaves glistening under the starlight.

'After all,' he thought to himself, 'my grandfather must have had plenty of troubles with the Indians, and all.'

He felt strong and invincible, that May night; and the end of his life seemed to him to stretch off unimaginably far. What could he not do between now and then? Especially, he reflected, with Lucina to help him — Lucina with her great, dark eyes and her black, shining hair. He began to think of her now, picturing her as living at Sunny Fields, welcoming his guests, offering them syllabub and wine, offering him — he did not dare to think what joys.

Chapter 4

Next morning, before Shelby was awake, Uncle Jed hitched a long, lank, cadaverous mule, too old for army use, to a wagon with rickety wheels that screaked at every wavering turn. Then, tucking a quilt neatly around the sides and bottom of the vehicle, he stepped back to observe his work. Yes, it would do — it would have to do. He was waiting outside the gate when Shelby and his sisters stepped out on the porch for breakfast.

Soon afterward, they started off, with Shelby holding Eagle back in order to accommodate his pace to that of a poor old mule, pulling a load uphill.

Lucina soon grew tired of sitting over the creaking, bumping wheels, and she spoke appealingly to her maid. 'Maria, why don't you move back here and let me put my head in your lap?'

Maria giggled, as she shifted her position. 'Lawd, Miss Lucy,' she exclaimed, 'it's a pity I ain't good an' fat. I been gittin' bonier and bonier ever since dat 'ar thievin' arm of Satan you calls Sherman come by heah. I hopes he starves some day, his self.'

'Maria!' Lucina exclaimed, thoroughly shocked. 'That's a wicked way to talk!'

She looked reproachfully up at the colored girl, whose brown face first wilted under her mistress's censure, and then brightened. 'Well, anyway, I'se gwine-a call him po' white trash. Dat ain't wrong, 'cause it's Gawd's truf, an' you knows it yo'self, Miss Lucy.'

Maria's mother had died the same day that Lucina had come into the world, and Beauford had given the black child to his daughter, transferring his title in Maria to the baby that lay by Susanna's side. As children, the little girls played together, and quarrelled and made up, and dressed paper dolls and picked berries, indifferent to the color of their skins. Then, as the years passed, their relationship slipped, imperceptibly to them both, into that of mistress and maid. Maria began sleeping on a trundle bed in Lucina's room, in case she should wake and want anything in the night; she began listening to her mistress's confessions of infatuation with this beau or that, replying with protestations of her own fondness for one or another of the strapping young slaves on the place. She undid Lucina's slippers at night; washed her hair and dressed her; poured Florida water lavishly into her bath; fanned her when it grew sultry. Sometimes Lucina would take the fan and wave it for a while over Maria's hot body.

All during the war, whenever Maria heard that one or another of the field hands had run off to join Sherman's troops, she would exclaim in horror: 'Laws-a-mussy! Whutebber did dey do dat fur? Gawd knows whut'll happen to 'em now.' She would not have been surprised to see vagrant slaves returning with their noses and ears cut off or their eyes gouged out. Like the Arab women who warned their sons that the Christian Crusaders were known to eat their enemies alive, Maria put nothing beyond Sherman's men.

She had a thin and sensitive face, with large, meditative eyes which she now bent affectionately upon Lucina, who lay with her head in her maid's lap, her full skirts over her ankles,

and her gaze on the scudding clouds. The future at least
promised to be interesting, she was thinking; for, like most
young people, she was less depressed than excited by changing
circumstance.

Maria smoothed her mistress's hair into place and looked
critically down at the bridge of her nose. 'Buttermilk'll bleach
out dem freckles, I reckon,' she observed hopefully.

Lucina told her, then, about the perfumed mutton tallow
that John had brought her; and they fell to discussing how other
beauty lotions could be prepared. They thought they might
try steeping elder flowers in honey; or extracting the juice of
green cucumbers just off the vine.

'Dey says,' Maria suggested earnestly, 'dat if you browns
flour a little, it makes pretty fair powder, atter it's sifted. But
lawdy me! Who's got de flour to projeck wid? Ef'n us had
some, I reckon us'd eat it.'

Lucina agreed with her, although she had almost forgotten
what flour tasted like.

Aunt Lottie and Jed seemed sunk in that placid satisfaction
with the moment of which the white race is so seldom capable.
They felt no need to worry; the Lord, in due time, would provide; if He didn't, Mas' Shelby would.

Shelby's thoughts, however, went round and round worriedly.
He had slept on the hard verandah; he had slept on frozen
ground. But the girls! What would they do for chairs to sit on,
tables to eat on, beds to rest on? Had Sherman's troops made
off with *all* of the furniture?

'You better send Uncle Jed right down to the old cotton
shed,' Margaret said suddenly, seeming to read his mind.
'Mother hid some things down there — and in the old flower
pit.' She smiled up at her brother, sensitive to his mood. 'We'll
get along somehow, Shelby.'

They had begun the curving approach to the house before anyone realized how near home they were. Then they were startled to see, as the wagon drew up, that a soldier in a rumpled private's uniform was sitting on the verandah step, with a colored boy about his own age sprawled out on the matted grass beside him. The soldier's light hair was pushed back off his face and lay, a shining, yellow mass in the morning sun, above his lively, roving blue eyes. His under lip was thin and narrow; and his upper lip hung over it, a little pendulous and heavy. When he grew older, he always wore narrow chin whiskers which made his mouth appear more symmetrical. His face was long, and well shaped; his ears lay flat against his head, and his nose had not yet taken on the beaked curve at the end which, in time, it assumed. As he stood up to explain his presence at Cedar Ledge, it was obvious that he had grown too fast for his bones to be covered by the thin fare of a soldier. Still, he bore himself with a kind of gangling, confident ease, as he approached his cousins. 'I'm Cavin,' he said, and saw at once that they did not recognize him.

He was smiling, enjoying the questioning surprise that he read in his relatives' faces. Their expressions hovered perilously between the open delight they once would have revealed at seeing a guest and the hesitancy occasioned by their now very limited ability to entertain one. Cavin always took pleasure in observing the perplexities of others, not in any mean fashion, but in a kind of humorous amusement that people allowed themselves to be disturbed by the trifles which he had learned either to ignore or to overcome. He knew exactly what his cousins were thinking now, as they watched him occupying their verandah, as if by some right which they had not yet admitted.

He went forward to meet Shelby, holding out his hand. His

uniform was stained and spotted, rather more brown than gray, and it was too short for him in the legs and in the sleeves, although it still met around his body. His feet were tied round with rolls of sacking and he stepped on them gingerly, placing his weight where it would hurt the least.

He smiled at his relatives, admitting their puzzlement as natural. 'I'm your cousin, Cavin — Cavin Darcy.' He smiled again, more broadly. 'I thought I'd like to see you all again, so I stopped by.'

'Why, of course!' Shelby responded warmly, grasping his cousin's hand. 'We're delighted to see you. We've talked about you often. Where've you been all this time?'

'My mother died the summer after we were here, you know.' Cavin paused and looked away. Ever since Mary Hartwell's death he had walked warily, conscious that the earth could shake and open beneath him.

'Since then,' he went on, 'Pa and I have been in Texas — that is,' he corrected himself, 'when we weren't in the army.' He waved his hand toward his black boy. 'Jake here and I've just come down from Virginia.' There seemed nothing else to say about himself, so he looked around at Cedar Ledge undaunted by what he saw. 'Before you drove up,' he remarked, 'I had just told him he'd better start raking the yard, but we couldn't decide what to use for a rake. I'll think of something, though,' he promised cheerfully.

As he talked, he was trying to recall Lucina's name. Finally he pronounced it and swung around to face her.

'You're Lucy! We fell in the river, that summer, and nearly drowned. And we have the same birthday, to the day, only I'm a year older!'

Margaret did not wait for him to address her. She put both hands on his shoulders and kissed him affectionately. 'You were the sweetest little boy!'

Cavin grinned and returned her kiss.

'What you want me to do first, Shelby?' he inquired genially 'Jake's a good worker, when he's awake.' He nodded toward his servant, who shuffled his feet and ducked his head, conscious of no desire on earth to go out into the world and call himself free.

'Free?' he had asked Cavin once. 'Free? How's a nigger gwine-a be free, ef'n he still has to wuk? And how's he gwine-a eat, less'n he does wuk?' As he stated the dilemma, he fixed Cavin with perplexed, intelligent eyes, unaware that he was neatly rounding a problem that was to trouble profounder minds than his.

'Lawd, Jake, I don't know,' Cavin replied irritably. 'The Yankees must spend all their time thinking up fool ideas.'

Jake acquiesced heartily in the opinion. 'Ain't it de gospel?' he replied in a judicial tone. 'One dem dar Yankee boys ast me 'tother night, whilst I'se down fishin' in de creek, right spam up to dair lines, didn't you an' Mas' Philip make me scrabble atter bones, 'long wid de bird dogs.'

Jake shook his round head, completely puzzled by all the strange talk he had heard around the campfires ever since Mas' Philip had written Miss Lettie, down in Texas, to send him, Jake, up to take care o' Mas' Cavin, in Virginia. Miss Lettie had given him a couple o' gold pieces, to jingle in his pocket, and had put him on a blockade runner sailing out o' Galveston for Chesapeake Bay.

Lawd God! it had taken him a million years, it seemed like, to find Mas' Cavin. He had run all over Virginia, climbing more hills than he had supposed the world could hold, begging everybody he came across, please, suh, to tell him whar'bouts could he find Mas' Cavin and the Fourth Texas.

One young officer had looked at Jake strangely, when he had stopped him and asked the usual anxious question. Then he had answered in a liquid Virginia accent which Jake immediately recognized.

'Tawks jes' lak old Mas' Archibald Bland down home,' he had thought to himself, listening carefully.

'Boy,' the officer had said solemnly, 'if you're looking for the Fourth Texas, you just stop dead still, and listen. Wherever you hear guns a-booming, right there you'll find the Fourth Texas — that is, if any of 'em are left alive.' Then he had wheeled his horse and galloped away down a long, red road.

Jake kept on after him, and, pretty soon, he'd heard the guns all right. Now there wasn't much he didn't know about war — except why the Yankees got so fighting mad that Mas' Philip and Mas' Cavin had to go out and whip 'em. Still, he meditated, white folks were always up to sump'n you couldn't understand. Finally, he had stopped thinking about the matter at all, and had put his mind on important things, like ketching a rabbit or a bird for Mas' Cavin's supper, or on softening his shoes — as long as he had any — with wagon grease, or laying out some old blankets or some pine boughs or some croker sacks for Mas' Cavin and him to sleep on. Now the war was all over, thank the Lord; and here he was in Georgia waiting, like always, to be told what to do.

Cavin put his question to Shelby again. 'What you want Jake and me to do, first, Shelby?'

'Well,' his cousin replied uncertainly, 'Margaret says Mother hid some of our furniture down in the old cotton shed back of the thicket——' Then he threw a sharp glance at Cavin. 'Have you had your breakfast?'

Cavin laughed. 'I'm plumb out o' the habit. Come on, Jake.' The negro followed him, close at his heels.

The winter rains had seeped into the pit, but the water had

drained out through the loosely boarded walls and floor, and the damage was considerably less than anyone had expected. The sheets and blankets were yellow and mildewed, but whole, safe in the trunk; and the heavy leather cover to the family Bible had shed water like the hide on a cow's back. Even the portraits that had hung on the parlor walls were unharmed. Andrew and Cecilia still smiled out of their frames, little changed by the dampness.

There was a keg of grape wine in the pit, and trunks, a lamp half-filled with oil, some candles, a barrel of silver and dishes, and some seeds — seeds that Susanna had carefully saved. But she had been too busy and hurried to label the stone jars in which she had stored them, and when Maria and Lucina tried to separate the vegetable from the flower seed, they were not completely successful. Before the summer was over, okra was growing in the rose garden and marigolds in the kitchen garden; but, after all, they consoled themselves, okra blossoms were almost as pretty as those on the flowering hibiscus.

After they had been working in the pit several hours, Aunt Lottie took a squint at the sun and climbed hurriedly out of the sloping hole. 'Mus' be gettin' on toads dinner time,' she announced. 'I'se gwine-a take a look aroun'.' She walked off proudly, with her usual free stride and her head held firm. 'I'll fin' sump'n or udder,' she told the girls, and before long they smelled smoke rising in the still, sunny air — smoke and a pleasant odor of poke greens and boiling ham.

All morning, until Aunt Lottie called them to dinner, the girls worked in the pit, laying out jars and linen and books to dry, while Cavin and Shelby and Jake made repeated trips back and forth from the cotton shed. When, after a rest at noon, the men started down the hill again, Aunt Lottie laid firm hold on Jake's arm.

'You ain't gwine,' she informed him, 'not you. I'se got plenty
for you to do right heah. You go git you a pile o' sand and scrub
up dese heah old rusty pans I found in de trash back o' de stable.
Atter dat, you kin rar' yo'se'f back an' try ter figger out sum
kin' o' way to git water out'n de well, widout no bucket. Lawd!
Mas' Beauford would tuhn ober in his grave to see de way us
has to live!' She fell to polishing vigorously with soft red clay
the silver spoons she intended to use at the next meal. 'Atter
you gits thu all dat,' she amended her instructions, 'you git out
an' skeer us up a rabbit fur supper.'

That evening, the old woman dressed herself in a clean apron
and wrapped a fresh, white bandanna around her head.

'Yo' rooms is ready,' she told Shelby and his sisters as they
came in from work, 'an' dar's hot water aroun'.'

That night, when the frogs had commenced their hoarse
croaking down by the creek, Lucina came out on the verandah
and dropped down on the steps next to Cavin. Above them,
her brother and sister were sitting, looking out over the darkening valley where the fireflies had begun to flit back and forth
in the brown night shadows. They could hear Aunt Lottie,
in the back yard, scolding Jed, who at supper had relinquished
his job of serving to Jake.

'Dat worfless boy don' know no mo'n nothin' 'bout waitin'
on a table, Jed,' she was protesting. In the still night, Jed's
answer floated back to them, but they could not see the long,
ominous glance which he cast at Aunt Lottie, from under his
wrinkled lids.

'He'll larn,' he was saying. 'Us has all got a heap to larn,'
and they caught the determined scrape of his chair as he
pulled it across the bricked floor and settled his old bones in it.

'He's right,' said Shelby, glancing down at Cavin. 'Dead
right!'

For a long time they sat there in silence, all of them sunk in the lethargy which follows physical labor. Shelby roused himself at last and turned to his cousin.

'Cavin,' he suggested, 'I've been wondering why you don't just stay on here with us.'

Cavin considered his answer, pushing his lower jaw forward as he thought, in a mannerism he never lost. Lucina noted it, as she also noted the amused glance that he darted in her direction when Shelby paused. All evening she had watched Cavin jotting down, from time to time, some notes in a little book he carried. He passed it over to her now, as though she were some sort of a fellow-conspirator. Opening it, she read:

1. Ask Shelby if it would be a good idea to train Eagle to pull a plow.
2. See whether we can exchange a ham for a setting of eggs and a hen.
3. Try to get vegetable seed planted by next week.
4. How can we get some paint?

'Looks like I'm counting on staying awhile, anyway, wouldn't you say?' Cavin asked Shelby, who took the book from Lucina, and ran his eye down the page.

'Not Eagle,' he said instantly. 'Plowing'd spoil his gait.'

Closing the little book, he handed it back with an approving nod. 'Then you'll stay?' he asked hopefully.

'Well,' Cavin hesitated, 'I don't know how soon I'll have to get back to Texas.'

'Texas!' Shelby exclaimed. 'How're you ever going to get way out there?'

'I don't know. I thought I might happen to run into Pa in Savannah, or maybe catch a boat to Galveston.'

Lucina was puzzled. 'Don't you know where Uncle Phil is? How long have you been living in Texas?'

Cavin looked down at her with a smile that invited her to accept whatever happened, without surprise or agitation.

'Well, you know,' he replied equably, 'Pa's a surgeon and he's been all over, wherever the fighting's been hottest; but he never happened to be anywhere I was, at the same time. I don't even know where he was mustered out. But I reckon if he's all right, he'll go straight home and he'll need me when he gets there.'

'Oh,' Margaret broke in, 'I remember a note Mother had from him, in Texas. We had forgotten he had a place there; maybe we didn't even know it.'

'You must have enlisted out there, then?' Shelby surmised casually, stretching out his legs in front of him. 'I met up with some o' the Terry Rangers in Tennessee and Kentucky. Lord! how they could ride!'

'Enlist?' Cavin was amused. 'I never enlisted, and,' he added with a wide grin, 'I never surrendered either!'

Shelby stared at him. 'You didn't?' he exclaimed. 'Didn't you have any officers? And,' he demanded sceptically, 'where'd you get that jacket you got on, if you weren't in the army?'

'In the army?' Cavin repeated the question mildly. 'Yes, I was in the army.' He looked off across the valley, his eyes narrowing. Seven Pines! Sharpsburg! Gettysburg! Chickamauga! The Wilderness! Cold Harbor! Petersburg! Williamsburg Road! The names drummed on his brain. He raised his head and nodded, answering his cousin's perplexed gaze. 'In the Fourth Texas,' he said simply. 'Our officers didn't last long; sometimes we didn't have *any*. I was big for my age when I sort of took up with 'em,' he explained. 'That's why I figured I didn't have to surrender at Appomattox. I never had exactly enlisted, so to speak.' Tilting back his head, he smiled amiably at Shelby. 'Wouldn't you 'a' figured it out that way? Jake and

I just lit out, befo' they started stacking their guns.' His lips tightened, as he spoke.

'The idea didn't appeal to me, somehow,' he went on.

Shelby thought of the morning in Carolina, a month ago now, when he himself had stood staring at Joe Johnston's notice, with despair settling around his heart. Getting up, he walked down the low step, the better to see his cousin who was leaning back negligently against one of the pillars that supported the overhanging verandah, with the dusky light masking his features.

'I don't wonder,' Shelby said dryly. 'I don't wonder you felt that way.'

'Stand up!' he suddenly invited Cavin. 'Let me look at you! Did you know,' he asked slowly, 'that General Hood always had your engagements posted up in our camp, when you were ordered back up to Virginia, after Chickamauga?'

'He did!' said Cavin softly. 'He did!' A light shone in his round blue eyes. 'General Hood did that!' He drew in his breath and then let it out. 'When I was wounded ——'

'Wounded!' exclaimed Lucina, sitting up sharply. 'When were you wounded?'

'Oh, at Chickamauga!' Cavin answered carelessly. 'It wasn't much, but it kept me down so long I pretty nearly didn't get to the Wilderness.' He hastily amended his remarks, with a glance at Shelby. 'Not but what I wasn't sorry to be there, after I got there — plenty sorry.'

'You must have a guardian angel,' Shelby responded, 'or you wouldn't be here now.'

'Well,' Cavin admitted judicially, 'there were plenty o' times I thought I'd 'a' showed a lot more sense if I'd 'a' picked out some other regiment to take up with. After Pa sent me Jake. though,' ' added reflectively, 'I got along better. That boy can rustle up a dinner out o' air,' he boasted.

Lucina interrupted him. She had heard enough about battles, she thought, to last her the rest of her life. She was more interested in what had happened to Cavin in Texas. She had read letters from people living on the Brazos, where a number of Georgians had settled. She wanted Cavin to tell her more about his life out there in that strange new country where, she had heard, toad-frogs grew horns. In fact, she had seen one of the ugly creatures which a Texas regiment had carried through Georgia for a mascot. Her mother had entertained several of the Texas officers — gay young boys they were, too, she remembered. After dinner they had asked her to show them an anthill.

'An anthill?' she had inquired, startled.

'Yes, ma'am — to feed Billy,' they had answered, hastening to tie Billy to a tree where he could gobble up hundreds of his chosen victims.

They had produced him out of a cigar-box, she recalled, and, with big, solemn eyes, had assured her that horned frogs could live forever on air, if they had to. 'That's why Billy belongs in our army,' they had said, laughing heartily. Ever since that day she had been curious about a state that could produce young men as nice as these and frogs as odd as Billy. Therefore, she leaned forward and asked Cavin eagerly to tell her some more about Texas.

'What'll I tell you?' he inquired practically.

'Oh! I don't know,' Lucina replied, and asked the first question that came into her head. 'Who keeps house for you and Uncle Phil?'

'Letitia,' Cavin replied, and then saw that Lucina was puzzled. 'Maybe you didn't know Pa married again?' he asked.

Lucina's interested eyes urged him on.

He looked at her, blinking. 'I never thought much about it before, but Letitia's not much older'n you, Lucy.'

'Well! For pity's sake!' Lucina said, leaning back with her hands clasped behind her head, and listening to Cavin's account of his life in Texas.

Never loquacious, he soon brought his story to a point. 'So you see,' he said, 'I don't know when I'll hear from Pa or what he'll say. I'll send Letitia a letter tomorrow, though, telling her where I am, so she can let him know.' He yawned and stood up. 'I believe I'll go up to bed. I'm plain tuckered out.'

Shelby stood up also. 'I'm waiting for John,' he explained.

'John?' Cavin inquired, catching up the stray shreds of his own information. 'Who's John?'

'John Martin,' Shelby answered. 'He's riding over to bring Lucina a book and to talk about organizing a guard unit in the county.'

Cavin laid light fingers on Lucina's sleek, black hair.

'Come on to bed, too, Shelby,' he advised his cousin in a teasing drawl. 'You ought-a know you're not wanted.'

'Cavin!' Lucina jumped to her feet. 'You're talking foolishness. I've known John ever since I was born; he's almost kin to me.'

'I *am* kin to you,' Cavin replied, stooping to plant a firm kiss on her lips. 'You've been owing me that since this morning,' he told her, his bright eyes twinkling.

'I'll be up soon,' Shelby called absently.

When John arrived, he lingered only long enough to extend him a welcome. John, however, put out his hand.

'I've asked everybody who's back to come over home next Tuesday night. I hope you'll bring your cousin?'

Shelby accepted the invitation and made another move to leave, but John again detained him.

'There's something else,' he began hesitantly, 'something I want Lucina to hear, too.'

He turned to her, with an expression she could not misinterpret, but as if he were surprised to hear himself at last putting his feelings into words.

'John!' Lucina exclaimed urgently. 'Don't say any more!' The words burst forth before she had time to think, marking an instantaneous reaction that puzzled even her.

Shelby glanced at her and raised his eyebrows, as if to say who on earth could understand a woman. 'You know how I feel, John,' he said, laying his hand affectionately on his friend's shoulder. 'Not that that matters, of course,' he added, and then, smiling at his sister, went inside.

John looked once at Lucina's face, and, taking her hands, dropped his cheek on her hair, waiting for her to speak.

But she had no words to explain the reluctance she was feeling. Last night she had counted the minutes until she could expect to see John riding his old mule down the drive. Now, she wished he had stayed home.

She was silent so long that at last John lifted his head, and raised her face till he could look full into it. 'I'll love you till I die,' he promised her solemnly. Then his voice suddenly flamed, lilted, sang, 'Till I die,' he exulted, 'and after that, too, Lucina. Nobody ever loved a girl the way I love you.' His arms closed tight about her and the passion in his voice shook her, almost persuaded her, but some deep caution prevailed.

To her surprise and to John's, the tears began to roll down her cheeks, fast and then faster. She could not have explained why her heart felt riven and heavy, why at one moment she wanted to take wings and fly for joy, and the next knew that she had never been so sad, never in all her life. John saw that some emotion she could not conquer held her in its grip.

The flush left his olive skin, as he struggled to win back his own composure. Lucina, he realized, could not possibly be so certain as he was about what she wanted in this world; she had not received life back, as he had, an unexpected gift from the gods. How could she understand that never again would existence seem to him safe, certain — a rich gift with which you could afford to dally, confident it would be renewed every morning, every night? He understood her, understood himself, as he saw she did not, could not; and he loved her enough to refrain from seizing the advantage he momentarily had won. If she came to him at all, he wanted her to come all the way alone, and because she could not stay away, could not even imagine a life apart from his.

Pulling out his own pocket handkerchief, he unfolded it and dried her eyes. 'Darling!' he exclaimed in the quiet, quizzical tones she was familiar with. She looked up gratefully. This was the boy she knew and loved, not the strange, quivering man who a little while ago had stared down at her with such demanding eyes.

Now he was watching her, as if from some far distance, and with a sad, thoughtful air. 'I'll never change, Lucina,' he was telling her quietly, and again her heart rose in her throat, the tears again into her eyes. 'Never,' he declared. 'You know that. You have my whole life, to find out how you feel.'

He seemed to be talking to her out of some half-dream, some place she could not enter with him. Then he smiled, and she recognized his smile — the smile that always appeared, first, in his dark blue eyes, and then moved slowly down to his sensitive lips. Yes, this was the John she knew. Waveringly she smiled back at him. He had himself well in hand now, and she saw that he would not push her, hurry her.

'Shall I tell you what I've been doing today?' he asked her, and reached down to pick up a pillow Aunt Lottie had left sunning on the grass all afternoon. 'Sit down, here by me.'

He sat there, holding her hand lightly pressed against his cheek. He might have been a hundred years old, the way he felt. War, he thought, gives a man some sort of strange power — a power to look at life like a ghost removed from this environment, a ghost hovering around in time. In war, a man learned too much about life to trust it or expect to twist it to his own purposes. He was glad Lucina had never had, would never have, that kind of searing knowledge to haunt her. Then he glanced down at her, and closed his eyes, dizzy with her nearness. He had only to put out his arm —— A fever ran in his veins, but he only stooped and smiled into her eyes.

'I've been planting black-eyed peas,' he told her tranquilly, 'thousands, millions of them. That is, I did until I got to thinking. Then,' he confessed, 'I forgot the peas. You know, Lucina,' he said, expressing only a part of what was in his mind, 'a man's got a plenty to think about when he gets home from a war.'

Lucina felt thoroughly acquainted with the John who was now talking. All her life her mind had followed his easily, without any effort.

He paused for some time, collecting his thoughts. The moon was now well up in the sky. Watching it, he vaguely recalled reading somewhere that moonlight must always bring to everyone's mind the cold thought of death, and, casting about for a safe topic of conversation, he began to tell Lucina about what he had read. 'The man who wrote that,' he argued, 'could never have lived down here.'

'Of course not!' Lucina answered him dreamily.

Years later, he was to understand the allusion, when on a visit to the North he looked out across a wide, white landscape lighted only by the full moon in the frozen sky. Then he knew why some people think naturally of death and the moon in the same breath. Sitting there, at Cedar Ledge, on this May night, though, he wondered how anyone could ever have had such an idea.

He looked down at Lucina meditatively, slowly bringing his attention back to what he had been saying. Lucina did not hurry him; she knew he would pick up the thread of his thinking when he was ready to do so. She sat quiet and relaxed, now, waiting for him to begin. The turmoil she had felt within her had subsided, as if it had never risen.

'You know, Lucy,' John said, 'this morning I got to reading while I rested my leg.'

'Does it hurt you often?' she interrupted.

'Oh!' he said, waving the question aside. 'You expect that. Well,' he went on, 'while I was resting, I started looking through a book Father used to read out loud to me when I was little. I thought it was a fairy story, then.'

Lucina, watching him, could see a gathering excitement kindling his quiet eyes.

'I wish Athene would come down just *once* in my cornfield and tell *me* what to do,' he continued after a moment. 'Listen. I'll read you what she told Telemachus one night by the sea-shore — "by the gray sea water," it says. That's just how it looks, too, at night, don't you remember?'

He pulled a leather-bound book, chased in rich colors, out of his pocket, and began to flip the pages. 'I thought I could see by the moon, but I can't. Maybe I can remember about how it goes.'

'Wait a minute,' Lucina said. 'I'll be right back.' When she returned she was carrying a lighted candle protected by a storm chimney.

'Now!' she urged him, holding the flickering light low.

'I'll have to read the translation,' he apologized, frowning a little. 'You remember I was just learning Greek when the war started.' He began to read aloud in his slow, rich voice, savoring and tasting the smooth flow of the words.

> Athene drew nigh him and spake:
> Telemachus, ever hereafter shalt thou not be craven or witless, if indeed thou hast a drop of thy father's blood or a portion of his spirit.

'I'll skip,' said John. 'Here's how the rest of it goes.'

> If thou art not hereafter craven or witless, so is there good hope of accomplishing thine work. Wherefore, take no heed of them who are senseless, in no way wise or just. They know naught of death and black fate. They shall perish.

Lucina held the candle closer to the book, peering around its flame to see the pages herself.

'Read some more,' she urged. 'Maybe they *will* perish,' she suggested. 'The Yankees.'

'It's late,' he said regretfully. 'I better go, but I'll find one more place.' He laid the book down, with his finger held in it to mark the place, and sat watching her. 'You remember that summer before the war when your family and ours were on the island, off Brunswick? Well, there's a passage in here that made me think of how I loved sailing our boat, with the waves beating against it and the wind blowing in from the sea.'

'Oh!' said Lucina, 'I remember! When I was on your boat, I always felt as if I had wings and was floating up into the blue sky. I've never enjoyed anything like that summer! Never!'

'Nor I,' John replied. 'I used to think about it when I was ramming guns,' he went on absently, turning the pages. 'Here it is! I've marked the best parts.'

> Athene sent them a favorable gale, a fresh West Wind singing
> over the wine-dark sea.... So they raised the mast... and
> hauled up the white sails with twisted ropes of oxhide.

'Like the harness we make for mules,' Lucina interpolated
breathlessly.

'Why, yes, probably so — I never thought of it,' John answered. 'Like the traces the negroes plait in the winter?' He
stopped to think over what she had said, but she urged him on:

> And the wind filled the belly of the sail and the dark wave
> seethed loudly round the stern of the running ship and she
> fleeted over the wave, accomplishing her path. So all night
> long and through the dawn the ship cleft her way.

John closed the book and sat still. From somewhere, a peace
had fallen on his spirit. Lucina was as close to him as she had
always been; between them there was a sympathy nothing
could destroy. He would not hurry her; she must find out for
herself what he already knew — that their lives were meant to
flow on and on, together.

Taking her hands again, he held them between his own,
studying her face. This time she smiled confidently back.

'One day, my darling,' John told her playfully, 'you are
going to sit on a cushion and sew a fine seam, and I'm going to
feed you on strawberries and cream.' How much else, he
wondered, did he dare utter, out of all his rushing thoughts?

'You are *my* goddess,' he said, at last, in the same controlled,
whimsical voice. 'Supposing she did have gray eyes? I like
yours better. Good night, darling Athene — sweet, darling
Athene.'

This time Lucina's serene gaze did not falter, and his heart
gave a great leap. 'Tomorrow,' he promised himself. 'Tomorrow.' Dropping his head, he turned her hands over and,
for a moment, buried his face in them, kissing her soft palms.

Lucina stood there on the verandah a long time, following Samson's muffled tread on the hard clay road — a tread so unlike the quick, ringing sound from a horse's hoof.

'I do love him,' thought Lucina, leaning her back against a white pillar and turning puzzled eyes to the moon. 'I'll never love anybody on this earth the way I do John. I know it. Whatever was the matter with me tonight?'

She picked up the candle that she had brought out to read by, and, with a last look at the gleaming valley below her, went inside.

Chapter 5

May passed, and as summer came on, some of the slaves began drifting back to Cedar Ledge. Most of them came in sheepishly, slinking home without saying a word, and Shelby adopted the policy of never remarking on their absence.

However, he varied his practice when he came out of the door one morning and saw Uncle Peter, the family's former coachman, holding Eagle for him to mount. Jed was standing by, grinning, but Peter looked tired and worn and would not lift his eyes.

Shelby stopped, took his hand, and asked him anxiously where he had been.

'How did they treat you, Uncle Peter?'

Jed burst out: 'Lawd, jes' look at 'im, Mas' Shelby! He's so skinny his old bones is stickin' out clean thu his skin. Dem houn's o' Satan must-a used 'im hard.' Jed looked imploringly toward his master. 'Whut you goin' to do with him, suh? He served yo' Pa a long time.'

Peter's brown eyes drooped, and his yellow eyeballs twitched nervously. He could not summon the courage to look up at Shelby, who stood quietly, watching him, thinking, in some bitterness, that he would as soon have expected Jed to run off as Uncle Peter.

Then the old negro at last raised his head and a fierce pride blazed up in his wrinkled face.

'Mas' Shelby,' he began, 'I don't know how bes' to explain
it to you. Free!' he said, lifting his gaze, as if toward some magnificent vision. 'Dat word kep' ringin' in my min' lak a tinklin'
bell an' a soundin' trumpet. I *had* to see whut it was lak to be a
free man in dis wurl. I *had* to fin' out.' His voice sank. 'I foun'
out,' he said, 'an' 'twarn't sweet. 'Twar misery and pain.
Ef'n yo' wants me, I'll serve you twell I die.'

Shelby's expression softened. 'I'm glad you're home, Uncle
Peter,' he said, and turned to Jed. 'Give him a good breakfast,
and let him rest up a day or two.'

Uncle Peter handed him his reins, then stooped and rubbed
both his hands with appraising care up and down Eagle's long
legs, saying softly, 'Ho, boy! Ho, dar now,' to the animal, who
first started at feeling a strange hand on his bridle, and then
steadied, recognizing it as sure.

Shelby rode off in the direction of the fields, considering what
he had better do. He had to have some cash, but he could not
think how to get it. All day, he turned the problem over in
his mind, but each possibility that came to him he rejected.

There seemed nothing else to do except to go down to
Savannah and arrange for credit, if he could. He did not think
of going into Atlanta, for the Shelbys and the Hartwells and the
Lyttletons had always carried on their finances through Devereaux's cotton house in Savannah. He had kept putting off the
trip, all summer, both because he hated to think of laying a
mortgage on Cedar Ledge and because Sherman had pulled
up every train track along his way to the sea, burning ties,
depots, churches, and schools indiscriminately. 'A crow could
not find a square meal in all of Georgia,' Sherman had
said, proud of his work. Now, it would be a long hard
trip, to Savannah and back, just when he was needed at
home.

Shelby and Cavin arrived early on the night appointed for the meeting at Sunny Fields, but when they got down off their horses there were a number of other young men already on the verandah talking to John's mother and sipping the rice wine that her family always sent up to her from Charleston every Christmas. When the Northern army approached, she had sunk the bottles in the bed of the shallow creek that flowed through her land, marking the place by a great tree on the bank.

The troops had set her house afire, but her servants had succeeded in beating out the blaze before it had damaged more than the kitchen ell. The place stood now, in full view of the road, no longer screened by the tall hedges which, before Sherman passed by, had cut off the drive from public view. Sometimes Mrs. Martin wondered what the soldiers could possibly have wanted with the entrance gate that she had had copied, at so much trouble and expense, from one in Charleston — a gate that flashed under the sun like a phalanx of gleaming swords. She had never looked at it without being stirred by its beauty. Where was it now? She often wondered.

When the glasses had been refilled and drained, she rose to say good night.

'Bring your sisters over, Shelby, as soon as you can, won't you?' she said, turning from him to hold out a small, steady hand to Cavin. 'You must come over often while you are here, my dear. Please be sure to give your father my love, when you see him.' Reaching up, she playfully tapped his cheek. 'Are you as devoted a lover as he was? La! La! I can see him yet, when we were all young together.' For a moment, she smiled up at him, lost in her thoughts.

When she had gone inside, Shelby threw himself down on the ground with his eyes on the drifting stars. The others followed his example, sitting or lying on the grass in a circle, talking, or ceasing to talk, as they felt like doing.

All were gaunt and brown and tired, as tired as they had been on long retreats. But still the strange confidence of youth was theirs, although it was not based on any of the usual illusory hopes common to their age. There was extremely little about life that they did not understand; and only one of them was over twenty-five.

John sat silent for a long time. Then he began to speak cautiously, feeling his way.

'There's no use planning anything exactly, is there? Who knows anything?' he demanded. 'Where to vote, or if we can vote, or even' — he laughed shortly — 'how to get married? Why,' he went on, his voice rising, 'we have no notion whether our own land's ours. There's nothing to do, is there, but gamble and guess, and guess again, and gamble some more?' He looked around the circle, with narrowed eyes. 'One thing is certain; there's going to be plenty of gambling and guessing to do in this county, and we'd better hang together.'

The rest of them nodded, understanding that John had said all there was to say, for the present.

Riding home that night, Shelby's thoughts milled around the issues of the election. Lately, he had been reading his father's books and the pamphlets that Beauford had collected and Susanna had stored in the pit along with other valuable papers out of his office.

The more of these documents that Shelby read, the more convinced he was of one thing: that Appomattox and Bentonville had only postponed, not settled, the questions discussed with such heat in these thin papers. He did not yet suspect that past and future had met head-on, in the war, and that for many a weary year no man alive could tell in what direction that impact had set the course of civilization spinning. He did not even know that behind the issue of slavery lay the whole long debate on human freedom — an argument that, by its very nature, must be debated again and again by every generation of men. Shelby never once thought of the intricate matters about which Calhoun loved to argue. A man is free, he told himself simply, when he can choose his own way of living — and that choice the North had not been willing to let the South make. Why, he did not yet surmise. But the fact was plain to him; and he was confident that the fundamental points of view which separated the sections had not been brought into agreement by force of arms.

Take the single matter of classes, for instance. Northerners, he reflected, seemed to want to destroy all the lines that marked off the different groups in a population, whereas he and John and Jed, too, always thought naturally, almost instinctively, of persons as belonging in this class or that. The classification, he realized, as his thoughts ran on, was a convenience, not a judgment. One spoke of clergymen, planters, farmers, tenants, storekeepers, lawyers, white people, black people, for instance, just as simply as one named variant animals, lions, elephants, or tigers. It was no more, no less than that. Where did Northerners get all their ideas, anyway? he asked himself irritably.

At first Cavin went regularly with Shelby to the meetings and to the long consultations that took place, but gradually he began to turn his attention more and more toward Cedar Ledge, leaving the formation of policies and the molding of public sentiment to his cousin.

Cavin was one of those fortunate people, born so seldom into the world, who seem to know instantly, without giving any apparent thought to the matter, what they must do in any set of cir-

cumstances. He knew exactly — as exactly as Nathaniel had
known — what kind of life he wanted to lead. Indeed, he had
never pictured any way of living different from the one in which
he had grown up; he could not imagine himself in a city, or off
his own land. So now he applied his efforts, not to formulating
possible compromises with the powers in charge, not to devising
political programs and formulas and parties, but to stubbornly
reshaping in Georgia the only kind of life he knew anything
about.

This obstinate perseverance, this instinctive will or purpose,
Cavin possessed in supreme measure. A more imaginative
man, or one more willing to compromise and argue, might very
well have failed where he succeeded.

He went over and over the things that needed to be done on
Camp Mountain, where gradually a daily routine had sprung
up, Margaret and Aunt Lottie looking after the house and the
garden, he and Lucina planning the work on the place.

He was continually hampered, however, by his inability to
buy the few supplies he needed — but those few were nearly
indispensable. A start, he thought impatiently, was all he
asked. At last he came to the conclusion that he himself would
have to go down to Savannah, if Shelby could not.

One night he met his cousin on the drive just as he was leaving for Sunny Fields.

'Would you see if anybody at the meeting can lend me some
pants and a pair of shoes?' Cavin inquired abruptly, forgetting
that he had not previously mentioned his plan of going down to
Savannah.

Shelby's brown face crinkled and his eyes lit up in amusement. 'Who is she? Whyn't you tell me about her, anyhow?
Has she a sister?'

For a moment Cavin was puzzled. Then he laughed, waved
the suggestion aside, and stated his real desire.

'What I want to do,' he explained, 'is to go down to Savannah, if you can't get away.' Dropping down on a low bank beside the road, he clasped his hands around one thin knee, and leaned back, watching Shelby's face. 'These clothes ——' he began. 'Are you in a hurry?'

Shelby pulled out his father's watch. It was a heavy, round object from which, if you set a spring, the sound of a music-box would come forth at proper intervals. It had to be wound with an enormous key that had always lain on the table by Beauford's bed. Once, when he had been looking for a locket for Susanna, he had picked it up in a shipment of jewelry just come to Savannah. It had amused him, as it did Susanna on his return. Shelby had taken it off Beauford's dead body, and had been wearing it ever since.

'I've half an hour. I was riding down to see what kept you. Any trouble?' he asked quickly.

'Not exactly. I was wishing we had some mules ——'

'And some plows, and a million other things,' Shelby broke in impatiently. 'I've been trying to figure out what to do,' he continued, with less heat. His anxious eyes held Cavin's. 'I've been intending to talk to you. Maybe you have an idea?'

'Well, a sort of one,' Cavin answered, stripping a twig off the bush that hung over his shoulder.

Shelby looked at his cousin expectantly, and, alighting, took his seat beside him, holding Eagle's reins in his hand.

Sitting there beside each other, the two cousins could not have looked less alike. Cavin's straight, almost yellow hair had not come down from old Nathaniel, nor had his bright, darting blue eyes. Nor did he hold his shoulders with Shelby's easy, negligent assurance. His whole carriage was more tautly drawn, his eyes less thoughtful, more keenly observant. Yet anyone looking at the two of them would have known they were close kin, not only by the assurance with which they turned to one another, but by the identical curve of their cheeks, and by the way their small delicate ears lay flat and carven against their long heads. These were Hartwell characteristics that Susanna would have recognized and admired.

'What would you say about my going down to Savannah and trying to get an advance on Cedar Ledge?' Cavin asked slowly. 'That's why I wanted you to borrow me the pants.'

He smiled, holding out a leg on which his faded gray trousers struck him midway between knee and ankle, and waited for an answer.

For a long time Shelby sat with his hands knotted together in front of him, between his knees, gazing off across the pines toward the house that was just around the curve.

'I've been fighting off the idea for a month,' he replied hesitantly. 'Last night, though, I gave up,' he admitted. 'The place is going to rack and ruin this way; and how are we going to take care of the servants this winter? We are obliged to get a start somehow — obliged to.' He rose suddenly, his mind snapping to a decision. 'Yes, go on. There's nothing else to do. Of course,' he added soberly, facing the situation without false hope, 'there's more than a good chance that we won't be able to get a cent on the place, anyhow.'

Standing up suddenly, he put one foot in his stirrup, then took it out, and stepped back toward his cousin. 'Cavin, how do you think Lucy feels about John?' he inquired, in some anxiety. 'She's got me puzzled.'

Cavin had started up the hill, hurrying to get his supper, but at the question every thought of food left him. He halted in his tracks, and, as he did so, an unexpected and vivid recollection struck him, arresting his stride.

All at once he remembered something that had happened a

few nights before when John had asked Lucina, as he was leaving the house, to walk down to the road with him. Lucina had gotten up laughingly and gone along, and Cavin had met her, on her return, halfway up the drive. At the time, he had given no particular thought to the circumstance; but now it came back to him in sharp remembrance, full of significance.

That afternoon, as he learned to do in the army, he had marked out on an old plank the squares of a checker-board, and, being unable to make round counters, had whittled out small, square pieces of wood for men. After supper, he had invited Lucina to a contest of skill, which, he now recalled, she had given up to accompany John down the avenue. On her return, she had been silent and preoccupied and had soon gone inside, refusing to finish the game. Cavin was puzzled and amazed now by the perturbation that shook him both at Shelby's question and his own recollection.

Lucina and he had played together affectionately and tolerantly all the summer when he had been nine and she eight. They had fallen in the river, that summer, had hunted birds' nests and eaten their suppers together on the long verandah in the cool of every evening, shunning their elders so as to continue some game between them. When he returned this time, they had both taken up their relationship just where they had left it off, years before. Never before had he known a girl, Cavin thought now, in surprise, to whom he would trust the running of a plantation; nor one with whom he enjoyed being for hours on end, either. Yet — for the first time he thought of it — all summer he and Lucina had spent the better part of every day with one another.

He faced Shelby, frowning. Some deep agitation was going on within him, but what it was he did not himself know. Therefore he was surprised to hear the sharp words that fell explosively out of his mouth.

'Lucina's not going to marry John,' he declared. 'Of course she's not.' Then the next words rushed, leaped into his startled consciousness. 'She's going to marry me — me,' he repeated emphatically.

Shelby was hardly more surprised to receive this information than Cavin was to hear himself giving it. He stared back at his cousin, scarcely believing his ears, unable to absorb the idea, so precipitately put forward. Then he clapped Cavin heartily on his shoulder, shaking him back and forth.

'Why not? Of all the idiots! It simply never occurred to me, not once!' He gazed at his cousin with speculative care, another notion working through his thoughts to utterance. 'I'll bet it never occurred to you, either, till right now, you old blunderbuss!' He was amused to read in Cavin's face the confirmation of his conjecture. 'Hadn't you better think it over?' he demanded sceptically.

Cavin's eyes began to take on the look of settled purpose that, later, his friends and enemies alike learned to recognize as final. His lips tightened and he met his cousin's question head-on.

'I don't need to think it over,' he declared firmly. 'I was a fool not to know, in the first place — a plain fool,' he insisted. 'But it's all right now, I'll talk to Lucy about it right away.' Turning, he started briskly up the hill.

Shelby reached out a hand to stop him. 'Don't you think,' he asked, with a slight frown between his brows, 'that you ought to go on down to Savannah, first, and try to get some news from Uncle Phil? Lucina ought to know what your plans are, oughtn't she?'

'No,' Cavin answered positively, 'all that'll take care of itself.'

Shelby held out his hand. 'Well, I hope you know what you're doing,' he said, and smiled warmly at Cavin. 'I'll have to admit you usually do.' Eagle pulled restlessly on the reins. 'You'll let me know?' Shelby inquired, holding in his horse.

'You already know,' Cavin answered soberly. 'It's got to be that way. How else could it be?' Shelby leaned over his saddle and laughed until he shook.

'Cavin,' he gasped, 'you can't ask a girl to marry you, out of the air like that, and expect her to do it!'

Cavin shifted his stand, and eyed his cousin doubtfully. For the moment all his certainty left him. In some matters he had the most profound respect for Shelby's opinion. Maybe this was one time when he had better take his advice. Briefly he reflected on that possibility. What! Wait for weeks to know the answer to the tumult that he felt burning hotter in his veins every minute? No! Very soon he realized that was impossible, altogether and utterly impossible.

'I'm going to find out tonight, before I eat my supper,' he informed Shelby grimly, his face looking anything but loverlike.

Shelby raised his free hand in mock honor.

'Well, don't say I didn't warn you!' he called back over his shoulder, as Eagle galloped off.

Cavin watched the horse's feet disappearing around the curve of the hill. Then he walked steadily up the drive, noticing as he moved along that it needed repair. Where had he seen a pile of sand and gravel, mixed? Jake could carry some of it up in buckets and fill in the worst places on the road. He had seen that pile somewhere, he was sure of that. Lucina had been with him; they had built castles in the sand, he remembered, trying to copy the magnificent ones they had molded together in their childhood. 'Where on earth did I see that gravel, now?' he fumed.

He was still puzzling over the matter when he made the turn

into the circled drive, which retained its measured outline, though flowers no longer bloomed around it. Then he caught sight of Lucina sitting on the verandah reading the last book John had left her.

She was following the fortunes of the prisoner of Chillon, holding out her book to catch the waning light. Thus bent over, with her dark hair tied back under a ribbon, she looked like a child intent on a fairy story.

Glancing up, she saw her cousin approaching. Her eye had become accustomed to his stubby hair, clipped short with scissors, to his open, sunburned face, his shoes cut out of rabbit skins and old carpet, his short, faded trousers, to Beauford's shirts on his wide shoulders. All she noticed now was that his long jaw was set in a way that had become familiar to her. She knew, as she saw him, that he was studying some problem for which he had not yet found a solution that even remotely satisfied him.

'Cavin!' she exclaimed, when he stood beside her. 'Listen to this!' She spoke the lines aloud, in a soft, vibrant voice, while he stood watching her.

> O'er it blew the mountain breeze [she read],
> And by it there were waters flowing,
> And on it there were young flowers growing.

'That might be Cedar Ledge, mightn't it?' she inquired eagerly. 'Wait! There's another place up here.' She ran a searching finger up the page.

> Bend upon the mountains high
> The quiet of a loving eye.

'That's how I feel about Cedar Ledge, don't you?'

Cavin looked critically at the light which covered the trees across the road with a kind of unearthly radiance, as their stiff branches swayed against the darkening sky, like shadows on a brilliant background. 'Yes,' he said, slowly examining his surroundings, 'that's a pretty good description, Lucy. Only,' he argued, 'we ought to set out more flowers, to make it look like it used to.'

'Used to!' exclaimed Lucina passionately, closing her book, and gazing sadly across it at the mountain's slope. 'Used to! It'll never look the same again, never! Nothing'll ever be the same!'

'Yes, it will!' Cavin promised her. 'Yes it will — you'll see,' he repeated, stubbornly resolute.

Lucina turned her head, to meet his blue and shining eyes. Recalling his expression as he had walked up the drive, she thought absently that, whatever it was that had been bothering him then, he had settled it now, in his mind.

Suddenly she sprang to her feet.

'Why, Cavin! You haven't had any supper.' Her mind flew back over the day's work. 'What kept you? Is everything all right?'

'Yes,' Cavin reassured her. 'Everything's all right, everything.' His eyes followed her every move, and, reaching out, he took both her little brown hands in his — hands browned by the summer sun.

'Tell me something, Lucy,' he asked her, looking directly into her face with a kind of puzzled intensity. 'Do you remember where we saw that gravel pile the other day? I want Jake to patch up the road with it tomorrow. Do you?' He looked at her inquiringly, disturbed as always by his failure to recall something he needed to know.

'Oh, yes,' she replied instantly, 'I know. It's right at the mouth of the cave. We sat under the bluff, there, while it sprinkled, don't you remember?'

It all came back to him, now. 'Of course!' he replied. 'Now, how'd I come to forget?' He wrinkled his brow in disgust with himself. 'I'll set Jake at it soon in the morning.'

'Hadn't you better eat your supper now?' she reminded him again, slipping her hands out of his. Whatever was the matter with Cavin tonight? Always she knew what he was thinking before he did himself, but now she felt uncertain, a little baffled. He kept looking at her with a suppressed gleam in his eye, as if he knew something she did not, something he half wanted and half feared to tell her. 'I'll go tell Aunt Lottie you're here,' she said, suddenly shy, with a delicious shyness she did not understand.

'No,' said Cavin firmly, 'not yet.' He caught her hands again and his usually keen, impatient gaze was soft and ardent.

'Not till I've asked you to marry me.' He peered earnestly into her upturned face. 'Had you ever thought about it, Lucy?'

Her pupils widened, turning her eyes jet black. Cavin looked, she thought, about the way he had when Uncle Jed, years before, had tied a string to his tooth to pull it out. Torn between laughter and tears, she laid her head on Beauford's shirt, and her shoulders shook.

'Why, of course, silly, lots of times I've thought about it,' she confessed. 'But,' she added tremulously, 'I thought you never would.'

He gripped her hands tighter. 'You don't mind about John?' he asked her, bending tensely forward.

Lucina was honest. 'Yes, I do. I mind terribly. If he had come back one night this summer ——' She stopped and took an impulsive step toward him.

'You're sure, now?' Cavin held himself still, almost rigid. 'I've got to be certain.' Never, he thought, in his life would any answer ever matter to him so much as this.

With a joyous, confident movement Lucina held up her face. 'Kiss me,' she said softly. 'Kiss me and see.'

Till the day of his death, Cavin never forgot the smile she gave him at that moment. He flung out his arms and lifted her till her face was level with his.

'You see?' she whispered tremulously, when she had caught her breath. 'You see?'

Neither of them remembered his supper crisping over the dying coals. The stars came out gleaming through the mist, and the soft breeze stirred in the tree-tops. The night closed over them — the warm Southern night, so radiant and pulsing, yet always so mysteriously sorrowful, as though marked by the tears as well as the ecstasy of lovers. Cavin and Lucina would not have felt the world shifting on its foundations had it moved perilously out of its course that night.

'Perhaps,' thought Lucina dimly, 'heaven will be like this.' But Cavin felt no need to compare the present with any future bliss.

When Shelby galloped up the drive at midnight, they did not hear him. Glancing at them, he tiptoed around the side of the house, and let himself in at the front door, feeling all his own activity go stale and flat in his mouth.

As he was undressing, a letter fell out of his pocket. It was one Brooks Gardner had given him for Cavin, one Captain Baker, of the merchant ship *Mary Frances*, had been instructed to leave at Devereaux's in Savannah. Shelby guessed at once that Philip Darcy had chosen this method of getting in touch with his son.

He hesitated. Should he dress and take the letter down now to Cavin? He chuckled to himself and decided not. Already it was a month old. Any news it bore would keep another night.

Chapter 6

Next morning, when Lucina woke up, she felt shy and a little afraid to face her brother and sister. What would they think of her sudden decision? Probably they would still regard her as a child, and she might have to win them over to her plans.

She dressed herself with great care, smoothing her hair and dusting her face with starch she had boiled out of field corn, drying it in the sun and adding jasmine petals to sweeten its smooth texture. When she had finished, she looked in the glass, inspecting every strand of her hair and the color in her cheeks. Never had she wanted so much to be beautiful. But she wanted to see no one, no one at all. Not until she had had time to think over all that had happened to her.

She slipped out the door before anyone was awake except the servants. Hearing Aunt Lottie stirring around in the kitchen, she hastily skirted it, and, making her way down the avenue, began to walk across the fields still wet with dew.

She knew exactly where she was going. Many a time, the first year of the war, she had gone out alone through the rose garden, past the snowdrops, past Martha's cabin and the kitchen garden, into the fields that sloped down to the brown creek. Sometimes she would lie among the oats, flat against the earth, her body hidden by the grain. Then, as she lay looking up straight into the floating clouds above her, the war would at once begin to seem remote and unreal, and, for a time, her perplexities would drop away from her. Or, sometimes, toward evening, she would catch her wide skirts around her and quickly climb the huge oak that stretched its arms so invitingly out over the creek's banks. From there she could look across the water to the cotton growing fresh and green in long, plowed rows, to the tall pear trees and the feathery wild plums from which the cook made tart jelly, flavored with orange peel and sealed in brandy, to eat with the ducks that Beauford regularly shot in the fall. As she sat there, hidden among the leaves, she could hear dragonflies fluttering their gossamer wings against the water beneath her, or pigeons flying past her, their soft feathers glistening, whirring in the air. She liked to sit there watching the sunset changing the gray earth to rose or to a deep glowing purple; and she liked to walk back dreamily to the house, content and quiet, suffused with a peace like that the choir in church was always praising — peace like a river, they chanted, Sunday after Sunday.

That was the spirit in which she wanted to make the choice that she had made the night before. She wished that the strange and turbulent emotions which stirred her whenever she thought of Cavin would pass into a less tempestuous joy. So she sat waiting for the kind of rest and quiet to fall upon her that hitherto she had always felt behind the swinging doors of their pew in church, or high up in this tree, looking up into the clouds or far away toward the horizon.

She watched the sun rise, large and golden, out of the quiet, dark earth, but she had no sense of the passage of hours. Not until she saw the negroes moving slowly across the fields did she realize that, by this time, they must have missed her at the house and would be worrying. Hastily she glanced at the sun; it was, she judged, at least nine o'clock. She roused herself then, and began to climb down.

She had just reached the lower limb, from which she could easily step to the ground, when she saw Cavin coming down the narrow path that led to her retreat. Suddenly, as she caught sight of him, the quiet that she had been seeking stole over her.

'Why, there was never any other way it could have been,' she told herself, now perfectly calm, as he came toward her. 'This is how it had to be.'

Cavin was whistling softly. He knew where to look for her. They had spent, this summer, a good many hours in this tree planning what needed to be done, or resting in its cool shade during the heat of the day while he dropped a fishing line into the water beneath them. Nothing would have surprised him more than a bite on the hook, but he never gave up sinking his bait.

Looking up, he smiled easily at her. 'I knew you'd be here.' Then, putting a foot on the low limb where she was standing balancing herself, with one hand on the branch above her, he drew himself up beside her.

She could not see that he seemed to feel any difference in their relationship. Had she dreamed all that had happened last night? Cavin's hand, as he held it out to her to steady herself by, was as cool and firm as it had ever been.

When they were seated on the lowest limb, his feet were planted on the ground, but hers swung a little above it. Cedar Ledge loomed high above them, through the ambuscade of trees; and in front of them lay the creek, flowing in languid curves through the rolling meadow. The sun was now high in the sky; its warmth fell on their cheeks. Lucina did not then know it, but the imprint of every leaf and plant around her that morning was stamped forever into her memory.

Cavin looked at her as if again he knew another secret that she did not, a new secret that pleased him mightily. 'What would you say to marrying me next week, Lucy?' he asked her suddenly.

Then, catching the dismay in her eyes, he put his arm quickly around her and smiled down at her, inviting her to share his own confidence. 'Kiss me, Sweet?' he asked her.

Lucina breathed deeply and, laying her hand on his cheek, lifted her face to his.

For a second, Cavin held her off from him to look at her — at her dark, shining head, her curving lips, her luminous, tender eyes. Then, certain that life would always be as joyous as he now felt it coursing in his veins, he drew her exultantly into the full circle of his arms.

'Don't you think,' Lucina asked him, in a small, shaken voice, 'that we ought to go up to the house and tell them?'

'No hurry,' he replied comfortably, settling his warm cheek against hers. 'They already know. I told them, myself, when I came back from John's this morning.'

'John's?' she inquired, a shadow appearing in her eyes. 'Have you been over there?'

'I forgot. I haven't told you, have I? I went over to see him the first thing this morning, before he got off to the fields.'

'Cavin!' cried Lucina, interrupting him, 'I was going to tell him, of course.'

'Yes, I knew you were; but I wanted to see him myself,' he said positively. 'He was just leaving, when I got there. I didn't have to say a word. He guessed right away why I had come.'

He sat staring across the open land to the creek, whose brown waters lay gleaming, like silvery metal, under the bright sun.

'We stood there looking at one another until ——' He

glanced down at Lucina inquiringly. 'You know that horse-block by the front gate? Well, all at once he sat down on it, the way men collapse in the army when a bullet hits them. I dropped down by him, waiting for him to say something, any-thing.'

'Oh!' cried Lucina, drawing a quivering breath. 'Oh!'

'Finally, he stood up,' Cavin went on. 'I'd better tell you. "You love her?" he asked me. "You do love her? Better than anything on God's earth? You'll take care of her?" He never even waited for me to answer him.' Cavin's voice was low, as he finished his story.

Lucina's head lay still on his shoulder. There swept over them both, then, some dim dread of the future that ruthlessly and re-lentlessly takes from one and gives to another. She shivered, for the first time in her life acknowledging the sorrow that is so strangely implicit in nearly every earthly joy. She thought she knew, now, what the negroes meant when they sometimes said, with gasps of horror, that they felt people walking over their graves. Stirring restlessly, as if to shake off some unexpected pain, she lifted a troubled gaze to Cavin's.

His arm tightened around her. 'Don't you see, Sweet,' he said, meeting her eyes, 'that there was nothing we could have done to make it easier for him? Nothing!' he declared again, and, feeling in his pocket with his free hand, laid a piece of paper between her flaccid fingers.

'There's no sense to life!' she exclaimed, making no move to open the folded slip.

Cavin lifted her face. 'Yes,' he reminded her steadily, 'there's sense, Lucy; there's how we feel, too. John understands that.' How could a soldier help knowing he didn't always get what he wanted in this world? he thought, but did not say.

With a long sigh, she held the white sheet up in front of her eyes, and then, without a word, handed it over to Cavin.

> Dear Athene — dear, darling Athene:
> In the months that I have loved you and dreamed you might be mine, I have had more joy than a man has a right to expect in this world. You will forgive me, I know, if I do not come to Cedar Ledge for some time. God bless you, always.
>
> Ever thine,
>
> JOHN

'Athene?' asked Cavin, folding the note. 'Athene?' But if Lucina heard him, she gave no sign.

For a long time they sat there, without stirring, and gradually there stole over them both the quiet that follows upon every deep surrender, every full acceptance or commitment.

'Where?' she asked at last, smoothing his bushy eyebrows with one finger. 'Where am I going with you?'

Cavin's thoughts were far afield. 'Oh,' he explained in amusement, 'I forgot.'

This time he felt around in his pocket in vain. 'I must have left it at the house,' he said. 'Shelby gave me a letter from Pa, when I got back from Sunny Fields this morning. He's back in Texas,' he informed Lucina. 'When he went into Galveston for supplies, he found old Captain Baker just putting off for Savannah and Old Point, so he gambled on my having stopped here, and got his cotton firm in Galveston to write Devereaux's, in Savannah, to extend me enough credit to get home on. There's a letter from them, too, up at the house. Captain Baker is sailing back on September 4th.' He stopped suddenly. 'That means — do you know what that means?' Leaning over, he kissed her joyfully. 'That means' — he smiled a broad, happy smile, carefully spacing his words — 'you — are — going — to — marry — me — about — a — week — from — today.'

Straightening himself, he gazed down at her, frowning. 'And that's too long,' he observed positively.

They went back to the house together, their hands swinging as they came up the narrow path that led steeply up the face of the cliff to the front verandah. When they were nearly at the top, Cavin stood still, and began to laugh, his shoulders shaking. His eyes were deeply blue and clear as he looked at Lucina.

'Do you know what?' he reminded her. 'I forgot my supper, and here it is going on twelve o'clock and neither of us has had a bite o' breakfast yet.'

They began to laugh together, because the world was a fine and happy place for lovers, because, for a fleeting instant, they felt themselves invulnerable, armed against any woe.

'We'll manage,' Cavin thought to himself. 'We'll manage, no matter what.'

Margaret hurried down the path to meet her sister, feeling some curious change of relationship between herself and Lucina, as though she were now the younger sister, as though, since the night before, Lucina had passed over into a wider knowledge that had so far escaped her, Margaret. 'Justin!' she was thinking as she went to meet Lucina. 'Justin! If only you had lived!'

'Well, of all the surprises!' she said, aloud. 'How long has this been going on?' Glancing from one to the other, she studied them with an earnest scrutiny that belied her light words. Then, as if reassured, she put an arm around each of their shoulders and walked back between them to the verandah where Shelby was standing on the long, low step, holding out his hand to his cousin.

'You're a man of your word, Cavin,' he exclaimed, and drew Lucina under his other arm, chuckling.

'I knew about this before you did, Lucy,' he told her affectionately.

'Oh, no!' she corrected him, smiling at Cavin. 'Not before I did — you mean before Cavin did.'

The sun was growing warm, and they went inside through the long windows to the cool of the parlor where they sat down, waiting for Aunt Lottie to announce dinner. Cavin, however, could not stay still and walked about restlessly.

'I can't seem to settle down!' he remarked, in humorous surprise. Shelby and the girls laughed, but they all felt the same way.

After dinner Shelby rode over to Orchard Hill; and when he returned, shortly before supper, Mrs. Connor was with him, on the bay mare that she had hid in a thicket of briars for three months before Sherman's army ever rode down her avenue.

'I'm going to stay till after the wedding,' she informed Margaret, who came out to meet her. Setting her foot on Shelby's outstretched palm, she dismounted, pointing to a large bundle behind his saddle. 'Some old dresses,' she explained, 'for the trousseau.'

When they rode up, Cavin was sitting with his back against one of the square, white pillars that faced the valley, carefully watching the changing light on Lucina's face, as the twilight passed into early dusk.

Mrs. Connor dropped down beside him, kissed both him and Lucina, and then fell at once to planning. 'Um-m-m.' She began counting on her fingers. 'This is the tenth. What day do you have to get off?'

'I've been trying to persuade Lucy to start next week,' said Cavin, smiling.

'Too soon,' said Mrs. Connor at once, shaking her head. 'It'll take us at least two weeks to get the sewing done.' Laughing, she patted Cavin's cheek. 'Don't you know a girl has to have a wedding dress? That'll still give you time to visit around in Savannah a little, if you want to,' she consoled him.

'Of course the child has to have a wedding dress,' said Margaret, looking reproachfully at Cavin. Leaning over she kissed her sister with affectionate care on the precise centre of each flushed cheek.

'Darling, you are going to have a lovely wedding,' she promised her.

'It seems a far way for you to go, Lucy,' Mrs. Connor remarked, with some hesitation in her voice.

But Lucina had no doubts.

That night she slept as calmly as a baby. She knew now what she was going to do; it seemed as though she had always known it. Once, however, she wakened for an instant, and saw a bough of the tree outside her window waving back and forth across the slatted panes. Then she wondered what she would see in the strange Texas dark, when she looked outside. She felt suddenly bereft when she thought that the shadow she was now watching would not then amuse and comfort her, as it had for eighteen years whenever her eyes opened in the night.

Next morning, before she had her breakfast, she ran downstairs and laid her cheek against the tree's rough trunk.

During the next two weeks, Mrs. Connor and Margaret and a sewing woman from the quarters ripped and basted and dyed old garments until they began to feel that Lucina might have enough to take with her. There were silks that had belonged to Susanna; a cape that had been Beauford's; pieces of lace preserved so long that no one knew who once had treasured them; and velvet dresses from Mrs. Connor's own trousseau. Laying all these together, they contrived a travelling dress for Lucina, a cloak, and a tiny velvet bonnet to match. They made her a wrapper of soft silk, too, with a cascade of lace falling down its front, and a dress of wine-red moiré, dipped in dye made from wood berries.

Then they packed her trunk for her and laid on top the cotton frocks she had worn all summer at Cedar Ledge, and the riding-habit that had been Susanna's, and the black velvet hat, with its sweeping plume, that went with the riding-habit. As a last thought, Mrs. Connor dropped in among the clothes a handful of leaves from the sweet-smelling balsam that had sprung up again in Susanna's garden, and bags of dried rose petals gathered from the bushes in the cemetery.

'Thank goodness she can wear my shoes. There's only one little tiny hole in them,' said Margaret.

Then they called Lucina in and laid out before her a bedspread. Inside, the coverlet was lined with a delicate blue brocade, which, although it had lain in the pit, was almost as fresh and clear as the day it had been made up. Outside, the spread still looked like heavy gold.

'Take your choice, darling,' said Mrs. Connor. 'Which side will you have for your wedding dress?'

'I'll go ask Cavin,' Lucina answered breathlessly.

She was laughing when she returned. 'He says maybe we'd better not cut it up at all, that I look all right in this.' Amused, she pointed to the plain blue percale she had on.

Mrs. Connor put down her scissors with a clatter and looked at Lucina severely. 'Now, isn't that like a man! If you ask them, they say something like that; and if you don't ask them, they ask you why you didn't ask them. Put that down to remember in your married life, Lucina,' she advised her crisply. 'Come over here to the window. Let *me* see.' She laid the pieces of silk up against Lucina's cheek.

'The blue, I think, don't you, Margaret?' she decided.

'I'll declare, child,' Margaret remonstrated, 'you act like you don't know your wedding day is only four days off! You haven't even said *where* you want to be married!' She looked at her sister lovingly, but a little impatiently. Her eyes against her creamy skin seemed very gray, and her hair hung in loose, vivid tendrils around her face. She was too young and pretty, thought Mrs. Connor, to be settling down the way she was doing since the war.

Lucina sat down and folded her hands in her lap. 'Honestly, I hadn't thought about it,' she confessed. Her ideas began to take swift shape. 'The front verandah,' she decided. 'Jed and Jake can set up evergreens at one end, and Mr. Curtis can bring over his lovely gold cross.'

That night, Shelby laid in Cavin's lap a couple of mysterious bundles tied up in newspapers, and stood back to watch him open them.

'Wedding presents!' he announced magnificently, 'and Mrs. Martin sent word wouldn't you like to drive her horses in Cousin Ella's carriage down to Savannah?'

'Like to!' cried Cavin. The idea sent prickles of delight down his spine, up into his hair. In Savannah, with Lucina all his own! He looked down at her, where she was sitting just below him on the lowest step, and forgot the packages in his lap.

'Open them!' urged Shelby. 'The big one's from John.'

Cavin untied the string then, and saw an almost new uniform carefully folded between the printed pages.

For a long time he sat looking down at the gray cloth spread out over his knees. Then he glanced up and smiled at Lucina.

'I ought to look pretty grand in an officer's uniform,' he remarked, 'pretty grand.'

'Well, yes,' Shelby admitted, his eyes twinkling. 'Considering you never were in the army. Go on, you old slow-poke, open your other package!'

'Boots!' exclaimed Cavin, magnificently holding them up. 'Boots!'

'I'm going to be all dressed up at your wedding, Lucina. You *better* look pretty,' he warned her.

Shelby smiled. 'From Brooks. You can send them back from Savannah.'

The conversation died away. Mrs. Connor found it hard to believe that it was Lucina's wedding and not her mother's that was in prospect. She supposed, however, that Lucina was not thinking of Susanna.

Pondering over the strange fact that the dead are so often remembered more warmly and frequently by their friends and relatives than by their own children, she sighed.

'That's life, I suppose,' she reflected. 'That's the way life goes on.'

Her eyes misted over as she sat watching Lucina. In her mind, she was seeing Susanna on her wedding day, joyous and excited, and herself with her own young husband, Robert, walking beside her. Now Susanna lay in her long grave, her dancing feet forever still, and Robert was, where? Resting, like his son and Beauford, under a cold, gray slab marked by a wreath of laurel and the inscription that covered so many new graves in Georgia — *Soldier of the Confederacy, Servant of Christ.*

'Ah! what does it all mean?' she wondered. 'What can it possibly mean?'

Suddenly she understood why the old are always lonely. 'They know so much they can never tell,' she thought.

But as she watched Cavin smiling at Lucina, she saw that they were conscious only of themselves and of the summer night. That was how it should be.

'It's all right, Susanna,' she said, addressing her friend in her thoughts. 'Everything is all right. You don't need to worry about your child.'

The next day, Shelby carefully extracted a wide sheet of white paper out of the back of one of Beauford's map-books. Working carefully, he pulled, through two slits at the top of the sheet, a piece of broad white ribbon that Margaret had had among her clothes since before the war. Tying it in a neat bow, with the short ends hanging, he began to write in a careful, shaded hand:

> You and your family are cordially invited to attend the wedding of my sister, Lucina, to Mr. Cavin Darcy at Cedar Ledge at ten o'clock on the morning of August twenty-third.
>
> SHELBY LYTTLETON
>
> CEDAR LEDGE, *August* 19*th*, 1865.

He signed his name precisely, drawing beneath it a graceful, intricate whorl.

Then, calling Jed to him, he instructed him to mount Eagle and carry the invitation around to all the neighboring plantations.

That done, he called Margaret and Aunt Lottie into anxious council.

'We haven't touched Father's wine,' he said, doubtfully— 'the wine we found in the pit. But there's nothing to go with it, is there?'

Aunt Lottie darted a scornful glance at him. 'Don't you worry none,' she cautioned him. 'Dar'll be a cake fur de bride to cut.'

Before the close of the war, she had worked out a way of making flour out of cornmeal ground very fine and sifted innumerable times through tightly meshed gauze. Now, she calculated shrewdly, she had on hand honey and blackberry preserves, and eggs; and for some time she had been depending on a fairly successful yeast powder made out of powdered corn-cobs fermented in the sun. In the next few days, using these ingredients, she filled a pan with rich dark batter, and Margaret sent Jake to gather trailing vines in the woods to lay around the wedding cake.

The morning of the twenty-third broke fair and cool. Maria woke early and put her head out the window to see the sky, where masses of pink and lavender clouds were piled in feathery confusion just above the horizon. As she watched them, they broke into thin spirals of color, marking the eastern sky with shifting, interlacing streamers. The air smelled fresh and washed, and in it the sweet, luxuriant odors of late summer lingered. Slowly, the sun appeared, its rays lighting up the tops of the tallest pines, and falling on the tree outside Lucina's window.

Then Lucina opened her eyes; and seeing the broad waxen leaves shining in the quivering light, she breathed deeply in gratitude that the day was fine. She lay there for a few mo-ments, quiet and composed, amazed that on her wedding day she felt no more excited than this.

Maria hurried down to the kitchen and returned with a break-fast tray.

'You better hurry up an' eat, Miss Lucy. Mas' Cavin is a-pacin' up an' down in front, dressed up fit to kill.' She sat down on the foot of the bed, watching her mistress; then got up and pushed a pillow carefully behind her back.

'Who's here?' said Lucina, nibbling at her breakfast. She wasn't hungry, but never, she thought, had she felt less hurried or excited. She lay back, calmly watching Maria pour hot water into a large white bowl, with a sponge beside it.

'Nobody yet, but dey'll all be comin' along putty soon, now,'

Maria returned confidently. 'Miz Martin sont you over a rose-bush by one o' her niggers dis mawnin' — one o' dem putty yellow ones she grows in her garden. It's all packed in a heap o' wet clay and wropped 'roun' wid millions o' croker sacks. She say I is to water it evy day, on de trip, an' it'll do fine fur us's garden in Texas — ef'n us ebber gits dar,' she complained. 'Looks lak us ain't nebber gwine-a start, eben, de way you lays dar an' won' git up.' As she spoke, she sniffed luxuriously at a small bottle she held in her hand and then, in a single lavish gesture, poured all its contents into the hot water in the bowl. 'Cologne,' she said. 'Miss Susanna gin it to me a long time ago.'

Lucina held out her hand to her maid. 'Why, Maria!' she exclaimed. 'You ought to have kept it yourself.'

Rising, she thrust out her small feet, waiting for Maria to draw on her slippers. 'Maria,' she asked suddenly, 'do you reckon you're going to get lonesome in Texas?'

'Ain't you gwine-a be along?' answered Maria. 'You better hurry up,' she grumbled. 'Mas' Cavin been fussin' aroun' a hour.'

A little later, Lucina began hearing the buzz of arriving guests and excited feet flying up the stairs. Then her door was flung open by a group of girls with flushed, happy faces.

'Why didn't you tell us?' Ellen Saunders from Fox Hill demanded, embracing Lucina.

'Write me what Texas is like, won't you?' asked Vivian Carter from Carter's Grove. 'Maybe I'll come out and see you.'

'Find me a beau in Texas, won't you, Lucy? I need one,' sighed Marilyn Hargreaves from Red Gates, wrinkling her short, little nose, and telling the sad truth. 'There aren't enough boys to go around any more.'

They sat down on the floor in a circle at Lucina's feet, looking at her with round, expectant eyes, feeling that she was being separated from them by a passage as wide as death. Soon she would be a married woman, no longer free, like them, to dance and flirt, and sit out under the stars. Soon she would settle down, deep in some mysterious content that they could neither share nor fathom.

'Lucina, you aren't really going way off to *Texas?*' Vivian asked in astonishment, shaping her tongue around the word with as much surprise as if she were saying 'New Guinea' or 'Borneo.' Still, the Texas boys had a way with them; she had met a few of them during the war. 'Invite me, too,' she urged Lucina.

'How did you know you wanted to marry him, for sure?' Ellen anxiously inquired. 'How on earth can you tell?' she pressed Lucina. The other faces around her reflected an extreme interest in the question. Lucina stood up and sent a quivering smile around the group.

Below, the sound of the young men's voices came floating up the staircase. Brooks Gardner's voice had a carrying quality which penetrated the heavy door. They all recognized his rollicking laughter, as he stepped up on the back verandah. He seemed to be conversing with Ned Devoe and with Hugh Pendleton, who, before they went to war, had been counted the best dancers in the county. Then Lucina's ears caught the echo of Cavin's deep voice.

Her cheeks flushed, and, lifting her head, she smiled confidently at her friends, flinging out her little hands to them in a sudden wide, impulsive gesture.

'You'll know,' she assured them. 'You won't have to ask *anybody.*' For a moment, her mind swept back to the night on the verandah when she had been so reluctant to let John speak, so uncertain of herself. No, it had never been like that with

Cavin. 'You'll know,' she said again, so softly that the girls scarcely caught her words.

They kept their eyes fixed on her; and all at once some transient intimation of how quickly life's best moments fade swept over them, some dim understanding that they were witnessing a miracle not destined to endure. They rose and gathered around Lucina, with unshed tears in their eyes; but her face was radiant, like that of a person who has seen a vision.

So Margaret found them, when she knocked and opened the door, with Cavin and Shelby just behind her.

'Mr. Curtis is waiting, and everybody's here,' she announced.

'I'm going down now, Lucy,' said Cavin, stepping past his cousins into the room.

He was as composed as if he were accustomed to being married every day in the week. He stood ten feet away from her, but Lucina felt that he had never been closer.

'I'm ready,' she told him, in a steady voice. Behind her, she caught the sound of her friends' soft breathing and the rustle of the leaves outside her window. She could hear the tick of her father's watch in Shelby's pocket, as he stood by the door; and she noticed a little flicker of sunlight falling on Cavin's forehead. 'I'm ready,' she repeated firmly, and took Shelby's arm.

As she stepped out of the door onto the verandah, she glanced at the valley spreading out wide and misty in front of her, with the rim of blue hills marking off its distant boundary, and the wide creek flowing through it. All her life, she was to recall every shadow passing, like smoke, over the land below her that morning. Then, shifting her glance, she saw Mr. Curtis standing in his robe and cassock in front of the tall gold cross, with his red prayer book open in his hand.

Suddenly, she felt a curious sensation, as if she were outside her body, with all her senses dormant and her consciousness independent of all her external surroundings. She wondered if she were breathing, and then, with a start, realized that she was kneeling on a silken cushion that belonged in the parlor, and that Mr. Curtis had laid his hands on her head and Cavin's. 'World to come . . . life everlasting . . .' she heard him saying, and then felt herself rising and turning. Still, she felt as though she were floating, not walking; as though she were dreaming, not awake.

Then she heard Jed strike up his first gay notes on his violin, and the strange sense of unreality began to desert her. Cavin's glance was confident and clear, and his new uniform brought out the color in his cheeks. Under the cloth, his shoulders moved easily, and his waist, belted in by a silken scarf, was slim and straight. His feet stirred to the music, and a smile broke over his face. He made a swift bow to Lucina.

'Mrs. Darcy, I believe?' he said lightly, his blue eyes twinkling. 'May I have this dance?' Suddenly intent, he looked down at her and drew her closer. 'No longer cousins,' he told her under his breath.

Lucina felt her heart fluttering, her voice disappearing in her throat, as she suited her step to his.

'Go away!' said Cavin to Ned Devoe, waving him firmly aside, when he came up to beg the second dance with Lucina. 'Go right along!'

'Come on, Lucy,' Ned jested. 'You better cure him of being jealous, while you can.' He offered her his arm invitingly.

Cavin smiled at Lucina and relinquished her.

'I've just thought of something I want to do,' he told her.

When she could slip away, she went out to find him, and came upon him stowing away a number of bundles in the carriage. He drew his shoulders out from under the top and, straightening himself, turned around to look at her.

'I thought,' he said, almost shyly, 'that you might like some of your own bulbs to put out in Texas. I've cut a few slips, too,' he added. 'They're stuck in sand in that old iron pot over there.' Pointing to a kettle on the floor of the carriage, he stood watching her. 'I never thought about doing it,' he admitted, 'until just a little while ago. When I get to Savannah, I'll probably remember a heap of other things I forgot,' he predicted ruefully.

'Oh, Cavin!' said Lucina, laying her hand on his sleeve. And then again, 'Oh, Cavin!'

'I brung along sum of dem seeds dat was in de pit, too, Miss Lucy,' Maria put in. 'Jake kin dig us up a flower garden quick as us gits dar, cain't he?' She was sitting beside him on the front seat, and, as she spoke, she turned toward him, ready to expatiate on her plans.

'Lawd, 'oman!' Jake remonstrated unhappily, 'whut you talkin' 'bout? Diggin'!' he exclaimed, repudiating the idea, with a firm shake of his head. 'De prairies an' de bottoms is plum' carpeted wid flowers, whar us's goin'!'

Uncle Jed ceased playing, and the guests began to troop out through the hall to the back porch, where a table, with wine and wedding cake on it, was standing. For a moment there was silence. Then Shelby held up his empty glass invitingly, and Lucina began to cut the cake, the slices falling in thin, waxy perfection upon Susanna's silver platter — the platter that had so long rested in the pit. It seemed to her, she tremblingly thought, that she had never known what happiness meant before.

When everyone had filled his glass, Mrs. Connor took her and Cavin by the hand, and led them out into the garden. Jed, seeing what she had in mind, clucked to his horses and drove on down the avenue. They stood there together in the middle of the circled drive, with their friends gathered close outside it and, as the conversation ceased, Shelby stepped in beside them, raising his glass high.

'Uncle Jed has fortunately provided me with a toast, ready-made,' he began, standing relaxed and at ease. 'I give it to you! "May their love grow twell it reach de sky o' hebben and may de Lawd smile on 'em and nebber frown." '

'Drink it down!' replied Brooks Gardner happily, clinking his glass against his neighbor's. 'Drink it down!'

'Come to see us,' Cavin invited them, his eyes sweeping full around the circle — 'all of you.'

'Come soon,' Lucina echoed. 'Soon!'

Jed backed the carriage up the drive and climbed down, his long whip held stiffly by his side. His face was beaming, though, and he made a wide bow. 'Miss Lucy, kin I gives you one piece o' advice?'

She looked at him expectantly, with a smile on her lips.

'Wheneber you gits mad wid Mas' Cavin — an' you will,' he assured her, holding up his hand. 'You don' believe it now, but you will — when you gits mad at 'im, you jes blame de Lawd fur makin' us po' mis'able men creatures de way we is, don' you blame Mas' Cavin.' He stood looking earnestly at her. 'Dat's de God's truf I'm tellin' you, Miss Lucy.'

'It is, Lucina, it certainly is,' observed Mrs. Martin, coming close and kissing Lucina. 'Be happy.' She kissed her fondly again. 'And write often!'

'Write often!' Lucina's friends cried out together, echoing Mrs. Martin's words. 'And be happy!'

Cavin stopped Jed as he raised his reins, and, putting his head out of the carriage, motioned to Shelby to step closer.

'I'll see about the business at Devereaux's and send you a letter back by Jed. There was a gate I wanted to get fixed ——'

His cousin nodded. 'I'll 'tend to it.'

'Shelby, I'll miss you!' cried Lucina, holding up her face for another kiss.

Her brother patted her on the shoulder and looked over her head at Cavin. 'Take care of her!'

'I will,' Cavin promised confidently. 'You come out soon.'

'Go on, Jed,' said Shelby, stepping back.

Before they reached the curve that hid the house from view, Lucina turned around to look back at it.

'Look, Cavin!' she urged him. 'Look!' Susanna's and Martha's houses were behind them, outlined in the noonday sun. One of Jed's understudies had taken up his fiddle, as the carriage drove off, and they could hear the music and the laughter coming down to them through the still air.

It passed through Cavin's mind that his life in Texas was beginning just where Nathaniel's had, in Georgia, nearly a century before. Suddenly, he was extremely anxious to land in Galveston.

Lucina noticed how bright the sunlight was against one side of the tree that stood beside her window, how the vines had begun to grow again over the west window of the summer kitchen, and her slow gaze fell at last on the cedars that marked where Susanna and Beauford lay. She felt grieved with herself that she had almost forgotten her parents on her wedding day, and a tremulous foreboding seized her. 'Some day Cavin and I will grow old and die,' she felt rather than thought.

Glancing down, Cavin saw that her eyes were full of tears.

'Don't look back, Sweet,' he said ardently, gathering his bride into his arms. 'Look at me!'

Part II

Texas: 1865—1867

Aye, with new quality imbued, the vast
World seems but ... voracious change.

LUIS DE CAMOËNS
Translated by Richard Garnett

Chapter 7

IT WAS the middle of October and Philip Darcy reflected, as he rode homeward through the gathering dusk, that the nights were closing down all too early. He shivered slightly, twisting his shoulders in discomfort as he felt the first cool breeze of the fall upon his neck. He was a tall, spare man, with hair as dark as when he had courted Mary Hartwell in Georgia; but his clean-shaven face was now marked by tighter lips and by a more austere expression than it then had borne. Only his eyes were the same — a deep, dark, misty blue that contrasted strangely with the general severity stamped on his expression by the passing years.

In one hand he held the reins slipped through his first and second fingers and gathered loosely into his closed palm. The other hand swung straight at his side, and he carried his shoulders squarely erect, as his body followed instantly and gracefully his horse's pace. 'Gentlemen never slouch in their saddles,' his father had warned him when first he put his son up on a horse alone. Now the position had become automatic and Philip no longer remembered the instruction.

He was extremely tired, for he had sat up all the night before watching a patient die — an experience that always strongly affected him — and, this afternoon, with no rest, he had attended a county gathering to consider a communication from the provisional governor's office.

In his letter, Governor Hamilton informed all Texas citizens that, since negroes were now free, their testimony would have to be accepted in court along with that of white men. Smiling a little wryly as he listened to the stipulation, Philip wondered how a poor negro, unable either to count or to read, could be expected to give accurate testimony. In the Southern courts his ignorance had hitherto protected him, but now — well, who could tell? The next item interested him more profoundly. The governor's letter stated bluntly that every citizen owning property to the value of twenty thousand dollars would be required to obtain a special pardon before he could vote or hold office. Philip knew the last regulation applied to him and to all his friends. When he got on Pilot, his great black horse with a blaze of white between his wide, intelligent eyes, he was tired to the bone, sad, and discouraged. Until this afternoon, he had hoped that the governor, who was Southern born, would under-stand Texans better than he seemed to. He admitted now to himself that the past few months were only the beginning of worse to come.

'Tomorrow,' he reminded himself, checking his mount again in surprise at the thought, 'tomorrow I shall be sixty-five.'

Since he had come home from the war in June, he had felt increasingly the fatigue that now began to overtake him. From the first day of his return, he had been engaged in political con-troversy of the most wearing, exhausting kind. He did not deceive himself; he did not expect he would live long enough to see free government restored in his county, but he hoped his children would inherit the fruit of his labors. It was a good thing, he thought, that Cavin would soon be coming home.

His medical practice, which extended well over a hundred miles in all directions, was beginning also to tax his strength. He sighed and admitted it to himself tonight. Ever since his return he had insisted, as he had always done, on his servant, Matt, keeping a horse bridled and saddled for him every hour of the day and night. He had made no more concessions to his age than he had in the past, and — no matter what the summons — he still galloped off across the prairie or the bottoms to answer it. Sometimes he was called out to attend sick servants or cowboys hurt in a gambling fracas, sometimes to consult with physicians in Houston and Galveston, sometimes to close the eyes of a friend. Never in his life had he refused to attend anybody, rich or poor, black or white, friend or enemy. Now at last he was beginning to feel the strain of a life lived at other people's beck and call.

On these excursions, he always carried, behind his saddle, two leather bags full of medicine which, before the war, he had regularly replenished from abroad; but now his supply of essential drugs was reduced to the danger point. Lately, he had spent as much time as he could in trying to work out substitutes, and he had succeeded in extracting from a common yellow prairie flower a powder that he had found useful in treating fevers. For some time it had also been in his mind to investigate the feasibility of producing opiates from poppies grown in Texas. Hadn't another Georgian discovered how to use ether, he meditated, undaunted by his meagre equipment for scientific research? In his little unpainted box of an office beside his low gray house, he was now carrying on a number of other experiments that interested him greatly. He wished, as he rode homeward, he had more time to devote to them, more time to read. There was a book on his table which an English friend had sent him — some notes by a man named Darwin. He ought to get at that. Then he fell to wondering what was the curative agent in the herbs the negro women boiled up to assuage the pain of burns. What was the magic in the brew they used to swab out their children's sore mouths? Philip had a mind that scorned no source of knowledge, and he was as willing to learn from his slaves as from the men who had instructed him in a London hospital.

The illnesses he encountered most often were simple malarial chills and fevers which he patiently treated with liberal doses of calomel and quinine measured out expertly on a knife blade. But, in general, he depended more on other factors than on drugs to cure his patients.

At intervals Philip was apt to spend hours looking over the neat notebooks that he kept for each of his patients. In these he recorded the date and number of his calls, as well as each patient's family history, previous ailments, and church membership. For he was firmly convinced that a man's religious convictions often determine the event of his life or death. He would take more operative chances with a man who possessed a steady, sustaining faith than he would with a drunkard or a rampant unbeliever.

'Too shaky,' he would say of such patients; 'no foundation to work on. Better not.' His judgment was usually right, and he learned to trust it.

Philip often wondered exactly what his own faith was. He could not have said, exactly. He only knew that something sustained him on his long rides, when his strength was gone, and gave him rest when his soul was most deeply torn. From somewhere he was conscious, too, that he often received a kind of illumination that thinking alone never yielded to him. It was that illumination — that sudden flooding of his mind with light and certainty — that Philip called God.

He was not aware of it, but his religion, such as it was, was as much composed of fragments from pagan thought as it was an outgrowth of Christian experience. His mind was quite as

full of Greek and Roman echoes as it was of Jewish mythology.
In his thinking, Jehovah and Great Jove dwelt together in
amiable companionship, and he was conscious of no incon-
gruity when he slipped the Prayer Book and Horace or Virgil
side by side into his pocket. He had trained himself, on long
rides, to read as his horse moved beneath him; and when spring
came along, he often opened his little volume of the Georgics and
murmured the lines aloud with exactly the same thrill that the
poetry of the Psalms always afforded him. Thus, though he
called himself a Christian, he was drawn more to religion by
the beauty that was in it than by any definite set of theological
beliefs.

Of these he had practically none; and felt no need to state
his religion in exact terms of argument. But all his patients
knew that, before he left their beds, he was apt to take out his
Prayer Book and read aloud the prayers for the sick, or sometimes for the dying, rolling the words over his stern lips with
constantly renewed appreciation of their beauty. He had no
sense of separation between his mind and his spirit. That cold
chasm, which was to engulf the world in time, had never opened
in front of him.

Philip was not only thus engaged in public discussion and
effort and immersed in the demands of a wide practice, but he
had also a large plantation to look after — a plantation which,
it appeared, he would now have to work with free labor.

All summer the negroes had been restless and sullen, ever
since the issuance of a proclamation in Galveston on June the
nineteenth informing them that they were free. During the
summer months, the regular army officers had made rather
consistent efforts to urge the field hands to work and harvest
the crop; but of late they had begun more and more to idle away
their time, engaging in crap and dice games, or assembling

along the roads in dangerous groupings which the planters knew could not long be safely ignored. And some planters, sizing up the situation, had packed up and moved into Houston, deserting their land.

Philip felt that any day might set off a chain of circumstances leading to riot and bloodshed. He could see no hopeful omen, no matter where he looked.

'Yes, I'm glad Cavin's coming home,' he reflected, his mind turning again, after a long circle, to his son. 'He can take over the plantation; he was good at it, even as a boy. He's probably much changed.'

Philip wondered, in amusement, if he would recognize Mary's child, now, if he were to come upon him in a crowd.

'Time the boy's coming home,' he meditated, 'full time. How old is he now?' He counted back, and in so doing revived the thought of his own impending birthday, tomorrow.

'Sixty-five!' Philip meditated. 'What if I should soon die?' He shuddered at the prospect, but forced himself to consider it, nevertheless, through to the end. 'It is not improbable that I shall,' he concluded, 'not at all improbable.' So thinking, he rode slowly on, trying to recall a passage he had read a few nights before, where he could not remember. 'But it's true,' he thought. 'The years revolving *do* steal from all their powers!' Then, in sudden and unexpected clarity, the whole passage returned to him. 'Ah!' he thought again, 'it's true. At my age, "my jests, my loves, my sports, my taste for festive hours — all, all have worn away!"'

'At my age!' The phrase startled him. 'Why it seems no time at all since I was a boy tracking birds in Georgia.'

He could feel the cool swamp mud under his feet, oozing through his toes as he hunted eggs and mosses for his collection;

could hear the baying of his favorite hound, Dexter, as the dog accompanied him and the negroes on dark nights, to hunt possum. He remembered the excitement that used to course through him when he heard the dog's barking in the distance ahead, and how, as soon as he heard it, he would begin to run, almost dropping his lantern. Now, more than fifty years afterward, the blood coursed hot in his veins at the memory.

'God!' he thought, 'to feel like that again! To feel like that again! To be young with all my life ahead of me!'

With a sudden jump, his mind passed over the years of his boyhood, skirting his education at home with a tutor, his decision to read medicine in Savannah, his one year in a London hospital. He remembered now in curious detachment, as though it had happened to another man, how, on his return from England, he had found the girl he loved married to another man, his best friend. He knew then that he would never live in Savannah, and had soon set up his practice in Florida.

For years afterward, he never thought of marriage — not until he was recalled to Savannah by his father's death. Then, at a friend's house one night, he met Mary Hartwell.

Now, as he rode alone through the silvery Texas night, her face rose before him unspoiled by time — her gray eyes, her sweet, curving mouth, the carriage of her dark head, and the tilt of her rounded chin. Even now, after he had had two other wives, his heart turned over in his breast as he recalled the little curls that clustered around Mary's neck, her tender, laughing voice, her sweet generosity of spirit. She was eighteen when he married her in 1830; he was, therefore, almost twelve years older than she, but he thought it had never mattered.

Once, before they were married, he had urged her to consider carefully how much sooner he would become wrinkled than she. Still too young to think seriously of death, she had answered him playfully, hardly knowing what she said:

'Why, I might die before you. And then you could marry a sensible, middle-aged lady to look after your rheumatism.'

He was too well acquainted with death to take the words negligently, and a sudden horror shook him as he heard her speak. He remembered, in the blowing Texas dark, the pink camellia that was in her hair that summer night, and its sweet fragrance as he had bent his head over hers, crushing her quickly to him as if to ward off the death about which she so lightly jested. Death and he were old enemies; he was not one to underestimate his adversary's power.

He counted back. That was — how many years ago? Thirty-five? It seemed impossible.

'And the last ten, nothing but tumult and pain,' he thought sadly, 'all tumult and pain, and soon the end. The end,' he repeated sombrely, and the thought weighed him down. He dreaded to think of a spring when he would not be alive to smell the soft breeze, of an autumn when he would no longer see the blue smoke of burning cotton stalks floating low and film-like over the black trees along his bayou.

He fell to recalling the years in Florida when his life had seemed, for a long period, to take shape under his steady hand — the years after he had married Mary. There, when his first child was about a year old, he had received a letter from his cousin, William Charlton, who, a few years before, had gone out to establish himself on a cotton and sugar plantation in Texas, near the Gulf. In his letter William described the enormous number of acres which settlers with families and slaves could secure almost for the asking, and the quick returns that a moderately small investment of capital would afford.

But that was not all he had written. He had taken time to

tell also of the glowing purple light that fell on the prairies at sundown, and of the flowers that covered the endless grass; he had traced the deep, yellow river that flowed, mile upon mile, through the bottom-lands, a river bordered by cypresses and live-oaks and pale wood flowers; and he had tried, but he had failed, to indicate the kind of life the planters enjoyed — the dangers that called out the best in them, the unlimited possibilities that fascinated the imagination of the bold and barred the timid from membership in a free society, wherein a man's right to live his own life in his own way went, as yet, unquestioned.

'Come, see for yourself,' William had urged him, and Philip had accepted the invitation, as Mary had wanted him to do. That was — he counted back — in 1832. Yes, he remembered that he had thought, looking at the baby in his cradle, it would be a fine thing to acquire a share in the new cotton lands to add to the child's inheritance.

After four months on the Brazos, Philip stocked part of William's acres with slaves, tools, and supplies, and went back to Florida and Mary. The agreement between the cousins was that William was to develop the land as opportunity afforded and his judgment dictated, making such returns on Philip's investment as was possible after deducting a reasonable charge for services.

For years after that, Philip thought only intermittently of his Texas property. The Texas Revolution came and went, and Philip, engrossed in his practice and in the management of his Georgia and Florida lands, was hardly aware that it had taken place. Occasionally some surprisingly large deposits were made to his account at Devereaux's; then there would be a few years when little or nothing came in from his investment. Long ago, however, Philip had decided he had buried his money in a nap-

kin in Texas, and that only time could tell whether it would increase or not. He thought of his lands there oftener, though,
when the papers began to be full of heated argument as to
whether the United States should welcome another slave state
into the Union. When at last the matter was settled, over the
protests of Massachusetts, Philip again almost forgot his acres
on the Brazos.

He never thought of living there himself until the summer
of 1855, when Mary and his two older children succumbed to
the yellow fever that was spreading, that year, from New
Orleans around the coast. Cavin only remained to him then —
Cavin, Mary's last child, born in 1846, almost ten years after
his brother and sister.

'Ah, well!' Philip thought, shifting his weight wearily in his
saddle, 'we had twenty-five years. How short a time, though!'
he sighed. 'How short!'

After Mary's funeral, Philip's world fell to pieces. Then,
clinging by a kind of blind instinct to the life that he no longer
treasured, he left Cavin behind with his Grandmother Darcy
and, in 1855, put off for Texas with only his servant, Matt,
for company. After his arrival, he concluded his former arrangement with William and took over, himself, the operation of his
plantation. Still, he had no expectation that he would be buried
there on it, beside the Brazos. A strange river, he had always
thought, sometimes so slow and red, laden deeply with clay
and phosphates from the up-country, sometimes so wild and
torrential, its yellow, whirling torrent taking everything before
it. It fascinated him, but he never loved it as he did the
Chattahoochee, which flowed so deep and dark and still between
its low banks.

Philip's horse moved suddenly beneath him, shying, as he
always did, at a tall dead sycamore beside the road. The white

trunk, overtopped by great gaunt limbs, reminded Philip of a picture he had seen as a child in a fairy-story book — a picture of a haunted wood. It never ceased to surprise him, however, that Pilot, whose intelligence was nearly human, always shied at this particular spot. He reined the horse in, and patted his neck, aroused now to the present and to the ache in his tired bones. He shook his shoulders vigorously, and, as if awakening from a dream, realized he was in Texas, not in Georgia or Florida, half a lifetime ago.

With the patience born of old habit he began to try to close his mind to memories which, he knew from experience, could not be too long dwelt upon. He had learned, by repeated trial and error, how to use his past to lengthen out his consciousness of having lived without at the same time opening full the floodgates of memory. Always some instinct warned him where he must stop. He had reached the point now, he thought. As one draws a cloth over the face of the dead, he began deliberately to let down the curtain in his mind between his past and his present, closing out agonies he could not endure to recall.

Pilot, recognizing the turn, took the side road leading home, and as Philip looked down the white, sandy stretch ahead of him, he remembered that he had first seen it on a night as cloudless as this, when he had come down the road with his cousin William, and had reined in his horse to sniff the heavy, sweet air he was always to associate in his mind with the Texas summer.

'Yes,' he thought as he rode along, his eyes wandering over the field beside the white road, 'yes, it looks tonight just as it did the first time William and I rode down it. Who would have supposed then that I would ever come here to live in this little shack of a house, to operate on kitchen tables with knives sharpened on bricks?'

He frowned, remembering his army experience when his supply of morphine was exhausted, and the difficulties under which he had always practised in Texas, having endlessly to invent procedures and treatments to meet the new conditions of life he encountered on the Brazos.

'And yet most of my patients live — God knows why,' he ruminated, resolving to make a further study of why he so often succeeded in saving life, even when he least expected to.

'Of course the books are often wrong,' he reflected. He intended to write a manual himself, if he lived long enough, embodying what he had learned — it had been considerable — about the treatment of wounds in the army. He had filled many notebooks with case records during the years when he had hurried from one battle field to another. The trouble was he could not bear to open them now, to call to mind again the boys he had been unable to save. He thought perhaps he might do a little general reading first, and played with the idea a while. But he had practised medicine too long to put much confidence in what he read.

'There's a plenty not in the books,' he thought, suddenly agitated. 'Nothing I have ever read explains why Caroline died so suddenly.'

His thoughts circled hesitantly around that sore spot in his life. Should he let himself think about it?

'Maybe she didn't want to live.' He put forward the idea tentatively, comparing her reactions to those of a very sick woman he was at present attending who seemed to have no desire at all to get well. 'It makes a difference.' He was certain of that.

'Heaven knows,' his thoughts ran on, 'I never treated poor Caroline right. Well, there's no use thinking about that, either,' he concluded, drawing shut another door to another set of recollections. But the door would not stay shut, try as he would to push it to.

'What's the matter with me tonight?' he said to himself, surprised at the torrent of memories that poured over him. 'It's a long time since I've let myself go like this. It's a good thing I don't have birthdays often.'

Caroline kept returning to his mind. He had been in Texas a year when he met her, in 1856. She was then a spinster of about forty, who had accompanied her brother, Rhoades Cunninghame, to the Brazos from South Carolina. Oftener and oftener Philip found himself going over after supper to pass the time between dusk and bedtime with him and Caroline. When, after about a year, he was killed in a fall from a horse he was breaking, Philip offered his hand to Caroline — Caroline as tall and spare as a rail, and without a gleam of humor in her dreamy gray eyes.

He was honest with her. 'I shall never love anyone again,' he told her, and he believed what he said. 'I am too old for that,' he went on amiably and reasonably; and, guessing her age, 'if you are not, you soon will be. We can make a home for each other, anyway.'

He did not once think, until after he was married, that people might accuse him of courting Caroline in order to share in the considerable property that she inherited from her brother, and which he, in turn, received from her.

From the beginning, he realized his marriage had been a mistake — a complete and total mistake. This was Caroline's first marriage, and it was soon apparent that she expected from him what he no longer had, or thought he had, to give — romantic affection. If she had been a widow, with a life already behind her, the venture might have succeeded; both of them in that case might have counted half a loaf better than none. But this was all the romance that poor Caroline had ever had, and she knew, when she looked in her mirror, that it was all she ever would have. She was possessed to make Philip live up to the descriptions of young love that she was always reading about in novels.

Finally, when the tension was becoming unbearable for them both, she sickened with some sudden fever that he could not diagnose, and, to his surprise, for she did not seem very ill, died suddenly one morning about a year after their marriage. He buried her in a plot that he then set aside on his plantation for a family cemetery, and erected above her a plain, white stone reciting simply that she had been his wife. He was surprised and deeply ashamed to acknowledge how happy he was to be free again.

That same winter — the winter of 1858 — William Charlton's widowed sister, Letitia, died in Natchez. When she was only eighteen she had married Talliaferro FitzHugh, and gone to live in the Delta with him, and after his death she began to die also, by slow degrees. During the few years she lived on after his funeral, she had twice come out to visit William, and William had grown fond of her only daughter, his niece, another Letitia. Therefore, when he heard of her mother's death he sent her an urgent invitation to come and make her home with him. He and his wife were childless, he wrote. Would Letitia come and be their daughter now?

'We need more girls in this county anyway,' Helen, William's wife, commented crisply. 'I'm always telling you that, my dear. Now, where is that delightful young gentleman, Povey Blount, for instance, going to find him a wife?' She looked reproachfully at her husband, as though the circumstance she deplored was his fault.

Povey had been in Texas for over a year, now, having come out from Henrico County, Virginia, to claim his land from an uncle who, on March 2, 1836, at San Felipe-on-the-Brazos had signed his name to a document declaring that the people of Texas would never submit to 'consolidated central despotism.' The language did not sound strange in a Virginian's ears, and Povey soon made himself at home on the Brazos. William and Helen both had grown to admire and like him, and they were always telling him he needed a wife, though he gave no sign of thinking so himself.

'Let me see, my dear,' said William, his wits springing into action. 'Let me see. How old would Letitia be now? The last time she was here, two years ago with her mother, you remember, she was pretty as the mischief, but a little rangy and impulsive. Don't you recollect,' he asked his wife, 'how she insisted on learning to ride Nero, as soon as she knew he had never had a woman on his back? She did, too,' he chuckled, 'and she kept at it until he ate out of her hand. And never cried when he threw her. Who would have imagined there was so much spunk in her?' he inquired, leaning back and looking reflectively at Helen. 'She's about as big as a minute, as I recall. Probably, though, she's a demure young lady by now,' he ended.

In April Letitia arrived, one fine sunny morning when the air sparkled like wine, and the flowers were white on the dewberry vines.

Thinking of that day, Philip pulled Pilot up sharply. He sat motionless, staring off through the night toward the light he could now see, ahead of him, shining down the road from Letitia's room, turning the rising mist to gold.

'Ah! How well I remember that morning.' The words were

so clear in his mind that for a moment he thought he had said them aloud.

Povey and he had both been sitting their horses, he remembered, waiting outside William's swinging white gate and picket fence for him to join them on a trip over the fields. They had laid a wager, he recalled, about whose cotton had the best start for the season. William had already mounted when he turned and saw, down the avenue behind them, the carriage he had sent to meet the boat.

'Excuse me, please, gentlemen,' William said to his guests. 'I had no idea they could get here so soon.'

He galloped down the drive to meet his niece, while Povey and Philip waited, their reins drawn loosely through their arms. They were throwing corn to the pigeons, Philip recalled, which picked and cooed at their feet. Startled by the rumble of the approaching wheels, the birds rose in wide circles, flying in excited groups high over the carriage, as Letitia stepped to the ground. She paused, and, shading her eyes from the sun, looked upward, as excited as a child by the whirring wings above her. She was wearing a yellow dress that morning, its wide skirt trimmed round and round with tiny bands of black velvet ribbon, and its waist fitted snugly around her young, almost childish, figure. She stood in precarious balance, with one black-mitted hand holding fast to the carriage door and one small foot already out on the step. She had on a black velvet bonnet, too, Philip remembered, with a single yellow rose fastened under it. Where it lifted off her face, he caught a glimpse of eyes so deeply blue that, at first sight, he thought they were as dark as her bonnet. The hair around her small, eager face was light, almost golden, and as she stood looking up at the pigeons she reflected some exciting vitality, some pulsating energy, as if life flowed through her at a quickened pace.

Something in the quality of the light that streamed over her or in the questioning youth that shone out of her eyes stayed with Povey and Philip to their dying day. Neither of them wanted to break the spell; they could have stood there forever watching her as, unconscious of their presence, she gazed upward at the flying pigeons.

'How many moments there are in life like this,' thought Philip, 'that one could wish would endure forever, never broken by change!' But Povey did not think at all. He stood motionless, unable to collect himself enough to offer Letitia his hand, and feeling only a great surge of happiness suddenly pulsing through him.

Now, living over, in sober recollection, the moment when he first saw her, Philip told himself that the same qualities in Mary and her had called forth his immediate response to them both. It was not that they looked alike, feature by feature, Philip said to himself; for Letitia had hair as light as Mary's had been dark, and eyes of a deep, sparkling blue, whereas Mary's had been as misty as his, and gray. He always thought of them in the same breath, though, he decided, because out of them both had flowed the same exuberant, vital joy in existence that one felt, if one stopped to think about it, in the surge and rise of spring over the fields.

'Yes,' he said, as he sat still on his horse watching the light from Letitia's window, watching the cleared space in the front of his house where her garden grew clear up against the thickets beyond it. 'Yes, that is it. That is why I love them both.' He paused, trying to frame in words what he could not easily express. 'Virgil has it,' he thought, his mind running back over a passage he had read the night before. ' "What the moon foreshadows, what the south wind secretly sings" — that's what Mary knew and that's what Letitia knows. If they

had both been ugly and deformed, it would have been the
same.'

In his mind he went back now over the months after Letitia's
arrival, when it had been as clear to him as to anyone that
Povey had won her heart as quickly as he had lost his to her.
He recalled Povey's glowing gray eyes, his brown hair, shot
through with gold, his thin, straight nose, his smiling mouth.
No wonder, he thought, that Letitia had looked at him and
loved him.

The whole spring came back to Philip now — the weeks
when she and Povey had ridden through the April woods
exploring the country, choosing trails that led along the dark
river, out under the live-oaks to open spaces where bees buzzed
thickly around blue bonnets and wine-cups. Once he, Philip,
had chanced upon them when Povey was down from his saddle
plucking a red blossom to share with Letitia its sweet, pungent
honey. Across the flower their eyes had met and clung, a spark
passing between them. Philip had pulled up his horse then,
hoping they would not see him. When they moved away,
unconscious of his presence, he did not know whether to be
glad or resentful.

He reminded himself now of how he had stayed away from
William's plantation, Holly Grove, cursing himself whenever,
on rare occasions, he did see and talk with Letitia. 'You are
seven times a fool,' he told himself when, as he sat beside her,
his heart would begin to pound. 'Seventy times seven, one,'
he would add relentlessly. Soon, he would get up and go home.

Before long, he realized to his utter amazement and consternation that he was no longer willing to put life aside, passing
out the remainder of his days in such senile quietude as he
could muster. No one could possibly have been more surprised

than he when he fell in love with Letitia — fell in love with her suddenly, madly, furiously, with the quick, springing passion that had drawn him to Mary so long before. At first he did not recognize what had happened to him; it had been a long time since he had felt that sweet flow of excitement within him. Finally, when he admitted the truth, he cursed himself roundly for his stupidity. He knew as well as anyone else that it was absurd, for he was more than three times Letitia's age.

'Three times her age,' he told himself sternly night after night, forcing himself to stay at home, alone, away from William's, where Letitia, he guessed, would be sitting under the wistaria vine that grew over the arbor talking to Povey.

'How old is he?' Philip wondered. 'About twenty-four, I should think,' he concluded, making an accurate guess.

'I'm an old fool,' Philip told himself, 'a dad-blamed idiotic fool. Who would have believed it?' he asked himself. 'Here am I, an old man, feeling what I thought I was through with forever. Well,' he reminded himself, 'at least I've got enough gumption to know what to do about it.' And he stayed away from William's house, stayed away until William sent over a note to see if he was ill.

'What have I to offer her sweet youth?' he told himself bitterly, facing the truth. 'A tired, worn spirit, and a body soon to lie in the grave. She would consider me crazy — and she would be perfectly right,' he admitted. 'Well, I can think of her, anyway,' he said, 'as much as I like.'

With a frosty smile, he would put his feet up on the railing of his gallery, and, clasping his hands behind his head, would gaze off across the Texas prairies rolling white in front of him, under the great, round moon.

'When she was born,' Philip commented to himself with distaste and surprise, 'I was forty years old, the father of two

children, and I was deeply in love with another woman.
Yes,' he reminded himself, not dodging the truth, 'deeply in
love, as much so or more than I now am with Letitia, who was
not even born when I met Mary. Why, O Lord, did you make
men such utter fools?' he groaned, impatient of his folly, but
not cured of it. 'I'd better go home, after Cavin,' he told himself, still thinking of Georgia as home.

One night in late August, William sent for him in great haste.
A slave had been kicked on the head by a mule and was still
unconscious. Philip hurried over, resolved to go straight to the
quarters, not to the house. But William was there beside the
injured negro, and invited Philip, when he had finished, to
sample a new case of apricot brandy that he had just received
from New Orleans. He could think of no excuse for declining.

They went up to the house and poured themselves a drink
out of the decanter that stood on the long sideboard. Passing
out onto the back gallery, they sat down, slowly sipping the
fragrant liquor, turning the thin glasses under their noses as they
drank, and holding them out to test, in the bright moonlight,
the rich, glowing color of the brandy. Suddenly the door
opened from the inside and Letitia stood, quivering, beside
them.

'Uncle William,' she informed him tensely, not at first
noticing Philip on the shadowy gallery, 'I've sent Povey home
and told him never to come back.'

Philip sat stock still, watching William's face, which betrayed,
successively, surprise, regret, and then amusement. Obviously
he thought that this was some quick lovers' quarrel, soon over.
'Go to bed, honey,' he told Letitia, patting her hand. 'Povey'll
be back apologizing in the morning, first thing.'

'He can't apologize,' she flared. 'There's nothing he can

ever do or say,' she said, proudly raising her head. 'He's
engaged to a girl in Virginia.' She looked at them as though
she did not see them, as though she were talking to herself,
trying in vain to explain to herself what had happened. 'Oh,
yes,' she continued, waving the fact aside as of no consequence;
'it was all a long time ago, and of course he has written to
tell her how he feels. But that makes no difference to me.'
Her young voice flamed in sudden anger. 'I never want to
see him again, never — not as long as I live.'

Philip and William exchanged a glance full of the bitter
knowledge which at their age they shared. How was it possible,
that glance said, to make Letitia understand, at nineteen, that
change is the law of life, that nothing ever remains fixed or
permanent, that what has been must always be forgotten and
put aside in favor of what is, or is to be? How inform her so
that the knowledge would not too rudely break in upon her
young dreams? They quailed before the task, as well they
might.

William stood up and put his arms around Letitia. 'There,
darling, there. It doesn't mean a thing. I'll go see Povey.
It'll be all right.' They could see she was hurt to the quick,
and resentful, blaming Povey because, at her age, she found
that easier to do than to admit to herself with what tragedy,
stupidity, and error the course of life is so often cast about.

She raised her head and flung it back, shaking her fair hair
out of her eyes. 'I'd marry anybody who asked me,' she told
William passionately; 'marry them tomorrow.' The color was
so high in her cheeks that even in the moonlight they flamed.
Had the child a fever? Automatically, Philip laid his hand on
her pulse.

As he did so, he felt his heart knocking against his chest.
'She is a child,' he reminded himself fiercely, wondering why,

knowing that, he still loved her as he had loved nothing on earth but Mary. 'A perfect child.'

It seemed to him, then, that he spoke because he could no longer help it.

'Miss Lettie,' he heard himself saying as he rose and stood beside her, 'I would be proud and honored to have you marry me.' It was out at last.

Over her head, William's face loomed, startled into immobility. 'Do you know what you are saying, Philip?' he demanded, sharply.

'I'm asking her to marry me, William,' Philip responded quietly. 'Just what you heard me say.'

Letitia took no notice of their conversation; if she heard it, it seemed to make no impression on her.

'Jumping Jehosophat!' exploded William, glaring at his cousin, and falling back on an expletive that he was apt to use under stress. 'You've had two wives already; you're old enough to be the child's grandfather!' He blurted out the truth, stung to a biting fury that knew no pity.

'Very true,' answered Philip, refusing to lose his temper. 'Too true. But need that matter to her?' he inquired reasonably. 'She is not in love with me; I am in love with her,' he explained. 'It's the truth, William,' he added, meeting his cousin's incredulous gaze.

Letitia stirred against William's shoulder, and raising her face, she looked straight at Philip.

'He said that he thought he had loved her once. He wouldn't deny it. He said that would be like denying he loved me now.' She was silent, but they could see she was repeating his words to herself, that she had not finished what she had to say.

Suddenly she moved over to Philip and, standing straight and still in front of him, with her hands clasped tightly together, replied to the proposal that he thought she had not even heard.

'I'll marry you tomorrow,' she told Philip in a clear, dead voice, and, turning, went rapidly into the house.

William sat down abruptly and studied Philip's face.

'You must be crazy,' he said, gazing intently at his cousin, 'entirely crazy, but I believe you are telling the truth. I never knew you to do otherwise,' he admitted. He was puzzled and irritable, as people and ants become when they do not know how to get around obstacles suddenly set up in the path they wish to follow.

Philip stood with his hand on one of the posts supporting the steep overhanging balcony. He could just catch the murmur of the river flowing over the twisted cypress roots that deflected its current and caused it, ever so often, even to shift its bed. He felt old, remote, and, suddenly, extremely weary; yet he was more at peace than he had been for many a day. The die was cast, at any rate; but he had lived too long to allow himself to hope that his desires would necessarily determine the outcome. Such a state of mind would have been impossible for Povey, a younger man, to summon.

'Of course,' William went on firmly, 'she didn't mean it, and if she did, I wouldn't expect you to take advantage of her excitement. She's upset now; she'll think differently in the morning.'

He stood up, deeply perturbed by the turn his plans had taken. 'Go on home, Philip,' he said, studying his cousin's face. 'We are all tired and worked up. This can't be settled tonight — you'll see how foolish the whole thing is in the morning. Go to bed. That's best. If you stay, we're both apt to say something we'll regret later on.'

Without moving, Philip answered. His back was still to William, and he spoke almost as if he were dreaming, his words

dropping from his lips without emphasis or emotion. 'You're
quite right, William. I'd better go home,' he assented. 'They'll
both think better of it, overnight. I expect Povey'll be over
before daybreak.'

He smiled a slow, reminiscent smile; then he swung around
abruptly facing his cousin with an expression that William
recognized. In their boyhood when he had noticed Philip's
eyes narrow, and harden, as they now did, he had learned there
was never any use arguing further.

'Listen and mark what I say, though, William. If she is
willing to stand by what she said, nothing on God's earth can
prevent me from marrying her.' Suddenly, he put out his hand
and shook William's spare frame vigorously. 'It's absurd; of
course it's absurd. I know it. We're both a couple of doddering
old idiots. They'll be certain to make it up tomorrow. Good
night. I'll take your advice and go to bed.'

William sighed in relief, almost pushing Philip off the steps.
'Go on,' he said urgently; 'go, while you're talking sense.'

Philip mounted his horse and rode homeward. When had
he felt such lethargy and utter fatigue as now overtook him?
Such dead and desperate certainty that there was no longer any
use either to hope or to grieve. Remembering that night now,
eight years later, he thought that only twice in his life had he
felt as he did then: the day Mary died, and the day he heard
General Lee had surrendered.

He did not open his eyes, he recalled, until the sun was well
up. His servant, Matt, was standing by his bed, touching him
lightly.

'Dar's a young lady outside, suh,' he was saying apologetically.
'She tell me she hatter see you, right straight away, and cain't
wait.'

Philip was instantly awake. He reached out for the cup of

black coffee in Matt's other hand, thinking at once that some of his patients had taken a turn for the worse.

Pouring it out in the saucer to cool, he hastily drew on his clothes. 'It's probably the Miller child,' he decided. 'Lockjaw, too, I'm afraid. I suspected it yesterday.'

He lifted his saddlebags, where bottles neatly labelled in Latin rested in small leather pockets. Then, picking up his surgical case, he checked over its contents carefully, counting his instruments one by one, lifting them in their clean white cases. Looking at his watch, he saw it had been less than ten minutes since Matt had called him; and then he stepped out onto the gallery through the long window from his bedroom.

Sitting on his horse with the October night shutting him in, Philip watched, without moving, the light now falling from that window. Remembering the morning, seven years ago, when he had passed through it to find Letitia waiting outside for him, he felt again the metal handle of his instrument case cutting into his hand as he saw her; felt again the weight of his long saddlebags on his shoulder; and recalled, as though it were this minute in time, the way her hair had glistened in the sunlight as he had bent over her, at first incredulous and then, suddenly, caught up in the strange, exciting sense of everlasting youth that always possessed him whenever he came near her.

'Letitia!' he remembered he had asked her instantly. 'William didn't let you come alone?'

'I got off before anybody else was awake,' she replied, waving the question impatiently aside, and hurrying on to what occupied her thoughts.

'I saw you didn't think I knew what I was saying last night,' she told him, as her breathing quickened. 'I came over to tell you I did mean it. I'll marry you today, if you want me to —

today,' she repeated. Her voice, to Philip's ears, sounded unnaturally tense and excited, like a sleep-walker's.

At the recollection of that moment Philip sighed long and heavily; and Pilot, feeling his rider stir in the saddle, picked up his feet to move on to the warm stall and mash that lay, he knew, in the stable ahead. Philip checked him absently. 'Not yet, boy; not yet,' he said aloud, rubbing Pilot's shining, arched neck, the muscles of which broke, under his touch, into a curious rippling motion.

Philip stared off over his horse's head, his eyes recording, not the night shadows that now lay thick upon the gallery in front of Letitia's window, but how her face had looked as the light fell upon it that morning seven years ago. Even yet he could feel her body relax like a child's against his as he caught her and held her, for the first time, in his arms.

'What would any man have done?' he asked himself fiercely now, as the falling leaves began to swirl around him in the rising wind. 'I would have been less than human had I not done what I did. Never a day since then that I have not loved her more!' he thought passionately, wishing that he might see her shadow moving across the light.

The light in the window went out. 'She has taken it in to see whether the children are covered,' he hazarded, watching the now darkened room with bright, intent eyes. 'That's it,' his attention automatically registered, as the light reappeared in the window. As though there had been no interruption in his thought, his mind went back to the day they were married.

He had ordered his trap hitched up at once; he remembered that now, and they had set off immediately to Berryville, the county seat, to obtain a license and a minister. He knew, then, as he knew now, that what he was doing was rash, impudent, and preposterous; but, even with all that had happened since in mind, he admitted, as his eye waited for Letitia's shadow to cross the window again, that even now he would do the same, that he had not had the strength in him to resist, would not have it now.

He remembered that they had hardly spoken, all the way to the village. A frenzy of excitement had possessed him; they could not get there quickly enough to suit him; he was hardly aware of the unbroken silence into which Letitia had sunk.

After they had secured the license, the clerk offered his surprised congratulations and remarked: 'I suppose you're looking for Bishop Gregg, Doctor. He's just been in, asking the way out to your place.'

'The Bishop?' Philip echoed in astonishment. 'Where is he? Which way did he go? I didn't know he had left South Carolina, yet.'

'Well, he's here,' the clerk beamed, pleased to be the bearer of good news. 'He said he was going to baptize somebody's baby. Let me see, now, whose was it?' he meditated, raising his forefinger to forestall any interruption of his thought. 'Couldn't have been Jim Greene's; no, they're Baptists. Must have been the Briscoe baby — they're in town today.'

'Yes! yes!' Philip had answered hurriedly. It seemed to him a good omen that the Bishop, whose salary he had offered to help guarantee, should have chosen this day, of all days, to arrive in the county. For the moment the anxiety that underlay his excitement was stilled.

'I'll just look in here,' he said to Letitia, as they passed by their small white church, with a gleaming cross above it. 'There's a chance.' She nodded, holding out her hand for the reins, but said nothing.

He met Bishop Gregg at the door, with Mr. and Mrs. Briscoe, whose land joined Philip's, on its western edge. He smiled and bowed to them and took a peep at their baby boy, who was still asleep, unmindful that his sponsors had renounced for him the vain pomp and glory of this world and all covetous desires. Then he turned to the Bishop.

'I'm Philip Darcy,' said Philip, cordially holding out his hand. 'It's good to have you here. We've been at loose ends in this state. I wish I'd known you were coming so soon,' he apologized. 'We'd have met you, of course.'

From a glance, he knew what manner of man he was addressing. 'Just what we expected,' he meditated, taking in the Bishop's thoughtful eyes, set a little unevenly in his head, his head of thick hair brushed off his fine brow and then combed around his ears; his lips set somewhat aslant, like his eyes, in a face distinguished by the reserve of a scholar and the resolve of a man who has, once and for all, put his own desires aside.

'I am glad to be here,' the Bishop replied and looked keenly at Philip. 'I have had letters from you.'

Philip smiled. 'A good many. I didn't dare to hope you'd leave Cheraw. A beautiful place, as I remember it,' he said sincerely.

'It took me a while to decide,' the Bishop admitted. 'The opportunity at Sewanee interested me profoundly.' For a moment his gaze was abstracted, as if his mind were still torn. Then a warm flashing smile lit up his reticent face, and he turned to Philip with the expression of a man who has burnt his bridges behind him. 'I see now,' he said, his glance meeting Philip's, 'why you wrote as you did. The Church has an opportunity to win an Empire here — an Empire.' He stood watching Philip, his meditative gray eyes bent, not on him but on a kingdom like that which the abbot, Augustine, foresaw, when he first knelt on English soil, with his monks bowing in a long line behind him.

Philip was conscious that Letitia was outside, waiting for him to return, that Mr. and Mrs. Briscoe were standing in the doorway anxious to get started home. He saw that he must make his desires known at once.

'I'm doubly glad you've come today,' Philip remarked, and threw a glance in the direction of the baby's parents; 'and I hope that Mr. and Mrs. Briscoe will consent to stay and act as witnesses.'

'Witnesses?' The Bishop raised his eyebrows and smiled pleasantly at Philip, waiting for an explanation.

'We want you to marry us,' Philip said simply. 'Miss Letitia FitzHugh and me.'

Mr. and Mrs. Briscoe could not conceal their surprise, but Philip refused to recognize it, and, taking the Bishop's arm, led him down to meet Letitia.

He seemed startled by her youth. 'My dear child,' he began, taking her by the hand, and glancing doubtfully back and forth between her and Philip. The gold cross against his black cloth glistened in the sun, and Letitia watched it with a feeling that she could not take her eyes away from it. Then she roused herself and, stepping down on the ground, looked straight up into the Bishop's face. He saw then that she was not quite the child he had taken her to be.

Taking the license that Philip offered him, he examined it closely, making up his mind. There was probably more to this than he knew, he reflected. He studied them both carefully and decided on his course. They were not people whose intentions you could easily suspect; and this was the man who had first invited him out to Texas.

'Come in,' he told them, 'and God bless you both.'

At sunset they drove up to William's house, Philip remembered, forcing his thoughts relentlessly back through the day that he had married Letitia. Povey was on the gallery, seated beside William. Letitia walked straight up to him, not waiting for Philip.

'She didn't quail,' Philip thought, and marvelled now, as he had marvelled then, at the strange combination of gentleness and courage that dwelt side by side in her. 'And she hasn't since,' Philip admitted; 'not once.' He could hear her low voice now. 'Povey,' she had said clearly — Philip remembered her exact accent — 'I told you last night I would never marry you. I have just married Doctor Darcy, and, if God will help me, I am going to be a good wife to him.'

William's face registered the surge of anger that seized him, as he hurried to meet Philip. It was a long time, Philip recollected, before he and William had resumed their old association — not till after the twins, Felicia and Letitia, were born, and he had come back from Savannah with Cavin, just before the war broke out.

'I don't blame him; I didn't blame him then,' Philip reflected, remembering that time. He recalled, too, as if it were happening under his eyes, how Povey, hearing what Letitia said, had jumped to his feet, throwing a sudden horrified glance at her. It was enough to tell him that what she said was true, past undoing.

'God help us all!' he had cried out, and had flung himself on his horse. One day in the army when Philip was operating on a man without chloroform, he suddenly remembered how Povey had looked that night when he brushed past William's outstretched hand.

'As far as I know,' Philip thought, 'since then she has never spoken to him, nor he to her.' He corrected himself. 'I know they have never met. But all the time, all the time, I look at her and know it will never be any different. He's back, now. I hoped — God forgive me, it's true — I hoped he would die in prison. What do I care now what becomes of me?' he asked himself vehemently. 'What does anything matter?'

There flashed into his mind the old saying that all men succeed in killing what they love the most. 'It's true,' he thought. 'God! How pitifully true. Why are we made as we are?' It was not the first time Philip had asked himself that question.

'Never a day that I have not regretted that I married her,' he added grimly, 'never a day that I have not acknowledged my mistake. For her sake' — he corrected himself — 'for her sake only.'

He wondered if she had ever heard what William had told him — how before Povey's letter could have reached his fiancée in Fredericksburg, he had received one from her announcing that she, like Povey, had mistaken her youthful infatuation for something more lasting. She was marrying another man, she wrote Povey, in a month. If Letitia knew, she had never revealed her knowledge. But Philip had recalled the fact many times.

'Yes,' his mind ran on, facing the truth that his experience and his training caused him always to admit to himself, 'I had no business marrying her — none on earth.' His stern face grew gentle as he thought of the years he had had with her, years broken by the war and by his knowledge that Letitia was, in a sense, as much a stranger to him as on the day he had met her.

When he saw the twins, in their crib beside their mother, he had had a hope — how vain it was he had soon realized — that they would rouse Letitia from the apathy that had taken increasing hold of her since the full realization of her actions had swept in upon her.

'Not that she hasn't always done her full duty by them and by Cavin and me,' Philip admitted to himself. 'She loves the children — too much so, I sometimes think. FitzHugh has been a constant care to her, too, and he gets no better. Strange, I can't think what holds him back.'

For the moment, his mind wandered to the baffling illness of his youngest child, FitzHugh, now almost three, who had been born after Philip had returned to the army with the wound healed that had sent him home, quite early in the war, on leave. FitzHugh had always been a delicate child, finicky and exacting. Letitia had been tireless in her care of him, but Philip knew what it had cost her to bring him to this age. 'How on earth did she manage,' he thought, 'with a sick child and a plantation to run? And a war going on besides! It's a good thing,' he meditated, 'that our overseer had only one leg and couldn't go in the army.' For a moment his mind wandered to this man, Dennis Giles, whose leg had been so badly mangled in his youth by an infuriated alligator that it had had to be cut off at the knee.

'Even so,' thought Philip, 'he was the best overseer in the county.' He thought of him kindly and regretfully, and wished that he had been able to save his life when, in the middle of the past summer, he had suddenly fallen in the fields, seized with a heart stroke. Since then, Philip had tried to manage alone.

He gathered his thoughts together, and resolutely swung them back to the problem that faced him and never let him rest.

Inexorably, he forced himself to go over again the circumstances that were never quite out of his thoughts. He felt that he could not bear to go home with his mind as unsettled and torn as it had become these last few weeks.

'Great God!' he cried aloud in the dark, falling into the language he had taken to using in the army. 'Am I willing to let her pay for my happiness?' As he spoke the blood seemed to run out of his heart, and an actual physical weakness shook him, like an ague, in the saddle.

Relentlessly, however, he dragged the thought out and faced it. 'I must decide, and soon,' he groaned. 'But how?' He was back at the old impasse that the war had not settled.

His jaws clamped together as he recalled the events of the past few months.

In August, William had met Philip and, after some hesitation, had informed him that Povey was back, released from prison, and, for the time being, until he was stronger, was living at Holly Grove.

Until then, after his own return from South Carolina, where he had been invalided during the last months of the war, Philip had not allowed himself to think of Povey. Since then, he told himself, he had thought of little else.

It had been a week now since the day he had sought out William in his cotton fields.

'How does he feel about it?' he asked his cousin abruptly when, after some search, he came upon him. William was off his horse, testing out the fibre of the white fluff in the brown bolls.

'The rain's ruined it,' he replied absently, glancing up. 'The damned negroes say they have to have a contract now. What's going to happen, Philip?' He looked up, and what Philip had asked him at last penetrated through his own depression. It required only one glance at Philip's face for William to understand the implications of the sudden question put to him. He knew his cousin too well either to evade his inquiry or to try to soften his own reply.

'I don't know, Philip. He's never mentioned her name to me,' he answered quietly, 'not once since that night.' He saw that Philip knew instantly to what night he referred. Laying his hand on his cousin's saddlehorn, William's hesitant voice went on. 'But I think I ought to tell you. I have a note for her from him, to be delivered if I survive him.'

William's eyes searched Philip's face anxiously. For a long time Philip sat motionless, with his gaze clinging to a lone tree some distance away in the field.

'There are six forks to that branch,' he counted. 'Six.' Endlessly he went over the number: 'Six forks; one, two, three, four, five, six. Count again. Yes, that's right — six.' Once, in his training period, he had encountered a patient who had incessantly counted his fingers aloud, only ceasing when he slept. All at once Philip recalled the man's face; he had not thought of it in forty years.

With an immense effort, he dragged his eyes down to meet William's. His tongue was dry, and his voice sounded strange to him, as he opened his mouth.

'There are the children.'

'Yes, I know.'

'My God, William, what must I do?' The words seemed to take visible shape and float before him. 'What *can* I do?' he asked; and again, 'What *can* I do?' He was unaware that he was repeating the question.

He had been sitting so long on his horse watching the light in Letitia's room that one entire leg was asleep. He moved it impatiently, slapping it until the circulation began again to flow into it in long, prickly waves like, and unlike, actual pain.

Settling back in the saddle, he recalled how William had looked off over the field of cotton that morning, studying his reply. At last he raised his hand off the saddlehorn and laid it on Philip's arm.

'I can't answer that question, Philip. God knows I've tried to often enough.'

Philip knew now, as he sat in the dark, meditating his course that ever since that day he had known what he had to do, that there was nothing else, indeed, that he could do. 'Longer than that,' he admitted the truth. 'Since the day I married her, I've known.'

Suddenly he took a deep breath, and straightening his shoulders, gathered up the reins and put Pilot to a gallop. 'Right now,' he said, 'so I won't have to go through it all again.' Pilot jumped clear off the road, startled by the spurs that so seldom touched his coal-black sides.

Philip threw the reins to Matt, who, hearing the horse's hooves, had come out with a lantern to take Pilot to his stall. Hurrying up the steps, he entered the house and hung his saddlebags on a low chair that always stood beside the door. He had his hand on the doorknob to his right when Letitia turned it and, passing out, held up her finger, pointing to the room across the hall.

'All asleep,' she said. Then she glanced at his face. 'You've had no supper?' she asked. 'And you're tired. Sit there by the fire,' she said, motioning to a room at the end of the hall where a lamp was burning. 'I thought, when the norther blew up, you'd be chilly. I'll have something brought in.'

He paid no attention to anything she said; if the words registered in his brain, he gave no sign of having heard them. Letitia was moving off to summon the cook, when Philip reached out and drew her into his arms, cradling her there. His eyes roved over her face, examining it intently; he pushed her soft hair back off her forehead, and touched it lightly with his lips.

'You've a beautiful brow, Lettie,' he told her. 'The first time I saw you, I noticed it.' It was the first time he had spoken since he came in.

'Is that what you stopped me to say?' she asked him lightly. 'I should think ——'

He interrupted her. 'No.' He drew a breath, and hurried on. 'No, I stopped you to say that I intend to give you the children and your freedom. You know Povey is back?' he added quietly. It was over, now. Would he feel like this the rest of his life? 'Sixty-five,' he thought. 'Not long.'

His arms were still around her. He could feel her stiffen, till it seemed as if she had no breath. Her eyes stared up into his face, her own devoid of expression, and her lips, which were slightly open, whitened, but did not move. He was afraid to speak, as he watched her.

Suddenly, FitzHugh awoke and began to cry in a loud, terrified wail, as if dreaming. The sound aroused Letitia, and she tried to draw herself together.

'Sit down, darling,' Philip persuaded her. 'I'll go.' They had been standing beside a large chair, covered with red calico and padded with cushions. Philip remembered, as he had looked at it, that the first time Letitia had entered the door as his wife she had dropped into it, exhausted. 'Sit there,' he told her, motioning toward the chair.

She shook her head and leaned against him for a moment, trying to control the trembling that all at once began to shake her, like a chill.

'Come,' she said; 'he may be running a fever again.'

Together they went in to the child, soothing him back to sleep. A night lamp burned on the table beside the bed filling the room with a gray, cheerless light. Philip took up Fitz-

Hugh's little hand and felt his pulse carefully, timing it with his excited breathing. 'Just starting in the world as I'm leaving it,' he thought. 'Strange that I should have a child this age.'

'Nothing wrong,' he said aloud, in relief, studying the child's face. Letitia had been rearranging the covers on FitzHugh's bed. Now she raised herself and, putting one hand out to the bedpost, stood silent, satisfying herself that he was asleep. Philip marvelled at her composure; he felt his own slipping from him, and started out of the room.

'Philip!' Letitia's voice recalled him. He took a step backward, and faced her beside the child's bed, bracing himself for whatever he was to hear. It seemed to him that, as he waited, time splintered into fragments and reassembled again before his eyes.

Letitia's face, however, was calm and drained of feeling. Seeing her, Philip recalled a group of young nuns he had once met on the street in New Orleans. He had never forgotten their young eyes, so clear and childlike, under their flaring headdresses. They too had renounced joy before ever they had tasted it, he thought now.

Letitia looked past him, seemingly occupied with some knowledge or purpose that he did not share. At last she spoke quietly, as if what she had to say was of no special importance.

'Philip, I must tell you. In the spring, we are going to have another child.'

He stared at her, startled into immobility. Could it be true? He knew, as he looked at her, that it was.

A phrase that he had lingered over the night before, as he lay awake reading began to drum in his brain. 'What gods rule human destiny? What gods? What gods?' He repeated the words with no room in his mind for any other thought, feeling vaguely that, so long as he permitted nothing else to enter his consciousness, he might ward off the pain that already he felt pushing against the thin barrier thus erected between it and him.

Letitia turned toward him, with a sudden rush of pity. She wanted to tell him what she had already learned, what he was never to learn: how to build up around the core of his soul a region that would be numb, impervious to agony — impervious because hope and desire had already passed out of it.

But as she reached her hand to touch him, she knew that he would never walk on that road with her. As long as he was alive, he could not — would not — cease to struggle, or cease to wrestle with pain.

She dropped her hand. There was no use. How could she tell him all this? And if she could, how was he to understand, without the knowledge increasing his own despair? One thing she could tell him, though.

Laying her hands lightly on his cheeks, she stood watching him, it seemed to him hours, before her lips opened. 'I'll never leave you, Philip, never while I live,' she said at last.

He drew a sudden breath and dropped his arms around her, conscious that a stronger bond than young romantic love united them, for they were drawn together by a proud and common spirit that scorned to grovel before the chances of life. Each loved the other, in that moment, not as lovers, but, Philip suddenly thought, for the reason that God must love mankind — because they were poor, blind human beings set down in a world of mystery and confronted by questions that they could never hope to answer. There in the child's dark bedroom they clung together, like worn travellers on a long desert march, and each drew from the presence of the other a strength that sustained and comforted them both.

How long they stood there, they never knew; but at last

Letitia stirred. 'Come,' she said to Philip gently, as one urges an invalid who is recovering to take up his accustomed round of life again. 'Come and get your supper.'

'Yes,' Philip answered. 'Yes, of course.' But he did not move. Then she felt his muscles slowly growing tense, and his shoulders resuming their usual firm carriage. Stooping, he kissed her long and tenderly and stood at last erect. 'Yes, my dear; yes, of course,' he said again, more distinctly, and followed her to the fire, where a pot was bubbling on the coals which had been dragged out on the red hearth from beneath the blazing logs.

'When do you expect Cavin?' she asked him, trying to make her tone casual, as Aunt Emmy appeared in the door with a plate of hot biscuits.

Chapter 8

I⊤ was September 26, and a fine clear day. For almost the first time since the *Mary Frances* had put out from Savannah, she moved easily through long, gentle swells with the graceful motion that sail boats always appear to have in pictures. But most of the way the little vessel had pitched and rolled in heavy waves stirred up by the edge of an equinoctial storm into which she had run.

The first day out, the wind was high, blowing not in gusts, but with an increasing steady force which pressed the sea almost as flat on top as though a roller had passed over it. But the comparatively quiet surface masked a deep, surging motion that deceived only people unfamiliar with the usual course of such hurricanes. Cavin and Lucina noticed nothing strange to begin with, for the storm was accompanied by none of the roar they had learned to expect on land. At first, the long swells rose and fell in heavy, oily motion with only a sibilant, hissing sound as the wind bore down upon them, like a solid weight. Stripped of white caps, they rolled, like molten quicksilver, under the wan, yellow sky.

By morning on the second day, however, the ship was trembling and straining, torn between the gale and the waves; and, looking out, Lucina saw that a fine veil of spray covered the vessel, shrouding it from view. She shuddered. This was a phantom ship flying through some dim waste of eternity. Almost she expected to see the ancient mariner standing at its helm, with icicles hanging from his 'long gray beard' and from under his 'glittering eye.' She felt now the same uncanny, prickling fright that had always possessed her whenever Beauford, on winter nights, settled himself in his chair and began to read: 'There was a ship, quoth he.' Then the sailors took to making hurried trips up the tall, swaying mast, and Captain Baker, who had previously been the most agreeable of hosts, went by them in the passage with only a short, curt nod. Lucina fell into her berth, racked with seasickness; and Cavin went to hunt up the captain, whom he found intently scanning the sky, with his head turned sidewise, and his long nose pushed out to sniff the wind.

He looked excited and yet confident, like a man who might enjoy any kind of conflict. He glanced briefly at Cavin, and decided that Philip Darcy's boy would probably not be easily frightened.

'Looks like we're edging into a hurricane,' he remarked in an unhurried, conversational tone.

'Edging into it?' Cavin replied, and grinned. 'I supposed we were right in the middle of it.'

'Haven't you ever seen a blow?' the captain inquired. 'No? Well, I'm pretty certain we've missed the big storm,' he remarked critically, running his narrowed eyes across the sky and the waves, 'but there'll be enough going on as it is.' Throwing another appraising glance at Cavin, he continued: 'The devil of it is that after the wind dies down, then the waves try to suck you under. Best get your wife to bed. Maybe she'll sleep through the worst of it.'

As Cavin turned to go below, it required all his strength to pull the door open against the wall of wind pushing against it.

The storm endured and endured, day after day, while the

rain was blown, not in drops but in actual curtains of water against the boat, which, almost bare of canvas and stripped for battle, was yet sailing far off its course. The sailors had intended to catch fresh water for drinking, but so high had the spray been blown by the whipping wind that the rain was salt, like the sea.

It was a week before the heavens broke entirely free of cloud, under such circumstances as Lucina was always to remember. The whole occurrence was so strange and curious that, seasick as she was, and too weak to stand, yet, when Cavin came down to tell her what was happening, she dragged herself to the porthole to look out. He had to carry her back and lay her down among her pillows, but she never forgot what she saw.

The moon was shining in the clear night sky, floating as tranquilly over the turbulent ocean as it had floated over the fields and pines around Cedar Ledge. Yet, although they could not see a cloud, a downpour was falling from somewhere underneath the moon. They puzzled over the occurrence in vain until next morning Cavin came upon the captain studying his charts and asked him for an explanation.

Captain Baker hesitated, then with a wave of his hand invited Cavin to sit down beside him. 'I don't know exactly what happens,' he answered, 'but it looks like the rain, or the ocean spray, is blown so high and so far by the wind that it comes down, days afterward, in some other place, out of a clear sky. Plenty of queer things happen on the ocean,' he remarked, after a moment's silence. 'Once we picked up a baby floating in a trunk far out in the Gulf — a live baby, sound asleep. More than once I've wondered what story was behind *that*. Oh, yes,' he said, fixing his sharp blue eyes on the water and then on the horizon. 'There's plenty of things happen on the ocean — more'n you can make most people believe.' Pulling out his pipe, he eyed his listener closely. 'Would *you* believe it,' he asked with a half smile on his thin lips, 'if I told you that out from Old Point one day I saw a ——' He waited a moment, puffing hard and inspecting Cavin with a cautious eye. 'A sea serpent, I suppose. I don't know what else you'd call the damn thing.'

Cavin's face registered no surprise. 'Yes, I'd believe you,' he returned without hesitation. 'Of course I would. No man's been through a war ought to be fool enough to say what can happen and what can't.'

The captain threw an amused glance at his passenger, a glance that said as plainly as words that here was a man who knew how to talk sense.

'There's plenty of people don't like to admit the world's full o' surprises, though — plenty of 'em, sir.' He rose, put his pipe decisively in his pocket. 'Mostly city people and those that know too much.'

'Oh, city people!' Cavin remarked in a tone that matched the captain's.

Captain Baker stood watching him for a long moment, and then he began to chuckle, his eyes meeting Cavin's in complete accord.

'As for the smart ones,' he hazarded, 'do 'em good to live on a ship a while, I always think when I hear 'em talking.' His face, lighted by sharp eyes narrowed from much watching, slowly resumed its impassive lines. 'Or,' he conceded, 'fighting a war'd likely do 'em good, too.' A moment longer he stood meditating, and then took Cavin into his confidence. 'Lawd! I hate 'em worse'n poison,' he exclaimed explosively, 'all the people who know just four words, *'Tis so* and *'Tain't so.* Do you know what I think?' he asked dryly, but with a hot flash in his usually cool eyes. 'Give people like that the world to run, and they'd steer us all right square onto the shoals.' Shaking his finger in Cavin's face, he repeated his words, giving them added emphasis: 'Right square on the shoals. It'd never occur to 'em their charts might be off — never!' He rocked reflectively back and forth from toe to heel. 'If you ask me, that's what's the matter with the Yankees. They always know what's so.'

Cavin grinned. 'Yeah. I've met 'em,' he drawled ruminatively. 'One Yankee wanted to bet me a month's pay alligators didn't lay eggs. 'Twarn't reasonable, he said.'

Their eyes met and held, in thorough agreement.

'That's it.' Captain Baker's thin lips clamped together. 'That's it! How we're goin' to live with 'em, now? Can you tell me that?'

Cavin shook his head. 'I reckon we'll make out.' An odd smile crossed his face. 'Looks like we got to!'

'Well yes,' the captain agreed. 'I've always noticed a man does what he has to in this world.' A moment longer he sat still, looking at Cavin, then rose and stuffed his pipe in his pocket.

Two days out of Galveston the waves fell, and a light, steady wind began to blow. Cavin was so well trained to the sea by this time that he could tell by the feel of the ship's movement beneath him that only the surface of the water was now disturbed, not the great depths beneath. The air against his cheeks was warm and friendly; the sunlight glanced back into his eyes from an ocean that no longer was dull and leaden but blue and sparkling, with light, running waves dancing joyously across it in the same rhythmic motion that bends the grass on the prairie or dips the yellow daffodils to earth in spring.

He did not consciously think of the day as beautiful, or rejoice in their safety. He was not made that way. But as always in his life — in the war, in the longer war of Reconstruction, in his old age — a difficulty or danger once over and surmounted induced in him a kind of growing, heady excitement and a deep, almost passionate, joy in being alive, in breathing the sweet air, in moving his limbs upon the earth that he loved.

Unlike Lucina, who drew in the world through her eyes and ears, and, like Mary, the mother of Jesus, meditated on these things in her heart, Cavin had a more elemental kinship with the earth and the stars and the swift-flowing winds. He did not ever consciously take note of them, nor did he ever in his mind call anything beautiful or lovely. His feet seemed to draw up from the soil the strength of Antaeus; and he had no need to think about what he saw because he responded to it instantly, without thought. If he had lived to hear the expression creative evolution bandied about, he would have understood its meaning, drawing his knowledge not out of philosophy books, but straight out of his own sensations, the way John Locke believed men must.

For had he not always felt life flowing through him, defying death or any other obstacle? After Chickamauga, even while the dead lay unburied around him, and he himself lay on the rocky ground with a bleeding hole in his shoulder, he knew that he would live. How could he die — a man who touched the earth, as he did, with such warm, groping, loving fingers and caressed the sky with his eyes, even while the blood poured out of him? He did not think then that the earth was too lovely to leave, and Hades probably a dark and dreary place. Philip might have meditated on these matters, but not his son, Cavin. He never even thought of dying. He was only aware, as he lay there, of a kind of intoxicating delight in being still alive; it was as though some magnetic current from the earth passed directly into him, unifying his separate impressions into a strong and vivid sense of the life that flowed through him and (though he did not think of it in such terms) through the wide universe around him, too. It was a sense that he felt but never analyzed, and it burned like a flame within him after danger, after happiness, after even death or loss.

When he felt like this after his marriage, he always turned to Lucina, finding in her the completion of the strange and curious heightening of his own feelings. In time she learned to allow for the appearance of this fever in him, but never to understand it. Life flowed through her by a different channel altogether. She took it in, not so much by instinct as by thought and by prayer, though she did not often call it prayer.

She was therefore unprepared for the energetic delight that animated Cavin, who was usually so calm, as he burst into their cabin early that first morning, the third week in their voyage, when the sky cleared and the waves began to run steadily, like horses trained for a long race, toward the shore. Suddenly he felt, as he stood on deck and watched the sunrise, that there was nothing on earth he could think of that he wanted. To be alive was a joy, a thrilling pulse in his blood. Lucina must come up on deck with him, and feel what he was feeling. He forgot that he was returning without shoes to his feet; he forgot that he had a wife to support, that the years ahead promised no least security, none of any kind. He was conscious only of a fierce, exultant happiness that he wanted Lucina to share; and thinking so, he went down to get her.

She had awakened that morning, feeling refreshed and hungry for the first time in many a day. It was late when she stirred, and Cavin had been up for some time. When she heard a knock on the door she thought it was he, but it was Maria, who, pale but determined, came in with a jug of hot water and a dish of oatmeal.

'Lay still,' she cautioned her mistress. 'The cap'm tol' me to feed you lak a baby befo' you tried to get up. Warn't it awful?' she asked, gesturing vaguely with her full hands to indicate the terror she had felt.

Lucina swallowed the hot, salty gruel meekly, but stopped halfway through. 'There, Maria, you finish it.'

Maria rolled her eyes, and leaned against the narrow bunk, taking the dish from Lucina as she spoke.

"Fo' Gawd,' she told Lucina, 'I thought I was daid. Ain't you surprised to be alive? Jake's still a-prayin'; he's afraid de Lawd'll let de storm come back again, I reckon, ef'n he stops.' She held her spoon in the air and drank the last drops from the upturned bowl. Then, leaning back, she surveyed her mistress with an air of visible displeasure.

'Yo' har needs fixin', Miss Lucy, don't it?' she asked, cocking her head on one side so as to get a better view. 'An' I reckon I better git out de Florida water an' de sponge an' de towels. Dis heah is de fust water dey'd lemme have,' she remarked, glancing at the jug, 'an' dey says us has to be mighty sparin' wid it.' She looked at Lucina brightly, suddenly hopeful. 'Is dey right, Miss Lucina? Is we gwine-a land today at — whut's de name of dat ar place we's gwine to?'

'Galveston.' Lucina stretched herself, yawning. 'Galveston.' How marvellous to be married to Cavin, she thought, and to be exploring the world like this, with him! She hummed a tune, no longer missing Cedar Ledge, as she had in the long nights when the wind tore at the ship and she lay terrified and seasick in her berth, with Cavin up above helping the sailors.

'Galveston!' Maria repeated the word slowly. 'De name of dat place soun' plain indecent to me.' Lucina was never able to erase that impression from her maid's mind, try as she might. The first time that she took Maria back, to spend a summer

there, Maria cast óne horrified look at the swimming beach
filled with men, women, and children and agitatedly exclaimed,
'Didn't I tell you, Miss Lucy, dat dis heah warn't no decent
place? Jes' look out dar!' That later reaction was based on
this, her first attempt to repeat the name after Lucina, who
burst out laughing at sight of her maid's shocked face.

'Oh, María, how absurd! It was named, Cavin says, for a
man named Galvez. He was a Spanish governor, or something,
in Louisiana.'

Maria accepted the correction, but remained obviously un-
convinced by it.

'Don't you 'spect I better git you dressed an' ready now?'
she asked, politely turning the conversation. 'No telling when
us gwine-a git dar. Who gwine-a meet us, anyway, an' den
whut does us do, whar does us go?'

'I don't know!' Lucina cried, springing out of bed, 'and
what's more, Maria, I don't care.'

'Well, how's I gwine-a do yo' har when you jumps aroun'
like a flea? Tell me dat,' Maria retorted severely, and then her
face relaxed, and she smiled in anticipation of a surprise she
had been reserving for Lucina. 'Did you know,' she inquired,
her eager, dark eyes lighting up her thin, brown face, 'did you
know I brung along some cornmeal mixed wid some orris
powder Miss Ella gin me, fo' us lef' home? Set still, now, an'
I'll bresh it in and out yo' haid. Lawd, Miss Lucy, you'se sho
got a putty lot o' har,' she exclaimed as she began sifting the
cornmeal on her mistress's long black hair and brushing it out
in repeated, even strokes.

She had just finished dressing Lucina and was fastening
Margaret's slippers on her feet when Cavin put his face eagerly
in at the door. When he saw Maria, he chuckled.

'Well, Maria! The Lord spared you, didn't He?' inquired

Cavin. 'Last time I saw you, you were getting ready to die. Where's Jake? Go tell him he better quit praying now and come on up and help me.'

'Hurry up, Sweet,' Cavin urged her, when Maria had left.

Lucina caught the excitement in his voice and responded to it.

'Land'll be showing up before you know it, now.' His eyes were bright and his smile wide. He was standing with his back against the door and his arms held out invitingly. 'You better come kiss me, while you got a chance,' he advised her. 'I'm going to be a powerful busy man after we land.'

'How do you know I want to kiss you, anyway?' Lucina demanded, tilting back his head with her hands and pushing his hair away from his forehead. 'Maybe I don't,' she warned him, raising herself on tiptoe to smile into his eyes. Never, she thought, had she seen anybody's eyes so blue as Cavin's, with not a fleck of gray or brown in them.

Cavin laughed happily, dropping his arms closer around her. 'Oh, yes, you do,' he answered confidently, smiling down at her. 'Don't you?' He held her there for a moment, with his face above hers, taking in the white curve of her brow, her soft brown eyes, her smiling lips, and the poise of her head as she gazed provocatively up at him. The fragrance of her hair and the warmth of her slight figure poured through him like wine, and his arms tightened about her.

'Lucina!' he cried, looking at her with his heart in his eyes while he groped falteringly for words. 'You're sweet,' he told her at last, with the awkward shyness that all her life she loved in him.

What it was she could not have said that both hurt her and set her heart to pounding whenever Cavin looked at her like this, with all his defences down. Some vague, inexplicable sadness overtook her, but as quickly as it came, it went, leaving her swayed by a sweet and unfamiliar ecstasy that she could not name.

Upon deck the sun was high, and the air was like summer in upper Georgia. Lucina and Cavin stood by the rail, peering into the distance ahead where they could just make out the wavering outline of what appeared to be land. Like a narrow sandbar, the shadow stretched across the water, steadily growing broader and clearer as they watched it, until finally they could see its outlines plainly under the noonday sun.

Lucina, looking out across the water, was struck by the quality of the light that fell in blinding brilliance everywhere. 'It hurts my eyes,' she complained, blinking.

'It's always that way, unless it rains,' Cavin replied, laughing a little. 'Wait till you get out on the prairies; there the light sparkles on the grass, just the way it does on the Gulf. That's why Pa built his house on the Brazos in a grove of trees — so as to get shade. Though it's not much of a house,' he warned Lucina with a slight anxiety replacing his amusement. 'Big enough, but kind of bare and unfinished compared to Cedar Ledge. It's never even been painted,' he said slowly. 'I don't know what you'll think about it. Pa's never done much to it.'

'Still' — his memory groped hesitantly back to the time before the war, when he had lived in that house — 'still, there's a something about it — well, I don't know, I liked it,' he ended, unable to explain his liking. 'There was a fig tree by my room; I used to reach out through the window and pull figs, before I got up — big purple ones. And there used to be an owl in the chinaberry tree outside my other window.' He tightened his arm around her. 'You'll like it. I know you will,' he prophesied.

'Yes,' she said, 'I expect I shall.' She felt in a humor to like anything, as she leaned against him, watching the curving shore appear.

His eyes twinkled as he looked at her, and crinkled into folds at their corners. It was a perfect world, as far as he was concerned — an entirely perfect world.

Today, on the twenty-sixth of September — he put the date down in his mind to remember — he was starting his married life in Texas.

The land loomed ahead of them maddeningly close, but it took them until late afternoon actually to reach it. They drew in slowly, sounding every few moments for the shifting sandbars that sometimes unexpectedly appeared after a storm in the channel. Just when Lucina had decided they would never reach shore that night, they picked up speed, and before she expected it to happen the boat was creaking against the wharf of the warehouse, where thousands of bales of cotton and huge barrels of sugar-cane syrup and various wooden crates lay piled in great confusion, all awaiting shipment.

While the deckhands were making fast the ropes to the pier she looked around her curiously, noticing half a dozen ships besides theirs drawn up at the long wharf. She stared with intense interest at the banners above them. What countries did they represent? she wondered. This was a foreign land, indeed, this Texas Cavin had brought her to. Then, with a thrill of pleasure, her eye fell on one flag that she recognized. It was one which Beauford had many times pointed out to his children in the big map book that lay in his office. Lucina touched Cavin's arm.

'There's an English ship,' she told him, not knowing why the sight gave her a certain pleasure. Amidst all this strangeness, it was a symbol to her of old, remembered things, and far less alien to her now than the Union flag floating above the warehouse — a flag she associated with more recent enemies than the English.

'Cavin!' she said again; 'an English ship!'

'Oh,' he replied, indifferently, glancing in the direction where her eyes were turned. 'There are always lots of them here in dock.'

He watched carefully to see whether their luggage was being brought up, and then, when he knew exactly where their few belongings were stacked, he turned to her and amplified his last remark. 'They say that the Republic couldn't decide for some time whether to join the British Empire or the United States. Anyway, there are always plenty of English about.'

Lucina listened, slightly mystified. What was this Republic Cavin was always referring to? Everything about this bright, burning land was only a kind of diffused buzzing in her mind.

She did not know, as yet, that Texans were apt to refer to San Jacinto instead of Yorktown as the symbol of their liberties, and to speak of Spain and Mexico as easily as of England. She did not realize either that, as a boy, Cavin had listened hour after hour to men talking who had helped to establish the Republic, men who had entered the Union under a treaty, expecting to withdraw when, or if, it pleased them to do so. It took her months to see that this fact explained why the sadness of defeat in Georgia blazed in Texas to a hotter, more defiant wrath. All she felt as she first stepped on Texas soil was that this was a strange land to which she had come, a land whose history was not yet laid down in her bones, as it was, apparently, in Cavin's.

Yet, her heart acknowledged, not altogether a strange land. For were there not Georgians already in it? And did not Texans and Georgians lie buried together from Virginia to Tennessee? Soon, she resolved, she would know what Cavin was talking about whenever he casually mentioned, as he so often did, the names every Texan seemed to have at his tongue's end: San Felipe. The Alamo. Goliad. San Jacinto. Travis. Houston. Fannin. Lamar. She called them off, like a roll. The Republic — soon she would be able to use the word as easily as Cavin.

Cavin had been leaning over the railing, impatient to be on shore. Almost before the boat was made fast to the dock he was on the wharf, holding out his hand to Lucina. Her knees shook beneath her, but she raised her head and walked firmly ashore.

Captain Baker followed them, approaching Cavin with a slight frown between his brows.

'Galveston's swarming with Yankees,' he remarked. 'Has been all summer, of course. But I've just been told that General Gregory is here setting up the Freedman's Bureau' — he made a gesture of distaste — 'and things are especially wild right now.' He looked from Cavin to Lucina, thinking how he had best state the facts without alarming her. No use beating around the bush, he decided. She'd have to learn how things were, sooner or later. 'Every Unionist in the state has rushed down here to get his name in for the pickings, and the town's running over with drunk negroes,' he explained. 'You all better plan to stay on board tonight, hadn't you?' The way he put the question showed that it was his own opinion.

Cavin was eager to be off, but as the sun was near setting, he realized they would not get far, even if they started, that night. Besides, was there anyone to meet them? He turned the possibilities over in his mind.

'Maybe I better go out and look around a little,' he decided. 'Lucina can stay with you, I suppose, Captain?' he inquired.

This business of having a wife made a man mighty cautious, he thought, taking out his pistols and looking them over.

'I'm coming along,' Lucina answered firmly. 'Though I appreciate Captain Baker's courtesy, of course.' She smiled at the captain and laid a determined hand inside Cavin's arm. 'I'm coming right along with you.' He saw, as he glanced doubtfully at her, that her mind was made up. 'Well,' he said, dropping his pistols back in his belt and tightening it, 'I reckon I can look after you.' Then he turned to Jake.

'Don't you get off this boat,' he warned him. 'Stay right here with Maria. We'll be back in a couple of hours, at most. If we don't, you'll look us up, Captain?' he said to his host. 'I don't expect any trouble, though. Come on, Lucina,' he said, drawing her hand closer. 'I expect Pa's sent a wagon to meet the boat, but Lord knows where the drivers are — probably all drunk. We better round them up, or figure out some other way to get started in the morning.'

They walked to the front of the warehouse, from which a long wooden sidewalk led across the sandy beach to the town, which lay some distance back from the shore, with the cathedral looming high above it. Approaching it, they soon realized that Captain Baker's information had been correct. The place was crowded with half-drunken white soldiers in blue uniforms and with entirely drunken negroes who had rushed down to Galveston expecting to receive, not the freedom the Bureau offered, but money, horses, mules, land.

The Northern officers were unprepared for this evidence of how frequently those who have cast off their chains prefer booty to redemption. Nor were they used to handling importunate black men who demanded the moon, and who, not getting it, curled up on your doorstep and promptly went sound asleep. Or else became drunk and violent. The responsible officers reflected uneasily that half of these negroes ought to be in jail; but wouldn't *that* move make a fine impression on the Reconstruction authorities? And in case Sheridan, sitting down at New Orleans in charge of the Fifth Reconstruction District, took a dislike to you, where could you get a job half as lucrative as this promised to be? The upshot was that the town was on the verge of a riot.

Cavin could not help but laugh out loud when he saw all the negroes milling around.

'La!' he said to Lucina. 'They act just like our hands at a good old shouting revival!'

It was clear to him that they regarded this occasion as some kind of a celebration like Christmas Eve, or a barbecue. The few who were sober stood around in groups with good-natured, expectant faces, looking exactly like the servants at Locust Hill, Cavin remembered, when his father was distributing new garments or an extra issue of rations. Most of them, however, had had far too much liquor and lay stretched out too drunk to move, their woolly black heads flat against the white crushed shell that covered the sidewalks.

'Gosh! They'll have a time getting that out of their hair,' Cavin remarked to Lucina, laughing as he passed the recumbent figures.

A few Union officers were trying desperately to maintain order, but their efforts made little impression on the crowd, through which Lucina and Cavin walked almost unnoticed, for Confederate uniforms were still too commonly worn on the Galveston streets to arouse the least notice. Cavin felt no special alarm until they passed a company of black soldiers parading in the street, all heavily armed.

He then urged Lucina around a corner, toward the residential section, planning to return to the boat by a longer route that would skirt the offices of the Bureau where the largest crowd was gathered. He would leave her there on the boat, he decided, and start out again, by himself, to see whether he could find the wagons, which, he felt confident, Philip had sent to meet him. The town was in worse confusion than he had thought possible when he agreed to let Lucina accompany him.

Along the quieter streets, however, there was little excitement; all of the noise and rioting was apparently centred around the offices of the Bureau and the waterfront. Here on the back avenues, children were playing in large yards enclosed by white palings or wrought-iron fences, and a few people were setting out to town, walking unconcernedly along under the chinaberry trees.

Cavin felt his anxiety slacken, and lingered to point out to Lucina how many houses in Galveston were set up on extremely high pillars, with the space underneath them paved in red brick and used for cool outdoor sitting-rooms. Some of the houses, she noticed, had graceful, curving steps which led up, by a double approach, to high, wide balconies screened with vines and overlooking side gardens still full of brilliant color. The streets seemed vaguely familiar, and all at once she knew they reminded her of Savannah. So did the white houses with double galleries onto which long doors, flanked with green blinds, opened, and the rows of palms and oleanders, and the grassy lanes between the curbs. Still, there was something different about the place. As she walked along, she decided that it was less planned, less elegant, perhaps; and certainly there was an even more luxuriant growth of foliage here than at home. Lemon trees, banana plants with long, glossy leaves, and roses were everywhere — deep yellow roses, almost golden, lightly tinged with crimson. Their heavy fragrance hung suspended in the warm evening air, and, with it, the smell of mint and sweet lavender. Ah! yes, there was something in this strange country she could call her own — the air she breathed. No, even that had a latent aroma that she now began to sense more and more, as the rising breeze blew in from over the water. 'Salt,' she thought. 'Of course, that's it, salt.' She drew closer to Cavin, and they stood watching the sunset, listening to the booming sound of the surf against the shore, a mile or more away.

As the coolness of night came on, and the Gulf breeze swept over the island, people began to come out on the streets in increasing numbers. Avoiding the district where the Bureau was located, Cavin and Lucina walked along the back avenues that he remembered from his boyhood when he had accompanied Uncle Matt to Galveston to receive supplies shipped in from New Orleans and London — oatmeal and smoked fish and bitter marmalade, brandy, coffee, bananas, and Jamaica rum.

'It's not like this out in the country,' Cavin warned Lucina, waving his hand to take in the gardens and the streets bordered with flowering shrubs, the immaculate white houses, and the freshly dressed children guarded by black nurses in white kerchiefs. 'Galveston is the' — he hesitated, not knowing just how to make his point — 'the Savannah of Texas,' he went on, repeating Lucina's own thought. 'It's full of people from New Orleans and Pass Christian, and English cotton firms have representatives living here. Still, I like it better on the plantation,' he said, already feeling the uneasiness that cities never failed to arouse in him.

Lucina's ear picked up what Cavin's had missed — that among the people they passed on the street there were some speaking a tongue she had never heard before. She pulled on Cavin's sleeve and spoke so softly that he had to bend his head to hear her.

'Who are those people?' she asked him. 'Listen.'

'Who?' Cavin responded, taken by surprise. 'Who do you mean? Oh,' he went on, following her eyes, 'they're Germans. There are lots of them in Galveston, nearly all Unionists, too, though not all,' he explained. 'There were some Germans — as brave as anybody — in Hood's army, and they hadn't a slave to fight for.' He paused there, meditating. 'Most of the Texas people who voted four to one for secession had no slaves, anyhow. Well,' he shrugged his shoulders, 'I was talking about the Germans. Most of them go on out to West Texas, where they like the climate better. Pa came in once to get a gardener out of the crowd that landed from one boat, but they were all teachers and people like that. No gardeners.'

The account aroused other memories in Cavin's mind, which he proceeded to share with Lucina. He smiled as he remembered some Germans who had settled in a corner of Cypress County, trying to raise huge blue turkeys for a living.

'They used to drive droves of 'em into Houston and Galveston, pushing them along with crooked sticks just like cowboys driving cattle,' he told Lucina. 'You've never seen cattle drives either, have you?' he asked her, struck with the thought. 'You've got a heap to learn about this country, haven't you?' He stopped short, suddenly conscious of all the things he ought to explain to her. Where should he begin? He seized on the first thing that came into his mind. 'Texas cattle now — you mustn't treat them like milch cows in Georgia. You'll see them on the prairie, on our way home — big, rangy beasts with long horns. They'll run you through in a minute and stomp you to death, if they get a chance. Well that wasn't what I was talking about, either, was it?'

Intent on what she saw around her, Lucina was only half listening. She was so absorbed that Cavin, too, fell silent, and be-

gan closely scrutinizing the people that they passed. He noticed, then, that nearly all those who were not in uniform, men
and women alike, wore on their clothes some mark to indicate
whether they were Confederates or Unionists. In their lapels
or on their shoulders they had pinned small flags or twisted
ribbons, and strangers exchanged quick, searching glances as
they passed, to see whether they were approaching friend or
foe.

'Look, Lucina!' Cavin said, pointing out what he had observed. 'Probably they don't want any more arguments than
they can help. Wonder when the Yankees took possession of
this town, anyway?' He realized, all at once, how long it had
been since he had received any Texas news.

'Well!' she exclaimed proudly, throwing up her small, sleek
head, 'that's one thing we don't need to do in Georgia. Everybody knows what side we are on.' She could not imagine existing, as the citizens of Galveston had had to learn to do, under
the very heel of their foes, and surrounded by people that had
opposed secession from the beginning. In her county in Georgia,
she had never met a single Unionist in her whole life.

But Cavin could understand how the citizens of Galveston
had worked out a way of living together, without drawn battle,
even under the circumstances that now surrounded them.
During the war, encamped before Chattanooga, he himself
had crept down, night after night, on his stomach to talk, across
a narrow creek in whispers, to a Northern boy only a little
older than himself. Now, recalling that boy and the food he
had sometimes saved from his own supper to offer to his Southern enemy, Cavin tried to put his feelings into words.

'Some Yankees are all right, Lucina,' he hazarded. 'If they
just don't push us too far, we ought-a could manage to get
along somehow with them.'

He wished that he knew what had become of the blue-coated boy who, one night, had silently handed him, across the creek, a sandwich and an apple. Even yet, his mouth watered as he thought of how good the food had tasted, as he lay on his stomach in the mud biting into it, and how it had, for a time at least, assuaged the terrible craving inside him.

'Ugh!' cried Lucina, suddenly shrugging her slight shoulders in writhing disgust. 'They're like flies — everywhere. Let's get started, Cavin, right away. See, it'll be moonlight.' She threw out her hand to where the moon now hung, enormous and golden, low over the town, and shuddered. 'I can't bear staying here.' It was the first time she had seen so many blue uniforms since Sherman's troops had marched into the garden at Cedar Ledge, trampling it under foot.

Suddenly Cavin felt the same haste to leave Galveston, to get out into the open prairie, to reach Locust Hill Plantation. Unconsciously he still thought of it as unchanged by the war. Once there, he felt, with his feet on his own soil, he could begin life in earnest. Here in Galveston he felt disturbed and uneasy. The sight of so many Yankee soldiers about was beginning to make an impression on him that he could not shake off. Maybe a man couldn't even farm to suit himself, with all these soldiers about. 'Well, we'll see,' he thought; and rubbing his chin thoughtfully, he met Lucina's anxious eyes.

'I'd like to move out of here, myself,' he admitted, 'but I haven't located our wagons yet.' Quickening his steps, he said: 'Let's get back to the boat. Maybe Matt's already there.'

As they drew close to shore, Cavin looked up and down the waterfront, scanning it closely, to see whether he could pick out Philip's mules from among the wagons and teams tied to hitching posts beside the wharf. So occupied, they were almost upon the *Mary Frances* before he was aware either of their nearness to it or of the negro soldier approaching them on the narrow plank walk, reeling as he walked.

Lucina saw him, however, and stopped dead in her tracks, fearing what she knew would happen if they met him on the passage that was, at best, barely wide enough for two. She knew that one of the men would have to step down in the sand, and she was positive that Cavin would not be the one to do so, nor would he permit her to move aside by so much as a hairsbreadth. Her sudden pause halted Cavin also, but only for a moment. Taking his decision almost unconsciously, he threw Lucina behind him with one hand, and with the other drew the pistol from his belt.

The huge negro saw the gesture and, inflated with arrogance, was just drunk enough to defy it. He took several uncertain steps, weaving a crooked course back and forth across the walk, waving his gun in front of him, and cursing in a variety of expressions that amused Cavin even as he pulled his pistol.

Realizing instantly that the Freedman's Bureau would probably hold him in jail for so much as touching one of their charges, Cavin first hoped, as he watched the soldier, to shove him off balance and seize his gun, but with Lucina behind him, he dared not risk missing his hold. Also he knew — and he did not have to take time to formulate the idea — that white people could not long continue to live in Texas if they once began stepping aside for their former slaves.

Almost automatically, his mind made a clear path through the choices he had, and, raising his pistol, he called out to the soldier to halt instantly where he was. His voice penetrated through the mist that covered the negro's mind, and some old habit of obedience reasserted itself in him. For a second he paused, motionless, and his arm fell.

That instant was enough, however, to give Jake, who had

watched the encounter from on deck, time to reach the spot and fall upon the colored soldier from behind, throwing him fiercely to the ground. His head hit the boards with so loud a thud that Cavin thought it must have cracked, and he lay still, stunned by the fall.

Stooping, Cavin unstrapped the negro's cartridge belt and gun, handing them to Jake, and slipped his own pistol back into its holster. Pushing the soldier off onto the sand with his foot, he turned a surprised face to Jake. 'Well, for the Lord's sake! How'd you happen to be here?' Then, for the first time, he observed that they were almost at the boat, where Captain Baker was standing on the gangplank, his rifle now dropped to his side and his face expressing the relief he felt, as Lucina and Cavin reached the wharf where he was anchored.

'By George!' the captain exclaimed, 'I thought I was going to have to kill that damned nigger, but I was afraid I'd hit you, too, if I started firing. Then I saw Jake making for the brute and I figured that was the best way out of it. Lord! you ought to have seen your boy,' he said, addressing Cavin. 'He made the distance between here and that creature' — he pointed to the still motionless soldier — 'in one jump, I do believe.'

'Sho,' said Jake, ''twarn't nothin' else *to* do.'

Cavin put his hand on Jake's shoulder and breathed deeply, three or four times. 'Boy,' he said at last, 'you've earned your freedom all right.' Jake seemed unimpressed by the remark and gazed mildly at his master, his blue-black face suffused with a grin.

'Dat nigger was plain lookin' for trouble,' he announced and grinned wider, showing all his white teeth in a pleased smile. 'Us gin it to him all right, didn't us?'

Cavin continued to stare at his servant and then smiled as broadly as Jake. 'Well,' he said, 'I reckon you've earned the shirt I've got on, besides, if you want it.'

Jake's face brightened perceptibly. 'Dat shirt *is* gittin'' mighty thin and old, Mas' Cavin. Dat's de truf,' he agreed, joining heartily in the laughter that followed his response.

'Here, Cavin, take this,' Lucina said, handing back his pistol.

'Where'd you get it?' he asked her in astonishment, feeling under his coat.

'Why,' she said calmly, 'I slipped it out while you were drawing yours.' Suddenly she was conscious of a creeping terror coming over her.

'Let's start, Cavin,' she implored him. 'Right away.'

Captain Baker leaned back, throwing his weight on his firm brown hands and clasping the boat's railing behind him. His eyes were narrowed and speculative under his eyebrows bleached almost white by the sun and wind. He pursed his lips, whistling softly. Obviously he was making up his mind. Suddenly he turned toward Cavin and addressed him directly.

'You've brought the right kind of wife to Texas, sir,' he said admiringly, 'and I expect her judgment is pretty nearly right about leaving tonight. When that nigger starts to making trouble, you'd better be out of town. They'll never send after you — too much to do here.' He took his hands off the railing and leaned forward, fixing his blue eyes soberly on Cavin's. 'Last time I was in port,' he announced in a cold, dead-level tone, 'they were trying a man for shooting a black soldier who had dragged his daughter off her own front gallery one night. Only reason they didn't hang him was because his friends rubbed the nigger jury's palms with gold.'

Cavin listened without comment.

'Yes,' Captain Baker went on, eyeing the black figure that lay stretched out on the white sand in the moonlight, 'I expect you better get out, quick as you can. No use deliberately courting trouble, in these times. There's plenty you can't avoid,' he concluded.

Cavin nodded. The advice sounded reasonable to him. 'I'll go see whether any of the mules and wagons tied down there by the wharf are ours. No, not this time, Lucina,' he said firmly, as she half-rose. 'I'll have to hunt Matt up, too,' he informed the captain.

'I'll take *you* along, Jake,' said Cavin, abruptly turning to his servant. 'See if that pistol you've got's working. Don't draw if you can help it, though,' he cautioned him sternly.

As Lucina watched Cavin reloading his long black pistols, she suddenly recalled the pearl-handled ones that always lay in a purple velvet case beside her father's bed. Many afternoons, before the war, as she began to grow out of childhood, he had taken them out and had her aim at a target, under his direction, showing her how to place her weight and stretch out her arm. In Texas, apparently, she meditated, guns were not laid away in velvet cases.

She watched Cavin and Jake moving in and out the mules and wagons some distance below her on the sand. They were carefully examining the mules' ears, why she could not imagine.

'Two long slits and one short, in the middle. That's our mark. Remember, Jake?' Cavin asked his black boy. 'Check up on this row, and I'll take the next.'

'Reckon dey's branded?' Jake answered, peering at the brown flanks of the animals. 'Most of our'n was branded, warn't dey, wid dis-heah mark?' He drew in the soft white sand with his toe a figure made up of the initials L H for Locust Hill.

Cavin looked down at the firm white sand and saw drawn in it the brand ⊢. 'Yes, of course, that's it; that's Pa's brand. But mostly he uses it on his cattle, not his mules. Still, you might look; it's plenty light to see.' He threw a glance upward at the full moon now riding overhead. 'No trouble travelling this kind of night,' he remarked to Jake.

'Naw, suh,' the negro replied uneasily. 'I plain don't like dese-here nigger soljers dey gots aroun' heah. Looks lak dey's layin' fur trouble evy time dey turns aroun'.'

Cavin was too occupied to answer. He moved up and down the long rows of animals, now unhitched from their wagons and tied with long ropes to cedar posts set some distance back from the high-tide mark. Their front feet were hobbled, so they could not wander far, even if they managed to work their halters loose. There were water troughs close by, and places for feeding the animals. In some of the wagons, their negro drivers lay asleep, guarding their masters' property, and ready for early loading when the sun began to rise over the water.

'Here's Colonel Brashear's team,' Cavin called out to Jake, recognizing a neighboring planter's wagon-train by the three short slits in the mules' ears. 'Lord! I'd forgotten all about tassels on bridles.'

Cavin felt vaguely excited and pleased to see the Brashear mules bridled, despite the war, as they had always been — with good steel bits in their mouths, instead of rope, and red silk tassels floating below their ears. Yes, they were fat and round, too, well cared for. Obviously food supplies were not so scarce in Texas as in Georgia, and not all the work animals had been seized by the Confederate government.

'Ours ought to be along here somewhere, Jake. Pa and Colonel Brashear usually sent their hands in together. Look sharp, now. I know Pa was expecting me on this boat. He'd have had somebody here.'

But their search was fruitless. No Locust Hill mules were on the beach, and no wagons either.

'We'll have to go up in town and find Uncle Matt, Jake,' Cavin decided. 'You run back to the boat and tell Miss Lucina where we are going, and not to be worried if we don't get back till late. I'll stay here,' he concluded, throwing himself down on the sand to await Jake's return.

He lay with his hands under his head staring up at the moon, over which now and then white clouds were floating, momentarily gleaming like silver against the vast dark sky. The waves broke with an incessant rushing hiss and roar upon the long white beach, and the warm October air was so full of salt that when he put out his tongue he could taste the brine on his lips. He stretched out his long legs and yawned, settling his hips comfortably into the white, drifting sand.

While he could, he took his rest, just as, in the army, he had always been able to sleep undisturbed by thoughts of coming battle or of past misery. But deep inside him, unknown to him, his attention kept guard. This was an attribute he shared with Philip — the ability to take momentary rest in the centre of turmoil and then to spring up instantly at call, ready for action.

Before Jake reached him, he heard across the sands the echo of the negro's quick running steps and knew, before he arrived, that he had news of some kind to report.

'Uncle Matt's at de boat, now, waitin' fur us, wid de teams an' all de hands whut ain't run off. Miss Lucy is already a-settin' in de wagon.' He paused to catch his breath, then added, 'Matt's been havin' a heap o' trouble o' some kine.'

Cavin was on his feet and had started toward the boat before Jake had finished his recital. Uncle Matt saw him coming and hurried to meet him on the sand, his long white whiskers blowing in the breeze and his hair shining like a halo under the moon.

'Lawd Gawd! Mas' Cavin. I nebber would a knowed you!' he exclaimed, his face expressing the relief he felt at being able to turn over his responsibilities to Cavin. 'I wuz lookin' fur a boy lak you wuz when you run off to de wah,' he continued, in an apologetic, surprised tone, 'an' heah you is, as big as yo' pa, comin' home wid a wife to boot. Well, I be doggoned, it do beat all.' He stood off, admiring the man Cavin had become.

Cavin laid his arm around Matt's shoulders. The old man had often sung him to sleep, singing over and over again, till his own eyes closed, some melody that Cavin had never known by name.

'My gran'pa, or some o' my folks way back yonder wuz a king in Af'ica,' Matt always told him before he began to chant, 'an' dis heah song I'm singin' you is whut de witch-gals uster sing in front o' him, in de dark o' de moon to raise sperits. Don' ask me no mo', caze I ain't gwine to tell you.' And he would remain stubbornly silent, despite all Cavin's pleadings.

'Well, I reckon I am most too big for you to sing to, now, Uncle Matt,' Cavin admitted, 'but I'm mighty glad to see you. How's Pa?'

'Dey's well; dey's all well, Mas' Cavin, all 'cep'n FitzHugh. He mighty po'ly.'

'FitzHugh?' Cavin broke in. 'Who's FitzHugh?'

'Ain't you heared? Lawdy-me!' Matt grinned. 'Time you wuz comin' home, when you don't know your own brudder.'

'That's right,' agreed Cavin. ''Tis time! Well,' he laughed, 'they don't know I have a wife either, for that matter. Tell me about Pa.'

'Um-m-m,' Uncle Matt answered regretfully; 'yo' pa ain't as young as he wuz when him and me took off fur Texas, an' dat's de truf.' Then his recent experience flooded over his lips. 'I'se mighty sorry to be so late gittin' heah, suh; but my Gawd-a-mussy!' he declared in a burst of wrath, 'dem Yankees is de Dickens an' Tom Walker. Dey's struttin' aroun' lak dey owns de roost, an' a man cain't tuhn aroun' widout bumpin' into 'em. Dey had me tied up wid dem agents till right now, wid all yo' pa's cotton waitin' to git on dis-heah boat.' His indignation boiled completely over. 'Dey oughta roas' in hell, all dem mens at de whut-you-may-call-it-place.'

'Bureau?' Cavin supplied the name and saw that it was correct. 'I knew something was up.' He looked inquiringly at Uncle Matt. 'You better tell me just what happened.'

'Well, suh,' Uncle Matt groaned, 'dey tuck charge o' me on de aidge o' town, as I was a-bringin' in de waggins full o' cotton, an' dey got me in a little bit of a room about so big ——' Here he threw out his arms in disgusted measurement.

'Whut do you reckon dey wanted me to swar?' he demanded, eyeing Cavin with indignant scorn in his eyes. 'Dey wanted me to swar 'twarn't Mas' Philip's cotton *a-tall* I wuz bringin' to de boat, but some dat belonged to de Confedrig govament; an' den dey said ef'n I'd swar to de fack dat it was govament cotton, dey'd pay me so much.'

He turned a puzzled face toward Cavin. 'Dey says now a nigger's swar is as good as a white man's, an' yo' pa say so, too. Is dat right, Mas' Cavin?'

Cavin nodded shortly. 'They seem to think so, Uncle Matt.'

'Lawd Gawd!' sighed Uncle Matt. 'All dat soun' pow'ful curious to me.'

Cavin smiled. 'To me, too,' he agreed. 'Well, go on, Uncle Matt. What'd you tell the man?'

Uncle Matt replied hotly. 'I tol' him I raised dis cotton, an' it was dis yeah's crap, when dar ain't no Confedrig govament no mo'; an' dey said I wuz a crazy ol' fool, an' I kep' worryin' 'bout meetin' you, an' dey kep' on sayin' dey wuz gwine-a mark it U.S.A. anyway, but dat it would set better wid dem up above 'em ef'n dey had *my* swar, to hand in wid *dair* papers. I reckon I'd a' been dar yet,' he concluded morosely, 'ef'n Cunnel Rutherford — you remembers him, Cunnel Wharton Rutherford whut handles yo' pa's cotton? — hadn't dropped in. De Lawd sont him, dar ain' no doubt about dat.' Solemnly he nodded his old white head up and down in confirmation of his last remark.

Cavin controlled his impatience, knowing there was no use on earth trying to hurry Uncle Matt's account.

'What happened then?'

'Well, he say he walkin' by an' notice Mas' Philip's waggins out dar in front, an' he ask me, "Whut's going on here?" But he seem to know widout askin', case right off, fo' I kin say a word, he turn aroun' to de men at de desk an' say sort o' snappy and short-like, "How much?"'

'De man study him a minute an' den say, "Same as las' time." Den Cunnel Rutherford say, "Come 'roun' to my office an' git it in de mawnin'. Now let dis ole nigger go put his cotton in my shed." Dey seems to know he takes keer o' yo' pa's business. Den dey lemme go,' he said with a long sigh of relief, 'an' I lit out, an' heah I is.'

Pausing, he began to run his fingers through his pockets. 'I mos' forgot,' he explained. 'Cunnel Rutherford gimme a bunch o' papers. Heah dey is,' he said, stretching out his black hand, with the papers resting on his pinkish-yellow palm.

Cavin took them and scrutinized them closely. 'You can mighty near read by this moon, but not quite,' he concluded, sticking them in his own pocket. 'I'll look 'em over, quick as I get to the boat.'

'I suppose you brought a tent along and some cover?' Cavin asked, as they turned back.

'Yas-suh. Yo' pa saw to all dat de las' thing fo' we started.'

'And are the hands all at the boat?'

Uncle Matt's face lengthened. 'Dat wuthless Ned got drunk fus' thing, an' three-fo' mo' o' de young hans wid him. Eph tell me 'bout it, when I come out de treasure agent's place. You remembers Eph? Ole one-eyed Eph? He's heah, an' I reckon dars a plenty men lef' to drive de waggins, but I'se los' some o' Mas' Philip's hans. You reckon I better go hunt 'em up?'

'No,' said Cavin, hotly. 'Let 'em alone. They'll be coming back quick enough, same as they did to Cedar Ledge, soon as they get hungry or sick.' He started impatiently toward the boat, with Uncle Matt and Jake following him. 'I had a little run-in myself, Uncle Matt, with a drunk soldier just before you turned up,' he explained, 'and I reckon I better be getting out o' here.'

'Lawd Gawd!' Uncle Matt exclaimed in open horror. 'Us better hurry! Dey throwed a white man in jail las' week, I heared 'em sayin' tonight, jus' fur talkin' rough to some impedint nigger.' He caught up with Cavin and passed him. 'I better see, is us ready to pull out.'

Cavin stopped him. 'You must have some supplies to get, don't you? Let me have your list.' He held out his hand and the negro, after fumbling around in his clothes, produced a dirty slip of wrinkled paper.

'I done got eveything,' Uncle Matt assured him. 'De man at de supply-house called off de order to me, an' I put 'em in de waggins myself.'

'Then we're set to go?' Cavin inquired.

'Yas-suh, ef'n my young mistis is.'

'Looks like she's all ready.' Cavin pointed to Lucina, who was seated on the first wagon in line, with the baggage piled behind her and Maria sitting beside it. Captain Baker was standing with his foot on the wagon hub and the lines in his hand, chatting with her.

'She kine o' quick-on-de-trigger, seem lak,' Uncle Matt grinned.

Cavin paused only to smile at her in passing, and then went below to examine the papers in his hand.

'Coffee, salt,' he read, holding the paper to the flickering yellow light of an oil lamp screwed into the cabin's wall. 'Thread, lavender soap, mackerel, blue denim, red calico, chewing plug.' His eye ran down the page and he smiled. The list was not much different from the ones he had carried into Galveston before the war. Texans, he thought suddenly, could still send for salt and expect to get it. Yes, everything was checked off, as Uncle Matt had said. He was up the narrow steps in three leaps, and, after shaking hands with Captain Baker, climbed up beside Lucina on the wagon seat.

'Hop in behind with Maria, Jake. Uncle Matt, you better get some rest. Tell the other hands to fall in and I'll see 'em all when we make camp. Holler when the last wagon's ready to start.'

'Wait a minute,' Captain Baker said, and hurried below. On his return, he handed Cavin a shotgun and a rifle, and some ammunition.

'You have only your pistols?' he inquired. 'I thought so. You better take these along, too. No telling what you'll run into between here and the Brazos. Good luck!' He seized Cavin's hand and bowed to Lucina. 'I hope you'll honor my ship by sailing with me again, Miss Lucy.'

Matt, from the end of the wagon-train, waved his hat in the air and whooped twice in a high sharp voice that the mules recognized. At the same instant the drivers cracked their black, snake-like whips, making a sound like exploding firecrackers, and immediately the teams began to pull. Cavin, looking back, signalled to Uncle Matt, who motioned to him, however, to wait and came running up, breathless, as the mules stopped, quivering, in their tracks.

'Maybe us better take de ole road down to de ferry, Mas' Cavin, so's we don't run into so many soljers. Whut you think?'

'Is it muddy?' Cavin inquired, with his mind on the heavily loaded wagons.

'Wall, dar's been right smart o' rain, but don' many people know 'bout dat road. De Yankees,' he explained, 'ain' foun' it yit. Dey all takes de wide shell road down to de new railroad crossin'.'

Cavin wrinkled his brow and laughed. 'By George, Uncle Matt,' he confessed, 'I been running around so fast all over Virginia I don't remember what turn you take out o' here.'

Uncle Matt chuckled. 'Lawd, ain't dat de truf? When me an' Mas' Philip fust got back fum de wah, I kep' tuhnin' aroun', myself, lak a chicken wid its head off. I'll go tell Eph to take hol' in de back,' he told Cavin. 'I better climb in wid you.'

He hurried to the back and then pulled himself up into Cavin's wagon, leaning back against the seat, ready to fall instantly asleep when he had got them on the right road. Cavin took up the lines, and looked at Lucina. 'Why don't you wrap up in some of those blankets and go to sleep like Maria?' he suggested.

'The idea!' she said. 'With a moon like this, and everything to look at! Go on, Cavin.'

He smiled into her dark eyes, and, sitting back, pulled on the reins. 'Gid-dap!' he called. 'Gid-dap there, doggone yo' tough hides!'

'Cavin!' Lucina remonstrated. 'Cavin!'

'I forgot I wasn't in the army,' he apologized, offering an excuse she was to grow very familiar with.

When the wagons were all in motion and the mules had fallen into the steady jog trot that they could follow uninterruptedly, hour after hour, Cavin slid his arm around Lucina.

'Here,' he said, 'lean back on my shoulder. Pa would have sent the carriage to meet us, if he'd known I was bringing a pretty young lady home.' When he looked at her again, she was asleep, with her dark head pressed against John's gray jacket.

Chapter 9

I$_T$ was nearly midnight, Cavin decided, squinting at the stars, before they were across the ferry and on the mainland. It would be long after that time before they could hope to reach the camp site where he planned to rest until some time next day.

As they drove onto the shaky ferry, Lucina awoke. At first, as her eyes slowly took in the gleaming water, the mules, and the fantastic shadows on the narrow arm of the bay across which they were passing, she thought she was dreaming, and lay quiet against Cavin's shoulder, expecting soon to see the familiar walls of her room at home taking shape before her. Soon, however, she realized that she was in a wagon headed for the Brazos, and sitting up, looked anxiously back across the bay toward Galveston, then up at Cavin.

'Do you suppose they'll send after us?' she inquired. Somehow the prospect seemed more terrifying to her, as the night wore on.

He considered his reply for some time, whistling under his breath as he meditated. 'No,' he said finally, 'I don't believe there's a chance, now we're out of town. I've been thinking about it as I drove along.' Shifting the reins from one hand to the other, he began to lay before her the various possibilities he had been canvassing. 'We had just landed, you know. Nobody in town ever saw us before, and that fool darky was too drunk to stir before daylight, anyway. No,' he concluded confidently, 'we'll never hear any more from it. Are you very tired?' he inquired solicitously, and yawned. 'I am! I'd wake up Jake and make him drive, but I want to get where we're going.'

The ferry creaked and came to rest. They were across the bay at last, and Cavin jumped off the wagon to lead his mules on shore. Then, holding out his arms to Lucina, he said: 'Hop down. We'll have to wait here till all the wagons get across.'

They paced back and forth, watching the ferry moving on its cable back across the bay, which, at this point, was hardly wider than a river. Lucina thought how strange it was that she, Lucina Lyttleton, should be here, under the night sky of Texas, walking on a sandy road with a man who, until four months before, she had never thought of as a lover, much less a husband. And, stranger yet, she felt no surprise at what she was doing; she felt that always she had known she would be here, on the white earth flooded with moonlight, walking, with Cavin's arm around her, to the bend of the road and back. It seemed to her that, if the night never ended, she could live on happily forever in its changeless, eery light.

With every sense heightened and alert, she stood listening to the brown grass rattling in the breeze and to small fish jumping in and out the silvery water. As she listened, an enormous white bird, aroused by the clatter of the mule team, rose, startled, from the marshes, and, flapping its angular wings, circled upward over the deserted beach. Lucina followed his curving flight and her eyes stayed fixed on the sky, as Cavin drew her to a fallen tree beside the narrow road marked only by two wheel tracks, with a wide swathe of grass growing between. They sat there for hours, it seemed to her, conscious of no hurry and no anxiety, filled with a content so deep that they had no need to speak.

'Cavin!' she exclaimed, struck by the appearance of the sky; 'there aren't any stars!' She pointed upward to the moon, floating alone, it seemed, in a sea of white and brilliant light.

'They'll come out directly, when the moon goes down,' he assured her. 'On the Gulf, you don't notice the stars if there's a moon. There's one.' Low toward the horizon, a single flaming sun whirled in space.

Intent on their search, they failed to hear Matt approaching. The negro, noticing their absorption, stood waiting, and at last Cavin caught sight of him and stood up.

'Ready, Uncle Matt?'

'Yas-suh. Dey's all acrost.'

As they started off, Cavin explained to Lucina how, for miles on end, the mule drivers would sleep sitting up in their seats. 'Just keep an eye on 'em,' he advised her. 'You'll see they wake up if a mule so much as switches his tail, or steps a foot out o' line.' Then he folded a blanket and, laying it on the wagon floor between the seat and the front panel, invited her to sit there and rest her back against his knees.

As they drove along under the wide night sky, he began telling her what he had been thinking about all summer at Cedar Ledge, what plans he had made for working his Texas land with free labor, what hopes he had for the future.

He must have talked for an hour, almost without stopping. She listened carefully, but he could see she was faintly troubled.

'Maybe Uncle Phil won't like your bringing home a wife?' she suggested.

Cavin turned her face up to him and looked at her reproachfully.

'Now you're talking foolishness. Time you got to bed!' He leaned forward, peering through the moonlight which covered the prairie like a misty blue-white cobweb. 'Here we are, I think.'

He hauled up the mules sharply and leaned further forward, scrutinizing the spot. 'Yes, there's the creek, and the lone split pine. Must be,' he hazarded, looking up at the sky, 'must be around two o'clock. Sleepy, Sweet?' he asked, as he lifted her down from the wagon.

'Not sleepy,' she answered, 'but, my goodness! I'm stiff.' She took a few painful steps and stopped. 'Whatever's the matter with me?'

'It's the jolting,' Cavin told her, knitting his heavy brows.

'Oh!' She was relieved. 'Is that all?'

Cavin threw a blanket around her and folded up another for her to sit on.

'Lean back against this tree and watch Eph get breakfast. Or maybe it's supper?' he suggested, with his eyes on the other approaching wagons.

The drivers had dozed in their seats all the way across the prairie, but they came to life at once when the motion ceased. One by one they jumped off the wagons and gathered around Cavin, smiling expansively, their white teeth gleaming in the moonlight. Lawd! How Mas' Philip's boy had growed, they thought, bringing home a wife, too. How Mas' Philip gonna take it, you rekkin? they had asked one another, coming across the prairie.

Cavin stood waiting for them all to assemble, picking out the drivers he recognized, as they drew their mules to a halt and, throwing down the heavy irons that held the teams anchored, made their way stiffly toward him.

'I'm mighty glad to see you all,' he told them, offering his hand to Uncle Eph, who stood in the forefront. 'Especially Uncle Eph,' he continued. 'I been hungry for some o' his batter-cakes ever since I joined the army.' Reaching out his arm, he drew Lucina to her feet.

'Boys,' he said to the negroes gathered in front of him, 'this is your new mistress, Miss Lucina. I expect you all to show her how well Miss Lettie has trained you to wait on her.'

'And this is Maria,' said Lucina, laying her hand on Maria's arm, and smiling. 'I've been hearing about you all the way out here.'

'Uncle Eph,' Cavin suggested briskly, 'how about starting a batch o' cakes to frying? And, Jim, you and Jefferson set up my tent, right away, won't you? Uncle Matt, I suppose you'll 'tend to the mules? Jake, you better help him. Who's this boy?' he asked, catching sight of a colored man he had not before noticed. The negro stepped forward, pulling off his hat.

'I'se Job, Miss Lettie's hunter, suh,' he told Cavin. 'Yo' pa done got too busy to hunt, an' me, I keeps the table supplied. Miss Lettie sont me along to bring back some game, dis trip. She say she pinin' fur some.'

'So'm I,' said Cavin enthusiastically. 'So'm I.'

Soon they began to smell coffee and bacon and wood smoke, and saw Eph flipping battercakes into the air. Cavin sank down beside Lucina, leaning his head against the tree, and clasping his hands around his knees, while Jake brought a seat out of one of the wagons and set it down in front of them, with a clean towel laid out on it for a tablecloth.

'Cavin!' cried Lucina incredulously. 'Do I smell coffee? And is this *butter?*' she demanded, as Maria set a plate of cakes before her. 'Impossible!'

'Well, Sherman never got to Texas, that's certain,' Cavin agreed, lavishly buttering his hot cakes. 'Thank the Lord,' he ended.

When they had finished, they sat for a time watching the servants putting up their tent and unhitching the mules. Then Lucina caught sight of Maria leaning disconsolately against a tree, and went over to comfort her, while Cavin walked over to a wagon looking for a coil of rope. Finding it, he hung it carelessly over his arm and dropped it just inside the door of the tent. Then he went over and spoke to Maria, too.

'Maria,' he promised her, 'you're going to like it here.'

'I hope I is,' she replied, so doubtfully that Lucina had to laugh.

Cavin stood for some time at his tent door looking out at the dying campfire, at the men huddled around it, and at the wagons and the mules gathered to one side. Then he unstrapped his pistols and laid them carefully on the canvas floor beside his pillow. 'It's a good thing you're along, Lucy,' he remarked, chuckling, 'or I'd think I was in the army.' Then, uncoiling the rope, he began to lay it neatly around the mattress.

Lucina watched him curiously. 'Whatever are you doing?' she demanded. Already she had seen many strange sights in Texas, but this was the strangest.

Cavin laughed. 'The rope's to keep off snakes,' he explained, smiling at her expression of startled distaste. 'Sometimes, this time of year, they'll crawl in any old place it's warm.' He stood looking down at her, his smile broadening. 'I don't know whether there is anything in this rope business,' he admitted, 'but the cowboys swear a rattler won't cross over one.'

'Well,' exclaimed Lucina, sinking back on her pillow. 'I've a lot to learn.' Snakes! All night she dreamed of black, creeping bodies writhing over ropes.

When they awoke, it was late morning, and the warm sun streamed out of a cloudless sky over an expanse of tawny grass that stretched away and away, endlessly Lucina thought, to the round horizon. The prairie was broken here and there in the distance by clumps of white bois-d'arcs and scraggly pin oaks which arose, like oases in a desert, out of bare open space. Lucina's eyes, however, did not linger on these trees. The prairie's wide loneliness crowded in upon her consciousness, blotting out every other impression. As she watched, the wind swept through the grass, giving it the undulating appearance of the ocean itself, and her the impression that the very ground under her feet was rocking. Detecting salt in the thin bright air blown inward from the Gulf, she drew a deep breath and, narrowing her eyes, stood watching the light that fell in sparkling brilliance upon the dun and sandy earth. The whole prairie lay drowsing under such warm and shifting color as she had never seen before. Like light through a prism, the sun's rays covered the dead grass, breaking against it into every shade of the spectrum. She felt overcome, beaten down by the effulgence that surrounded her. It seemed to her almost unearthly, as though it fell redly from some other sun than that which blanketed the Georgia valleys in a whiter, dimmer radiance. She had a momentary feeling that she had been set down somewhere on a strange and deserted planet, that she drew into her nostrils air from some old, forsaken world. Yet the sight stimulated her imagination; and this flat land seemed to her, despite its strangeness, somehow familiar and cherished, like something she dimly remembered out of a past so remote that she had almost forgotten it.

Cavin, who stood behind her looking out over her shoulder, took an exultant breath, as his eyes fell on the open prairie. Lucina leaned against him and began to speak slowly, trying to put into words her half-formed thoughts. 'I know why you feel the way you do about this country,' she began. 'It's — well, it's mysterious. It makes you shiver, like a dream that you keep dreaming over and over at night — a dream in which everything is new and strange and, yet, old too, old as time.'

'That's it,' Cavin said, delighted with her immediate under-standing of what he had always felt but could never express. 'That's it, exactly. How do you know everything you do, Sweet?'

'Oh,' she replied lightly, 'I read it in your mind.' He laughed and released her, throwing a warm glance at the endless prairie sky, unbroken by mountains or forests.

'Eph's carried out Pa's orders never to wake anybody up, short of fire or murder. It must be time for dinner, not break-fast!'

The scent of burning wood drifted toward them, and the aroma of browning meat. 'Well,' Lucina responded, 'whatever it is, I want some.'

Cavin followed her to the fire, where Eph was anxiously inspecting a hollow in the ground banked with leaves and ashes, and heaped over with red coals.

'Mawnin', suh,' the negro said, looking up from his work. 'I was mighty worried fur fear you wouldn't wake up befo' dis heah hen was too done, and my hoe cakes all burnt up.' Lifting his black face, he leaned back, squatting on his heels, while an expression of triumph rose in his one good eye. 'Dere's some preserved figs,' he announced proudly. 'Miss Lettie sont 'em along fur you to eat wid yo' breakfus, an' I picked up some collards an' turnips in de market yestiddy in town. I ain't gwine let Miss Lucy git hongry,' he announced, rising and bowing to Lucina.

'You'll spoil me, Uncle Eph,' Lucina answered, dropping down on the blanket before the wagon seat that she saw was again to serve as a table.

'How'd you get the prairie chicken, Uncle Eph?' Cavin in-quired, holding out his hand for a plate. 'I didn't hear any shots.'

'Naw suh, we didn't wants to wakes you all up. Matt sont Jim out, quick's he got up dis mawnin', to bring one in, an' here 'tis,' he added, holding the bird, stripped of its clay covering, up to view.

As they ate, they could hear the drivers gathered some distance away around their own campfire, talking and laughing, and the hobbled mules munching their way through the rustling grass. Around them, small, brilliantly colored birds rose on fluttering wings from the thick-matted blackberry bushes that followed the creek's course a little distance away.

'Redbirds and wild canaries,' Cavin told Lucina, pointing them out to her, 'and see that dull, gray bird amongst them? You never saw anything in your life fly so high as that little bird,' he laughed. 'We've another funny bird here — no bigger'n a minute, but it'll tackle a hawk and get the best of it, too. I used to lie in the grass and watch 'em fight through Pa's field glasses. There are all kinds of snakes and ants and spiders and scorpions and things I ought to show you, besides,' he said, eagerly drawing on his pleasant boyhood memories, unconscious of her shrinking.

'Come on,' he said, rising briskly and pulling her up beside him. 'Let's go take a walk while Matt's hitching up.' He stood still, eyeing her with a gleam of amusement in his lively eyes. 'Bet you never saw a sensitive plant that folds up if you touch it, or a plant that eats flies? Or a tree whose bark'll cure your toothache? Or' — he grinned — 'a cactus that grows pears and nuts on it?'

For an hour they walked along the creek bed, resting here and there on fallen logs, while they watched vultures circling and dipping, under a sky so wide and blue that it was almost black.

'Look!' said Cavin. suddenly noticing a flower that grew

just out of reach of his hand. 'Here's one o' the plants I was telling you about.'

It grew on a damp spot sloping down to the creek, its pansy-like red blossom studded thickly with tiny hairs tipped with drops of sticky dew.

Moving closer, Cavin dropped his finger in its centre, and the petals curled quickly around it. 'Gosh! It has a grip,' he cried, as delighted with its behavior as when he first had tested out its curious, tensile strength. 'Watch it; it'll let go in a minute, soon as it finds out I'm not a fly.'

'Does it hurt?' she asked, watching the leaves unfold. 'Oh, no,' he answered; 'try it.' But when she did, her delicate skin turned fiery red and burned as though it had been blistered.

'You have to get used to this country. I see that,' she told him, as they returned to camp. 'Even the flowers bite you!'

Ahead of them, the six wagons stood in line with Matt in the front driver's seat.

Cavin tucked Lucina's hand inside his arm and hurried toward the teams. 'The rest of the way is pretty tough going, as I remember it,' he said. 'You just have to cut across the prairie, and hope you don't run into a bog hole. Wish I had some boots.' With a lugubrious grin, he held out his foot for Lucina to look at. 'Imagine what'll happen to those contraptions if we strike deep mud!'

Uncle Matt had been worrying about the same contingency. Sometimes, he meditated, Mas' Philip sent into town for a soft pair of new boots, hand sewed and turned — boots finely traced in red, with tops as pliable as silk, and heels as red as the tracery. Lawd Jesus! Wouldn't it be just right, now, if there happened to be a pair like that in the wagon? Maybe Mas' Cavin could wear his pa's boots! Patiently, he felt around among the various parcels, until at last he came upon what he was searching for. Then, raising himself with an expression of absolute felicity on his black face, he laid the boots out in Cavin's wagon.

'My Gosh-amighty!' Cavin exclaimed, when he saw them. 'Talk about answers to prayer!'

With a little padding in the toes, they fitted fairly well, and all afternoon he lay back in the wagon, lifting his foot from time to time to gaze, like a child, at his brand-new boots. They had not yet reached the part of the route that was hard going, so he had little to do but rest and call Lucina's attention to things she should notice as they moved slowly along across the monot-onous plain.

Toward evening, the whole prairie began again to reflect the shifting tints of the sky; and suddenly the yellow crimson light passed into a quick and settling dark. A little later, as they sat under the pines waiting for supper, the moon rose, a golden disk, out of the edge of the world. They ate their boiled eggs, and their yams baked in ashes by its light, with the glow from the fire playing over them.

Cavin's hand groped for Lucina's. 'I don't want a thing in this world, do you?' She laughed softly. 'I can't think of a thing!'

Then, as they sat there, they heard a slow humming from the servants' camp, and saw the drivers approaching through the trees. Jim held a jews-harp to his lips and Eph a comb, with its teeth wrapped in tissue paper. Jefferson was carrying a banjo, on which he strummed lightly as he walked. Behind them were the other drivers, all humming in a deep, resonant chorus. Eph stepped forward and addressed Cavin diffidently, his old, stooped body etched against the flames, and his single eye giving him a weird, Cyclops-like appearance.

'Mas' Cavin,' he said, shuffling his feet, 'us thought maybe you and our young mistis might lak a little song and dance.'

'Fine!' Cavin responded heartily. 'Fine! Go ahead!' He drew closer to Lucina, whispering to her that, as a boy, he had often tried in vain to imitate Uncle Eph's skill.

As he spoke, Uncle Eph began to play a slow, haunting tune on the fine teeth of the comb, expertly bending it toward one angle or another, and his head with it. The sound was at one moment like the rustling of leaves or the movement of dried grass, at another like the whirling of water in a small pool. Then Jim joined in with his mournful jews-harp, and, a little later, Jefferson struck up his tinkling banjo. Almost immediately all the men began a low humming, which rose at the end to a magnificent crescendo that left Lucina breathless, filled with some deep, aching pity, for what she could not tell.

Then two of the drivers began to clog to the rhythmic clapping of the others' hands and to the strumming of the banjos, their figures moving like shadows back and forth in front of the fire, as they followed minutely the lilt and flow of the music. No one noticed how late it was growing until they stopped, breathing hard and bowing elaborately.

'Well,' said Cavin heartily, rising, 'that was a fine show. Uncle Eph, I'll have to get you to give me some more lessons.' He smiled at Jim and Jefferson. 'Why don't you all see what you can do about showing Jake some o' yo' tricks?'

Lucina slid her hand in his, and they walked slowly over to their tent, standing for some time in front of it watching the light on the prairie and listening, in the warm night, to the soft scuffling sounds of birds and rabbits in the thick grass. All her days, she was to remember those few moments, when life seemed to her to lie out in front of her as clear and plain as the vast prairie that stretched before her eyes, flooded with moonlight and sunk in a strange, fathomless peace.

Some time later, in the night, she woke to hear a roaring wind that howled and tore at the tent, and, shivering, heard above that sound a chorus of long, penetrating wails rising and sinking, rising and sinking again. It seemed to her that all the sorrow and suffering in the world was condensed and expressed in the dreary, dismal cries that echoed endlessly over the wild and vacant land. What could it be? The noise sounded like nothing so much as the weeping of banshees that she had heard described by old mountain women, or like the wailing of ghosts who, the negroes said, deserted their peaceful graves every year on the eve before All Saints' Day.

She lay petrified by fear, too frightened to move, and then she heard rain falling, in violent gusts, upon the roof of the tent, and again, above the rain and the wind, the long, mournful cries coming, it seemed, from some soul beyond the reach of pity. Never in any nightmare had she experienced the terror that possessed her as she heard again, high and piercing above the rain and wind, the sounds that had awakened her.

The wind grew to such intensity that it roused Cavin, who usually slept indifferent to almost any disturbance, and Lucina asked him, in a voice that quivered and shook, what the noise was. He had heard only the rain, but, as he listened, there floated over the prairie again the long, shrieking wails that had terrified Lucina.

'Oh,' he chuckled, 'coyotes out running before the wind. They'll probably carry on like that till daylight.'

'Are they dangerous?' she asked him, feeling flow through her, at his touch, the same happy security that always overtook her as a child, when, after a bad dream, she opened her eyes to feel her mother's arms around her.

'Dangerous!' he laughed. 'To calves! Hear that norther!' he said, drawing the blankets tighter. 'I hope the rain lets up before daylight.'

But it was five days before it stopped, five days before the storm was spent. Cavin and the men put on slickers and got the wagons started, raising hoops and canvas over several of them, and spreading tarpaulin over the rest. The rain fell in a steady drizzle, and the air was so damp that Lucina's hair dripped moisture.

She could hear the mules' feet splashing in the wet, where a sheet of cold water lay over the prairie; and all day long she listened to the sucking sound of the wheels as they pulled in and out the sticky soil. Sometimes the wagons sank up to their hubs in mud, and then Cavin and the negroes would have to get down in the rain and unload the pine branches which Cavin, anticipating the difficulties ahead, had had the men cut and pile into the back wagon. Running these under the wheels that were stuck fast, the drivers would crack their long black whips, and usually the mules, hearing the sound, would pull and strain until the wheels were loose. Sometimes, though, Cavin would have to order the mules of one wagon to be unhitched and added to the team that could no longer move. So, by slow degrees, they made their way across the dismal prairie, with the rain falling and the cold, wet wind forcing its way into every open crack.

'Maybe we ought to stop and make camp till it blows over?' Lucina asked one night, as Cavin entered, dripping, into the covered wagon where she was sitting, with Maria huddled close beside her.

'Trouble is, you never know how long it'll last,' he replied. 'No, I think we'd better keep on. If you can stand it?' He threw a commiserating glance in her direction.

'I?' she responded in a surprised tone. 'Why, of course! But I don't see how you manage, out in the rain!'

He sat down, eyeing her with a slow, amused smile.

'How do you suppose they kept me nice and warm and comfortable in the army?' he asked her. 'Here,' he said handing her a cup of coffee from the pot that was brewing on the brazier in the wagon, and adding a ration of rum to his own portion. How you making out, Maria?' he asked the negro girl, sipping his hot drink in satisfaction.

'I'd be shamed to complain, ef'n Miss Lucy don't,' she told him primly, and Cavin threw his head back and laughed at her unhappy face.

'Never mind, Maria,' Lucina consoled her. 'Nothing lasts forever.'

She was surprised herself that she minded the shaking and the jolting, the wind and the dampness so little. It all seemed part of some large drama being enacted around her that she watched, rather than shared — watched with the keenest interest.

She would peer for hours, out of the slit in her wagon, at the long-horned cattle standing hunched together in the opaque mist, with their tails between their legs and their necks drawn back into their shoulders, as if to present as little body surface as possible to the driving wind and rain. Sometimes groups of them, looking almost like wax figures, would drift along in one direction, seemingly pushed by the wind. Days later, when the weather was again mild and warm, Lucina was amazed to see the agility with which these enormous beasts moved, and the eager attention with which they raised their heads and stared across the grass at the approaching wagons. Watching them, in the slow rain, she had no impression of the ferocity that later she was to learn often distinguished them.

Peeping through the slit, she also noticed droves of wild

horses standing huddled together with water running off their tangled manes and tails. Every now and then a deer with antlers would flash by; or prairie chickens and wild turkeys, disturbed by the passing wagons, would fly agitatedly into the air, squawking as they settled again on the ground, or on some lone tree or shrub.

Sometimes it seemed to Lucina that they had been pushing on like this, in wind and cold rain, ever since they had left Savannah, and that the rest of her life would be spent in this endless procession leading nowhere, it seemed. For they passed no houses or settlements; and the wet prairie looked yesterday exactly as it did today, and would, she supposed, tomorrow.

Eventually it cleared, as suddenly as the storm had fallen; and that day they paused, made camp, and dried out their belongings, enjoying a better meal than any they had had since the outset of the rain.

'Six days out,' remarked Cavin at supper that night. 'How many miles do you think we've made, Uncle Eph?'

The negro was carrying a plate of hot corn dodgers and a platter of birds wrapped around with bacon, which he had roasted in a black skillet set over the coals, and their brown and succulent appearance pleased him mightily. Taking another approving glance at them, he offered them, with a proud flourish, to Lucina. 'Lawd! Uncle Eph!' Cavin exclaimed, 'you're the best cook twixt here and the Rio Grande.' Then he cast a searching glance at the prairie, which offered so few landmarks. 'Where are we?' he inquired again. 'I've kind-a forgotten the way.'

'See dat-ar row of trees yonder?' Uncle Eph pointed to a shadowy black strip ahead. 'Us ought-a git dar tomorrow, or maybe next day. That's some less'n half way.'

'It'll take us about two weeks in all, then,' Cavin calculated.

'Well,' Uncle Eph responded prudently, 'I do' know, suh. Mebbe, mebbe not. Us most generally makes it in dat time, but we's had a streak o' wedder dis trip, an' I specks dar'll be a powerful heap of mud twixt heah an' de Brazos. Dar too,' he added, grinning.

There was no more rain, not until the last day, but the ground was wet and sticky and progress slow and halting. Lucina might have thought the last stretch monotonous if the negroes had not caught in a trap, overnight, a cotton-tail rabbit which they intended to cook in a stew to be eaten with lye hominy. She was so much amused by the little creature's blinking eyes and its absurd white tuft of a tail, that she would not let Uncle Eph have it and took it for a pet. Soon she and Maria had it eating out of their hands, and, as they played with it, the hours passed and another day was gone.

As Lucina jolted across the flat prairie, it seemed to her that she was existing in some separate section of time and space, into which the ordinary cares and duties of life did not enter, and that these days, from the beginning of her life, had been set apart for her to pass through. She felt like a traveller on a train who, for the time being, is removed by his passage through space from any temporal demands; and she understood that, as long as she travelled in this creaking, jolting wagon, she could enjoy a world in which she and Cavin seemed to be almost its sole occupants. Now, at least, they could move as they pleased regardless of other people, or of a government that, at Galveston, had seemed to them insupportable and intolerable.

But at last they emerged from the open plain into a different region altogether — a region full of sprawling trees, enormous in width, heavily laden with moss and mistletoe, and Lucina observed, looking at the ground, that it was no longer gray, filled with shell, or white and sandy, but a deep, rich black, a loam going down, Cavin told her, so deep they had never reached its bottom with any plow. For, he explained, an overflow of the Brazos, while disastrous in its immediate effects, in the long run replenished the soil so well that it had never been necessary to use fertilizer on his father's place. And the millions of leaves that fell annually kept the ground loose and pliable.

'Pa wrote to my mother,' Cavin remembered as they drove along, 'and described this land as "lovely and fertile, with water and pasture for cattle and with deep soil for cotton and sugar cane." ' The words rolled over his tongue almost automatically, coming, Lucina realized, out of the depths of some old memory that she did not as yet share with him.

They were following the turns of a yellow river that flowed in and around sand banks in its bed, on and on, in monstrous curves, to its wide and gaping end. On each side of the river great cypress trees extended their huge and groping roots out into the river that flowed over them, indifferent to their presence. 'This isn't a bit like the prairie,' Lucina commented.

'It's the river bottom,' Cavin explained, 'and there's no better land anywhere.' He threw out his hand to the river. 'Look at it, running along there as peaceful as you please. But you ought to see it when it goes on a rampage. The Spaniards who were here first called it the River of God, as they watched its capers, but in the spring you'd think it belonged to the devil. They say, though,' he smiled at his bride, 'if you once drink out of it, there's a spell on you so you can never leave these bottoms. Well,' he sighed comfortably and stretched his long legs out in front of him, 'mighty few ever do want to leave. It grows on you, somehow; you'll see. Stop, Jake,' he ordered. 'I want Miss Lucina to see the woods along here.'

'Snakes?' she questioned fearfully. 'Spiders?' Hesitantly she put her foot down on the crunching leaves, and followed him.

'There's a live-oak grove I want you to look at,' he told her, 'nothing but live-oaks, bigger than any trees you ever saw anywhere.' A little further on he came to a dead stand, looking down at a bent tree by the road. 'Why it's the mad-dog tree!' he exclaimed. 'The tree I climbed, the day a mad dog got after me.' He stood staring at it. 'There's been war, and surrender, and everything else going on, and here's that very tree, still here by the side of the road!' He blinked at her, for a moment feeling time move mysteriously around him, and then, shrugging his shoulders, went on. 'And here,' he continued, picking her up and setting her down in a grapevine swing, 'here is the vine I used to hang onto and try to touch the top of that tallest tree yonder. See? Want me to push you?' he asked, giving her a light shove.

'Not that high,' she begged him, as she began to sway, going higher and higher, until he could easily run beneath her and catch her on the return.

She jumped out of the swing into his arms, and he gave her one of the grapevine's sour leaves to chew. Its tart flavor reminded her of their childhood, when they had kept their pockets filled with grape leaves, munching on them all day.

He stood looking around him, happy to be at last on his own ground. 'There are wild grapes and wild plums, too, in these woods,' he told her, 'and all kinds of persimmons, and dewberries, and blackberries, and thorn-apples, and pecans, and walnuts, and I don't know what all.' Gesturing magnificently, with a wide swing of his arms, he observed, 'The Lord never intended for anybody to go hungry in Texas.'

'Whose land is all this?' she asked him, remarking that some of the foliage, even in the warm autumn, was beginning to shrivel. Cavin told her that the live-oaks and the holly trees, the cedars, and the graceful rounded haws kept their leaves all winter, changing their color during the colder season from a lighter shade to a green so dark it was almost black; but that the other trees, obeying a rhythm that seemed insensible to climate, were by Christmas standing stark and bare along creeks filled with still, brown water. And, then, she asked him again whose land they were on.

'Ours,' he answered absently. 'Ours. We've been travelling on it since early this morning. As soon as we hit the road back there, we were on it.' He was studying a clearing filled with black stumps. 'They ought to all be pulled up. That's tough work, though,' he told her.

His eyes roamed over the fields, and Lucina knew that he was planning some particular task, overcoming its difficulties in thought, before he undertook to do so in fact. Soon, however, his face lighted up and he began to try to tell her how the bottom land looked in spring, when the ground was covered with violets and white Mayflowers and with sweet-smelling shrubs borne down with blossoms, when the locusts and the red buds, the magnolias and crêpe myrtles were at their best, when blackberries hung thick on their bushes, and dewberries crept lushly along the ground.

Then it came to him that, after all, there was no need to try to describe to her what she would be seeing with her own eyes in a few months. The thought brought him a sudden sharp satisfaction. He had only to stretch out his hand and, forevermore now, there would be Lucina.

'I'll bring you back down here in the spring,' he promised her happily, picking her up and carrying her, high over the tangled bushes and damp ground, back toward the wagon.

'Cavin, put me down!' she remonstrated. But he did not pause until they were almost out of the trees.

'That's to show you you'd better not ever try running away from me,' he warned her, in mock ferocity, as she lay limp and laughing against him.

'Do you suppose I'm likely to want to?' she asked him, amused at the idea, as he carefully set her down.

Standing there in the circle of his arms, listening to the river flowing through the quiet woods, she felt again the certainty that had come over her the morning she sat waiting for him in the tree at Cedar Ledge. He dropped his cheek on hers, and they stood there without moving, unconscious of the restless movements of the teams halted on the road close by.

'No, Sweet,' he replied gently, 'I don't think you are going to want to leave me. But,' with a sudden change of mood, 'it wouldn't do you any good if you did! Come on! If we're going to get home by dark, we'll have to hurry.' Taking her hand, he led her through the tall berry bushes that screened the road to the waiting wagons.

It was — Cavin glanced quickly at the sun — probably four o'clock. They jolted and bumped along the winding road all the rest of the afternoon, making slow and tortuous progress through the sticky mud left by the heavy rains of the past week. For even though it had been clear for a week or more, the rains did not quickly drain off this flat, heavy soil. Toward dusk, the road dipped into a slough. Lucina shuddered as she glanced down at the black water which still stood well above the ooze in which the mules struggled, and hoped she would never have to put her own foot into it. Dark fell long before they were clear of the mire. Uncle Matt lighted a lantern and went ahead, with his hand on the bridle of the mules hitched to the front wagon. Then the rain began to fail, in a slow, steady drizzle, which, already Lucina knew, could keep up for days on end, in this coastal country.

Cavin buttoned his slicker around her, and threw a blanket over his own shoulders.

'Almost there now,' he said. 'No use trying to put up the top. See that light through the trees? A little further and we turn into a lane, and then we're home.'

But when they had entered the lane, their wheels once again rolled into a deep mud hole. One of the mules lay down in his traces and refused, even at the crack of the whip, to budge, and the wagons behind drew up with a loud clatter.

The noise penetrated Philip's office, where, since supper, he had been sitting, going over his experiments. Grabbing the lantern he had used to light his way from the house to his office, he threw a long yellow slicker around him, and, guessing at once what the commotion meant, started hurriedly off down the lane, the light bobbing against his thin knees. His riding horse, he remembered, had stumbled in that hole a few days before.

'Damn my carelessness,' he thought irascibly, 'I ought to have had that place filled in. I can't seem to get around to doing all I ought to. Now, I knew when Pilot stepped in that hole that it had to be fixed! Why didn't I do it?' he fumed, angry with himself and resentful of the lassitude that, more and more often, overtook him. For the moment, having long ago become accustomed to Cavin's absence, he forgot he was expecting his son home on the wagon-train.

He reached the mud hole and took in the situation. It was after nine o'clock and raining; it would probably rain all night. They could not hope to get all the wagons pulled past the hole now, in the dark, with exhausted teams in the traces. He made his decision quickly.

'Matt,' he said quickly, not taking time to ask about the trip, 'tell the men to unhitch and be sure to cover up the supplies. Then you better go tell Aunt Emmy to make you all some hot coffee and issue dry clothes, all around. Here,' he fumbled in his pocket, 'give her the key to the storeroom. I don't want you all turning up with pneumonia, just when I need you. How'd you get along?' he asked, almost as an afterthought, as he came closer, edging his way around the hole.

'Fine,' said Cavin, coming to meet him and throwing his arms around his father. 'Fine, Pa!'

Philip held him off with one hand and raised his lantern, scanning his son's face.

'My God-a-mighty, boy! For the minute, I'd forgot you were coming!' He put down his lantern and seized Cavin's hands. 'Are you well?' Laughing, he ran his hand up his son's sleeve until he touched his shoulder and saw that it was level with his own. 'I was looking for a boy, and here you are, tall as I am!'

'Well, I reckon it's about time I was,' said Cavin, shaking his father's hands and gazing cheerfully at him in the flickering lantern light. 'Full time, because I've brought home a wife!'

'A what?' Philip almost roared, his surprise lifting his voice beyond his expectation.

'A wife, Pa,' repeated Cavin. 'I don't blame you for being surprised. I was myself,' he admitted, his eyes twinkling. His father thought suddenly as he watched him, 'There's something — what is it? — something about the boy that's like Mary?'

'Where is she?' Philip demanded. 'Cavin! Are you serious?'

'Certainly, Pa, I'm serious. And here she is,' Cavin said, moving over to the wagon and holding out his arms to Lucina.

'I hope you don't mind, Uncle Phil,' said Lucina, in a small, shaky voice, as Cavin handed her over bodily to Philip.

Again Philip took up his lantern, throwing its beams full on Lucina's face, holding her to him with one arm while he studied her features — her mouth, a little too wide for the delicate chin beneath it, her black, shining hair.

'I'm Lucina,' she told him, shyly, smiling at his bewilderment. 'Lucina Lyttleton.'

'Mary's niece?' Philip asked in astonishment, and saw as he looked at her that she was. 'Well, I declare! But I'd have recognized those big eyes anywhere!' he said, and pinched her cheek. 'Cavin, how did you ever persuade this sweet child to accept you?' he demanded. 'I hope we can make you happy, my dear.'

'Cavin,' he said, turning to his son, 'any woman puts a man eternally in her debt by marrying him! You've got to remember that!'

Smiling down at Lucina, he stooped to kiss her. 'This is a mighty muddy lane. We're going to carry you into the house, young lady.'

Letitia was sitting at her piano, when she heard steps on the gallery. Hurrying to the door, she opened it and stood there framed in the yellow light, with her blue dress blowing about her and her light hair standing out, like a nimbus, around her face.

'It's Cavin!' she cried; and a moment later they stood in the lighted hall, with the water running off them in rivulets to the floor. 'Why, Cavin! I'm so glad you are back! And——' She turned expectantly toward Lucina.

'My wife,' said Cavin, smiling. 'My wife, Lucina. I've been telling her about you, Letitia.'

Letitia was as startled as Philip had been. She put her arm around Lucina's waist and looked at her searchingly, remarking with a sudden uprise of emotion, how young she was.

'Wife, Cavin, did you say?' she said aloud, kissing Lucina's cold cheek. 'Why, you had just left off flying kites when you went to war! And here you come home with a bride!' She smiled at Lucina, who, she felt certain, must be wet and tired.

'Philip,' Letitia said briskly to her husband, 'wouldn't it be a good idea for you to give Cavin some dry clothes and a toddy? I expect Lucina could stand a glass of wine herself, and a hot bath, and bed. Couldn't you?' she asked, feeling a sudden tenderness arise in her as she turned toward Lucina. Once, years and years ago, she had been as young as this child.

Lucina glanced at the hall, with its wide board floors, and at the long gilded mirror, with four candlesticks attached, that hung on the bare, wide wall.

'That *would* be pleasant,' she confessed, realizing all at once, that she was exhausted.

'Philip and Cavin'll be discussing crops and the state of the country in a minute!' Letitia predicted. 'You come along with me, Lucina.'

'Maria!' Lucina cried, hesitating. 'I must see what she's doing. My maid,' she explained to Letitia.

'She's all right,' Cavin answered. 'I told Jake to take her around to Aunt Emmy. She's probably laying out your things by now.' He looked toward Letitia with an apologetic smile. 'This trip's upset Maria more than it has Lucina. Maybe you could put her in with Aunt Emmy,' he suggested.

'I'll put her in with Callie, my own maid, and fix up some way for Lucina to call her when she needs her,' Letitia replied. 'I always tap three times,' she said, handing Lucina a small bronze bell, 'to tell Callie I want her. You arrange something with Maria.'

'Don't think it'll stay this damp and cold,' she remarked as they moved off. 'It may be hot tomorrow, hot as summer. I hope you'll be comfortable and get a good rest tonight,' she added, opening the door to a room where Maria was standing in front of a small fire warming her mistress's damp nightgown on the fender.

When Lucina lay warm in her bed, Maria, looking happier than she had in days, brought her in a glass of blackberry wine, a plate of thin tea cakes, and some cold chicken, flanked by hot buttered biscuits.

'Us is gwine to like it here, ain't we, Miss Lucy?' she asked at once, her eyes shining gently. 'Does you need any mo' tonight? Ef'n yo' don't, Jake say he gwine-a make me acquainted wid de servants.'

'No, Maria,' said Lucina. 'Thank you. I don't need anything more. Just open that window, though, before you go, will you, and pick me one of the leaves off the tree? That one, I think,' she said, indicating the window closest her bed.

'Lawzee! Whut on earth, Miss Lucy? Is you gone plum' crazy?' began Maria, puzzled, but doing as she was told. 'Here 'tis. Still wet as all get-out,' she grumbled, handing Lucina the leaf. 'I'se mighty glad we ain't sleeping out in dem waggins tonight, ain't you?'

Lucina wasn't listening. She glanced once at the fig leaf and handed it back to Maria.

'I knew it,' she said, falling back on her pillows. 'Throw it in the fire, Maria.'

Chapter 10

Aᴀ̆ꜰᴛᴇʀ Letitia and Lucina had left them, Cavin and Philip sank into padded rocking-chairs on each side of the dining-room hearth, where tonight there was a snapping blaze.

'You feel the first norther,' said Philip, glancing keenly at his son, his face taking on the withdrawn watchfulness that characterized it at a patient's bedside — a gathering of all his senses to ascertain what manner of man and ailment he was dealing with. Then he struck a bell that brought a little negro girl running in from the kitchen to answer it.

'Ask Uncle Matt to bring in the toddies right away, will you, Milly?' Philip directed her. Then as she turned to go, he stopped her. 'Tell him to bring along a plate of sandwiches too.' The boy was tired and cold — anybody could see that; and thin, yes, far thinner than he ought to be.

Cavin, who was ordinarily ready to sleep early, was tonight as wakeful as Philip. The anxiety that he had been able to lull in Georgia had sprung to life in Galveston; and now he was beginning to feel more and more anxious about the kind of existence that he had asked Lucina to share.

This was an attitude that she never fully understood. From the beginning of their life in Texas, Cavin put her aside, as it were, in a secure corner in his mind, and applied himself to building around her a community fit for her to live in. Even

to himself, he never put this idea into words, but all his life
he was unconsciously affected by it. Like a craftsman who
designs a jewel case, with little thought for the diamonds it
may contain, so, from the beginning, Cavin set his mind, not
on Lucina, but on the circumstances that surrounded her.
How, he felt rather than reasoned, could she be safe in a county
dominated by negroes and alien military rule?

'Well, Cavin,' Philip remarked, leaning back in his chair and
carefully cradling his pipe's ivory bowl in his palm while he
gazed at his son, 'we have to get acquainted, it seems.'

Matt, entering the dining-room at that moment, laid some
pieces of fat kindling on the fire and drew a round table with a
fluted edge directly in front of the hearth. On it he placed a
small silver bowl containing several whole lemons boiled in
thick sugary syrup the color of amber — a preparation always
on hand in Philip's house. Then he set a bottle of rum on the
table, a silver pitcher of hot water, a saucer of cloves, and two
julep cups with long spoons in them. He had slipped on the
white coat that always hung behind the kitchen door and stood,
with a bootjack in hand, waiting for a pause in the conversation.
Standing there, with his head thrown up, in a gesture reminiscent of Philip's own carriage, he chose his moment and then,
kneeling before his master's outstretched feet, changed his
boots to crocheted slippers.

'I told Jake I'd take keer o' you, too, Mas' Cavin,' he said,
turning to Cavin.

Cavin glanced at his father, and laughed. 'Good thing you
sent in to Galveston for some boots, Pa,' he remarked, holding
out his foot to Matt. 'These are your new ones.' He looked
down at the muddy, worn leather, and then up again at his
father. 'I've been wearing skins on my feet,' he explained, and
grinned. 'They're all the style in Georgia. I had to borrow a

pair o' boots to get married in. I reckon they were the only pair in the county, too.'

'Yes, I know,' said Philip. 'I was down to hides myself, toward the end.' He looked Cavin over from head to toe, observing his mud-soaked uniform.

'Matt,' he directed, 'go see if there's not an extra pair of pants in my closet.'

Matt came back with them in his hands. 'Dey could stan' a pressin',' he remarked critically. 'I'll sen' 'em in by Jake when he stahts yo' fiah in de mawnin', Mas' Cavin.'

'What's Jake up to, anyway?' Cavin inquired, reaching over to mix himself a toddy, and raising his feet comfortably up on the fender.

'Here, son!' said Philip, staying Cavin's hand and offering him a drink already prepared. 'My compliments, and welcome home!' He smiled across the cup. Yes, this was Mary's boy all right. He knew just how he felt, young and a bridegroom. It seemed no time at all since he was that age himself.

How little he knew then — how little! Sometimes he thought the more a man learned, though, the less happy he was. Like Adam, he smiled. As soon as you eat of the tree of knowledge, you find it's bitter fruit. He kept his eyes on his son, and his thoughts sealed inside his lips. Strange, he thought, that light yellow hair on the boy's head. His grandfather's, Mary had always said. This heredity business had lots of queer kinks in it. A man's a fool who thinks he knows too much, he meditated.

'It's a pity he can't keep on feeling the way he does tonight, all his life — just the way he does tonight,' thought Philip sorrowfully, gazing on his son.

Matt stepped forward and mixed a cup for Philip.

'One for you, too, Matt,' Philip said absently, stirring together a pungent drink like his own and holding it out to his

servant, who bowed in gratitude and then stood erect, holding
the cup, hot and untouched, in his hand. Never, in the years
he had served Philip, had he ever poured out a drink for himself in his master's presence without being told to do so; nor
had he ever in his life drunk his potion before he retired to the
kitchen.

'Will dar be any mo' tonight, suh?' he asked, addressing
Philip.

'No, thank you, Matt, I think not.'

'Matt,' Cavin halted him, as he was turning to go, 'you tell
Jake if he's not on hand early in the morning, I'll break his
trifling neck.'

'Yas suh, I'll tell 'im,' the negro replied. 'I hopes you bofe
rests well,' he added from the door, closing it noiselessly as he
went out.

'I don't know what I'd a done if you hadn't sent me Jake,'
Cavin remarked, as Matt withdrew. 'You know, Pa, that nigger
could rassle a meal out o' air. I reckon I'd have starved if he
hadn't been around — plain starved. Mighty nigh did anyhow,' he said, taking an appreciative sip of his toddy. 'I got so
I was afraid to ask him what he was cooking. Once he told
me it was crow, and after that I quit asking. It's curious,' he
said, lowering his cup and fastening his eyes meditatively on
his father, 'mighty curious, when you think about it. The
Yankees started the war to free the niggers, they say, and, now
the war's over, but Matt and Jake are just exactly where they
were when the fighting began.' He shook his head, puzzled.
'What difference on earth can freedom make to them?'

Philip set his cup down on the table, and, leaning over, poked
the fire till it flared up and threw a rich glow over his and
Cavin's faces.

'You know, I've thought that a thousand times,' he said

slowly. 'And that's exactly what William Charlton said when he refused to vote for secession in the Texas legislature. He said it all through the war, too, although he fought as long and as hard as anybody, after the fighting once began.' He was silent for some time staring into the fire. Then he roused himself and continued. 'God knows,' he added wearily, 'it's hard for any man to set another free, or make him a slave either, when it comes down to it. Freedom's not a thing you can pass around like a basket of apples, the way the Yankees seem to think. It's nothing you can give to anybody; it's what every man alive has to want, and take, and keep, for himself. Isn't that so, Cavin?' He fixed his thoughtful eyes on his son, but it was plain he expected no answer, that he was thinking aloud. 'Besides,' he went on, 'what's one man's freedom is another man's slavery in this world. Now, you take all those shoe factories they're building up north. Don't you suppose Matt would *feel* more of a slave in one of them than he does here, doing most of the time what he pleases?'

Leaning over he tapped his pipe sharply against the inside of the hearth, and, as he did so, the firelight flamed against his face, bringing out his sharp nose, the deep hollows in which his eyes were sunk, the high plane of his cheeks, and his straight eyebrows, which lifted noticeably upward where they joined his temples. Straightening himself, he sat leaning slightly forward with an ironical smile on his thin lips. 'Yet,' he went on, 'that's what we're all willing to die for — to stay free! And not one of us knows what freedom means for anybody, white *or* black.'

He stopped and gravely studied his son. 'You've been fighting, boy, when you ought to have been at your books. You'll need 'em to lean on, too, as the years go on. Well,' he sighed, 'you've learned what life is like, anyway, and that's all book-learning can teach you — what life is like, and how to take it when it knocks you down, as it will. Still,' he meditated, 'it's comforting to read what somebody like you, thousands of years before you were born, thought about problems like your own. Sometimes identically like your own, too,' he said, setting his cup down, clasping his hands behind his head, and putting his feet up beside Cavin's on the high brass fender. 'Now, take Horace,' he went on; 'that old Roman had thought a lot about freedom, as was natural in the child of a man who wasn't free-born. Or Plato. Plato had no illusions at all — he knew there are mighty few men fit to bear the burdens that freedom calls for.'

Feeling inside his coat he shook his head. 'I thought I had my Horace here in my pocket. Must be out in my saddlebags.'

Going into the hall, he returned with a small, scarred brown-leather book in his hand. Then, turning up the wick of the lamp that stood on a crocheted mat in the centre of the dining-room table, he laid the thin volume open, running his finger up and down the lines as he turned the pages. 'Here,' he said, 'here is what Horace says makes a man a slave — Listen!' He began to translate.

> Who, then, is free? The wise man who is master of himself, whom poverty or death finds unafraid, who scorns unworthy ambition.

Closing the book, he took his seat again.

'The Prayer Book speaks of service that is perfect freedom, doesn't it? I serve my country, or my creditors, or my family, don't I? Matt serves me, Jake you. Horace is right. Who is free? I don't know.'

'And yet, Cavin' — he stood up and began to pace agitatedly back and forth across the space in front of the hearth, with his long fingers interlaced behind him. 'Man's an unreasonable fool. Just the sight of one of those damned black rascals they've

sent out to police this county riles me to a point where I stop
thinking.'

Suddenly he stood still, studying Cavin's passive form, while
a deepening despair settled over his own features. 'It looks,' he
observed slowly, 'as though the Yankees intend to enslave *us*
now, in place of the poor darky. God knows why they think
that'll improve matters any!' He stood so long silent, staring
at his son, that Cavin at last urged him on. With a start, he
shrugged his shoulders lightly and began to speak again, in a
tired, remote voice.

'If we'd had any support at Richmond, we might have rallied
the Western armies —— Oh! well, no use talking about that
now,' he dismissed the idea gloomily. 'Maybe it wouldn't have
worked out anyway. When they gave out the order in Texas,
late in May, for the soldiers to reassemble in Houston, nobody
turned up but a few officers. Thousands were on their way to
Mexico, after looting all their own supply depôts.'

His expression was like that which always flooded his face
whenever he met with an illness he could not cure. Why did
the Creator make men subject to pain and frailty? he always
asked himself angrily on those occasions, as he did now. Shrugging his shoulders again, as though to shake off a persistent
gadfly, he went on. 'Some say they intended to join the French
there, but nobody knows. Even Governor Murrah scuttled
across the border. And those who stayed at home have mighty
strange advice to offer. Just look at this letter from John Reagan,
for example — and he was in our cabinet! Have you seen it?
It's here in one of the papers.' He got up and went over to a
black iron safe in the corner, where a stack of papers lay folded
together.

He stood scanning them hurriedly, till he found what he
wanted. 'Listen!' he exclaimed. 'This is what he advises us

to do.' Philip began to read slowly from the open page: 'To admit testimony of negroes in court, and fix qualifications for voting applicable to both races alike.' Speechless, he laid the sheet down.

'Cavin,' he said at last, standing still on the rug in front of his son, and looking at him earnestly, 'you've come home to a hell of a job. I can't see any end to it all. They say there's going to be an election and a constitutional convention; but if there is, all of us will have to apply for a special pardon before we can vote. That means, of course,' he observed, with a bitter smile, 'we'll never vote. Governor Hamilton called for a registration of voters in August, but not one single man worth killing has been allowed to qualify in this county — not one.'

His eyes burned and scorn rose in his voice. 'We've all held some kind of office, they say, or' — he grimaced — 'we own too much property. Since when was it a crime in this country to make a living?' he demanded. 'Or to serve as justice of peace, or on a school board?' He threw his long thin hands out hopelessly and his blue eyes were no longer misty, but flaming under his black brows. 'I've been four times to register, and each time they've turned me down.' For a moment he was silent, sunk in thoughts too bitter to express. Then he dropped into a chair and leaned forward to face Cavin. 'I'll be damned if I'll apply for a pardon,' he announced. 'A pardon for what? President Davis is right in his stand.'

For another moment, he sat still, until his gathering wrath again burst out. 'Twenty thousand dollars! It's absurd! Who do they want to run this country anyhow? The scum o' the earth?' The question seemed to answer itself and he went on, in gathering wrath. 'My children have to live here — and yours too!' he added, resuming his pacing up and down. 'Their children, too, after you, and I, and they, are all dead.'

'What do they think we are made of?' he asked, turning in
his tracks. 'Water? I tell you, Cavin, men who went through
four years of the army, and came out alive, will not endure
what's going on now in this state. And it's getting worse every
day.'

He paused, apparently trying to subdue his mounting emotions.

'Go on,' Cavin prompted him. 'I'd better know how things
are.'

'The rule now is,' Philip continued, almost as if he had never
paused in his recital, 'that planters have to draw up contracts
with their negroes — contracts satisfactory to the government
officials at Galveston.' He paused, with a significant smile.
'To get them approved, of course you have to bribe everybody
concerned. I simply haven't bothered with any such foolishness,' he asserted, moving over to the window and staring out
into the night, with his tall, severely erect back turned to Cavin.

The flames in the fireplace were reflected in the shining panes,
and he seemed to be looking out into another room full of light
and warmth, a room more strangely real than the one in which
he stood. 'Yes,' he thought suddenly. 'Who knows what is
real, what fancy?'

He sighed and turned sharply from the window. 'Cavin,'
he asked his son, emphasizing every word, 'Do you realize that
if any black negro should take a notion to make a complaint
against me, for any reason whatever, the military could throw
me into jail without so much as a warrant for my arrest? God
knows whether they'd ever let me out, and, even if they went
through the formality of trying me, I'd have to come up before
both our courts and theirs, and the military court'd be dead
certain to convict me. At least,' he amended his conclusion,
'that's their record so far — for white men of any reputation.'

He stopped in front of Cavin, turning toward his son a face marked now less by anger than by ironic, bitter amusement.

'The army claims control over all disputes involving soldiers or Union employees,' he explained. 'That takes in most of the cases, of course. The regular civil courts are supposed to be operating, but' — he drew his lips tight — 'they might as well be closed. The Governor has ruled explicitly that the state courts have no jurisdiction over federal agents. Now that the Freedman's Bureau is in Texas, things'll be worse yet, I suppose, because they tell me that organization has its own courts, too.'

'Well,' he said, sitting down heavily in his chair, 'there it is. There's nothing to do but get along the best way you can from day to day, knowing you are sitting right on top of a volcano.'

He sat groping for any facts he had left untold, and, drawing a long breath began again. 'We drew up a warning last week, after the negro troops tried to kidnap a white child, warning the military that if they cannot stop such offenses, we can and will. Every planter in the county signed his name to it,' he sighed, 'but God knows whether they'll pay any attention to us. More likely, they'll throw us all in jail for posting the notice.'

Cavin listened without comment, nodding from time to time. 'They sent a garrison of armed negro troops into this county in August,' Philip went on. 'Fortunately, they stay too dead drunk, most of the time, to do as much damage as they might; and they spend most of their time hanging around town, shooting craps in gambling dens. But they'll steal your hams and horses out from under your nose, if you turn your back. They would have cleaned Colonel Brashear out one night last week, if most of his teams hadn't happened to be in Galveston.'

'Yes, I saw them,' Cavin replied, 'when I was looking for ours. And I had some first-hand acquaintance myself with the Freedman's Bureau.' He threw a quick glance at his father.

'That reminds me. I better give you these.' He hunted in his pockets until he found and handed over to Philip the cotton receipts that Matt had given him at Galveston.

'I've already run into their fine soldiers,' he continued, emphasizing the word sarcastically. 'In fact, I barely missed killing one of 'em before I got out of town. He *may* be dead, for all I know. So,' he smiled grimly, 'I have some idea what's going on. It's worse than I expected — a good deal worse. Georgia seems to be quieter than this state. Here, sir. Finish your toddy,' he suggested, refilling the pitcher on the table with hot water from the kettle that hissed on the coals at their feet. Draining his own glass, he set it down, and reached out for another sandwich.

'In Georgia, Shelby and John Martin —— I believe you know the Martin family?' he broke off, tapping his breast. 'This uniform I have on is John Martin's.'

'I do, indeed.' Philip settled back in his chair, his youth rising again before him, and his voice dropping to a pleasant, reminiscent level. 'She was Celeste Daingerfield. They used to make an extraordinary kind of wine on their plantation just out of Charleston.'

'I know,' said Cavin. 'Rice wine. I had some this summer at Sunny Fields.'

'Yes,' Philip nodded. 'Your mother and I have visited there.'

In his slow, resonant voice, he began to inquire about what had happened to his son since he had seen him last.

'I simply made a jump in the dark,' he declared, 'when I sent you that letter in care of Devereaux's. Still, I felt pretty sure you'd make for Savannah, or Cedar Ledge. That is, if you pulled through.' He stuffed his pipe again, and held out his tobacco pouch to Cavin, inviting him to help himself.

Cavin shook his head, smiling. 'You'll think this is funny,

Pa, but it's the honest truth. I never learned to smoke in the army. We used to turn over all the liquor and the tobacco to the wounded men, and, when I was in the hospital ——'

'When? Where? How badly were you hurt?' Philip interrupted.

'Oh, it wasn't much.' With a wave of his square, muscular hand Cavin dismissed the subject and returned to one that interested him more. 'I didn't know how to smoke then, when I had the chance, and I haven't learned since,' he admitted with an apologetic smile which made him appear more of a boy than, until now, he had revealed himself to be.

For a long time Philip sat watching his son between half-closed eyes. Then he roused himself. 'Let's get to sleep the way we used to,' he suggested, 'with a game of checkers to settle our minds. They need settling all right,' he commented. 'You'll agree to that, I suppose. It's too late for any more talking to-night.' He glanced at the clock above the mantel, which already stood at twelve o'clock.

He rose to get the checkerboard which rested on top of the tall iron safe, where he stored his valuable papers, Letitia's jewelry, and such money as he kept on hand.

'I must show you how to work the combination to this safe tomorrow,' he told Cavin, picking up the board as he spoke. 'And here' — he indicated where a large pile of newspapers and pamphlets were piled inside a rack above the safe — 'are some *State Gazettes* and *Houston Telegraphs* and old copies of the *Galveston News* and the *Brazos Signal* that Letitia's been saving. If you'll look 'em over, you'll see how things have been going.'

He pulled the table squarely between them, and, drawing his chair up against it, set the checkers down, with a slight rattle, upon its polished surface.

'One round,' he told his son, 'for a nightcap.'

They played, intent and quiet, until the clock began to strike
the half-hour, and, instead of stopping at one metallic clang,
went on until Cavin counted twenty strokes.

He looked over the board at Philip and chuckled. 'Same
old clock. Once I heard it strike thirty-seven times before it
stopped.'

Rising, Philip leaned across the table and touched his son
lightly on the head with his sensitive fingers.

'I'm glad you're back, boy. Give my apologies to Lucina for
keeping you up so late. You'll blow out the lamp and bank
the fire?'

After he was gone, Cavin sat for a while in front of the blaze,
letting the familiar room again soak into his consciousness. He
looked around, noticing the long, cheap yellow table, with
six rickety legs, which Philip had picked up at the county seat
before he married Letitia, intending to use it only in the kitchen
for the servants or on outdoor occasions, like barbecues, when
he might need an extra stand. It had served now, though, for
seven years, in his dining-room, with a long rude bench, made
by one of Philip's carpenters, drawn up its length, at one side.
On the other side, ranged against the unpainted, unpapered
wall, were a number of finely designed chairs that Rhoades
Cunninghame and his sister Caroline had brought into the
bottoms from Carolina, and a tall highboy, with a pineapple
carved upon each drawer, which, Cavin knew, Mary had
taken with her from Savannah to Florida, and which Philip,
on his last trip back, had brought out to Texas.

Over the fireplace, hung a little crookedly, was an oil painting of Letitia's grandfather, old Brewster Charlton, her mother's father. His head was held high above a tight stock and a
black cravat, and the rich ivory tones of his skin and the flashing

blue of his eyes were amazingly lifelike. Cavin studied the face without recognizing it, and then his glance fell on the wall where hung two crayon drawings of Letitia's twins which a passing soldier, on leave, had done for some small compensation. They were execrable pieces of work, and the children stared out of the frame like stuffed dolls, lifeless and misshapen. Cavin wandered over to look at them, suddenly aware that he had not yet seen his little sisters.

He laid his hand on the door, and looked back at the room, remembering that his father expected him to bank the fire and blow out the lamp. The chair he had just vacated was still swaying slightly. It was a plain, pine rocking chair, with a sagging cowhide seat cushioned over with red sprigged calico, like its mate. Cavin sank down into it and leaned over the fender to rake together the ashes — a fender of fine brass, delicately designed, matching the tools by its side. The andirons, however, were of black iron, forged in Philip's own blacksmith shop by the man who made shoes for the horses and metal rims for the wagon wheels. And the stool in front of the hearth, on which the children sat to warm their feet, was only a wooden box covered with padding. Cavin recalled it from his own youth, but then it had had a different covering, he thought.

Going across to the table to blow out the light, he turned its wick low, and was leaning over the tall chimney with his lips drawn together for a vigorous puff, when his eye chanced to fall on the rack above the safe where the newspapers were stored. It had a solid black front broken in one corner by a sketch of a branching tree, and, in the other, by a round, yellow disk rising out of a dark background. Suddenly he realized that the painting on the front of the rack was intended to represent a tree lit up, in the black night, by the rising moon.

'By George!' he exclaimed aloud, slapping his thigh, 'all my life I thought the dark part of that picture was an enormous pig rooting in the ground.' He remembered as a child lying on the round rag rug in front of the fireplace warming himself before he got into bed, and studying, as he lay there, the progress of the pig. 'I'd have sworn it was a black Berkshire pig,' he said. 'I must tell Lucina about it.'

Laughing, he went to his own room, that was down the passage from the dining-room. Fourteen steps — he counted them, yes they were the same — turn to the right at the end of the hall; one step up, and bend your head. He was inside. The fire was almost out, but the coals threw a soft glow over the shadowy room, with its walls sloping down to meet the floor.

He moved silently over to his bed, with its twisted posts and its white ruffled canopy from which always hung, in season, an enormous mosquito net. There, with her head on a long bolster lay Lucina, sleeping as he had often watched her sleep on the grass on hot summer afternoons in their childhood at Cedar Ledge, with her hands crossed upon her breast, and her long dark lashes quiet upon her cheeks. As he stood watching her, he forgot the reports that Philip had been giving him, forgot the war, and remembered only that he was home at last with Lucina. He touched her fingers lightly, as he bent over her, and, feeling their chill, he drew the covers awkwardly higher. Opening her eyes, she smiled up at him, and was almost instantly asleep again.

At sunup, Cavin was wakened by the loud clanging noise of a heavy iron hammer striking against a plowshare — the signal which on their plantation always summoned the field hands to their work. Half an hour later, Aunt Emmy appeared with a tray on which were orange sections laid open like fans on paper napkins, hot black coffee, and buttered biscuits. Cavin held up a warning finger, as she knocked gently and entered the room.

Setting the tray quietly on a table beside him, in easy reach, she asked, in a sibilant whisper: 'Does you remember dar's two bells, Mas' Cavin? One fur dressin', one fur eatin'?'

Cavin nodded, folding his hands under his head. He wondered if he would ever get over remembering the hunger that had almost never left him the last year of the war. To the day he died, he thought, he would never cease being grateful for good hot biscuits and coffee.

He looked at the oranges and remembered how, every chilly night, Aunt Emmy always peeled the morning's supply and thrust them, in their white skins, on a shelf outside the kitchen window, leaving them there to crisp in the cool night air. Reaching out his hand, he picked up a stiff section and slipped it into his mouth. He knew exactly how it would taste, with the skin bitter and tough, and the fruit inside sweet as honey, yet slightly bitter and acrid, at the same time.

Years later, eating sweet California oranges, he told Lucina how much better the ones tasted that Philip took off English ships at Galveston, along with huge bunches of bananas, and brought across the bumpy prairies to his storehouse on the Brazos. He did not ever know that most of the oranges he ate then, in his youth, grew in Spain and were part of the lot that had been shipped to England for marmalade, before ever they were put on ships for Galveston.

He picked up another slice, and, leaning over Lucina, tickled her lips with it, watching her in amusement. She sat up suddenly, and he slipped behind her one of the big extra pillows which, during the day, always stood in hemstitched, buttoned cases on top the long bolster.

'I thought I was dreaming!' she exclaimed.

Lifting the tray, he set it down on the patchwork quilt. 'Pa says there's plenty of trouble brewing in Texas; but one thing sure, there's enough to eat.'

He bit into his biscuit, luxuriantly tasting the sweet butter that was churned daily in the big wooden dasher always left to sun out beside the well. Then he noticed two small white packets on the tray and pointed them out to Lucina. 'With Pa's compliments,' he told her, smiling at her puzzled look. 'It's quinine,' he informed her, pronouncing the vowel long. 'You pour it in your first half cup of coffee. Everybody in the bottom takes a dose every day.' He stopped and laughed. 'Everybody but Letitia. Pa's never been able to get her to swallow the bitter stuff. Says she'd rather have chills and fevers. Letitia's like that,' he commented thoughtfully. 'No bigger'n a mite, but dead set in her ways.' Taking up Lucina's packet, he poured it into her cup. 'Here, drink it,' he urged her. 'You'll hardly taste it, in this black coffee.'

They were out walking around in the yard before the second bell rang. It had cleared during the night, and, though the ground was wet, the air was already warming under the sun, and the wind had died down altogether.

'I ought to set out my flowers,' Lucina said, looking uncertainly around at the clean, sanded yard, with its precise beds marked off in slanting bricks, and filled in with rich black soil from the river bottom. The rosebushes, however, she noticed, were standing, like her mother's at Cedar Ledge, in beds of clay and loam. Now, in late October, they were weighed down by yellow blossoms delicately veined in pink. The night's wind and rain had lashed them about, however; and their petals were wet and torn, dripping incessantly over thorny leaves stained a soft brick red beneath their shining, green surface. The space under the cedar trees, where Letitia's bulbs came up in the spring, was raked and clear; and the ground under the large, shiny holly tree by the front gate was packed down and smooth.

The light that had blinded Lucina on the prairie seemed diffused and subdued, here on the river. It fell glaringly only on the white board fence enclosing the garden, on the white benches with trellised backs which edged three sides of the yard, and on the similarly trellised gate. Above it, there hung a copper bell that tinkled whenever the latch was lifted. Then, Cavin told her, Philip's enormous dog, George, who always slept on the door-sill, would rise on his tawny haunches and growl ominously, relaxing into friendly affability only when certain that the entering caller was white, not black.

The room in the garden seemed already taken up, Lucina thought, as she looked around. At that moment the bell rang for late breakfast.

As they approached the house, the sun came out from under a passing cloud, fully illuminating the long, gray building. Unpainted, it sat low on the ground, barely off it, indeed, with the front gallery covered by a sloping, projecting roof supported on six square, rough posts. Four dormers looked out over the porch, and a wide ell at the back provided space for a kitchen, a dining-room, and a sitting-room opening out, by long windows, on a side yard planned for another garden, but given over, in fact, to chicken-coops. Philip had added this ell the year that he had married Letitia, and they had kept the two front rooms for quiet bedrooms. Soon, Philip had built an office for himself outside, adding to the house, at the same time, an extra hall and a bedroom down it for Cavin. The war came on, and the upstairs remained unfinished — a place in which to store odd bureaus and broken rockers.

Philip and Letitia were already behind their chairs when

Cavin and Lucina came in through the front door, down the hall to the dining-room.

'Chicken hash!' cried Cavin, pausing on the threshold. 'And waffles!' Lucina echoed his delight, catching sight of Aunt Emmy as Letitia's fat cook entered the room, bearing a plate of waffles and two pitchers — one of fresh sugar cane syrup, the other of honey mixed with melted butter.

'My dear,' Philip asked Lucina, as he took his seat, 'is there anything you had in mind to do today? If not —— ' He paused, smiling pleasantly, with a reservation of some kind in his tone.

Lucina hesitated. 'I've some rosebushes and bulbs in the wagon that ought to be set out somewhere. I thought perhaps here by the kitchen —— ' She glanced out the long windows toward the back yard cluttered with dog-kennels and chicken-coops.

Philip leaned back in his chair and fitted his long fingers together into a precise triangle.

'How about it, Lettie?' he asked his wife across them. 'Shall we break the news? As well now as any time, perhaps?' She nodded, smiling.

'News?' asked Cavin, as Lucina laid down her fork. They both sat watching Philip's face, sensing that he was enjoying his unspoken thoughts.

'Well,' he began, looking at Cavin with a ghost of a smile curving his thin lips. 'It's been over thirty years now since I came out to Texas to visit your Cousin William. I was a young man then,' he said, in an aside to Letitia, but his glance immediately returned to his son. 'I remember that William and I rode all day long up and down the river, but toward sunset, we came out on the prairie to a place where the ground rose up from the river in a long slanting plateau, lightly wooded.

From the top of that slant, we could see off in every direction, toward the river close by and, further off, toward the prairie that seemed to me then so endless and forlorn.'

He leaned across the table, and his glance sought and held Cavin's.

'Always, ever since that evening,' he concluded, 'I've known that some day, if I stayed in Texas, I was going to build a house to suit me on that hill.'

His audience remained silent, realizing that his story was not yet finished. Taking out his pipe, Philip filled it and addressed his wife.

'My dear, you've no objections? Lucina? Cavin, no use learning the filthy habit.' Thoughtfully, he walked over to the fire, rolled a piece of paper beside it, and, lighting it, applied it to the tobacco in his pipe. Then, after settling himself again in his chair, he rose again, and, laying his hands on the table in front of him, smiled at his listeners.

'Wait a minute. I'll get a map and show you.'

Burrowing in the pigeonholes of his safe, he held up a folded, yellow paper, and, opening it, spread it out on the dining-room table, pushing aside the dishes to make room for the rattling sheet.

'See there,' he said, pointing to a firm black cross. 'Well, that's a sign I made thirty years ago to mark the place where I expected to build a house some day. I remember writing Cavin's mother about it.'

'Yes,' Cavin broke in, 'and I know what you wrote her, too.'

'No doubt,' returned Philip equably. 'I've reminded you often enough. Well,' he continued, sitting forward in his chair, with his hands on the table, 'I think it's time to start building that house, if I'm ever to see it finished. What do you say, Cavin?'

He turned squarely toward his son. 'The twins are coming
on, and there's FitzHugh. I sold my land in Florida before the
war and leased your mother's place in Georgia. I figure that
income — if there is any, now — is yours, outright, but' — he
smiled gently — 'we can pool our resources, I suppose? Even
with the war going on, Colonel Rutherford was able to ship
some cotton out of Mexico — and he got a good price for it,
too. Most of that money went into Confederate bonds, of course,
but there's a little on deposit in London — passage money,
about. I thought, if the war went against us —— ' Shrugging
his shoulders, he lifted his hands, spreading his fingers apart.
'When it came down to it, though, I couldn't persuade myself
to pull up stakes.'

He leaned closer. 'This place is clear. We can get an advance
from Colonel Rutherford — all we need, I expect. How does
it look to you, son?' he inquired.

Cavin stood up, pushing back his chair.

'I think we'd better start building,' he said decisively.

'Well, then,' said Philip, with an easy smile, 'that's settled.
In that event,' he went on, 'Lucy better get her garden started
up there, on the hill.'

It was mid-morning when they set out, and the air had lost
its chill, but not its freshness. In the woods, the odor of fallen
leaves and wet stumps followed them, but as they came out
into the open, the sunlit air was marked by some pungent,
exhilarating perfume that it took Lucina years to identify and
name hesitantly to herself as the sweet smell of open space.
They crossed a little creek, the water coming up to their horses'
knees, and then Philip drew Pilot up, sharply.

'Here's the very tree I tied my horse to, thirty years ago.'

The sun lay warm on the dry, brown grass which covered the

spot. Toward the west, the rich, black bottom land was cut by the river and a small creek; to the east, the dun and dreary prairie stretched out to the Gulf. Toward the north, a grove of dark trees rose, like an open fan — a grove of oaks, cotton-woods, and bois d'arcs rising in an enormous half-circle, and spreading above them, along the creek, a line of grotesque cypresses.

Letitia, Philip saw, was inspecting the location like a visitor, with a tranquil, impersonal interest.

'She doesn't care,' he thought, reading her mind, as if she had opened it to him. 'She simply doesn't care.' He tore his attention from her, taking such comfort as he could in Cavin's delight.

'He has no idea,' Philip meditated, 'that you can give every-thing you have on earth to a venture, and yet lose, in the end. Like President Davis,' he thought, remembering, as he often did, the man who lay in Fortress Monroe, growing weaker every day. His eyes followed Cavin's movements with a kind of still, passionate interest. Yes, it would be harder to see his son frustrated and baffled by life than to endure defeat him-self.

'Lettie,' he said, strolling over to his wife who stood leaning both arms on a low limb of a mulberry tree, looking absently down the sloping hill. 'Having children is like offering life several places, instead of one, to hit you a mortal blow.'

She raised her eyes and he saw that she understood him. Suddenly he was sad because she did. 'Ah! well,' he said gently. 'Even great Jove wept over his children.' He took her hand, and they stood watching Cavin pacing out a square.

'We'll have to keep the rabbits off somehow,' they heard him saying to Lucina. For a moment he seemed to have no solution for the problem. Then he set two of the negroes to cutting small straight limbs which he had them stick, like staves, into the ground around the plants.

Philip smiled. Over and over he had read how Odysseus, on his return, had stood back for some time, watching his son moving capably about amongst his roistering guests. Now it came to him afresh how unerringly right that story was, how in accord with human nature. 'I'd have done the same,' he thought, with his eye fixed on Cavin, 'exactly the same. Any father would have.'

That night, Lucina and Cavin sat on each side of the dining-room table drawing separate sketches. Philip leaned over them, studying the sheets.

'Lettie,' he called, 'come here and look.'

She glanced over his shoulder, and quickly, while Lucina watched, drew two long lines to indicate a wide avenue leading straight from a gate to the house. 'That would be a nice place to scatter all your bulbs, wouldn't it, Lucy? What kind of trees had you thought of setting out?'

Almost before she thought, Lucina answered.

'No, no,' Philip corrected her. 'Not in Texas, my dear. Cedars don't do so well in dry years, and, young as you are, you'd never live to see live-oaks full grown. Better stick to locusts. They spring up quickly after a hurricane —— '

'Hurricane?' Lucina asked, catching her breath.

'Yes,' Philip responded firmly, meditating on the point, 'locusts are your best choice.'

'Anyway,' said Cavin, a grim mask dropping over his features, 'a man who's been at Chickamauga can do without cedars, all the rest of his days.'

'I'd think so,' said Philip, a glance of understanding passing quickly between him and his son.

After a moment, however, he smiled down at Lucina, and, laying his hand affectionately on her head, sent an inquiring glance at his wife.

'Lettie,' he said, 'we must invite the county to meet this child, next week.'

Chapter 11

DESPITE the difference in their ages, Povey Blount and William Charlton enjoyed a close friendship. William often said to Helen, his wife, that, since the night Letitia had driven away from their house with Philip, Povey had ceased to be young, anyway. Then, as time went on, he almost forgot the years that separated them. After they both returned from the army, they would sometimes sit together for hours, speaking rarely, and then about rain and weather and growing crops.

'Povey acts as if some spring's broken in him,' William worried. 'When he gets well, I must try to stir him up somehow.'

He tried, and continued to try, long after Povey had partially recovered and had moved back from Holly Grove to his own plantation, Land's End — named for the spit of land projecting into the Brazos, where Povey's uncle, young Tobias Blount, had built his rambling whitewashed house when he first came out to Texas, in 1827.

'Povey,' William would inquire, riding over from his own fields to interview his friend, 'why don't you go and call on the two charming young ladies visiting Colonel Brashear's girls?'

Povey would smile a slow smile that never rose into his quiet eyes.

'I'm sorry,' he would invariably say, 'but I must see to planting the West Field tomorrow.' Or to building a levee, or to repairing fences, or to something else — William could seldom persuade him to leave his plantation.

'It's unnatural,' William would storm to his wife. 'It's against nature for a handsome young man to live like a hermit. I thought if he came back he'd come back changed; but he's back, and everything's just the same. They walk around like ghosts — all of them. Helen,' he would sigh wearily. 'I don't see how it's going to end.'

Then, her eyes, as black as the long jet earrings she always wore, would grow thoughtful, and she, too, would begin to fret. 'He never goes to church with us, any more!' she would complain, sighing.

She recognized this omission, however, as a sign of apathy, not a turning toward sin; for, on the Brazos, she knew that people regarded their church not only as a road to salvation but also as a component part of their social system — as component a part, indeed, as their courts or their plantations. Therefore, she understood that Povey was not necessarily renouncing his faith when he stayed away, as he did, from the little church where Letitia's children had been christened respectively Felicia, Letitia, and FitzHugh.

There, on Sunday mornings, the white people always seated themselves downstairs, while their servants occupied the balcony. Afterward, family groups were apt to join their relations, all driving together to the little creek and spreading their dinners out side by side on long, white tablecloths laid flat on the ground.

Time after time, in the past, Povey had sat by, while cold fried chicken was being exchanged for minced chicken salad, covered over in a neat star design of sieved egg yolk; or while pear chip preserves were being passed, or yellow pound cake. Time after time, he had sat listening to all the county gossip, as he watched his friends pouring grape and blackberry wine out of great brown jugs. But not any more; he had given up going to church altogether, now, it seemed.

Even the Bishop no longer made any effort to persuade Povey to accompany him, when he arose, as he often did, at Land's End early on Sunday mornings and started off to early service alone. Sometimes, though, they would sit for hours under Povey's lacy chinaberry trees talking of war and, after that, of men's strange passions and dark fears and long unanswered prayers. Theirs was a companionship which drew from two different sources, which met and merged in a poetic faith based less on theology than on a strong sense of the mysterious beauty moving in this world — a beauty which, they both agreed, men need as they need the air and the sun, and the wind, and the rain.

'You know,' Povey admitted late one black night as they sat talking together, 'I can't follow you all the way. Take your creed, now —— ' he protested, leaving his sentence half finished.

'What are creeds but words?' the Bishop replied, in his clear, flowing voice, turning a thoughtful face toward the leaves above him. 'And what are words? There's nothing stranger than a word, Povey — that frail net in which men try to enclose every kind of meaning. "The Word was made flesh" — that is the eternal mystery.'

The Bishop's gaze wandered slowly out across the dark sky and his ear caught the sound of the wind moving thinly in the cypresses by the river — a sound quite different from the heavy bass with which it sang through the oaks. He listened a moment wondering how to explain what had brought him to Texas and kept him there. Could any man ever explain his dream to another — even to his closest and dearest? — he pondered.

Then he remembered a line he had read and marked a few days before in an old book of English sermons and he repeated it to Povey.

' "To hold a flickering candle in Time's dark hall" — that is what the Church has to do, isn't it?' he asked in a voice that revealed how often he had argued this same subject with himself. He paused, and his eyes, set strangely aslant under his high brow, glowed with some urgent conviction.

'I am in Texas to hold up that candle,' he said, at last. 'The priests of Isis and Buddha have had the same duty to perform.'

Povey smiled in the dark — a sorrowful, fleeting smile. 'I have not so good a reason for being here,' he said. '*I* am in Texas because I first loved one woman, and then another, and have since loved nothing, not your God, or Isis, or the Lord Buddha either.' His low voice ceased, as he peered through the dark into the Bishop's face.

'You married her to him!' he exclaimed, sitting upright in his chair, as the words poured suddenly and hotly across his lips.

The Bishop spread out his slender, brown hands and dropped them in a weary gesture.

'I've always known you were going to say that to me, Povey. Because a man wears my cloth is no reason he won't on occasion be a fool and a sinner, too, unless the Lord prevents him. I know. I've been both — and that was one of the times.' He locked his thin fingers behind his back and began to walk back and forth in quick, impatient strides.

Povey sank back into his chair, as still as he would be when he was dead. It was the first time he had ever spoken his mind, the Bishop reflected, and probably it would be the last time, too. Therefore, when his pacing brought him again in front of Povey's silent figure he stopped and faced him.

'Povey, tell me — I had hoped the war and her children——'
He broke off, interrupted by a short, harsh laugh out of the
darkness.

'What difference do her children make? I've sense enough
to know that now — though I didn't at first. As for the war
——' Leaving his sentence unfinished, he began another in
the cold, quiet voice of man uttering a simple fact. 'I never
dreaded death as much as I do life.'

'Yes,' the Bishop thought with one part of his mind, while
the other followed Povey's voice, 'that's why confessions are
heard in dark churches — a man will not talk in the light.'

'When I saw how things were,' he ventured, 'I was afraid——'

'Yes,' Povey interrupted, 'I know you were. I'll admit I
thought of that possibility, myself. I still do. Yes,' he said,
suddenly rising and falling into step with the Bishop, 'I'll tell
you the truth, there's never a day yet I don't think of it. I'm
not such a fool as to suppose that God — if there is a God —
would count it an offense.' He kicked away a stick that had
fallen in his path, and laid his hand on his friend's arm,
swinging him sharply around.

'Can't you see?' he demanded. 'We were too young to understand that nothing in the past or in the future mattered; she
was hurt and I, too — unbearably hurt, I thought. Your God
should spare mankind from being young, my good Bishop,'
he ended bitterly, and then, after a moment's silence, began
again to move restlessly back and forth across the wide yard.

'I saw from the very beginning that there was no answer, no
way out for any of us — all of us being what we were. If we
had been savages, it would have been simple. But being what
we were' — he sighed deeply and explosively — 'being what we
were — what is the answer?' Breaking his step, he moved over
to the fence, leaning on the white top rail.

'Over there,' he pointed, 'she is. Here am I. Can you suggest what to do, my friend? No,' he said slowly, 'don't answer. I know you can't, but a Hottentot could.' He gazed out into the night. 'Plenty of men in this state, too, would call me a fool, and sometimes I think they are right,' he admitted, lifting his gaze across the dark and vacant fields. 'Sometimes I despise myself.'

They stood there together, without speaking. The frogs began their nightly croaking in the river flat, and an alligator's deep muttering roar broke across the quiet.

'That's why we're friends,' said Povey, 'because you don't know any sure answers, either. Come on in to bed.' He laid his arm around the Bishop's broad shoulders, and they stood, for a few moments longer in utter silence, each following his own thoughts out into the blackness that surrounded them.

The Bishop sighed and stirred at last. 'God knows I wish I did, Povey.' They were at the doorstep when he put out his hand and touched his friend.

'I hope you'll go tomorrow, Povey,' he said in his most persuasive voice.

Povey stared at him. 'Go? Go where?' Then in a flash he understood. Of course. Philip would be welcoming Cavin home. The boy was back, he had heard, with a wife.

Suddenly his old despair quickened within him, and on an unreasonable impulse, he made a sudden decision.

'No,' he replied sharply; 'I'm not going; I'm not even invited. I'm going down to Berryville tomorrow, to the dance Judge Symington's giving for his nieces.'

It was the Bishop's turn to stare. He could hardly have been more astonished.

'You've been advising me,' said Povey sternly, 'to do just that. Well, I think it's good advice and I'm accepting it. That's all.'

As the Bishop prepared for bed, he meditated on how little he liked the turn his advice had taken. All night, he was restless; but when he left early in the morning, he decided that it was best not to reopen the conversation of the night before.

As he rode away, he found himself thinking of his home in Cheraw, and was suddenly homesick for it. This was a strange country, Texas. Every day here, he ran into a problem he couldn't solve. There had been months in Carolina, after he had given up his legal practice and entered the Church, when nothing more urgent than a christening had come up, when he had even had all the time he needed to write a history of the Cheraw Indians.

'This won't do,' he said, and fell to planning his work. 'Now,' he thought, 'I might just *try* holding service in the saloons. If they can sing drinking songs, they can sing chants,' he mused, and made a sudden decision. 'A bar-counter ought to make an acceptable altar.'

He touched his mare, Firefly, lightly with his spurs. He was due at Locust Hill by noon, and he had three or four sick people to visit first.

A few hours later, when he turned into Philip's lane, he saw ahead of him a long procession of Philip's friends. Some were riding Kentucky mares, decorated with the faded rosettes and ribbons which they or their sires had won in old, forgotten races. Some were on tough little mustang ponies, with tangled manes, hard mouths, and resentful, rolling eyes. Others came in gigs pulled by nervous, wiry horses with delicate, twitching ears and long, well-shaped legs.

In the midst of this procession, one figure stood out, like Sancho Panza, from the crowd — the shrivelled figure of old Mr. Archibald Bland, who sat his freckled, gray mule, Gabe, as erectly as if the animal were a charger, and from time to time shifted the greenish tails of his long black coat more evenly across the creature's rump. He owned a three-acre island in the river, deeply shaded with live-oaks, and there he lived with his dogs and his chickens and his old mule, Gabe. 'What more does a man need?' he would ask Philip, whenever they fished together from his leaky boat. He kept Gabe's mane roached and upright, but even then the cockleburrs would get into it, and at last he let them stay there — just as he let the steps to his house fall down and stuffed the hole in his skiff with rags. For not since his wife and children had been trapped in a burning house had he considered life worth taking much pains about.

He was accompanied by young Doctor David Armstrong, only two months home from the war, who was reining in his prancing mare to keep pace with Gabe's stiff legs. He had inherited his father's plantation, Shadow Point, where, on an arm of land jutting out into the yellow river, he and his younger brother Byrnes lived alone. Byrnes was running the place, David informed old Mr. Bland, and he himself had not yet decided whether to practise medicine here in the county, or in Harrisburg, where the crumbling capitol of the Republic still stood, overlooking Buffalo Bayou. He remembered, as he rode along between the locusts, that the man beside him had also lingered, on spring nights, under the shadow of the Rotunda at Charlottesville, and began at once to talk to him about the University. David had enlisted in Virginia, where his father had sent him to study medicine; and he had not been in Texas for now nearly six years. His listener had not been in Virginia for twenty; but they soon found they shared many recollections.

'Yes, yes,' responded old Mr. Bland absently, as though he were recalling a familiar dream. He too knew how the Univer-

sity lawn looked between midnight and morning, with the white
colonnades gleaming in the moonlight and the wavering shadows crossing the damp grass.

A carriage drove up behind them. William Charlton, in the
seat beside his driver, raised his carriage-whip, with its flowing
red ribbon, high in salutation.

'Fine day, gentlemen!' His hair was combed away from his
face in front, but he still wore it long in back and about his ears,
where, despite vigilant clipping and brushing, his short sideburns curled against his cheeks. Lowering his whip, he lifted
his wide hat, and his keen blue eyes gleamed pleasantly as he
passed his friends.

With him were his wife and two guests just then visiting at
Holly Grove — Judge Duval White, from Berryville, and his
sister, Miss Clarissa, a little wisp of a woman with a wide, firm
mouth. She had learned music in South Carolina and was
teaching it now in Texas. 'Clarissa,' her brother sometimes said
to her a little anxiously, 'you just missed being strong-minded.'
She looked after him with meticulous care, and every day had
his servant brush his sleazy black coat and press the narrow black
tie that he wore with the ends crossed, but never knotted, under
his flaring wing collar. The Judge would never have thought
of such matters himself. His mild gray eyes stared out too absently on the world to take note of creases in a coat. 'Does a
man have to tie his cravat if he doesn't want to?' he would
demand mildly, but firmly, whenever his sister remonstrated
with him.

Judge Toombs Dickerson, from Austin County, was standing
on the gallery at Philip's house when Judge White arrived.
Stepping modestly out of the carriage on a box provided for that
purpose, Miss Clarissa threw a sudden searching glance at her
brother. In her mind she was comparing him, to his advantage,

with the tall man who stood lounging against Philip's gallery, stroking a flowing brown moustache.

Toombs Dickerson was born at Velasco and had never yet put foot out of his native state. His father — a Georgian — had been massacred with Fannin at Goliad, and, as a boy of nine, Toombs himself had taken part in the celebrations which followed Santa Anna's capture at San Jacinto. At seventeen, he began to read law and, later, served as county judge before the war broke out, when he was assigned to the defense of Galveston. In April, 1865, he saw no reason whatever for Texans to surrender because Virginians had. Still he was, above all, a man of common sense, and when the troops failed to reassemble at Houston in June, 1865, he realized, at last, that the struggle was over.

Returning home, he found a deputation of citizens waiting to welcome him back. Next day, without the formality of an election, he resumed his former office, sitting with two pistols in easy reach and the flag of the Republic nailed high up behind his chair. Never, except in court, was he ever seen with his wide hat off his head; and even there he wore his tight trousers stuffed inside his high boots — and, in the hottest weather, tore off his collar. Yet Duval White, his sister had to admit, did not know more law than Toombs Dickerson, nor could he bow more politely to a lady.

Miss Clarissa surveyed Toombs now, however, with a vague air of distaste which he recognized. It was a warm day for November, and he wore no coat over his pleated white shirt, only a striped vest made with a high, turned-down collar edged round with silk braid. This buttoned up under his brown chin, almost hiding the ready-made cravat which, in deference to the occasion, he had snapped on beneath his soft collar. He had discarded his boots, for the day, in favor of a pair of shoes with comfortable toes and elastic insets at the ankles; and as he had left home that morning, he had lifted his enormous black hat off its cowhorn rack thinking he did very well.

This, however, he saw at once, was not Miss Clarissa's opinion. Smiling, he came forward to swing open the gate for her. Long ago, they had agreed to a kind of prickly, armed neutrality, so now he began, in his deep, drawling voice, to tease her, his alert eyes, more yellow than brown, twinkling as he spoke.

'Miss Clarissa,' he demanded, 'when you reckon you're going to get me all dressed up slick and fine, like the Judge here?' He held out his hand, as he spoke, half-winking at Judge White across his sister's thin shoulders.

The two men shook hands heartily. A few weeks before, they had planned a couple of days' shooting together, but a riot had prevented them from carrying out their intention. 'Too bad we never got those partridges for breakfast, Judge,' said Toombs now, recalling the emergency which had arisen in the narrow section where their counties joined.

The three of them now walked over to speak to Letitia and Philip, who were standing in the yard, with Cavin and Lucina beside them.

'Good morning. Good morning ... Lucina, my dear, ... let me introduce ...' Philip repeated time after time, 'Glad to see you. ... How are you?'

A good many of his guests thought, as they passed him, that with his straight back, his shadowy blue eyes, and his still dark hair, he was handsomer than his son. His long black coat, held together at his throat with a large single button, just escaped his knees, accentuating his height. His trousers, with their tight legs and very wide cuffs, had been made before the war, and likewise his frilled white shirt, but they became him well. Cavin's shoulders had yet to fill out, his thin body to take on more weight, before he would make as impressive a figure as Philip. Perhaps that time would never come.

The next man to ride up was young Mr. Alexander Winston, who, like Cavin, had fought in the Fourth Texas and had left an arm in Virginia. As he saw him dismounting, Philip remarked under his breath to Letitia that the boy was the spit and image of all the Winstons he ever saw — the same shining, black hair and cold, gray, searching eyes, the same narrow head and furious, reckless temper that never seemed to smolder out. He came alone and was eager to talk with his stocky young neighbor, Mr. Thomas Abernethy, whose connections at Shelbyville, Kentucky, had been kind enough to entertain him, Alexander, during a brief furlough between battles. He wanted to ask Thomas, too, how the fighting had been on the Border, where Thomas had been stationed throughout the war; and whether he had seen any of the camels President Davis was said to have turned loose there during the Mexican War, twenty years earlier.

'Lord! How I'd-a hated being stuck down there!' Alexander groaned, and then smiled as he saw Thomas approaching with his two stoutish, older sisters, whose figures revealed their strange passion for cake and pickles at unaccountable hours.

Alexander paused.

'How are you, Miss Minerva, Miss Eliza?' he inquired, beaming. That night, Miss Minerva recalled his smile in her dreams; but next morning, being a realist, she took a stern glance at her near-sighted eyes and her pudgy figure, and put aside her dream.

'Somebody's got to run this plantation,' she told herself resolutely, and set about doing it with energy and competence. Already she could tell that her young brother Thomas was going to be better at books than at cotton-planting. She didn't mind. She had plenty of ideas herself about managing the place. If the Lord didn't make a girl pretty, she reflected thankfully, He nearly always gave her good sense. Not that it was altogether a good exchange, but still — there was that new Hungarian grass everybody was talking about, for fodder. She resolved to plant some.

As Miss Minerva passed by Philip, old Mr. Tripp Cuttross approached — old Mr. Cuttross, who could lift his hat like a prince and often boasted that he lived on a dollar a week.

'Sober, for once,' thought Letitia. 'Thank goodness.'

He was followed by Mr. Davidson Rideout, who, after the war, had started up a tiny store on the road that passed his place, where he never remembered to dust the shelves. He wore a spotted pair of trousers, but he was known to have his boots polished every day and never — not even in August — to leave off his coat at meals. His wife, like himself, was brought up in Annapolis, where, except for the war, their daughter, Evelina, would now have been in school. Now, of course, she would never go, a fact which distressed her parents far more than it did her. Her father had never had a large plantation in Texas — only a few hundred acres, and nobody knew how he held on to that, nowadays.

Mrs. Horatio Spurlock, coming up behind Evelina, paused to admire the fit of the young girl's dress. She had reason to do so, for she had made it out of one of Mrs. Rideout's old ones. Mrs. Spurlock's husband was a better soldier than a business man, so, since the war, she had quietly taken to doing fine sewing, being careful to put it out of sight whenever dear Horatio was around. She examined Letitia's frock also, finding no fault with the numberless rows of narrow tucks which she had stitched into its wide skirt, nor with the smoky blue velvet ribbon with which Lucina had laced her basque. She stood back a moment admiring the taste which had dictated exactly that combination of blue with ashy rose.

'I do declare, Lettie,' she told her, kissing her, 'you get prettier every single day. You'll have to,' she added, kissing Lucina too, 'to keep up with this young lady.' Stopping in her tracks, she smiled at this bride of Cavin's — this slight, dark, glowing girl, with such shining, dark hair, such happy, brown eyes and smiling lips, lips almost as red as the dress she was wearing. 'Hum!' thought Mrs. Spurlock expertly, 'that silk's been dyed, but,' she admitted, 'whoever dipped it knew how.' She leaned over and, on an impulse, kissed Lucina again. 'Cavin,' she remarked severely, 'you stole a march on us. And all the girls in the county setting their caps for you, too!'

Two men came late, John and Kirby McGaughey, with their wives and sons. They were middle-aged brothers, with a great deal of iron-gray hair, loud, rumbling voices, and extremely active feet inside their high boots, which they wore everywhere, their spurs clanking at every step. Since the war they had taken up cattle-raising on a big scale.

They were always telling Philip that, with things the way they were, it was a heap better sense to turn to white labor. When the bush fall season was over, now, most of their cowhands would go back to working in stores in the German settlement at the far end of the county, or back to the little, sandy tracts of scrubby prairie land where their fathers tried to raise potatoes and beans. And the Freedman's Bureau, they devoutly hoped, would never come poking around demanding contracts between free white men.

'Philip,' John said, shaking his host's hand, 'better come into the cattle business with us. These fool contracts they're talking about now'll drive you plumb crazy, if you keep on planting cotton.'

The Bishop fell in behind him. There was nobody he enjoyed talking to more than Philip, but he passed on to get acquainted with Cavin.

'I knew your mother,' he told Lucina, 'when I was a young man visiting around in Savannah.' He began to tell her about those days now, with evident relish and no sign of hurry.

'Don't you go monopolizing the belle of the ball, Bishop,' said Colonel Rutherford, who had come in from Galveston. 'I haven't spoken to her yet.' He smiled at Lucina and spoke hastily to Philip. 'Colonel Ashbel Smith sent you his apologies and regrets. He's down again with the fever he picked up at Matagorda.'

'Ah! I'm sorry,' said Philip. 'Lucina, you must meet the Colonel later, when he recovers. He is one of our Texas proselytes,' he informed her, 'a Northerner who served both in the Republic and the Confederacy.'

She held out her hand to Colonel Rutherford, smiling; and Philip turned to welcome a tiny lady just approaching.

'How do you do, Mrs. Dyess?' Philip said warmly. 'And Miss Winnie Lee!' he exclaimed, holding out his other hand. 'How are *you*?'

Colonel Rutherford smiled and bowed, too. He admired Mrs. Dyess without reservation. She had a delicately formed body; and, although she was well on to fifty, an eager, childlike face. But her looks were deceiving. All alone she had come out from Mississippi, a widow with her three boys and her slaves, and had taken out an extensive head right at Oyster Creek to equal that of her brother, who, at his death, had left her all his property besides.

'It's a pity she isn't a man,' Colonel Rutherford often thought, and then wondered why he thought so. She made a better job of cotton-raising than most men, and she was, he admitted, remarkably punctual in meeting her obligations.

'You're looking well, Miss Winnie Lee,' said Philip cordially, directing his attention to Mrs. Dyess' companion. 'Still sleeping late?'

Everybody knew Miss Winnie Lee, who, despite ten years of matrimony, had all the characteristics of an old maid. Men, she sniffed, were poor creatures — all except John Kemper, whom she had married. He was as poor as Job's turkey and had had only one thing to offer her — the privilege of sleeping as late as she pleased in the morning. Miss Winnie Lee had never combed her own hair until she became his wife. But they had been happy. Now he was buried in Virginia, in deep red clay; and she lived with each of her friends in turn, teaching their girl children to paint on fine china, and their boys to keep their feet off other people's chairs, and to look a questioner straight in the eye.

Last of all, came Colonel Carpenter Brashear, a widower, with his two pretty, vivacious daughters, Miss Sabra and Miss Alice. His rusty carriage-top was folded back, and carpet no longer covered the floor of the swaying vehicle, but the horses that drew it were rubbed down and shining, and the coachman that drove it knew how to hold up his reins.

'Sorry to be late, Philip,' Colonel Brashear apologized, taking out a hemstitched pocket handkerchief and dusting his strong, brown hands, 'but I met up with a couple of rascally soldiers who took a fancy to my horses. Fortunately Howard Blakely came along with his boy, and here we are,' he concluded, '*with* the horses.'

'I hope we all have as much luck,' Philip congratulated him. 'Letitia, you remember Ruthven, of course?' he said, laying his hand on Howard's son, who, since Cold Harbor, had been sunk in perpetual melancholy, with the sight of one eye gone entirely, and of the other nearly so.

Bishop Gregg had been in Texas only a few years. Therefore gatherings like this interested him immensely. He took his seat in a rocking-chair on the front gallery and watched the people moving amongst the rosebushes. A stranger, he thought, might well wonder what common tie all these friends enjoyed. But he had lived long enough in the state to know that those who had had a similar bringing up in the older South naturally flocked together in Texas. Whether newcomers possessed money, or lacked it, was of far less importance in this bottom, he reflected, than whether they were disposed to fit easily into the pattern of life already established on the Brazos.

He had tried, without much success, to explain these matters to Major Bradford, a Northern army officer recently sent into the county — a man who was a member of the Bishop's church and had, therefore, sought him out. Soon they discovered that they had met before, when the Bishop was on a summer's visit to a classmate's home in New Jersey. Now Major Bradford was stationed, not at Berryville, where the largest garrison was, but down the river ten miles, at a small outpost where cotton claimed for the Federal Government was stored.

'And yet I've never been able to make him understand the situation here in Texas,' the Bishop thought. 'Never.' For a moment his mind hovered anxiously around the case. 'Maybe I'd be wise to ask him if he ever read Burke's great chapter on how often folly and madness are perpetrated in the name of liberty,' he mused, and immediately rejected the idea. 'He'd be certain to quote Carlyle back at me,' he decided, a half smile appearing on his lips. 'How'll I ever explain this country to him?'

There were so many things Northern people in Texas had to be told, the Bishop reflected unhappily, entirely too many. No wonder it was easier for Southerners to flock together.

'For instance,' the Bishop went on thinking, 'there is the

county judgeship. The planters on the Brazos seem to reward their judge exactly as they do their bishop — when they market their crops.'

The circumstance had bothered him when he first came to Texas, but not any longer. He had learned better how to interpret events on the Brazos, where the planters preferred to lay their own roads, and pay the costs of justice direct. Wasn't it cheaper, they reasoned, to look after things yourself than to pay a lot of clerks at the county seat to do it for you? So they kept the tax rate low, and burned the notes with which the judge sometimes supplemented his meagre salary. Yet they would not have elected a judge whose integrity they held in doubt.

'Yes,' the Bishop thought, his mind returning to the point from which it had circled, 'that's why we all get along — we don't have to stop and explain things to each other. Things like Mr. Cuttross's habit of sitting on his front gallery in his nightgown on hot days; or' — his eyes grew sad — 'Povey's absence here today; or why nobody ever mentions his family to Tazewell Barclay.' His eye fell pityingly on a man just then talking to Philip — a man whose wife never accompanied him to gatherings, whose son, as everyone knew, had fallen on evil ways in New Orleans.

'Why,' thought the Bishop, rising, 'I'm getting to be a regular Texan myself!'

He was going over to inquire how FitzHugh was when he saw that Philip seemed to be explaining something to a group of people gathered around him. The Bishop got up and strolled closer.

'If you will all be so good as to walk back to the river,' Philip was saying, 'the cowboys from Lost Island Ranch will proceed to demonstrate what poor riders most of us are.'

As he paused, a number of cowhands on horseback began to file out of the lane, passing through the open stable gates, to the field behind the barns, where Philip had raised enough tiered seats to accommodate his guests, and a stout board fence to protect them from the plunging horses. The riders advanced, with their blue-checked gingham jumpers swelling backward in the breeze. They were all wearing bright handkerchiefs loosely tied around their necks, and wide hats with jagged holes cut in the crowns to let in air. They wore no chaps, however, such as were needed in west Texas where thorny bushes tore incessantly at a rider's legs. Their boots and spurs were dull, and their ponies' sides had never felt a currycomb; but each man sat his horse with a slouching, easy poise; and horse and man, by some indefinable sympathy, seemed to move as one.

Lucina took her seat on the tiered benches and leaned eagerly forward, as Cavin warned her to keep an eye on the men, who were limbering up their muscles in the field in front of them.

She sat watching the ropes ascend and drop in wide, graceful circles precisely where those who wielded them expected them to fall. Some of the men were sitting idly on the fences whirling their ropes with easy, negligent gestures, making amazingly intricate loops and whorls. Others were walking carelessly about, throwing their ropes upward in various involved figures, their bodies swaying in perfect balance with the fall of the coil. A stranger, observing the facility with which these tricks were performed, might have supposed them easy to imitate, but Philip's guests were not so easily deceived.

One of the McGaughey cowboys, in fact, spent most of his spare time trying to make a rope stand up straight and stiff, like a pole, in the air. Somewhere, he had heard, there were Indians who could manage that trick. 'Now, if I could do that, it'd wake 'em up,' he told himself, relishing fame in his own way, and meditating on the fact that no Indian *he* had ever laid eyes on could even rope a calf. But today he did not dare attempt that final feat, and had to content himself with shaping a perfect figure eight into the air.

Then the horses were let in the pen. Lucina saw at once that they were exactly like those she had watched huddled in the driving rain, as she had bumped across the prairie from Galveston. But now, excited and quivering, they were running in long circles, neighing and whinnying for an exit they could never find, for all their frantic searching.

Each cowboy carefully aimed his rope at a particular animal's two front feet, and, edging forward with infinite care, approached his chosen mount, crooning in a gentle singsong as he advanced. Some of the men were determined to get saddles on the wild ponies which stood drawn back, quivering in every muscle, pulling away from their tormentors. Others waited only to slip a bridle into their ponies' mouths before mounting them. Lucina felt sure every man on the horses would be killed, for the frantic creatures either dashed toward the high board fence or stood snorting with their noses to the ground and their hind feet in the air, their eyes rolling red and furious in their heads. But before long she heard the people cheering around her, and saw that the men who were attempting to ride these wild horses could actually do so. Soon horse after horse began to tire; and soon one rider after another was leading his subdued mount back and forth in front of the grandstand, bowing and sweeping his hat to the ground in recognition of enthusiastic applause.

From time to time, all afternoon, Matt had been cocking his ears, cupping them with his square, black hands, to listen. As soon as he heard the cheers slackening, he started stirring the coals in the barbecue pit. The company would soon come chattering down the path to the river expecting dinner, which was usually served at three o'clock, and it was now nearly four. Young niggers like Jake and Maria, Matt meditated importantly, might manage to get off and watch the festivities; but — he tested the sizzling beef with a long, slim fork — as for him and Aunt Emmy, Mas' Philip was depending on *them*. Carefully he mixed up a fresh batch of spicy, hot, red sauce with which to baste the browning meat and sniffed, with expert care, the aroma pouring up from the hole.

''Bout right,' he first congratulated himself, and then shook his head. 'A mite more pepper.'

Looking up, he saw Aunt Emmy coming down the path to join him, swinging her broad hips, and carrying in her arms a basket of rolls. Since early morning she had been baking them, using the yeast that she always kept rising in a crock where bubbles continuously formed and broke in a foamy mixture of cornmeal and potato water. She began singing a slow, rising chant as she walked, bringing buttered rolls to lay on the long tables that were arranged near the pit.

'Lawd! Look at dem tables!' she said to Matt, appreciatively sucking her lips at sight of the full boards. 'Dar Miss Winnie Lee's dried apple pies, an' Miz Rideout's mashed potato salad, an' Miz Spurlock's minced chicken. Who brung dat ar' batch o' stickies?' she asked, critically sampling one of the round crusty circles sprinkled liberally with cinnamon and sugar. 'Dey'll do,' she decided, chewing reflectively, 'but I'd a made 'em a mite shorter, ef'n I'd been makin' 'em. Lemme taste dat cawffee, Matt. Las' time you made it — fo' de war, warn't it? — you biled it too long.'

'Get away fum heah, woman,' Matt replied. 'I knows my business; you 'tend to your'n.'

Matt imagined he could hear the company all talking now.

'Philip, you must send Matt over right away to show my cook how to barbecue meat. . . . Uncle Matt, I'll just watch you mix up that sauce. . . . Philip, my cook can't equal yours, that's certain.'

'Lawd! Dey *better* hurry up,' Matt grumbled worriedly, 'dis heah meat's gwine-a git too done.'

The ladies began coming down the path first, taking their seats on chairs and blankets spread around the tables. The men followed them, in groups of two or three, discussing the rope throwing. As soon as they smelled the roasting meat, however, they quickened their pace, suddenly aware of a great hunger. Matt glanced importantly at the younger negroes who were helping him, and they fell into action, passing thick, aromatic slices of beef, brown and crusty on top, shading toward pink in the centre, and steaming cups of black, bitter coffee.

For a few hours, the war seemed a long way off, like a bad dream receding into the past. After supper, when Philip's colored singers appeared, nobody remembered that Sheridan sat at New Orleans, carrying the fate of every listener in his impatient hands. Or that, nearer yet, an enemy garrison of black troops was at their very doors.

Just at sunset, the Bishop arose, apologizing to Philip. 'I've an appointment with Major Bradford,' he explained.

'I marvel at your patience,' Philip replied, accompanying him to his horse.

Dark fell early in November, and the light from the fires began to flicker lower and lower. The ladies moved back up the path to the house where some gathered on the porch, exchanging news, and others around Letitia's square old Chickering piano.

The men remained seated in a circle, waiting for Matt to appear with a wide japanned tray full of silver cups ringed round with curly orange peel. They were not disappointed. Toombs Dickerson lifted his cup, dropped his nose over it, and rolled his eyes upward, sinking back against a tree with a sigh of utter content.

'Philip!' he exclaimed. 'If you asked me for my best saddle horse right now, I'd likely give him to you.'

Philip smiled, and stood up, running his eyes over the group, with the smile slowly fading off his lips. The light from the coals illuminated only his face, which, against the shadows behind him, gleamed white and ghost-like, as if separated from his body.

'Gentlemen,' he began, 'I will waste no words. When a convention is called — if it *is* called — we've got to be ready to elect a delegate. Who is it going to be?'

John McGaughey laughed, shortly.

'You mean, who *can* it be, Philip!' Rubbing his hand across his lips, he asked scornfully: 'Who's even applied for a pardon? I know I haven't. What's the use, anyhow?'

Philip looked at William Charlton. 'You've applied for a pardon, William, I believe,' he began, tentatively.

'Who else?' asked Toombs Dickerson, speaking suddenly from his place next to Cavin. 'Let's get this straight.' He searched the circle anxiously. 'Nobody, except William? Well, then,' he concluded, 'William will have to run.'

His face hardened, as his eye roamed from one man to the next.

'Hadn't we all better start trying to get on the amnesty list?' he demanded. 'Oh! yes,' he said, hotly, getting up and moving about with long, restless strides, 'I know. I'd rather drink poison myself, but who's going to run this country if we let ourselves get euchred out of our votes? They're certain as hell to keep

right on thinking o' slick ways to keep us away from the polls.'
He swung around on one heel and faced his friends, and the
firelight accentuated the heavy creases around his mouth and
eyes.

'Don't you see?' he demanded harshly. 'We've got to be
slicker than they are. Whatever they ask us to swear, we've got
to swear, even if it's to deny our own names!' He stood looking
at them while his face set in a cold, hard mask, out of which his
eyes glittered dangerously. 'We've got to vote, no matter how.
We've got to hold office, no matter how. That's the long and
short of it. General Lee's told us that,' he concluded abruptly.
'I nominate William Charlton as delegate.'

Cavin leaned over and touched his father.

'Even the Yankees must know Cousin William wasn't raring
to secede, like the rest of us.' Philip nodded and rose to his feet.

'I hope you'll accept, William.'

John McGaughey conferred with his brother and stood up.
His body swayed vigorously, as he expressed his mind, pounding
his broad fist into his open hand. He was never one to hesitate,
but acted instantly on his first conviction.

'If you will,' he declared, turning to William with his eyes
snapping, 'my cowhands'll roll up the German vote for you,
and the Yankees are dead certain to let anybody through who's
got a name you can't pronounce. Jesus Christ!' he thundered.
'It's come to that in this county!' Disgustedly he ran his heavy
fingers through his abundant hair till it stood up around his
angry face like a halo. 'You'll have to run, William,' he concluded abruptly, 'whether you want to or not.'

'My friends,' began William, rising, 'as little as I welcome this
responsibility at my age, when a man naturally craves rest, yet
if you think I should take it, I accept it, in your name. Of course,
there's not a dog's chance we'll win.'

Judge White answered him in his calm, deep voice.

'They'll probably unseat you at the convention, William, even if you should get elected,' he agreed, with a slight smile on his lips. 'Just as they are now preparing to fill my office with a loyalist — a former bartender, I am told.' He spoke entirely without rancor, but as he looked around the circle, the smile suddenly left his lips. 'Of course,' he added, 'we have to remember we may *all* be in jail this time next week.'

'One trouble at a time, one trouble at a time,' said Mr. Tripp Cuttross firmly. 'I've found that a good rule in life.' Rising as he spoke, he gestured toward the house. 'This is a party, gentlemen, not a misery meeting. I propose we join the ladies.' Turning, he addressed Cavin. 'You young rascal, where'd you find such a charming wife? She's an ornament to the county, much too good for you, sir, much too good.'

'Of course,' said Cavin. 'That's true, sir.' He smiled. 'I've told her so myself.'

'No man's good enough for a woman, when it comes down to it,' Mr. Spurlock exclaimed heartily.

Philip spoke to Matt, who passed around another tray, this time of small thimble-sized glasses. They all stood up, waiting for Philip's signal.

'To our wives,' he said, raising his glass, 'our mothers, and,' he smiled at the young men, 'our sweethearts.' Still his glass was high. 'God save the South.' He drained his cup and sighed. 'Calhoun put it another way, on his deathbed, do you remember, gentlemen? — "*The South, the poor South, I don't know what will become of her.*"'

Some of the young people who were due at Judge Symington's ball in Berryville left early; and, toward midnight, William and a few others who lived close by went home. A good many, however, planned to stay all night, for Philip's friends took it for granted that any who found it convenient to sleep at his house would find extra cots and mattresses laid out for their convenience. If it was a good day, and the mood seized them, there might be good shooting tomorrow, perhaps the next day too.

As the night wore on, however, it seemed that everybody preferred conversation to sleep. In the early evening the servants had come up from the quarters to finish up the barbecued beef, and, a little later, the fiddlers and dancers among them had appeared in Philip's drive, to amuse his guests. Then, when the musicians had retired, the conversations and reminiscences began — conversations which Philip well knew might keep up till any hour.

He yawned behind his hand. He was sleepy and tired, and suddenly he wished his guests were. He glanced at the stars. At this rate it would be daylight before he got to bed. He yawned again. Cavin could do the honors from now on, he decided. At sixty-five a man needed his rest. He slipped off to his own room, and dropped asleep instantly. Soon afterward, the guests began one by one to follow his example.

Chapter 12

POVEY gave himself no chance to change his mind about going to Judge Symington's ball. Early the next morning after his midnight conversation with the Bishop, he called in his colored boy, Horace, and set him to work steaming and pressing his clothes and shining his softest boots. He asked Aunt Cindy to wash and iron a white pleated shirt he had in his trunk, and to another servant he gave the task of polishing his saddle and of currying and rubbing down his dappled roan, Xanthus. When he was dressed and ready, it was the middle of the morning. The dance was not until evening, but he decided to leave home early, for he had business to transact in town — wines and brandies to order at Horst and La Farque's, a pair of mules to look over at Heilschmidt's Livery, and other matters of more or less importance. He got on his horse, and threw an appraising glance at Horace. Yes, he was turned out very well in one of Povey's own discarded suits, with a broad black cravat, exactly like his master's, knotted under his brown chin.

They started off, riding along at an easy pace through the warm and sunny autumn morning, following a narrow one-way road that dipped and curved through prairie and bottom land — a road bordered by tall bushes bearing many long black pods.

'Coffee beans!' thought Povey, leaning over to strip the bushes as he rode by them. 'Black jaundice!'

The two ideas naturally followed one another in immediate succession, for it was common knowledge that in the years when the coffee beans were thickest, black jaundice was most common. No one guessed, however, that the rain which nourished the bushes also provided extra fine breeding holes for the striped gray mosquitoes which distributed malaria impartially between black and white alike, sparing only those liberally dosed with quinine.

They began to meet travellers mounted on sleek animals, or riding in light gigs behind high-stepping horses, all on their way to Locust Hill, Povey knew. Passing them, he reflected that in no other Southern state — certainly in none where Sherman or Sheridan had been — would it have been possible to come across so many good horses in a single morning. The reflection took his mind back to Virginia, where, when the war came on, he had expected to join Jeb Stuart's cavalry — the pride of the Southern army; but in the end, he had stayed with Terry's Texans, who would never even so much as try to keep their horses' necks in line. They had more important things to think about, their officers said; and, after their first engagements, even General Lee agreed that they had. Povey began to smile, remembering how, once at a review in Richmond, Wade Hampton had had to throw his Carolinians between the hot-tempered Texans and the crack Virginia troops who were supposed to be demonstrating near perfection in drill and accoutrement. Well, he'd never regretted his decision, though he knew if his mother had been alive, she would never have understood it. All that was long ago, though, he reminded himself; and now he was riding not into Richmond, but into Berryville, Texas.

The nearer he arrived there, however, the less inclined he felt to carry out the purpose he had so suddenly formed the night before. In fact, he wondered if he still knew how to dance. It had been a long time since he had whirled around a polished floor with a pretty girl on his arm. His delicate nostrils dilated. The last time he had escorted a young lady to a ball, he was still young and foolish enough to believe that a man might expect to be happy in this world. Since then, there had been no dances for him — only marches, victories, retreats, and finally capture at the battle of Green River, where the Texans had fallen row upon row in a charge so hopeless that other veteran troops had refused even to attempt it.

He shook his head impatiently. How long, he wondered, did it take a man to learn to stop thinking about the war? He might as well get on with his life, he thought with an ironic smile. There seemed to be a good deal of it left, as men counted time — that strange mystery in which they lived and breathed, like fish in water, never knowing how to measure it. For, according to the way a man felt, a second sometimes stretched out to feel like hours; or, again, sometimes — especially if you were happy — an hour shrivelled down to a second. Well, for him, at least, there was not apt to be much shrivelling of hours, he thought, with a certain wry amusement.

When they rode into the village, it was almost deserted. Later on, some of the young people who had spent the afternoon at Philip's party would come riding in to dance at Judge Symington's, but at present the streets were empty. The square, once optimistically planted in grass, was now littered with paper, and the hedge around it was neglected and scraggly. Along one side of it, there was a long row of black hitching posts, with horses' heads at their tops, and to these Povey and Horace tied their horses. After reminding Horace to keep a sharp eye on Xanthus and to feed and water him well at the livery stable, Povey started off to complete his round of errands.

'You know where the servants are dancing, don't you, Horace?' he inquired. 'Across the creek, in the old cotton shed?'

'Yas-suh.' Horace's white teeth gleamed. He knew all right. Lawd! How dat black gal of Judge Symington's set his heart to jumping.

Povey reached in his pocket. 'You'll want to treat Sally to plenty of frozen custard, I suppose.' He turned an adamant eye on his servant. 'And don't you get to drinking so much beer that you forget to bring Xanthus around at one o'clock sharp. If you do,' he warned Horace, 'I'll have you beat in an inch o' yo' life.'

Horace grinned again, amiably and expansively. 'No-suh. Yas-suh,' he promised Povey. 'I gwine-a be right dar when yo' steps out'n de do'. You see ef'n I ain't.'

'You will, if you know what's good for you,' Povey said severely. Relenting, he reached again into his pocket and flipped Horace another coin.

'No use telling you to lay off craps, I suppose, Horace, but try to hold onto your front teeth.' Laughing, he turned down the street toward the wine house where he traded. Horace, he knew, would bet the shirt off his back.

His business in town, with all the details attending the selection of wines and brandies and the critical examination of the mules he was buying, took so long that it was after dark before he left for Judge Symington's square, red-brick house.

It stood well back in a wide yard full of stubby grass, rosebushes, and glossy magnolia trees. A damp herring-bone walk, thickly shaded by cedar trees and crêpe myrtles, led from the entrance gate to the high flight of white steps by which one entered the front door. Judge Symington's grandfather, on arriving in South Carolina from England, had expected to have his kitchen in his basement, where he had had it at home. When he found that water lay too close under the top soil for basements in the country to which he had come, he had quite simply built his cellar on top of the ground, instead of under it, left his kitchen where his ancestors had had it, and provided a rising flight of steps up to his front door, with its long sidelights. His grandson continued the practice in Texas and also kept the title that he had acquired in Carolina — how, no one had ever thought to inquire. On the Brazos he raised cotton and corn and left the law to his neighbor and fellow Carolinian, Judge White. Still, everybody called him Judge, agreeing that if he didn't actually sit on the bench, there was no reason at all why he couldn't.

Povey made his way up the walk and pulled the brass knocker out as far as it would go — the knocker delicately molded into the shape of a squirrel, which, in the bronze, seemed almost as lithe and eager as the agitated little animals climbing up and down the trees in the yard, flirting their tails. As he waited, he heard a young girl's voice in the parlor and wished he had stayed home. He was too old, he thought, to dance with a girl who had a voice like that — a child's voice, almost.

'Too old to dance with anybody,' he said soberly to himself. Well, he would leave early. 'Though I suppose Horace won't welcome the idea,' he smiled.

A servant opened the door, and ushered him into a large, square room, with a very high ceiling, where Judge Symington stood, with his wife, and his two nieces in front of French windows opening out into the raised gallery. As he entered, a few young couples were already testing out, on the polished floor, the steps of the schottische, and the negro musicians were tuning up.

'I hardly dared hope you would come, my dear Povey,' Mrs.

Symington said, laying her hand lightly on his coat-sleeve.
'You're too handsome a young man to shut yourself up as
you've been doing since the war. It's high time all of us thought
of something else — if we can,' she added sighing.

Harriet Symington was a plump little woman, with tiny feet
and hands, and only lately, at fifty-five, had she given up
struggling to keep a tiny waist also. Her husband was well over
six feet, with a fine head of flowing gray hair and a beard that
he kept carefully clipped. He had lost an arm riding, like
Povey, with the Terry Rangers, but he seemed never to notice
its absence.

He waited till his wife and his nieces were occupied with their
guests. Then he drew Povey aside, using a significant tone and
glance to stress the importance of his few, low words.

'Maybe it'd be good sense, Povey, for you to go around and
see that none of the men have left their pistols in their saddlebags?'

'I'll check up,' Povey agreed instantly, in a voice as low as
the Judge's.

Soon the guests began arriving more rapidly, and by nine
o'clock the dance was in full swing. Young ladies in tarlatan,
with flowers behind their ears, moved across the lighted windows
as lightly as though they had never heard of a war; and young
gentlemen who, until recently, had stumbled wearily along on
muddy roads stained with blood, now stepped across a polished
floor as gracefully as though they had never lifted aching feet,
or shouldered a gun.

The music sank and rose, rose and sank again, and as the
gay young couples whirled by, Povey began more and more to
feel that he did not belong where he was.

'There's no use,' he told himself; 'not the slightest. Why am
I here? I'll get Horace and start home.'

Just then, the long clock struck twelve, the dining-room doors were thrown open, and Judge Symington's houseboy, Franklin, began ringing a bronze bell with a long handle — the same bell the boy's father had rung in Carolina to indicate that supper was served on the same long table at the customary hour of midnight.

There was a buzzing of many voices, as the couples entered the room.

'Syllabub!... Pecan cake!... Beaten biscuit!... Chicken salad!... Um-m-m! Jelly pie!... And sweet-potato pone!... Franklin, which of these sandwiches do you recommend?... That's what I said, honey-angel... Blackberry wine!... Custard... More syllabub?'

Upstairs in the hall a few negro maids peered over the bannisters, but most of them were dancing in the cotton shed, where those upstairs would soon take their turn at swinging around its rough floor.

After supper the musicians had scarcely picked up their instruments when suddenly they laid them down, and the dancers stood still on the floor, tautly listening. In the distance, they could hear a loud confusion coming nearer — a confusion of shouts, and shrieks, and galloping hoofbeats mingled oddly with running human feet.

It was so quiet in the parlor that Judge Symington had hardly to raise his voice above its natural tone.

'Ladies, upstairs, please.' He ran his eyes coolly around the room, where the dancers were standing motionless in their places. 'Tarrant, kindly take the staircase. Gordon, to the back, if you please. Goodwin' — he turned to his nephew — 'the rest of you to the front gallery. I'll go to the gate. Franklin,' he ordered his servant, 'put out the lamps.'

There was not a sound except the swish of their skirts as the girls moved upstairs, gathering around their hostess in the wide hall at the top of the flight.

'There, my dears, don't bother!' she said easily. 'Sit down. The men will manage, of course. It is pleasant to have you here with us tonight. We must have more parties.'

Stooping, she calmly arranged a displaced curl on one of the girls' heads. 'Lavender, you have on a lovely dress. You, too, Lorena.' Her pleasant-blue eyes moved over the group. 'Don't be alarmed. I am quite certain Judge Symington will know what to do.'

The girls sat on the floor, in a close circle, as quiet as death, not moving or uttering a sound. As they listened, they heard a rising murmur of excited voices in the hall below them.

'Mas' Tarrant! . . . Dey's atter us! Dey'll kill us all . . . Mas' Goodwin! Mas' Goodwin! . . . Lawd Jesus he'p us! . . .'

Then several negro girls came stumbling up the stairs to their mistresses, panting and crying, gray with fright. Before they could calm themselves enough to tell what had happened, Mrs. Symington heard a negro answering Judge Symington's sharp questions.

Peering out into the dark through the upstairs window, she held her breath. She could barely see her husband's erect figure behind his swinging gate, in front of which stood three colored soldiers.

'Officers, probably,' she thought, her lips curling. Behind them, other shadows were moving and surging in restless confusion. Listening intently, she heard the Judge warning the soldiers not to come a step closer.

They stopped, irresolute. There were not many of them in this party, for their group had scattered in several directions. They were all halfdrunk, but not too drunk to realize the mat-

ter had gone farther than any of them had planned when they
entered the cotton shed intending merely to drag off a negro
girl for each soldier. They had not expected the negro men to
resist; nor, least of all, had they expected them all to rush pell-
mell to their white masters. Then, when it had become clear
that that was exactly what they were doing, the soldiers had
decided it might be amusing to break up a white dance, too.
Now, they were beginning to wonder whether that idea had
not been, perhaps, somewhat overambitious. For a minute,
while Mrs. Symington heard her heart beat, the three soldiers
at the gate paused.

Then, in the stillness, she heard another negro voice. Horace
had dashed into the yard, hunting for Povey, and, seeing what
was going on, now rushed over to the Judge. It was his girl,
Sally, Mrs. Symington's maid, who had caught the colored
captain's eye as he rode past the cotton shed.

'Kill 'im, Jedge, kill 'im!' Horace shrieked. 'Dey's run off
wid my Sally.'

Hearing Horace's voice, Povey swung around sharply, addressing the Judge's nephew, Goodwin Breckinridge.

'Goodwin!' he exclaimed. 'That's my boy, Horace!' Already,
as he spoke, he was halfway down the walk.

Emboldened by Povey's and the Judge's presence, Horace
suddenly leaped over the fence and knocked one surprised
black soldier to the ground. Immediately, the other two fell
upon him and dragged him off their companion, striking him
furiously about the head with their pistol butts. Without an
instant's hesitation, Povey flung open the wicket gate.

'Turn him loose!' he commanded them, in a low, abrupt voice.
The negro soldiers were unaccustomed to men who dropped their
voices when they expected to be obeyed. Therefore, instead of
turning Horace loose, they began kicking him with their heavy

boots and, at the same moment, put out their hand for the gate, thinking themselves fully covered by the soldiers behind them. But their support had had considerable experience in Texas and, the moment they saw one of their leaders on the ground and all the white men drawn up on the porch, they decided it was time to retreat to the garrison. Hurriedly, before anybody was aware of their intention, they turned their horses and galloped off.

The two colored soldiers, however, pushed forward as Horace scrambled up and bounded to his master's side, shaking but determined.

'Lawd Jesus! Gimme a gun an' lemme at 'em!' he gasped. The soldiers, the Judge saw, were too drunk for caution.

'All right,' he said, nodding to Povey, and both negroes dropped in their tracks.

The men on the gallery closed in, as Povey and Horace stooped to disarm the men who lay, cursing, on the ground.

Leaning over them also, the Judge looked up at Horace, smiling wryly. 'You put one of 'em to sleep all right, boy,' he exclaimed, stooping more closely over the other two.

'It's nothing,' he said and glanced at Povey. 'We intended only to stop them.'

Standing erect, he looked gravely around the circle of men. 'I suppose we ought to take them back to the garrison. There's a bare chance the new white officer there may be responsible.'

As he spoke, they all heard a renewed clanking of sabres and hurried marching, and realized that the soldiers who had galloped away had returned, this time with reinforcements. The Judge again stepped to his gate, and Povey and Goodwin Breckinridge fell in beside him.

Seeing that the white officer did not draw his pistol, they kept theirs also lowered. One look at him, however, told them why

he was so negligent. He was swaying on his feet, but his eyes
flashed dangerously. Two pompous colored lieutenants stood
silently beside him, holding lanterns.

'I request you, sir, to remove your men from my premises,'
Judge Symington said curtly. The shifting yellow light of the
lanterns threw his massive head into sharp relief against the
night.

'Who shot my men? Who shot 'em?' the officer roared. His
round face was red and apoplectic, his voice furious. 'I'm
Major Richards, and I'll jail every damned white man in this
crowd unless I find out.'

The men in the yard stepped closer, but Judge Symington
dropped his pistol into its holster and held up his hand. Gesturing contemptuously toward the officer, whose brain appeared
to be clearing somewhat under the night air, he reminded his
friends that the only authority operative in the state was standing
there in front of them.

Stepping forward, then, he eyed Major Richards firmly.

'I have the honor to report, sir, that I wounded these drunken
criminals' — he inclined his head slightly toward the negroes
at his foot — 'who trespassed on my property and abused my
servants. I give you fair warning, I'll kill the next ones who put
foot on my land.'

'And this is my negro,' said Povey, pointing to Horace.
'Your men have made off with his girl, and God knows what
they've done with her. I shot one of your drunken cowards
there, and I'll shoot the next one that steps in my path.'

The patience of the officer in charge of the troops was exhausted. He had not the slightest understanding of the people
with whom he was dealing. Putting out his hand, he yanked
the Judge around.

'Come along, now,' he said, and spoke curtly to the colored

soldiers at his side. 'Take 'em both on down to the garrison.'

At the words, all the men in the yard suddenly fell in around the Judge and Povey, brushing the officer aside.

'Get out of this yard and get out quick,' Goodwin Breckinridge warned him.

The Major was taken off guard; he had thought the sight of so many armed soldiers would prevent any resistance. He had not even pulled his gun; and, as his brain cleared in the cool night air, he realized that the soldiers drawn up outside the fence were awaiting his order, would not fire without it. Taking a look at Goodwin Breckinridge's face, he decided not to give the order.

'March your men back to the garrison double quick,' Goodwin commanded crisply. 'And don't waste any time about starting, either.'

The Major hesitated, but not for long. He was beginning to see his course. He had been firmly instructed at Galveston that, if he wished to fatten his purse as his predecessor had done, he must refrain from stirring up bloodshed. The citizens, he had been assured, were prepared to pay well for peace. And wasn't money what he had come South hoping to get? It took him only a moment to make up his mind.

Then he removed his hand from the Judge's arm and ordered his colored bodyguard to pick up their wounded comrades and return with them and the troops outside to their posts.

Goodwin Breckinridge waited until they had turned the corner two blocks away before he stepped forward and addressed the Major.

'Now,' he said calmly, 'we can talk turkey. Come to think of it,' he added slowly, 'might not be a bad idea to hold you, ourselves.' Eyeing the officer with extreme and obvious distaste, he considered the prospect with pleasure. 'Only, God knows, I'd hate to associate that long with a skunk like you.'

'I'd thought of that plan myself, but we'd better give it up,' said Judge Symington regretfully. 'It would prejudice our case.'

'Case?' Goodwin blinked at his uncle.

'Yes,' repeated the Judge calmly. 'That's exactly what I mean, Goodwin. Don't you see, this is a test case? We've got to find out whether there are any courts operating in this state — any courts of justice, that is,' he argued in a steady, restrained voice.

A murmur of dissent began to spread through the gathering, when Povey raised his hand to silence it.

'I think the Judge is right,' he said firmly. 'More is involved than our personal fortunes. Don't you see that, gentlemen?' he pleaded, supporting the Judge's decision. 'How can we demand the restoration of law and order in this county, and refuse to submit ourselves to the only visible constituted authority?'

'When you think it over,' continued Judge Symington, taking up the argument, 'you will all agree with us.' He stood facing the group, judging their reaction by their silence. Then whirling on his heel, he addressed the Federal officer sharply.

'We are at your service, sir.'

'Mightn't it be a good idea,' Povey suggested dryly, 'to find out right now how much it'll cost per week to — er — board the prisoners. I presume that is the point you are interested in, sir?' he said, turning to the Major.

Now they were talking sensibly, that officer concluded. He ran over several possible figures in his mind, but he had a certain canny sagacity that warned him what was possible and what was not. They would likely pay more, if the matter was left unsettled and they were allowed to make a free-will offering, weekly.

'Whatever you hand me every Monday morning, gentlemen, will be applied to the comfort of the prisoners,' he assured them. Gentlemen! That was a word they seemed to be fond of; he must remember to use it, as the Judge was already doing, with a kind of easy, intimate warmth in his tone.

'Well, gentlemen,' said Judge Symington, 'my thanks to you all. Tarrant, will you be good enough to hand a note to my wife?' Moving over to the steps, he sat down and wrote a few words on the back of an envelope he took from his pocket.

Rising, he addressed the blue-coated officer as pleasantly as if they were starting off together for a short stroll. 'Shall we be starting, sir?'

'Of course,' Povey broke in, 'Sally must be returned.'

'Sally?' the Major inquired.

'Your men ran off with her,' Povey bluntly informed him. 'Sally, the Judge's housemaid.'

The Major took time to think about that demand. 'My men ——' he began, shaking his head.

'How much?' Povey inquired tartly, without wasting words.

'I have already instructed my wife to' — Judge Symington bowed and cleared his throat — 'to sufficiently reward the soldier who brings her back.'

'Very good, very good indeed,' the Major commented. It was becoming clearer and clearer to him that he had been well advised at Galveston. Still, he couldn't understand these people at all. He threw a suspicious glance at the Judge and Povey. They had disarmed him; and, yet, here they were, walking along to the jail with him as politely as you please, and of their own free will, too, asking him what kind of crops they grew, up where he came from.

Nobody at Judge Symington's closed an eye, but as night

wore on, it began to look as though the soldiers were sleeping
off their spree. By daybreak, the men on guard began to feel
their tension relaxing — too soon, however, they discovered.

Jackson Tarrant was standing with his long arm raised against
the pillars of Judge Symington's high porch, when he caught
sight of a flame leaping around the corner of a building that
faced the square, two short blocks away. Then he smelt the
sharp odor of burning pine.

'The horses!' he thought instantly, his dark, sleepy eyes suddenly springing open. 'They're all tied down by the
square.'

'Gordon!' He spoke quietly to the man next him. 'I'm going
down to the square a minute to look around.'

Cox Gordon nodded. 'I'll come along.' His round face was
boyish, but not his eyes, for, though he was barely twenty-one,
he had been at Gettysburg and Cold Harbor.

They crept along, hiding themselves in every shadow. It
took only a glance for them to see that the horses were gone
from the square. Cox had raised his cream-colored mare,
Butterfly, on a bottle, from a colt. He began to swear incessantly,
tingling from head to toe, racked with the anger that had been
gathering in him all night. Butterfly's back would be full of
sores, if he ever found her again.

But soon he had more to think about than a horse's back.
For flames were beginning to roar around the square; and
soldiers were running in and out the smoke applying fresh
torches wherever the fire seemed to be dying down. The air
was thick and choking, and sparks were flying everywhere —
like Roman candles bursting at Christmas, Cox suddenly
thought. It was plain that the business section of the town was
doomed. There was no breeze, however. Swiftly Cox and
Jackson calculated the chances. It did not seem likely, unless

the soldiers also began setting fire to the residences, that the flames would leap the empty square.

But the garrison where the Judge and Povey were!

'Do you reckon they'll fire that, too?' whispered Cox.

'No, I don't think so,' Jackson whispered back, flattening himself against the wall around which he peered. 'It's a good ways out, and the wind's the other way.'

'Right!' agreed Cox. 'We'd better get back.'

As soon as they stepped on the gallery, they realized affairs had taken a more serious turn. There, in deathly stillness, stood the men they had left, surrounding Goodwin Breckinridge's servant, Aaron — a tall, slim black who, breathless and panting, was trying to tell his story.

Aaron, like Horace, was in love with Sally, who had not yet made up her mind between them. When he saw a colored soldier dashing out of the hall with her, Aaron had rushed outdoors, and mounted the first horse he came to. It took him some moments to find a mount, however, and in the confusion he lost track of the man he was after. He rode aimlessly around the town and out into the side roads and into the woods for hours, it seemed to him, looking for the officer who had carried his girl away. He would know him, anywhere.

Finally, it occurred to him that if he would hang around the garrison, as many negroes did, he might hear what had become of Sally. He put out of his mind the fact that he was on some white man's horse. Plenty of black men were doing that nowadays and getting away with it, too. He spurred his horse on, and had just drawn up in the shadows behind the guard-house when he saw Judge Symington and Povey entering it by the front door, with the officer in charge of the garrison.

'Well, I be doggoned!' Aaron said, moving cautiously closer. 'Ef'n it ain't Mas' Povey an' Jedge Symington! My Lawd!

Whut kine o' trouble is stackin' up now?' Watching, he saw
the officer set off for town again, alone.

Aaron had a little money and soon fell into a crap game
with the sentry on duty, who at intervals would break off the
game and walk his beat, wandering in and out the prison house
and the barracks. Aaron sat back and waited. He was ahead,
so he had no doubt that the soldier would soon return.

'Sho look mighty deserted aroun' heah,' Aaron commented,
carefully shaking his dice, when they had taken up their play
after one of these interruptions.

'Ought to look deserted,' the darky observed. 'Dey ain't
nobody heah hardly a-tall.'

'Where is dey all?' said Aaron, innocently.

The soldier chuckled. 'Lawd, nigger, de soljers is riflin' all
de sto's an' settin' de whole place on fiah; an' dem whut ain't
in town is got dair gals out in de woods. An' heah I sets! Got
a mind to let out de niggers dey was gwine-a hang.' Putting
down his dice, he turned the possibility over in his thoughts.
''Twouldn't be no trick at all to do. Dat'd leave jes' dem two
white men. Reckon *dey* might as well hang as not.' The longer
he thought about his idea, the better it seemed to please him.
'Ef'n I don't make way wid 'em, de udders will, soon's dey gitt
thu firin' de town.'

Aaron had heard enough. Mas' Goodwin would help him
get Sally out of the woods. He better hurry back, too, and tell
him about Judge Symington and Mas' Povey maybe getting
hung. He tossed a few more throws and then rose lazily,
stretching himself. The sentry, who had been winning for the
last quarter-hour, did not urge him to remain.

Until he was out of sight, he rode slowly. Then he put his
horse to a frantic gallop, circled the blazing town, and came by
a back route into Judge Symington's yard.

Cox and Jackson had just stepped back on the porch when Aaron began his account.

Goodwin listened to only a few sentences before he began to shuffle matches around in his hand.

'Draw!' he said, quietly stepping from man to man.

Chapter 13

THE house was quiet when Philip woke suddenly, and looked at his watch. Half-past four, and the night was still bright with stars. What had wakened him? His ear, attuned to a lifetime of listening, caught the sound of a horse's galloping feet in his lane. He sat up, instantly awake. Then, certain of what he heard, he grabbed up his pistols and, hurrying down the stairs, stepped outside the door onto the gallery.

'Whose horse is that?' he asked himself, before he could see the rider's face, and then, with a start of surprise, recognized the animal. Surely that was Povey's mount, Xanthus, at his gate. In the dark, he saw a negro throw himself on the ground and run rapidly toward him.

'Stop!' Philip's voice was sharp. 'Who is it?'

'Horace, suh. Horace. Mas' Povey's boy,' the darky panted. 'Mas' William sont me ahead to tell you he gwine-a be along any minute now.' Horace jumped at every moving shadow. 'I'se afeard dey's gwine-a hang 'em,' he quavered.

'Hang 'em?' Philip inquired, startled. 'Hang who? What are you saying, boy?' He grasped the negro by the shoulder. 'Be quiet,' he cautioned him. 'Don't wake up the ladies.'

Then his thoughts began to take shape beneath his mounting anxiety. He watched Horace narrowly. 'Now, tell me!' he said, as soon as he saw the colored boy could speak coherently.

'Mas' Povey an' Jedge Symington, suh,' Horace explained. 'Dey's gwine-a hang 'em, I reckon. Dey wuz a shootin',' he gasped, 'an' de soljers took 'em, an' I lit out de back way to git Mas' William.'

Philip pushed the shaking negro down the steps. 'Go back to the servants' house,' he commanded him, 'and tell Matt and Jake to saddle every horse in the barn, quick.'

As he swung open the front door, he saw Letitia standing there, just inside the hall.

'I heard a little,' she said, holding him with her eyes.

He could not spare her; he knew that. Better get it over with. 'The soldiers have put Povey and Judge Symington in jail,' he informed her, with pity in his voice. 'This boy says they've threatened to hang them.' He put out his hand, but she did not notice it. 'We'll be leaving immediately,' he finished. Still she did not move.

Philip took her by the shoulders and spoke to her firmly. It would be better for her to have something to do, something to focus her attention.

'Get my saddlebags, my pistols. Take them to Matt. Put in something for bandages and a bottle of brandy. Right away. Do you hear me, Lettie, do you hear? I can't wait.'

She nodded, and, with an effort, repeated slowly after him, in a dead, automatic voice, 'Pistols. Bandages. Brandy. Yes, Philip, of course.' Then he saw her quiver and heard her draw a long, slow breath. 'This minute,' she added more firmly. 'Go!' She shoved him. 'Go!'

Later, after William had galloped up with reinforcements, she stood peering out at the men assembled just outside the gate in the bleak, cold light of breaking dawn. Two or three of the ladies had waked up and were standing, tense and quiet, beside her. This was likely to be bitter and bloody business, they all knew, as they listened in anxious, strained silence to the men's low voices and to the sharp click of revolving cartridge barrels.

'Cavin,' Letitia heard Philip saying, 'I don't think there'll be any trouble here, but somebody'll have to stay. I'll ask you and David' — he chose rapidly — 'and the McGaughey and Dyess boys. The rest of us ——' Before he could complete his sentence, the men were climbing on their horses and, in another moment, their saddles were creaking under them and their spurs clanking.

'Draw up under the big live-oak a mile from town,' said William, taking the lead as Povey's closest friend. 'If we meet any soldiers, fall behind your horses, and don't fire unless I raise my arm.'

Letitia saw Philip whirl, dig his spurs into Pilot's black sides, and be off, just as light began to brighten in the East. She stood at the window until the last hoof beats died away in the chill, damp air, watching the horses, with their necks stretched out, their ears laid back, and their manes flying, and the men leaning forward in their saddles, lifting their weight. Often Philip had had to dash off like that, in the middle of the night, to save a patient. Now he was galloping off to save Povey and — Letitia pushed her hair back off her face — she had forgotten even to tell him good-bye.

Lucina opened the door and walked straight across the gallery to Cavin.

'I can hit a target,' she told him steadily. 'Mrs. Dyess has her own pistols. Mrs. Spurlock has a box of red pepper.'

'Red pepper?' Cavin raised his brows, smiling.

'Yes,' Lucina nodded wisely. 'She says she's going to throw it in anybody's eyes that dares to touch her.'

Cavin began to laugh. 'My gosh! that's an idea,' he chuckled.

'It's a pity Hood didn't have some ladies on his staff!' Then suddenly he became sober and serious. 'You get your company together, Sweet,' he warned her, 'and stay inside that room.' He pointed to where Letitia was standing. 'I don't believe anything's going to come up,' he said slowly, 'but you can't tell what they may have up their sleeves.'

They sat there until full daylight, keeping guard — against what danger they did not know.

'Just boys!' Mrs. Dyess thought, watching them through the window. 'Just boys!'

She turned to Miss Winnie Lee. 'Just sleepy boys! And they've fought a war!' She pointed through the blinds. 'See my two! Sometimes, when I go to wake 'em up in the morning, I can't believe they've been through what they have.' Her voice broke and she looked at her friend, with slow tears welling up in her sad, gray eyes. 'But they've been up Little Round Top, and buried their brother at its foot. What a world, Winnie Lee!' She swallowed and shook her head. 'What a world!'

Mrs. Kemper's eyes followed her friend's finger, and her own eyes blurred. 'Yes,' her heart echoed, 'what a world!'; but she did not trust herself to speak. What was there to say?

As William raced along the road now beginning to lighten ahead of him, with the men pounding beside him, he felt an exhilaration in definite action which the last hard months of marking time had taken from him. As day broke clearer, he saw that the man next to him was Povey's servant, Horace, on Xanthus.

The negro, catching William's eye, pressed closer and cried questioningly above the clatter of the hoofbeats, 'Ef'n I rode in to town ahead, suh, dey might tell me ——'

Instantly William saw that it was a good plan. They had only a handful of men against a garrison of soldiers. It would be far wiser to draw up under the live-oak tree just outside of town and see what news Horace could bring back.

He pulled his horse slightly, and signified his assent. 'Hurry back, as quick as you can, to the big live-oak at the fork of the road, a mile from town,' he told the negro. 'If we can't wait there,' he warned him, 'we'll be at the garrison.' God only knew what they'd find going on, when they got nearer, he thought.

Horace nodded in quick understanding. 'Yas-suh. I better take de swamp road, and cut acrost to de back o' town,' he calculated, and was off as quickly as he spoke, disappearing into the fog that enveloped the low bottom land.

But long before they reached the tree, William saw they could not pause under it. Some miles back, he had caught the smell of smoke in the air, but had laid it to a prairie fire. Now he knew he had been mistaken, for great clouds of smoke were pouring in acrid gusts down the road from Berryville.

'My God! There's hell to pay!' he heard John McGaughey exclaiming and saw the other men draw up a moment, in horror, and then dash on at redoubled speed.

Swiftly he recast his plans. The sky seemed ablaze, as they came out of the wooded road into the clear stretch leading to the village. The yellow smoke drifting across the bushes burned their throats and stung their eyes. Already the heat had caused their horses to turn their heads; and when the sparks began flying thickly around them, they became almost unmanageable, nickering in fright and rearing, with the white foam pouring off their legs. The garrison was now in plain sight, on the edge of town.

William's mind worked quickly. The best plan, he thought,

would be to hide the horses in the thicket off the road, leaving two or three men to guard them. The rest would proceed on foot, in small groups, at least as far as the guard-house. They would be less noticeable that way than on horseback, and in the confusion might just chance to slip into town, unobserved. He jerked out his watch. Two hours and a half since they had left Locust Hill. He had thought the route impossible to cover in less than three.

He signalled for the men to draw up and explained his idea, asking for suggestions. Several of the men had already considered the same possibility. They got down, speaking in short, jerky sentences, under their breath, tied their horses, and separated. Proceeding cautiously, they made their way by twos and threes, cutting through the thicket that lay parallel to the strangely empty road. But at the garrison they halted, dumbfounded, in front of an open door. There was no one about; the barracks were deserted; even the fires were out in the kitchen. They might have been ghosts walking around an empty battle field. What had been going on there?

Philip glanced at his companions' faces and saw that he was not alone in the sudden, dreadful certainty which took possession of him. Laying a plank slantwise against the low sloping wall that led to the roof, he was about to climb up it and reconnoitre, when he felt a hand pulling at his sleeve. Horace had managed to slip through the town, and was on his way back to the appointed place, when, passing the garrison, he saw that Philip and his friends were already there. Xanthus's reins were drawn through Horace's arm, and the negro's brown skin looked gray and ashen.

'Mas' Philip,' he implored, 'you-all ain't got a minute to spare.' His face was contorted and his eyes were twitching.

The other men pressed close, to hear what he was saying.

'Dey was gonna hang some niggers this mawnin',' Horace repeated, his eyes moving in jerks from face to face, until he found William's — 'some niggers ——' He stopped and began to explain to William, 'I met some soljers, lak I tol' you ——'

'Yes, yes,' William hurried him on. 'Where's your master? Didn't you find that out?' He was frowning heavily at the shaking darky.

'Yas-suh, yas-suh,' Horace waved a trembling hand toward the bayou. 'Dey tuhned de niggers loose, and dey's plannin' on hangin' Mas' Povey an' Jedge Symington in dair place.' He was climbing on Xanthus as he spoke.

William put out a swift hand and pulled him back. 'Get up behind me,' he commanded him, and dug his spurs into Xanthus's dripping sides. 'Horace'll bring out your horses,' he called back to the men on foot.

They followed as fast as they could down the deserted road back to the thicket, grabbing their reins from Horace. Across the fields, they could see, galloping furiously ahead, William and the men who had been left to guard the horses. They followed, spurring their mounts over the low rail fence. William's party, they saw, was floundering in wet, red mud, and they, therefore, swung their own horses to the right, up a slight incline where the ground looked sandy. Now they were all together again, racing across deep furrows, where a horse could easily stumble and break a leg; and then out of that field into a mule pasture cut with gullies; and at last, there in front of them, was the bayou flowing thick and red with mud stirred up by autumn rains.

William plunged in first, and his horse's head went under. Up it came, and the creature snorted, shaking his mane clear. Now Philip was in. Pilot laid his delicate ears back and swam ahead with long, sure strokes. Soaked to the waist, they all scrambled up the slippery bank, making for the cut through the woods, where hangings were always carried out. They knew the place — a dark, sinister, open spot curtained by gray, swinging moss, and surrounded by trees with long, straight-spreading limbs. The negroes would not go past it by night; and now, as Horace thought of the dark, haunted circle, he pressed closer to William.

They galloped on through the woods, jumping stumps and dodging limbs. 'If the soldiers are drunk, we can probably scatter them,' William thought, but he knew they could make no plan. Each rider would have to rely on his own wits.

The trees were thinning now, and through a cleared space, William caught a glimpse of soldiers — how many he could not exactly determine — around two other men on horseback. Now, he could see a little better, and he made a rough estimate. There did not seem to be over forty or fifty men under the trees. There were, he supposed — he had not counted them — eighteen or twenty in their own group. Probably most of the soldiers were in town looting and burning it, he thought.

Suddenly, strangled sounds of which he was hardly conscious began to roll out of his throat. There in front of him — for the first time he could see clearly through the trees — was a new dangling rope, but — his eyes bored through the brush — swinging free. Yes! thank God, still swinging free and empty. He dug in his spurs with all his strength, and out of the corner of his eyes saw Philip tearing the bowie knife that always hung on his saddle out of its case. It was sharp as a razor, he knew. Only last week he had helped Philip whet it, himself. The men behind him closed in. There, not a hundred yards away now, sat Povey and Judge Symington, on horseback.

Povey's hands were tied behind him, and Judge Symington's one arm roped to the pommel of his saddle. Their shirts were hanging in strips, torn off their backs. Hearing the crashing in the bushes they both turned their heads to see what was happening; and, seeing, took instant action. Povey struck his horse's flanks sharply with his heavy boots, just as Philip raced by, knocking over a guard and, in a single sure movement, cutting the ropes that bound his hands together. William missed Judge Symington's bridle and seized hold, instead, of his horse's mane. Then, without more than the briefest momentary slackening of speed, the rest of the men charged upon the colored soldiers, breaking, as they galloped, into the shrill, high piercing yell that had scattered the Yankees at Manassas. These black soldiers had never heard that sharp yell before, but something in its fierce, wild cadence terrified them. They were dismounted, all of them, and more than half drunk. The sight of these galloping, plunging horses, with their bold, furious riders, was too much for them. Taking to cover, they disappeared in the woods, as if devils were after them. Letting them go, the riders raced on after William and Philip, this time boldly coming out on the main road.

They met no one. The soldiers were in town, their commander drunk and asleep on the saloon floor.

On and on they galloped. Suddenly William remembered a narrow path to the left of the road, which led to an old Indian fort, long ago abandoned. But the heavy walls were still there, and the hole in the ground where the gunpowder had been stored. He turned and the rest followed. There they could safely draw up, he thought. Their horses came to a sharp halt, their back legs bending and their front feet coming up in the air, their breaths escaping in long, tearing gasps.

Mr. Archibald Bland, not on his mule this time, but on one of Philip's horses, got down, walked over to Judge Symington, and untied the Judge's hand from his pommel.

'Well, I be doggoned, Judge,' he said casually. 'You didn't ride with the Rangers for nothing.'

Judge Symington's face was pallid, and his eyelids twitched, but he straightened his shoulders, and looked at his friends calmly.

'My gratitude, gentlemen,' he said, in a warm, steady voice. 'My very deep gratitude, indeed.' Then a quizzical expression crossed his face. 'I trust that none of you will ever be in a position to require a similar service of me.' John McGaughey offered him a hand, but he waved it away, and, unassisted, swung his stiff legs to the ground.

Philip felt in his saddlebags and walked silently over to the Judge and Povey. Without a word, he unscrewed the silver top of his flask, filled it with brandy, and offered it first to Judge Symington, then to Povey. The Judge took it at once and sipped it slowly, as the color returned to his cheeks; but Povey stood looking for a long minute straight at Philip, who returned his gaze without a flicker of his eyelashes. Then, suddenly, Povey turned the cup up and swallowed its contents in one impetuous gesture. Handing it back to Philip with a slight, formal bow, he began swinging his arms.

'This is a pleasant surprise, gentlemen, I assure you — a very pleasant surprise. By now, I had confidently expected to be trying out my wings.'

He sat down on the low, mud wall of the old fort, and the sunlight dappled the dry leaves at his feet, and gleamed against his horse's wet sides. Then his gaze fell on Horace standing in the background, energetically rubbing Xanthus down, and he looked over toward William, a sudden idea crossing his mind. That's where Horace went to, then. And he'd been ready to break his bones!

William met his eyes and nodded. 'Horace woke me up before day.'

Povey got up and walked straight over to his servant. 'Horace,' he said, clapping him on the shoulder and turning him around in his tracks, as, somewhat abashed, the negro returned his gaze. 'I reckon there's nothing I've got, boy, you can't have.'

'You remembers dat time in de army when you jumped in an' pulled me out de ribber?' asked Horace. 'Well, suh,' he said, looking straight at Povey, 'I ain't done no mo' fur you, no mo' at all.' Then he handed his master the reins he was holding. 'You better take Xanthus, hadn't you, suh?' he asked. The horse, recognizing Povey, nipped playfully at his sleeve.

Judge Symington stood up. 'William,' he decided, 'I've got to get on home. God knows what's happened there since one o'clock last night. Apparently they can't even control their own troops.'

He threw a tentative, inquiring glance at his friends. 'Perhaps, though, gentlemen, it would be wiser for you to scatter,' he suggested.

For answer, Povey sprang on Xanthus, and William on his horse. Philip spurred Pilot until he was just behind the Judge, and the others pushed through the underbrush after him. Their horses' knees were caked with mud, their nostrils dilated. Over ditches, into gullies and up again, through the slough, past the Judge's cornfield, out by his pasture — there at last was his white back fence in sight, on the edge of the village from which black smoke still poured sickeningly out in hot, curling waves. They threw their reins over the fence, and Philip grabbed his saddlebags.

The Judge paused a second on the back gallery. 'Aaron, Franklin, blanket the horses, walk 'em slowly about, and don't let them drink for an hour.' Then he was inside.

Goodwin Breckinridge threw open the back door, but there

was no time for questions or explanation. Goodwin had barely recognized his uncle and the men with him, when they all heard the same sound — not the uproarious rioting that had been going on for hours, not the crackling flames, but the steady tramp-tramp of disciplined, orderly feet, pausing again in front of the garden gate.

'I'll go,' said Goodwin, laying a restraining hand on his uncle's arm. He did not know what had happened, but he saw that Judge Symington had been under heavy strain.

The Judge smiled and shook off his hand. 'No, thank you, Goodwin,' he said briefly, and strode firmly out to the gate, pausing only to lay his hand on his wife's in passing, as she stood on the bottom stairstep unable to believe her eyes and her ears. Would this strange and terrible nightmare never pass? She had thought the Judge was in jail. She stood rigid, clinging to the rail for support, and stared after him, in complete silence, understanding that this was no time for a man to have to stop and comfort his wife.

The Judge walked down the path toward the gate, where he saw a group of white soldiers standing at ease behind two men in the foreground. Their officers, he supposed. Then as he drew nearer, he recognized one of the men.

'My dear Bishop!' he exclaimed, hardly believing his own eyes, and looking long and hard at his friend.

'Thank God!' exclaimed the Bishop, seizing the Judge's hand and shaking it as his features brightened in relief. 'We've been looking for you.' He turned his head toward the officer at his side. 'Judge Symington, Major Bradford.'

The Northern officer bowed courteously, and Judge Symington returned his salutation with cold precision, maintaining strict silence, as Major Bradford leaned across the gate, addressing him in short, crisp sentences.

'Judge Symington,' he began, 'the soldiers who have fired this village are as dastardly a bunch of renegades as I have seen under uniform.' His cold blue eyes snapped, and he held his head, with its dark clipped sideburns, as high as the Judge's own. 'They are a disgrace to the army in which I have the honor to serve, and I intend to see that not one of them escapes court-martial. In the name of the United States Government, sir, I apologize for their conduct.'

The Judge's expression did not alter, and Major Bradford leaned closer.

'I have just had the pleasure of arresting a company of drunken cowards who had trussed up some of your young men' — he lifted his eyes and looked briefly over the group now assembled behind the Judge — 'and left them in a building directly in the path of the fire.' His clipped voice went on. 'The soldiers in question are under guard, and your friends should be along safely at any minute now.'

'Ah!' said Goodwin, aloud, breathing easier. 'That's why they didn't come back.' He moved nearer the gate, as did the other men around him.

The officer was still speaking, holding his steady gaze on the Judge's attentive face.

'I had known Bishop Gregg well in a happier time,' he was explaining in his harsh, precise accent, 'and I, therefore, wrote and asked him to confer with me about the administration of this county. We were talking together, when a young officer from this post galloped up asking for assistance in quieting this damnable outrage that our troops have committed here.' For a moment, he stood silent, with his watchful eyes still on the Judge's face, which, he saw, had taken on a somewhat less severe cast. 'I trust you will do me the honor, sir, of permitting my men to guard your family and friends.'

'That, sir,' replied the Judge promptly and decisively, 'is
hardly necessary.' The officer's eyes lifted and dwelt on the
group of determined faces drawn up behind the Judge. He
saw that the men were all armed and, he judged, soldiers
themselves, accustomed to handling their weapons. He addressed them directly, raising his voice slightly.

'Gentlemen,' he said clearly, 'I urge you to put up your
guns, return home, and let me assume full responsibility for the
restoration of order in this village.'

John McGaughey spoke hotly across the Judge's shoulders,
and the scorn in his rumbling voice brought a sudden flush to
Major Bradford's cheeks.

'Your infamous gang of horsethieves couldn't be trusted to put
a stop to a yellow-dog-fight,' he taunted the Major, his huge
voice leaping like a bullet across the space between him and the
Northern officer. 'Besides,' he went on, clapping his hands
suddenly to his cartridge belt, 'we want to hear your ideas
about these gentlemen.' He swung his large head as he spoke
toward the Judge and Povey.

The officer did not flinch. He moved forward and addressed
Judge Symington.

'It is my disagreeable duty to inform you, sir, that you are
again under arrest, you and' — he consulted a list he held in
his hand — 'Mr. Povey Blount, and the other leaders of the
group, who, I am happy to say, were successful in rescuing
you.' He paused and spoke emphatically to the men now
gathered close around the Judge.

'The United States Government will condone no defiance of
its authority in this province — none whatsoever. The sooner
that fact is accepted in this state, the better for all concerned.'
His keen, cold eyes swept the gathering.

John McGaughey sprang suddenly forward, with a furious

lurching movement of his whole body, but the Judge put out his arm to stop him.

'I am at your service, sir,' he informed the officer coolly. 'Permit me to speak to my friends, myself.' He swung around with vigorous precision, and the Bishop pulled open the gate and stepped inside the yard.

'Judge,' he said quietly, laying his hand on his friend's shoulder, 'you can accept Major Bradford's word.'

The Judge returned his long glance, nodded twice, and stood silent, waiting for quiet. In a moment the yard was so still that, as the Judge began to speak, the Bishop could hear the sound of the squirrels scurrying among the oak leaves on the grass.

'Put down your guns, my friends,' the Judge was saying in an unimpassioned, deliberate voice. 'This matter goes beyond any of our personal desires.' He stopped, and the men who stood listening were conscious that his mind was made up. 'I said last night,' he reminded them, 'that the issue was this: Is there any responsible, orderly government in this county? I still think that is the question at stake,' he concluded, his voice rising slightly. 'In order to put the case to a test, gentlemen, I am prepared to stand trial on the right of any American to defend his home and family from attack by a gang of drunken ruffians.' His eye sought the Bishop's. 'I will ask Bishop Gregg to see that the truth is laid before the Governor.'

'And Sheridan, and the President, if need be,' the Bishop replied, extending the list. 'I have already so informed Major Bradford.'

There was a moment's quiet broken by Povey's cool, mocking voice. Leaning slightly across the fence, he looked into the Major's face with elevated brows and a disdainful smile on his lips.

'I trust, sir,' he inquired politely, 'that your prison accommodations in this state excel those I enjoyed in Illinois?'

He stepped back then, with a light, easy step, and the officer waited, with a frown between his brows. He would never understand these people, never. Were they never reasonable? They laughed when he expected them to be serious, and were deadly serious when he expected them to laugh. 'A strange people,' he thought, 'a strange people,' and glanced out of the corner of his eye at the Bishop, remembering the advice he had received from him that morning. Well, he supposed he had better try to hold his temper, if he could.

John McGaughey could no longer contain himself. He strode forward and shook his large fist across the gate, under the officer's very nose. His face was no longer red, but deadly pale, as it always grew when he became sufficiently angry — shooting mad, his cowboys said.

'I give you fair warning,' he roared, 'any time your black baboons lay hands on us, they'll get what they got this morning.' His eyes glittered — like a rattlesnake's, Philip suddenly thought — and his thick hair stood up around his white face. 'Do you think we're going to let your god-damned bunch o' hell-cats go on hanging our men and kidnapping our women?' He stopped, shaking with anger, unaware that William was just behind him, with his finger raised as a signal to Major Bradford.

'John,' said William, speaking quietly, without a flicker in his calm, blue eyes, 'John, you're wasting your fire.' He laid his hand firmly on his friend's elbow. 'Judge Symington is right. What we have to find out now is whether the men who settled these bottoms have any legal rights at all under this' — a brief, scornful smile crossed his thin face — 'this so-called government.' He straightened his shoulders and faced Major Bradford. 'I am prepared, sir,' he said firmly, 'to defend, in any court in this land, my right to ride to the assistance of my friends.'

Philip stepped forward, and, seizing shrewdly on the one appeal he thought might move John to accept his decision, he laid on his shoulders two obligations. 'I am counting on you,' he said slowly, 'to help Cavin take hold. And,' he continued, 'there's the election. Somebody has to stay out of jail.' He stood for a moment watching John with the same close attention that he gave to a man just coming out of a congestive chill. 'Besides,' he reminded him, 'your turn may be later.' He saw the blood coming back to John's face, and, with a nod of satisfaction, he turned toward Major Bradford.

'I am ready, sir,' he said composedly.

The Bishop shot a warning glance under his lids toward Major Bradford. His finger-tips felt cold as he clenched them. If only the Major would remember a little of what he had been telling him this very morning, when the sentry galloped up! Only a little would be enough.

Major Bradford looked straight into the faces of the four men in front of him, and saluted sharply.

'You are, sirs, I believe, all officers of the Confederate Army?' he inquired, looking from Judge Symington to Povey, and from them to William and Philip.

They bowed, returning his salute.

'Then,' said Major Bradford, 'I will ask you to meet me at my quarters at' — he seemed to be weighing the hour — 'at nightfall, gentlemen. I trust that will give you time to arrange your affairs?' he inquired courteously.

'By nightfall,' Philip responded slowly. 'You may expect us, sir.' He snapped open his watch and held it against the Major's. 'It is now nearly midday.'

Major Bradford signalled to a junior officer in line. 'These gentlemen will require no escort and no protection,' he informed him, and turned again to the men in front of him.

'I wish you good day, gentlemen.' His eyes sought the Bishop's. 'Good day, Bishop Gregg,' he bowed. 'Accept my appreciation of your generous advice.'

The Bishop's hands fell open. Somehow the Lord must have put the right words into his mouth this morning.

'Well,' said Judge Symington, watching the troops depart, 'that gives us good time to get all the ladies home safely.' He closed the gate carefully and went inside. 'Harriet,' the men on the porch heard him calling to his wife, 'Harriet.'

Philip glanced again at his watch and then sat down by Povey on the steps.

'Hardly time to make it to Locust Hill and back, I suppose,' he remarked easily. It was the first time they had spoken together since the night Povey had flung past him in William's yard, now over six years ago.

'It seems,' Philip went on, holding his calm gaze steady, 'that we are going to be together for some time. We might as well settle on some suitable topics of conversation, don't you think?'

Povey's eyes never varied. At last he spoke, as evenly as Philip.

'Are you by chance sending a note home? Perhaps, in that case, you will be good enough to include in it some mention of my heavy debt to you.' He stopped, but Philip understood he had not finished.

'That fact,' he added, emphasizing his words carefully, 'makes any topic of conversation possible between us, I should think.'

'Except one,' Philip said, after a long silence.

'Except one,' Povey agreed slowly. 'Except one.'

Chapter 14

Two weeks later, the county had quieted down — temporarily, at least. Cavin decided to try to see Philip and, after that, to ride out on the prairie and take a look at his long-horned steers. When he returned at dusk, Lucina and Letitia were rocking by the dining-room fire, and a fresh norther was whipping around the house, sending the dust in fine showers of sand against the windows. The twins and FitzHugh, on low stools at Letitia's feet, were holding out their wide yellow bowls for Aunt Elvy to fill with the grits she was scooping out of a black iron pot steaming on the hearth. Cavin paused at the door, liking the picture he saw.

He had been out all day with Jake and his father's cowboys, gathering in the range cattle with Philip's brand on their raw-boned hips. He intended to drive the animals down into the shelter of the woods before the cold winter rains began, for he knew that one December day might be balmy, like June, and the next freezing, with a heavy, sleety rain miring the cows in their tracks. The cowhands, too, understood the tricky weather, and every day they pushed farther and farther out onto the open, unfenced range to find Philip's wandering long-horned steers. When spring came, Cavin decided he would send them out for a whole month to round up all the Locust Hill cattle that had strayed into other herds.

He was tired and cold, but exultant, when he reached home.

Already Lucina had learned to keep a pot of coffee hot by the hearth, and tonight, when he came in, shaking the wet from his clothes as irascibly as old George, on rainy days, shook the damp from his fur, she reached immediately for the cup that stood waiting on the window-ledge. In it was a mound of sugar and some grated orange peeling. Pouring a careful measure of brandy over the sugar, she lighted it, watching the mixture turn to caramel. Then, without a word, she filled the cup and handed it to Cavin. He drank it, stretching out his spurred boots to the fire with a luxurious sigh of utter relaxation.

Soon he stirred himself and pulled a roll of damp newspapers out of his pocket. As he did so, FitzHugh finished his supper, got up from his chair and climbed up into his brother's lap, confidently lying back against his chest and sticking out his thin little legs in ridiculous copy of Cavin's own posture.

'I met a wagon coming in from Houston,' Cavin said, settling FitzHugh more comfortably in his lap and peeping around at his face. 'How are you, old chap?' he interrupted himself to ask. The child smiled widely and burrowed deeper.

Cavin continued, 'There's plenty of news.'

Lucina held out her hand for the *Telegraph*, but Cavin could not wait to have her read what he already knew.

'Wait! I'll tell you!' He held back the papers watching her face. 'Would you believe it?' he demanded, 'the Governor's come to his senses! He's not only calling on the citizens to form their own guard units, but he's actually set the date for an election. Let's see ——' Opening the paper, he consulted it briefly. 'January the eighth,' he said slowly. 'That gives us nearly two months to get in our work.' Leaning back in his chair, he pulled the child closer, and began to shape his plans, whistling softly between his pursed lips.

Lucina took the paper from him and scanned it.

'You talk exactly the way Shelby did all summer, Cavin!
I can see right now that Letitia and I might just as well get
ready to run this plantation until the election's over, anyway.
We've just come in from the quarters,' she informed him.

Cavin held out his cup to be refilled. 'How'd you find
Uncle Claib? I was afraid he wouldn't be alive, today, when I
was down to see him last night.'

'We took David along, but' — Lucina smiled — 'Claib
thought he was too young to be much of a doctor. He thinks
the old fellow'll pull through, though. Aunt Mattie's nursing
him.'

'She'll look after him,' Cavin agreed. 'I see you are beginning
to know your way around here, Lucy.' His eyes rested on her
approvingly.

'Did you go by to see Philip?' Letitia asked him suddenly,
laying down a paper.

Cavin's face grew suddenly serious.

'They wouldn't let me see him,' he declared, in an anxious
tone. 'I left the clothes. God knows if they'll give 'em to him.'
He sat looking at Letitia, trying to interpret the events of the
day. 'Major Bradford's been recalled to Galveston. The higher-
ups seemed to think he'd been too lenient, I gathered. Nobody
knows yet what the new man's like — like all the rest of 'em,
I reckon,' he concluded disgustedly, and then went on with his
news as Letitia fixed her eyes on him, listening with tense
attention. 'They haven't set the date of the trial yet.'

He turned his gaze moodily toward the fire.

'Of course,' he continued, 'the best thing would be to get
Pa's case transferred to Judge White's court. That's what we
had all been hoping to do, but look here!' He reached over to
Lucina's lap and hunted through the roll of papers till he found
the *Galveston News*.

'Here's the Governor's latest ruling — in big letters on the front page. Listen!'

Cavin began to read aloud, emphasizing each word, as he spoke it with a stroke of his brown forefinger.

' "*There is no constitutional state government.*" ' ('We already knew that,' commented Cavin dryly.) ' "*Therefore I not only see no objection to the trial of offenders before military tribunals, but believe it to be a necessity.*" '

'Well,' Cavin said, laying down the paper, 'that's clear enough.' He began to whistle softly again, drumming one set of fingers on his chair-arm. Then he glanced toward Letitia. 'Don't worry too much,' he advised her. 'There's always *some* way to beat the old devil around the stump.'

Lucina sat quiet, watching a slow smile appear and spread over Cavin's serious face. She wondered what could possibly be amusing him, as he suddenly began to laugh aloud.

'Did Maria tell you?' he asked. 'She and Jake want to get married — right away.'

'I've been expecting it,' Lucina replied. 'She's been mooning around for weeks. Well,' she decided, 'it's a good idea.'

'I thought so too,' he agreed. 'I promised Jake a fine wedding.'

'Why, yes,' Letitia said. 'Philip usually sets the servants' weddings for Christmas Eve, along with the fireworks.' She glanced up smiling. 'The Bishop is apt to be in the neighborhood around that time.'

Lucina tapped a bell on the window-ledge beside her.

'Maria,' she said to her maid reproachfully when the girl stood in the doorway, 'whyn't you tell me?'

'Lawd, Miss Lucy,' Maria giggled, fingering her apron, 'you knowed it, all de time.'

Just then, Jake came in with an armful of wood for the fire, and, seeing Maria, paused uncertainly at the door.

'Jake,' said Cavin, 'how'd you and Maria like me to build you a new cabin, down by the creek?'

'And,' asked Letitia, 'how about a wedding Christmas Eve?'

Jake cast a broad smile at Maria.

'Us been thinkin' dat-a-way ourselves, ain't we, Maria?'

She nodded, and looked toward Lucina.

'Ef'n Miss Lucy laks de notion.' Her soft, liquid eyes dropped and she glanced shyly at Jake.

Lucina laughed. 'Of course, Maria.'

The next week, Cavin was almost never at home, and, as Lucina had predicted, she and Letitia soon had to take over the management of the plantation. As the weeks went on, however, most of the task fell to Lucina; for, as the winter approached, Letitia felt less and less like moving around. Cavin was often away, looking after the cattle or electioneering for William, and in his absence, Lucina had to help Uncle Matt plan the work and attend not only to giving out supplies from the commissary but also to looking after the sick, the old, and the young children on the place. Now, she thought, she knew what had kept Susanna always so busy.

During the late fall, following Letitia's advice, Lucina set the negro women to making work garments and cotton comforters and quilts. Matt kept the young men busy digging up stumps, repairing rail fences, clearing new fields, or grading new roads, and the old men busy whittling new hoe handles, and plaiting mule collars out of corn shucks, or harness out of hides.

Cavin had had it in mind ever since he returned home to drain a swamp that covered several acres down by the river.

'If you ever get a place like that drained,' he told Lucina reflectively every time they rode by, 'it'll grow a plenty cotton.'

About the first of December he began the task, selecting his men carefully for the work, and going with them himself instead of sending Uncle Matt alone.

'Why are you always down there?' Lucina asked him, when he came in late to supper one night.

'Well, I figured I'd better be around,' he told her, and frowned. 'That swamp is alive with rattlesnakes. I saw one old fellow there as big as my arm yesterday. We counted his rattles after we killed him.' He looked at her significantly. 'There were twenty left on his tail, and the Lord knows how many broken off.' Seeing that she did not seem impressed, he began to laugh. 'Don't you know,' he asked her, 'that a snake grows a rattle every year of his life?' Leaning over, he kissed her lightly. 'You've still got a lot to learn about this bottom!'

Next day, Lucina insisted on accompanying him down to the swamp.

'Thought you were afraid of snakes,' Cavin said to her, as he knelt and held out his hand for her to spring from into her saddle. She was wearing Susanna's velvet riding habit, and looked, he thought, though he did not say so, as pretty as anybody *could* look.

'I am,' she answered. 'I'm scared to death of them.' She did not lift her reins, but sat looking anxiously down on him. 'What do I do, if you get bit?'

He turned Pilot's head toward the river, and reaching over from his saddle, rumpled her dark hair. 'Listen! I'm taking you along for company, not for a nurse.'

But she was not satisfied.

'Well,' he warned her, 'you won't like thinking about it. You tie a string just above the bite, and take your knife and slice deep down to the bone. Then you suck out the poison, drink a lot of whiskey, and send for a doctor — and pray, if you're not too drunk from the whiskey. That's about all.'

'It's aplenty,' she shuddered, and poked tentatively at a package on his saddle. 'That's your medicine case, I suppose.'

Cavin pulled up his horse some distance from the swamp.

'Horses are nearly as scared o' snakes as you are,' Cavin explained. 'Better tie 'em here.' As he spoke, he was unstrapping from the back of his saddle a pillow that he had brought along for Lucina to rest on.

'Watch out!' he warned her as they took a narrow trail running between low bushes. 'The snakes are all stirred up now, though when we started in they were nearly dormant.'

She threw her long riding skirt over her arm and followed behind him with wary steps, her eyes on the ground. When they reached the place where a ditch was being dug, she climbed thankfully into a high wagon standing there.

'Be careful,' she begged Cavin.

He stood with one booted foot on the wagon tongue, and his strong, brown hands clasped lightly around his bent knee. 'Now, maybe you better wrap me up in cotton, Lucy, I might break,' he teased her, cocking an innocent blue eye up at her. 'Here, hold this.' He handed her his kit. 'I have to start the hands to work.'

She sat there in the wagon, leaning back against her pillow. It was a warm day, like early summer in Georgia, and there was not a breath of chill in the air. She felt deeply content, and half penitent because she felt so.

'I ought to be worrying about Uncle Phil. And I thought I'd be homesick,' she meditated. 'Yet, here I am sitting in a wagon in the middle of a swamp full of rattlesnakes, feeling perfectly happy.'

She leaned further back and closed her book, staring up through the branches at the drifting masses of white cloud above her. Here on the Gulf coast, where the moisture hung so thick in the air, the sky was almost never clear and solidly blue, as she remembered it in the mountains. Her eye fell on the limb above her, where a bunch of mistletoe studded with tiny pearl-like berries hung suspended in the still, bright air. Jake would have to climb up and haul it down for Christmas. She watched a squirrel jumping from one tree to the next, with its fuzzy tail serving for a rudder, and she heard crows cawing lustily in a cornfield across the bayou, and the steady chop-chop-chop of the negroes' shovels dipping into wet black ooze. Then, just as she felt her eyes closing, she sat up with a start, alert and listening. What had wakened her?

'Jake!' she heard Cavin calling. 'Jake!' The sharp warning in his voice roused her to sudden attention.

She raised herself to look, and saw Jake poised for a tremendous leap, pushing out his free hand to balance himself. But the footing was slick and he fell sideways with his extended hand striking the ground just in front of a thick brown coil that moved, at first, with sickening jelly-like motion and, then, suddenly with darting, angry speed. Jake lay still, as if paralyzed, and the negro working beside him stood drawn back in horror, unable to move.

Cavin took two strides, and, as Matt came running up with a heavy stick, aimed his pistol at a snake writhing off into the bushes.

Then he hurried to the wagon and reached for his bag, which Lucina handed to him without a word. Leaning far over the wagon's side she watched to see what he was doing.

'Where'd he get you?' he asked Jake briefly. The negro lay where he had fallen. His eyes moved to his thumb, but he was too terrified to speak.

Kneeling beside him, Cavin said, 'Just a minute, boy.' Lucina saw the red blood spurt and the flow die down. Then she saw Cavin push Jake's thumb between his lips and suck vigorously, spewing out his mouth, from time to time, on the black, wet earth.

'There!' she heard Cavin saying, and then saw him reach out his hand to a stump against which he had laid his whiskey bottle.

As he did so, there was a sharp rattle and a flash and he sprang up, looking at his own hand.

Before he could speak, Matt was pounding the second snake to death, and Lucina was out of the wagon at his side, holding up her long skirts around her.

'Whar'd it come from?' Matt exclaimed.

Cavin peered into the stump and pointed. 'Hollow,' he said, briefly. 'Probably the mate.'

Already he had cut deep to the bone and was squeezing his own hand, forcing the blood out. Matt was kneeling by him twisting a cord above his wrist, but Lucina pushed him aside, and applied her own lips to Cavin's palm.

He pulled his hand away, in a sharp and sudden gesture.

'Let me see your mouth.' She opened it wide and he peered inside. 'All right,' he said, and gave her back his hand. She sucked till she thought her lungs would burst.

'There, that'll be enough, I guess,' he said finally, and turned to Jake, who was now sitting up weakly, white showing in strange, gray patches through his black skin. Tipping the whiskey bottle, Cavin drank half of its contents himself and handed the rest to Jake. 'Finish it,' he told him, shortly.

They climbed into the wagon, to which one of the hands was already hitching a pair of mules.

'Matt!' Cavin leaned over the wheel. 'You know what to do.'

'Yas-suh,' Matt answered, fastening the traces to the wagon.

'I better stay here. Asa'll drive you home. I done sont Henry to fetch Doctor David. Go on, Asa!'

Cavin laid his head on Lucina's lap, and grinned at Jake, who was shaking as if he were in a malarial chill.

'Cheer up, Jake. You'll feel a heap wuss by night, but you'll be up in plenty o' time for your wedding.'

They were both out sooner than that, although they both suffered for a long time with aching heads and swollen arms.

There was never much use trying to get work out of the hands around Christmas-time, Cavin knew, especially with a wedding in prospect. Therefore, he gave up draining the swamp until after the holidays.

Lucina set some of the women to sewing for Maria, and others to baking cakes, using dozens of the eggs Aunt Emmy had been accumulating in a big tin bucket against this time of extra need. She had taken them out of their nests, greased them carefully, and laid them away between layers of clean straw. Now, when she wanted them, she triumphantly produced them.

'Gwine-a make you a big wedding cake,' she told Maria.

She made a three-tiered one that sat like a king amid the lesser cakes arranged in the dining-room cupboard. For weeks, seated beside a long table in the back yard, the negro women had been seeding raisins by hand, washing currants, candying orange peeling, grating coconuts, and picking out pecans and walnuts, while their babies lay in a row on the back gallery, wrapped in blankets.

Every morning Lucina and Letitia would go around stooping over each bundle, inspecting the black baby inside each cocoon. Lucina wondered how anybody could be so blind as to imagine that because babies were black, they all looked alike. Very soon she was able to tell at sight which child belonged to which mother.

The cakes were finally baked and ready — the black wedding cake high above all; and below it, packed solidly on the broad shelves, were the pecan and coconut cakes, the jelly, and fig, and pound cakes for which Aunt Emmy was famous.

Ten days before Christmas the Bishop returned from Austin. The Governor had been firm, he reported. Cases like Philip's had to be tried in the military courts. But he had promised to bear the circumstances in mind and to review the decision. 'Right after New Year's I'd better start for New Orleans,' the Bishop concluded his report. It was plain he did not expect much help from Governor Hamilton.

'Well,' Cavin said slowly, darting a suggestive glance at the Bishop, 'there's another possibility. Better come to the county guard meeting at Holly Grove this evening. We are appointing road patrols and' — his eyes twinkled — 'taking up a collection.'

'Collection?' asked the Bishop, dully. He was very tired after his long ride.

'Oh, for charity,' said Cavin lightly. 'It's down on the books like that, anyway. *The Helping Hand: A Society for the Assistance of the Sick and the Poor in Cypress County.*'

This time, the Bishop's mind quickened. 'Ah?' he said, lifting his brows.

'Exactly,' responded Cavin, a slow smile appearing in his own eyes.

'Permit me,' said the Bishop cheerfully, 'to remit your usual contribution to my salary, the amount to be applied to the purpose you mention.'

Cavin shook his head. 'I believe there's enough on hand. No telling when we'll need more, though — or how often.'

Christmas approached, and the wagons returned from Galveston loaded with firecrackers and Roman candles and skyrockets and stockings for the old people and with balls and harps for the children.

All day in her big kitchen, Aunt Emmy made batches of white taffy candy and yellow molasses chips, and popped corn, while Letitia filled many red gauze bags to hang on the holly tree just outside the garden gate. She counted them; there was one for each colored child on the plantation and identical ones for her own three children.

The day before Christmas, Lucina looked hopefully out at the early sky and laid her hand on the fig tree outside her window.

'Cavin! It's nice and warm.' Her tone was surprised. Georgia Christmases were often chilly.

'It usually is,' remarked Cavin, pulling on his boots. 'I can remember only a few times when it was too cold to hang the presents outside. Better set Jake to tying all the bags on early,' he warned her, 'and to clipping on the candles and fixing up the cleats to hold the sky-rockets. That'll keep him from getting nervous,' he suggested, and drew Lucina down on his knee. 'A man does, you know, black or white. Didn't you see my legs shaking at Cedar Ledge?'

Lucina kissed him lightly. 'Foolish!' Then more soberly, 'Aren't you going to be home today, Cavin?'

He looked up at her, worried. 'I know I'm leaving a lot to you and Letitia.'

Lucina rose firmly. 'When you get back, Letitia will be practising the wedding march and the Bishop will be putting on his robes. Come on to breakfast.'

Letitia had preceded them to the table, and was pouring their coffee when they sat down.

'Don't ask me any questions,' Cavin said mysteriously, smiling at her and beginning on his toasted cheese, 'but I'm thinking about buying you a present while I'm out.'

Toward evening, Lucina went out on the gallery several times, looking anxiously down the long drive. Soon it would be time to light the candles on the holly tree, and Cavin was not yet back. There was no wind stirring; it would be a nice night. The sky was filled with the warm, almost golden, light she had learned to expect in Texas at sunset; but already the shadows which so soon followed the orange glow were falling over the tree-tops, whose branches seemed to merge in a violet mist — a color much warmer than the intense blue which at dusk fell over the Georgia mountains. Lucina remembered that Shelby and Margaret were far away on Cedar Ledge, and that Susanna and Beauford were farther yet — so far, indeed, that she might never hope to reach them. Her thoughts saddened her, for she was too young to take comfort in remembering those she had lost, thus briefly calling them back to transient life. She wished for Cavin, but he was not in sight. At length, she gave up her vigil and turned inside, to supervise Maria's dressing.

She was pinning down her veil, which she had contrived out of an old mosquito bar, when she heard Cavin's step on the gallery. Already, she could pick it out of a thousand treads, that quick, confident step of Cavin's. Then she heard a slower and heavier footfall than his, and Letitia's piano was suddenly silent.

'I'll be back in a minute,' Lucina cried breathlessly.

When she reached the hall, Philip had the twins in his arms, and Cavin was standing back of him, with the light from the lamp on the wall shining directly on his hair, turning it to a pale golden yellow. He was smiling, manifestly happy, but Philip looked immensely weary, and his shoulders sagged, although his eyes were bright.

'Didn't I tell you I'd buy you a present?' Lucina heard Cavin reminding Letitia.

Then Philip noticed Lucina leaning against the shadowy wall.

'Buy's the right word, Lucy,' he said, sending her an affectionate glance. 'Cavin did a right smart bit o' buying today.'

'How on earth ——' asked Letitia, her voice returning to her.

The Bishop appeared in the parlor door, his robes falling around him in long, draped folds, and his wide sleeves scraping the door-jamb.

His eyes caught Cavin's.

'The charity fund, I suppose?'

Cavin smiled. 'Pa was sick, wasn't he? And they seemed to be needing money.' He slapped his pockets, enjoying the telling. 'I happened to have it, that's all.'

Continuing, he smiled cheerfully.

'Judge Symington's coachman was waiting outside for him, and Horace was there to drive Cousin William and Povey home.'

'How — how are they?' asked Letitia, suddenly.

Philip glanced at her, and waited a perceptible moment to answer.

'Well,' he replied, equivocating, 'nobody could consider the place we've been living in a health resort, exactly. Still,' he remarked comfortably, 'we may have time to get well before the officers in the Freedman's Bureau decide they want their rake-off, too. They will, of course, Cavin,' he said, dropping into a chair, and addressing his son.

'You're worn out!' Letitia exclaimed, noticing his pallor. 'You ought to be in bed.'

The Bishop opened his large gold watch with the picture of a leaping deer on its case.

'I've promised to hold service at the garrison at midnight, and early church at Berryville in the morning.'

Cavin beckoned to Lucina.

'Find Maria,' he suggested. 'I'll hunt up Jake.'

Letitia sat down at the piano. Philip took the walnut chair, with grapes carved on its high curved back, that was drawn up close to the keyboard, and Lucina and Cavin fell in behind him. The house servants filed in through the hall door and Jake, entering through the long window of the gallery, took his place in front of the Bishop. From time to time he looked nervously toward Cavin, but the smile on his black face never varied.

Milly, carrying a basket of rose petals, halfway opened the door into the parlor from the hall, peered hesitantly in, and finally, in response to Lucina's signal, entered, scattering petals as she walked. Behind her walked Maria, under her white veil.

'Dearly beloved.' The Bishop's rich voice filled the parlor.

'... Who giveth this woman?' he asked.

'I do,' said Philip, rising stiffly.

'Bless ... preserve,' the Bishop read. 'Amen,' echoed Lucina and Cavin. For a moment, it had seemed to them that they were back on the verandah at Cedar Ledge.

Then Cavin shook Jake's hand, and Aunt Emmy bustled forward to congratulate and kiss Maria, while Matt went out to ring the ploughshare summoning the field hands to the house. He was shaking his head as he walked, and grumbling beneath his breath.

'Lawd! Lawd!' he said to himself. 'All dat fuss about a weddin'. An' none o' de fo' wives I'se had in my life wuth killin', not ary one of 'em. Lessen it wuz Hallie, now — she warn't so bad.'

His mind went back to the lithe brown girl that he had married before Philip brought Mary to live in Florida. Now she lay, under the hanging moss, as silent as Mary. But Matt remembered her, this Christmas Eve; and he thought of her, not as his present age, but as fleet and light-footed, unchanged by time.

Soon the colored children began streaming across the fields toward the drive where the holly tree gleamed like a shower of stars against the dark sky. Lucina leaned over the front gate watching Cavin, in his rôle of Santa Claus. She laughed silently, remembering how she had had to stuff the red suit with pillows, to pad out the thin figure beneath it. Now, Cavin looked jolly and fat standing in front of the tree, as a line of colored children, escorted by their mothers, filed past him, lifting wondering, eager eyes. Lucina knew exactly what would now take place. Every Christmas Eve of her life she had watched Beauford in the part that Cavin was now assuming. She was a big girl, though, she remembered, before she ever once suspected that it was her father behind the white, flowing whiskers. Now, she stood with her eyes on her husband watching him go through the familiar ritual that she knew by heart.

Cavin was stooping over a very black little girl, with wrapped pigtails of hair standing up straight and stiff all over her woolly, round head.

'Have you minded your mammy and said your prayers?' he was asking her earnestly.

Lucina knew he would put that question to every single child who paused, with wide eyes, in front of him. If the invariable answer, 'Yas-suh, Mas' Santa Claus,' went unquestioned, then he would drop the expected present into the child's outstretched palm. But if some mother had a complaint to make, he would sternly withhold his hand.

'What's that you say, Mandy? This child talks back, and won't say his prayers? I *am* surprised. Well, well. Of course, he can't have a present. Santa Claus only visits good children.'

Cavin would drop that child's gift back into a pouch at his waist and frown severely on the miscreant.

When the gifts were finally distributed, however, Lucina knew that Santa Claus would begin to look around him, as he soon did. She leaned further over the gate, to hear better.

'Where are all those bad children?' Cavin was inquiring. 'Bring 'em up!' he ordered. 'I'm goin' to give 'em one more chance. Liza! Jimmy! Fanny! If I give you these presents, are you gwine-a be good this whole next year?' Falling unconsciously, at the end of his inquiry, into the children's own dialect, he awaited the usual affirmative reply.

Then he began handing out firecrackers and Roman candles, and went himself to superintend the setting off of the skyrockets. Soon they sprang, sizzling high above the trees, exploding in a burst of final glory that both delighted and terrified FitzHugh, who was clinging to Aunt Elvy's hand, with his small, excited face turned upward toward the stars.

As Cavin walked down the lane, he could see fireworks going up from William's plantation, and from Colonel Brashear's too. 'What a fine Christmas!' he thought, recalling the one he had passed, the preceding year, in mud and cold.

Philip and Letitia were sitting on a garden bench, looking on, while the black children ran up and down the long lane shouting and shooting firecrackers, completely unaware that thousands of white boys, who loved their fleeting youth, had marched to their deaths because of them. In their midst, Felicia and Letitia were running about, entirely unconscious of the pallor of their skins.

Philip sat with his arm around Letitia's shoulders, remembering, in the darkness, the children who had died in Florida, and how Cavin had looked the first Christmas he had stretched out his tiny hands to the Christmas tree Mary had set up by his cradle. All this was a past in which Letitia had had no part, and yet he felt it was true that she had somehow shared in it. Again he wondered, as he so often had, what is past and what is present in what men call life, never once knowing what the word means. The candles slowly burning out there on the holly tree might have been those that Mary had lighted her first Christmas Eve as his bride. 'Nearly forty years ago,' he said to himself now, and the words startled him.

Cavin slipped into the house, and left his Santa Claus suit where Philip always kept it — in the locked cedar chest. Then he came out and joined Lucina, handing her a long Roman candle to match the one he held in his hand. For an hour, then, they lighted firecrackers and shot off Roman candles, pausing now and then to watch the bright balls of fire going up from the quarters where Jake and Maria were celebrating their wedding. They did not notice when Letitia and Philip left their seats in the garden and went inside. But finally they tired themselves; and, when at last the women began taking their sleepy children home, they dropped down on the long gallery step, breathless and laughing.

It was a warm night and the stars seemed low enough to touch as they moved, mysterious and brilliant, across the sky. The musicians were fiddling in the quarters and the sound of dancing feet drifted across the silent fields.

'Christmas Gift!' Lucina cried, suddenly, leaning back to look at Cavin. 'I've caught you!' she exulted.

'Christmas Gift!' Cavin returned, only half awake. 'I must-a been asleep,' he yawned, 'to let you catch me.'

'I — I have a present for you,' she said softly.

'What?' he answered, scarcely interested. It had been a long day. He wanted to get up and go in, but he felt too lethargic to move. To think it had been as easy as that to buy Philip's freedom! 'The scoundrels!' he thought. 'The rascally scoun-drels!'

'*What* have you got for me?' he asked her again, with his mind less on his question than on her face, which lay on his knee, quiet against his hand.

'Your son,' she told him, in a voice so low that he had to bend low to hear what she said.

Chapter 15

CHRISTMAS DAY, Philip kept to his bed. He was not sick, he told Letitia, only resting. He did not want even a sip of the eggnog she brought to his bed.

'I'll get up tomorrow,' he promised her. But the next morning, and the next, he felt no inclination to rise. Still, no one was especially alarmed, least of all Philip himself. It seemed to him, as it did to everyone else, that his experiences had been such as to induce fatigue and prostration in a man of his age. He did not even suspect what was the matter with him until he began to study the rise and fall of the fever that soon began to turn his head giddy.

Then he sent for Cavin. 'Find out whether Judge Symington and William and Povey are down.'

The Judge and Povey were, but they had not thought much about the matter. 'Slow fever,' they had guessed, perhaps, and, if so, a person had to wear it out. David had been to see Povey, but the Judge had not sent for him. He was waiting for Philip to get up and doctor him, he told Cavin in a weak, querulous voice.

'What does a young whipper-snapper like David know?' he inquired irritably, shaking his buzzing head.

As soon as Philip heard how both his prison companions were affected, he knew what ailed them and him. He had thought vaguely of the possibility of typhoid while he was in the garrison. Now he was certain what fever burned in him, hotter every day. At first he consulted with David about his treatment, but soon he was delirious, floating away, like a feather on a current of air.

January the eighth was the day set for the elections. It was pouring rain and dismally cold. Cavin was reluctant to leave his father, but Philip seemed no worse, so he and the McGaughey brothers rode off together to round up William's supporters. The weather was bad and the roads so treacherous that many Unionists, feeling certain of victory, simply stayed home. And, as John McGaughey had promised, the German vote went, almost in a body, to William — a contingency that the loyalists had never expected. Furthermore, for weeks Judge White had been riding up and down the county urging the planters and their sons to take all the required oaths and appear at the polls, even if they were turned down. The registrars were strangers to the county, and there were no birth records to search. How were they to be sure of either the age, the possessions, or the actual sentiments of a returned soldier? The upshot was that William outran his opponent by a large majority.

But neither he nor Cavin had it in them to rejoice, for it was now clear that Philip was a dying man. David visited his bedside, Judge Symington's, and Povey's in turn. Of the three he thought only Povey would recover. Philip and the Judge were almost beyond the reach of the Freedman's Bureau. Looking at his father's sharp, worn face, Cavin reflected, however, that the military had caused his death quite as effectively as if they had hanged him, and a slow, burning hate took possession of him, dulling his grief.

Philip slept most of the time and was seldom conscious, and

then only for a few moments at a time. Day in and day out, Letitia sat on one side of his bed, Cavin on the other, and the management of the place devolved more and more upon Lucina and Matt. As the rains kept up and a dizzy wretchedness began to overwhelm her, it seemed to Lucina a long time — a century — since the Christmas Eve when Philip had first returned home, and they had all been happy.

Cavin and Letitia, she saw, were too much occupied with Philip to realize what she was suffering. She had had no idea that bearing a child involved so much physical misery. Only Aunt Emmy had time to gather her in her wide and comfortable lap and assure her that soon she would be feeling better.

'How soon?' asked Lucina feverishly. A day more seemed too long for her to endure what she was enduring. Each morning she dragged herself out of bed, white and desperate. She realized this was no time to add to Letitia's and Cavin's troubles, but if he remembered that Lucina was going to bear his child, he gave no sign of it. For all she could tell, he had no thought of anything except the election and the progress of Philip's illness. She believed that he had not even noticed her yellow pallor and her dizzy, shuddering exhaustion.

And, indeed, Cavin did not suspect that Lucina was really suffering. He supposed — and Letitia's uniformly good health supported this belief— that what Lucina was passing through was a normal experience and nothing to be alarmed about. He did notice that she had little to say, but he put her taciturnity to the long strain of Philip's illness, which had driven every other thought out of his own mind.

For between Philip and Cavin there existed a stronger bond than unites most fathers and sons. Their thoughts fitted together like hand and glove, the mental processes of the one vivifying and energizing those of the other. Since Cavin's return, they had enjoyed one another, less as parent and child than as two companionable men interested in working out a set of common problems. As Cavin watched Philip wasting away, the sharpest pain he had ever yet felt closed around his heart and gripped it.

Philip had been sick almost a month when he awoke one night, feeling light and free, cured of suffering. He was entirely conscious, but he was aware that some strong force was drawing him out into a void; whatever it was on which he floated, he knew it felt like the undertow that at certain points on the Galveston beach could carry the strongest swimmer out into the Gulf. Once caught in that steady flow, resistance was useless. Now Philip, as he lay on his bed, felt that a current of similar strength was pulling him away. Where? He had not even strength to wonder.

But the old habit of inquiry was aroused in him. Is this death? he thought quietly. Was it to creep upon him, unawares — upon him, who had watched so many others die? How strange, he thought, that even a physician never knows what death feels like — to the one who is dying.

'That's it,' he thought. 'I'm seeing it now from the inside.' He felt keenly interested in what was happening to him, not frightened, not even rebellious, only very curious.

He opened his eyes with much difficulty and, having opened them, it seemed they would not close. No matter. Perhaps he could manage to open his lips too. He saw Cavin leaning over him. He had not been there, Philip thought, a moment before.

His mind worked clearly and precisely. Always he had wanted to feel sure how long the dying were conscious of sensation, how long their muscles obeyed their will.

Words came easily to his lips. To his own ears, his voice sounded high and shrill, piercingly high. He did not know that

Cavin caught only the faintest whisper, reading his father's lips rather than hearing the words that fluttered faintly out of them.

'I'll move my finger as long as I can,' Philip said.

By the most tremendous effort of will, he forced his forefinger to begin its slow swing, and he strained every faculty he possessed to keep it going. The fate of the universe seemed to him to hinge on whether he could move it ever so slightly. He watched its motion slow down, pause, then start again, and at last cease entirely. As it stopped, Cavin saw plainly the surprise that flared in his father's eyes, and then, almost instantly, like the snuffing of a candle, they were blank.

Cavin sat there a long time, feeling wearier than he had supposed a person could feel, conscious as yet of no other sensation.

Should he wake Letitia? No, she would know soon enough. He walked over to where Matt was asleep on a pallet, aroused him, and told him to send Jake for David and to bring hot water and his father's uniform.

Together they bathed Philip and dressed him, and closed his eyes, and stretched his thin limbs straight and crossed his graceful hands upon his breast. Then they made up his bed and laid on it the long firm board that every planter kept in his storeroom to remind him that life is a perilous adventure. When Philip's emaciated body was at last covered with a sheet and a bedspread and lay decently, as he had always said a man's body should, in his own bed, under his own roof, Matt could no longer hold back his grief.

'Mas' Cavin,' he said brokenly, when they had finished, 'yo' pa an' me ain't never been separated befo'.'

Cavin felt a deep pity for Matt. For himself he felt nothing at all, not all night as he sat beside the bed, not even when the morning broke and he saw that Philip's face was ashen and

gray, the very color of the faces both he and Cavin had passed
on battle fields, innumerable times.

He called Letitia, at last, at sunrise when David had come,
and left her there beside Philip, while he stumbled in to Lucina.
Not until he felt her warm body breathing beside him, did he
really grasp the fact that Philip, who lay so cold and still down
the hall, was really dead.

'You have a son,' he promised Philip, in his heart, 'a son who
will not forget what you planned to do.' And after a moment,
he added, his heart leaping, 'A grandson, too.' For the first
time, the night his own father died, Cavin understood what it
felt like for a man to have a child.

He could not sleep; soon he gave up the attempt and dressed
himself and went to Philip's tall desk which had a writing
drawer in the middle. There he found what he was looking for
— a long sheet of white paper. Letitia, hearing him moving
about, entered the room and saw what he was doing. Silently
she went to her own room and returned with a black ribbon
which Cavin inserted through the top of the blank page. Under
it he wrote the notice of Philip's death and the place and hour
of his funeral. Today he would send Matt, with a crape band
on his coat-sleeve, to all the near-by plantations with the notice;
and tomorrow Philip's friends would come to bury him, with
his head to the West. Under the great magnolia, in the en-
closure by the river, Cavin supposed, where Caroline already
lay, the first Darcy buried in Texas. Philip would be the second.
Who would be the third? Cavin asked himself. Yesterday the
question would never have occurred to him.

Jake and Matt dug Philip's grave, and the day after his
death they helped lay him in it. It had rained for days before
the funeral, and the ground was sodden, the foliage dripping.
But as the little procession started through the back yard, down

to the plot by the river, the sun broke through the clouds and the trees shone in that strange, unreal illumination which sometimes falls upon the earth after water has washed it clean — an illumination that seems to shine from within every plant and bush, as if they were radiating light already absorbed. But the clouds soon closed over the sun again, and rain was falling in fast, heavy drops before William had finished reading the service. The Bishop was gone on one of his long trips, but Cavin knew that, as fond as Philip had been of him, yet he would still have preferred to have one of his own blood saying the last prayers over his body. It was fortunate, Cavin said to himself, as William's voice rose and fell, that his cousin had kept well, and that he had not yet left for Austin, where the Constitutional Convention was to convene early in February.

Before they got back to the house Lucina was drenched and shivering with cold and with a vague, impalpable terror that left her helpless before it. Not fear of death so much as a horror of the tragedies and losses that threaten every life. 'Ours too,' she thought. 'Ours too.' Cavin was busy with Philip's friends. Letitia had gone straight to her room, as Lucina wanted desperately to do. It had been days since she had swallowed more than a few mouthfuls of food, and she felt sick, dizzy, and cold. But she did not like to desert Cavin, even though he did not seem to notice her; and she therefore stayed up until the last carriage had drawn away in the rain, and wet dark settled over the trees and rosebushes outside.

Then, as she at last prepared for bed, she began to shake in an ague that seemed to spread to her heart and stop it. It was not possible, she thought, for anyone to be as cold as she and yet remain alive. Maria packed hot bricks around her and hot salt bags and sent for Cavin, who poured half his whiskey flask into a glass and held it to her blue, chattering lips. And when finally she did grow warmer, soon she was too warm, soon she was burning up with a fever that mounted and never ceased to mount. And every breath she drew was biting agony.

David, who was lingering on after the others had left, remained all night; but he knew there was little he could do. That variety of pleurisy was certain to develop into a pneumonia that would have to burn itself out, like a fire. Only too often, as already he had learned, the battle was over before it had well begun.

All her life Lucina was to remember the next week when she begged incessantly for water and always begged in vain. For David had been taught that water was not to be given to pneumonia patients. Therefore he doled out to her at stated intervals thimblefuls of water, no more, no less. After she was well, she could never get enough water, and always kept a glassful beside her bed at night.

It took her a long time to recover, for after her fever left her, her dizziness increased, and she lay racked and helpless day after day in her bed. When at last she became fully conscious and knew that she might live, she wondered whether, considering the way she felt, life was worth the effort. She lay for days stretched out almost as still as Philip in his grave. Her watchers could see her dark lashes occasionally moving and her slow breath rising and falling, lifting the sheet, but otherwise, with her pallid, clouded skin and her thin, sunken cheeks, she seemed scarcely alive herself.

Aunt Emmy made her wine jelly, and custards, and chicken soup, and every delicacy she could think of; but all Lucina would swallow was a few sips of hot cornmeal gruel. Once it crossed her mind that that was all she had been able to take on her seasick voyage from Savannah, and she smiled a little. But usually she scarcely thought at all, conscious only of an unendurable sickness and prostration which seemed to have no end.

David tormented himself trying to remember what his professors at Charlottesville had taught him about cases like Lucina's. Nothing, he thought. Apparently men physicians expected women to bring children into the world without fuss, or else to die, also without fuss. He read all of Philip's books, and all his own too, time and again, but he found no least suggestion in them to tell him what to do.

Cavin turned the place over to Matt and Jake to run, and sat all day and most of the night by the fire in Lucina's room, helping Maria lift and nurse her mistress. It seemed to him that it must have been in another world that Lucina had sat, gay, and well, and happy, on a branching limb in Georgia, the first morning they were engaged, and had promised to go anywhere on earth with him. Well, this was what it had all come to, he thought wretchedly. He wished only for Lucina's quick recovery, and scarcely remembered the son she had offered him for his Christmas gift.

He had no heart for following the course of affairs in the state, but at intervals he was glad to remember that William was at Austin. Sometimes he would open a *Galveston News* for a few moments and read briefly and hurriedly about the Convention, where they seemed to be haggling endlessly as to whether the people did wrong 'knowingly and willingly' in attempting secession. Cavin's every instinct rose up in hot answer to that question. Yet that was the admission the Radicals were trying to obtain up at Austin. 'They'll never get it,' Cavin said to himself, with bitter emphasis, and wondered why sensible men could not see that the thing to do was to leave the past alone, and go on from where they were.

What did he care, though, what they did up at Austin?

Lucina was still lying white and sick on her bed, wasting away under his eyes. During the month of February, Cavin wandered desolately around the house, never still, never satisfied.

He was worried about Letitia, too, increasingly worried as March wore on. Since Philip's death, she had sunk further and further into the impassive quiet which had so long marked her attitude. She was fond of Lucina, Cavin knew, but she often sat for hours by her bed, saying nothing, hardly stirring, her face like a wax cast. She seemed to be thinking, to be in a long, deep study, to be waiting, listening.

Waiting, Cavin supposed, for the birth of her child, in less than a month now, he gathered. Well, if Lucina was going to look like that when she got better — *if* she got better — he did not see that the end was going to be much different from the beginning. He decided, as he watched Letitia and Lucina, that the pleasures of parenthood were greatly overrated.

He could not tell how Letitia felt about Philip's death. Indeed, Letitia would have found it hard to put her own emotions into words. During the years they had been married, there had grown up between her and Philip a sense of respect and confidence based on mutual need. Without him she felt helpless, stripped, and forlorn; but sometimes at night, thinking of him, she grieved that she was not more desolate. The very warmth of Philip's affection for her seemed to demand a deeper grief than she actually felt for him. She missed him, as she would have missed any companion on whom she had learned to rely, but she knew that the sorrow she experienced when she thought of him was nothing at all like the anguish that had racked her the first year of her marriage, before she had painfully taught herself to deaden her feelings. Now, she did not permit herself to look beyond the few weeks remaining before her child's birth.

As March wore on, Lucina grew slowly, almost imperceptibly, better. One clear, sunny morning in the middle of the month, Cavin picked her up and carried her out into the garden, slowly walking with her in his arms between the rose-bushes and the beds where the bulbs had already ceased blooming, a month before.

'Is Jake taking care of my flower garden?' she asked him weakly. It was the first interest she had displayed in anything since the night she had come down with pneumonia. Slowly, and with many backsets, from that day on her strength began to return to her.

But when Letitia's second set of twins was born, on a night in late March, she was still unable to sit up. She had short stretches of bliss now, though, when, if she lay perfectly quiet without moving so much as a finger, her wretched misery would leave her. One night, when she was enjoying a rare period of ease, she heard the servants moving about and David talking, in hushed tones, in the hall to Cavin. But she was afraid to lift her eyelashes or to raise her voice, lest she fall back into the agony out of which she had just climbed for a brief respite. With desperate purpose she prayed for sleep, for forgetfulness, before the room should again begin to sway and turn around her. All through the night she slept, in the deep insensibility that now overtook her whenever she closed her eyes.

She was, accordingly, unprepared to have Cavin come into her room early the next morning, as she was regretfully opening her eyes, with two bundles in his arms. He looked pleased and less strained than he had at any time since Philip's death. Putting the bundles down carefully, one on each side of her, he stood back, smiling at her surprise.

'Philip and Philippa, two hours old and ready to fight the world,' he announced, playfully engaging the four tightly closed tiny fists that waved in the air.

From that time on, Letitia's twins spent more time on
Lucina's bed than in their own. Watching them, as she grew
better, she began to wonder what her own child would look
like, and to think of it with the delight she had felt at first
instead of with the apprehension that her long illness had
induced in her.

Soon she was sitting up in a chair, out on the gallery; and,
a little later, she began to walk around slowly in the garden.
By the time William arrived home from Austin, about the
middle of April, and came over to see the twins, she felt almost
well again, though no longer agile and lightfooted.

The afternoon that William and Helen drove over from
Holly Grove, Letitia was up and around for the first time and
Lucina was sitting, pale but comfortable, on the front gallery.
Seeing them there, as he turned into the gate with his cousins,
Cavin thought gratefully that it looked like his world was
beginning to fall again into some kind of order.

William admired the twins and congratulated Letitia on
their looks and health. But it was plain, despite his affability,
that the months of wrangling at Austin had worn on him, for
he seemed tired and weary.

Yes, he told them briefly, the Convention had done the work
expected of it. It had passed the ordinances nullifying secession, slavery, and the state debt. It had provided for delegates
to go to Washington, and for a general election to be held in
June. The candidate that he and Cavin would naturally support in this election, he said, was J. W. Throckmorton — a man
who had been president of the Convention just ended, and who,
although he had voted against secession, had served loyally in
the Confederate Government as commissioner to the Indians.

'Looks like it might be possible for us to elect him,' Cavin remarked, after considering the political alignment behind the conservative ticket.

'Well, we can try,' replied William more doubtfully, 'but it'll be a fight, I think, Cavin.'

Lucina listened with a sinking of her heart. She realized that Cavin would soon be immersed in another long political campaign, and she dreaded it. But in William's election he had learned the wires to pull, and they had only to be pulled over again, this time for John McGaughey, who, after William's refusal to run again, had permitted his name to go on the ticket. In late May, the campaign drew to its doubtful close.

To the surprise of even the most optimistic Conservatives, the Throckmorton ticket was elected in June by a majority of four to one, and John McGaughey prepared to go up to Austin in August. When Lucina heard the news, her first thought was that at last they would all be free to turn their attention to their own personal affairs. She was tired — tired to death — of war and elections, she thought vehemently.

Cavin, however, began, now that the election was past, to wonder whether it would not be wiser openly to recognize the changed state of affairs by entering into a contract with his hands. He was encouraged in this conviction by reading in the *Galveston News* of June the nineteenth a letter from the Freedman's Bureau warning Texas negroes, on the anniversary of their freedom, 'to stand by their contracts and to work early and late.'

One night, he went over to consult William. Might it not be a good idea, he suggested, for them all to go ahead and draw up some kind of contracts with their negroes? Certainly, they must all act together. After some talk, they mounted their horses and rode over to sound out Povey, whom they found stretched out on his old couch, with Horace lolling beside him.

This was no time, Cavin had decided, with the directness
that usually characterized him, to dwell on personal differences.
Besides, as much as he loved his father, he had often thought,
since his own marriage, that it was a pity for a pretty young
girl like Letitia to have married a man of Philip's age. He had
pushed the matter out of his mind, however, as he did now,
in his conversation with Povey.

'The Freedman's Bureau,' Povey agreed dryly, 'seems at last
to be grasping the idea that colored people are not all born
with wings' — a remark which caused Horace suddenly to
clutch his sides and rock.

Povey was smiling, himself. 'Do you recall, William, General
Gregory's observations the first time he took a tour through
this county?' he asked.

William recalled very well how the head of the Bureau had
enthusiastically informed the President that the colored people
in Cypress County were fully equal, if not superior, to the
whites in industry, moral worth, and ambition. William
chuckled at the recollection.

'Well!' he remarked charitably, 'they seem to be learning.'

The three men talked until late, and, during the next week,
invited the McGaughey brothers and David and other planters
into conference. Most of them agreed that the time had come
to make the best of what would have to be a perilous time of
readjustment, and Cavin was instructed to carry down to
Galveston a sheaf of contracts to register at the Bureau.

He prepared to start one morning toward the end of June.
Since he was not taking a loaded wagon-train along this time,
he expected to shorten the trip by riding on the new Galveston,
Houston, and Henderson Railroad that now extended from the
Gulf to Buffalo Bayou. He and Jake set off in good spirits. He

was riding, not Pilot as he usually did since Philip's death, but a new and skittish bay horse named Star, because of the white marking just above his eyes.

It was about eleven o'clock when they galloped off, their horses keeping step in swinging, easy stride across the woods to the prairie. They intended to arrive before dark at Lost Island Ranch, where the McGaughey brothers lived together with their families in a huge rambling house built around an open square in the centre, and flanked by wide porches on three sides. It was a big house, and needed to be, for it was always full of visitors. There was a man there now, Cavin remembered, who had come out from North Carolina long before the war to do a little shooting; and, now that the war was over, had returned, still a welcome guest.

The sun was hot and the sky was cloudless, but Jake and Cavin were used to heat, and Cavin's skin was already, this early in the summer, a deep reddish tan which, before fall, would turn to brown. The grass hung limply to the earth and would not revive until the cool gulf breeze of evening sprang up, as it usually did, at sunset. Like a sponge, the ground absorbed and muted the sound of the horses' galloping feet.

Cavin and Jake wrapped their handkerchiefs around their necks, feeling, if anything, exhilarated and stimulated by the intense light and heat that enveloped them. Visitors, Cavin knew, always grew depressed and wilted by the summer sun, but Texans liked to feel it tingling along their backbones, exciting them, when they were actually out in it. Afterward, of course, he admitted, a chair felt good, or a rest under the trees, with a long, cool drink, but the sun itself was nothing to dread. During his war experience, he had heard Northerners talking so about blizzards and ice and snow. As for him, he would take the sun, with all its heat, every time. He knew he could never

endure a frozen world five or six months every year, the way
Northern people had to.

The stillness that surrounded them was intense, a deep,
brooding silence that hot afternoons always induce on the
prairie. They drew up to rest about three o'clock under the
first shade they had passed since they left the bottom that morning. Beside them, a little stream seeped slowly in its shallow
bed through the marshy grass, barely moving across the flat,
level plain.

Cavin and Jake tied their horses, and flung themselves down
on the grass, their hands under their heads for pillows, and
their knees upraised. Unconsciously they assumed the position
which permitted the most air to flow under and around them
— the air that, at this time in the afternoon, was as still as the
prairie around them. Cavin listened intently, but he heard only
the thin slithering of grasshoppers' legs against the leaves, or
against the shallow, glassy water, and that sound was so low
and so brief as to be almost imperceptible.

He lay stretched on the grass, vaguely conscious, without
putting the thought into words, that the rhythm beating up
through the earth flowed in his own veins also. If he had been
an introspective person by nature, he would long ago have
understood that he had fought, and marched, and hungered
not to preserve slavery, not even to preserve state's rights, but
simply in order that a man might continue to work the earth
as it pleased him, leading his life according to his own taste,
not some stranger's. He could not imagine living where he
could no longer throw himself upon the ground when he
pleased and feel the whirling earth beneath him, and himself
moving with it. He could not even picture a life where some
other man ordered his comings and goings, his sitting down
and his rising up.

They lay there a long time, until the shadows began to slant on the grass outside their resting place. Then, just as the light on the prairie turned from the blazing brilliance of mid-afternoon to the softer, duller glow of evening, they started again on their way, loping easily in the pace that Texas horses were trained to keep for hours on end.

Toward sunset, Cavin saw to the right of him a herd of cattle, and he signalled to Jake to follow him as he altered his course to pass directly by them. If these cattle bore the McGaughey brand, he thought, he and Jake could slow up, for supper and a bed would then be in sight. Cavin knew the direction he was taking well enough; but in a country without landmarks miles are hard to check off, and cattle will serve as well as trees or creeks to indicate position.

He spurred his horse, failing to notice that between him and the cattle there lay, covered over with new grass, a deep furrow that had been plowed up in the fall to guard against prairie fire. Star's front feet slipped into the ditch, and he made a crouching backward movement, digging his hind feet frantically into the slick grass. Cavin, feeling which way the horse was falling, threw his weight almost automatically in the opposite direction, but before he could pull his left leg over the saddlehorn, Star had fallen and lay, with his heavy body full upon Cavin's hip, and his own front legs snapped at the knees.

Hurriedly reining in his own horse, Jake jumped off and ran over to his master. There was no chance of Star's ever rising again; Jake saw that at once. What was the quickest way to quiet him and get Cavin out from under his desperate plunging? There was only one answer, and both Jake and Cavin knew what it was.

One arm was free, and Cavin pointed to his saddle where his pistol hung, fortunately, on the horse's exposed flank. Jake had a steady hand, and in a moment, after a few violent jerks, Star lay still. But strain as he did with all his might, Jake could not budge the heavy body and Cavin was caught beneath it.

Soon both saw they would have to have help. Cavin felt himself losing consciousness, as he had on the battle field. He had just strength to point, again; and, as his eyes closed, he caught a blurred glimpse of Jake frantically spurring his horse toward the ranch, which lay, he could only hope, closer than he thought.

When he woke, it was to pain, darkness, and thirst such as he had never known, for at Chickamauga his canteen had been full. He lay there an endless time, it seemed to him, alternately conscious and unconscious, forcing his mind, whenever he could, to the surface, so that he might call out if he heard horses approaching. How else would they find him, a small dot, in the dark night, on the bald prairie?

At last, faintly transmitted along the earth's sounding board, he heard the running tread of horses, and some time later, a low rumble which he interpreted as the turning of wagon wheels. When the sounds grew close, he began to whoop as loud as he was able. Then, just as he felt his mind again becoming blank, and knew he had no more strength left in him to call out even once again, he heard Kirby McGaughey's voice coming, it seemed to him, from a distance as far as the stars.

As he left home, Kirby had snatched up a canvas cot that was standing on his back gallery and had shoved it in the wagon, telling one of the cowhands to jump up in the driver's seat. Now as he and Jake sat on the grass beside Cavin, waiting for the wagon to come up, he was glad of his forethought. When at last it reached the spot, he slid the canvas as gently as possible under Cavin, uncertain whether he was still breathing.

Should he take him on to his own ranch, only an hour's ride

ahead, he wondered, or start back with him to Locust Hill and
David, who was the nearest doctor? It took him only a moment
to make up his mind. He gave Jake his own fresh horse, telling
him to ride ahead and hurry back with David, and he took his
seat in the wagon beside Cavin, pouring whiskey down his
throat, at intervals, and washing his face with the water he had
brought from the ranch in a jug. There was nothing else he
could do. Somehow the night passed; and the wagon moved
slowly across the dark prairie, and still Cavin breathed. It was
late morning before Kirby caught sight of two rapidly moving
specks on the horizon which he had been so anxiously watching.

David had just come in from a call when Jake woke him.
Within a few minutes he had grabbed a cup of coffee and his
saddlebags, and had supplied Jake with another mount. As
he galloped off across the prairie, it suddenly occurred to him
that, since Philip's death, he had had no chance to wonder
whether he was going to practise in the county or hang up his
shingle in Harrisburg. He was never again to think of the
matter as unsettled — never in all his life.

He took only a few moments to examine Cavin. Bending his
brown head over him, he said only, 'Better get him home,' and
handed his horse's reins to Jake, taking a seat on the wagon bed.

It was long past dark, so slowly did they move, before they
turned into Philip's lane.

Old George rose growling on the front gallery as he heard
the wagon approaching, and Byrnes Armstrong, whom David
had sent over to Locust Hill, came out to meet his brother,
swinging a lantern.

'I'm taking him to the office,' David told him hurriedly.
'Send me out all the lamps you can find.'

He was grateful now for the experience he had had in hospital

tents, and, with his mind on Cavin, did not at once notice that
Lucina had come out from the house and was following along
beside the cot, with her eyes on Cavin's face, not on the dark
path in front of her. Nor did she notice that the men carrying
the stretcher raised their feet and stepped across a wide plank
that had been laid sideways between the gateposts which separated the front from the back yard. Had she stopped to think,
she would have recalled telling Jake to lay the plank there, to
keep out the brood of baby chickens that followed behind her
every time she opened the gate. Now she completely forgot the
barrier and stumbled against it in the dark, falling her full
length across it.

She cried out in pain, and David, turning instantly, cursed
himself for his stupidity. Why had he not watched out for her?
There was only — he counted back swiftly — a few more weeks
before the end of her painful period of waiting.

Motioning to Byrnes to go on, he helped her up, questioning
her carefully. No, it was nothing, she said; she was sorry to be
so careless.

Doubtfully, he relinquished her to Letitia, who had lingered
behind to quiet FitzHugh but had come hurrying out when she
heard Lucina's sharp outcry.

Then for the next hour he leaned over Cavin, his fingers
moving precisely where his mind, intently concentrated on the
task before him, told them to go. Always, when he had a job
like this to do, he was oblivious to anything that happened
around him. Always he was conscious of that slow heightening
of power within him, that sharp focussing of energies that any
artist experiences whenever he throws himself into his work.
He did not permit his thoughts to wander to Lucina until he
had done all he could for Cavin, and had got him onto Philip's
bed.

Then David stepped out of the long window that led from Philip's bedroom onto the porch and sank into a chair, resting his head for a moment against its high back. Almost as soon, however, as he had relaxed his muscles he saw Letitia standing in the doorway, looking anxiously out into the dark.

'Lucina?' he asked, instantly on his feet. She nodded.

'I was afraid ——' he began, and saw by Letitia's face that he had good reason to be.

For the next two days, David never left the house, and never once took his clothes off, as he moved back and forth between Lucina's and Cavin's rooms. He warned Byrnes to tell anybody suffering only from malaria that he could not leave Locust Hill. 'Tell 'em to take a black pill and go to bed,' he said. 'I'll get around when I can.'

Toward dark, the next day, Lucina's tiny son was born; David had no hope that the child would live, and not much more that Lucina would revive from the exhaustion and shock through which she had passed. He told Maria to wrap the child in cotton wool and lay him in a deep basket between warm bricks, but that he did not think it likely they could save him.

Leaving Letitia to watch Cavin, and, warning Maria to call him if Lucina stirred, he managed to sleep an hour. Then he hurried back to Lucina's room, only to see Aunt Elvy dipping a clean rag into a saucer and then dropping the end of it into the baby's small open mouth. 'Ah!' he thought, 'the child's still alive, then!' Surprised and pleased, he stepped to Aunt Elvy's side.

'What you giving him?' he asked her quickly.

'Sugar an' warm water an' a drap or two o' whiskey,' Aunt Elvy answered, without looking up. 'Didn't seem lak it could hurt him none,' she explained, testing the cooling bricks with her finger and exchanging them for two warmer ones from the hearth in which she had started a small fire.

'Good enough!' David responded. 'You know what to do.'

Aunt Elvy sniffed.

'Knowed whut to do fo' you wuz bawn,' she told him, in injured pride, her sunken, old eyes snapping.

David smiled for the first time in several days. He had a ruddy face, with an abundance of straight brown hair and keen eyes, oddly matched, for one was almost brown, the other almost green. They did not look out of place, however, in his face, but instead gave him a curious appearance of perpetual watchfulness. Now, his glance brightened.

'Not more'n a few drops at a time, Aunt Elvy,' he warned the old woman, leaning over the child to listen to his faint breathing.

'Know dat, too,' said the old woman crossly. 'Me an' Maria'll watch 'im,' she promised. Turning her wrinkled face to David, she explained her nursing plans. 'Hatter git ole Aunt Mattie up f'um de place to take keer o' my well babies, and Rachel to help Maria nuss Miss Lucy. Jake an' Matt ain't gwine-a leab Mas' Cavin, dat's sho. I gwine-a take keer o' dis chile, myself.' She paused and looked David over, studying him critically and at length. 'Don' seem mo'n yistiddy when I was watching yo' nuss make sugar teats fur you,' she observed. Then she added, seemingly satisfied by her scrutiny, 'Ef'n yo' tells us whut to do, suh, us kin do it.'

David learned, as the days passed, that the old woman had made no idle promise. He found that he could rely on her and on the other nurses to carry out his instructions exactly, with anxious care. And, whenever the weights were changed on Cavin's leg, Uncle Matt would fall on his knees and pray while his master groaned aloud.

The days passed, and still all David's patients lived. He slept now, and ate, at Locust Hill, leaving only when he had to. But it was a full month before he dared tell Cavin that his son had been born, and almost that long before enough life flowed in Lucina for her to care whether either she or her child continued to draw breath in this world.

One hot, still morning, late in July, David was feeling Lucina's pulse when she opened her dark eyes and smiled weakly up at him.

'You're getting better every day,' he said evenly, not shifting his fingers.

After a moment she spoke again, barely opening her lips.

Her eyes were insistent, but, although he stooped and listened, he could not make out a word of what she said. He sent a puzzled glance across to Aunt Elvy.

'Humph!' said she, and lifting Lucina's child proudly out of his basket, laid him on his mother's arm.

'Whut else would she a-wanted?' Aunt Elvy snapped, later, talking to Maria. 'Mens — even ef dey is doctors — is mightily lackin' in plain, awdinery gumption.'

Chapter 16

All August and September Cavin and Lucina slowly improved. And the child, whom they had decided to name Beauford Cavin, since Philip's own son already bore his father's name, was keeping a firm hold on life.

'Miss Lucy,' Maria told her mistress one morning, 'two months ago, you could-a put dis-heah boy in a pint cup an' run yo' weddin' ring up his little arm.' Proudly she laid him in his mother's lap. 'Now, look at 'im! He's gwine to be as big a man as his pa, ain't you, sugar-pie?' she predicted, addressing the baby, who gazed up out of the cocoon of wrappings that enclosed him as placidly as if he had never had to struggle for life.

Lucina looked down at her son. She was even yet too weak to feel certain that she could lift him.

'Give him to me, Maria,' she said, holding her arms open. Maria knelt and laid her own strong brown hands firmly under Lucina's white ones.

'Dar now,' she said; 'look at 'im as long as you please, Miss Lucy.'

Lucina saw that the baby's hair was as black as her own, and as thick, but the eyes that stared up at her were Cavin's. She touched his hand — it seemed to her unbelievably tiny — and noticed, with equal surprise, that, though his hair had come down from her and his eyes from Cavin, his fingers were like Susanna's — long with thin, flattened ends.

'He don't hardly ever cry,' Maria said, extolling the virtues of her charge.

Lucina held her son to her, startled by the torrent of tenderness that poured through her. It seemed to her that a part of herself — some inner essence of her being too fragile and exquisite to face this world — had, nevertheless, entered into it. This child was not something different from herself, he was her thought externalized, her breath, her heartbeat. Suddenly she knew — and the knowledge racked her — that every sorrow he felt would be hers twice over, every pain, every loss.

'Oh Maria!' cried Lucina, hugging the child to her, 'take care of him!'

'I feels dat way 'bout him myself,' Maria answered gently. 'And 'bout my own baby, too,' she added, after a minute's silence.

'Maria!' exclaimed Lucina. 'I've been sick so long, I never knew.' She looked penitently at her maid.

Maria threw her head back and laughed. 'I figger I been practising up on dis-heah lamb,' she declared, peeping over Lucina's arms. 'Beauford's a mighty big name for such a little fellow. I'se gwine-a call 'im Beau.' And soon that was what they all began to call him.

Cavin was able, now in September, to hobble around, but not without pain. During his long illness, he had grown so resentful of the weight hanging from his aching limb, that, despite David's remonstrances, he had discarded it.

'I'd rather be lame than fool with that damn cannon ball on my foot any longer,' he said, twisting irritably in his bed. 'Take it off, Jake.' And it had remained off. Now he walked with a limp that was never remedied until Uncle Matt built up a thick inner sole inside his master's boot.

During July, while he lay ill in one room and Lucina in another, William had gathered up the labor contracts, and had had them registered at Galveston. But Letitia, who was running the place, with Uncle Matt's help, decided to pay no attention to them. There would be no settlements, anyway, until the crop was in; and the negroes on Philip's place, she knew, never had understood what their marks on the contracts implied, anyhow. Some more white folks' notions, they supposed, and obediently set crosses beside their names, as Cavin told them to do. Most of them stayed at home now doing their work about as usual. True, a few of the younger slaves interpreted their freedom to mean freedom from labor; and these Letitia told to leave, making one firm rule from which she never varied: no work, no rations. She was quick, however, to supply extra food and bright new clothes to any who kept their cotton clean, and, on the whole, had little trouble with the field hands. She was glad, however, when August came to an end, and Cavin was able to lie on his bed and confer every morning with her and Matt.

After this part of the day's routine was disposed of, the remaining hours seemed to him intolerably long. He was not a reader, like his father; by instinct he was fonder of action than of meditation. But with time hanging on his hands, as it now did, he found himself thinking oftener and oftener of what was going on in the state.

'Well, at least we're making some progress,' he meditated. 'The way we carried the Throckmorton election showed that. Now if we can only get the best element on both sides to pulling together.'

He recalled hearing William say that certain citizens of the Republic always kept three flags flying on the masts of their sailing vessels — those of the Republic, of England, and of the United States.

'But they always flew the Lone Star at the top,' he meditated, remembering how, ever since the war, the Confederates had taken to raising the flag of the Republic in all kinds of places. The Yankees seemed either not to recognize the banner or not to object to it.

'That's the flag Judge Dickerson nailed up in his court,' Cavin recalled. 'That's the flag that flies from the post in the square at Berryville.'

'I don't know why I didn't see how to manage before,' his thoughts ran on. 'We've all got to think about Texas, now, not about the United States or the Confederacy. We've got to go on from where we are, whether we like it or not. God knows we don't like it,' his sombre thoughts flowed on, 'but that can't be helped.'

As he lay there sorting and arranging his ideas, he was exasperated by his inability to be up, putting them into operation, now that they were fully clear to him. It never occurred to him, as it so often had to Philip, that his undertakings might as easily fail as succeed. Because he had read so much less than Philip, his vicarious experience was more limited, and his optimism, not his courage, more exuberant.

He was too tired and in too much pain to follow with any degree of accuracy the reports that began to come in from John McGaughey sitting in the legislature at Austin. Even so, he rejoiced, like everyone else, when he heard that President Johnson had declared Reconstruction over in Texas. August 20th was a day, he thought, that Texans would have to put down on their calendars to celebrate like San Jacinto Day.

'Now we can go about our business, thank the Lord,' he reflected, with a satisfying sense of release. 'I must talk things over with Lucy,' he decided, and then remembered with a shock of surprise and regret that the last time he had tried to talk to her she had not been at all interested in his plans for testing new varieties of cotton.

He could hardly believe that the pale, listless, and hollow-eyed girl who answered only 'Yes' or 'No' or 'I suppose so' to all his remarks was the same Lucina whose agile mind, before this, had usually expanded his ideas before he had clearly formulated them, himself.

His son was over a month old before he saw him, still in a basket between warm bricks. And then he was afraid to touch him. Whenever he looked at the baby or its mother, he was forced to meditate on how many drawbacks there were to the usual method of populating the world.

As September passed, however, he realized thankfully that he was learning how to manage his crippled leg. By the end of the month, he was able to mount his horse, and then he began to feel a whole man again.

He was well enough, now, to follow the debate going on in the legislature over the Thirteenth and Fourteenth Amendments to the Constitution of the United States. The legislators showed good sense, he thought, in accepting the first measure, thus conceding slavery to be a dead issue, but he admired them for rejecting the second entirely, declaring it dictated by 'passion and malignancy.'

'This is a white man's country,' he declared, 'and they might as well learn it, first as last.'

He also approved of the new law by which a young negro could be bound out to long service, and fined for leaving his employer without the consent of the county judge. 'You can't have black boys running hog-wild,' he reflected, and smiled. 'White boys either.' But some of the new labor laws irritated and puzzled him. 'They must be trying to satisfy the Freedman's Bureau, up at Austin,' he surmised shrewdly. 'Half the crop for the labor! And fines for cruelty! The Bureau'll call it cruelty, of course,' he predicted glumly, 'if a man puts his negroes to work at all. Well, there's no use trying to follow out such fool measures. They'll never stand up in practice.'

He went, then, to look over his own contracts, drawn up before he fell ill. He saw that a few called for cash payments, but that most of them provided for his supplying his hands in full and allowing them one-quarter or one-third of the crop as pay for their labor.

'That's somewhere about right, I reckon,' Cavin ruminated. 'How's anybody to know? It's bound to be hit and miss for a long time. Already it's pretty clear that I'm going to have to look out for my people — the same as always — and pay 'em besides.' He sighed. 'Well, there's nothing to do but keep on.'

One Saturday morning, about the middle of October, he told his field hands to begin coming up to his office next day to go over their accounts.

'Accounts?' they inquired. 'Whut's dem?' Most of them had no idea what he was talking about.

One of the younger negroes, however, had been riding into town at night, and he began to grumble. 'How's I gwine-a know whether I'se gittin' all's comin' to me?' he demanded, putting the justifiable question in an insolent and impudent manner.

Cavin looked him over calmly. 'Get off my place, Jupiter,' he warned him. 'I'll leave your pay at the army post in the morning.'

The negro was startled at the turn affairs had taken. 'Whar's I gwine?' he inquired, dropping his hoe and his insolence in one gesture.

'That's no business of mine any more,' Cavin replied. 'Hurry up, get off my place.'

'Well,' said Cavin to himself, watching Jupiter's retreating figure, 'once I'd-a had to go to the bother of selling that rascal. He's been swelling up, looking for trouble for a month.'

He watched the negro until he was out of sight, then turned to the other hands. 'Anybody else want to quit?' he inquired. 'You're free, now, you know, free to stay or to go. Well, get this straight, then,' he warned them sternly, seeing that nobody made a move to go, 'as long as you stay on this place, you do what I say — the way you always have.' Catching a loud murmur of assent, he smiled. 'All right, I see you understand. We'll get along,' he said comfortably. 'If we don't, you're fired, that's all, and you'll stay fired, too. You remember that,' he cautioned them. 'You can quit, that's true, any time *you* want to, but I don't have to take care of you any more unless *I* want to.' He sat his horse, watching them, until he saw they had taken in the tenor of his remarks. 'You all know I'll do the best I can for you.' There was a vigorous nodding of heads.

Then he began to explain to them the system he had devised while he was bedridden. He showed them the ledgers in which he had set aside a page for every man and woman on his place. Then he told them how, under present conditions, they would work the fields they had always worked, but he would have to figure out, according to the contracts, the share of the crop which belonged to them. He would also have to figure out, he told them, what each man owed him, at current prices, for the supplies advanced since the contracts were drawn up.

Already Cavin knew that there was not going to be much difference, in actual practice, between operating his plantation this way and in the old way. 'Only a lot more fuss and bother — and bookkeeping,' he thought half in amusement and half in irritation, as he rode homeward. 'I wish to God the damn Yankees who thought up all these fancy ideas, had to keep my place going for about a month.'

Automatically, he began to estimate
of his year's profit would now be taken
had had to pay to a young official at t
get the contracts he carried with hir

'From now on,' figured Cavin, 'v
count on more and more of that kin
tell me he had to bribe the port insp
put on the boat?' His mind nourish
people'll get onto the racket,' he th
well acknowledge it.'

As he got down from Pilot, using no
the ladies mounted their horses, he ru
tively. 'Maybe it'll turn out they did do
long run, by freeing the slaves. That is, i.
They won't, though,' he reminded himse
though the Freedman's Bureau had set a
sick negroes, yet this charge had been laid
individual planter. 'If they're so hell-bent
ought to have to pay for their pleasure, same as
tated grimly. 'Slaves cost plenty of money and ti

Flinging his reins to Jake, he walked toward the
ing the ground. He had lifted the latch before he sa
cina was coming down the path to meet him, with the
her arms.

Quickening his step, he stooped to kiss her, and together
bent over the child, who searched his father's face with eyes th
narrowed, like Lucina's, to an oval at their corners.

'Lucy,' said Cavin, straightening himself after a long scrutiny, 'I'm about ready to say this chap's worth what he cost.'

He tucked his son under one arm, with careless surety, and
drew Lucina under the other.

That night, as twilight began to gather, he went in and took

:n joined Letitia and Lucina in the
re sitting, playing with the young-
    It was as warm as summer, but
in of the year a norther might be
; down on the long bench that
d Beauford critically up against
, all right,' he said, pleased with

id Lucina. Glancing up, he saw
nue down which a man was gal-
ed roan horse. He and Lucina
ment, for the twins, and, rising in-
nt inside the house together, with

ey stepped out into his garden, he
streaming warm and golden over his
race, on a sudden impulse, to saddle
ponded at once to the rising inflection
d looked up swiftly.
appy, Mas' Povey?'
his servant with a brief smile.
nd out, Horace. Tell Aunt Cindy I'll take
ly Grove.'
drinking his coffee in the arbor when Povey rode

g his hand in salutation, he invited Povey to get down
have a cup with him.
'Breakfast too,' Povey replied, alighting and opening the gate.
'I didn't stop for it at home.'
William spoke to the darky who was working around the
flower beds in the yard.

'Tell Aunt Mary to send back the spoon-bread and bacon, Ranse.' He leaned forward to scan Povey's face.

'What's on your mind?'

'William,' Povey began, sitting down in a chair directly opposite his host and gazing straight at him, 'I'm alive and talking to you this morning because of Philip. I'm not forgetting that.' He paused while William looked unsmilingly at him across the huge saucer in which his own coffee was cooling.

'I had decided,' Povey began tentatively, 'that perhaps in the summer ——' Stopping again, he gazed off across the cotton fields where the dead, brown stalks now followed one after the other, like soldiers drawn up in long lines. 'Then the way things were, I saw it was no time — thank you, Ranse,' he said interrupting himself to take the tray the darky handed him. Putting it down on the seat beside him, he forgot it, as he laid both hands heavily on William's knee.

'I've come over to tell you ——'

William put down his saucer. 'The minute I saw you get down off your horse, I knew what you had in mind, Povey.' His voice was not happy. 'You'll have to remember she's my own blood — the closest I've got in the world. Five children — I don't know.' He hesitated. 'You've been separated a long time.'

Povey met his eyes steadily.

'I know. You don't suppose I haven't thought of all that? What does it matter? Seven years ago, it might have, not now. I'm no boy. I know what life's like.'

William leaned back in his chair, looking so long at the horizon that Povey impatiently got up and started for his horse. He had not believed he would ever again feel the eager expectation that now possessed him.

William called him back, and rose to meet him.

'Go on, Povey,' he said, looking at him intently. 'You seem

to have thought it all out.' He detained him for a moment longer, seeming to be uncertain how best to say what he had to say. Finally he put his thought into slow words.

'Tell Cavin I had a long talk with his father about this very thing, one morning in my cotton field last summer.' His eyes searched Povey's face, and then he held out his hand. 'God knows, I hope it's not too late.'

Povey was halfway home before he realized the implication of William's concluding remarks. Then he drew Xanthus to a sudden stop, watching the sunlight advance over his dark fields, and feeling an odd, harsh sympathy welling up in him for Philip, for himself, for every man alive. A moment longer he sat still. Then he lifted his reins, and Xanthus fell into the quick, pacing step that he usually followed.

When Povey got home, he sent Horace back to tell Aunt Cindy he had not, after all, had his breakfast at Holly Grove.

'Fust he say he won't an' den he say he will, Aunt Cindy,' Horace reported. 'Sumpin' brewing aroun' heah, but I cain't make out whut it is.'

Aunt Cindy looked him over scornfully.

'You is a plum fool, den,' she told him. 'You better clean up dis-heah yahd tell it shines.'

Horace's mouth fell open. 'I declare fo' Jesus,' he replied, 'I is a fool, lak you say.'

He went out meditating, and, a few hours later, when Povey sent for him and told him to polish his boots and press his clothes, Horace grinned.

'I done 'tended to all dat, suh. An' put a extry shine on Xanthus, an' raked de yahd, an' swep' de galleries.'

Povey looked up at his servant, with an amused smile hovering on his lips. 'No use trying to keep anything from you, Horace.'

'Naw-suh,' Horace agreed. 'Dat's so.' He paused on one foot, uncertainly. 'Aunt Cindy want to know, is you 'specting company fur supper?'

'Go on,' said Povey. 'Go on, you imp o' Satan; I'll let you both know in plenty of time.' He began to hum as he went into his office to look over some papers. It had been years since he had felt so young and happy.

'Tonight, after supper, I'll ride over,' he planned.

When he came out of his room in the late afternoon, Xanthus was tied at the gate, ready for him, and Horace nowhere in sight.

'He knows I won't want him tonight,' Povey thought, and mounted his horse, breaking into a swift gallop.

'Seven years since I spoke to her!' he thought, spurring Xanthus — a thing he seldom did. His throat and mouth were dry, every muscle tense, when he got down at Philip's gate.

For a moment he stood there completely still, as Letitia rose to her feet, with one hand half outstretched. Taking a step toward him she too paused, motionless.

'Am I dreaming?' she asked herself. 'I must be.' Slowly, life began to pour back into her.

'If it's a dream,' she told herself, 'I'll wake up. I always do.'

At sight of her, a quiet that Povey had forgotten stole over him, and, opening the gate, he walked toward her, holding out his arms.

She took a single, halting step and touched his sleeve; and then raised her hand to his cheek, in a groping gesture, as if to test her sight. Suddenly joy broke across her features like a flood of blinding light.

'There *is* a glory not of this world,' Povey told himself as his arms fell around her.

The soft dusk passed over into night, and the stars moved across the dark sky, but they scarcely spoke.

This is how the dead must feel on the Resurrection Morn, Letitia thought once, and then she thought no more, as, caught up, like Elijah, in a chariot of fire, she felt the heavens opening and closing about her.

When Povey reached home that night, Horace was asleep. Povey did not wake him, but unsaddled his horse himself, and went in to bed, but not to sleep. Finally toward daylight he got up and dressed and began going through his house, carrying a lighted lamp with him. Looking around at his office where books, maps, and papers were mingled in dusty confusion, he was suddenly ashamed to show it to Letitia.

'I always told Aunt Cindy to let this place alone,' he fumed. 'It didn't seem to matter, until now.'

He passed, then, into his parlor — a square room full of an odd assortment of furniture that his uncle had accumulated. There were peacock fans in the centre of the mantel and dried grasses in white fluted vases at each end, but the room was as dead and cold as all unused rooms come to be.

'I'll send to New Orleans for wallpaper tomorrow,' he resolved. 'Letitia will know what to do.' At the thought, his heart pounded within his breast.

When light broke, he was in a fever. 'Anything might have happened,' he told himself unreasonably, and swung himself up on Xanthus.

'Anybody up yet?' he asked Aunt Emmy, walking into the kitchen at Locust Hill. 'I'll be here for breakfast.'

'Miss Lettie,' she answered him. 'Looks lak she ain't slep' none. Mas' Cavin's stirring. Is you well, Mas' Povey?' she inquired politely. 'I'll set you a plate.'

'I never felt so well in my life, Aunt Emmy.'

'Dat's good.' The old woman paused in her tracks and, darting a sharp glance in his direction, laid her hands on her enormous hips.

'I ain't got de sense of a jay bird. Lawd bless you, Mas' Povey, you an' her bofe.'

Povey ran his hand in his pocket. 'Take this for a wedding present, Aunt Emmy,' he told her, and went out whistling.

He found Letitia in the flower garden, and took her in his arms so urgently that she was startled. 'Are you all right?' he asked her. 'Look at me, Lettie. Let me see if you are.' He kissed her again and again. 'Darling,' he exclaimed brokenly, holding her off. 'Every minute I'm away from you, I'm in torment.' His gaze caressed her face. 'I never shut my eyes, after I left,' he told her, more quietly, watching the pulse in her white throat. 'Seven years I was dead,' he told her; 'now I'm alive,' and dropped his lips on hers.

Letitia laid both hands on his cheeks. Her eyes were deeply blue. 'I know,' she said softly. Her bright hair shone under the sunlight, and fell about her face.

Povey bent his head closer. 'The Bishop's in Berryville. I could ride down ——' His voice implored her. 'Don't you see, I can never leave you again?'

She was smiling, running her fingers lightly over the outline of his face. 'The same eyes,' she thought, loving the way the pupils widened and darkened the clear gray that surrounded them. 'The same hair!' Lightly she touched it, brushing it off his forehead. Still she could not tell whether it was more brown than red. She traced the delicate oblong of his lips with her finger-tips, and then his question penetrated her consciousness.

'Here in the garden,' she breathed.

His eyes darkened and his breath caught in his throat. 'This evening?'

She shook her head. 'You'll get back too late. In the morning.'

'No,' he said, '*whenever* I get back. It's been too long, already.'

'Too long,' she echoed. 'Yes, too long.' The past flooded into her mind. Since last night, it had dropped out of her consciousness. For twelve hours, now, she had been nineteen again, unconscious of sorrow. She clung to him now, suddenly cold and shivering.

'Seven years — seven eternities!' exclaimed Povey, holding her off from him to look at her, and to feel again the joy that shook him whenever he drew her back into the circle of his arms. 'A day's too long!' he whispered. 'An hour's too long!'

She leaned against him, shivering again, feeling faint and dizzy, and he saw that she was pale, with a grayish pallor, and that her lips were blue.

'It's nothing.' She laughed up at him. 'Happiness, maybe.'

Lifting her, he carried her in to the dining-room. Lucina wrapped her in blankets and Povey made a fire in the fireplace. After she had swallowed a cup of hot coffee, the color began to come back to her cheeks.

'Go on,' she urged him, then. 'Go on, Povey, so you can hurry back. Get your breakfast before you start,' she said, smiling up at him with lips that were beginning to be warm again.

'Breakfast!' he exclaimed. And again, 'Breakfast!' He laughed down at her, his eyes shining. 'What do I need with breakfast?' He felt on fire, like a man with wings.

'Go on, then,' she urged him again. 'Go on, while I can let you go.'

She was too tired to move. All morning she lay there, up-lifted into another world of pure and passionate joy. She thought she knew now what the saints were always talking about when they spoke of a new heaven and a new earth. This floating happiness must take you there.

But toward afternoon another chill began to shake her — this time so relentlessly that the movement of her clothes over her skin was agony. Lucina tapped the bell for Aunt Elvy.

'Help me get her to bed,' she said, frightened by Letitia's pinched face. Aunt Elvy groaned, and hurried to heat salt and to wrap up hot stove lids in newspapers and towels. It would take more than that, though, she knew, to drive away the con-gestive chill which precedes black jaundice — a disease she had too often fought now to mistake its symptoms.

Cavin sent Jake on Pilot for David. No telling where he would find him; he might have to ride after him all day. He himself set off for Berryville to overtake Povey.

David, however, was just dismounting at his front gate when Jake galloped up, spurring Pilot down the road.

'My God!' David exclaimed aghast. 'What else can happen at Locust Hill?' Grabbing his case, he shifted to the fresh horse that was always tied at his gate, and he and Jake raced back toward the river, their horses' necks stretching even.

When he entered the room, Letitia smiled wanly up at him, and he saw that she knew this was no ordinary illness she was suffering from.

'Don't let me die,' she pleaded with him. 'I can't die now, David.'

As he galloped into Berryville, Cavin met Povey and the Bishop just starting home. At sight of him, they pulled up their horses sharply, and Povey looked once into Cavin's face, then spurred Xanthus till he plunged in fright.

'What is it?' he asked, leaning out of his saddle. 'My God, man, what is it?'

'Letitia,' said Cavin. His tongue was heavy in his mouth. He could say no more.

'Let him go,' the Bishop said, laying his hand on Cavin's pommel as Povey dashed ahead, leaning low across his horse's neck.

'Cavin,' the Bishop asked, his shoulders drooping, 'how is a man to understand God?'

They followed close behind, and saw Povey throw himself out of his saddle and pause for a moment in front of the long window that opened onto the gallery from Letitia's room, and then go in.

David glanced up as he entered.

'You'd better stay,' he said.

Povey dropped into a chair by the bed, feeling cold and stunned, as if every emotion had suddenly drained out of him.

'There's nothing I can do for him,' David thought, and centred his mind on Letitia, the progress of whose illness he seemed unable to halt. He had a feeling, as he had had with Philip, that he was beaten, from the beginning. But he refused to acknowledge defeat to himself. Almost, he thought, you could see Letitia rallying her forces, when, for brief instants, she opened her eyes and recognized those around her.

'Povey,' she said once that night, and David could feel the resolve that strengthened her fluttering pulse. For three days, the unequal battle kept up.

The last night, she looked straight up into Povey's face, and smiled as he lifted her into his arms.

'I can do no more,' said David, and left them. Not since he had practised medicine had he felt the despair that overwhelmed him now. What had he left undone? What had he not tried?

He sat in the dark, just outside the room, sunk in a bitter, unavailing grief. Why did he pretend to be a doctor at all? he wondered, forgetting other lives he had snatched from the grave.

The Bishop joined him there, and Cavin and Lucina. Together they watched the stars grow pale.

'We'd better go in,' said David at last, and, entering the room, knelt to look closely at Letitia's face.

The Bishop thought he had never seen more compassion in anyone's gaze than was in David's, when he looked up at his friend.

'She's gone, Povey,' he said. 'She's already gone.'

For a long time Povey sat there, unable to move, but at last he rose slowly, like a man in a trance, and with infinite care laid his burden in Cavin's arms. Then, without a word, he walked out of the room with the swaying motion of a drunken man.

The Bishop followed him, and, when he caught up with him, said gently, 'Let me come with you, Povey.'

The swaying figure kept straight on, and the Bishop laid his hand again on his arm, repeating his request.

'Yes, certainly,' Povey said courteously. 'If you like.'

All that night he rode his horse through the bottoms, and next day he stood at Letitia's grave so far withdrawn into his grief that no one ventured even to speak to him.

His demeanor never varied, during the next few days or the next few months. The Bishop often had the feeling that Povey lived, if he lived at all, in another world, that only his body walked and moved about on this earth. He seemed more like a wraith than a man. Sometimes he would get up and sit motionless, till the sun rose, under his live-oaks and his chinaberries. He talked very little, and always gently. His friends did not know how to break the silence that even the Bishop was unable to penetrate before he was called back to Carolina by illness in his family.

'He don' eat an' he don' sleep,' Aunt Cindy moaned to John McGaughey, who, after his return from Austin in December, came over to call at Land's End. Povey welcomed him, but it was clear that he preferred to be alone. John soon rose and left, and Povey did not appear even to be aware of his going.

On his way home, John stopped by David's.

'What can we do for him?' he demanded, with his usual brisk efficiency.

'Nothing,' David replied, sadly. 'Nothing. I don't know what to think,' he confessed. 'Of course there's his old wound and his cough——' He broke off despairingly. 'Everybody's read about a living death, but mighty few have seen it.'

John rode home deeply despondent. When you look at life straight, he reflected, what sense does it make?

After Christmas, David spent more and more time at Land's End, where Povey lay day after day scarcely stirring in his high bed. One morning the bright warm blood took his breath.

'How long?' he asked David, and appeared to welcome the answer he received. Then he asked for a piece of paper and a pen. 'Land's End is for her children, of course,' he said, 'but I'd better make it clear.' Handing the pen back, he sank on his pillows, relieved.

'Don't bother,' he said often in the next three months. 'What does it matter?'

'There's nothing to work on,' David reported to William, one night when he came to take his turn nursing.

William sighed heavily. 'I've known that for a long time.'

Early in March, Povey failed so rapidly that David moved over to Land's End, but his patient clung to life with a tenacity that surprised them both.

'It's a long time coming,' Povey said one morning. It was the only complaint he ever made.

The last night of his life Cavin was with him, and David and Aunt Cindy, his nurse, and Horace. It was a pouring night late in March, and the rain slashed against the windows. They turned down the light and put an envelope in front of the chimney to shade his eyes. Toward morning, he began to talk a little, lightly and happily. Aunt Cindy leaned over him, listening.

'It don't make no sense,' she said, lifting a face in which the separate features seemed curiously broken down and softened, as if merged by the tears that had flowed over them. 'Seem lak Mas' Povey jes' talkin' 'bout pidgens — pidgens flyin' in de sun.'

But when William entered the quiet room, just before daylight he understood what recollections were crossing Povey's mind. 'Lord, if he has to die, let him die now,' he prayed. And, as if his prayer were answered, Povey breathed a sigh, opened his eyes and smiled, a happy, peaceful smile, and never moved again.

Cavin rode home just as the sun was beginning to climb in the sky. The air was soft and warm and wet, full of the odor of pushing shoots and new green leaves and freshly ploughed earth. Never, he thought, had the world looked more beautiful; and suddenly it seemed to him strange past all belief that nature should be so indifferent to the death of a man like Povey — a man, young and strong, like himself. It was a waste, a wrong, for anybody to find life harsher than death. Deep in Cavin, something revolted at the idea of extinction, of ceasing to be able to move upon the sunny earth and subdue it to his will. He had not lived close enough to the ancients, as Philip had, to acquire something of their fatality, of the detachment which enabled Lucian to poke jibes at the gray, aimless shades he was so soon to join in Hades. Against any event in nature and life that oppressed him, he was accustomed to set the whole weight of his strength, confident that he would succeed; but death — how could anybody dispute an invisible enemy? And with all the youth in his pulsing body, he admitted death to be an enemy, not an enemy that he feared, for nearly every day of his life he had to defy it, but one he loathed and hated, never despised.

He was thinking of Povey, as he rode along the narrow road that shone clear and golden in front of him, covered over, beneath the dark tree-tops, by the low, spreading rays of the orange sun. Of Povey, and of Philip, and Letitia. Povey's uncle and aunt lay buried at Land's End, he knew, far away from the yellow James they always called home. Povey would lie there beside them, he supposed; but he would not feel lonely in a Texas grave.

Then Cavin paused and sat still in his saddle, struck by a compelling thought. Of course. That was what Povey would want, and Letitia too, exactly that. But what would people think? Cavin brushed that idea away as of no consequence. What kind of man was it who pandered to other people's fancies? He could not be sure, though, of how Philip would have responded to his impulse, whether it would hurt him, if somewhere, out in illimitable space, he ever chanced to look back on this world.

Cavin would not have said that he believed in any kind of future life. Too often he had looked at dead men turned to horror to think that people were apt to survive dissolution and decay. But so strong was his sense of life stirring in him, so sure the beat of his own heart, that he could not imagine a personality like Philip's simply going out, like a candle. Cavin was an unconscious sceptic, and a thoroughgoing one; enough of a sceptic, indeed, not entirely to scout the *possibility* that Philip's spirit *might*, even now, shrink back from knowing that Povey, in death, lay under the live-oaks at Locust Hill, as close to Letitia as he himself.

Still, surveying all the past, Cavin could not shake off the thought that there was where it would be right to bury Povey — there by the river where Philip and Caroline and Letitia already lay. As soon as he got home, and went into the house, he told Lucina that it was a mercy Povey had never waked from his dream. And then he asked her how she felt about what had been passing through his mind, on the road.

'Lucy,' he said in his slow voice, 'I've been wondering — maybe we ought to lay him next to Letitia.' His eyes sought hers in puzzled uncertainty. 'Do you think Pa ——?'

She stood on tiptoe to put her arms around his neck. 'He'd say it was right,' she replied immediately. 'I know he would.'

And William agreed with her judgment.

Next day, Povey's friends draped one of his own wagons in white sheets, ignoring the hearse that had recently been brought into the county, and laid his long, wasted body on it. It seemed to them that no man would want to be borne to his grave in a hired carriage, or want a stranger to drive him there. Therefore, when the procession started off from Land's End, William rode at its head, and Horace, with a broad band of crape on his arm, climbed sadly onto the driver's seat. One on each side of the wagon, Cavin and David took their places; and just behind it walked old Uncle Godfrey, the black preacher on Povey's place, leading Xanthus, with an empty saddle on his back.

The sun was bright overhead when William opened his Prayer Book, and it was still full daylight when Povey's friends drove away from Locust Hill. They got into their carriages silent and preoccupied, unable either to explain why the innocent should suffer or to be reconciled to the fact. And yet they felt there was beauty, terror, pity somehow implicit in Povey's death, that grief could elevate and ennoble a man as well as torture him.

The problem of evil represented no remote abstraction to them, but one that life itself puts to every living being, one it was impossible to avoid. They did not, therefore, try timidly to twist away from it, but, driving home that April evening, they wrestled with it, offering answers no more varied and contradictory than those supplied by sages.

When they had all gone, Cavin sank down in Philip's chair by the dining-room fireplace. He was depressed and weary, Lucina saw, as she looked at him anxiously. She could not endure seeing him lose the vitality that usually flamed in him, sustaining her too. Drawing up a footstool, she sank on it at his feet, laying her head on his knees.

'Lucy,' Cavin remarked, 'there's a lot a man can't make out about this life.' He leaned over to look into her eyes. 'We've got each other.'

'Yes,' she repeated after him, 'each other.' Her voice shook. 'Cavin!' she cried, 'we're still young — we're still alive. After all that's happened, it doesn't seem right for us to be happy.'

Suddenly he stooped low and lifted her impulsively into his arms.

'It's right,' he told her. 'It's mighty right.'

He sat looking down into her face for a long time before he spoke again. She could not tell what he was thinking.

'Six children!' he said at last. 'That's quite a family, Sweet. Had you thought about it?'

'Yes,' she answered, 'I'd thought about it.' She laid her warm soft arms around his neck. 'We'll manage,' she told him, and held up her lips. Her eyes glowed as she looked at him, and as his arms tightened about her, his courage came pouring back into his veins.

'I hope we live a thousand years,' he said, dropping his face on hers.

'Two thousand!' he exclaimed, on second thought. 'Two thousand!'

Part III

*For now it standeth on a razor's edge
Either pitiful ruin . . . or life.*

Iliad, BOOK X
Lang translation

Chapter 17

CAVIN soon began to realize that he had fallen heir not only to Philip's land, but to his obligations as well — a fact which was first borne in upon him one morning in early April when William's servant, Ranse, appeared at his dining-room door.

Cavin laid down the spoon with which he was dipping warm milk over split, toasted biscuits and turned toward the darky. On the smooth-painted floor his chair moved with him as he shifted his weight. Laying his hands on its arms, he leaned forward with his head thrown back, and his eyes narrowed.

Ranse shuffled his feet and repeated the usual greeting.

'Good mawnin', Mas' Cavin. I hopes you's well.'

'Yes, thank you, Ranse,' Cavin replied. 'Anything wrong at Holly Grove?'

'Naw-suh, not dar, but Mas' Willyum say he down in bed an' he speck you better go right ober and see whut's goin' on at Little Creek Plantation.'

'Little Creek Plantation? That's Colonel Tazewell Barclay's place!'

'Yes-suh, 'tis,' Ranse agreed. 'When Naomi whut cooks fur 'em couldn't wake 'em up dis mawnin', she come hot-footin' ober fur Mas' Willyum, an' he sont me runnin' fur you.'

Cavin thought suddenly of Philip, who, until now, had always answered such calls as this.

The fact that he was now called upon to fill his father's place gave him a fleeting sense of his own maturity, but never again was the idea consciously to occur to him. In time his friends learned to send for him, as they had done for Philip, and to ask his advice on all occasions of stress — when a child was ill or a wife dying; when an obligation could not be met; when an election was in doubt; when a relative strayed; when a fine horse was seized with colic; when worms were taking a crop. But all that came later. This morning, when Ranse stood before him advising him to hurry over to Little Creek Plantation, was the beginning of his county stewardship.

Jake came to the door, carrying his and Maria's child — a boy, Josh, now nearly four months old — on his arm.

'Pilot's at de gate,' he told Cavin.

Cavin stood up with his coffee-cup in his hand, and Jake waited while his master came to the decision that he was obviously reluctant to reach.

'I expect I better take Miss Lucina along, too, Jake,' Cavin said slowly. 'Here, give me Josh. I'll carry him in to Maria. You go hitch up the gig.'

He went into the bedroom, where Lucina was watching Maria bathe Beauford.

'Maria,' Cavin said, standing by her as she soaped Beauford's head, 'you got a fine baby.' He laid him down carefully on the bed. 'He's going to be just the right age to take care o' Beau, when he grows up.'

'Yas-suh, he'll do,' Maria returned, with proud negligence, lifting Beauford out of the tub and rolling him in a towel. 'You's Maria's booful, angel-pie,' she told the white child affectionately.

Cavin was wondering how well Lucina would relish the task that lay before her. Somewhat hesitantly he told her that he thought she might be needed.

Maria looked up aghast. 'Lawd! Miss Lucy!' she exclaimed in consternation. Then she sighed. 'I reckon you has to go.'

'Yes, of course, I have to,' Lucina agreed, opening her wardrobe door. 'Let me get my cape, Cavin.' She pulled a heavy net over her hair. 'I'm ready.'

On the way, Cavin explained to her that Colonel Barclay's first wife had died soon after Philip's arrival in Texas. The Colonel had then taken to drinking — 'and worse,' Cavin went on haltingly, reluctant to name such matters outright to Lucina. There had been one child, Frank, who the year after his mother's death had gone down to celebrate Mardi Gras in New Orleans and had remained there, finding gambling more profitable than cotton-raising. Whenever he returned — which was seldom — he always behaved circumspectly himself, remonstrated with his father, and then, after a brief visit, returned to New Orleans. When the war broke out, Colonel Barclay and his son were among the first to enlist and everyone hoped that, if they came back, they would have changed their habits. Nobody was surprised, however, that, on his way home, Colonel Barclay married one of his passing attachments and brought her back to his empty house. She had had a child when the Colonel took her for his wife.

'A pretty boy, named James,' Cavin remarked. 'God knows where she got him.'

Colonel Barclay never mentioned his new wife to his friends except to announce his marriage, after which he continued to go in and out of their homes as usual, alone. His hosts refrained from asking him questions, and he volunteered no information. All they knew was that his wife's name was Marie.

'Marie what?' old Mr. Tripp Cuttross had asked one night, without thinking, soon after the Colonel's return.

The Colonel fixed him with a long, meditative glance, and at length replied, in a cold, level tone, 'Marie.' No one had ever repeated the question.

'Well, there it is, Sweet,' said Cavin as they drove along. 'Any way you look at it, it is not a pretty story.' He drew his mouth down as they pulled up at the gate. 'Looks like we might have bad business here. Maybe you better stay outside.'

Lucina did not hesitate. 'No,' she decided, 'I'll come along.'

She put out a firm foot to the high step of the gig, and Cavin laid his arm around her to lift her down. For a moment, as he held her, the same odd sense of guilt overtook him that he had experienced the morning they were first engaged when he had thought that, in knowledge of life, Lucina was a child compared to him.

He glanced down at her shining black hair, now caught resolutely back under a net, at her brown eyes, and her soft skin, no longer rosy, but still unmarred by the dark splotches which the Texas sun so often brought out on the smoothest cheeks. She had on a blue-and-white cotton dress, freshly washed and ironed, and Cavin noticed that it was becoming to her. For the hundredth time he experienced an indefinable satisfaction in her appearance. He did not know that twice a day, throughout the hot season, Maria laid out for her mistress a complete change of clothing and was careful to see that there was never a wrinkle left in the cotton frocks that Lucina almost now wore altogether.

'Some married women take to wrappers — but not Lucy,' Cavin meditated, looking at her as she stood poised on the narrow, precarious step, conscious only of the air moving gently around them, and of the April sky stretching above them, wide and immense. Danger and death seemed far away — abstractions removed from the sense of warm security that enveloped her, as she stood there in the circle of Cavin's arms.

Reluctantly he set her down, and turned, with an intent gaze, toward the house.

'I hope Ranse's mistaken. Well' — he drew a breath — 'we'll have to go in and find out.'

As they walked up the path, they saw that a boy about three years old was huddled on the front steps crying hopelessly, as if he had long ago given up any expectation of being heard. Lucina dropped on her knees beside him, and he snuggled into her arms, his wails falling to sobs, and then ceasing.

After a few moments, Cavin came out of the house, his usually bright eyes remote and veiled. 'I had to drop Naomi's boy through the transom, to open the door,' he said.

Lucina shuddered, dreading what was to come.

'He must have shot her first,' he went on. 'She was lying on the floor beside him, with a pillow under her head.'

'Oh!' Lucina felt her muscles turning to jelly.

Cavin took no notice of her trembling, but drew a long sigh and stood up.

'I'll have to go back in. I've sent after David and Judge White, and I asked them to bring Miss Clarissa to help you.'

'Help me?' Lucina echoed faintly. But as she spoke, she realized what she would have to do when Miss Clarissa arrived.

That night, she and Cavin and the Judge and Miss Clarissa sat until daybreak on the gallery that edged the house. They had little to say, for each of them felt the same reluctance to discuss the Colonel's affairs that had silenced their inquiries during his lifetime. But toward morning, Cavin leaned forward and touched the Judge on the knee.

'Maybe if we had known more ——' he suggested, in a puzzled voice from which the rising lilt of youth had disappeared.

The Judge was a small man with a sensitive face in which was written the continuous conflict that went on inside him between his tender heart and his logical mind. For thirty years he had sat on the bench, and long ago had admitted to himself that death was the only possible answer to some situations. Now he looked at Cavin and wondered how long it would be before this young man, too, would give up expecting to work miracles in this world. Contenting himself, however, with a nod of response, he pointed to the dawn beginning to break over the tree-tops in a shadowy, eery radiance which was neither light nor dark. A bird hushed its young with a low, querulous twitter, as the Judge listened, and a star that he had been following as it moved on its mysterious path through space suddenly flickered and went out.

'Rosy-fingered Dawn arising from the couch of night,' the Judge murmured as he watched the heavy mass of cloud in the eastern sky turning from gray to gold. 'Saffron dawn!'

The words came automatically onto his lips from somewhere out of his past. He was old and he was tired. What was the use, he decided, of trying to tell a man Cavin's age what he had learned about living? He turned to him with that sudden compassion, oddly mixed with envy, which so often overtakes the old when they try to talk to the young.

He looked at the vigorous lift of Cavin's shoulders, at the poise of his head, at his smooth muscles that moved so easily under his bronzed skin, and sighed, uttering only the lesser part of his thought.

'Cavin,' he said, throwing his hands apart in a gesture which indicated his own ignorance of Colonel Barclay's motives, 'a man has a right to keep his own counsel.'

It was an opinion that all who came to the funeral seemed to share. Next day, one man after another climbed silently into his carriage and drove away respecting the Colonel's privacy in death as they had in life. Judge White looked at the large rosewood desk in the parlor at Little Creek and regretted that he would probably have to pry into it in order to find Frank Barclay's address. When he turned back the heavy writing lid lined with green felt, however, he saw that he would be spared the searching he dreaded.

For his eye fell immediately upon a note enclosed in an unsealed envelope addressed to Frank Barclay, Esq., at a New Orleans address. The Judge drew his tongue across the flap and with a sigh of relief went out to tell Cavin what he had found.

No one had given any thought to the child, James, till, after the funeral, everybody had left for home except Lucina and Cavin, the Judge, and Miss Clarissa. As they walked together down the brick path to the gate, there pressed flat against the white pickets was a little figure dressed in a blue apron.

'We can't all go off and leave that baby here!' Lucina exclaimed.

The Judge glanced apprehensively at Cavin. Miss Clarissa, everyone knew, would not allow a dog or a cat in her neat home. Cavin stooped and swung the boy up on his shoulder.

'We've six already at home. What do you say, Lucy?'

That night, as she and Aunt Elvy prepared a bed for the child, Lucina asked herself what else could she have said except yes. How could she evade a responsibility so clearly laid on her shoulders? It was her plain duty, Lucina decided, to look after this child; and he was a prepossessing boy, too, she admitted, as she kissed first him and then FitzHugh good night.

Very soon Cavin had little opportunity to give more than a passing thought to the family he had so suddenly inherited. For by April, 1867, it was as apparent to him as to everyone else that Congress, in passing the Reconstruction Acts of March,

1867, had intended not only to paralyze the state government that President Johnson had recognized in Texas the previous summer, but to break the people's pride. Now that the government had been forced, by aroused Northern sentiment, to consider freeing President Davis, Congress seemed determined to retaliate by putting his countrymen in irons, all over the South.

'Now what?' thought Cavin, stunned as the full meaning of the measures adopted at Washington sank in upon him.

He read the news aloud to Lucina, on fire with a resentment bitterer than any that the war had called forth.

'To free a group of ignorant colored people, they are proposing to enslave *us!* And they rant about freedom!' He paused and glared at Lucina, as if she had some part in the outrage.

'A pretty pair!' he stormed. 'Sheridan in charge at New Orleans and Griffin at Galveston!' His eye ran impatiently down the page. 'I see Sheridan is proposing to fill all the regular state offices with military appointees. They're going to oust Throckmorton and make Pease governor, it seems. Do you know what that means?' he demanded. 'It means they'll be putting that bartender Judge White was talking about in his place, too.' Cavin ground his teeth as his rage flared up in him. 'My God! Lucy,' he went on, pacing up and down angrily on his crippled leg; 'we surrendered too soon.'

Lucina had none of the complacency about the processes of government that characterizes those who have lived in fairly settled periods of time. She looked at Cavin in horror.

'What will we do?' she gasped. She had a vision of him languishing in jail as Philip had done, of his being hanged by infuriated, drunken soldiers.

He sat down heavily and his under jaw shot out in a gesture that she remembered from his boyhood.

'Do?' He glowered at her, repeating her question. 'Defy 'em; that's what we'll do!' His eyes were cold as they fell on her. She thought she had never seen Cavin in this mood. 'Defy 'em! We've tried trying to get along with 'em. I'm through.' He restrained his anger and forced himself to pick up the paper and consider the situation more calmly.

'Grant seems to have a glimmering of sense. The *Telegraph* reports that he is opposed to Sheridan's whole plan. Well' — he concluded, his voice shaking with indignation — 'we might as well fight soon as late — the sooner the better. You can't argue with a den of rattlesnakes. I'm through trying to.' He laid the page open between his knees and leaned over it, scanning its narrow blurred columns with close and eager attention.

He turned savagely to Lucina. 'Griffin has ordered the Governor to turn loose every colored convict in the state penitentiary! That's a sample of what they intend to do.'

He read on further and, as Lucina sat watching him, she saw his body stiffen and his eyes pause on a paragraph.

'My God!' he announced, 'they are going to bar us all from jury service.' Slowly he read the notice over again, unable to believe what he saw in front of him, and his eyes swept down the page. 'Here's why!' he exclaimed. 'Now it's as clear as crystal! They couldn't enforce a regulation like this with free juries!'

'What regulation?' Lucina asked fearfully.

'This,' he replied, tapping the page as he read. 'This damn nonsense. Listen — here's exactly how it reads':

> Any person who subjects any inhabitant of the state, by reason of his previous condition of servitude, to punishment, pains, or penalties except as a punishment for crime whereof the party shall have been duly convicted, is liable to a year in prison and a thousand-dollar fine.

'Anybody knows how they'll twist that,' Cavin said slowly.
'There won't be a negro turning up for work.' The tension
behind his words brought him again to his feet. 'With the
courts filled to order and the new jury provisions in effect,
there's nothing left for us to do but fight 'em, and go to jail,
then get out, if we can, and fight 'em all over again! There's
nothing else on God's earth to do but that.'

His thoughts came to accurate focus. 'There won't be *any*
juries,' he concluded grimly. 'How can there be? The state
laws will disqualify the negroes and most of the poor whites, and
the military orders will throw out the balance of the voters.
That's what we're coming to — all to make some poor black
devil think he can turn into a white man. Well,' he said, 'let
'em have it. They've asked for it.' He felt a sudden surge of
elation. 'They'll get it, too.'

Lucina was immersed in the immediate consequences of his
decision. 'I suppose, then,' she ventured, 'we won't start the
house.'

Cavin brought his nose sharply up from his paper. 'I'm
sending the wagons in for lumber next month,' he announced,
and stared at Lucina with a curious drawn look around his
mouth and eyes. 'It's none o' their damn business what I do,
is it?' He struck his fist into his palm. 'That's what they've got
to learn — and learn mighty soon! What I do — what any
Texas citizen does — is none o' their damn business.'

The next week Colonel Rutherford came out from Galveston,
in a mood that matched Cavin's. It was a hot day for May and
he was fanning himself with his big white hat when he came up
the steps, but soon Cavin saw that something more than the
heat had brought the Colonel's temper to boiling point. Cavin
pushed forward a chair.

'Sit down, sir!' he suggested. 'I'll have Jake mix up a drink.'

The Colonel paused for no amenities. 'Have you run up against Griffin's new orders?'

'Not yet,' replied Cavin, and a glint of humor shot into his eyes. 'I expect to — soon.'

'You will,' prophesied the Colonel gloomily. 'You will.' He glared upward at Cavin, pulling fiercely on his short goatee. 'They've thrown me out,' he announced. 'What do you suppose the damned idiots asked me when I went up to register? Whether I had not at one time been on the board of a charity hospital.' He began to chuckle bitterly. 'I reminded him the hospital was for negroes — but they don't care what happens to the poor darky. All they want is power — power and graft.' His mouth fell into a straight hard line. 'Of course, they refused to accept my registration.' He laughed aloud mirthlessly.

'I hear,' he went on after a brief pause to ease his anger, 'that they are inviting the negroes to a big convention in June.' He closed his account with a prophecy. 'Watch what I say: There's worse to come. They'll remove Governor Throck-morton as soon as they dare, and the Lord only knows what they'll do then! I hear they're even considering organizing colored people and arming them — to enforce their rights, they claim.'

Cavin sat with one conflicting thought after another passing in and out his mind. 'God knows,' he said finally, throwing out his hands in a gesture of despair, 'they're crazy — crazy as loons.' Then he shrugged his shoulders and leaned back in his chair. 'I reckon we'll get along somehow. Right now, I'd like to know how much money I can get from you to build a house, clear some more land, and buy some more cattle.'

Colonel Rutherford's excitement visibly dropped from him.

'Well, by the Lord Harry!' he exclaimed, staring at Cavin.

'Is it possible you are serious?' He leaned forward, examining his host's face intently. Then his eyes kindled and, putting his feet on the floor with a thud, he leaned over Cavin, laying both his hands on his shoulders, and rocking his chair under him. 'By Gad! boy,' he exclaimed; 'you're a gambler after my own heart!' Straightening himself, he lit a very long, thin cigar, with an odor like dried apples.

'Go on,' he said. 'Draw on me for whatever you need. You'll pull out,' he prophesied confidently. 'We'll all pull out.'

He began to laugh, his huge frame shaking. To look at his round and ruddy face, lengthened by his clipped goatee, no one would have imagined how, under stress, his ruminative eyes could change and harden to a cold, slaty gray.

'By George, Cavin,' he chuckled, 'it takes gamblers like us to keep a state like this going. You gamble your way, and I'll gamble mine!'

He glanced at Cavin out of the narrowed corner of his eye. 'Even the Bishop's got his own special form of gambling.' Holding his cigar out in front of him, he sat thoughtfully watching the white ash form on the end of it. 'Gambling's the right word, Cavin. If it isn't a gamble to count on making men better, what is? By George,' he said, again, pleased with his idea, 'we're all gambling in this state — that is, everybody who amounts to anything.' His voice sobered. 'But it looks like the dice are pretty well loaded against us at present.'

'At present,' Cavin answered with his eyes on the horizon, 'at present.' Then a thought struck him. 'But, Colonel,' he protested, 'I'm no gambler, not any kind of one. This is no gamble I'm undertaking,' he insisted. 'I'm certain to win. You ought to know that.'

Colonel Rutherford sat down in his chair, rocked back, and laced his hands across his broad breast. 'Yes?' he asked politely.

'Yes? Well, God knows I hope you're right.' The chair under him shook with his laughter. 'It's a pity the Bishop's in England. I'd like to see his face when I tell him he's a gambler.'

Cavin looked serious. 'I told him he'd better stay here. What was that meeting he went to anyway?' he asked, somewhat exasperated. 'What business has he got in England?'

'He went to the Lambeth Conference,' Colonel Rutherford explained.

'Never heard of it,' Cavin answered. Losing interest in the topic, he tapped a bell.

'Jake,' he said, when his servant appeared, 'where's that Bourbon I got in last week? If you've been at it, you damned rascal, I'm going to skin you alive.'

Jake grinned. 'I'se got a couple o' drinks ripenin', Mas' Cavin.'

'Is this whiskey any better'n the last lot?' Cavin inquired, winking at the Colonel.

'Yas-suh,' Jake answered positively, 'it's a heap better.'

As Jake left the room the Colonel and Cavin both began to laugh.

'Lawd! Lawd!' the Colonel exclaimed, tilting his chair backward, 'what a terrible time the po' niggers are going to have when the Yankees start reforming *them*. They will,' he predicted confidently. 'It's the first thing a Yankee thinks about — reforming somebody. When they get through with us, they'll start on them. Lord help the poor, ignorant creatures!'

Jake returned with the frosty silver cups which, except on Communion Sunday, when Lucina took them to church wrapped in fine linen, were always kept against the ice. For Cavin was now having ice shipped into Berryville by the ton, keeping it carefully buried under cotton-seed hulls in his ice house.

'Did you cut the mint bed back today and water it?' Cavin
asked Jake. Then, smiling across the green sprigs at the Colonel,
he breathed deeply. 'Here's to you, sir!'

They leaned back, drawing easily on their straws, and stirring, at intervals, with their long spoons.

'A little more lime,' said the Colonel. 'Pass me the syrup.'
He glanced over his cup at Cavin. 'Met a man in Virginia who
objected to lime.'

'You don't say?' replied Cavin absently sipping. 'Never saw
a Yankee yet could remember to smell before he swallows,' he
observed, reopening the conversation after a long silence. 'Or,'
he went on, 'who could sit still long enough to enjoy a drink.'

'Not a bit o' use in the world wasting prime Bourbon on 'em,'
the Colonel remarked, tipping his cup. 'Where'd you turn up
this kind o' liquor, anyway, Cavin?'

All that summer, from early in May until September, Cavin
sent his wagons back and forth to Houston and Galveston,
hauling, across the prairie, glass and window-blinds and screws
and latches and nails and great piles of heavy lumber and brick
the color of Georgia clay.

The undertaking was one that pleased and delighted him,
and he always liked to remember that he began his hauling the
very day Jefferson Davis was at last allowed 'the liberty of free
locomotion.'

'What a fool way to put it!' Cavin thought when he read the
news, and then grinned. 'It's the way Yankees talk, though,
exactly.' The knowledge that his President was no longer in
prison released his spirit more than he would have believed
possible. The Brazos planters met one another and could
hardly speak for emotion as they exchanged information about
the trial at Richmond. The very fact that ten eminent Northern

citizens, including Horace Greeley, had gone on the President's bond seemed to promise that there was sanity and justice still alive in the country, somewhere. In this atmosphere of renewed hope and confidence, Cavin began to build his house.

On one of his trips to Galveston after supplies, he ran across a man who had only just arrived in Texas — one Jeremiah Blake, whom he chanced to overhear criticizing the building of a house just then going up on the Avenue facing the Gulf.

Cavin stopped and looked the man over. He had blazing red hair, a freckled face, and rapidly moving pale blue eyes, and he walked with an eager stride that gave him the appearance of being considerably younger than he was. Suddenly, he approached one of the carpenters and suggested a better way of raising the heavy timbers he was handling. In his eagerness, Jeremiah scarcely noticed the coldness with which his suggestion was received, but Cavin paused, with an amused smile on his face, expecting exactly what happened. The carpenter was plainly resentful and suspicious of Jeremiah's intentions, and made no bones about saying so.

Jeremiah Blake smiled broadly at the irate man. 'All right, brother,' he said, good-humor in his eyes. 'Have it your own way.' He put his foot up on the piling, then, and leaned closer. 'You couldn't use an extra hammer, I reckon?' The carpenter was mollified, but not to the extent of being willing to share his job.

At the moment Cavin made up his mind, and strolled over to the newcomer, examining him carefully as he approached him.

'Maybe *we* can make a bargain,' he said quietly over Jeremiah's shoulder.

Jeremiah flung himself around and cast a glance at Cavin as searching as that with which Cavin covered him.

'Maybe,' he returned non-committally. Then after another brief scrutiny, he smiled, 'What at?'

Cavin explained that he was putting up a house and needed an expert carpenter.

'Well,' Jeremiah began, 'till I went in the army, I was a tol'able fair builder.' He looked closely at Cavin. 'My pappy built houses in Charleston, and my grandpappy before him. What I know, they learnt me there. But,' he added, examining his heavy hands with aloof care, 'I been totin' a gun quite some time, now.' He faced Cavin frankly. 'Shootin' it, too. I got in some trouble in South Carolina an' lit out. That's why I'm here, I reckon I better tell you straight.'

Cavin took count of the humor in Jeremiah's eyes, his competent carriage, his broad, steady fingers. 'Well, I reckon that's your business,' he observed. 'I'm leaving town tonight. If you care about riding out in the country with me, we might see how we get along till the next time I send in for more lumber.'

Jeremiah took no longer than Cavin to come to a decision. 'What kin' o' place you thinkin' 'bout buildin'?'

Cavin stooped and drew on a piece of white board a rough sketch. Jeremiah studied it with approving interest.

'Whut time you leavin' and where from?' he asked.

Not until they were well out on the prairie did it cross Cavin's mind that he had made no terms with the man. 'Time enough later,' he concluded.

He soon found, after he got home, that Jeremiah's eye was as straight as a measuring rod. By the time the rough outlines of the house began to take shape, he was convinced that he could safely leave the building of it to Jeremiah and to Lucina. Otherwise it might never have been completed; for, as Colonel Rutherford had predicted, Governor Throckmorton

was removed from office in July of 1867, and all summer affairs
in the state mounted to feverish intensity.

The first week in August, Cavin came in late one afternoon
from a meeting of the planters at Berryville. Flinging his hat
down, he dropped into a chair on the shady east gallery where
Lucina was sitting, reading. He was hot and, she could see,
holding down his temper. 'Well,' he said finally, answering the
anxiety in her face, 'they've made Pease governor now, Lucy,
and I suppose everybody we sent up to Austin last year will
be put out — the attorney general, the Supreme Court justices,
the treasurer, everybody.' Reaching out his hand, he took the
glass of cold water Jake offered him and began to relax as
Jake stood fanning him with a huge palmetto fan. 'There's
one chance — Pease made a pretty good governor of this state
in the fifties, they say, even if he was a born Yankee. He may
have *some* sense.'

'You oughta not get so hot, Mas' Cavin,' Jake observed.
'Some day it gwine-a make you sick.'

'Lawd, Jake!' Cavin replied, 'I've heard enough today to
make anybody sick.' He shook his head fiercely and turned
his chair to face Lucina's. 'John McGaughey swears that when
he was in Galveston last week he saw a petition with eighty
signatures on it asking for a whole new set of loyal county
officers.' He studied her from under his lids while his lips
tightened. 'The signatures were all in the same handwriting.
That's the kind o' skulduggery we're up against!'

As the summer passed, it became apparent that the confusion
in the state was growing worse. Governor Pease had at first
acted on the assumption that all state laws not specifically
annulled were still in force. Soon, however, the extremists in
his party began to advance the idea that every law passed since

the war began was void, and before long they were quarrelling hotly among themselves over this issue. Under such an interpretation of the law, who, the moderates demanded, could know where he stood in the most everyday concerns of his life?

Cavin dismissed all such argument as theoretical in the extreme, and gave it little thought. 'Still,' he decided, 'it may keep 'em from thinking up worse mischief. While they're at all that foolishness, maybe I can get a chance to tend to my crop.'

He had now all of Philip's land as well as Povey's to look after; and, since William had noticeably aged during the year, he was often called on to take charge of Holly Grove, as well. And the settlement of Letitia's interest in her father's Natchez Plantation had also begun — a settlement which, though Cavin did not then know it, was to extend over many years. If Cavin had not been able to count on Matt to keep things going on his plantation and Horace to do the same on Povey's, he would have been harder pressed than he was.

Lucina, also, had her hands full and running over. With seven children to be looked after, a house to be built, and a garden to be planned and planted, time did not oppress her with its slow passage. Every day, after she had conferred with Aunt Elvy and Jeremiah, she looked at the bare ground around Locust Hill and sighed, wondering how long it would take her to learn what plants would thrive under the long Texas summers. Still, the bulbs Cavin had dug up in the garden at Cedar Ledge were doing well, and yellow roses bloomed as freely in her Texas garden as they had at Sunny Fields.

The summer was wet and muggy and hot. 'Yellow-fever weather,' the oldest people in the county predicted, taking care to burn all the letters that arrived from New Orleans, where the fever was raging.

Lucina looked at Beau in terror every time she heard the

words. When in August all the children came down with
measles, she lived in agony until she found out what it was that
had turned Beauford's usually pink cheeks to a pale yellowish
pallor.

She was too much alarmed over the children to take much
note of how seldom Cavin was now at home. At intervals he
would be out nearly all night meeting with the Council of
Safety which the white citizens of the county had been expanding all that summer. A direct outgrowth of the guard units
legally set up the preceding year, it had now expanded to
include people who had little or no property to protect, but
who had come to understand the dangers for everybody in
Radical rule. A few white tenants were already in the group,
all of John McGaughey's German cowboys, who treasured their
jobs well above the Unionist principles of their fathers, and
Jeremiah Blake. The dangers that threatened every white man
had begun to consolidate all classes.

'The truth is,' John remarked, opening a meeting one night
at Locust Hill, 'they'll drive us out, or we'll drive them out.'
He surveyed the men grouped in front of him with care, singling
out each man's face as he recognized it. 'We are forced to protect our lives and property and to take over our government.'

Old Mr. Joseph O'Fallon, who lived with his wife and eight
children on twenty acres of David's land, stood up in the back
of the gathering, and cleared his mouth of tobacco juice. His
dark blue eyes glowed under half-closed lids and his wrinkled
face was burned and spotted by the sun and wind. The
poise of his body suggested a youth that was disproved by
one glance at his leathery neck, where heavy lines were deeply
grooved in the sagging flesh. He looked out on the men in
front of him with the distant gaze of a man more accustomed
to scanning the prairie and the horizon than to focussing his

attention on an audience; and above his rough blue jumper, thrown open at the neck, his lips smiled amiably, almost like a child's. He glanced at David, who sat attentively listening from his seat on the steps that edged the gallery. If there was anybody on earth Joseph O'Fallon loved, it was David — David who had sat up all night with him and his children when they were all down with slow fever, David on whose father's doorstep he had placed, every Christmas morning for a quarter of a century, a fat pullet and a dozen brown eggs.

'I ain't got one thing on God's earth to pertect,' he began in his slow drawl. 'But,' he asserted with rising vigor, 'I hate being run over worse'n pizen.'

Meditatively he took out his long black pistols and examined them, with careful affection. Then he observed, in a gentle, reminiscent voice, 'I didn't keer much 'bout having the Mexicans rarin' aroun' in this state and' — suddenly his words came out of his mouth like a growl — 'I ain't no whit better disposed toward these buzzards.' He stopped and made a promise. 'Next time we meet all my boys'll be here and some mo' white men who been at me to jine 'em, now fur some time. I ain't intendin' to, but they don't know it.' Throwing his head back, he replaced his quid of tobacco, but, on second thought, took it out again, uneasily shifting his muddy feet in their heavy brogans. 'You ain't asking fur church membership in this group, I reckon?' he inquired, looking toward Cavin as the elected leader of the county defense. 'David would-a been a heap better choice,' he thought critically, while he waited for an answer.

Cavin smiled. 'A man's religious convictions are his own business, I should say, Mr. O'Fallon.' Turning his face toward his friends, he announced, 'Next week, the same time,' and the men began to mount their horses, their spurs jingling as their feet fitted into the stirrups.

Cavin went inside, too preoccupied to remember that the night marked the second anniversary of his wedding.

A week later, he learned that President Johnson had removed Sheridan from the military command of Louisiana and Texas.

'Now what's up?' Cavin wondered. This constant shift in officers was puzzling and disconcerting. 'You no sooner get on to one variety of deviltry,' he reflected, 'till they spring something new on you!' He grinned tolerantly. 'I suppose the same man runs out o' mean ideas, though Lord knows Sheridan seemed to be full enough of 'em to suit anybody.'

But when cotton-picking began in full force, he put aside his anxieties about the state. Looking over his white fields, he judged that, even under present conditions, his crop would bring in good returns.

'Colonel Rutherford'll get some of his money back right away,' he told himself. 'But not too much,' he calculated swiftly. 'I need a herd of Jerseys — maybe Holsteins — to milk, and some beef cattle, too. It might be a good idea to saw off the horns of these range cattle I've got, then feed 'em and cross 'em with better stock. I'll write to Shelby and ask him if he knows anything about raising fine cattle. No' — a better thought struck him — 'the Yankees are all time talking about their fine, fat cows. Next time I go to Galveston, I'll ask around.'

He went to bed planning what portion of his prairie land he would have to fence in to keep his cattle together, and failed to notice either the strange coppery color of the late evening sky or the sultry air that hung, as still as a vacuum, over everything, with a faint whiff of sulphur in its still depths.

About midnight, however, he was wakened by the blinds banging against the house which shivered under the fierce wind, almost like the ship that had brought him and Lucina to Texas.

'It's the equinoctial storm,' he told her, instantly on his feet. 'The double chimney in the dining-room will hold up the walls.'

At that moment they heard Jake and Matt entering the kitchen, with Maria and the other house servants at their heels. Cavin called to Jake to get ropes from the carriage house, and watched him almost blown off his feet as he stepped outside.

'Stay away from the trees,' Cavin warned him, but his voice was carried away by the wind.

Jake fell flat and crawled along, hugging the ground. When he returned, Cavin hauled him in the door and began to cut the rope into pieces.

'Quit that shivering,' Cavin said shortly, 'and help me tie the blinds and doors shut.'

Aunt Elvy made a pallet in the corner for the children to sleep on, and then, falling on her stiff old knees, began to pray aloud.

'You keep right at it, Aunt Elvy,' Cavin encouraged her; 'we're goin' to need the Lord's help a-plenty before this blows over. You keep a-prayin'.' He went himself to test the knot he had tied around the doorknob, drawing it tight to the heavy iron safe in the corner.

Lucina sat by the fireplace, holding Beau in her arms, her shoulders bowed over him. She was conscious only of one thought: his safety. Cavin may not have felt much difference in the affection he bestowed almost impartially on his little brothers and sisters and on his own child, but from that night on Lucina knew what a gap there was in her own heart between them. She would have seen the river rush in the door and sweep away every living soul in the room before she would have relinquished her grasp on Beau.

The house shook with a sudden quiver more violent than any that had gone before, and Cavin went to see which windows were out. He returned to say that books were floating in two feet of water on the floor of Philip's room. As day broke through gray rifts of cloud, the tree-tops were still bending almost to the groun

Lucina thought Cavin seemed almost proud of the violence of this Texas wind. 'You never saw anything like it in Georgia, did you?' he kept asking her.

The storm, she saw, induced a strange excitement in him, as if he found it pleasurable to match his wits and energy against its force. She, however, felt exhausted and frightened by its fury, and was aware of a passionate uprising of the homesickness that for months she had been suppressing.

About nine o'clock in the morning the storm died down, and the air was still, with a strange, menacing calm.

'It'll blow back the other way,' Cavin said. 'In between, you better hunt up the stock, Matt. Good thing they warn't in the barn.' Glancing out of the window, he saw that the structure which had held his hay and corn was now only a pile of lumber.

'Yas-suh.' Matt rose, 'Come on, Jake.'

Cavin followed them. 'I better see if the river's rising.'

When he came back after half an hour, his face was white.

'There's not a shred of cotton left in the field, Lucy, not a shred; even the stalks are blown away.'

He dropped down in a chair, laid his face in his hands, following repeatedly the pattern of the wood in the board under his gaze. He did not move when the wind returned, in diminished force, but sat there in complete silence, as the afternoon wore away. Not until the wind had blown itself out at dusk and Aunt Elvy laid their supper before them did he speak.

'Probably,' he said, rousing himself. 'Probably it has.'

'What do you mean?' Lucina asked.

'The house has blown down, too, I suppose.' He sat looking

at her, with heavy, tired eyes, as a knock sounded on the side door, and Jeremiah Blake walked in.

'By George, Mister Darcy!' he exclaimed, 'I didn't know how bad it was till it was all over. I thought I better ride down an' see how you all made out.' He was rubbing his broad, red hands together, smiling.

Cavin asked sharply, 'I suppose it's on the ground?'

'Whut's on the ground?' Jeremiah replied, surprised by the tone of the question.

'The house,' Lucina put in; 'the house, Jeremiah.'

Jeremiah folded his arms, leaned back against the door, and stared at them both.

'My house down? A house I built? Why, Mister Darcy, I'm surprised, I really am, that you thought so.' His round, freckled face was grieved. 'You must-a forgot I been born and brought up on the coast, an' know what the kind o' air we been havin' means.' He turned reproachful eyes on Cavin. 'For a couple o' days, now, I been bracin' my timbers. No-suh, there ain't a thing blown down. Well, maybe a few pieces of siding,' he corrected himself.

Cavin stood up. 'That's good news; but the cotton's gone, every damned stalk.' He turned to Lucina.

'I'm going out to ride over the place.'

'Now?' she asked, surprised, for it was nearly dark.

'Now,' he repeated. 'Come along, Jeremiah?'

Jeremiah shook his head. 'I'll be gettin' back.'

Lucina did not begin to worry about Cavin until nearly morning, for as soon as she realized the storm had blown past, she and Maria began trying to set the house in order. Every rug, carpet, and curtain, she soon saw, would have to be put out to dry, and most of the books. She fell into her bed sodden with fatigue.

About four o'clock, however, she waked with a start. Where was Cavin? He had not yet come in.

'He tried to swim the river. He's drowned.' At the thought, her teeth began to chatter, and she shook in a nervous chill.

Getting up, she dressed and called Matt, who had made himself a pallet in the kitchen. He went to get Jake and together, in the gray hour just before full daybreak, they set out to find their master.

It did not take them long. To Lucina the minutes were torture, but within half an hour they had come upon Cavin riding toward home.

Jake laid his hand on Matt's rein.

'I been followin' Mas' Cavin all dese yeahs, an' I ain't nebber befo' seed him wid a drap too much inside 'im. Gawd-amighty! Dis gwine-a kill Miss Lucy, near-bout. Whut you reckin got into 'im?'

'De Debbil,' Matt responded, with positive conviction. He meditated. 'Us better see kin us sober 'im up 'fo us takes 'im home.'

But Cavin passed them on a sudden gallop and they did not dare to try to stop him.

'When a Darcy man gits liquor in 'im, he's wusser'n a pack o' wildcats,' Matt commented, 'but long's I'se known 'em, I ain't nebber put 'em down as whut you'd call drinkers. Now, Mas' Philip warn't one to rassle much wid whiskey; but I remembers he tried it onct or twict, when he wuz a young man, an' I wouldn't-a knowed 'im when he had it in 'im.'

Keeping Cavin in sight, they drew up their horses in the lane, just as he entered his door.

Then they consulted together.

'Miss Lucy ain't gwine-a lak it,' Jake reasoned. 'Maybe us

better kine-a hang aroun' a while, an' den go in an' say us couldn't fin' 'im.'

'You got sense, Jake,' Matt agreed slowly. 'Us better go by yo' house fur breakfus!'

When they returned an hour later and rapped cautiously at the kitchen door, Lucina met them.

'Your master's home. Pilot sprained his ankle in a hole and it took Mas' Cavin a long time to get back. Go to bed, now, and get some rest, yourselves,' she said in her usual kind voice.

'But she don't look right,' Matt worried. 'Somepin' funny about de way her eyes works.'

He stopped in his tracks.

'Us ain't seen nothin',' he said solemnly to Jake. 'Nothin' a-tall.'

'Yeah,' Jake agreed, 'dat's right. Us couldn't fin' 'im no-whar.' They separated, each nodding wisely.

When she had dismissed the servants, Lucina went to her room. She was glad there was nobody there, that Maria had gone back to her own cabin and the other servants were yet asleep. She was filled with a cold, calm fury, and felt, as yet, neither grief, pity, nor regret.

At the thought of Cavin such disgust rose in her throat as she had never suspected she could feel. She had known, ever since she came to Texas, that there were plenty of men who thought nothing of coming home reeling, and plenty of wives who put up with it — men whom everyone respected except for their single weakness. But never had it so much as entered her head that such an eventuality might ever befall her, Lucina Lyttleton. Beauford had taught her to despise a man who couldn't drink like a gentleman, without taking too much. She thought of the matter less as a moral issue than as one of taste and manners, like eating with your knife or beating your wife. She shuddered, revolted by her recollection of the night's events, and a desolate, settling despair closed in upon her.

'I'm married to him! He's Beau's father!' she said, in stark amazement.

Throwing herself on her bed, she lay there too miserable to move or to think. How could she go on living, she thought, always feeling like this? Cavin — where was he? The man she had helped in the door was a stranger. Nothing would ever be the same again between them, nothing. She was shocked to the depths of her being. But at last she fell asleep in the complete exhaustion that nature often grants to those who have borne too much.

When she awoke, she moved like an automaton, but her course was clear before her — a course not so much of her deliberate choosing as it was the only one that presented itself to her. She felt stricken, dumb, but some deep instinct warned her that any words she might utter now would be irrevocable. Besides, she had a sense of dignity that prevented her from accusing Cavin. If he did not accuse himself, what would any recriminations from her amount to? She knew that this was a moment between them that would better pass in silence. Then what? What next? She had no idea, and was conscious only of a sick, spreading misery within her.

She sent word to Aunt Emmy that she wanted no dinner, but toward evening she rose and dressed herself with even more care than usual and met Cavin at supper with the courtesy she would have accorded any guest. She spoke to him, however, only when she had to, and returned, after the meal, to her room and shut her door tight. Every time she thought of him as he had looked foolishly drunk, a nausea arose in her throat and suffocated her.

After one glance at her, as she took her seat across from him, Cavin had taken his cue. If she wanted it that way, so it would be. Hers was the choice, not his; he acknowledged the fairness of that and he would not beg or cringe, even to Lucina. She did not even dream that his impassive face masked an inner disturbance as profound as her own.

Not that Cavin thought of his yielding as sinful. The word never entered his mind; he was too well acquainted with men and the world, anyway, to use that easy word often. Rather — and this thought agitated him to his very centre — he had acted, he admitted to himself, like a plain fool with mighty little judgment, and this picture of himself did not please him. For the first time his natural confidence in himself — a confidence that was far from being conceit — was rudely and severely shaken. Couldn't a man count even on *himself* in this world? he asked himself with a strange surprise. That eventuality had never before occurred to him.

Apparently Lucina had decided he wasn't worth putting any confidence in, and this realization stung him in his tenderest spot, where, unadmitted even to himself, he kept the thought of her hid. She was — he knew it now — the spring that controlled his energies, that gave zest and meaning to his efforts. Without her — a black, merciless despair settled on him too. He was as silent as Lucina, not because he intended to be, but because he knew no words to express the turmoil going on within him.

'It'll be like this forever,' Lucina told herself, as day after day passed in this painful deadlock of wills. 'Forever,' she reiterated, too young to pronounce the word with anything except finality. A cold fright settled upon her. The feelings that gripped her were beyond her control as she watched Cavin rise from the table morning, noon, and night and go his way with no remarks of any kind for her. 'Forever!' The word began to ring in her ears.

The days dragged on, till nearly a week had passed. It was the middle of September, and they had hoped to move into their house before Christmas. But now she gave it no thought, neither it nor the children, but shut herself up day after day with Beau, alone in her room.

One afternoon, while she lay on her bed fanning him, lightning began to flash across the swiftly moving black clouds which had filled the sky since morning. Lucina listened to the rumbling thunder and to the hail that accompanied it with an indifference that surprised her.

'Once,' she thought idly, 'I was afraid of lightning.'

There was a hurried knock at her door, and she sprang to her feet to find Maria there, her face working in fright.

'Jake jes' rid in. Mas' Cavin's done been struck by lightnin'.'

Lucina took a step, moving automatically, without feeling. Her breath fluttered in her throat.

'Here,' she said to Maria, handing Beau over to her.

Then she caught sight of Jake in the doorway and motioned to him to go ahead. Suddenly she began to run, but she was not conscious of so doing, as she followed Jake's hurrying steps. Her body and her mind seemed to her to have no slightest connection. She felt light, freed from the dominance of matter, as if her muscles had taken wing from her thoughts.

A little way off, in the stubble of the oatfield across the lane, she saw that a horse was down, his legs stretched out stiff in front of his huge, quiet body.

'Cavin's under him,' she judged, and began to run faster than she had ever supposed she could move across the ground. The dead misery that had filled her mind for the past week was replaced by a fear which tore at her heart.

'Oh, God!' she moaned. 'Let him live. I don't care about anything else. Only let him be alive.'

She caught her breath and flew on, and then, looking up, stood suddenly still with her hands to her lips and her eyes staring. Who was that running across the field to meet her? Not Cavin? Not Cavin? Oh, not Cavin!

She was in his arms, straining him to her, kissing his eyes, his ears, his lips.

'I had just got down to see about a calf,' he told her, dropping his arms around her with a long, deep sigh.

'My darling! My darling!' she repeated over and over. 'You're alive. I thought you were dead.'

'I've been in hell,' said Cavin brokenly, lifting her in his arms, and burying his face in her neck. 'In hell,' he said again, with complete conviction. 'I won't ever need to go there again.' After a while, he raised his head and threw it back, looking at her with shining eyes.

She touched his cheek. It was firm and warm. 'He's alive,' she thought, 'not cold and dead.'

He stooped over her with a sudden, shuddering gasp.

'Kiss me!' he said. 'Kiss me! Again!' he demanded. 'Again!' He felt whole, restored. The blood coursed through his veins like a torrent.

After supper, before it was quite dark they rode over to see a new field that he was clearing for cotton. Cavin pulled up his horse by the curve of the river that separated old Mr. Archibald Bland's island from his land.

'That night,' he began, darting a glance sidewise at her, 'I was cold and tired and plumb discouraged and I ran across old Mr. Archibald and Mr. Cuttross.'

She laid her hand on his lips. 'Don't ever mention it again.' She shuddered violently. 'It makes me sick even to think about it.'

Cavin looked at her a long time without speaking or smiling.

'Listen, Lucina,' he said at last. 'Listen to me. Once is one time too many for a man to play a fool.' Reaching over, he raised her face, so he could look full into her eyes. 'You can count on my remembering that.'

Chapter 18

THE fall of 1867 was hot and dry and the air lay flat and heavy, with the life burned out of it, over the fields. Every afternoon Lucina undressed herself and lay resting on a sheet spread over the matting that, in the summer, replaced the carpet on her bedroom floor. She always sighed with relief when, toward evening, the breeze from the Gulf began to stir in and out the closed shutters, but she never felt its cool flow without wondering whether it brought with it the yellow fever that was spreading in Galveston, though not so far, on the Brazos.

It was a trying period, for the people's patience was threadbare; and the military rule imposed by Congress the preceding spring had been enough worse than that which had preceded it to exhaust the hopes of the most optimistic. The tension grew until the steadiest felt their nerves cracking under the long strain.

When General Griffin, in charge at Galveston, died in September, after hardly six months in office, even William lost his usual calm. 'Vicious as Griffin was,' he commented to Cavin, 'the next one may be worse.' All they knew was that the new commander was named Reynolds, and was reported to be an extreme abolitionist.

'God help us, then!' groaned William. 'Nobody's as dangerous as a man with some kind of a conviction gnawing in him. I'd rather deal with an out and out sinner, any day!'

William was in bed now, most of the time, and more and more, as the fall lengthened out into winter, the care of his place fell upon Cavin. One evening, just before Christmas, Cavin stopped by to see his cousin. He found David and Colonel Brashear and Judge White already there, and noticed, as he entered the door, that David was carefully measuring out some kind of powders and folding them up in neat, white papers.

Then he saw William wave away the glass that David handed him and lean his thin elbows on the four pillows stuffed behind his back. His beaked nose loomed unusually prominent, and the skin across his forehead was stretched so tight that it seemed transparent. His white hair accentuated the sharp, clear blue of his eyes, and the hand with which he repelled David's offer of medicine was pallid and thin to emaciation. His fingers, however, spread apart in a firm gesture of disdain; and the expression that appeared in his eyes was tolerant, even humorous, as though something in the idea of his infirmities amused him. As Cavin watched, William laid his hand lightly on David's wrist.

'I assume, David,' he asserted rather than asked, 'that these powders you are giving me are to satisfy Helen?' He kept his eyes fixed on David's, reading his face.

Soon his hand dropped back on the bedspread and it was several moments before he spoke. 'I see,' he said at last. 'I thought as much.'

He lay silent for some time, his face illumined by the red glow of the wintry sunset which fell upon his bed. Then he looked up at David, who was still standing beside him. The expression in his eyes was as tranquil as though he were commenting on wind or weather. 'I watched my father's heart slow down, David,' he remarked. 'Then of course it seemed to me my own would last forever.'

His lips above his curling gray beard broke into a brief smile, and he included Cavin in the gaze with which he swept the room, meeting each of his friends' eyes with a mild reminiscent glance. He spoke quietly, casually, as if his recollections interested him more than present circumstances.

'Do you know, gentlemen, I hadn't thought of it in sixty years, but I remember once hearing my father say to my mother that Charltons ought to know how to die. I wonder if I do?' The question seemed to puzzle him, like some theoretical matter about which he had little personal concern.

He turned his head toward the window, where already the shadows were forming like deep black pools beneath the great magnolia that swept the western window beside his bed. His friends watched him as thoughts of which they were unaware rose in his breast and flowed upward, altering the lines of his face until it glowed with a soft warmth they did not know how to account for. How could they understand that, as he lay there, his mind was out in his fields following every curve and line of the river where it cut through his black soil? Following the border of crêpe-myrtles that his own hands had set out beside the bayou, the forest of pecans that he had always treasured as much for their stately height and their lacy leaves as for their fruit, the grove of live-oaks that he had slept under on the bare ground, his first night in Texas. He chuckled and smiled gently as he brought his gaze back from the falling dusk outside.

'It was amusing, that night,' he began; and his listeners, sitting still and attentive in their chairs, waited to hear to what night he referred.

William smiled again, and a gleam flashed in his shadowed

eyes. Momentarily the memory of the youth he had enjoyed so long ago stirred in his veins, and exhilarated his spirit.

'It was really amusing,' he explained. 'Ranse and I rode onto this place in the late evening. There we were,' he said, lacing his hands in front of him on the white counterpane, and leaning his head back on the pillows. 'There we were, in the pouring rain, without a bite to eat. I owned then — oh! I don't know, probably half the county.' Lifting his hand negligently, he dropped it again. 'But just the same, Ranse and I had to crawl under a dog-tent together and wait for the rain to let up, so we could fish for our supper. It was a catfish that we finally caught, I remember; but to us it tasted like manna. Don't you remember, Ranse, that I told you it tasted like manna?'

Ranse was sitting close beside his master's head, ready to lift or move him. At the question, his blurred eyes brightened under their drooping lids.

'Yas-suh, I recollects dat fish, an' how us took mos' de night gittin' a fiah stahted wid wet wood. Sho', I recollects dat fish. Milk an' honey ain't gwine tase no better.'

'Well, Ranse!' William observed pleasantly, 'I'm likely to know about that before you do.' He moved his eyes from his servant to Colonel Brashear. 'You'll look after Ranse, Colonel? His joints are getting stiff, like ours.' He studied his friend's face reflectively. 'It's been a fine life, Colonel, we've shared together here on the Brazos. A fine life. Worth fighting the Indians and the Yankees for.'

The Colonel blew his nose deliberately, nodded vigorously, and rising with sudden abruptness from his chair, stalked out of the room, the red heels of his tall polished boots clicking against the painted floor. Soon he returned, shaking his thick white hair back out of his face.

'I sent my boy home, William. I'm staying.' He swallowed and unashamedly wiped his eyes with an enormous white pocket handkerchief. 'There's a damn lot to live for, William. You better hang on as long as you can. We're better acquainted here on the Brazos than we are across the river.'

'Oh! I don't know, Colonel,' William replied easily.

Judge White got up, walked over to the bed, and leaned over his friend.

'Your will and papers are in good order, William.' His spare frame looked unusually thin against the waning light, and his straight shoulders drooped. William laid his hand on the Judge's arm and his eyes, under their waxen lids, twinkled. 'Judge,' he said, 'I haven't forgiven you for that time — do you remember? — when, unbeknownst to me, you entered a mare for the races and took the ribbon over my colt?'

The Judge smiled. 'Lord! That mare o' mine was a born trotter, William. It would-a been a sin and a shame to have let your Touchstone walk away with the purse.' He sank down into the chair opposite Ranse. 'La! La!' he sighed. 'It was a pretty race.'

William looked around the room for Cavin, as a more anxious expression than had yet appeared on his face gathered around his eyes and lips.

'This place — you might as well take it over for Helen, Cavin. It was all one piece, anyway, once.'

Cavin got out of his chair and walked across to his cousin's bed with a long, firm stride.

'I'll look after your land, Cousin William.' He seemed to be thinking as he laid his firm fingers on William's how he could best ease his cousin's passing. 'We'll get rid of the Yankees, too,' he promised. 'Don't you worry about anything.'

'No,' said William placidly, 'I don't intend to.' His eyes that were even now clear and brightly blue drooped shut while his friends stood watching him. They thought he was asleep, but after a moment he opened his lids.

'I've had a fine life,' he said in a serene voice, and turned his head on his pillow. 'A fine life,' he echoed, drowsily.

It was late when Cavin slowly lifted the latch of William's white front gate and told a young negro lounging by the fence to bring his horse around. He rode a different mount, now that Pilot was gone, a beautiful gray that he had named Derby because, as he frequently told Jake, 'he would run a good race anywhere.' He rubbed the animal's neck, now, before he climbed on him, and Derby, sensing the temper of his rider, began to move in a slow, careful trot.

Cavin's face was preoccupied when Lucina met him on the steps, in the dark.

She laid her hands on his shoulders, sensing his dejection. 'Oh!' she exclaimed sadly, 'he's worse then?'

The muscles of his arms, beneath her touch, seemed to Lucina to lack their usual vigorous firmness.

'He's dying,' he said, and his other worries flooded over him, intensified by his grief.

'There won't be a penny coming in from the crop to meet even the interest. I dropped Colonel Rutherford a note last week to tell him so.'

'There's a letter from him in the mail,' Lucina said. Cavin followed her inside.

She leaned over his arm as he unfolded the single sheet, holding it close to the lamp to read.

'I've been in New Orleans.' The easy handwriting stood out black and sharp on the heavy white paper. 'What kind of gambler do you take me for, Cavin? Besides, who am I to set myself against the Lord?'

That was all. Lucina could feel Cavin's courage pouring back into him. She leaned against him, warmed by the content she had felt ever since the day she had watched him, strong and alive, running toward her across the oatfield.

'Jeremiah ought to make a good overseer,' he began to plan. 'Why don't we let him live in this house when we leave it? He'll be finding him a wife pretty soon; or he will, if he's got as much sense as I think he has.'

Lucina smiled gently and rubbed her face against Cavin's sleeve. She was learning how to take his sentences apart in order to discover the thought of her that was often wrapped up in them, unsuspected even by himself.

Early in January they moved from Philip's long gray dwelling to the hill, where a fair copy of the white house on Cedar Ledge was being completed.

Lucina was jubilant as she drove up the sandhill and down the avenue, that was yet little more than a wagon track through weeds. 'It's the same,' she thought at first. 'No, not quite,' she added quickly. 'Not quite.'

To allow for the heat of the Texas summers, the house had been built higher off the ground than the one she remembered; and, instead of an upper verandah running full across the length of the house, two overhanging rooms rested on the square, white pillars that in Georgia had supported a verandah alone. Susanna, however, would have recognized the side-lights at the door and the fan above it, as well as the long central hall opening onto a verandah identical with the one facing the driveway. In general outline, Lucina saw, the house was almost a complete reproduction of the one she had grown up in, in Georgia.

She paused, as she mounted the three steps, instead of the

one which at Cedar Ledge had separated the low verandah of the house from the ground. What was it that this entrance door lacked? It did not take her long to remember. Climbing on a chair, she sketched, below the fan, the wavering outline of stars and a moon that Uncle Abner, so long before, had carved above the Georgia doorway.

'You see,' she explained to Jeremiah, 'it looks like this.' She turned around anxiously. 'Where's the paint? There's blue here' — she ran her hand around the curving lines of the fan — 'a deep, misty blue, like the night.' She told him what Uncle Abner's idea had been, as she had heard it from her mother. 'And the same up there,' she said, pointing to the gallery's ceiling.

Jeremiah smiled up at her with his slow, steady smile. 'I see,' he said.

The next week, when she entered the door for good, Lucina had the impression that the house on Cedar Ledge had been transposed, only slightly altered, to Texas. From that time on, she began to think of the Brazos without always remembering the hideous, armored alligators that bellowed in it, or the huge, fat spiders, with groping hairy legs, that lived in damp under-brush.

'Maybe we'd better finish the attic,' she suggested to Cavin, when he came in at three o'clock, for his first dinner in the new dining-room. 'We're going to need a schoolroom and a governess, and, later on, a tutor for all these children.'

'Yes,' he agreed, 'that's so.' He lifted Beau from her arms to his. 'How you goin' to like studying, boy?' he asked the child who nuzzled his dark head under his father's chin. 'You'll have to learn enough for yo' pa, too,' Cavin warned his son, holding him high above his head and shaking him while he gurgled.

He set Beau down, and laying his hand on the door through which floated the aroma of spicy cashew and barbecued pork, turned interested, amused eyes on Lucina.

'They tell me the army's setting up schools for colored children. I'm going to advise Jake to send his Josh to one of them, when he gets bigger.'

She smiled, and opened her eyes wide. 'Really?'

'Well, why not?' he demanded. 'If the government's bound to turn the po' niggers loose, helpless, they ought to teach 'em to take care o' themselves, and that means some kind of education, I suppose.'

He lifted his hand, this time with more determination, and drew Lucina through the door with him.

'Well, as old Mr. Tripp Cuttross always says: "One thing at a time! One thing at a time!"' She took her seat beside him at the pine table they had brought over from Philip's.

The children were outside on the long back gallery, and they were alone. Halfway through the meal, he took up their earlier conversation.

'Why don't you ask Margaret to come out and teach the children?' he asked, splitting and buttering a triangle of the hot corn bread that was always placed at his elbow. Lucina saw that the idea grew in his mind, as he thought of it. 'Didn't you say Shelby was going to marry Vivian Carter?'

'Well,' Lucina temporized, 'I hadn't meant to tell you, till she got here.'

'Got here?' Cavin demanded, with startled interest. 'What do you mean?'

'I wrote her to come out if she could — as soon as I knew I wouldn't be able to take care of the children this winter.' Her voice was low and Cavin leaned forward, his fork held in mid-air, and his eyes riveted on her troubled face, while the possible meaning of her remark penetrated his mind.

'The devil!' he groaned. Aghast, he pushed his plate aside and leaned closer. 'The devil!' He stared at her in dismay.

'Yes,' she said calmly, and raised her lids. 'Don't look like that, Cavin.' Pouring herself out a glass of water, she drank it down slowly, but suddenly her composure left her. Rising from his chair, he lifted her into his arms and his grasp tightened fiercely around her. 'If I'd been making this world, Lucy,' he exclaimed bitterly, 'God knows I'd have made it a different place!'

She lifted her head and looked despairingly at him.

'It can't be any worse than it was before.'

But it was soon apparent that it would be at least as bad. By the end of January, she no longer even inquired how Beau was, but lay on her bed in a stupor of pain and dreary weakness. This time, David thought, she seemed less inclined than before to exert any energy. If he could have read her mind, he would have known that the certainty of all that lay ahead of her reduced her spirit to a hopeless level.

'There's a doctor at San Antonio I'd like to consult,' David told Cavin. 'He's a teacher of mine, out here from Charlottesville for his health.'

'Write him,' Cavin replied instantly. 'Write him at once.' He glared angrily at David. 'The Creator's foot slipped when he thought up this way of keeping the race going,' Cavin declared. 'I could have done better myself.'

A smile appeared momentarily on David's sober young face. 'I've heard that before, Cavin,' he said. 'Your idea's not original.'

Cavin felt the confused irascibility that always overtakes active natures not given to abstract thinking in the face of some disaster that only time can cure. He had no answers to the questions which tormented him like gnats in the back of his brain;

in fact he did not even formulate clearly the dissatisfaction that possessed him. He felt beaten by a combination of circumstances that he did not know how to defeat; and, uninclined as he was to indulge in speculation, yet he turned, with a kind of sullen fury, against any order of nature that afflicted Lucina.

In his mail that day there was a letter from Colonel Rutherford suggesting a Conservative convention in Houston late in the month. The next morning, he set out in a cold rain across the prairie.

'Take care of her,' he said to David. Desperately he resolved that at least he could make the state fit and safe for her to live in; and in action he found, as always, a relief to his tension.

Lucina was hardly aware that he had gone, for the misery that afflicted her body had produced in her mind a melancholia so acute that she felt life was hardly worth struggling for. Too weak to care very much whether the doctor from San Antonio could do anything for her or not, she was too despairing even to hope that he might.

One morning early in February, David entered Lucina's room and found Margaret there taking capable charge. He smiled, first in relief, and then in surprise.

'We were expecting to hear from you,' he said, guessing at once who she was.

'My letter would have come on the same boat I did,' she replied. 'When I got off at Galveston, and heard there was a Democratic convention going on in Houston, I took the first train over, expecting to find Cavin there. I did,' she smiled, 'and he sent me back with Jeremiah. Here I am,' she concluded.

David's eyes dwelt on her in warm approval, and he gestured toward the door. She followed him outside. He studied her a moment gravely and decided she could bear the truth. 'She seems to have no resistance left,' he said, waving his hand toward the closed door. 'No hope she'll ever improve.'

'I'll encourage her,' Margaret replied, meeting his gaze without flinching. 'She'll get better.'

And, indeed, Margaret seemed to supply the assurance that gradually began to conquer her sister's depression. She told Lucina how much in love Shelby and Vivian were, how John was studying to learn enough to go into politics and be governor of Georgia some day, how Cedar Ledge looked with its coat of fresh paint. Lucina listened and, leaning her spirit on her sister's strength, soon felt her own resolve rising hesitantly within her. But she still looked like a very sick woman when Cavin returned from Houston a few days before the election.

David tried to rally him out of his discouragement. 'At least, you can be glad you aren't in bed with a broken hip!'

'That's all I can be glad about, then,' Cavin retorted. He surveyed his friend with desperate eyes. 'What use are doctors?'

'I've asked myself that,' said David slowly. 'Tell me about the meeting.'

'It was hopeless, of course,' Cavin returned, shrugging his shoulders. 'We're bound to lose this election. Half the decent people didn't even try to register last summer and fall. What chance on earth is there of getting them accepted now when Pease is appointing negro registrars right and left?' He sat down heavily and turned a glum face to David. 'She looks worse'n she did when I left.'

When the returns from the election came in toward the end of February, 1868, Cavin studied them with bitter care.

'We've lost, of course,' he said to Margaret, 'and it's certain the negroes know damn well what the election means. They are all over the roads now, carrying pistols and bowie knives.'

All through March, he went about oppressed by a gloomy foreboding that was accentuated both by Lucina's failure to improve and by the substitution at New Orleans of yet another Commanding General to rule over them — two changes in a few months.

'They treat us the way a cat does a mouse,' he thought in morose resentment, and began to wonder whether open battle would not be preferable to continued submission.

'Not yet,' his common sense told him. 'Not yet. When things get so bad people'd as soon die as live — then'll be the time.'

His anxiety was too deep to permit him even to rejoice that, by April, Lucina began to enjoy hours of ease and to show a slight improvement which continued, with several setbacks, through the spring months. By June, when the new Convention, composed almost entirely of Radical delegates, assembled in Austin, she was moving weakly about, able to be up all day.

She had ceased to wonder that Cavin's mind seemed to have no room for any other thoughts than those of political expediency. Now, all at once she herself realized there were twice as many negroes in the county as there were whites.

The hands on Cavin's plantations, however, seemed to give no thought to anything that was going on. He put their continued tractability down to the fact that he refused to allow a restless negro to stay on his place, or to return, if once put off it. And his negroes knew, even if Matt and Jake had not often reminded them of the fact, that the Freedman's Bureau was far less generous to good hoe hands than Cavin was.

He wished many times, that June, as the Convention got under way, that William were still alive for him to consult. But William had dropped off to sleep one blustering night in January and had never waked again. Cavin thought sometimes that he missed him as much as he did Philip.

'No sense to the way they're carrying on up at Austin, Lucy,' Cavin grumbled, studying with painful care the first dispatches that came out from the Convention. 'They're still trying to decide whether laws passed under the Confederacy are valid.' Then he rose from his chair in utter horror. 'My God-a-mighty!' he roared in a voice shaking with anger, 'they're proposing to make us all pay enough taxes to distribute a bonus to every Texas Unionist. And if they don't get enough out of us that way, they say they're going to divide the state and sell off a part of it to pay for increasing their own doggone salaries.' His paper fell from his hands and he stared at Lucina in stark amazement. 'They call themselves reformers!'

'West Texas, they claim, has a right to secede!' he went on. 'That's too much for even some of the Radicals to stomach.' He laughed aloud, but it was a bitter laugh. 'A bunch of Radicals turned Secessionists!'

By July, the feeling in the county had become so intense that the men gathered late one night at Locust Hill for a conference. As David stepped up on the gallery, Cavin drew him aside.

'David, they say the Convention's actually turned loose all the colored convicts.'

David nodded. 'I was going to tell you. Last night one of our own negroes came back — a negro Judge White sent up several years ago for murdering his wife. He told me two hundred and forty-seven convicts were let loose when he was. God knows what the truth is.' He leaned back against the white pillar behind him and a slow smile crossed his face. 'I'm not saying his wife didn't deserve it, Cavin. Henry's really a good nigger; he wouldn't hurt a fly. The convicts can't be any worse than the soldiers we've got quartered on us.'

'That's the truth,' Cavin assented, and, turning, faced the men assembled on his gallery. Their horses were tied at the gate, and, in the stillness, he could hear their slow, heavy breathing and the creaking of the saddles on their backs. He began to speak, holding his temper down. The facts seemed to him sufficiently inflammatory to require no comment.

'Here,' he said, holding up a folded sheet in the semi-darkness, 'is the report turned in to the Convention by the Committee on Lawlessness. Have you all read it?'

'I presume,' answered young Thomas Abernethy, rising, 'that we are the men to whom it refers — "the disloyal, desperate men intent on murdering Union men, on intimidating the freedmen and on protecting their own members from the military courts."' He had read the report so many times that day that the words rolled easily off his lips.

His listeners stamped their feet in vigorous approval, and old Mr. Archibald Bland stood up, pulling on the long tails of his coat as he spoke. He held his heels closely together and rocked energetically on them, but his thin, wheezing voice neither rose nor fell.

'Smarter than I thought they were, gentlemen. By jiminy, a good deal smarter. They've got it figured out about right, I should say.'

Old Mr. Joseph O'Fallon was sitting on the steps with his back hunched up against a pillar, and around him were grouped a number of other men. Cavin ran his eyes over this group. He could see them fairly well, now, for the night was radiant with starlight, which covered the men on the gallery with a subdued, unreal illumination only a little less vivid than that of the moon.

He was aware that for some time there had been forming in the bottoms a band of men without money or resources who had

drifted in from all sections of the South, anxious to repair or
acquire their fortunes while they could be fairly safe from the
law. In the state that Texas was now in, what officer would
pause to arrest a man for petty stealing, or who would protest
if funds derived from gambling in New Orleans or Indian
Territory were used to buy up land on which the taxes remained
unpaid? Was there not in Cypress County right now land to be
had for a dollar an acre, land as rich as Egypt? The Army
of Occupation knew it, and so, he thought, did these men. Here
was an opportunity that might never be repeated for landless
soldiers to get a foothold up in the world. Obviously they would
have no desire to divide pickings like these with an enemy they
had fought on the battle field. In his own mind, Cavin was
positive that some of the men facing him belonged to these
bands of adventurers.

He saw, too, by his brief glance, that some of the men in
front of him were small white owners of prairie land and a few
others, tenants. He knew that their right to the possession of
their one mule and a few chickens had been no more rigorously
respected by the Northern soldiers than the planter's right to
his many mules and many fowl. All around them, now, these
small farmers and tenants were seeing black men and carpet-
baggers elevated to posts they might well have expected to
fill themselves. Repeated experiences of this kind had convinced
most Texans with white skins, whether planters, tenants, or
robbers, that they had common cause, temporarily at least.

'How about introducing us to your friends, Mr. O'Fallon?'
Cavin suggested when he had finished his brief scrutiny. Old
Joseph shuffled his feet and seemed to be considering his
answer.

'Ain't hardly no need to call names, I reckon, Mr. Darcy,'
he said, hesitating. 'To tell the truth,' he drawled, 'most of

'em ain't usin' their own names. They ain't no fonder o' interference in their business, though, than the rest o' us is. You can count on that.' He sat staring at the worn toes of his boots and then lifted his candid gaze to Cavin's. 'I ought to tell you, they're all more'n tol'able shots.'

Cavin eyed them carefully. He was by now convinced that the desperadoes who were beginning to operate in the bottom were gathered together, here on his gallery. They were more fearless than the Yankees, he knew, and were bound to cause trouble as soon as they acquired a little more confidence. Already they had held up Colonel Rutherford on the prairie and had made off with his best horses which they had promptly sold to a high officer in the Freedman's Bureau at Galveston. The Colonel swore with determination, proficiency, and fluency every time he saw his horses pulling the Union officer's carriage.

Cavin turned to the planters grouped around Colonel Brashear, who sat next the door.

'What do you say, gentlemen?'

His own mind had immediately snapped to a decision. They needed reinforcements on any terms. These lawless men could be dealt with later on, when the Yankees had been disposed of.

Colonel Brashear arose and walked over to the group of strangers. He leaned close, giving them a long, thorough inspection which they returned with interest. They formed a curious collection of men. Not one of them, Colonel Brashear judged, was over thirty; all were hard-faced, with tanned, leathery complexions, against which, even in the starlight, their enigmatical eyes stood out very bright and piercing. Their broad, white hats, with rolled-up brims, were pushed back off their faces, and, tucked inside their muddy, spurred boots, they wore battered trousers, topped by checked gingham jumpers, unbuttoned at the throat and hanging loose over the hips. Their waists were encircled by cartridge belts, and some of them had tied blue or red handkerchiefs around their necks. Every single man sat with his feet well apart, poised for instant rising on his high heels.

Colonel Brashear studied the faces before him until his eye had picked out the man who appeared to be the leader of the group. His name, he had heard, was Warren Hughes, and now he noticed, with some surprise, that he carried his head well. Then Colonel Brashear's black eyes narrowed till only a gleam of light came through them, like a quick spark of fire in the night.

'Where are my mules I lost last week?' The question was pumped out with a ferocity that promised little for the alliance Cavin had in mind. Involuntarily, he turned, throwing out a warning hand toward the man whom Colonel Brashear had addressed.

He was a lithe individual, not very tall, with a reckless expression and a sharp, defensive glance. He arose, with a shrug and a bow that included both Cavin and Colonel Brashear. As quickly as Cavin, he had grasped the virtue of the arrangement under discussion. There was plenty of good stealing to be had from the Federals, even from the negroes at present. And there was plenty of deserted land in the county too, to be had now without a fight. Later, when his men had gained more strength, they could take over the black river plantations if they wanted to.

He returned Cavin's gesture, holding up his own thin hand with a polite smile of appreciation as if to admit that he and Cavin fully understood one another. Then he addressed the Colonel, using a voice which his men failed to recognize. Colonel Brashear's mind, however, clicked as he heard it.

'Tidewater! How in hell'd he get in with this gang?' But his eyes never wavered.

The young leader held himself erect, well set on his feet, and was speaking in a surprised, inquiring tone.

'How should I know, sir, where your mules are?'

His lips broke over his evenly spaced teeth in an ingratiating, impudent smile.

'You might just look in your barn in the morning, though, Colonel,' he suggested. 'They might happen to wander back.'

His cool gray eyes moved from one stern and forbidding face to another. The men in front of him had as yet given no sign of their purpose, but he did not underestimate how far he could push them. He made another polite, swinging bow, which took in every man in the group around Colonel Brashear.

'That goes for all of you, gentlemen, all of you — until we've got rid of the damned ravening pests that infest this county. My men hate 'em as much as you do. Besides,' he chuckled significantly, 'they get in our way.'

Colonel Brashear was still standing. Now he leaned across Mr. Archibald Bland's shoulders, and gave Cavin his decision.

'I vote to take 'em on,' he said, with decision, and sat down.

David spoke from his chair, gently and nonchalantly. 'I'm voting with the Colonel.'

'How about the rest of you?' Cavin demanded.

There was an intense stillness on the gallery, which remained unbroken for some time. Cavin and Warren stood estimating one another's qualities. After a moment, Warren stepped forward.

'For the present,' he announced, 'I'm following your lead.'

'Gentlemen,' said Cavin, 'you all heard that remark?' He waited a moment.

'How do you vote?' he asked again. This time there was a concerted chorus of ayes.

Warren's lips quirked derisively. 'I better make myself clear. You notice I don't say how *long* I'll follow on a halter.'

Cavin studied him with an impassive face. 'You don't need to say,' he replied. 'Good night.'

Warren eyed him mockingly.

'Ah?' he inquired. 'Well, time will tell. Good night' — for the fraction of a second he hesitated — 'gentlemen.' With a flourish he swept his hat around the group, and, as he started toward his horse, his men rose in a body and followed him with steps as rapid as his.

Cavin was in Houston when his second son was born on the eighteenth of August, 1868. He had gone there to confer again with a group of Conservatives, expecting to return by the first week in the month; but the reports coming in from the Convention in session at Austin varied so sharply from day to day that the men gathered in Houston dared not separate until they knew what action the Convention would finally take. They began to suspect, at last, that the Radicals would disband before any agreement could be reached between the moderates under the leadership of the former Provisional Governor Hamilton and the extremists led by the President of the Convention, E. J. Davis.

'God knows they ought to disband,' Colonel Rutherford gasped when John McGaughey, whom the Conservatives had sent up to Austin to find out what he could, returned with his report. He had heard, he said, that the Unionists proposed to organize a loyal state militia to supplement the Federal troops already in Texas and to fill every office in the state with their own appointees.

'They ought to swing,' Colonel Rutherford again asserted, pale with fury, 'swing as high as Haman. The *Telegraph* is right,' he concluded, turning to Cavin and pointing to an editorial in that paper. 'If they try to arm our negroes against us, they ought to die.'

As the month wore on, it was apparent that since there were no more funds available to support the Convention, the Radicals at Austin would have to adjourn, without even agreeing on a constitution. The planters in Houston went home, then, on the last day of August, 1868. They too could mark time, they had decided.

Riding homeward, Cavin faced the truth. There was now no law in the state, no recognized authority of any kind. For the local Unionists had found the reconstructive fervor of even the Federal district commanders too mild for their tastes and had revolted against it, finally splitting into two unreconcilable camps themselves.

'It's every group for itself now, and the devil take the hindmost.' He shut his mouth in a straight, firm line. 'There's only one thing to do.'

He began to lay his plans. He would turn the group that had met on his gallery early in the summer into an active branch of the organization that General Forrest was sponsoring all over the South — an organization variously known as the White League, or the Knights of the White Camelia, or the Order of the White Rose, or — as was beginning to be common — the Ku Klux Klan. 'It's dangerous, of course.' His mind acknowledged the fact. 'It may turn out like a prairie fire — beyond control. But this is no time to be squeamish. Great God, no!' His mind ran on. 'What'll we call the group on the Brazos?' Considering the different possibilities, he rejected them all. 'Might as well keep on being The Helping Hand, or, better yet' — he threw his head back laughing at his own humor — 'The Hunter's Club. We can run that sort of notice in the *Signal*, right under their noses.'

Not until he was almost in sight of Locust Hill late that afternoon did he remember that his second child might have been born. Indeed, he had scarcely thought of his family since he had left them late in July in David's and Jeremiah's care.

He raised his quirt, and Derby plunged ahead. He was all at once in a fever of anxiety and fear. What would he find at Locust Hill, if he ever got there? He called to Jake riding behind him. 'Don't try to keep up with me.'

Jake whipped his horse till he was level with Cavin's ears.

'I'm gonna ride like de debbil, too, Mas' Cavin. I been worryin' 'bout Maria.'

Cavin drew his reins tight, and gazed questioningly at Jake. 'You too?' he asked. His shoulders shook.

'By all the saints, Jake! We are a fine couple of husbands. We don't even know how many children we've got.'

For a moment longer he held in his horse.

'The Lord help me! What she must be thinking!' The words escaped him, and Jake heard them.

'Maria, too,' he sighed dolefully, shaking his head. 'I'se skeered to see her!'

The two men looked for a long moment at each other; then simultaneously they laid themselves low on their horses' necks, spurring them on till their sides bled.

At sunset, they rode up the avenue and flung themselves stiff and weary to the ground. There, sitting on the front step was Maria, in her dark gray dress, with the glow from the western sky falling on her brown skin and turning it to a strange, coppery rose. She was nursing two babies, one white and one black, while Josh and Beau looked on, leaning against her.

Cavin paused, with Jake falling one step behind him. He was terrified, afraid to ask the question on his lips.

'Miss Lucy been lookin' fur you,' Maria said, and dropped her eyes to the babies in her arms. 'Mine's a week de oldes'.' Her smile was proud and possessive. She did not seem to notice Jake, who eyed her gingerly and cautiously. But as Cavin strode past her, not stopping so much as to glance at Beau, he heard Jake talking to his son in a low, affectionate rumble, and Maria's answering murmur.

At the door to Lucina's room, he paused, and laying both hands on the door-jamb, stood watching her. She was asleep; her hair was dark against the white bolster under her head, and her breast rose and fell in long, deep breaths. Moving quietly across the room, he stood over her, gazing down at her peaceful face. He had a fleeting, indefinable impression that her own spirit had again resumed the flesh so long pre-empted by her child's demands. Slowly she opened her eyes, and seeing Cavin, smiled uncertainly at him.

He stooped and laid his head on her breast. 'You must hate me,' was all he could say. She made no answer until she had put her arms around his shoulders, and pushed his face up till it was level with her own. Then before she spoke, she lay looking at him, while an expression he had never seen in her eyes gathered there. 'I did at first,' she admitted at last, 'but not now.'

'How could I bring up children in a state run over with Yankees?' she asked him. 'How could I? Tell me that.' Pulling his head down again, she laid her cheek comfortably against his. 'He's not as pretty as Beau was.'

Cavin felt a desperate uncertainty seizing him; he knew that he was going either to laugh or cry, and he chose the first alternative. His whole body shook and Lucina's with it, as he raised her to him, covering her with his broad shoulders.

'Lucy,' he began, and his amusement choked him. 'I don't even know his name.'

She laughed with him. 'We'll have to think up something to call him.'

He kissed her with such long tenderness that she was certain he had forgotten the child. But soon she realized he had not.

'I've always admired old Nathaniel for going up into the mountains, the way I've heard you tell about,' he said slowly. 'Nathaniel — Nathaniel Lyttleton Darcy. How's that?' He laid her back on her pillows. 'I better go take a look at him.'

Chapter 19

COUNTING Nathaniel, there were now eight children under Lucina's roof. It was true that she divided their care with Aunt Elvy and Maria, who undertook, as the old woman told her one day, to 'wash and watch' their charges, leaving 'the praying and the learning' of them to their mother. But Lucina, of course, carried the responsibility for their upbringing; and she was nearly always oppressed by a vague, lowering fear of what might happen to them. For, despite the most vigilant watchfulness, hardly a day passed that some child did not give her a bad fright. Once Felicia and Letitia were lost for several hours in the thick woods back of the house, where wildcats with shining, green eyes roamed at night; once Philip stepped under a horse's hoof; and, another day, FitzHugh fell into the deep underground cistern over which he had leaned to call down a taunting echo to the old devil who, he confidently believed, lived there. Lucina tried to teach herself to stop anticipating such dangers, but back deep in her mind she was never free from a sense of anxiety and haunting strain.

'Suppose,' she asked herself, 'suppose Jake had not heard FitzHugh floundering in the water? Suppose Matt had not hauled Philip back?' She felt sometimes as if any personality she had ever possessed was being slowly ground and shredded into bits between the children's claims.

She knew that they did not weigh upon Cavin's mind as they did upon hers. He seemed to feel some certainty about them that she never possessed.

'Make 'em all drink their pot-likker, down their quinine, and say their prayers,' he always answered cheerfully, whenever she asked his advice about them. 'They'll be all right.' One thing only seemed to worry him — that one of them might step on a nail and die of lockjaw, as he had once watched a colored child do. Sometimes, he would come back as he was leaving the house to remind her not to let the children take off their shoes. This one evidence of anxiety both amused and comforted Lucina — amused her because, coming from Cavin, it was so unexpected, and comforted her because she felt a desperate need of someone to share the uncertainty that oppressed her day and night.

Sometimes she wondered why, at her age, she had been given charge of all these children not her own, and whether she would ever find the wisdom and strength she needed to meet all their needs. There were moments, days, when she felt strong and competent; at other times she was weary and irritable, full of nerves and that strange depression which so often overtakes mothers.

It seemed to her that she did not recognize herself in all the rôles that she had been called upon to fill in Texas. She had even a new name, which she heard much oftener than she did her own, for all the children had taken to calling her Nannie. Lucina had wanted Letitia's children to remember her as their own mother, and had tried to teach them to call her, Lucina, Auntie — a word which Beau as well as they quickly twisted into Nannie. Anxious also to keep Philip's memory alive in his children's minds, she had urged the twins to address Cavin as Brother. To her surprise, Beau found that title also pleasing

and could not be persuaded to give it up, while the twins persisted in calling their brother Papa. It was a confusion that was
never cleared up, for in the end, Cavin's own children regularly
referred to him as Brother, his brothers and sisters as Papa.
Finally, even Lucina gave up trying to persuade them to do
otherwise.

Cavin was apt to lump all the children together in his mind
almost as he did his young calves. But Lucina understood that
already they were developing traits and personalities which at
times deeply perplexed her.

The oldest twins, now eight years old, were twins only in
name, she often told herself. They could scarcely have differed
more widely in appearance or disposition, for Felicia's head was
as dark and steady as Letitia's was fair and restless. Some
intangible, hidden bond, however, united them, Lucina judged,
for, if one fell ill, the other was certain soon to come down with
the same ailment.

'And FitzHugh!' Lucina often exclaimed. 'What a strange
child he is!' Still, he was growing steadily stronger and developing a passion for curing sick animals. He was always bringing
in a pet to be nursed back to health, and once — to Cavin's
utter amazement — he had coaxed the life into a chicken that a
cow had stepped on. For several days he had sat by the poor
creature watching it with the listening, intent expression that,
Cavin recalled, always appeared on Philip's face whenever he
was called in to see a very sick patient. The child had Philip's
clear-cut features, his misty eyes, but Letitia's light, waving
hair. Lucina felt closer to him than to any of the children
except Beau.

'Then there's Philip and Philippa!' Lucina's thoughts would
run on, 'as much like one another as the other twins are
different.'

Both of them had inherited not only Philip's ways, but his looks also. Sometimes at bedtime, when they resisted Aunt Elvy's authority, standing adamant at first and then yielding without fuss when they saw they must, the old woman would turn to Lucina and exclaim: 'My Lawd! Seems lak Mas' Philip's sperit's done come back in de flesh!' And Lucina would nod. Sometimes she felt the same way.

It was James on whom she spent the most anxious thought, however — James Barclay, whom they had brought home from Little Creek Plantation and still had with them. He was now nearly five, a boy with a graceful, winsome air, a thin, dark face, eyes so deep they were almost black, and thick, curling hair. 'Now what are we to do with him?' Lucina asked herself many times, never once knowing the answer.

About Beauford, she felt none of the perplexities that often puzzled her regarding the other children, for she understood him with a clarity of intuition which she could not explain even to herself. She could tell, days before, when he was coming down with some illness, and she loved him with a passion that was more like agony than joy, loved his dark hair, his way of suddenly darting a smile at her from out the narrow corner of his flashing, blue eyes. She always felt, whenever she looked at him, that she held him by some precarious title and that, if she relaxed her vigilance for an instant, he might slip away into the darkness out of which she had drawn him, with so much peril and pain.

With her first child Lucina had been conscious of creation moving stubbornly through her, striving to take shape in her weary, reluctant flesh. But that same sense of exaltation never fell upon her before Nathaniel's birth; and, though she loved her second son with a deep and steady tenderness, which even she suspected was more normal than her feeling for Beau, yet the sight of him never stirred her so deeply and strangely as did the briefest glimpse of her first-born.

Cavin, however, she soon began to see, recognized in his second child his own impulses springing to life; and because this child was well and sturdy from the beginning, he was able to handle him with the natural, spontaneous ease that Beau's troublous babyhood had prevented.

Every morning, now, when Margaret led the older children up into the garret, which Cavin had fitted up as a schoolroom with desks and blackboards and slates, Lucina would wonder what she would have done if her sister had not come out to Texas. It was fortunate, she thought, that Shelby had married. Margaret could see that she was more needed now at Locust Hill than at Cedar Ledge; and her visit lengthened out imperceptibly until, at length, she stopped even talking of sailing back to Georgia.

The equilibrium which wiser men on both sides had been trying to build up for three years in the state crashed to the ground in the fall of 1868, as Cavin, the previous summer, had foreseen that it must. All that season he had been busy organizing the band of men who had gathered on his gallery in July. Since most of them had been soldiers, they found it easy to transfer to the Hunter's Club the habit of acting in concert and responding to orders. Therefore, by fall the organization had developed into a tight, effective unit which the Unionists at Galveston knew enough not to despise. Soon they began to suspect that Cavin was the head of the opposition they were so actively encountering in Cypress County; and, therefore, night after night for weeks during the fall they sent soldiers to search his home.

For the time being, then, he turned his post over to old Mr.

Joseph O'Fallon — a man whose sympathies the Yankees would not be likely to guess, and whose leadership the white tenants would be certain to welcome — and for several weeks made it a point to be home asleep in bed every night, rather enjoying the game of hide and seek. It always amused him to hear the Yankees talking. They seemed to think the men wore their strange white garb in order to hide behind it, whereas the truth was they had adopted it in order to frighten the super-stitious darkies. Sometimes it even amused him to watch the soldiers throwing open closets and drawers looking for his own regalia, which he knew was simply a sheet and a handkerchief plucked at random from the stacks of white linen on Lucina's shelves.

Lucina, however, found nothing to smile about in the soldiers' visits. She came to loathe them as she would have a roving pest of rats or locusts. At last, they gave up coming. Then Cavin again resumed his command and was again gone nearly all night, leaving Jeremiah on guard at Locust Hill when he was away.

Sometimes during that fall — the most uncertain and danger-ous since she had come to Texas — Lucina wondered how it was that she had become enough accustomed to perpetual fear to wear it so lightly. If she had counted her years — she was barely twenty-one — she might have been surprised that she was not yet an old woman, so long ago did her girlhood seem to her.

There were times even now, though, when she forgot her anxieties and felt again the irrational happiness which had glowed within her, that morning during her first months in Texas, when she had sat in the wagon watching Cavin at work in the rattlesnake den. The whole autumn of 1868 her spirits rose — why she could not possibly have explained. Certainly the circumstances of her existence and the conditions that surrounded her were not such as to invite the exuberance she felt even through the slow, chilly rains of fall.

The first two weeks of October reminded her of the weather she had endured on her first trip across the prairie. The month came in with a sudden squall of cold blustering wind which sent the rain beating in gusty force against the windows. One afternoon she was sitting in the warm sun on one end of the gallery, when, around the other end, she felt a sudden rush of cold air out of the black clouds that had been gathering all afternoon in the north. For a few days after that, Jake had to build fires night and morning; and even in the daytime the chickens climbed high in the chinaberry trees to roost, mistaking the dull gray skies for the lowering night. Hour after hour they would perch there, outside Lucina's window, with the water pouring off their drooping feathers.

But now, however, she had been long enough in Texas to expect the weather soon to break, as it did. October came to an end with a week of the cool and brilliant air which always induced in her a kind of ecstasy and sharpened apprehension of all she saw and felt. The persimmons hanging ripe and orange between shrivelling yellow leaves seemed to her miraculously lovely; and the haze that floated across the horizon every evening always aroused in her a heightened awareness that her own life was a legacy from all the others before her who had paused at dusk, as she was doing, to watch blue smoke rising off the ground. Ruth among her sheaves, she thought, Greeks, Romans, Englishmen, and her own people in Georgia and, further back yet, in Virginia — all these must often have stood still, at the end of a day, taking in the beauty that hangs, so evanescent and wraithlike, over the world at dusk — over prairie and cotton field, over deep, slow bayous, and dark, drooping live-oaks.

'What does it matter,' she thought, 'whether they let us vote for President or not? Grant's certain to be elected anyway.' She knew Cavin was bitterly resentful of the order posted at Galveston announcing that there would be 'no election for President and Vice President in the State of Texas,' and 'no assemblages, proceedings, or acts' toward that end tolerated. But, as for herself, she put such matters aside and all day drew in her breath, exultantly tasting the cool, sweet air. One morning she sat with Beau under the leaves just beginning to turn faintly red and yellow where the sun sifted through, and thought that she would not be surprised to see fauns and dryads springing up out of the woods behind her.

The field hands, too, seemed to respond to the excitement of the changing season. They came one night, at the close of cotton-picking, to ask Cavin whether they might not begin their revival meeting in time for a baptizing before the river ran cold with winter rains.

The Bishop disapproved of these meetings, but Cavin took them for what they were — a festival of rejoicing when the crops were in, a festival (though he did not so think of it) as old as time. He liked old Uncle Arthur, the colored preacher, who, rotund and important in the long black coat that Philip had provided for him, came up to the house to talk about the revival.

'When do you want to begin your meeting, Uncle Arthur?' Cavin asked him, jotting the day down in his notebook.

The next Sunday when he and Lucina entered the bare, little church, the seats were already full of eager mourners. Beau and Nath would some day own this place, Lucina thought and — the idea gave her pleasure — they, in their turn, would then

be opening the annual revival meeting on Locust Hill Plantation, and shaking each darky's hand as he came up fresh and
dripping from baptism.

Cavin waited until Lucina was seated on the front bench
reserved for them, then ascended the low platform raised only a
few inches off the floor. He was wearing a pepper-and-salt suit
of Philip's which, a few months before, he had had cut down to
fit his more youthful frame; and, in deference to the occasion,
he had refrained from tucking his trousers inside his boots. A
thin black tie, like the one Judge White wore, flowed from under
his narrow collar, its long ends meeting his white, pleated shirt-
front. His clean-shaven face was firm and ruddy, and his almost
honey-colored hair was brushed back behind his small ears, as
though to get it out of his way. Lucina looked up at him, giving
him her undistracted attention.

'Why, he seems older,' she thought, noticing for the first time
how his jaw had squared and his lips tightened under the stress
of the past two years.

Sitting there, now, on the hard bench below Cavin, with the
negroes grouped behind her, Lucina wondered what he would
find to say to his people on this occasion. She looked around at
the dingy, unpainted walls, at the flickering lamps in rusty
brackets which cast a pale, uncertain light over the women
dressed in every shade of startling color, over the men in blue
and faded denim with bright handkerchiefs tied around their
necks. To Cavin, the negroes' eyeballs looked staring white, as,
in the semi-darkness, he gazed down into the faces raised expectantly toward him. The silence was unbroken, but, beating
against it, he felt the strong excitement of those who would soon
be wrestling in mortal anguish with their old adversary, Satan.

The negroes had pasted vari-colored tissue paper over the
window-panes — paper saved out of boxes shipped into Galves-

ton from London, from all the ports of the earth — but most of
the windows were thrown wide open to the fall night. Outside,
Lucina could hear the south wind moving in long, sibilant
sighs through the moss that hung thick on the trees; and the
river, flowing to the sea, made a faint lapping, gurgling noise
against the ferryboat tied close beside the church.

Between the river and the church was the slaves' graveyard.
For an instant a clear picture of it flashed into Lucina's mind
— the clean-swept paths, the unpainted wooden cross above
each mound with a name marked upon it, the broken pieces
of bright crockery and glass laid upon each grave, the rooster
feathers and charms hung upon each cross. Then she brought
her attention back to Cavin, who was standing, with easy
composure, before his people, who, in any emergency, would be
certain to turn to him for relief before they so much as thought
of calling on the distant God they had assembled to importune.

Cavin seemed to absorb the confidence they reposed in him.
His eyes found Uncle Arthur's, and, as he raised his hand, the
quiet that already prevailed except for a steady shuffling of
many feet, became yet more profound.

'Uncle Arthur, ask the Lord's blessing,' Cavin said simply.

Lucina slipped to her knees, admitting to herself that, for all
her white skin, she was as ignorant and lost in this strange
world as any of the black people praying there under the old
preacher's outstretched hands.

'Yea, Lord!' Uncle Matt groaned from his seat. 'Yea, Lord!
Stretch out yo' mighty arm!'

Lucina stole a glance at Cavin through her locked fingers,
and, as she looked at him, her cheeks flushed and her eyes
softened. She was surprised at the warm, sweet excitement that
the sight of him aroused in her. Three years and more she had
been his wife. She could scarcely believe it.

She caught her breath and reminded herself that she was no girl; she was a woman with two children. She was in a negro church listening to Cavin address his servants; and the moss she was watching sway outside the window was stirred, not by winds from the Georgia mountains, but by the Gulf breeze blowing across the bald and empty Texas prairie.

Cavin held his audience still with a gesture.

'I've told you,' he began quietly, 'that you're free now.' His eyes moved from one face to another. He recognized them all — Aunt Mattie, the best nurse on his place; Aunt Elvy, his children's mammy; Aunt Emmy, the cook; big Ben, the pace-setter in the cotton row; young 'Lijah, just promoted to be head mule-tender; old George Ann and Uncle Gabe, the best sausage-makers in the county. Behind them were rows of other faces gleaming under the yellow light, and in the bench directly behind Lucina, Jake and Maria sat, with Matt, who had aged a good deal this year, between them.

'It's true,' he repeated. 'You are all free now — in one sense. But in another sense, you are not, and never will be; nor will I, nor was your old master.'

The negroes leaned forward, following him with close attention. They were startled by his last words, and their eyeballs rolled in their sockets as they turned to look at one another in incredulous amazement. Not free? Mas' Cavin and Mas' Philip not free? Whatever did Mas' Cavin mean by talking such foolishness?

'We are all of us — you, and me, and Miss Lucina and everybody else — servants, servants of one Lord,' Cavin explained.

An audible sigh of relief went up from the audience. Now they knew what Mas' Cavin was talking about. Hadn't Mas' Philip always told them the same thing — that, black or white, free or slave, they all served one Master, all had to do His bidding?

Cavin leaned across the pulpit, across the enormous Bible which rested there, although Uncle Arthur could not tell one word on its pages from any other. Just the same, regularly every Sunday morning he opened it, and recited ponderously from memory what he purported to be reading aloud, as he slid his heavy, black finger up and down the lines.

'The way I figure it out,' Cavin continued, 'is that Lijah, for instance' — he waited until he had drawn Lijah's attention from the slim, black girl who sat beside him — 'Lijah, over there, has a big job to do for the Lord in taking the best care he knows how of his mules; and Ben' — he raised his finger and levelled it at the large figure in the back of the room — 'Ben is serving the Lord when he keeps his cotton clean all summer.' He looked around the room. 'Whoever sticks at his proper business is glorifying the Lord,' he concluded. 'We're all His servants.'

'Amen!' Uncle Arthur's bass voice rolled through the church and was echoed back to him, as loud and vigorous Amens rose from all the benches.

Stepping down off the platform, Cavin offered Lucina his arm. Uncle Arthur held open the door for them to pass out into the night, suffused with the eery glow of suns swinging unimaginably far in space. The moon above the black tree-tops was hardly brighter than the single great star that burned low on the horizon.

'Lawd bless us!' they heard the negroes begin to moan, as they went down the steps. 'Lawd save us!' And soon the shrill, high shriek of women filled with a glorious vision, and shouting because of it, cut through the silent night air.

Cavin glanced at Lucina and began to chuckle, as he lifted her into the gig.

'That old rascal, Uncle Arthur! Before he left the other day,

I looked in the back of his wagon, and what do you think I saw?' His chuckle changed to open laughter. 'A couple of the biggest hams in our smokehouse!'

He stepped in beside her and drew the reins tight, while he bent over to look in her face. She had become accustomed to the darkness and she could see the twinkle that always appeared in his eyes before his deep, low laugh began to rumble over his lips. 'Looks like the louder Uncle Arthur prays, the better he steals,' he commented with no resentment.

He relaxed the reins, and the bay mare he was driving pricked up her thin, sensitive ears.

'She knows the way home,' Cavin said, knotting his lines around the whip socket. Turning, he put his arms around Lucina; but he took careful note of the mare's paces. 'I bet you she takes the ribbon this fall,' he predicted.

His glance swept upward across the sky, where the Milky Way streamed, a broad band of starry, iridescent mist. 'It's a pretty night, Sweet,' he said, drawing Lucina closer, feeling content in every bone. As much as one of the great live-oaks by the river, he belonged where he was; he, too, drew his strength from the rich, black soil under him — soil that had never known any plow but his. He was suddenly glad Lucina was his cousin as well as his wife, that the same blood flowed in their veins. He felt as if he drew in through the pores of his skin the delight that possessed him — delight in the starry night, in the damp, sweet air, in his own strength, in Lucina's fragrant hair against his lips. He always enjoyed the whiff of the delicate perfume that lingered about her head after Maria had brushed it with cologne or Florida water; and now he laid his lips lightly on her cheek and, then, with sudden eagerness, on her lips. Raising her eyes, startled out of her passive quiet, she took firm hold of his head with both her hands, and held his face away from hers.

'You forget, sir,' she teased him, 'that you are an old married man with two boys at home, a state to rescue, cattle to buy, and a mortgage to pay off.'

He looked down at her with deepening warmth and his usually silent tongue found husky words. 'I'm just your lover — your lover,' he repeated, and kissed her till the night whirled around her. She put her arms around his neck, and breathed a long sigh, as ahead of them the house loomed up white in the misty starlight.

They did not notice until they were almost at the gate that the gallery was full of robed figures, for, motionless in the shadows, they had melted against the walls.

Cavin jumped out of the gig. What was going on? He had called no meeting for tonight.

As Lucina sat watching, Warren Hughes, accompanied by another figure, walked toward Cavin. The young mare raised her head with ears sharply pricked forward, the way she always carried them past the graveyard, where, the negroes swore, she could see hants that were hid from them.

Warren spoke to Cavin with an open anxiety which Lucina could detect from her seat in the trap.

'Lucina,' Cavin said briefly, 'you have not met Mr. Hughes.'

Warren bowed gracefully. 'I am honored,' he said, and motioned toward his companion, who moved closer. 'I believe you are not acquainted with Mr. Barclay, either.'

Cavin started, looked closer and held out his hand. 'I've been sending you mail all over the country! Where've you been?'

'Oh, various places!' Frank replied non-committally. His lips smiled but not his eyes, and he watched Cavin guardedly.

'Ah!' said Cavin. 'You didn't get my letters, then?' He

touched Frank's arm. 'I'll have to see you after this business
is over.'

Then he turned with some asperity toward Warren. 'What's
going on here?' he demanded.

Warren's voice was low now and no longer bantering.

'I understand your people are starting a revival meeting?'
he began interrogatively.

'That's right.' Cavin watched Warren's face as, in the moonlight, it took on the stern, tight look with which the Hunter's
Club was familiar. 'What about it?'

'You know that damned son-of-a-gun, Weatherley? That
rascally carpet-bagger who lives with a yellow wench somewhere
down in the bottom and eats with the negroes — all to show his
Christian principles, he says?'

Cavin's face hardened, and he waved his hand with a barely
perceptible gesture backward.

'My wife's back there.'

Warren nodded understandingly and dropped his voice lower
yet.

'Well, he was ranting around half drunk with an insolent
bunch of black bucks in front of Mr. Rideout's store this evening;
and when Mr. Rideout warned him to move on, this Weatherley calmly raised his pistol and shot him — to show off before
his gang, I suppose. Anyway, that's what Miss Evelina thought.
She was inside talking to Byrnes Armstrong, and they had just
gone to the window to see what was happening, when her father
was shot down.' He paused, while Cavin waited, anxiously
leaning forward to catch the low words.

'I don't suppose even Weatherley would-a sicked his niggers
on to do what they did next,' Warren said, thoughtfully. 'They
must-a got away from him.'

'Go on,' Cavin urged him. 'What happened?'

'Well,' Warren continued, 'it seems that a couple o' Weatherley's black devils caught sight of Miss Evelina in her white dress
looking out of the window, but they didn't notice Byrnes. One
of 'em swaggered in at the door, laid his hand on her, and
asked her for a kiss, so her mother says, who entered through
the back hall just in time to see Byrnes taking aim. She thinks
he didn't see the second negro — a big, tall mulatto — who shot
him down and then made off hell-for-leather, with the whole
bunch galloping after him.'

The corners of Cavin's mouth were drawn down and his
nostrils were pinched in and white. 'How bad off are they?'
he inquired, holding his voice to a level tone.

'Evelina says Byrnes never moved after he fell. Mr. Rideout
lived about an hour — long enough to tell who shot him.'

Warren kept his eyes on Cavin. 'I heard, later on, that
Weatherley and his gang were figuring on stirring up the niggers
at your revival. They're counting, of course, on the military
never touching them, or else on a black jury freeing 'em.'
He reflected briefly. 'You just happen to be first, I suppose.
He's got some idea, I know, on organizing all the colored people
in the county, and offering them to the governor for state
militia.' A smile as bitter as it was brief crept up into his eyes
and curled his lips. 'I understand they are all paying him a
dollar a month, the poor ignorant fools, for belonging to his
uplift society.' Barely moving his hand toward the silent figures
grouped behind them, he explained, 'My men are all here, and
yours, too — as many as I could get word to.'

'There'll be the devil to pay,' Cavin said, glancing toward
the gallery.

Warren stood watching him, not moving. 'They're pretty
well worked up,' he agreed.

Cavin's voice quickened. 'Get your men together,' he said.
'We'll stop by David's.'

Then he remembered Lucina. 'I must take my wife inside,' he explained hurriedly. But she had passed by him as he talked, and now he noticed that she and Margaret were standing in the doorway.

Both of them knew that this was no ordinary emergency that had brought the men out. They heard Colonel Brashear remarking that his daughters were visiting in Galveston and Cavin asking him if he would, then, choose a few men and stand guard at Locust Hill; and while they were still ignorant of what had happened, they watched the white figures mounting their horses and vanishing into the darkness, Cavin somewhere amongst them.

Lucina listened till the last echo from the galloping hoofbeats had died away. As she stood there, straining to catch the least sound, she heard, in the chinaberry tree by the chimney, a screech owl's dismal hooting and, across the fields now shrouded in a dim gray mist, a dog's long desolate howling. Remembering that the negroes thought either sound foretold a death, she looked up at Margaret, wondering if she too recalled the old saying, and saw that she did.

Margaret put her arm around Lucina's shoulder, leaning protectively toward her, as if to receive first whatever danger there might be. She stood almost a head taller than Lucina, and the long white dress she wore accentuated her height. The graceful alertness with which she carried her head suggested a temperament not quite so composed as the lines of her face. Her hair — so like old Nathaniel's — was loose about her face, and her gray eyes were quiet. She might have been watching a reception or a ball from a comfortable chair along the wall.

Frank Barclay, standing in the shadow of a square, white column at the far end of the gallery, wondered idly, when his

glance fell upon them, who the two ladies were, in the doorway. Cavin's wife, he supposed and — he looked closer,
agitated by some quick emotion. What was it in the taller
figure that drew and held his attention until it merged suddenly into a sadness which he supposed he had conquered?
Yes, he admitted the fact; it was still true — the only women
who had ever attracted him were cut off from him, irretrievably
cut off.

He stood motionless, staring through the dark.

'Who is she?' he thought. He was about to put the question
to Colonel Brashear when, as the echo of the horses' feet died
completely away, the Colonel moved toward the doorway.

'Miss Margaret, I always forget you are a newcomer,' he
apologized. 'Have you met these gentlemen — Mr. Thomas
Abernethy, Mr. Ruthven Blakeley, Mr. Goodwin Breckinridge?
Of course you know Mr. Bland. Come over here, Frank.'
He motioned to the figure at the far end of the gallery. 'Let
me introduce Mr. Barclay, Miss Margaret — Miss Lucina's
sister,' he explained, somewhat belatedly.

Frank was almost six feet tall, with the assured carriage
and pleasing voice that his father had had before him. His
face was marred, however, by a mouth that drooped at one
corner, giving his whole countenance a definitely cynical cast.
But, to offset this first impression, his cold gray eyes sometimes
suddenly softened, suggesting that he was a man afflicted with
memories he did not care to share.

He took a deep breath. 'I have had the honor of meeting
Mrs. Darcy,' he said, and then plunged recklessly, heedlessly.
He had won big stakes in the past, he reminded himself, by
discarding the last vestige of caution.

'Will you sit out here on the gallery with me, Miss Margaret?' he asked. With a sidewise, graceful motion of his head,

he indicated two chairs drawn up where he had been standing. 'I have a lot to say to you, I think — I hope.'

Margaret moved a step backward and lifted her finely drawn eyebrows. Who was this impetuous young man?

Frank appealed to Colonel Brashear, using his most persuasive voice.

'Colonel, tell Miss Margaret I'm no ogre.' He took her hand and smiled at the Colonel, then at her.

Colonel Brashear noticed that, although Margaret was obviously puzzled and slightly displeased by this impulsive stranger, she had not withdrawn her slim hands from his.

'Well, Colonel?' Frank prompted, throwing across his shoulder a scornful warning that he would not beg for mercy. 'Tell her all you know.'

Colonel Brashear tapped his lips meditatively, and drew his black eyes half shut, before he answered.

'Miss Margaret,' he said at last, 'you can count on Frank's telling you the truth. Why don't you ask him to do so?'

Margaret had regained her composure.

'Yes, Colonel, I will,' she answered clearly, and turned her quiet gaze toward Frank.

He raised both her hands, then, and, with a sharp intake of his breath, looked straight into her steady eyes. 'It's true,' he said, 'I'll not deceive you. I've committed about every sin in the calendar and some that aren't there, besides; but I usually keep my word and tell the truth. If it's convenient to do so, of course,' he commented with a mocking gleam in his gaze. 'Now will you talk to me?' His voice pleaded with her, as he would not permit his words to do.

Margaret leaned over and touched her lips to Lucina's cheek. She knew that her sister wished this tempestuous young man were somewhere else.

'It's all right, darling,' she assured Lucina.

Then she stepped firmly out onto the gallery.

Colonel Brashear had a remark on the end of his tongue to make, but it was never uttered. For as he began to speak, he stopped, straightened his tall body, and listened intently, automatically dropping his hands on his pistols.

'What do you hear?' he asked her.

Lucina wished she could stop the beating of her heart, so as to make out better the faint sound that moved, shadow-like, through the darkness.

'Horses?' she whispered, after a moment's strained silence.

'Only two, I think,' he whispered back. 'Still, maybe you'd better get inside, and Miss Margaret, too.' Lucina's glance followed his in the direction of the couple at the end of the gallery.

Frank, she saw, was leaning far forward in his chair, with his dark head thrown back and his fingers clasped together. He sat in the dim light of the failing moon, Margaret in the shadow, and he was speaking rapidly, as if he feared she might get up and leave him before he had finished all he had to say.

'I'll have to disturb them.' The Colonel had taken two long steps in their direction when Lucina caught at his arm.

The sounds were closer now, and she heard the creak with which the big gate at the end of the avenue always swung open. It was a noise with which she had grown very familiar during the nights that she had lain awake expecting the Northern soldiers to come searching the house.

'Wait!' she cautioned the Colonel, and, keeping her hand on his arm, tried, with every sharpened sense, to identify the pace of the horses she first heard, and then saw, in front of her under the waning blue-gray light of the sky. 'They're out horses!' she exclaimed.

Her grasp relaxed. 'Why, it's Matt and Jake!' She watched them approaching, saw them spurring their mounts whenever their galloping slowed down, and, dropping the Colonel's arm, she ran down the steps to the gate. Colonel Brashear hurried after her.

'Uncle Matt?' Lucina almost gasped, leaning across the pickets to catch his reply. 'What's the matter?'

Matt made two or three ineffectual efforts to answer her, but his breath was coming and going, and Lucina saw that he could not yet utter the words he wanted to say.

She pushed on the gate and swung it open. 'Jake?' All the terror she had been suppressing that night was in the single word.

The younger negro had his breathing now under partial control, but his words tumbled out between long pauses. He reported that, in the middle of the revival meeting, a white man, with a company of negroes behind his back, had appeared in front of the little church and had begun exhorting the mourners.

'Lawd God! How he talked!' Matt broke in, now having partially recovered the use of his voice. 'The Lawd oughta struck him daid in his tracks, the way he talked!'

'Who was he? What did he say?' the Colonel inquired. No longer able to control his impatience, he began to reconstruct what he guessed had happened.

'Was he a Yankee, talking about loosening your chains? Was he?'

His hand fell again on Jake's shoulder in a tight grip and he explained to Lucina. 'That's how he usually begins, the confounded son-of-a-gun!' The words slipped out. 'I beg your pardon, Miss Lucy,' he apologized.

She flashed a straight look at the Colonel. 'What's his name? What's he doing on our place?'

She was dressed in white, like her sister, and had caught her heavy, dark hair back with a ribbon, instead of the net she had taken to wearing. She looked like a child, standing there in the faint light, with her indignant brown eyes turned up to the Colonel, and the color flaring in her cheeks.

'Weatherley's his name, I think; at least that's what he calls himself.' Colonel Brashear's lips moved contemptuously. 'He acts like he thinks he's old John Brown's spirit come to life. Am I right, Jake?' he questioned sharply. 'Was his name Weatherley?'

'Yas-suh, yas-suh. I hearn some o' de niggers sayin' dat was his name. He mus' be crazier'n a bedbug to talk de way he do.' Jake was plainly horrified at what he had heard. 'He down dar now promisin' all Mas' Cavin's niggers white houses to live in an' a lot o' land, an' hosses to ride instid o' mules, an — Lawd God, I'm skeered to tell it — white gals fur wives. Dar ain't nuthin' he ain't said! Nuthin'!' Jake concluded solemnly. 'De niggers wuz gittin' so worked up dat Matt an' me put out fur Mas' Cavin.'

'Whar is he, Miss Lucy, whar is he?' Matt demanded, still panting. 'He gotta git down to dat meetin' de fus' minute he kin.'

The Colonel said quietly: 'You'll have to know, Lucy. This Weatherley shot Mr. Rideout tonight, and one of the negroes with him killed Byrnes. Cavin and the rest of the men are out after his gang now. They expect to catch up with them at the church.'

Lucina put her hand to her heart and stared at the Colonel, speechless. Was it only yesterday she had congratulated herself on having gotten over being afraid all the time? — all the time, every minute of the day and night?

'It'll be like this, Colonel, it'll be like this ——' Her tense voice broke.

Colonel Brashear looked at her sorrowfully and finished her sentence, seeming, as he spoke, to be promising himself, as well as answering her.

'Until we're all free — or dead — Miss Lucy, it's going to be like this.'

She turned and cast a quick glance at the men standing beside the Colonel — at Ruthven Blakeley with his one blind eye; at Goodwin Breckinridge and Thomas Abernethy, whose young faces were too set and bitter, she suddenly thought, for their years; at old Mr. Archibald Bland, who seemed temporarily to have regained some of the alertness he had so long ago lost.

Slowly the blood came back to her face, and her thoughts began to take shape. It came to her, there in the night, that there is something oddly familiar to the human heart in terror, pain, and sorrow; that sooner or later they enter, like old occupants, into every life and settle there. Somehow she would have to learn how to live with them in possession of her own existence, learn how to set against them the strength of her own resolves. This was something nobody could do for her, nobody — she was old enough to know that, now. Old enough, too, to accept, deep in her inmost consciousness, the hard and painful truth that every human being, facing his own destiny, has no choice except to find his own way out of grief and fear. This, and nothing else, was the terrible spiritual isolation of which the saints perpetually complained. What she did not realize was that when she first thought of her life in such terms, she was, in that moment, leaving her youth forever behind her.

Nor did she think, then, consciously of her parents, or realize that, almost by instinct, she was reacting to the pattern of conduct they had laid down in her. She would be judged — she thought — would judge herself — not by victory over any kind of circumstance, but by the spirit with which she confronted it. The obligation never to falter lay as heavily and inescapably upon a woman of her group as upon a man; always she had known that.

Her tongue hung heavy in her mouth and her limbs were unsteady beneath her, but her mind seemed to her all at once to recover from the paralysis that had fallen briefly upon it, to grasp, without effort or dismay, the probable course of the next few years. Instead of fear, a pride in herself and her people welled up in her — a strange, stubborn pride she did not know she possessed; but, feeling it move within her, she was certain that, in the measure she scorned danger and death, in that same measure she had already vanquished them.

She raised her head to meet Colonel Brashear's anxious gaze fixed on the end of the gallery where Frank and Margaret were still sitting, deeply engrossed, it appeared, in their talk.

'They haven't heard a thing,' he commented, with sudden asperity.

'I don't like it,' Lucina replied slowly.

'Nor I,' he responded. Then he whirled on his heel with an agility that startled her, and looked down at her with an expression divided between anger and despair. His eyes were dark and piercing under his white eyebrows and the heavy furrows that ran straight up and down the sides of his long cheeks seemed to deepen.

'Miss Lucy,' he said, 'it's amazing how little it matters what we like or don't like in this world!'

She returned his steady gaze with one that matched it. 'I was just thinking that.'

'Lord help you, child!' the Colonel groaned. 'It's likely you're going to have to think more and more about it!'

It was almost daylight when they heard the even sound of
Derby's long, swinging gallop down the drive, and, after him,
the thud of other beating hooves. Lucina and Colonel Brashear
rose from their seats, and Jake hurried to take the reins that
Cavin flung him.

He came up the steps slowly, seeming for a moment to sway
with fatigue. Then he put his hand carelessly, hardly seeming
to know what he did, on Lucina's shoulder, and looked slowly
around at the group gathered so anxiously about him. Their
faces were pallid under the gray half-light of dawn; his own was
smeared with dust and curiously set, as if the resolve he had
held in his mind throughout the night had hardened into a
mask which he could not shift at will.

'Let 'em raise hell all they want to, now,' he said, spacing his
words, whether from fatigue or purpose his listeners could not
tell. 'We can handle 'em.'

'What happened, Cavin?' Colonel Brashear stepped closer.
'How'd you come out? Did you catch up with Weatherley?'

Cavin flung his arms wide, and his eyes brightened to a
strange, intense blue.

'Catch up with him, Colonel? David's got him and the mulatto we were looking for under guard in the church!' He began
to laugh, but it was a hoarse, cheerless sound. 'When the
scoundrels saw us, they cut and ran like rabbits, some of my
own hands with them — that fool, Lijah, who looked after the
mules was one of them, Lucy,' he explained, his gaze dropping
momentarily to hers, and then lifting. 'I reckon they thought
the angel Gabriel was after them, or ghosts, or God knows what;
but just as we planned, Colonel, that bugle-blowing was too
much for 'em. When they heard it, they broke and made for
the woods. Weatherley held his ground. You can say that much
for 'im; he's no coward; after we'd tied 'im up, he began to try

to harangue *us* with his crazy talk. Warren Hughes and his
men wanted to hang 'im and his outfit, then and there. I don't
know but what I would have agreed, if it hadn't been for David
insisting on a trial.'

'David?' The Colonel fired the question like a bullet at Cavin.

'Yes — David,' Cavin explained. 'We picked him up at
home.' He paused, trying to clear his thoughts for expression.
'What David said was true; I knew that,' he acknowledged,
frowning. 'How under heaven can we demand trials for ourselves and refuse 'em to our prisoners?'

'That's right,' Colonel Brashear nodded with a firm snap to
his gesture. 'Entirely right.'

'We sent a note to the garrison,' Cavin went on, 'and told the
officers there we'd give 'em a chance to do justice; that if they
wouldn't, we would. That's all,' he ended impatiently. 'Now
we have to wait and see what they'll do.'

'Do? My God-a-mighty, Cavin! You know what they'll do!
What's the sense o' talking like that?' John McGaughey strode
indignantly forward hitting his fist into his other hand — a gesture that always betrayed the tension inside him. 'Courts?' He
laughed in bitter scorn. 'When have there been any courts in the
county? Great God!' He laughed again in derision. 'What's
the use of turning murderers over to Pease's hired judges? You
act like you don't know that even the Supreme Court justices
are his tools.'

Judge White stepped out of the group and moved forward,
holding his small figure with the dignity which seemed to add
inches to his stature whenever he was on the bench. His words
boomed with astonishing sonority out of his thin, almost reedy,
neck.

'I would remind you, gentlemen —' he began and then
paused, casting a withering glance around the group. Brushing

his white hair back from around his thin temples, he raised his cupping, pointed chin in a way that young lawyers had learned to dread. 'Mr. McGaughey,' he remarked icily, 'seems to have forgotten that I am the last legally elected judge in this county. As long as I am out of jail, every criminal in my jurisdiction will be tried by due process of law — and not military law either.' The light of the rising sun fell on his face, throwing into relief his blazing, blue eyes and his head thrown proudly up. 'I have the temerity to suppose that we are able to preserve the courts which our ancestors set up in this county.' Facing his listeners, superbly indifferent to their approval or their disapproval, he went on, watching them with keen, attentive eyes. 'Because the military has no conception of liberty, are we to sink to that level ourselves? We, whose fathers devised and framed a free government?' His voice softened, and he began to plead with them. 'No! I warn you, my friends — the price of liberty is high, extremely high; and he who would enjoy it must know how to value it above his own passions and greed, above every other end or desire.' With a sudden unexpected movement, he turned toward John, directly. 'We'll hold court, ourselves, John, as we have every moral right to do, and call our own witnesses. I promise you that. They'll hang,' he ended gravely. 'But we'll give 'em a fair and free trial first.' His voice dropped. 'You'll agree to that, John?'

'No use agreeing to anything,' a new voice broke in. Cavin swung around to face a man he had never seen before. 'Slipped in that way,' the visitor explained, gesturing toward the border of thick vines which climbed over the fence along the western edge of the yard. 'You warn't expecting me, I jedge?' He drew himself up, important because of the news he had to tell, and paused at the bottom of the steps.

'They're already swinging,' he announced slowly, 'Weatherley and the nigger, both. You don't know me, brother?' He smiled lightly at Cavin. 'You better go untie your men. We trussed 'em up, to save us all a mighty heap o' trouble. In case you want to know, Warren Hughes sent me to tell you all you could take him on now or later, jest as you please, about this.' The man spat carefully. 'He was satisfied you warn't goin' to like what he's done. That is,' he continued thoughtfully, 'you can have two crowds in this county fighting each other, or one fighting the Yankees, jest as you like. It don't much matter to us, only we ain't disposed to fool with no military courts, or no other kind. When we catches a varmint, we wrings its neck, then an' thar. Now whut's your answer?' He surveyed Cavin with an impudent, inquiring gaze. 'I got to be gittin' back.'

Cavin inspected the man coldly, but at last grunted in a kind of reluctant approval.

'Well, you've got nerve, anyway, coming here like this,' he grudgingly admitted, laying his course.

'We could hold you, of course; but I don't think we will. What do you say, Judge? What do you think, Colonel?' He ran his eye over the group that surrounded him. 'I see you're o' one mind.' Turning to the stranger, he delivered his decision.

'You go on back and tell Warren Hughes that scoundrel Weatherley's not worth another killing. But you tell him something else for me, too. Get it straight, now. You tell 'im, as sure as God's in His heaven we'll settle with your crowd later on. And that after this, we'll plan on protecting our prisoners better. That's all.'

The man smiled sullenly. 'That's about what he thought you'd have to say,' he observed, backing out of the yard as he spoke. Once outside, he leaned across the white palings and, with an insolent flutter of his eyelids, remarked, 'We figured it warn't work any o' you'd keer about doing, yourselves.'

Colonel Brashear took a few enormous strides, and, reaching over the fence in a swift and unexpected movement, grabbed the man's shoulder, shaking him breathless.

'You better not count on that,' the Colonel warned him sternly. 'It'd be a bad mistake.' His fierce black eyes bored through the stranger's bold demeanor. 'A mighty bad mistake.'

Dipping suddenly, the man slipped out of the Colonel's grasp and disappeared, in a scrambling run, behind the locusts and the pear trees.

Colonel Brashear dusted off his hands and shrugged his shoulders. 'What do you say to getting a little sleep now, gentlemen?' he suggested.

'I hear the beds in the jail are plenty hard,' Cavin agreed, yawning.

Chapter 20

To Cavin's surprise, however, a week passed without the soldiers' arresting anybody. Apparently the fact that he had sent two messengers hurrying to the garrison removed him from the suspicious list. And the fact that the officers had found David and the other guards tied to the horse-rack in front of the church also helped to shift the blame for the hanging from the whole planter group. The Federal officials seemed genuinely puzzled and, for once, refrained from making dragnet arrests. This evidence of reason Cavin ascribed to the new Federal commander in charge at Galveston — a man of much less violent temper than his immediate predecessor.

Two years before, when he lay on his bed with a broken hip, Cavin had decided that it was time to put the nation out of his mind. Now, as he read the reports of the endless squabbling going on at Austin, where the Radical Convention had reassembled in December, he concluded in disgust that, for the time being, it might even be the best policy to restrict his interest even more — to his own county alone.

'Now's the time,' he calculated, 'to lay low and let the Radicals loose — plumb loose. They'll hang themselves, in the end. We know now we can hold down the county,' he reflected in relief.

Toombs Dickerson, however, Cavin soon found out, took a

different view of affairs. The Judge had just returned from a visit to Austin when he stopped by Locust Hill, late one afternoon about the middle of February.

It was a frosty afternoon, for the season, when Judge Dickerson rode up. He dismounted and rubbed his arms vigorously as he followed Cavin into the house.

'All stove up from sittin' still listenin' up at Austin,' he told Cavin, pulling on his long brown moustache, and carefully lowering his tall, angular body into a chair by the fire. 'Well, the Convention's adjourned,' he announced, spreading out his big hands to the blaze. 'You can guess what kind of a constitution they've rigged up for us to vote on.'

Flinging one booted foot restlessly across the other, he snorted: 'Vote on! They'll never let us so much as smell a ballot. I ran across a man in Austin who swore they cancelled his registration simply because he wouldn't swear to believing that his cook was his equal. And look at me,' he continued, 'I've had a pardon sewed up in my vest ever since the first election, but they turned me down like everybody else. "Washington's a long way off," they told me. Well, I know it now, if I didn't then — the further the better, I say.'

For a time he sat in silence, going over his thoughts, looking for some encouragement that was not in him.

Cavin had just come in from riding over his place. He put his shining boots up on the fender and his silver spurs jangled companionably with the Judge's against the heavy copper of the screen. Looking at his guest with placid, speculative eyes, almost entirely free from anxiety, he remarked:

'Do you know how I've got it figured out? If they can get along without us in this government, we ought to be able to get along without them. We began to do just that in this county, when we cleaned up the gang that murdered Byrnes Armstrong.'

The Judge inclined his head, nodding slowly and thoughtfully.

'As for the negro vote,' Cavin continued, 'it'll be a cold day in June when I can't count on my hands putting a mark where I tell 'em to, soldiers or no soldiers. It's the same with your colored people.'

He crossed one foot over the other and seemed to be critically examining the toe of his boot. Then he looked up and smiled cheerfully at his guest. 'Let 'em vote all the blacks they want to. Lord! Lord, we can beat 'em at that game; they don't know the first thing about how a nigger's mind works. It's actually foolish, some of the things they do.' He began to laugh again in slow, easy chuckles.

'You know old George Ann, who makes our sausages?'

'Best ones in the county,' the Judge observed with interest. Cavin did not dispute him.

'Well, one o' these blasted carpet-baggers we got around here drove down and left her a big pile of those fancy books Northern missionaries are always sending down here. What do you reckon she did with 'em?' Cavin demanded. 'Tore out the pages and papered her house all over nice inside with 'em!' He sat smiling at the recollection. 'I asked her how she liked the gentleman. "He ain't no gentleman!" she said, and, by George! she was mad as hell. "That low-down, worfless white trash wanted me to set down an' eat wid him!" she told me. Gad! Judge, it looks to me like we can whip 'em at their own tricks.' Cavin slapped his thigh and laughed aloud. 'What they don't know! Only thing they're smart at's graft!'

The Judge was not so confident as Cavin. He sat quiet, staring bleakly into the fire; then he raised his eyes and scowled under his heavy, bristling brows, the cleft in his chin seeming to deepen under the shadowy light of the fire.

'You know, of course,' he inquired, 'that old Governor Hamilton got through a measure allowing every male citizen, black or white, to vote? Provided of course,' he added, 'that they are not disqualified by Congress and are neither in jail nor in the insane asylum. It's two shots to one, of course,' he concluded, amending his remarks with a bitter certainty born of experience, 'that they'll pretty soon set out to prove we're all insane.' Suddenly the Judge's face reddened, and he shook till tears ran out of the corners of his eyes.

'By Gad! Cavin, we're reduced to such a state that I'm actually taking pleasure in being classed as a citizen on a par with a nigger! Wouldn't Mirabeau Lamar turn in his grave?' He sat darkly brooding until Cavin aroused him by thinking aloud.

'Why wouldn't our best move be to lay low now, and put up our real fight after they drag us back into the Union?' he inquired looking at the Judge questioningly. 'I suppose they won't be able to plaster military courts all over us, once we're citizens of the United States again, like everybody else?'

'They say,' the Judge returned acidly, 'that the Supreme Court still has some regard for the ordinary liberties of American citizens. What are *we* now, though?' he demanded in a sharp change of tone. 'Citizens? The Lord only knows! Something between carrion crows and vermin, they seem to think.'

Cavin was undisturbed. 'Let 'em have their head,' he said in placid unconcern. 'They're kinda like a bunch of stampeding steers. You cain't turn 'em till they're over the cliff. The Lord knows, though, I wish they'd hurry and break all their damnfool necks.' He sighed deeply. 'I've been expecting 'em to announce it's sinful for a man to have fried chicken for breakfast, because one o' his niggers might happen to relish it more'n him.' Then he grinned propitiatingly. ''Twouldn't make me so firing mad, if they'd leave off all their highfalutin phrases about equality, and democracy, and Lord knows what all. You might think they're all angels, and considerably smarter than the Creator.'

Judge Dickerson put both hands on his knees and leaned forward so anxiously that Cavin plumped his own feet down to the floor and sat in strained silence with his eyes on his visitor's face.

'Here's exactly how the land lies,' said the Judge. 'As I see it, anyway. The Republicans are certain to run two tickets; one headed by E. J. Davis, representing the most radical group, and the other by old Governor Hamilton, representing the moderates. Now,' Toombs asserted, leaning closer and putting his question firmly, 'this is the point. Ought we to support the moderates in the hope of a fairly bearable administration, or the extremists in the expectation they'll kill off their following by their folly? Or would it be better to push our own ticket to the limit? Those are the three choices, and every single one of 'em's damned uncomfortable. I think,' he concluded, 'we'd be wise to run a full ticket.'

Cavin meditated for some time, and his features, lit up by the fire which played over them, revealed the intensity of his absorption in the problem before them.

'It still seems to me,' he said at last, 'that the only thing to do is to stay out o' this row and let 'em haul us back in the Union any way they want to. Then' — He turned emphatically to the Judge — '*then* we'll cut in for all we're worth.'

Judge Dickerson yawned. He had been in his saddle since morning. 'Well, maybe you're right, Cavin,' he said with a weary gesture. 'God knows.'

For several moments they stood facing one another in complete silence. Finally, the Judge shrugged his heavy shoulders. 'Of course,' he remarked, 'it'll be hell the next two years, any way we play the game.'

'And after,' said Cavin gloomily. 'Confederates know what money'll buy same as Yankees, don't they? Look at the editor of the *Telegraph*. He'd sell his dirty soul, I reckon, if anybody was fool enough to buy it.' Striking his hands heatedly together, he announced an intention that had been smoldering within him for some time. 'I swear, Judge,' he exclaimed solemnly, 'I'm going to teach my children to trust nobody, especially nobody that's got any power over 'em. The man's not born that's wise enough or good enough to stand having much power.'

He looked at the Judge in consternation. 'The world's upside down. Here's Colonel Barclay's own son, a gambler and Lord knows what else, courting my sister-in-law right out on my front gallery!'

Judge Dickerson smiled under his long moustache. 'If I recollect aright' — the Judge's yellowish eyes twinkled — 'some time back you told me Colonel Rutherford called you a gambler, yourself.' He held up two fingers to still the protest arising in Cavin's face. 'Oh, in a different way, my dear Cavin, a vastly different way.' He yawned again, behind his hand. 'Excuse me! I've had a long day, and I must get on over to see how David feels. You'll let me know what you decide, I hope?'

'I decided some time ago,' Cavin answered. 'I'm not going to move one way or the other in this election. But we'll hold this county down; you can count on that.'

Toombs accepted the decision and moved toward the door. There was plenty of time for Cavin to change his mind, he was thinking.

But spring passed and summer came on, and still Cavin held to his course.

One evening in early June, Margaret came to the door of the

attic schoolroom where Lucina was sitting, with Nathaniel in her arms and Beau on a stool at her feet. For a moment she stood there silently, watching Beau drawing on his slate and Philip and Philippa, across the room from him, playing with large wooden blocks that Uncle Matt had carved out of a fallen cedar tree. The old man would sit for hours now, reluctant to move, whittling away at pieces of wood.

Lucina glanced up, feeling some tension in the air which a single glimpse of Margaret's face confirmed.

'You're going to marry Frank Barclay!' she exclaimed sadly, before her sister could speak. 'I've been expecting it!'

'Then I don't need to tell you!' Margaret held up both her hands and smiled. 'Don't say all you're thinking. Cavin's already said it for you — and more besides.' She put her arms around Lucina and kissed the top of her shining head.

'You don't suppose that at my age I imagine marriage is all sunshine and roses, do you?' she asked. 'Now, listen to me,' she went on. 'You happened to fall in love with Cavin, and he happened to stop by Cedar Ledge, so you could. But where was the man for me to fall in love with?' She pressed her small hands hard against Lucina's head. 'Dead in the war — that's where. Those that did come back — what had they but poverty to offer a woman? Well, they weren't offering it, not in Georgia anyway. Ned Devoe — you remember him — spent four hours one evening explaining that to me.'

She came around and took a footstool at Lucina's feet, leaning her head across her folded hands on her sister's knee. 'What's the use of life, Lucina, if you just exist on the edge of it all the time?'

Lucina had not said a word since she first spoke, but she kept her gaze fixed unhappily on her sister. Finally she asked, 'Are you in love with him, Margaret? That's what matters, you know.'

'You know!' Margaret flared back. '*How* do I know? If you are asking me whether I feel the way I did toward Justin, I'll tell you I don't.' Her eyes turned toward the gable window against which the leaves of the tallest locusts moved. Through it she caught a glimpse of the glowing western sky — a sky like the one she had watched fade the night Justin rode away from Cedar Ledge for the last time.

That whole night, Margaret remembered, she had not closed an eye, and life had seemed to her insupportably sweet. He was her cousin; she had kissed him many times before that last evening, when in a palpitant, exquisite moment she had lifted her face to him. The memory of that moment came back to her now, and of the days that had followed when she had walked on air, trembling with a bliss that she could not define, loving the whole earth because somewhere Justin was alive on it. How had it come about, she asked herself, that she had turned into the tired woman sitting here in Texas at Lucina's feet?

She shivered and raised a pale face to her sister. 'I'll never feel that way again,' she said slowly. 'I know that. The past is gone. I have to have something to call my own, Lucy.'

She got up idly and wandered across the room, picking up and putting into their places the children's books and slates, but Lucina saw that she was scarcely aware of what she was doing, that she moved almost automatically. She stood so long motionless by the window that Lucina was startled by the quickness of her movement when she turned at last, speaking almost angrily.

'Oh, I know I can keep on living here with you and Cavin forever, if I want to; or I can go home to Cedar Ledge.' She was suddenly still; and her voice, when she spoke, had dropped to almost a whisper.

'Do you remember, Lucy,' she asked, 'how the shadows fall just before dark, with the sun going down at the far edge of the valley?'

Locking her hands together, she stood watching her sister's face.

'Do you remember how the mist rises on moonlight nights and floats over the mountain? And how the house looks, and the garden, as you come up the avenue and around the curve?'

As Lucina listened, she grasped Nathaniel more tightly to her breast and laid her hand on Beau's head as if to tether herself to the spot where she sat. Before her eyes she saw, not the locust tree etched, through the narrow window, against the falling Texas night, but the glossy magnolia outside her bedroom at home. She saw, not the few bushes around her Texas door, not the flowers that Cavin had planted for her the morning after she arrived on the Brazos, but Susanna's white garden skirting a gray Georgia cliff.

Margaret took a few stumbling steps and knelt by her sister's chair, dropping her arms tight around her. For a long time neither of them stirred.

Then Margaret raised her face.

'I'm going to marry him, Lucy,' she asserted firmly. 'Nobody can live the way I've been trying to do — forever thinking of the past.' She rose resolutely to her feet, having regained her usual assurance. 'Don't think I've lost my senses.'

She stood reflecting, with her hand on Lucina's chair. 'There's something about him, Lucy — I don't know what it is. Sometimes I believe I'm more in love with him than I think.'

'I expect you are.' Lucina shifted Nathaniel carefully from one arm to the other and made a little face at Beau, who had given up his drawing to watch with wide, startled eyes the expression on his mother's face. Reassured, he picked up his slate pencil again. Then she gave her full attention to Margaret.

'I expect you *are* in love with him,' she repeated. 'Anyway, I know this much, Maggie; you'd better be if you aren't — that is, if you're determined on marrying him.' She turned a distressed, baffled gaze on her sister. What else could she say to her? What else was there *to* say? She sighed and gave it up. There were some things nobody could tell another person, chances one could not measure even for one's own sister.

Lucina had on a red cotton frock which accentuated her dark hair and eyes and the warm color, which, since Nathaniel's birth, was beginning to return to her cheeks. Margaret thought, as she glanced at her, that she had never looked prettier than she did now, with the yellow, sunset light filtering through the leaves on her and Beau, as he sat at her side dressed in his little, blue apron.

'Come here, Lucina,' Margaret cried suddenly, walking over to a mirror that hung on the sloping wall. 'Put Nathaniel down, and come here.'

It was just light enough to see as the two sisters stood, arm in arm, before the long glass.

'Look at your face,' Margaret said. 'Look at it! And then at mine. You're ten years younger than I am, that's true; but that's not all I see. You've been sick, and you've been unhappy — oh! yes, you have, at times,' she said, interrupting herself. 'But still,' she went on, 'your eyes don't look empty like mine — that's the word, empty. I've seen plenty of old maids with eyes getting bleaker and bleaker every day they live, and their noses longer and longer.' Laughingly she drew her finger down her own nose. 'Mine's plenty long enough, already.'

She held her head high, and her serious, gray eyes met Lucina's in the mirror. There were curls loose about her face, softening it until she looked scarcely older than her sister. On a sudden impulse, she pulled her hair straight back off her forehead, thus sharpening her features into a cold, hard mask.

'Do you want me to look like that, darling? I will in a few

years! No!' she protested, 'I'd rather take a chance on marrying Frank.' She held Lucina's gaze in the mirror, smiling provocatively.

'Maybe you'd rather I'd marry Jeremiah?' she demanded.

'Jeremiah?' Lucina was startled. 'What an idea!'

'You needn't laugh,' Margaret said, suddenly serious. 'Didn't Marilyn Hargreaves marry her father's overseer's son, just before I started out here!'

As if resentful of the expression on Lucina's face, Margaret demanded: 'Who else was she to marry? Tell me that — things being the way they are.'

Stooping, she kissed her sister as lightly as she might have kissed Nathaniel. 'You don't know what's going on nowadays, Lucy.'

'Well, I don't like what I do know!' Lucina replied with spirit.

Margaret looked at her, suddenly serious again. 'I don't either; but what good does that do?'

She stood watching Lucina with quiet, reflective eyes.

'Sometime in the winter, I should think,' she said finally. 'That ought to give me time to be sure.'

'Darling, you shall have a lovely wedding!' Lucina smiled. 'Do you remember saying that to me on the verandah at Cedar Ledge? If you don't, I do.'

As soon as the election notices were posted in the late summer of 1869, the lines of battle began to take shape. As Toombs Dickerson had predicted the Republicans ran two tickets — the ultra-radical E. J. Davis heading one, and the former Provisional Governor A. J. Hamilton the other. By contrast the latter seemed almost moderate, and some Democrats decided to support that ticket instead of their own, which they knew was bound to lose. The results of the election in late November, however, made it clear that a large proportion of the whites had followed Cavin's reasoning and simply stayed away from the polls.

'Well, Margaret,' Frank predicted when he heard that Davis had been elected governor by the small majority of eight hundred votes, 'we're going to have so much trouble in this county, now, that you won't have a chance to get tired of me, because I'll never be home.' He spoke more seriously than she realized, for as the time for their wedding approached, his conscience sometimes smote him.

'You deserve a better life than I'm going to be able to give you,' he warned her one night, drawing in his breath and waiting for her answer, while his heart stood still in his breast. 'What will she say?' he thought, knowing, as he looked into her face, that, in that moment, he loved her enough to release her from her promise, if she so much as hesitated in choosing her reply. But she had not hesitated; instead, she had smiled at him gently and surely, slipping her hand into his.

They were married in the parlor at Locust Hill at four o'clock on the first day of January, 1870. As Lucina dispensed syllabub and tiny currant cakes to her guests after the ceremony, she kept hoping the marriage would turn out better than she feared. But foreboding lay heavy within her.

By the time the legislature, so dubiously elected, finally assembled early in February it began to appear that the new Governor, Davis, must have received and accepted some sound advice. For he asked the legislature, in a conciliatory address, to do two things only: to confer equal rights of citizenship upon white and black alike, and to elect United States senators. With the membership made up as it was, these measures were soon rushed through, and the senators chosen were sufficiently radical to satisfy even Congress.

On April 16, 1870, therefore, General Reynolds issued a proclamation declaring the reconstruction period in Texas ended.

But there was little enough rejoicing along the Brazos. They had heard that kind of talk before, and what had it come to? Besides, no matter what happened at Washington now, there was hardly a man in Cypress County who did not understand that the real fight for state control had just begun. Ten days later, the Governor's first message to the special session of the legislature confirmed such a belief beyond any possible doubt.

'The Governor's asked for centralized control and for a state militia to establish martial law wherever the citizens feel like resisting him,' Cavin informed the Hunters. 'He'll get what he's asked for,' he predicted, 'maybe more, considering who the legislators are.'

He was right. The Governor, fattening on power, soon demanded and was allowed to appoint not only the district registrars and attorneys, but even the mayors and boards of aldermen in every city and village. The compliant legislature also permitted him to postpone for two years the regular elections, and, finally, to control the press by distributing only to certain picked journals the highly remunerative public advertising and printing. Nor did the legislators contradict the Governor when he declared military law still to be the law of the state. Nobody, by this time, was innocent enough to suppose that the moneys and bonds generously appropriated for railroads would actually be used for opening up the state to travel.

Cavin followed every move, each one, from his point of view more satisfactory than the last.

'They're playing right into our hands!' he exclaimed to the

Hunter's Club, pushing out his jaw and rubbing it thoughtfully.
'I was afraid they'd lose their nerve and not go far enough.
What we want to do, now, is to let 'em climb right out on the
end of the limb!'

During the next few months, he felt a boiling excitement as
he saw events working out almost exactly as he had foreseen.
In July, the Governor announced that he had just begun to
fight and gave out the names of his state police — half of them
negroes. 'The war is not yet over,' he wrote, 'the war to radi-
ate civilization into the darkest corners of the state.'

The night after the list of police was published, the Hunters
conferred till almost daybreak at Locust Hill.

'Don't you see?' Cavin demanded jubilantly. 'The scoundrels
are digging their own graves. I hear some of the Radicals
themselves sent a petition to Congress last week asking for a
republican form of government in this state. Why,' he declared,
'they are finding out they can't float any more bonds in New
York, and' — Cavin checked the items off on his fingers — 'even
they admit the Governor's gone too far in recommending
court martial for the people in Houston who broke quaran-
tine.'

He sat smiling, almost happily. 'Let 'em take their own
medicine,' he concluded. 'They'll find it good and bitter.'

The next few months were charged with uncertainty and
sadness, heightened by the death of General Lee at Lexington.
The Texans temporarily laid aside their own troubles and
grieved, not for a great public figure, but for a man they had
loved like a father, a man who had personified in himself the
virtues which they believed they had been defending.

However, they took new heart when, in November of 1870,
the returns for the special elections began to come in. Then the
most hot-headed saw the gains the Conservatives were making

even in the districts previously counted as almost completely Radical.

One morning in early December, however, Cavin received an urgent note from Judge Dickerson.

'The geese are flying low over Devil's Slough,' wrote the Judge in his note, according to a signal that he and Cavin had previously agreed upon. The hour and place of meeting were also indicated in simple code.

'Good hunting!' Cavin wrote back in return in his precise, angular script at the bottom of the page, and sent word around to the other men.

In the pouring rain, two nights later, they started off to join Judge Dickerson in a wet swamp known as the Devil's Slough because of the strange and fearful blue lights that from time to time floated, like bubbles, above the slimy water and ooze.

The men tethered their horses at different places in the woods, so that a passing sentry might not suspect a meeting was going on, and made their way on foot across the bog, toward a grove of dead trees where they had agreed to gather. Beneath their dripping slickers, they carried sheets, and masks, and carefully loaded guns.

'Jesus!' Jeremiah whispered to Joseph O'Fallon, who stepped along beside him. 'This place must be working with water moccasins!' As he tried to lift his boot, the mud closed around it. 'Feels like quicksand!'

''Tain't been cold enough yit for snakes to hole up,' old Joseph conceded and hunched his shoulders. 'Ruther step on a lion's tail than on one o' them-thar slimy devils.' Carefully he pulled his boot out of the mud, and at the sucking sound that followed his movement he jumped like a skittish young colt. 'Suffering tomcats!' he exclaimed, speaking into Jeremiah's ear, 'you cain't make a move without stirring up a racket.'

Leaning close, he offered an apologetic explanation of his timidity. 'Soon's ever I git to shooting I'll be all right. I remember when I was a Ranger, under Capt'n Ownsby, fighting the Comanchees right in these here swamps, my damn teeth'd always get to chattering, right before a skirmish. The Capt'n got so's he could figger on telling when a Indian was around by the way my jaws 'ud begin clicking together.'

He felt his sunken cheeks in the dark. 'Had somp'n to chew with then,' he chuckled, and took a few gingerly steps forward, peering through the darkness. 'Cain't see yo' nose on yo' face, kin you?'

'Lawd knows how we're ever goin' to find them trees,' Jeremiah whispered back.

'I'm a-headin' right thar,' said Joseph and patted Jeremiah's arm soothingly. 'I always feel sorry for a man like you that warn't raised in these here blasted bottoms. Me, now' — he jumped a foot in the air — 'Jesus Christ! One of 'em's got me! No 'twarn't,' he added hastily; ''twas a vine o' some sort.'

It seemed to Jeremiah it took them hours to get where they were going, but finally, through the rain that had now begun to turn into thick mist, they made out the outlines of a silent, waiting group. They fell in behind the rest of the men, scarcely drawing their breath, and old Joseph stuffed a little cotton under his upper lip.

'Larned that fighting the Wacos,' he said softly to Jeremiah, offering him a white wad. 'Keeps you from sneezing.'

By straining their eyes they could see three figures conferring together. They knew who they were — Judge Dickerson, Cavin, and Colonel Brashear, but what they were saying, what orders they would give, they could not guess.

After some time, Cavin strode back to a slickered figure standing against a tree. 'David?' he asked in a low voice. 'It's you?'

'Yes,' said David energetically nodding his head in the black dark. 'What's up?' Cavin's grasp tightened.

'Close in around the jail at sunup, will you, and if you hear three shots, rush the door.'

'Where'll you be?'

'Inside with Colonel Brashear and Judge Dickerson. Understand?' he asked.

'Sunup — jail — three shots — rush,' David whispered back.

Cavin dropped his hand, and David began to step softly from man to man.

'Separate,' he told them, 'and reform just before sunup, back o' the mill, half-mile from the jail.'

Then he moved back to Cavin, who was hurriedly mounting Derby, and repeated his question.

'I better know what's the trouble.'

'I just found out, myself,' said Cavin, taking his foot out of his stirrup. 'Do you know Judge Graves? Judge Graves at New Columbia?'

'Blown up at Petersburg, wasn't he? Yes, I know him. It's a wonder he's alive.'

'That's the one. Well, Alec Winston was over calling on the Judge's daughter, a week ago Sunday, when a couple o' drunk white police rode in the yard and called the old man out — said he was their prisoner, God knows what for. In the fracas that followed, Alec had to shoot one of 'em to hold him off — just a grazing bullet that barely brought blood. Alec went on back to his cousin's, Major Bowen's, where he was staying, and went to bed. Along toward daylight, a couple o' black police and a white lieutenant rode up and demanded the right to search the Major's house.

' "Where's your search warrants?" he asked 'em. Well, they hadn't any, of course, and the Major swore at 'em.

' "You can't search my house with your damned nigger police," he told 'em.'

David nodded in vigorous approval.

'Yes — but listen,' Cavin continued in a graver tone. 'The two negroes tied up the Major and dragged Alec out o' bed, with a couple o' guns stickin' in his ribs. Fortunately, a bunch o' young men were coming by late and saw what was happening. They made themselves out to be constables and hauled the police up before the Justice of Peace for illegal entry. The old Justice let 'em all out on a five-hundred-dollar bond — Lord knows what for — and naturally the damned police lit out for Austin.' Cavin stopped for breath.

'I see,' said David. 'What next?'

'Well,' Cavin continued, 'Davis sent his little banty Adjutant-General down to lay the whole town under martial law. Alec and Major Bowen are in jail, and old Judge Graves, to boot — the last two merely for resisting arrest. The Adjutant has announced he'll call it all off for $3000 cash,' Cavin concluded.

'I'd see him in hell first,' David broke out, as the rain began to pour thickly against his face.

'Exactly,' said Cavin heartily; 'but 'twouldn't be good sense, would it, David, to show our full hand right now?'

Cavin could feel David's muscles relaxing under his hand. 'Well,' he went on, 'Judge Dickerson has got together $2765. We're going to show it to the Adjutant.'

'Now,' Cavin went on, 'you better cover us, in case he refuses the money, or starts getting ugly. He might even take a notion to hang Alec for murder — seems the policeman he shot was so drunk he fell off his horse and rolled around in the dirt all night and the post doctor's afraid he's getting lockjaw. What's likely, though, we think, is that the General will hop the first train to Austin, where one of us'll meet him with the money. We'd be fools to turn it over to him here.' He stood silent a moment with the rain pouring around him, dripping down his yellow slicker off his wide, white hat.

'If we don't come out in half an hour — exactly half an hour — your turn is to come in and get us out,' he concluded.

David put his hand on Cavin's shoulder. 'Three shots,' he repeated. 'I'll keep my ears open.'

The red brick jail at New Columbia stood bare to the sun and wind under a single locust in a neglected, sandy yard. But not far away a thick cluster of trees grew along the creek which, at high water, turned the mill where the Hunters had planned to assemble. As Cavin, Judge Dickerson, and Colonel Brashear splashed through this creek, just before sunup, they could see, above the rise in front of them, that the jail was guarded by only a few sleepy sentries.

'Where you reckon the Adjutant is?' Cavin asked.

'You might know,' Toombs replied grimly, 'he wouldn't be there.' His head inclined to the jail as he spoke. 'Not there. He's quartered himself and his bodyguard on Major Bowen's wife, who has the best cook in town,' he explained. 'Probably he won't like being waked up.'

When they got down off their horses at Major Bowen's front gate, the soldier on duty was quite certain that the Adjutant wouldn't enjoy being roused, not in the least.

'He's expecting us,' the Judge answered curtly, and flipped a bill toward the guard, who at once smiled affably and drew out his watch.

'Well, sir,' he observed, 'maybe 'tis time the General woke up.'

In a few moments, the Adjutant appeared, suave and confident.

Judge Dickerson spoke to him briefly, and the General rubbed his very small hands together, beaming.

'Certainly, gentlemen, certainly. I'm glad you've come to your senses and brought me the money. Martial law is always an unpleasant duty to perform — always.' He smiled ingratiatingly at Colonel Brashear, who towered far above him.

'I have your personal word of honor, Colonel, to meet me at Austin with the cash a week from today?' The Colonel bowed coldly, and the Adjutant led the way toward the jail.

They had hardly stepped inside when Cavin saw the first ray of sunlight falling on the dark wall. He stepped to the window and nodded in satisfaction. Then he invited the General to take a look outside. He did so, and his face turned gray. 'The man looks like a corpse,' Cavin thought, watching him calculatingly.

What the General saw would have shaken a stouter heart than his. The morning mist was still heavy in the air, and the enormous red sun seemed to be floating, a deserted globe, in an opaque, mysterious sea. Under its diffuse light, the figures encircling the jail looked hardly like men. They sat almost motionless, each on his shrouded horse, their bodies draped in white, their own and their horses' faces covered, except for two staring eyeholes and slits at the mouth, with masks. Behind the ghostly riders, a dark thicket of woods loomed black against the gray cloud that enveloped it.

The Adjutant's legs trembled visibly beneath him, as he observed that every rider was holding across his pommel a rifle aimed, it seemed to him, directly at the window where he was standing. He could not move his eyes away from the glancing light that fell, blue and cold, off those shining barrels.

Watching him, Cavin smiled a slow, grim smile. 'You're perfectly safe,' Cavin assured him, 'perfectly — provided you hurry up and get out o' these bottoms — *and stay out.*' He emphasized his last words carefully.

'The men out there won't hurt you, General, unless you

should be foolish enough to call out your police.' He looked at him with cool, steady eyes. 'What we think you'll do is to get on the nine o'clock train and take your damned robbers with you. Our men out there,' he added, 'will stay where they are till *we* tell 'em to leave.'

He waited a moment and then inquired, 'Well?'

The General was a man of good common sense, and possessed of considerably more cupidity than bravery. 'You've got the draw on me,' he admitted.

Colonel Brashear held out a steady hand, on which was a black onyx ring. 'The keys, if you please, General.' Then he drew himself up to his full height. 'I wish you a pleasant trip, sir, and a long — a very long absence from this vicinity.' His black eyes narrowed, and he studied the Adjutant's face with care. 'It is an extremely unhealthful climate in this country for state police, General. You'd be wise to stay out of it altogether.'

'I believe you said $2765.25, Colonel?' the police officer replied. 'To be in my hand within a week?'

'Correct, to the cent,' the Colonel replied bitingly.

'Very well,' replied the Adjutant and drew his short figure up. 'But I would remind you that I was sent into this region not merely to keep the peace in this village' — he paused — 'this notorious village which has acquired a most unsavory reputation — people are even calling it Six-Shooter Junction.' His listeners moved no muscle in their faces and the General continued:

'I was sent here also to clean up a gang of horsethieves and brigands that are working in this county and the next. I should expect you, gentlemen' — he eyed them with close attention — 'to welcome any assistance in the way of law and order.'

His listeners never blinked an eyelash, and Cavin walked towards the door. 'If they *should* show up, General,' he said, pausing with his hand on the knob, 'we'll take care of 'em; you needn't put yourself to any bother.' He looked back pleasantly. 'We'll see you off. You've got' — he snapped open his watch — 'less'n two hours to get your men on the train.'

When Cavin got home, he had not shaved for a week and Lucina scarcely knew him when he walked up on the gallery in his rumpled, muddy clothes. She ran up to meet him, but he held her off.

'I'm too dirty to touch you, Sweet.' Then he caught sight of Jake in the doorway. 'Jake,' he said, 'fix me a hot tub right off, will you? Did you have any trouble here, Lucy?' he asked her.

'Why, no,' she said and smiled widely, touching his dusty cheek lightly with one finger. 'None at all — except I had to listen about a hundred times to old Mr. Archibald Bland telling about how smart his old mule is. What did you leave him here for?'

'He might-a taken to drinking with us,' said Cavin, smiling.

'*'Tis* a smart mule, Miss Lucy,' Jake put in, turning to go after his master's tub. 'He can set up on his hind quarters, Mas' Cavin, and beg, same as a dog.'

'You don't say!' said Cavin interestedly. 'I'm goin' to try training one o' my mules to do that.'

'Cavin!' Lucina laughed. 'You are a perfect child!' She ran her eyes over his face. 'Jake!' she exclaimed, 'I do declare, if your master hasn't started a beard.'

'A man wid all Mas' Cavin's business to look after *oughta* wear a beard, dat's de Lawd's truf,' Jake replied earnestly.

Cavin yielded. This was an old argument he had heard before. 'You two got a chance to fix me up any way you want to, now, Lucy. I'm too tired to bother.'

Then he threw back his head and smiled at his wife. 'You don't need to worry about the state police any more,' he assured her.

'I never have worried about *them*,' she replied. 'I'm busy enough worrying about *you*.'

'Ask Aunt Emmy to beat up some battercakes for supper!' Cavin called after her, as she left the room. 'Tell her Major Bowen's cook's nowhere near as good as ours.'

Lucina could hear him talking to Jake, as she started down the steps.

'We've got 'em whipped, Jake,' he was saying.

'Thank de Lawd!' Jake replied. 'De onery, low-down debbils!'

That night as they sat at the table eating battercakes and new sugar-cane syrup, Cavin began telling Lucina what had happened, but stopped short in the middle of a sentence to consider a circumstance that had not previously impressed him. He was still so long that his cakes grew cold, and Lucina at last touched his arm and asked what was on his mind.

He answered her absently. Resting his cheek against his uplifted fist, he seemed scarcely aware of her presence.

'I wonder' — he raised his head and began to tap one finger against his open palm, looking doubtfully at Lucina — 'I don't know — neither of 'em turned up — neither Warren Hughes nor Frank.'

'Know what?' Her brows puckered. 'Know what? Oh!' she exclaimed, at last following his thought, 'I forgot to tell you. Whatever possessed me? I know where Frank was——' Her eyes too became thoughtful. 'But *what* happened to Warren?'

Cavin's expression did not lift. 'Where was Frank, Lucy?'

She smiled again mischievously. 'He's got a lot better memory than some people I know,' she observed, and paused to let the point sink in. 'He's been nursing his wife and his new daughter ever since the morning you left, Cavin. He sent for me only a couple of hours after you rode off.' She watched him, with a teasing smile on her lips. 'Imagine a man staying home to see his new baby!'

Cavin grabbed her wrists and shook them lightly. 'I feel mighty relieved,' he said slowly.

For a moment longer he sat holding her hands. His skin was fresh and clear from vigorous rubbing; his eyes sparkled under his lids, and the beard that Jake had clipped neatly into shape gave Lucina the odd feeling that some strange man was making love to her across the table.

'In case you don't know it,' Cavin said, leaning over to scan her face, 'I never saw a lady who appealed to me the way you do!'

Chapter 21

ALTHOUGH the Democrats had gambled on Governor Davis's policies eventually producing a reaction against radicalism in the state, yet no one foresaw how rapidly the various groups opposed to the administration would be able to draw together. Cavin was frankly sceptical when, at a meeting of the central Democratic committee, a few days after Christmas, Colonel Rutherford proposed inviting 'all good citizens, whatever their past political preferences,' to meet with the Democrats at Austin early in January, 1871.

Colonel Rutherford had sat up a good share of the night before drawing up the paper which he now asked permission to read aloud to the committee. In it, he listed the usurpations of power which all honest Texans, he believed, were finding intolerable; and he closed his argument with an urgent invitation to 'every citizen to join the Democrats in their struggle to abolish the infamous dictatorship under which we all suffer.' When he had finished, he laid the two closely written sheets down on the table and called for suggestions and criticisms.

At first there was complete silence, while the Colonel sat gauging the reaction of the men gathered around the table in his office. The only sound was the soft swish and roll of the waves on the sandy beach below his window, as the tide, that had receded before daybreak, came pouring in. He knew all the men there — knew them well; knew that one of them — Ebenezer Yeardley — had ridden horseback sixty miles across the wet prairie to reach this meeting. The Colonel's eyes dwelt for some time upon this man. He had been chosen to sit on this committee both because he represented the smaller farmers who had followed Stephen F. Austin to Texas, and because, at the previous Democratic State Convention, he had presented, in strong terms, the claims of those who wanted more taxes returned to the counties from which they were originally drawn.

'It's absurd,' this man had stood up and contended, 'plain absurd for us to have to go way up to Austin and beg for money we ourselves turned into the general treasury. How do they know at Austin,' he had argued, 'what bridges we need in our county, what roads, what ditches? Like as not, the legislators'll use our taxes to raise their own pay; but,' he had observed acutely, to the Colonel's deep amusement, 'if ary dollar sticks to *our* hands, our neighbors'll know it and ask us how come we are able to go into town and buy fresh meat.'

After that speech, Colonel Rutherford had sought Ebenezer out, to congratulate him.

'Ebenezer Yeardley,' the Colonel thought now, as his eyes fell on him, 'was born with downright good sense, which is more'n most people are. I wonder if he knows his name is as good as anybody's.' He fell to meditating on how many people were breaking the sod in Texas, forgetful that their ancestors had once worn lace at their wrists. 'They won't stay down, though,' the Colonel reflected, 'not long. Blood'll rise in the end.' He smiled under his moustache, recollecting how one of the early families in the state, afflicted with the support of a worthless relative, had conceived the idea of making their dependent Governor. 'And,' the Colonel reflected, 'he surprised everybody by discharging his office to the credit of the

family. It was his mother's blood, though, showing up,' the
Colonel told himself complacently. 'Ebenezer's sure to rise.'

He glanced down the table till his attention settled on a
mild-mannered man at the end of the board — a man with a
very long brown beard, streaked with gray, over which from
time to time he absently passed a thin hand with strong, graceful fingers. He had straight features and melancholy, blue eyes
in which a humorous glint sometimes appeared and as quickly
passed, like light on a wave. The wind, blowing in from the
Gulf, ruffled his thick iron-gray hair, but he was completely
indifferent to its order and, at intervals, threw it back out of his
face with an irritable gesture as though he did not know what
it was that obstructed his vision. He had on spurs and high
boots shined to a turn by the Mexican who awaited him outside
the door; and his collarless white shirt, fastened together at the
neck with a button whittled out of wood, was fresh and starched.
Over it he wore a pair of red and black suspenders, in which he
found it easy and pleasant to rest his thumbs.

His name, Colonel Rutherford knew, was Titus Blackwood
and he owned the Mañana Ranch — a piece of land extending
for miles along the Nueces, which he had named as he did
because, he told his friends, he mortally hated to hurry.

'The Mexicans have the right idea now,' he always expatiated.
'What's the use o' doing anything today you can put off till
tomorrow?'

Colonel Rutherford had visited him there on his ranch once,
planning to shoot black bear and deer. He retained a vivid
recollection of how, instead of hunting, he had scurried across
the border with his host and his cowhands, to recapture a
hundred head of cattle that an incautious Mexican had driven
across the river into his own barren pastures.

'How far away is the fort?' he recalled leaning over to ask, as he galloped furiously through the night with the Mañana cowboys and the ranch's owner.

'Shucks!' old Titus Blackwood had responded; and, sitting there in his Galveston office, this bright October morning, Colonel Rutherford remembered the amused tolerance in Titus's voice, that black night. 'Shucks!' he had chuckled, with open scorn. 'Federals wouldn't dare cross over a creek without calling the Cabinet together in Washington; and by that time where'd my cows be?'

He had spurred his horse, and the Colonel had swum with him across the river. The next night, they had herded the bellowing cattle back across the yellow, turgid stream, the Mexican robber riding beside old Titus, with his arms roped behind him. Now that same Mexican was foreman on old Titus's range.

'There warn't a mite o' meanness in him,' Titus had explained to Colonel Rutherford before the meeting began; 'not a mite, sir. All he wanted was cows to run; and now he's got 'em. He don't really care whether they're mine or his'n.'

Colonel Rutherford nodded with assurance now, as he looked at old Titus. He and Ebenezer Yeardley, he thought, would be certain to see that the invitation he was proposing to send out would be good strategy at this time. How would Major Sewall Gresham vote, though, he wondered — Major Gresham sitting right next to old Titus Blackwood, in his stiff white wing collar and black frock coat, with one empty sleeve pinned back. There wasn't a finer man born, Colonel Rutherford reflected, than Sewall Gresham who, like Mrs. Dyess' boys, had plunged to the crest of little Round Top only to come down again without an arm. 'There's no fear in him,' the Colonel admitted, 'but he's sot in his ways, terrible sot in his ways.'

He had a plantation at Sugar Land, the Colonel knew, and a

supply house in Houston, at the foot of dusty Main Street, close onto the smooth, brown, oily bayou. Some of the merchandise that he unloaded at Galveston or Brazoria came from England and Scotland — his smoked fish and marmalade and thread, his Scotch and his oatmeal, his bitter oranges and his tea; other things he bought in New Orleans — wines, and liquors, and cordials, and fruit brandies, and pralines, and tasteful *filé* powder for gumbo, and green coffee for roasting, one grade for negroes, one for the masters. He had established his own credit everywhere, even in far-away Philadelphia where were turned out — who would imagine it? the Colonel mused — the big white hats the Texans cheerfully paid twenty-five silver dollars for. Sewall Gresham had closed his business, Colonel Rutherford recollected, and had set out for Richmond the very day the seceding Texans marched over to San Antonio to demand the surrender of the United States fort there; and, as the Colonel well knew, he had never excused General Lee for apparently forgetting at Appomattox that there were troops in Texas who had never smelled powder. 'Sot in his ways,' the Colonel calculated. 'He'll be dead set against having anything whatever to do with the Republicans.'

Cavin sat next to Colonel Rutherford, on his right. He was the youngest member of the committee, having recently fallen heir to William's seat. Directly across from him was a man — almost a stranger — from somewhere in the Panhandle. The Colonel did not know much about him except that he dealt in mules and wild horses and Brahma bulls and that he had been recently put on the committee to represent his section. The Colonel gave him a swift, appraising look. 'I recollect his name now,' he thought. 'It's James Hardenbrook.' Then he turned to Cavin.

'Well?' he asked him, 'what's your idea, Cavin? I'll begin on

my right and go around the table, gentlemen,' he explained,
addressing them all.

'You seem to think, Colonel,' Cavin observed in a dry voice,
'that a leopard's apt to change his spots.'

Colonel Rutherford returned his smile, with a shrewd upward
glance from under his narrowed lids.

'Well, not exactly, Cavin; but I'm fairly certain he'll try
right hard tc paint 'em over, when he finds they're costing him
money.' His accent changed abruptly. 'Republicans pay taxes
same as we do, don't they?' he demanded sharply. 'Look at
these figures!' He shoved a sheaf of papers across the table-top,
as he spoke.

Cavin's eye fell on the totals at the bottom of the long, straight
columns, and his eyebrows went up in astonishment.

'I didn't suppose it was that bad,' he commented, frowning
at the figures. 'Not nearly that bad.'

His black alpaca coat hung on the back of his chair, for, even
in October, the sun that fell on him through the window was
warm. His sleeves were rolled back to his brown, muscular
elbows, and his trousers were tucked inside his red-topped boots,
although he had faithfully promised Lucina to remember, when
he came to the meeting, to drop them outside. He smiled a little
as he chanced to look down at his feet, remembering how she
had come running out with his coat, just before he had left,
reminding him to be sure to wear it and his new black cravat to
the meeting — his first as committeeman. 'I better not tell her
I forgot 'em both,' he had just decided, when the Colonel
pushed the figures over to him to examine.

Whistling under his breath, he began to scratch down a few
notes in the thin book he always carried in his vest pocket, in
case he came across a good suggestion as to how to improve the
flavor of his hams or his wine, or how to increase his cotton or

corn yield. Anything and everything he recorded in this little book, writing out each note in a careful, accurate hand. Now he was jotting down, for future reference, the astonishing fact that state taxes had risen, since 1860, from fifteen cents on the hundred dollars to two dollars and seventeen and one-half cents on the same valuation, in the current year. 'One-half cent!' He smiled as he wrote. 'The Colonel's a close figurer.'

Colonel Rutherford continued, tapping his stout finger on the table as he spoke.

'I've been getting these figures together for months, gentlemen. Bear in mind that they don't include all the little niggling extra taxes, either; nor,' he went on impressively, 'do they make clear that the legislature is proposing to turn over about twenty-two million acres of good Texas land to two railroads alone, in case they should happen to prefer land to bonds.' He sighed deeply and threw up his hands. 'Why, railroads run on that scale,' he declared hotly, 'would cost more than they're worth — a heap more. We'd better stick to horses and buggies!'

He calmed himself by an obvious effort. 'When the Radicals see how much it's actually costing them to try to turn black men white, maybe they won't be so damned certain they can work miracles.' He squared himself around so as to face all the men gathered around the long table. 'When the Republicans get to studying these figures, quite a few of 'em'll be joining us.' Drawing his eyes into narrow slits, he looked thoughtfully out of the window with his hands pressing the table and his chair tilted back. 'At least that's how I estimate what'll happen. What's your opinion, Titus?' he demanded suddenly, bringing his chair down with a bang.

'You've got it figured out, sir,' old Titus Blackwood exclaimed admiringly, 'right down to a hair.'

The last person to vote was Sewall Gresham, who arose and

remarked in his slow, pleasing voice that, since his friends all seemed to differ with him, he deeply regretted his inability to consider association with Republicans as ever praiseworthy, or even remotely wise.

'Since, however, I appear to be the only dissenter, I defer to your combined judgment,' he said, and sat down.

'You may be right, Sewall,' Colonel Rutherford answered him at once. 'The majority's mighty often wrong, you know.' He cast his eye around the group. 'Major Gresham may have the pleasure of taunting us all.'

His voice fell to a deeper note. 'Is it your decision then, gentlemen,' he inquired, 'to seek support from the moderate Republicans in our effort to restore free government, honest elections, and unprejudiced courts to this Republic?' He counted the assents and, gathering his papers together, smiled down the table at Titus Blackwood. 'I notice your tongue always slips at the same place, Titus.'

Cavin was out on the white shell walk that bordered the front entrance to Colonel Rutherford's office — a white one-room building surrounded by oleanders — when he wheeled and went back, almost bumping into the Colonel on his doorstep.

'How much money do you figure we can count on to buy *our* votes?' Cavin asked, not softening his question.

The Colonel blinked. 'Well, I wouldn't put it quite that way, Cavin — not quite,' he chided. He was standing a step above Cavin, and his hand fell easily on his arm. 'Still,' he went on, smiling quizzically, 'everybody knows there's only one sure way to fight a fire that's out-o'-hand. You know what that is?' He fixed Cavin with a sharp look.

'I been at it all fall,' he returned. 'We're going to lay 'em out this time, Colonel. You watch!'

'And pray!' the Colonel added thoughtfully. He looked at

his watch. 'Come to dinner with me, Cavin? Aunt Mahaley's fixing up some crab gumbo, I believe, and I've got a case o' Bourbon that's nearly as good as yours.'

The invitations to what facetious and sceptical Democrats began to call the Love-Feast went out immediately, and met a more favorable response than even Colonel Rutherford had expected. Ex-Governor Hamilton, the leader of the Conservative Republicans, asserted in a public speech that 'the people of Texas, in circumstances like the present, care nothing whatever for party labels,' and the joint convention opened late in January, with a large number of moderate Republicans present. The delegates soon agreed to the necessity of establishing a network of committees throughout the state and a central party organ to be known as the *Statesman.*

'We'll print your tax figures on the first page of the first issue, Colonel Rutherford,' one of the Republicans insisted, and stood up and asked for guarantees to support the new Democratic paper.

When Lucina reproached Cavin, on his return home, for what she regarded as the extravagance of his heavy subscription, he countered by asking her what use there was in trying to raise cotton in a country run by men who, apparently, not only thought money grew on trees, but were willing to swap good black land for steam engines. The Colonel's revelations about the railroads had stuck in his mind.

'If we don't throw the Radicals out now, we never will,' he told Lucina. 'Next thing, they'll be taking our land away from us, and selling off the public domain, besides, to get money for raising their pay, or maybe' — he smiled acidly — 'for putting a silver teapot in every nigger cabin.' He sat looking at her a long time, weighing his next remark.

'Don't you remember,' he finally asked, 'hearing Cousin William tell how the men in the Republic had to mortgage their slaves and their land to get it going? Well,' he concluded, 'it looks like every now and then a man mighty nigh *has* to gamble that way on his country, or he won't *have* one to gamble on.' He shook his head in disgust. 'There are plenty of ninnies sitting around waiting to steal your country out from under your nose. If you want to run it yourself, you're going to have to pay for your pleasure. There's no way o' getting out o' that, is there?' he demanded.

To the surprise of the Conservatives, when the legislature convened in the spring of 1871, Governor Davis seemed to have taken warning from the special elections of the previous fall, which had plainly revealed the decline of Radical strength.

'The Governor must-a run out o' fool ideas,' David observed to Judge White one morning when he was attending him for some slight illness.

The Judge looked over his glasses and grunted sceptically.

'Didn't you ever watch a possum playing dead, David?'

The state held its breath and waited, but the legislature adjourned at the end of May without having passed any new oppressive legislation. Cavin then settled down to what he hoped would be an uninterrupted summer's work on his plantations, where the new variety of cotton that he had had Jeremiah plant was just coming into bloom.

For some months he had realized, with rising impatience, that, to get the best results from the three places he controlled — his own and Povey's and William's — he needed more time to think out his plans. When he had made Jeremiah overseer, he had given him some detailed suggestions, but since then he had never had any opportunity of trying out the other ideas which simmered in his brain.

'You have to raise enough food on this place,' he had warned Jeremiah positively at that time, 'to feed every man and animal on it.' This rule, though Cavin did not know it, had come straight down to him from men like old Nathaniel who had moved far enough out into the wilderness to know its importance.

Then he had told Jeremiah that, as soon as the cotton was baled, it had to be hurried across the prairie to Colonel Rutherford who would worry about selling it.

'That's his business. How's he going to get his money back if he fails to market my cotton? We make the crop, he worries about shipping it.' Jeremiah had nodded, understanding the arrangement well. 'Sometimes, though,' Cavin went on, 'if the price is poor, he'll naturally hold our bales over.' Jeremiah saw the point.

'And,' Cavin had insisted, 'don't forget to dose all the hands regular with quinine, and let me know right away when anybody turns up sick. You can't make a good crop with sick hands and sore-back mules,' he explained to Jeremiah. 'You can tell what kind of an overseer a man is by just taking a look at his teams.'

Cavin had stressed the next rule particularly. 'And don't go buying anything you can make, or do without,' he had cautioned Jeremiah emphatically. 'A man's sho' to land at the po' farm, if he keeps a-running into town all the time.'

Following these rules, Jeremiah had managed very well, producing some good crops; but always, inside him, Cavin chafed at his inability to make any faster progress with his plans for raising cattle.

Every time he looked at his prairie land, where cotton, if it grew at all, yielded scarcely any return, he thought how cows would thrive and multiply on this infertile soil. In his mind, he saw fine herds fattened on corn and cotton-seed hulls wandering about over the prairie grass, but as yet he had acquired only the barest beginnings of such stock.

He decided that a cotton planter had no business going in for driving range cattle up the Chisholm Trail to Kansas. He had met and talked with ranchers from around San Antonio, and he was acquainted with men in his own section, like John McGaughey, who had given up cotton-planting altogether in favor of cattle-raising. These men were looking for tough, wiry breeds able to stand long, hot drives and sudden changes of weather, cattle who would not mind living on grass and little else. But that was not the kind of enterprise which interested him. He already had as many cattle of that kind as he wanted — long cadaverous beasts, with spreading horns and gloomy, sunken eyes.

'The money,' he argued, 'is going to be in fine, fat beeves. I ought to dig wells and put in feeding-troughs and build shelters against the wind. Fine lambs might pay too. No, maybe it's too hot in this country for lambs. Goats, then. Down in Mexico, they say kids are mighty good eating.'

But during the years he had been mulling over his plans, he had been able to put none of them into execution. Only one step had he made toward doing so. One day, after observing how a heavy, pouring rain had accumulated in a few shallow ditches, it occurred to him how easy it would be to dig out wide, deep dams in the pliable prairie soil and collect water in them through the rainy season. He set to work at once to experiment in a small way, plowing deep furrows to drain the flowing water where he wanted it to go.

''Twouldn't seep out so fast, Mas' Cavin, ef'n you'd plaster the inside o' dis-yere hole wid clay and let it bake dry in de sun,' Jake suggested one day. 'Lak it tell 'bout in de Bible,' he continued. Cavin seized immediately on the idea.

Close to the house was a clay bed, out of which the servants mixed the soft, red paste which, every Saturday, Lucina had them rub over every hearth in her house. In a spell of hot, dry weather Cavin hauled great loads of this clay to the prairie and then, mixing it with dry grass, he showed his negroes how to plaster it over the sides and bottom of the hole. Before the next rains fell, the clay had formed a solid lining to his dam.

All winter and fall he watched this hollow in the prairie fill up and overflow. When, by June of the following summer, the water had not seeped out, he confidently dug two more dams — large ones, this time — several miles apart, and as an afterthought, stocked them with perch.

'Might as well have a little fun,' he speculated. 'Perch fried in butter is better'n chicken.'

Then a sudden idea struck him, and he began to dig again.

'What's dat fur?' asked Jake curiously. 'Ain't us got enough dams?'

'Jake,' said Cavin, 'I bet you anything we've gone to a lot o' trouble for nothing.' He looked at his servant with a sheepish grin. 'I'm going to find out whether water won't stay in a hole without plastering it with clay. Whyn't I think about it before?' he demanded. 'Sometimes a man don't have the sense of a jack rabbit.'

Every day he rode out to observe with great interest the progress of his experiment, and he didn't know whether to be glad or sorry when he found out that his conjecture was correct. By fall, water was standing quite as high in the bare hole as in the ones so laboriously plastered over.

'Now, don't that show you?' he asked Jake in chagrin. 'Don't that show you a man can let his ideas run away with him?' Sitting in the hot sun, staring at his venture, he turned a disgusted eye toward his servant. 'You'd think anybody who's been watching the Yankees ought-a know that much.' This was an experience he never forgot.

Now, he had the dams, but not the cattle to drink out of them.

This summer — the summer of 1871 — he hoped, since the Governor had apparently settled down, to get somewhere with the ideas that scurried around in his brain faster than he could unfold them to Lucina, who, he noticed thankfully, was getting to be like herself again, now that the children were growing up. On the rare occasions when he took stock of his feelings, he knew that what he had felt for Lucina at Cedar Ledge was nothing — a boy's emotion — compared to the sweet and tender torrent that sometimes now seized him when he thought of her. And then, at other times, there would be whole days when he was scarcely aware of having a wife at all.

Every night, when he tightened his reins and Derby fell into a swinging lope down the drive, Cavin gazed on his house with pleasure and satisfaction. There it sat, long and white under the falling shadows, its blinds straight on their hinges, its twin red chimneys rising wide and true against each end, with the sloping roof coming up exactly between them — a house fit for Lucina to live in, he thought.

He always turned his eyes away from the barn, as yet unpainted, that he had thrown together far to the right of the house, and from the sagging cotton-seed shed which faced the cow lot. These were only makeshifts, he told himself, displeased with their looks. But as he turned homeward, he liked to remember the cold, deep well he had bored in his backyard, and to listen to the chickens and turkeys cackling and gobbling in the turkey run to the left of the few peach and plum and pear trees he had planted — the trees that were only the beginning of the complete orchard he intended to develop. He liked, too, to watch how the peacocks' green feathers glistened under the long, slanting light as they spread their tails, marching in stately dignity up and down the avenue. Always, then, whenever he turned into his gate, he saw the drive as it would be, with rolled green grass and tall, straight rows of blooming locusts edging it.

'Now, that gate at the end of the avenue,' he meditated. 'Would stone pillars be better, or brick? And where can I find a man to put 'em up, and hammer out fine steel?' Always at dusk, as he got off his horse and looked down the drive, he thought of the entrance which would some day grace its further end. And always, then, he would remember the great sword gate at Sunny Fields. 'That's the kind of entrance I want — one exactly like that,' Cavin thought impatiently every time he stooped to open the plain, white, wooden gates that, as yet, marked the end of his lane. 'Like the ones Judge Symington used to always be talking about.'

The summer of 1871 was the sixth since his return from the war, but he took no count of how the years had passed. Time seemed to him like a deep well out of which a man could dip and dip without ever lowering the flow.

One hot afternoon in July, Judge White drove over to sample Cavin's watermelon crop and found his host busy with his long account books.

'Cavin,' he remarked, stuffing his pipe and turning his eyes in amusement to where Cavin was standing, impatiently moving his crippled leg, and figuring on top of Philip's black iron safe, 'you remind me of General Washington. Do you remember how, while he was President — even while he was in the army — he kept on making notes about his farm? It looks to me,' the Judge observed thoughtfully, 'that any Southerner worth a damn don't feel natural and right off his own land.'

Cavin looked up.

'I can understand that all right,' he declared. 'Now, take me. I'm as miserable as a sick cat in Austin or Houston, for instance. How on earth does a man ever get used to living on a piece o' ground as big as a pocket handkerchief?' He looked earnestly at the Judge. 'Lord, I'm thankful I'm not called on to do it.' Waving his arms in an expansive gesture, he added, 'Far as I can see, I like to know it's mine.'

'That's my feeling,' said the Judge, comfortably laying his feet on a footstool. 'I hope your melon's cold.'

'It's been on ice since yesterday.' Cavin slammed his ledgers together.

'I was just going over the list of the people at the taxpayers' meeting in Richmond last week. It was a lively gathering, wasn't it? Never saw so many sinners suddenly turning saints in all my life, did you?'

'That'll be mild compared to what the state meeting at Austin in September's going to be, I suppose,' the Judge responded. 'We're getting a lot o' converts I never on earth expected to see marching under our banner. Has your *Statesman* come?'

He held the first issue out in front of him, pointing to Colonel Rutherford's tax estimates. 'That's what's bringing 'em in — that and our' — he smiled — 'our white-robed angels.'

'Some call 'em devils,' Cavin grinned.

The Judge's thin face lighted up, losing its usual austerity. 'The Bishop's back. He spent the night with me. I told him to make a note of our methods, he might find a use for 'em in his own line o' work. Clarissa,' the Judge observed mildly, 'was shocked, and apologized profusely for my levity.'

Cavin's eyes twinkled under their long, light lashes. 'Unless the Bishop's considerably changed by his stay in England,' he predicted, 'he'll appreciate your suggestions — probably use 'em, too. How is he?' he inquired. 'I haven't seen him yet.'

'Fine, fine,' the Judge reported, and laughed. 'He'll be around to see you, don't you worry about that. He's come back all on fire with the notion of opening up a missionary diocese in north Texas; and that idea,' said the Judge shrewdly, 'is going to cost money.'

'It will, all right,' agreed Cavin, moving with his guest toward the gallery where, through the window, he had caught sight of Jake slashing a large, green melon.

'The Bishop,' said the Judge, pausing to choose with deliberate care a long, triangular slice of sweet, red fruit, 'the Bishop could talk a snake's head off, if he set out to do it. You know that as well as I do.'

'He'll show up at every meeting between now and the election,' Cavin prophesied, smiling, 'urging us to remember that the Lord loves old Davis, if nobody else does.' He smiled more widely. 'Well, it's certain nobody else does.'

Despite Cavin's hopes, the summer was far from peaceful, for in August Governor Davis issued an election order which revealed how fearful he was of Democratic success. There would be state police at every voting booth, 'to keep the peace,' the Governor asserted.

'Hunters, too, then,' the planters decided.

Therefore, when the October elections rolled around, they took their stand along the sandy road to the schoolhouse where the citizens living near Locust Hill always voted. In total silence, the hooded riders sat their horses, with their rifles pointed across their saddlehorns. Their intention was merely to hearten timid voters by their presence, but they were doubtful whether the state police ordered out by the Governor would accept any such comparatively innocent interpretation of their purpose. If they were not fired on, however, they had orders to take no action of any kind — merely to stand guard.

Cavin approached the schoolhouse early, with the same sense of enjoyable excitement that any contest of power always aroused in him. He counted the militia hurriedly. Some of the police were colored, he saw, and some white; but there were not enough of them, not nearly enough, to overpower the line of men back on the road.

'The Governor's made a bad miscalculation,' he said to himself, in satisfaction. 'They won't tackle us.'

He got down to take his place in the group of voters that was forming under the eye of a few indolent police.

'They think we're whipped and hogtied,' Cavin calculated and stepped into line between a double row of the Governor's henchmen.

'Move along there, now, one at a time down that plank lane.' The soldier on duty swore in a harsh, nasal voice that marked him as a foreigner. 'Step along now; you gotta do all your talking before you get here. Orders is, no talking.'

Alexander Winston was in front of Cavin and as he put his foot across the lintel, his progress was rudely barred by a colored policeman, who pushed him insolently back and slammed the door in his face. Cavin sprang forward and grabbed Alec's arm, holding it firmly down.

'That damned nigger was as swol up as an old spreadenadder,' Alexander remarked that night, as they rode home together. 'I'd-a shot him if it hadn't-a been for you, Cavin.' Falling back into the language he had used when, as a boy, he had run through the woods with the little negroes on his father's plantation, he turned somewhat apologetically toward his companion.

'You would have, all right, if I hadn't grabbed yo' pistol,' Cavin returned grimly. 'Then where'd we-a been? Where *none* of us could vote, that's certain. The Adjutant's still mad as hell at us for driving him out o' the county, to save yo' onery hide, Alec. He'd-a been delighted to slam us all in jail and plank down martial law.'

Cavin began to shake in his saddle. 'Lord! That nigger thought he was as good as dead and buried!' he laughed. 'I felt kind-a sympathetic with him for feeling so big-Ikey,' he went on, drawling. 'By George!' he declared enthusiastically, 'I was all set up myself. First time I've voted since the year I got home, and then I warn't of age. Maybe we're going to pull out o' this mess, Alec, without killing everybody in the county yet — that is, if we can hold onto our tempers long enough. Lord knows,' he confessed, 'my own disposition is to fill 'em full o' holes on sight. Now,' he went on with evident relish, 'the rascal at the head o' this particular bunch of hellions stationed here — I'd take a lot o' pleasure in seeing him swing, and I don't even know his name. Just to look at that yellow devil makes my hair rise!'

Alexander glared at Cavin disgustedly.

'You make me sick,' he said, 'always using yo' brains the way you do. What fun do you get out o' living? The worst part of it is,' he confessed, with a rueful smile, 'I have to admit you're nearly always right. Not always.' He looked grudgingly at Cavin. 'Not always. Right now, for instance, I think we're making a fool mistake riding hounds with Warren Hughes.' He studied Cavin out of his wide, gray eyes, now grown hard as nails, and moved his long head impatiently. 'Lord knows what he's up to.'

Cavin pursed his lips, whistling thoughtfully.

'Well,' he admitted, 'it's been kind-a worrying me, myself, lately. Several times he hasn't showed up when I was looking for him. The first time,' he said, darting a puzzled glance at Alexander, 'was that night we rode down to pull you out o' trouble at New Columbia.' Cavin took off his hat and ran impatient fingers through his thick hair. 'He's always got some airtight excuse. Come to think of it,' he went on, 'where was he last night?'

'I don't know,' Alexander replied negligently, 'but' — his pleasant voice sharpened — 'I know my best pair o' mules's missing today. The two things kind-a square off, don't they?' He seemed to be uncertain whether to go on. 'I hate to say this, Cavin, because the man's kin to you, but had you noticed Frank Barclay fails to answer roll every now and then too — and it's always when most of us are there?'

'Yes,' Cavin's voice was reluctant, 'I'd noticed it. It's bothered me a heap. You don't think——?' He stopped his horse and laid his hand on his friend's saddlehorn. 'It'd about kill Margaret. She's been looking mighty peaked and mis'able lately. I put it down to the fact that she's expecting her second child long about February, Lucy says.'

They sat there in the darkness going over the chain of circumstances together.

'Well,' Cavin said deliberately, after a long silence, during which he had chosen his course. 'Thieving's not apt to damage yo' aim any, is it? And,' he chuckled, 'there's no doubt on earth robbers are in high favor as voters right now. Alec!' His voice quickened. 'Send over your nigger. I'll spare you a couple o' mules. We got a bigger battle on our hands than tackling Warren Hughes — a battle we'll never win on earth without him and his kind. I've warned him,' Cavin ended. 'He knows what's due him.' He lifted his reins and then let them fall. 'Now,' he said emphatically, 'you take it at Atlanta — there was a regular dog-fight going on between the President and his generals. No,' he spoke slowly, his voice stiffening, 'anyway you look at it, votes are a good sight more important than mules, Alec.'

'I know it,' Alexander answered regretfully. 'But Lord knows I hate holding off of 'em like the devil.'

'You'll feel better after the election,' Cavin suggested confidently.

His prediction was justified. Every single Democratic candidate for Congress was elected, and many well-known Radicals went down under a shower of votes.

Cavin's delight at the result was so exuberant that Lucina hated to tell him that she was going to have another child.

Her third son, William, was born late in June, 1872, and Lucina thought as she lay in her bed so weak that the tears ran, at a word, down her cheeks that he had cost her even more pain and weariness than either of her other two children.

'It looks like I wasn't meant to have children,' she said to Cavin one morning when the baby was a month old, and she still could barely summon the strength to raise her arm. 'Nor Margaret either,' she went on, her face clouding, as she thought of her sister, who was recovering very slowly after her second child's birth. She touched the baby by her side. 'He's a sweet little thing. It would have been nicer to have had a daughter, though. Maybe next time ——'

Cavin's expression, as he leaned over her, surprised her. She paused, waiting for him to speak.

'Lucina!' His voice was hoarse. 'What sort of a double-barrelled fool do you take me for?' He put his hands on her shoulders and gazed down at her with intense earnestness. 'This boy here' — he tapped the bundle by her side lightly — 'is your last child.' He looked deep into her eyes and repeated his words: 'Your last child. Do you hear me?'

Slowly she put up her hand and touched his temple.

'Cavin!' she said, hardly believing what she saw. 'There's some gray hair on your temples.'

'It's a wonder it's not all white!' he groaned. 'Lord, these past few months! You don't know what they've been like!'

'Don't I?' she retorted with surprising spirit, smiling waveringly. 'Don't I?'

'Thank the Lord!' Cavin said gratefully. 'Smile again!'

He began to smile himself.

'I bet you'll never believe something.'

'What won't I believe?' she asked him, laying her cheek on his hand.

His eyes lighted up and he began to chuckle. 'There was a Democratic convention in Corsicana, Lucy ——' he began.

'You didn't stay home?' she interrupted him. 'I don't believe it!'

'I did,' he returned solemnly. 'I did.' He looked at her, suddenly serious.

'I never remembered it was going on!' he exclaimed with deep feeling. 'All I thought about was whether you were going to get well or not.'

She smiled luxuriantly up at him. 'I am,' she promised him. 'I'm going to get well fast now.'

But it was late summer before she was able to be up all day.

The outlook for the regular state elections of November, 1872, was less troubled than at any time since the war. The Democrats, therefore, laid their plans with some assurance. When they heard that the Adjutant-General had absconded with thirty thousand dollars of the state's funds, they were delighted, believing the news would redound — as it did — to their advantage.

'We know where he got nearly three thousand dollars of it,' Colonel Brashear announced dryly. 'Two thousand, seven hundred and sixty-five dollars, warn't it?' he asked Cavin.

'And twenty-five cents,' Cavin returned. 'Makes me boil yet.'

'No need,' said the Colonel amiably. 'Worth more'n that to get rid of a skunk like him.'

As the voting approached, both sides drew their lines tight.

'There's no use even campaigning in Cypress County. The election's already decided there,' Cavin told Colonel Rutherford a month before the voting. 'Even the Germans in the lower end of the county — and they're the only ones now who'll openly admit to being Republicans — are saying that Davis is killing their party in this state. I hope to God,' Cavin added thoughtfully, 'we don't push him out too soon.'

'His term's not up yet, you know,' Colonel Rutherford replied, consulting the reports that were coming in to his office. 'It looks like we are going to carry the election this time, Cavin.'

They smiled at one another, feeling like runners at the close of a long race.

'You've had experience,' Colonel Rutherford urged John McGaughey; 'it's your duty to represent this district up at Austin. We'll elect you, if you'll run.'

'Doggone it! That's exactly what I'm afraid of,' John replied. 'I've had that job once, I know what it's like.' But finally he had consented to allow his name again to be printed on the ballot and he was one of a decided Democratic majority elected to the legislature.

The night after the returns were published, Lucina stood at her front gate watching bonfires and fireworks flashing in the sky on every plantation; as far as her eye could reach, there was a celebration going on. The colored children at Locust Hill were puzzled by all the merriment, and, concluding that it must be Christmas, bewailed the absence of presents. Finally, Uncle Arthur explained to them that the white people were celebrating their freedom, the way the colored people had celebrated theirs every nineteenth of June since General Granger had posted the order at Galveston releasing them from slavery.

'Praise de Lawd!' the old preacher said to Cavin as he rode up to the house that night and, dismounting from his tattered, old, gray mule, whipped off his hat. 'We'se all free now, Mas' Cavin — de white folks and de niggers, too. Dis county is gwine-a be a plenty nice place to live in now.' He peered earnestly up at Cavin. 'Is you whupped 'em good, Mas' Cavin, so dey'll stay down? I sho hopes to de Lawd you has, de onery, no-account critters, always a-pokin' deir noses in whar dey ain't wanted no more'n a polecat.'

After the fireworks were over and the excitement had somewhat died down, Cavin told Lucina that, in his opinion, Uncle Arthur had stated the case quite neatly.

'The Bishop couldn't-a put it better,' he grinned. 'My Lord!' he exclaimed, 'I feel like a man let out o' jail.'

'Well,' Lucina replied slowly, 'people go right on sleeping and eating and raising children and crops, don't they, no matter *who's* running the country?'

'Pa said something like that once,' Cavin remarked, thinking of his conversation with Philip the first night he returned to Texas. 'It's been in my mind off and on ever since.' He looked at her in a puzzled fashion, struggling to clarify his own ideas on the subject. 'The way I figure it, though, Lucy, is, that if you don't watch out, you'll be raising your crops and your children, too, to suit somebody else and not yourself. There's something about holding office that seems to make any man alive hone to tell you how much salt to put in your soup.' He smiled broadly. 'I never was in any group o' people yet but that, sooner or later, somebody got the idea he was smart enough to run everybody else's business. Looks like it's human nature,' he asserted. 'That's why you've got to keep your eyes open.'

Chapter 22

THE Christmas of 1872 was the most cheerful since the war, and Lucina invited a good many guests to dinner that day. As she took her seat at the table, Matt was just bringing in the tureen of oyster stew for her to serve — stew rich with cream and full of the plump oysters Colonel Rutherford never failed to send out from Galveston every Christmas Eve. She glanced appraisingly down the long white cloth. There in front of Cavin was the huge turkey, its neck draped with hot, spicy sausages. In the middle of the table stood a golden chicken pie, delicately fluted around its edges; and, just back of the tureen, was a silver platter holding a large ham with a crisp, brown crust neatly marked off into diamonds punctuated by raisins and cloves. She leaned a little closer, to take a surreptitious sniff. Yes, Aunt Emmy had remembered to baste the big ham with sherry. Satisfied, she sat back in her chair and smiled at her guests.

There were eight of them — Margaret and Frank, Colonel Brashear and his two daughters, Judge White and Miss Clarissa and David. And, not counting the two babies, the children made nine more to eat Christmas dinner at Locust Hill. Glancing out the windows from the dining-room to the back gallery, where the children were seated around another table, Lucina heard old Aunt Elvy cautioning them — Aunt Elvy, who was now getting so old that she had several young nurses to help her.

'Set still, you all,' the old woman was saying. 'Don't yo' let me see 'ary one o' you pushin' and shovin' like little niggers.'

Cavin heard her, too, and laying down his long carving-knife, he turned, with a sudden impatient movement of his whole body, to Jake, who was standing at his elbow with another knife and a silver-handled sharpener in his hand.

'Go bring me those chillun's plates,' he told his servant. Then he looked back across his shoulder at his friends. 'I found out in the army what it's like to be hungry,' he explained, an apologetic note in his deep voice.

'Lucy,' he announced, swinging himself around again, 'from now on in this house, we're going to serve all the children first, beginning with the youngest, right straight up the line.'

Lucina smiled at his distress. 'Don't worry, Cavin. Aunt Emmy's baked a separate turkey for them. Maria'll be bringing it out in a minute.'

Cavin began to carve again in quick, accurate strokes.

'Be sure Josh gets a plenty,' he warned Jake, as the slices began to fall off his knife.

'Lawd, Mas' Cavin,' Jake beamed, 'dat boy been climbing all over Aunt Emmy's feets since fo' breakfus' dis mornin'.'

'Josh is getting along all right,' said Lucina. 'Look out there!'

The amusement in her voice caused the whole table to peer out the window.

Beau, they saw, had drawn up his own little table and chair for Josh, and, close beside the white children, Josh's black head was bobbing as contentedly as theirs over a mound of rice and gravy.

Jake laughed when he caught sight of his son, and then asked Cavin, 'You know whut Beau tol' Maria yestiddy?'

'No,' Cavin returned interestedly; 'what?' Ceasing his carving, he leaned back to listen.

Jake grinned, much amused. 'He say Josh dar ain't no nigger chile, he is a dark-skinned white gentleman.'

When the laughter that followed his account had died down, Cavin took up his knife and began to carve again, laying a slice of white meat and a slice of dark in neat orderly piles on the plate in Jake's hand.

'If they don't have Christmases in heaven,' he observed, looking up when he was half through, 'I'm going to quit and leave.'

'How you know,' asked the Judge with interest, 'that you're headed that way, Cavin? You warn't at church with Lucina last Sunday, I observed.' He leaned back, sampling with a careful tongue the dewberry wine by his plate. 'Some of Philip's, I take it?' he hazarded.

'Yes,' Cavin returned absently, 'it is. Laid down the first year he came to Texas.'

He regarded the Judge earnestly, his mind on his first question. 'I'm convinced,' he said, his bright eyes twinkling as he resumed his carving, 'that the Lord's got more sense than to expect a man to let his cows stand out in a norther whilst he's doing his praying.'

When the legislature convened in January, 1873, there was some talk of impeaching Governor Davis, but his message was mild and, as John McGaughey wrote Colonel Rutherford, 'to do so would take up the time we ought to put in repealing the infamous laws the Governor has inaugurated. We've set,' he wrote jubilantly, 'the first Tuesday in next December for the election that will sweep out this damnable administration. With renewed assurance of respect,' he signed himself, 'I am, my dear sir, Your obedient servant, John McGaughey.' As an afterthought he had added: 'P.S. We had ice here yesterday morning. They say it freezes, up here, right often. Rather live down where we do.'

Colonel Rutherford read the letter with some concern. 'John's too confident,' he told Cavin, when he came into Galveston after supplies. 'We haven't heard the last of Davis. He hasn't sense enough to know when he's beat. Cavin!' he sighed, 'when a man gets to thinking he's called on by the Lord to do some mighty work, it's apt to take the angel Gabriel to throw him out, no less.'

'Shouldn't be surprised.' Cavin looked out of the window at the whitecaps topping the waves, and laughed, pointing toward a shoal of porpoises which were rolling, with their enormous black fins upraised, in and out the comparatively peaceful water beyond the breaking surf.

'Still, look at those critters,' he went on. 'You might think they'd be as vicious as sharks, but a shoal of little bitty fish can scatter 'em. Maybe we'll get the whole Davis following on the run without much more trouble, Colonel.' He grinned complacently. 'Most of 'em got about as much horse sense as a jack rabbit, anyhow.'

'Cavin,' the Colonel said, fixing his blue eyes coldly on his visitor, 'don't you go getting optimistic. Not until we've won this next election. And not then. Not ever,' he advised him. 'Not ever. Man's a poor sinful creature who's considerably more apt to grow horns than wings,' he explained thoughtfully. 'There's no time you don't have to watch out for the horns, Cavin.' Looking at him meaningfully, he continued, 'Sometimes I've even seen 'em, myself, growing right smack out

from under a man's wings.' Leaning forward anxiously, he
laid his hands on his listener's knees. 'Don't you forget what
I'm telling you.'

Cavin felt the pressure of the Colonel's hands tightening.
'I won't forget,' he promised.

'Lord-a-mercy!' Colonel Rutherford went on, leaning back
in apparent satisfaction. 'Men have been murdering one another for many a long year over that very point — whether
men are by nature sinful or good. Or,' he meditated, 'over
other matters just as foolish, like whether the Lord takes
shape only in emperors and kings, or in every man alive. My
observation, in Texas ——' He broke off smiling. 'There's no
better place to do your observing. Well, I made up my mind
long ago, when I was a young man, from what I saw going on
in the Republic, that the Lord has a pretty hard job crowding
into *any* man's heart, be he black or white, king or common
man. Everybody living's plain full o' the Devil, I reckon, and
nobody's so good he won't bear watching. Once you come
to that conclusion,' the Colonel looked at Cavin soberly,
'you're fit to try to govern — provided,' he went on keenly,
'you don't forget you're just as tarred as anybody with an in-
born taste for sin.' He leaned back and sighed, gazing at
Cavin apologetically.

'I don't know what came over me to talk so much — except
that I've come to realize lately I'm not going to live forever.'

Cavin rose and stood watching Colonel Rutherford silently.

'I'm not, either,' he said and smiled as a look of surprise
crept into his face. 'But it's the first time I ever thought about
it, while you were talking.' Moving over to the chair in which
the Colonel lay comfortably stretched out, with his hands
clasping its wide arms, he laid his brown fingers lightly on the
Colonel's wrist. 'Don't get up,' he said, and stood a moment

longer looking down at him. 'I'm going to tell Beau what you've been saying, when he gets bigger.'

As the elections of December, 1873, approached, Governor Davis revealed that he by no means considered himself beaten. He had the blind courage that animates many fanatics, and he carried his fight openly into the very counties — Cypress among them — where he was most despised.

'I'm going to vote my negroes — every last man of 'em,' Cavin announced to David one evening after their return from a meeting at Berryville. 'What you going to do, Tom?' he inquired of Thomas Abernethy, who was sitting next to him on David's front gallery. They were sampling the fig wine which old James Armstrong had always declared was better than the blackberry that most of his friends made every spring and then bottled for their children to enjoy, twenty years later.

'How you know you can count on 'em voting the way you tell 'em to?' Thomas asked, still in doubt as to what course he himself would follow. 'Hits the spot, David,' he remarked, pouring himself out another drink, while he waited for Cavin's answer. Carefully he savored the taste and smell of the golden liquor in his thin glass. 'Still, there's a little bite in the blackberry——' This was an old debate, and Thomas lost interest in it. 'How you know, Cavin?' he persisted.

'They'll vote the way I tell 'em,' Cavin answered positively. 'They're used to doing what I say. Besides, we're still riding this bottom, ain't we?' He sat watching his friends without moving. They saw that some thought was taking shape in his mind. 'Listen,' he went on, 'we better get busy hunting up all the big, tall white boys in this county, too. You remember the first election after the war? We got a lot o' the under-age ones through then.'

An amused smile flickered across his lips. 'We're going to have to get out of a mighty lot o' bad habits, once this state's sewed up for the Democrats. It's going to be right hard to remember how to run an election by all the rules.'

Thomas laughed. 'And not near so much fun.' He sat eyeing his friends in sardonic mirth. 'They tell me in Galveston, they're having a panic up North, and the bottom's dropping out of everything.' Stretching his arms above his head, he yawned vigorously. 'Strikes me, there's some advantage in having nothing to lose.'

'Except the election,' Cavin put in, 'and that's a far chance.'

The total vote was surprising, even to John McGaughey, for the Democratic nominee for Governor, Judge Richard Coke, received almost double the votes cast for the Radical, Davis, and all the new state officials, as well as the great majority of legislators and county officers, were elected on the same ticket.

Cavin momentarily forgot Colonel Rutherford's advice against premature confidence; but soon he was aware that the Colonel had accurately gauged Davis's temperament. For the Governor flatly refused to accept the returns, and announced, not only that he was relying on his Supreme Court appointees to set aside the election, but that, if necessary, he would call on Grant to support him. 'I am resolved,' he wrote, 'at any cost to put down the slow civil war that is going on in this state.'

Colonel Rutherford sent out a letter, then, to the Democratic committee. 'We must act,' he warned them, 'without delay.'

A few days later they were seated around his table in his office, with the waves pounding unheard outside.

'Davis must be insane!' Colonel Rutherford began, in a voice marked by both anger and regret. 'He doesn't seem to have any idea how Texans respond to high-handedness.'

'He's digging his own grave.' Cavin spoke confidently.

'Ours, too, maybe,' the Colonel responded soberly. 'I've thought right along that he wouldn't give up without drawn battle. What is your advice, gentlemen?'

Titus Blackwood looked up from a piece of wood he was carefully whittling into shape. 'Colonel,' he said, 'you remember we had to ketch and tie up my Mexican before we convinced him banditry was unhealthy.'

'Mr. Yeardley?' The Colonel was withholding his own decision until he had discovered the sentiment of his committee. 'What course do you recommend?'

'I heard a lot o' different tales before I started out,' Ebenezer answered slowly. 'I thought I wouldn't make up my mind till I got the facts straight. Just what is the Governor threatening? I ain't seen a paper,' he explained, 'in the Lord knows when. I found out' — he looked around the board, apologizing for his ignorance — 'a man cain't believe anything he reads, so I quit taking a paper at all.'

'Good sense,' the Colonel agreed, 'plain good sense.' He looked toward the end of the table where Major Gresham was sitting. 'Major,' he requested, 'will you lay the case before us, exactly as it stands?'

Sewall Gresham arose. 'I will try,' he said, 'not to let my feelings distort my account.' He stood silent a moment, gathering his facts together in his mind. Colonel Rutherford thought, as he watched him, that he made a fine figure of a man standing there, with his firm, lean cheeks outlined by brown sideburns, and his very large, gray eyes overtopped by brows always slightly raised, as if he were perpetually surprised at what he saw going on in the world.

'As I understand the situation,' he began calmly, 'Governor Davis is asking the Supreme Court to set aside the December election because of a punctuation mark. He insists that, with a proper pause for a semicolon, the present Constitution calls for a four-day period for every state election. The last legislature, however, set aside only one day, instead of four, for the recent election, which Davis is, therefore, petitioning the court to declare null and void. Bear in mind, gentlemen,' he commented in a dry voice, 'the further fact that the court is packed with the Governor's vassals.' Then, leaning sharply across the table, he uttered his next words with more fire than he had yet permitted himself to display. 'I believe,' he continued in a rising tone, 'I believe Davis has no intention on earth of giving up his office. Furthermore, I expect him to be supported from Washington.' Pausing, he looked slowly around the board. 'I was always opposed to surrender,' he remarked emphatically, and took his seat in almost complete silence.

'Thank you, Sewall,' Colonel Rutherford said, lacing his stout fingers carefully together. 'There is how the matter lies, gentlemen. What stand do you think we ought to take?'

James Hardenbrook sat up straight in his chair, his black eyes snapping. It was almost the first time he had raised his voice in committee meeting. The Colonel was wondering what he would say, when he saw him rising impulsively to his feet, with his tall, spare figure bent slightly forward.

'Davis'll understand only one kind of election figures,' he said hotly. 'I'm in favor of ramming 'em down his throat. When does the legislature convene, Colonel?'

'The thirteenth,' the Colonel replied slowly, almost hesitantly. 'The thirteenth of January.' He turned his gaze soberly around the table.

'That's the conclusion I have reluctantly reached, myself, gentlemen — the identical conclusion. We have exhausted every possible avenue of peaceful persuasion.'

Cavin was on his feet.

'I've been holding our group back, Colonel.'

Titus Blackwood laid down his whittling and pulled thought-fully on his floating beard. 'It's quite a step back to the Nueces,' he observed. 'Our boys better bring their tents along.'

'You all seem to be of one mind,' the Colonel remarked. 'You understand it's touch and go?' he inquired carefully. 'Davis may get support from Grant, as Major Gresham suggests, and the police will be dead certain to remember who issues their pay. What we are undertaking is to defy the Governor and probably the President.' He sat meditating. 'Still, I repeat, I see no other course. Speaking for myself alone, I shall be in Austin on the morning of January the twelfth.' He paused, looking searchingly at the listeners. 'I may be wrong. I hope every man here will examine his own conscience and vote in the light of what he finds there.' After a long silence, he spoke again. 'I call now for a show of hands.'

He looked around the table, and with a deep sigh dropped his knuckles heavily on the polished board in front of him.

'It's unanimous, then?' He was apparently weighing their decision, as if oppressed by it.

Titus Blackwood darted a quick glance under his shaggy eyebrows in the Colonel's general direction.

'You act a little regretful about having to defy authority, Colonel,' he said in a surprised tone. 'You and me ought to be accustomed to doing that by this time, looks to me. Warn't we both red hot for a Republic, and then, after that, for seces-sion?' Resuming his whittling, he observed, 'I never had any complaint about being called a Rebel, none in the world.' He looked out across the Gulf with reminiscent eyes. 'Lord! Lord! I laugh yet when I think of how those po' Mexicans

hated to wake up from their siestas at San Jacinto. They seemed
to think 'twarn't really polite of us to spring a fight on 'em.'
Turning his gaze back on the Colonel, he studied him severely.
'Authority!' he snorted. 'That's a word I plain hate. The
matter with the Yankees is, they like it.'

Colonel Rutherford smiled.

'Mr. Jefferson, if I recollect aright, Titus, shared your aver-
sion. But,' he observed, smiling more broadly, 'I never noticed,
in reading about him in office, that he minded exercising
authority himself. You're kinda like him. I expect we all are.
Authority is all right, provided *we* exercise it.' He sent an
interrogative glance around the group. 'No harm in seeing
ourselves straight, is there?'

There was a ripple of appreciative laughter. 'Well, back to
business.' Colonel Rutherford's ruddy, round face seemed to
lengthen and harden.

'I've been remembering, as we sat here, gentlemen, Grant's
conduct at Appomattox. There's a chance — a bare chance,
I admit, but a chance — that he may refuse to support Davis.'
He came to a sudden decision. 'Would you approve my wiring
him tonight, putting our case before him?'

Titus Blackwood rubbed his square jaws, and then pulled
on his beard. 'I'll pay for sending that telegram, myself,
Colonel. Long's I've known you, I never saw you fail to turn
up a good idea when you needed it!'

The rest of the heads around the table nodded in warm
agreement. Colonel Rutherford stood up, rising with a sudden, decisive movement that belied his weight.

'Very well, gentlemen. Keep in touch with me and report
your progress. I'll lay the information before our new Adjutant-
General, McCulloch.' He looked straight down the table till
his eye found Sewall Gresham's. 'What was that song, Sewall,

the young people were singing at your house the other night when I was over there?'

Sewall Gresham rose to his feet, and the others followed his example. He seemed to be trying to recall the song to which the Colonel referred.

'Ah!' he exclaimed, 'you mean the one that ends, "Cry vengeance for Texas! and God speed the right." '

'Exactly,' Colonel Rutherford replied. 'Exactly!'

On the night of January the twelfth, 1874, very few people in Austin closed their eyes. That morning, the town began to fill up with angry, silent men, most of them dusty, unshaven, and tired; and all day they kept pouring in, on every road. By dusk, they were sprawled out over all the open space around the capitol, or hunched together, in sullen lines, along the boarded sidewalks. Hour after hour the crowd, so strangely silent, thronged up and down around the capitol, exchanging sardines and crackers and cheese, but extremely few words.

Colonel Rutherford, sitting beside the new Adjutant-General just outside his tent, studied the slowly moving throng which filled the capitol grounds and overflowed out from it into every adjacent street.

'What you going to do with all of them, McCulloch? There must be' — he calculated roughly — 'two or three times as many as we figured on. How'll we get 'em all organized in time? It's getting late. Morning'll be here before you know it.'

McCulloch's calm, blue eyes roved over the crowd which, in the misty half-light of evening, seemed to move, even to breathe, in unison. 'I'm not figuring on organizing them, Colonel. They're plenty riled up to act on their own account. Besides,' he added with a slight smile that barely ruffled his tight lips, 'I've had the Supreme Court's decision printed and circulated among them — the decision declaring the last election unconstitutional; and,' he concluded confidently, 'right now most of the men out there are studying the proclamation the Governor posted this morning, warning them not even to try to seat the officers they elected.' He darted a shrewd glance at the Colonel. 'If that kind o' reading don't stir up Texans, nothing will. Still — just to be certain — I've closed up the saloons tighter'n a bucket, and padlocked the gambling dens, and notified every last company of militia that they're responsible to me — and to me alone. I've called on the Governor's guard, the Travis Rifles, in particular, to support me — if I need 'em. But,' he concluded, 'I don't hardly believe I will.' He waved a negligent hand toward the crowd, from which some hard inflexible purpose seemed to stream.

'Those men out there know what they're here for, or they wouldn't be here,' he said. 'All we need to do is to make the first move. They'll be along right after us and use their sense doing it too.' Climbing up on a table beside him in order to get a better view, he looked out over the grounds, on which the early dark was beginning to fall, partially masking the white columns at the summit of the hill and the little balcony that projected, as in so many private homes, over the entrance door of the capitol.

'Come here, Colonel!' he exclaimed, dropping his hands from his eyes and pointing with a steady, brown finger. 'Look where I'm looking. Who do you see?' His face expressed utter astonishment. 'There's one o' the leading Radicals on our side, or I'm losing my eyesight!'

Colonel Rutherford climbed up beside him.

'You're right!' he exclaimed, and chuckled. 'You forget some of 'em have had a kind o' change o' heart lately. I heard one of 'em, myself, calling the state police wolves, last week.

But' — the Colonel's mouth hardened — 'it'll take more than that to convince me they've got religion.'

The General's laughter got the better of him.

'They're all going to be climbing up on the mourner's bench right soon now, I figure. They'll conclude it's healthier there, not to say more profitable.' He took off his white hat and waved it vigorously in the direction of a man he saw approaching through the crowd.

'Who's that?' Colonel Rutherford inquired.

'Oh, just one o' my boys,' the Adjutant replied casually. 'I told him he better pass the word around for all the men to keep their eyes on this flag.' He laid his hand on the folds of a large flag of the Republic floating just above his head.

'Let's set down,' he suggested.

They climbed down and McCulloch put his feet comfortably up on a camp-stool. 'It don't matter,' he observed, reflectively, looking upward, 'whether you are a Reb or a Yank under that flag. It'll cover you both.'

'That's true,' Colonel Rutherford assented. 'It's always been true.' Then he swung sharply on his friend.

'When do you figure on moving in?' he demanded. 'Coke's here and all the new state officers and legislators, you know, waiting on you to say when.'

'Yes,' McCulloch replied equably. 'They been telling me so every ten minutes all day. I'm aiming on waiting till plumb-black dark, Colonel, maybe longer. I figure on learning what Grant intends to do, if I can, before I start moving.'

'Grant wired me,' the Colonel replied, 'that he was considering the message I sent him. Lord knows what that means!' He turned impatiently, cocking an anxious eye at McCulloch.

'How you figuring on learning whether we're going to have to take on the whole United States Army?'

While he waited for an answer, the Colonel let his glance wander over the new Adjutant. McCulloch, he observed in some amusement, wore a rumpled pair of dark trousers, carelessly stuffed into his boots, and a white shirt, drawn together at the collar by a crisp, red handkerchief, dotted with large, blue stars. A slight norther was blowing, and the General had thrown on a jacket, as ill-fitting as his trousers. Where it hung open, a worn leather belt, sewn round with cartridges, was revealed — a belt from which hung also a bowie knife, and two gleaming six-shooters. The Colonel spoke disgustedly.

'Shucks! I've got on as many decorations myself as you're wearing, McCulloch. You ought to have on a uniform and badges and things, like that nigger policeman strutting up and down outside Davis's door. For an Adjutant-General, you look kinda humble to me.'

McCulloch was pained by the remark. He examined himself hurriedly. 'Why, Colonel,' he remonstrated, in his soft, unhurried voice, 'I got on a bran-clean shirt, and I spent two bits on this handkerchief just this morning.' He pointed to the blue stars in it and then to the star on the flag above his tent. 'Seemed to me kind of appropriate for the occasion. Besides' — he lowered his voice till it was a whisper — 'that nigger policeman you're talking about is going to turn over all his jewelry to me, as quick as he gets inside this tent. That's not saying I'm going to put it on though, Colonel — not even to satisfy you.'

'You mean —— ?' The Colonel was genuinely startled.

'Sure,' McCulloch drawled, stretching out his long legs. 'Sure. I went down to see him 'fo daylight, down where he sleeps. I told him we'd see he didn't get hurt when we started hanging all the other police right here on this square tomorrow morning, *provided*,' McCulloch explained carefully, '*provided* he'd come tell me what Davis said when he got that telegram back from Washington.' He laughed heartily. 'I put it on a little thick, I admit. I warned the darky we were planning on starting a blaze under every black policeman, befo' we hung 'em. I figured he'd spread the news. Then,' he explained modestly, 'I made it clear to him old Croesus wasn't as rich as we were — nor as generous. He saw reason,' the General observed, 'but I got a dozen men watching him. He'll come cutting through the crowd hell-for-Hallelujah directly, and then I'll know where I'm at, Colonel.' He stopped, eyeing his friend carefully. 'What's the use o' bringing down the whole United States Army on us by drawing too quick?'

'You don't suppose,' the Colonel inquired, 'that Davis'll get nervous and start shooting, himself?'

McCulloch turned his head toward the capitol, where, on the lower floor, all the windows were now aglow with light. Nonchalantly, he began to drone beneath his breath, 'Jeff Davis rides a milk-white steed, Abe Lincoln rides a mule,' repeating the words over and over like a litany. Then he broke off and answered the Colonel.

'That's a chance, of course — but I don't think he will. He can see, cain't he?' Again he waved his hand toward the crowd. 'And count? They tell me he's a well-educated man. Probably,' hazarded McCulloch, 'he's begun to suspect by now that there ain't a Texan alive'll stand being dictated to. No — ' he spoke more decisively — 'I don't think he'll make a move till he hears from Grant. He'll lay low till then; but God knows what he'll do after that, if he turns desperate. A pig-headed man like him's apt to lose his head under stress.' He reflected a few moments in silence, beginning again to murmur in a deep solemn bass, 'Jeff Davis rides a milk-white steed, Abe Lincoln rides a mule.'

'Only good thing I ever heard about the Governor,' he remarked, after some minutes, 'is he himself ain't no richer now than when he took office. You cain't say that about his lieutenants, though. Watch out!' His booming voice rose. 'Here comes my nigger!'

He dashed out into the crowd, shoving right and left, taking great swinging strides until he reached a panting colored policeman whose clothes had been almost torn off of him by the crowd through which he had passed. He was supported by two of McCulloch's deputies.

The negro was gray with fright. McCulloch grabbed him. 'Throw some water in his face, Colonel. We cain't have him fainting on us, not yet anyway, not till he tells us what we want to know.'

Seizing the policeman's collar, he shook him fiercely till his badge dropped off on the ground.

'What'd he say? What'd Davis say when he opened the telegram?' he demanded.

'Lawd God, Boss! You ain't goin' to let nobody hurt me?' The negro's voice was imploring. McCulloch stooped until his face was level with the black man's.

'I told you I'd protect you. What'd he say? What — did — he — say?' His voice grew ominous, and the negro's quick ear caught the intensity flowing through the low words.

'He didn't say nothin', Boss, nothin' at all; but he looked madder'n hell and all of a sudden he jumped up an' run out quick — whar to I don't know.'

'I do,' one of the lieutenants said shortly. 'I know exactly where he went — to call out the Travis Rifles. I followed him, to see.'

McCulloch sprang up, and, thrusting the negro toward the lieutenants who had brought him in, strode to the open doorway of his tent.

Hauling down the flag of the Republic, he lifted it above his head, swinging it slowly back and forth like a pendulum. The silence outside, already ominous, was broken by a dull, sullen roar, which McCulloch silenced by raising both his hands.

'Fellow Texans!' he began in a quiet, gentle, almost dreamy tone of voice, 'we have had enough strife in this state. I propose tonight to take over this capitol without shedding a drop of blood, if I can help it. I urge you all to hold your tempers and your fire as long as possible.' He stood, looking out over the brown, set faces in front of his tent. 'My plan is simple,' he concluded. 'The Governor's colored troops hold the lower floor. We will take the upper, entering by the back stairway. Once inside, the new Governor and the legislature will be sworn in.'

There was a rumbling murmur of assent from those who could hear McCulloch's words and then a whispering and a stirring like wind in the corn, as his instructions were passed back from man to man. McCulloch stood waiting until he could tell by the renewed silence, that his suggestions were understood by the crowd.

Then the new Governor, Richard Coke, motioned to the members of the legislature assembled about him, and they moved forward, taking their stand by McCulloch. Coke was a huge man, with a full, flowing beard and a head thrown up to meet whatever came his way. His hands and feet were so large that he had to have his shoes and gloves made to order, yet he did not give the impression of walking heavily. As he stood now in the full light appraising the situation, there was a certain alertness in his tall figure that marked him as a more wiry, nervous individual than his size at first suggested. His clothes fitted him precisely, as always, and across his broad diaphragm was draped a heavy gold watch chain which he absently fingered while he watched McCulloch's least move.

Standing out in the crowd, with David pushing against his elbow, Cavin carefully inspected the new Governor and, as he did so, he began to smile.

'You can tell by the set of his back,' he whispered to David, 'that he's remembering how old Sheridan pitched him off the Supreme Court.' Then eyeing him even more carefully, he commented, 'Makes me think of my bird-dog, Hector, scenting a bird. He'll be hot on their trail all right.'

David glanced at Cavin, surprised. 'I believe we're moving!'

The crowd pushed against them and flowed around them, shoving them forward, as McCulloch began his slow advance toward the capitol. Thump! Thump! Thump! Already, in the curious stillness, each man could hear the booted feet around him beginning to quicken, hear them moving in faster and faster rhythm until, when they began to ascend the stairs, the sound was like heavy surf beating against the shore. Ominously repeated, over and over again, the rhythmic echo of the ascending feet suddenly broke upon the night. The negro police, hearing it, shuddered and retreated out of the halls into the legislative chambers, seeking there the protection once afforded criminals by the high altar of the Church.

McCulloch's followers stopped dead in their tracks, listening to the confusion below. For a brief moment, from their places on the steps, they stared down into the rooms now jammed full of terrified colored police trying in vain to hide behind desks or behind one another. One glance was enough for the white men. A low rumble, more like a growl than a roar, broke from them, and, turning back, or vaulting over the low stair railing, they fell upon the negroes with a purpose as resolute as it was unpremeditated.

Without a word, they began stripping them of their badges and their uniforms, passing from one to the next with the inescapable efficiency of locusts clearing a forest of leaves. Then, grabbing the now almost naked black figures by any hold possible, they flung them, one by one, out through the broad, open windows onto the lawn below. Trapped and desperate, the negroes fought back, but soon the rooms were clear.

Still the crowd poured up the steps, where, in the upper hall, leaning over the rotunda, McCulloch was watching the struggle below. When he was satisfied of the outcome, he walked over to a window and looked out of it at the negro police scurrying across the capitol grounds. Negligently he kicked at a shining police badge on the floor at his feet before he turned and spoke to Colonel Rutherford.

'Po' ignorant critters!' he said, pointing out of the window. 'The Davis gang got rich off 'em, collecting three dollars for a two-bit piece o' jewelry like this!' Laying his toe against the badge at his feet, he sent it flying toward the wall. 'Not to speak of charging 'em fifty dollars for a broken-down horse not worth ten,' he continued in disgust. 'We're actually doing 'em a kindness in pitching 'em out o' the capitol.'

At daybreak, when the excitement had partially died down, the two houses convened in the dusty upper chambers of the capitol, and in the pallid light of dawn the officers took their oaths.

Governor Coke turned to face his colleagues, and slowly raised his hand. There was almost complete silence in the room, anyway, except for a vague shuffling of feet, and some coughing. But now even these noises ceased, and the Governor was aware that the men facing him were listening as men do only a few times in their lives, perhaps only once. He would be brief, but the words burning on his tongue must be uttered, now, tonight. He had a slight lisp in his speech of which he was usually conscious, but he forgot it entirely as he threw back his large head, and, with his hands resting on his heavy stick, began to talk.

'Tonight, fellow Texans,' he exclaimed in a voice leaping with the emotion which he held resolutely in check, 'tonight constitutional representative government, so long lost, is restored and the ancient liberties of the people of Texas re-established. The issues we have faced are not new in the world's history. Our ancestors before us fought and died to preserve the very same liberties we are this night celebrating. God grant our children, and their children, till time shall end, may treasure what we this day have won again for them to enjoy!'

'So,' thought Governor Coke, watching the grim faces around him, 'so must our people have looked when they faced King John at Runnymede.' Studying those brown, set faces, he found it easy to understand why the king had yielded to his barons. 'The spirit's still in us,' he reflected, remembering the history he had learned at William and Mary long before he had come out, with a descendant of the great Virginian, Judge Wythe, to practise law at Waco. Jerking himself back to the present, he stepped down from the platform, silencing the applause that began, after his deep, solemn voice had ceased. He turned tentatively to the Adjutant, McCulloch.

'You might, I suppose,' he suggested, 'try a little argument on Governor Davis, if he's still down there in his office?'

'Oh, yes, he's down there, sittin' tight as a snail on a log,' one of McCulloch's lieutenants reported, grinning. 'He's waiting for Grant's army to show up and having a fit because the Travis Rifles he ordered out ain't surrounding his chair.'

McCulloch glanced out the corner of a twinkling eye at the alert young captain of the Travis Rifles standing immediately beside him. 'What'll I tell him, Captain?'

'You might ease his mind a little, sir,' the young captain

suggested amiably, 'and let him know Sheriff Zimpleman summoned me here to keep the peace and' — his voice hardened —
'that I'm doing it. In the light o' my own conscience, o' course,'
he added, grinning, and shifting his gun.

'I reckon,' said McCulloch thoughtfully, 'that Davis must-a
forgotten the sheriff's a Terry Ranger. Besides,' he commented,
'he seems still to be figuring on persuading Grant.' Feeling in
his pocket, he produced a copy of a telegram one of his men
had just handed him. 'This is the last telegram the President
sent him,' he explained. 'What I cain't see,' he drawled, 'is
how as reasonable a man as Grant seems to be ever come to
take up with the Yankees. Here 'tis, Governor,' he said,
handing the message over to Governor Coke, who took it
from him and, going to the window, read it out in a firm tone.

'Wouldn't it be prudent as well as right,' Grant had wired
Davis, 'to yield to the verdict of the people as expressed in the
ballot?'

For the first time that night, the men gathered in the room
began to cheer and, throwing their hats into the air, they let
loose the high, piercing yell most of them had practised on the
battle field. But McCulloch held up a firm hand.

'Wait!' he urged his audience. 'Maybe,' he suggested, turning to Governor Coke, 'I *had* better go down and argue a little
more with the Governor. It'd be a downright shame to have
to pitch an old man like him out o' the window, the way we
did the niggers.'

Accompanied by a committee from both houses, he went down
the steps, but soon returned, shaking his head in disgust.

'Stubborn as a mule,' he reported. 'Well,' he added looking
again out of the window where the crowd that could not push
itself into the capitol stood waiting, 'we got as much time as he
has — and more men. He'll give in about tomorrow,' he pre-

dicted. 'You know,' he said thoughtfully, 'the Governor's got
a kind of tight, stiff face. Makes me think of somebody. Who
is it?' he asked the new Governor, and then struck his hands
against his sides in sudden recognition of the resemblance.

'I'll be doggoned,' he exclaimed, 'if he ain't the spittin'
image o' Old Joe Johnston — and just as stubborn.'

The Adjutant, however, had underestimated Governor
Davis's tenacity. It was not until four days later, on the afternoon of the seventeenth of January, that Davis walked out of
the Governor's office, and McCulloch's forces into it.

'Not,' commented McCulloch to Colonel Rutherford, 'not
until he got another wire from Grant refusing for the third
time to furnish United States troops. Looks like the General's
learned something since Appomattox,' he conceded, in grudging
praise.

Turning, he took his hat and, dusting off the chair where
Davis had sat, offered it politely to Governor Coke.

'Pig-headed man, Davis!' he remarked. 'Set down, Governor;
you must be all wore out by now.'

It was February and time to think about planting corn,
when Cavin got home from Austin where the Democratic
committee had stayed until the bill eliminating the state police
had safely passed both houses.

'I hope I never have to step foot off my land any more,
Lucy,' Cavin said with a long sigh as he alighted from his
horse. 'Nine years I been running around like a chicken with
its head off.' He was standing with one arm on his saddle,
the other around Lucina, who had run out to meet him when
she heard the big gate slam. 'I'd like to stay home long enough,
anyway, to get that grass rolled down to suit me,' he concluded,
as his eye fell on the rough green that edged his drive.

But, in spite of his wish, he soon had to leave again, when Colonel Rutherford summoned the entire committee back to Austin in an effort to persuade the new Governor to refrain from vetoing the bill that had put an end to the state police.

'Not till we've built up the Ranger force again,' Governor Coke protested. 'Look!' He pointed to the police record. 'Insufferable as the police have been, yet they've kept criminals on the run. We can't have a state with no Rangers, no militia, no police at all!' he argued.

The committee, however, persisted, stubbornly holding its ground, and the mail that poured in convinced the legislators that the entire state was determined to be rid of the hated police, at any cost.

On the twenty-second of April, the bill passed over the executive veto and Cavin sent Lucina an exultant wire telling her the news. 'Glory be to God!' his message read. 'We're free!'

When he got home late one evening over a week later, Lucina met him with a paper in her hand.

'If I hadn't known you were a sober man' — she looked at him severely, suppressing her smile — 'I'd have worried about your drinking too much, up there at Austin. Look!' The smile appeared again on her face, and broke over her lips. 'Here's the way the editor of the Dallas *Herald* reports what happened up at the capitol.' Handing him the page, she pointed to an editorial on the first column of the first page.

'The people of Texas,' the editor wrote, 'are today delivered from as infernal an engine of oppression as ever crushed any people beneath the heel of God's sunlight.'

Cavin's beaming smile covered his ruddy face and rose up into his sparkling, blue eyes.

'Lucy!' he exclaimed, exuberantly, 'that's nothing to the

way I felt!' He stopped, wondering how to make clear to her the sudden release of spirit that had swept across the state. 'When I passed through New Columbia on the way home, what do you suppose everybody was out doing? Shooting at anvils, to celebrate!' He flung his arms wide to the air. 'White and black, all of 'em out celebrating.'

'Lucy,' he implored her, 'come here and kiss me! I'm a free man!'

'Nine years!' he exclaimed. He held her close in his arms with his chin resting on her smooth, dark hair, but his voice was not that of a lover. 'Nine years a slave!' he exclaimed again, and drew a long, shuddering breath. 'Maybe no man ought to be a slave — not even a black man!'

Suddenly he swung her around with him to face the avenue, holding her absently in the hollow of his arm, as he stood considering what lay ahead of him to do. Then his grasp tightened and he laughed softly.

'Still,' he said, 'you can't say a man's altogether idle that's accumulated ten children in nine years!'

'Nine,' Lucina corrected him lightly, 'nine, darling.'

'Ten,' he persisted, apologetically. 'I picked up another boy on my way home. At the German settlement,' he explained, 'where I stopped to get my dinner. He was crying fit to kill, and nobody seemed to want him.' He looked at her uncertainly. 'He's an orphan. I thought just for a few days — till something turned up — one more wouldn't bother us any.' Feeling more and more on the defensive, he added, with a hesitant smile: 'He's a cute, little rascal, Lucy, no bigger'n Beau, named Heinrich, or something like that. Of course if you want me to, I'll take him back.' He leaned toward her impulsively. 'I ought to have known you had enough children to look after without this one.'

Lucina reached up and kissed his ear. 'Don't talk foolishness. Where is the poor little thing?'

Cavin swept her into his arms.

'Are you sorry you married me?' he demanded fiercely. 'I expect you ought to be,' he admitted, with a repentant smile. 'A man who lets his bird dogs run all over your house, and forgets to put on his coat for dinner and swears like the devil, and is nearly always gone, and, when he does come home, brings stray boys and wildcats and coyotes back with him!' Suddenly he stooped, and, resting his hands firmly on her arms, kissed her twice, and then went on as though he had never paused. 'And gives you ten children in nine years, and leaves you to run three plantations —— '

He caught his breath, arrested by the look on her face. When had he seen it before? The memory stirred dimly in his mind, but as he tried to recall it, it eluded him.

'Who am I?' Lucina was thinking, almost frightened by the importunity of the question. 'Who am I?' she repeated. 'Not the same girl who sat in the live-oak tree that August morning and promised to marry this tired, jubilant man.' She felt an affection, a kind of yearning tenderness, for that young girl, remembering her with the gentle, wistful pain that is aroused by recollections of one long dead. 'And yet,' she thought, 'I would not have her come to life — she knew so little, she was so ignorant.'

She raised her eyes to Cavin and studied his face.

'And who is he,' she thought, 'this tall limping man — no boy — with a few gray hairs on his temple, with lines beginning to show around his mouth and eyes, this man, who is Beau's father?'

For a moment Cavin seemed to her like a stranger, as though she were now seeing him for the first time in her life.

She shook her head in bewilderment; but so short was the time since Cavin had left off speaking, arrested by the expression in her eyes, that he was scarcely conscious of her faltering. Then, as suddenly as a familiar design sometimes flashes out of a mass of intricate lines, she saw that the face she was now looking at was the same one she had first seen peeping out of the carriage which had brought her aunt and cousins from Florida to Georgia; that this man on the gallery beside her was also the boy she had watched rising from the verandah at Cedar Ledge, one May morning so long ago; that in him some principle, some inviolable essence, of his own being had survived, and would survive, any change.

She smiled slowly and put her arms around his neck, sighing as if she were laying some burden down — a burden that had worn on her.

'What do you think, foolish?' she asked him, lightly shaking him.

For a moment he returned her smile, at peace with the world. Across her shoulder, his attention wandered off to his land, which lay slanting under long, black shadows, now, down toward the yellow bayou. Locust blossoms, past their prime, lay thickly strewn over the warm, moist earth, and their perfume rose cloyingly sweet on the evening mist.

Standing there perfectly still with his arm around Lucina, Cavin watched night closing down over his fields. Life welled up in him then, suddenly strong and sweet. What he had to do he could do; what he wanted he would have. He leaned over to look into Lucina's eyes.

'Listen!' she told him, holding up her hand. 'Listen!'

Inside the hall, her quicker ear had caught the sound of Aunt Elvy's approaching voice. She was talking to the children in a pleased, proud voice.

'Your pa's home,' she was telling them. 'He's done whupped the Yankees clean off their feet, and sont 'em all back whar they belong.'

Cavin bent a humorous glance on Lucina. 'I hope they stay there,' he said fervently, locking his arms around her with sudden warmth. This was living again — to feel Lucina's smooth fingers on his cheek, to breathe the sweet fragrance rising from her hair. Lifting her off her feet, he strained her to him. Then, with a sharp breath, he put her away from him and, turning abruptly, strode over to the edge of the gallery.

She followed, smiling up at him serenely, and locked her arm in his.

'I hope now you'll get around to straightening the drive,' she urged him. 'Do you reckon you will?'

'Tomorrow,' he replied emphatically. 'First thing in the morning.'

Part IV

Texas: 1874—1888

This was the last toil, this the goal of the long ways.

VIRGIL, *Aeneid*, BOOK III
Mackail translation

Chapter 23

Next morning, Cavin barely waited to drink his early morning coffee before he was up and out. The sun had not yet risen, and over the whole prairie to the east of him there lay that coppery, rosy glow which presages the Texas dawn, when earth and sky appear to merge, when grass and cloud are covered by identically the same warm and spreading light. To the west, the land still drowsed, shadowy and remote, under the spring mist, which hung, not blue, as in autumn, but gray and thin, like a dripping cobweb, over the twisting bayou and the purple tree-tops. The dew lay on the grass in tiny, crystalline globules, weighing it down.

As Cavin came down his steps, however, he was scarcely conscious of the ruddy light that fell upon him, or of the wet leaves that brushed against his cheek. He would not wait, he decided, for Jake to come up from his and Maria's cabin and saddle Derby. He would do it himself and start out at once to see what Jeremiah had been up to, all spring, in the cotton fields. He remembered a certain corner, where two rail fences came together. The last time he had seen it, on his brief trip home in early February, it had been full of weeds. And, thinking of it now, he put his foot into the stirrup and then impatiently over his saddle. The years he had been at war seemed to him, all at once, too long.

'Four years in the army,' he meditated, 'and nine more in the saddle, after that. All' — he considered the point carefully — 'all so I don't have to run my life to suit some Yankee full o' fool ideas.'

As he rode along, an unformulated uneasiness began to stir in the back of his brain. What remark was that Lucina had dropped last night about the children needing a better education than they were getting?

She'd been teaching them, the best she could, herself, since Margaret had married. The oldest twins, now fourteen, were ravenous readers; and, in Lucina's neat, round, flowing hand, they had already written out a long poem of their own composing. They could play on the piano, having practised with Miss Clarissa; and they could translate a little Latin; they knew their Catechism and their Bible, and Lucina had had them study a child's history of England that was among Philip's books — a history written by an author named Charles Dickens. Philip had some other histories in his library, too, illustrated histories of Rome and Greece, full of pictures of statuary and of buildings fronted with columns. He also had a thick volume in fine print called *Plutarch's Lives*, in which Lucina had started the twins to reading, before she realized how much of it was hardly suited to a modest young lady's understanding. Well, that was as good a way as any to learn about life, she supposed — that and Philip's big anatomy books they were always poring over, and his enormous dictionary full of pressed, yellow flowers that made dark brown blotches on the crackling pages.

It did not strike her as strange that this dictionary had been an engagement present from Philip's father to his mother. Not at all. Instead, she had said to the girls that it was a very proper gift for a young lady to receive from a young gentleman.

They were getting old enough, now, to think about such matters. They would have plenty of beaus, she could see that already, as who could not who looked twice at their pretty, bright faces? And everyone did look twice at them.

'Twins?' people would ask incredulously. 'But you'd never know it!' they would always end by exclaiming. Well, they were, thought Lucina, a trifle resentfully. They were twins, just the same.

She liked people and things to move along the way they were expected to do. That was why she found Felicia with her steady, dependable mind, easier to teach than Letitia, with her more uncertain spurts of interests.

And teach them Lucina did, stubbornly, persistently, although neither they nor she were aware that they were actually studying. Every morning she called the other children around her and set them to reading, to writing, to ciphering, or the girls to doing fine sewing — to rolling and whipping raw edging, to hemstitching with tiny, delicate needles, to making tatting or hairpin lace, to embroidering linen spatter-backs to pin up on the walls behind the washstands. For these were all things girls needed to know, as well as how to sing and play the piano. Whether they liked it or not, they had to run their scales, too, one hour every day, on Letitia's square Chickering, inset, along its dark front, with mother-of-pearl. Philippa, who was only eight, made a great fuss about practising; but where would you be, if you began paying attention to what children liked or didn't like? Lucina asked herself. There were certain things they had to learn, and nobody to see that they learned them, except herself.

So she began to teach them the various subjects of knowledge in a haphazard sort of way, as the occasion arose. They had come across a picture of George III somewhere, for instance, and that had started her to telling them what Beauford had told her about his great-grandfather Andrew's life — Andrew, who had regularly drunk a toast to his King, all the while he lived in Virginia. Thus, before they knew it, they were studying about General Washington and then about Mr. Jefferson in Philip's book *Great Men*. From there it was easy enough to pass on to telling them about how Mr. Clay lived at Lexington, where one of their grandfathers had often visited him, and about General Jackson's beautiful Hermitage, where General Houston and their other grandfather were always welcome. And thus, without a break, they were back reading Texas history, again.

She did not think she was doing a very good job, though, Lucina told Cavin. The children needed somebody, now, to keep them in school all day. And the boys — what, she asked helplessly, could a woman be expected to teach boys? Cavin agreed with her about that, anyway.

Neither of them was aware that Lucina had a genuine gift for teaching which she revealed by bringing all of Philip's books up from the parlor, where they had stood behind glass doors in his walnut secretary, to the garret schoolroom. Then she put them out on open shelves for the children to handle — Philip's twelve volumes of Shakespeare, his *Iliad* and his *Odyssey*, both in translation, his beautiful mythology books, the little Latin primers he himself had studied, his fairy-story books, his collection of English poets, his Virgil, his Horace, his many volumes of sermons and biographies, his Plato, his Plutarch, his volumes of Walter Scott, and Dickens, and Addison, his *Southern Treasury*, his *Tom Brown's School Days*, his *Vicar of Wakefield*, his copy of Darwin. That was nearly all, but it was enough. Lucina sent the children directly to these books because she had no others, never dreaming that she could scarcely have done better for them.

She made the big children memorize the Psalms and Shake-speare's sonnets, and lines from Byron and from a strange, dreamy poet named Donne whom they all liked, and made them look up every name and reference they did not understand, and spell every new word ten times over. In the same way, she had the little children learn to read out of Mother Goose and Grimm, and draw on their slates, using their pets as models, or the leaves fluttering outside the window; and she started FitzHugh to looking in Philip's surgery books when he wanted to find out how to put a splint on a calf's leg, or mend a turkey's broken wing. All this seemed to her only sensible, and her duty. She never suspected that she was a better teacher than any governess or tutor they would be apt to tempt out into the bottoms.

Riding along by the bayou, Cavin was thinking hard of what Lucina had said about the children's schooling. Letitia and Felicia were now — he stopped and counted up — fourteen years old. He could scarcely believe it. And coming along, right behind them, was FitzHugh, stretching up at eleven far above Beau, who, like Philip and Philippa, was only eight, just the age of little, tow-headed Heinrich. He mustn't forget James Barclay — about ten, he supposed. He never had known exactly how old that boy was, that little black, wiry streak of lightning who would be halfway down the drive before Beau ever waked up enough to start after him. Nathaniel, at six, Cavin reflected, was quicker on the trigger than Beau. Lucy kept that boy too spick and his hands too clean. That was all right with a baby like William, hardly out of his cradle, but Beau was a big boy. You could count on any woman — even Lucy — ruining a boy, he thought severely, if you turned him over to her entirely. Well, he'd be home more, now, thank the Lord.

Still, he told himself honestly, he didn't know much about
books; but he didn't deny that a boy needed to learn more
than how to ride a horse, and shoot a gun, and run a plantation,
and vote at elections. All that he had to know, of course, and how
to pick himself up when he got hurt, but he had to know more
yet — things like Judge White knew, how to quote learned
authority, how to stand up straight and make an eloquent speech
full of quotations on a moment's notice. Philip's respect for
books lingered on in his son, who seldom opened one, whose
reading was almost altogether confined to the *Constitution*, the
Statesman, the *News*, the *Telegraph*, and the *Farm and Ranch
Weekly*. He decided, yes, the boys would have to have a tutor
and then go off to school, and study law or something. And
Lucina would find a governess a big help with the girls, no
doubt about that. Time she was getting some rest. She hadn't
had much since he had brought her to Texas. Nobody knew
that better than he did. He determined, she was going to get
some now.

He began to figure his income. It took a lot of money to
support a family like his, and it was plain enough it was going
to take more. Not to speak of what it was going to cost to buy
a herd of Brahma cattle and set up a brand-new gin big enough
to press and bale all his own cotton, and his neighbors' besides.
Just to feed as many mules as he needed to run his place and
William's and Povey's, he would have to plant a lot of cleared
land in corn — land that could be bringing in good cash money,
if planted in cotton. And all the bookkeeping — think of it!
With Povey's land belonging now to Letitia's children, and
part of Philip's too, his little brothers and sisters would be
owning more land than he did. He'd have to keep all their
accounts separate from his own, from now on, he supposed.
As soon as he sold his mother's place in Georgia, he'd buy

William's land outright for himself. Helen would sell him Holly Grove, he thought. She had no near relatives to leave it to. Well, it would all work out somehow. He had a lot of time to live, yet. How old was he? Barely thirty!

'Lord! Lord!' he laughed aloud. 'I thought I was older than that!'

He leaned off his horse to open a gate leading into Povey's fields, for he had decided, as he rode along, to stop and see how Horace and Sally were making out, and how Jeremiah was managing to get along by himself in Philip's old house by the river.

'I'm through with politics,' he told himself. 'I've got business to look after.'

He felt relieved at the thought, and ideas about how to run his place began to simmer in his brain. He rode along, his keen eyes taking in every detail of Jeremiah's management. The moss drooped above him, swaying gray and ghost-like in the morning air, and from under it, the sweet fragrance of a thousand blossoms and leaves crept into his senses. He was following a path along the river, and beyond the turn, he knew, would be the first house he was looking for — the house he had built for Horace and Sally on the fifty acres of land that Povey had left his servant in his will. Horace was therefore a well-set-up darky, in his own name, but he had continued to follow Cavin's bidding. When Horace had at last persuaded Sally to accept him, instead of Aaron, Cavin had put up this house for them. That had been — why it must be all of five years ago now.

Well, a man let a lot slip when he got into politics, Cavin thought, with a sigh. For all he cared, anybody could run the state from now on — anybody that felt like it. So long as they weren't Yankees, he wouldn't quarrel with them.

In fact, if there wasn't so much stealing and low-down meanness going on, he'd be in favor of disbanding the Hunter's Club altogether, now. An organization like that, as he had fore-seen from the beginning, had no place in a state that was running along normally. He acknowledged, though, things were pretty far from normal yet. In a way, he admitted to himself, Governor Coke had been right about not giving up the state police till they had something better. Still, he had known, right off, as the Governor did not seem to, that the people in the state would never stand for keeping the police.

'Something about a man's being smart,' mused Cavin, 'makes him act *too* reasonable most o' the time.'

He was almost at Horace's house now. There it lay in front of him — a cheerful enough place with its gray sides and its red chimney tying it to the ground. The early sunlight covered it in a soft, yellow glow, and chinaberry trees hung over the low roof. The house had a long ell, for a kitchen, and two big rooms in front, divided by a generous hall. Wooden windows swung wide on their hinges, their openings covered with mosquito netting tacked against the frame. There was smoke coming out of the chimney, and a pleasant smell of frying bacon in the air. Cavin got down and threw his rein over the fence railings stuck close together in the ground.

The bare, swept, sandy yard was as clean as his own. Horace and Sally were a couple o' good niggers, Cavin thought, looking around at the cape jessamines and pomegranate bushes by the steps. On a shelf on the front porch were a lot of tin cans full of geraniums, and a broken-down old couch that had once been in Povey's office, Cavin suddenly remembered, as his eyes fell on it.

He put his hand on the gate separating the back yard from the front and paused, looking over it. There, way to the back, was a pig-pen, with two sows and a lot of little pigs wallowing in it; and, further off yet, was a good-sized vegetable garden protected by chicken wire against the hens that were, even now, pecking about under the house and around the back doorstep. Cavin laughed as he saw that one of the chicken-coops was covered over with Horace's coat, around which a yellow cur dog was prowling, sniffing at it.

'Just like a darky, for all the world,' he chuckled, 'to throw his good coat over a chicken-coop.' He wondered for the thousandth time why the Yankees got so excited about what they called the hovels the negroes lived in.

Why, this place suited Horace, exactly, and if he didn't mind putting his good coat out in the weather, whose business was it but his?

Of course, Sally and Horace were good, clean darkies — you had to allow for that. Plenty of field hands kept their places looking a lot worse than this, with no flowers, no vines, no vegetable garden. They didn't have to, though. If they wanted to, they could get along the way Horace and Sally and Jake and Maria were doing. That reminded him: he'd have to remember right away to put a clause in *his* will leaving Jake as much land as Horace had. That was only fair, the way things had worked around.

That resolution made, Cavin fell to meditating on a fact that had often puzzled him. Northern missionaries, now, seemed to have an idea you could take a dirty, no-count family of black people and put them in Horace's house and they would, right away, start in being clean and looking after the place. It just didn't work out that way.

He laughed. How could you even make colored people drink sweet milk, if they didn't want it? They could all come up and get clabber at Locust Hill, which they did, whenever they felt like it. They could raise vegetables, too, if they wanted any. But how many would eat anything out of a garden except turnip greens and maybe snap beans?

Cavin began to smile, remembering the horrified astonishment of one of the army inspectors who had come upon a negro cabin, where one of the rooms housed chickens and a calf.

'Lord! Lord!' he thought. 'The man like to-a had a fit.'

He had tried to calm him down by asking him why he minded, if the darky didn't, but it was no good. The man had rushed back to Galveston and wired up North for a dozen more missionaries to hurry on down there, he supposed.

At the recollection, he laughed to himself and then sobered. 'Maybe,' he grudgingly admitted, 'their ideas'd work out fine in their own country. Why don't they stay up there?'

He had gotten up early and that bacon smelled good. As he stepped foot on the back step, the kitchen door was flung open and Horace appeared with a child on each arm.

'Lawd God, it's Mas' Cavin!' he exclaimed, and called to Sally. 'Come 'ere, Sally, and grab dese-yeah chillun off o' me. How is you, suh?' he asked smiling, advancing toward the shaky steps.

Cavin reached up and took one of the black babies. 'This here's a new one, Horace, looks like.' He patted the child's round, brown face and chucked it under the chin. Colored babies were all eyes, he thought, as he always did whenever he picked one up.

'Gal,' said Horace. 'De udders is all boys. Us named her fur Miss Lettie,' he announced.

'Did you, now?' asked Cavin, obviously pleased. He looked again at the child, swathed, like the infants in Italian paintings, in many tight wrappings, and then handed her to Sally, who had come out of the kitchen.

'You're getting a nice batch o' chillun, Sally,' he remarked, 'and you take good care of 'em too.'

Sally beamed. 'Yas-suh,' she said; 'I tries to.'

'How 'bout fryin' me up an egg and a little o' that bacon, Sally?' Cavin proposed. 'And supposen you bring me out a piece o' corn bread and a cup o' coffee. I'll sit out here and eat it while I talk over some work with Horace.' He sank down on the steps. 'It's a long ways back home to breakfast.'

Horace looked at him questioningly. 'Dey's some squabs settin' in de safe — ' he began. 'I was fixin' to take 'em ober to Miss Lucy today.'

'Squabs!' exclaimed Cavin, and called to Sally to put one on the fire. 'Don't know when I had a squab. Nothing better,' he remarked glancing toward Horace as if to verify his opinion, 'less'n it's wild duck.'

'Or 'possum,' returned Horace critically, and then added, suspending his judgment, 'squirrel stew mighty good eatin', too.'

'Been ketching any fish this spring?' Cavin inquired, flicking his boots with his quirt.

'Plenty of 'em,' said Horace grinning. 'Catfish in de bayou and perch in dat-ar dam o' your'n out on de prairie.' His smile stretched wider. 'You ought-a seen Beau settin' in de skiff, throwin' out his line. Dat boy,' he concluded, 'is a bawn fisherman. I goes over an' gits him mos' evy time I starts out, myself.'

'Is that so?' said Cavin, interestedly.

Horace laughed, sending an understanding glance toward his master. 'Miss Lucy 'bout had a fit when I brung him back wid his pocket full o' worms.'

'I expect she did,' said Cavin, chuckling. 'Can he hitch a mule to a plow yet, and keep himself up in the bayou?'

'I been learnin' him,' Horace replied earnestly. 'Me an' Jake been taking him and Josh out huntin', too. Now Fitz-Hugh,' he continued, 'de Lawd gib him a stiddy han'. Dat boy kin hit a aig a hunderd yahds away. But,' he added in open disgust, 'he all time readin', stid o' tendin' to business.'

Cavin stretched himself. 'Lawd, Horace!' he exclaimed, 'chillun are a responsibility.'

'Yas-suh, dey is,' Horace agreed. 'Dey sho is.'

'Thank you, Sally.' Cavin reached up to take the tin plate on which a tempting brown squab nestled against a hot corn-dodger marked with the print of three fingers on its crusty top. The coffee in his cup was as black as ink and bitter as quinine, almost, but that was how he liked it.

'Sally, how you get birds to taste like this?' he asked her. 'I believe it's better'n the way Aunt Emmy fixes 'em up. But' — his eyes twinkled — 'don't you ever let on I said so.'

He listened attentively while Sally explained that, to her mind, a squab wasn't worth eating less'n before you cooked it, you rubbed it good with butter flavored with vinegar and thyme and red pepper.

'Lots o' red pepper,' she urged him. 'Dat gives 'em de taste; an' be sho' to hol' 'em low, so's dey ketches de wood smoke.'

He sat there for a while longer on the steps finishing his breakfast and listening to Horace's account of work on the place. The cotton was coming along, and the corn was up good, Horace said, but the Johnson grass was about to take everything. The new potatoes were about ready to eat, and the snap beans through blooming. They were figuring on planting watermelons and sweet potatoes before long. He expected there'd be a mess o' dewberries this year. They could stand some rain.

Then a worried look crept over his brown face. He was an intelligent-looking negro with a well-set head, covered with closely cropped, tightly curled, black hair, and now his expression grew anxious.

'You's gwine-a hab to git rid o' Pete, Mas' Cavin. Dat nigger's sho' been tryin' my patience dis spring.'

Cavin set down his plate, leaned back against the rough, round trunk of a small pin-oak that supported Horace's narrow porch roof. Stretching out his spurred boots, he crossed one foot over the other.

'How come?' he asked, returning Horace's anxious glance with a sudden sharpening of his own expression.

'Well,' said Horace, 'he been actin' mighty funny lately, runnin' aroun' wid a bunch o' no-count white men. He up to sump'n, I do' know whut.' He looked suddenly worried. 'You know it ain't no way fur a nigger to behave, Mas' Cavin — struttin' aroun' lak a ole gobbler.'

Cavin got to his feet. 'I'll see Mr. Blake about it,' he said.

There were other matters he wanted to talk over with Jeremiah — a good many other matters. For one thing, while he had lain awake in the dark, last night, planning, it had occurred to him to try raising more sugar cane and selling the syrup — the light first boiling — in Houston and Galveston. Philip and William had found out they couldn't compete on the Brazos with Louisiana sugar farmers, and had dropped back to planting only enough sugar cane to make syrup for themselves and the negroes. The stuff they gave you to put on your battercakes in Houston or Austin wasn't worth eating, Cavin recollected — thick blackstrap it was, probably the second or third boiling. There ought to be good money in clear sugar-cane syrup, yellow like honey, delivered in town every two weeks throughout the season. What was the matter with Jeremiah's starting that business? It wasn't exactly the thing a cotton planter would be likely to do, of course; but Jeremiah could do the marketing, and gradually add pecans, and turkeys, and yams, and good sweet butter, and fresh eggs to his list. The Buffalo Bayou, Brazos, and Colorado Railroad ran from Berryville to Houston now, and what was to prevent Jeremiah building up quite a trade? They had not used the train very much because the freight rates were too high, but if they wanted to get their produce into town in a hurry, probably they'd better begin depending more on the cars.

'Sausages, too,' thought Cavin, remembering how the town people liked his hot, fragrant sausage meat made from tiny pigs and seasoned with plenty of sage and red pepper. 'Lord, the tasteless stuff they always give you at the Capitol Hotel in Houston!' he thought.

Jeremiah could do all the necessary fiddling about, and take half the profits for his own. Then, when he, Cavin, got his fine cattle to going, he would have enough strings to his bow to get along, no matter if they did have an overflow, or the price of cotton dropped way down. In that event, Colonel Rutherford could just hold the bales in his warehouse till he could get a better price.

'The point is,' Cavin ruminated with a foresight the future was to confirm, 'I've got to get myself fixed so I can live without passing much money and without going busted if the cotton crops fail. Cotton'll bring in the cash, but I've got to be independent of worms, and flood, and the market.' It was an idea that never left him.

Jeremiah, he went on planning, could take over the marketing — 'Fig preserves,' thought Cavin suddenly. 'What's the matter with them?' Aunt Emmy made jars of them, the figs coming out clear and transparent, floating in an amber syrup delicately flavored with lemon or ginger. Jeremiah could sell those, too, in town; and maybe the pieced quilts the negro women put together all winter would please city people, also.

The more he thought of his notions, the better they pleased him. 'It'll keep all the young hands busy and out of mischief, besides,' he meditated pleasurably.

He was home now, for good, he hoped, and could put in all his time managing Land's End, Holly Grove, and Locust Hill. Horace was doing a good job as headman on Povey's place, but, with Jeremiah taking on all the marketing, there'd have to be a new overseer, and an engineer to look after the new gin, where, for a fair price, Cavin planned to bale other people's cotton beside his own. Jake was getting along very well with the cattle. He could keep right on running them.

Things would work out, Cavin had no doubt. He got down off his horse in fine humor and pushed open the swinging gate at Philip's old house. Jeremiah heard the gate-bell tinkling, and came out from the kitchen, his red hair flashing under the morning sun. He carried himself with the vibrant tension that always animated his stocky figure, and sent a swift, pleased glance toward his visitor.

'Well, sir,' he said, coming down the steps and holding out his hand, 'I'm glad you're back.'

'Mighty glad to be back, too,' Cavin returned. 'A town's no place to be in.'

'That's how it always seems to me,' said Jeremiah, in complete agreement. 'Come in, Mr. Darcy. Aunt Phoebe'll bring you out some coffee.' He led the way toward a couple of rocking-chairs on Philip's gallery. 'You oughta feel right at home,' he observed, as Cavin took his seat.

'Horace gave me some coffee,' Cavin explained. 'There's a

lot I want to talk to you about, Jeremiah. Glad you hadn't started off yet. I aimed to catch you.'

'Well, I wish you'd caught me in better shape,' Jeremiah apologized. 'Aunt Phoebe does her best, but things don't look right around here.' He leaned toward Cavin with sternly suppressed excitement. 'I been thinking about getting married,' he announced, watching his caller closely.

'And I've been wondering,' Cavin said, smiling broadly, 'how long it was going to take you to get around to that idea.' He rocked back and forth, eyeing Jeremiah. 'Got any objections to telling me who the young lady is?' he inquired.

'It's Miss Evelina,' Jeremiah answered, and began to explain. 'She and her ma've been all alone on their place, you know. I've been helping 'em out, some.' He paused, and Cavin sat waiting for him to bring out what was obviously on his mind. 'She oughta marry a better man than me, though,' Jeremiah said at last, looking straight at his visitor.

Cavin laughed and shot an amused glance at the man beside him. 'Don't you worry about that, Jeremiah,' he remarked with conviction, 'Miss Evelina'll take you in hand.' His keen eyes began to twinkle. 'And get lots o' pleasure out o' doing it, too. Ladies are like that,' he told Jeremiah, drawing the observation out of his experience.

'She's got her pa's two hundred acres,' Jeremiah went on, his face still troubled. 'I — I've got nothing but my two hands.' He looked down at them, where they lay on his knees — broad, red hands with stubby nails and grime ground into the skin. 'They're not fitten to touch her!' he cried.

'Listen, Jeremiah!' Cavin proposed. 'I'll sell you a couple o' hundred acres!' He stopped, thought over his plans, and decided to confide in his overseer. 'I can spare 'em. I'm going to try to buy Holly Grove for myself.'

'I thought you might,' said Jeremiah slowly, 'but I couldn't see no way to pay for 'em, lessen — ' He surveyed Cavin's face doubtfully. 'I had a kind of an idea.'

'Wait!' Cavin rubbed his hand across his lips, and pulled on the short chin whiskers into which Jake had finally trained his beard to grow. 'Lemme tell you mine.'

He went into it at length, as all the ramifications of the plan he had formed the night before came clear in his mind.

'People in town'll pay good money any time for things to eat, Jeremiah,' he assured him; 'and,' he concluded, 'Mrs. Rideout knows good food, from the ground up.' He sat studying his listener and then leaned over, plumping his broad, brown hands down on Jeremiah's knees. 'Dewberry wine!' he exclaimed. 'Dewberry wine, Jeremiah! Of course,' he added, ''twon't be any good now, but in about ten years —— ' His voice trailed off. 'You'll see. It'll be a success — the plan will. What was your notion?' he suddenly demanded. 'Maybe it's a better one.' He began to laugh. 'Did you ever think, Jeremiah,' he inquired, 'how much better off a nigger is than we are? They're not plagued by a lot o' ideas running around in their brains!'

Jeremiah rose suddenly to his feet, a half-smile on his lips.

'Would you step out to the back, Mr. Darcy?' he asked. 'There's something I'd like to show you.'

Cavin followed him through the familiar hall and dining-room, which looked stripped and bare without Letitia's things in them, out onto the back gallery, where a stack of small crokersacks lay against the wall.

'I've been having the women cut 'em down and sew 'em up again,' Jeremiah explained, 'so's to be all ready for the crop o' tiny, new potatoes. I thought I'd plant enough to rush 'em to the market, when they're not much bigger'n marbles.'

Cavin took a look at the sacks, saw they were washed and clean and marked, each one of them, with the brand his cattle carried, H

'Jeremiah,' he predicted, 'we're going to make a go of this! Both of us. By crickety!' he exclaimed. 'I'll throw in fifty acres o' land for a wedding present.' He stood jubilantly watching Jeremiah, while a sudden thought crept into his mind. 'I expect I owe you that much, anyhow, Jeremiah,' he inquired. 'How long you been workin' for me?'

''Bout eight years, now,' Jeremiah answered, counting up the years. 'That's about right, ain't it?'

'And have I ever made any kind of a contract with you?' Cavin persisted. 'Or a settlement? I don't believe I have.'

'No, sir,' Jeremiah answered; 'you just told me to keep out what I needed to get along on. I been doing it.' He smiled. ''Twarn't bothering me none, ever.' Looking down at his feet, he sent a swift, blue glance toward Cavin from under his white lids — the only white spot on his deeply tanned face. 'The kind o' people you gotta make tight contracts with,' he said sententiously, 'is them that'd be shore to do you dirt, anyway.'

'Exactly!' Cavin's voice was scornful. 'I'd never lend a man a penny, if I thought I had to depend on his note.'

He held out his hand to Jeremiah, smiling.

'There's about two hundred acres of uncleared land at the west end of this league. How'd that do? And forty-seven and one-half acres alongside it, as pretty a piece o' bottom land as there is.'

'That's mighty fine o' you, Mr. Darcy, mighty fine,' Jeremiah replied. 'If I cain't pay you, you can take it back.'

'You'll pay me, all right,' Cavin said, moving down the steps toward his horse. 'I'm counting on us both making money out of your marketing. They'll think I'm lost, at home,' he ended, swinging himself up on his saddle. Then he leaned down toward Jeremiah, lowering his voice.

'What's the matter with this nigger, Pete? Horace says you're having trouble with him.'

'I told him yestiddy,' said Jeremiah, 'he'd have to get off the place, if he didn't quit swelling up like a bullfrog.' He leaned closer. 'I'll tell you what I think, **Mr. Darcy**. This gang o' white trash that's running around this bottom is puttin' ideas into Pete's head. They need,' Jeremiah announced, 'somebody to sneak mules and cotton off of every plantation.' Lifting one foot onto the horse-block, he leaned his elbow on his knee, and turned a worried face toward Cavin.

Cavin took his hat off and hung it on his pommel.

'Jeremiah,' he declared, irritably, 'if it ain't one damn thing, it's another!' His mouth sagged at the corners, and two lines running from each side of it down to his chin suddenly appeared, as if etched in his tanned skin.

'I reckon so,' said Jeremiah, giving him a long look. 'That's about it.'

'Well, so long,' said Cavin. 'If you have any more trouble with Pete, lemme know.'

Jeremiah nodded. 'Good day, sir.'

Cavin put his hat on the back of his head and lifted his reins.

'Tell Miss Evelina I'm going to dance at her wedding,' he said. 'We'll ride over to see her and her mother in a few days.'

'Now what else was it I intended to do this morning?' he asked himself as he paced slowly down the lane. 'I know. Get a letter off to the *Telegraph* and the *News*.'

He began to compose the form of his letters. He would advertise for a tutor for — he began to smile — the five worst boys in Texas. No ninny would answer that kind of an advertisement. And he'd run one for a governess, too, to teach girls music, singing, elocution, fine embroidery, history, and literature. Then Lucy could concentrate on drilling them all in their manners, and helping him plan. Suddenly it seemed to him that Lucina had been too busy or too tired for years to give him her full mind.

'Well, I'm fixing things up for her, now,' he thought in sudden pleasure.

It was noon when he got home, and late breakfast was long over. Jake brought him a pitcher of cool buttermilk fresh out of the ice-house.

'I reckon I can make out till dinner,' he said, pouring out the thick, white milk, full of floating yellow globules and holding up his foot for Jake to pull off his boot.

'Jake,' he remarked, 'I been thinking. I'm going to get me a steam pump, or one o' those windmills I been seeing advertised, one o' these days.'

'Yas-suh,' said Jake. Then he looked up at Cavin, grinning. 'Whilst you's away dis mawnin', me an' Maria got us a new baby.'

'I'll have to be building you a bigger house,' Cavin exclaimed, wriggling his foot out of his boot. 'How many chillun is it you've got, Jake? Four now?' he asked.

'Yas-suh,' said Jake. 'Fo'. Two boys, two gals. Miss Lucy's settin' down wid Maria, now.'

'Oh,' said Cavin. 'That's where she is, is it?' He'd missed her, as soon as he came in, and thought maybe she was over at Margaret's.

For Margaret was very far from well, Lucina had told him. She was much worried about her; she thought she was running a slow fever, right along.

'I haven't got a mite o' confidence in Frank Barclay,' Lucina had declared, 'not a mite; but,' she had corrected herself justly, 'he *is* good to Margaret, there's no denying that. What do you suppose he was doing the last time I was over there? The nurse was sick and he was bathing the children himself, and getting them to bed. That's more'n you know how to do,' she had said, tapping him on his cheek. 'Now, isn't it?'

'Well,' he had countered, 'maybe.'

He was glad to hear anything good about his brother-in-law.

'You never can tell what a Barclay's going to be up to,' Cavin thought. 'They've all got a streak in 'em that'll bear watching.' In his mind, you could estimate pretty well what any man was apt to do, by the blood that ran in him. Such a judgment was as natural as figuring a trotter's speed by his sire's, wasn't it, he always argued. Northern people, though, seemed to think a man was born into the world without ancestors.

'They must-a never raised colts,' Cavin mused, calling to Jake to bring him the last *Statesman*. There wasn't any harm in just keeping an eye on what Governor Coke was about up at Austin.

He began to read the paper with the close interest he always gave it. La! la! Here was a good story about the new Governor. How he had faced and backed down a group of his enemies, marching, sole and alone, out of his office to defy them.

Cavin knew just how the capitol looked at night, sitting high and white up a steep slope, with a circular tower crowning its long base, and four columns fronting a small balcony overhanging the entrance door.

The Governor had stepped out on that balcony, so the account ran, estimating the number of his opponents in the square below. Then he had walked quietly back into his room, put his big, black hat on his massive, bald head, and picked up his knotted stick.

Cavin could imagine how the Governor's deep-set eyes had flashed, how high his bushy eyebrows had gone up, when someone tried to stop him. He had marched straight down to the group of men who were swearing at him, and called their bluff.

Cavin laid the paper aside. He could rest easy now and put his whole mind on his business. A governor like Coke could be trusted to run a state like Texas.

Sitting in his small white office, just off the side of the house proper, with his feet up on the window-ledge, he was reading, and humming as he read, when he heard the door open. He glanced up, and stopped his humming, and then almost immediately resumed it, as Lucina came over and sat on the arm of his chair. She was always laughing at him because he never could carry a tune and yet was forever trying to sing the songs he had picked up in the army.

He leaned his head against her arm and kept on repeating, in a low monotone:

> 'Come along my own true love
> And set you down by me.
> It's been three-quarters of a year or more
> Since I spoke a word with thee.'

She stooped and kissed him.

'*You* come along to dinner. There's smothered chicken and brown dumplings.' She put her hand under his chin and smiled into his eyes. 'Maria's named her boy after you.'

'Well, I'll be doggoned!' Cavin exclaimed, laying off his humming and plumping his spurred feet down. 'That's nice.'

Chapter 24

CAVIN almost never stopped, that spring, to look at the big calendar that hung over Philip's black iron safe — the calendar with the moon's phases emphasized on it in red sickles, quarters, halves, and full circles. He had no sense of the pressure of time, but each morning as he arose thought leisurely of what needed to be done. There were no other people waiting on his labors. His work was of his own choosing, and he found it hard to understand the haste that overtakes men who have been a long time away from the smell of rain, and smoke, and new, wet earth. Besides he had a steady, sustaining, though almost unconscious, awareness that his life would go on through his children and their children, who (he never thought otherwise) would live on the Brazos, would inherit and improve on his beginnings. Thus, time stretched out before him in an ever-expanding line, not limited and bounded, as his grandchildren would come to feel, by one life or by other people's demands.

Lucina shared with him this serenity and repose in the midst of incessant activity. She had married Cavin because she had fallen in love with him, and then the Lord had seen fit to lay all these children in her arms. Who was she to protest?

Was she happy? It was a question that would have struck her as entirely out of place to think about. Had she done well to marry Cavin? That was another question she would have put from her, like the plague. She had never thought, not once in all her life, of probing into her emotions to see if they still were fixed on the man she had married. She was Cavin's wife, wasn't she? And what sort of woman was it who asked herself whether she loved her husband? Not like those whose names were set down proudly in the big family Bible under her parlor table. She had never thought of not loving Cavin — of course she did, and his life, with all its burdens, ambitions, and dangers, was hers. Lucina had no doubt whatever about any of these matters.

She had never heard anyone suggest that, in following this compliant course, she might be inhibiting and stifling the free blooming of her own desires and capacities. Had she not a full measure of responsibility which exacted all her energies? Besides, she believed firmly, as Susanna had once told her, that one's natural instincts were apt to run toward sin, and usually had to be firmly disciplined. Sin and coarse manners were somehow joined together in her mind, and both of them quite simply offended her good taste.

When she looked every night at the stars whirling above her, endlessly drifting across space, she thought of those bright points of light as driven by some purpose, some law, some divinity. She never once imagined that chance might direct their course, or that she — as well as the stars above her — might be respond-ing automatically to errant stimuli, pulls, and forces. That chaos, not order, might be at the heart of the universe, she had never even suspected. And she always thought of her own life as directed by the same hand that turned the world, and set the great pole star immovably in its place. The pole star that guided sailors on the sea and cowboys lost at night on the prairie.

She had, however, a clear and active mind, which seized

interestedly on the material in the books out of which she taught the children. Reading in Philip's library, she began more and more, as time went on, to speculate on the strange course of human events and to ask herself shattering questions, in the abstract, which she never once attempted to apply to her own existence. These questions interested her merely as mental exercises, like the geometry problems she occasionally worked out, with her hands gloved to avoid chalk dust, on the blackboard in the children's schoolroom.

It gave her a certain pleasure to feel her mind shaping itself around a thought — a pleasure which Judge White and the Bishop shared with her, but who else? Speculation was not in Cavin's line, she knew that well enough; nor in the minds of most of the men around her. They were too busy doing all the things that needed to be done, and they enjoyed their activity, found it in itself meaningful enough.

She came across two minds like her own, though, where she least expected them — one in a blind German tenant woman of theirs, and another in an old, decrepit Indian fighter living alone just back of their woods.

In the beginning she had taken to reading the Bible to old Mrs. Gruber and carrying tea-cakes to old Mr. Wyatt because she thought she ought to. But soon she began to enjoy talking to them, for one was blind and one was helpless; and they both, therefore, spent a good deal of time thinking about this life, and the next, too.

One morning in the early winter of 1875, when the red berries hung heavy on the haws, and the bright sun sparkled back off the shiny leaves of the live-oaks, she set off to visit the old German woman. She took a pleasant path through the rutted sweet-potato patch and the pear orchard, and walked fearfully across the creek on a fallen tree-trunk. Then through the bushes up the slope, she saw the weathered house surrounded by fig trees, where the blind woman lived with her son, Chris.

He was a gaunt, silent, hard-working man who plowed his thin, sandy acres all day, and then came home to do all that needed doing about the three-room gray shack, even the washing. He seemed entirely content with his life, and took the greatest pleasure in the violets, and pansies, and bluebonnets, and creeping moss roses, and geraniums that grew around his house — such enormous, glowing, red geraniums as Lucina had never brought to bloom at Locust Hill. All day every Sunday Chris worked on his flower garden; and every night during the summer when his blossoms drooped, he would haul heavy buckets of water up on his creaking windlass and pour them carefully around his shrivelling plants. In the winter, his house was decorated, like any peasant's cottage in Germany, with pine cones and field grasses and red berries out of the woods, his kitchen windows full of red geraniums, and the rafters hung with long, swaying strings of dried peppers and herbs.

His mother sat most of the day in a rocking-chair drawn up to her fireplace, rising now and then to putter about the room, or to feel her way out to the little henhouse and back with a large, brown egg in her shaking old hand, or even to roll out a batch of tea-cakes against Chris's return. For that was one thing she could still do — prepare food for cooking, although she never ventured to lay a fire.

As Lucina put her foot on the lowest step this wintry morning, she saw Mrs. Gruber's little, bent, gnome-like figure at the kitchen window. Before she had time to rap, the blind woman threw open the door, and stood with her unblinking eyes fixed almost directly on the sun. Her knobby, old hands were white with flour and the steel rims of her spectacles, which she still persisted in wearing, were pushed up on her head, where the scant, gray hair barely covered the pink scalp.

'Vell,' she said, holding up her dusty fingers, 'I mek pfeffer-nüsse.' Her English was broken, but fluent, for though no one could have mistaken Chris's ancestry, he had only a feeble command of his mother's tongue. So Mrs. Gruber had fallen back on a kind of rapid patois that had become, through the years, as poor German as it was English. Lucina often asked her sympathetically if she had not had a great deal of trouble learning any English at all. She knew she could never imagine herself mastering the long-syllabled guttural words Mrs. Gruber often tried to get her to repeat. But the old lady answered no, what else was there to do? And though she kept a little German Bible, beautifully decorated in blue and gold, by her bed, yet she had no trouble following Lucina, when she opened her plain, black Testament and began to read aloud to her, as she often did.

Now she invited Lucina in, with a welcoming smile, and, looking at her, Lucina had the impression that she had somehow grown frailer, more shrunken since the week before.

'I tell you,' she said, 'you put in das wood und ve drinken kaffee und essen pfeffernüsse togedder.' She nodded her small head up and down, as delighted as a child.

When they had put aside their cups, Lucina went over to a walnut bureau where a little music-box stood beneath the swinging mirror. She turned the key and started the tinkling strains to going, and then, opening one of the drawers, took out a brush and comb.

There was one thing her son could never do to please his mother: his rough fingers never laid her thin white hair quite to suit her.

Lucina combed it now gently, arranging it in the neat, exact lines that Mrs. Gruber had taught her — in two tightly braided plaits wound together and pinned just above the neck, but

fluffed out a little above each ear. When she had finished, the
blind woman felt her head all over carefully and then turned in
her chair for Lucina to judge her work.

'It look gut?' she inquired anxiously, as she never failed to do,
and, after being reassured, sank back, content.

Lucina always smiled at this question coming from a shrivelled old woman with broad heavy shoes on her feet and a shiny
black shawl pinned around her stooped shoulders. But though
she smiled, she usually remembered every time she came over
to bring along a little powder and lilac water to please Mrs.
Gruber, whose vanity had not departed with her eyesight.

'Nor her mind, either,' Lucina often thought, admiring the
way the old tenant woman had of wrestling with the knottiest
passages in Scripture, applying to them the bitter experience of
a long life.

It was a real trouble to Mrs. Gruber that she could not admire
some of the Biblical heroes, and Lucina shared her difficulty
They both approached theology with a direct, groping interest
that was very far from superstitious credulity. It interested them
because it seemed to offer some explanation for the unhappy
events which so often blighted people's lives, no man apparently
being spared. Separated by years, and class — by that toughest
barrier of human society — and by a variety of possessions, by
education and training, yet these two women drew close together as human beings equally baffled by the mysteries of sin,
death, and sorrow. They both had the grim courage neither to
deny nor to push aside the facts of pain and evil; and they had
the temerity to face the unpalatable truth that, at best, men are
poor creatures hardly fit to walk the earth, much less to boast
incontinently about their puny efforts. People living in cities
might forget flood and peril and lightning and storm; might not
see their neighbors often enough to understand that the thunder-

bolts of the Lord fall where they will, on rich and poor alike.
But these were truths that both Lucina and Mrs. Gruber
admitted without argument; and, facing these ultimate mysteries, they were drawn close in a common effort to understand
them.

Saint Paul they could not take to their heart the way they
did Saint John — an omission which puzzled and troubled them
both. Except in his magnificent thirteenth chapter of Corin-
thians, he seemed to them too thunderous, too impatient for a
believing Christian. In the face of what they knew about life,
his vigorous, bustling energy somehow definitely repelled them.

'Saint Paul,' said Mrs. Gruber, turning an earnest face toward
Lucina, 'is *alvays* vorry. He vant to hurry up Gott.' She paused
and smiled. 'Er iss a Yankee, maybe — mek alles gut in *von*
minute.' She turned her worn, old hands around like a windmill. 'So I feel, ven I tink about ihm, all time running some-
vhere, scold — vat you say? — vuss?'

Lucina laughed quietly and rose to go. She patted the old
woman's cheeks, and told her somebody from Locust Hill would
be over again in a day or two. Mrs. Gruber said, 'Vait!' and
rising stiffly, groped her way into the kitchen, returning with
two brown eggs and a few pfeffernüsse.

'Ah! thank you!' said Lucina, accepting the gifts. 'Beau loves
your little cakes, Mrs. Gruber. I'm going to send Aunt Emmy
over to learn how to make 'em,' she said.

As she walked slowly back home, enjoying the crisp day, she
never thought about pitying this blind old woman, in a plain,
clean, calico wrapper, waiting for death. Indeed, if she had
thought about it, she would have known that Mrs. Gruber did
not pity herself. For was not this world but a gateway to another
where unimaginable treasures were laid up secure against moth
and corruption? Mrs. Gruber no more doubted her reasoning

than scientists doubt the evidence of *their* reasoning about things never seen, either, with any mortal eye. Nor did Lucina doubt hers.

Therefore their differences of station merged in a larger justice, to which they both acknowledged themselves subject. Neither of them, however, thought much about their positions in this world; they accepted them as simply and directly as they accepted the varying color of their hair, or the differing shapes of their bodies, and tried only to do their duty in the places they were called upon to fill. That was a hard and weary enough struggle for anybody, they would both have said, entirely unaware that the war had been waged to enforce a radically different social theory from the one they accepted — to enforce an equalitarian, levelling theory, born straight out of the Industrial Revolution. To them the whole struggle had seemed to circle about another problem altogether — a man's right to resist interference in his own affairs. And that was a right tenants held as dear as landlords.

Lucina, on her way home, was now in sight of the pear orchard, beneath which great, yellow mounds of sweet potatoes were thrown up, mounds behind which she could hear the boys yelling in a hot Indian foray.

They knew all about Indian battles first hand, and she did, too, now. Old Mr. Wyatt had seen to that. Crippled and alone in his old age, he was always ready to talk about his experiences as a Ranger fighting against the ferocious Karankawas and the more friendly Caddos, from whose confederacy, called Texas, she now knew, the state had derived its name. Hardly a day passed that Beau and FitzHugh did not get on their ponies and ride over to listen to the grizzled, old veteran. Often Lucina would go along too, and, she reflected, almost without knowing it she had thus become familiar with the Texas past, with all

the names that rolled off Cavin's lips as easily as General Lee's
or General Hood's.

Old Mr. Wyatt would sometimes tell about the great Ranger
captain, John Bird, and the battle thirty-odd of his Rangers had
put up against two hundred and forty Indians.

'Right down there back o' your sandhill,' he would tell the
boys. 'You know where the Indian graves are?' Yes, indeed,
they knew.

As he began to tell the story, he would forget his rheumatism
and would rise and fall on one stiff knee, squinting his bleared,
old eyes and pulling fiercely at an imaginary trigger. The boys
would hardly breathe while they listened; and even Lucina
would begin to feel her hair rising on her head when the old
Ranger would stand up, and suddenly assuming an Indian pose,
would begin the dolorous, haunting, Indian chant for the dead.

Always, when it was time for the boys to go home, he would
clap them fiercely on their thin, young shoulders.

'Listen,' he would say, 'and never forget what I'm telling
you: Thirty Texans can whup any two hundred other men, any
time, anywhere on earth.' The boys would nod, their eyes wide
and staring.

Now through the pear trees Lucina suddenly heard Heinrich
cheering on his men.

'Listen,' he was saying in the sputtery English he had learned
since Cavin had brought him home. 'Listen! Thutty Taix-
ands...'

She laughed to herself and made a wide detour to avoid disturbing their game. But she stood still a moment before she
turned, with her gaze fixed on Beau's hot, excited face. He must
be the Indian chief, she judged, from the rooster feathers stuck
in a string around his head.

He seemed to her entirely beautiful, every line of him, as he

stood there under the bright sun, with his long, oval eyes narrowed, and his straight, young legs tensed. Suddenly she hated
to think of his inevitable defeat in the coming battle. She
wanted him never to be defeated, never hurt. Then she realized
that, with his usual quick inventiveness, so much like Cavin's
own, he had seized on the precise way to exalt his necessary
fall.

'Ketch all the girls,' she heard him telling his men. 'We'll
hold 'em for gold.'

Lucina went on towards Cavin's office, where he usually was
at this hour of day, to tell him what she had just heard Beau
saying. She felt certain he would enjoy the account.

But she saw, as soon as she entered the door, that Cavin had
no time to listen to her story. He was talking to Jake.

'Better take a bunch o' cows along,' he was saying. 'They had
plenty o' trouble over at Lost Island Ranch getting their bull
home.'

Lucina knew what he was talking about — the huge, humped
Brahma bull that he had ordered out of the herd James Hardenbrook, of the Democratic Committee, was raising. She was
pleased, because for months Cavin had been talking about starting his own Brahma herd and she knew how he liked to see his
ideas working out. She couldn't understand, though, why John
McGaughey seemed so enthusiastic about the great, lumbering,
wild animal he already had in his own pasture — a bull with
mean red eyes, short, sharp horns, and a tawny, striped body
surmounted by a huge hump, like a camel's. They never drove
past John's pasture unless the beast was pawing the grass and
bellowing. She had thought Cavin would do better to go in for
pretty, gentle Jerseys and angular black and white Holsteins
like those on the green Georgia slopes, but he had said you had

to have a few of them, of course, for milch cows, but they couldn't stand the Texas heat and the prairie ticks. No, Brahmas were all the talk in the cattlemen's convention he had attended at San Antonio in the fall — Brahmas and Herefords. He had told James Hardenbrook, then, to send him down a young Brahma bull, the first chance he had. Now, she supposed from the talk, Jake had to go and meet the Hardenbrook cowboys somewhere on the prairie, and bring home the bull.

'Saddle Derby,' Cavin was saying. 'I better go along.' Jake, she could see, welcomed the information.

All afternoon she gave the matter no more thought. But when she looked out her upstairs window at dusk and saw Cavin riding down the avenue, his figure slumping in the saddle, she knew something had gone wrong. Running down the stairs, she met him as he got off his horse.

'It's Jake,' he said, flinging his reins around the gatepost. 'David's working on him now.'

He leaned back against the horseblock, telling her at once what had happened.

'That damn bull,' he said, 'was off like a streak o' chained lightning. We'd no sooner started back with him till he lit out, with his head down and his tail splitting the wind. Lord!' he said, shaking his thick head of hair. 'Nothing stopped him. He broke through fences and swam the bayou, with me and Jake putting out hot after him, but never once getting close enough to head him off.'

He stopped, throwing her a humorous glance. 'Promise you'll believe what I'm going to tell you?'

She nodded, and sat down on the block beside him. 'I always try to, don't I?' she teased him.

'Well,' he went on, 'you know what that fool critter did? He ran clean through a nigger house, through the hall and out the back door, and smashed the porch and a wall down doing it. They were all out in the field, thank the Lord,' he explained, 'the niggers were. We cut around a clump o' trees to head him off, and quick as he saw us, he made for us bellowing like a lion. Lord!' he exclaimed forcefully, 'it never even occurred to me Jake'd try to rope him. You might as well-a tried to rope a couple o' cyclones. Before you could say Amen,' he went on, 'he'd run his horns into Jake's pony, and turned on Jake to stomp him. I saw he'd kill him,' he said, 'and I reached for my gun.'

'Oh!' said Lucina anxiously, jumping to the ground. 'Oh, I must go find Maria.'

'He won't know her,' Cavin said ruefully. 'He's got a couple o' ribs broke and a leg, besides. David's bringing him home in a wagon.'

He was worried, Lucina could see, deeply worried. 'That black boy's been in a raft o' tight places with me,' he observed, 'and I never yet have seen a streak o' cowardice in him. Yet' — he looked at her angrily — 'you'll hear people saying niggers are all cowards. That's not what makes 'em different,' he insisted. 'It's not that. Jake's not scared o' the devil himself, with his spurs on. Well,' he sighed, 'we'll have to tell Maria, and get old Aunt Matty up to help nurse him. He'll be in bed as long as I was,' he predicted gloomily, starting toward the house.

On the steps he waited for her.

'Don't let me forget to send a check for a hundred dollars to old Mr. Chilton tonight,' he said.

'For pity's sake!' she exclaimed, aghast. What new project was Cavin up to?

'At the convention last fall he bet me a hundred dollars I'd be switching to Herefords,' said Cavin. 'Didn't you know,' he asked, noticing Lucina's puzzled face, 'that they raise Herefords

on the Chilton ranch?' He looked at her in surprise. 'There's
a lot you don't know about this state, even yet.'

'Yes,' she replied, 'there is.' At any rate, she knew she had
never ceased to feel a stranger, a visitor in it. She thought she
could understand how the captive Israelites, weeping by the
waters of Babylon, must have felt. Since she had come to Texas
she had read the Psalms with new understanding. But she tried
hard never to let Cavin see how homesick she was.

She need not have been so careful. He wouldn't have noticed
her disposition anyhow; for all that winter he kept his hands
busy stringing barbed-wire fences around his unfenced prairie
land. One day, nearly a year before, when he was in Houston
he had run across a sample reel of the new barbed wire he had
been hearing so much about. He had known, then, that it was
exactly what he needed. Now he wrote to Gresham's for reels
and reels of it and set his negroes to cutting down hundreds of
little trees for fenceposts — cedars, young oaks, and locusts.
Cedar posts, he was to find out, would last, while locusts would
take root and grow. What he was interested in then, however,
was in fencing in his prairie land, any way he could, and stock-
ing it with Herefords. By hot weather, Jake was again well
enough to drive Cavin's cattle — fat, short-horned creatures,
with white, open faces — down to drink at the dams scooped
out years before in anticipation of their huge thirst.

All fall Cavin attended to his plantations, and his beeves
and paid almost no attention to the matter of the new state
constitution which ninety delegates had assembled in Austin to
draw up. Was not Colonel Rutherford's judgment to be trusted?
Let him and Colonel Brashear, who was also among the delegates, puzzle over the just powers of government. The less of it
the better, he thought, and he didn't know a Texan who felt
otherwise. And from this time on, they were going to run their

own state. Even Grant had understood that. When, at last, he saw a copy of the new Constitution he read no further than the Bill of Rights which prefaced it. Texas, he read there asserted, is forever free and independent, and its people have the inalienable right to alter, abolish, or reform their government. He sighed in relief. That's all he had ever been fighting for, up and down Virginia and then home again, in Texas.

This was a time in which Cavin's plans seemed all to be taking root. His crop was as flourishing as any he had ever picked; across the bayou a four-hundred-acre tract was filled with tall, girdled trees, already dead, ready for clearing; and on his raw prairie land a herd of fat, red Herefords was now grazing. There was a new overseer on the place, Henry Reeves, and he was taking hold, fast. Jeremiah's trade was increasing week by week; and Cavin saw no reason why, when the cotton was sold, he would not be able to pay off a good share of his indebtedness to Colonel Rutherford.

At home, things were working out, too. There was a tutor, now, in the house — a young man who seemed to know how to handle boys. Lucina had wanted to engage a candidate from Charlottesville about whom Justin Hartwell's widow had written her, but Cavin thought young Texans would get along better under a teacher who wouldn't have to be told that the Travis who defended the Alamo was a Texan, even if his family home *was* only a street back of the Governor's Palace at Williamsburg. So they had finally settled on young Mr. Moseley Allen, who had been up in Kentucky with his mother's people, studying at Transylvania, but who had been born and raised on Buffalo Bayou. He had taken up his duties in October.

He was a handsome young chap, who knew as well how to jump on a horse and take the boys hunting as how to read Latin, who would sometimes disappear in the woods all day with his charges and return, at nightfall, with a collection of snails, cray-fish, lizards, and spiders, or a pile of leaves and folded buds. Then he would spend all the next day getting the boys to identify these specimens out of the natural history and botany books he had brought along with him. Perhaps the next day they would switch to geography, and wander up and down the creek all morning, hunting for islands, peninsulas, or capes; and the next day Cavin might come upon him and the boys reading Greek mythology, or Texas history. Well, he supposed the young man ought to know his business.

And he knew his, too, he thought. Boys who were going to have to manage a plantation had to be able to do every job that needed doing better than their servants. You didn't learn out of books how to boss a gang of field hands; or how to head off a wild steer; or break a horse; or always to lay down your gun, when you crawled under a fence; or how to arrest a crazy-drunk negro. These things a boy had to learn because there was no place in the world for weaklings. FitzHugh was old enough, now, to be taking charge, and Heinrich and James Barclay, too, who, he judged, must be nearly the same age. There were Beau and Philip also coming right along. And Nathaniel, it was already clear, was a born cotton planter. Cavin often picked up his second son and took him along with him when he went over the place. Yes, it would take young Moseley Allen and him, too, to bring up a lively batch of boys like these. After a while, he supposed, they'd all have to be going off to school somewhere; but he wouldn't worry about that, just yet.

As soon as Lucina took a good look at her handsome new tutor, she knew what kind of governess she would have to have — a woman old enough to have given up any idea of romance.

When she said that to Cavin, he glanced up from his paper and raised his sun-bleached eyebrows.

'La!' he had asked her, laughing. 'Where you going to find a woman like that? Not unless you cut her finger and blood won't run out of it.'

But she knew she had to, and one night the answer came to her in a flash — Miss Winnie Lee, of course. She was the very person. Within two weeks, then, Miss Winnie Lee began the task which was to consume the next ten years of her life — the task of teaching Lucina's and Letitia's girls to run their scales, to learn Latin (which she herself had about forgotten), to memorize poetry and read history, and never, never to cross their knees or drop their shoulders.

One disturbing event, however, took place during this time — an event which convinced Cavin that he could never allow a contentious negro to remain on his place. For Pete, about whom Horace had long freely expressed doubts, finally stirred up enough trouble in the county for Cavin and the Hunters to have to take to patrolling the roads again. Cavin felt responsible for the leniency that had precipitated the situation, and could not forgive himself for letting his heart overrule his head.

The truth was that Pete was Aunt Matty's boy — an enormous, gangling black man — and Cavin hated to separate the old woman from her one child. Besides, when Pete was behaving himself, he was a good worker, and Cavin figured, now that he was home, Pete would settle down.

One cold, rainy night in January, however, Cavin was wakened by Horace.

'Lawd God! Mas' Cavin,' he panted, knocking on the bedroom window under which he knew Cavin's small bed was drawn up. 'Hurry and get up!'

Cavin was already on his feet, throwing on his clothes. He drew on his boots and snapped on his cartridge belt before he said a word. Lucina sat up in her big, high bed, in the shadows across the room, listening, with her hands clasped tight to her heart. She was suddenly cold with terror, and afraid to stay alone. Slipping on a wrapper, she crept, shivering, to Cavin's side.

'It's Pete,' said Horace. 'Us followed him, Mr. Reeves an' me.'

'Just a minute,' said Cavin. He went upstairs and waked up FitzHugh. The boy was thirteen now, and a good shot. It would be an hour before the overseer could get back here to stay with Lucina.

'FitzHugh,' he said sternly, 'get your shotgun and come downstairs.' James was sitting up rubbing his eyes. He was quick as lightning, Cavin knew, afraid of nothing, and as stubborn as the devil. For a moment, he hesitated. Better get Beau and Heinrich up, too.

'James,' he said, 'you boys ride down and tell Jake I say to get up here as quick as he can.'

James already had his feet in his shoes. 'Yessir,' he answered, and began to shake Heinrich and Beau.

Lucina met him at the bottom of the stairs, dressed, with a lamp in her hand.

'Pete,' she told him, 'was hiding stolen cotton in the old fort down by Berryville.'

'Yes?' Cavin waited.

'Horace'll tell you,' she said. He could see her hands were shaking. 'He's saddling Derby.'

Cavin stepped to the front door and listened.

'All right, Horace,' he called, hearing Derby's familiar, low nicker. The negro took the steps at a bound.

'I know about the cotton,' said Cavin. 'Go on, tell me the balance.'

'Us ketched up wid 'im.' Horace suddenly groaned. 'Oh, my Lawd! Den we saw him skedaddling under de house——'

'What house?' Cavin interrupted.

Horace threw a hesitant glance at Lucina.

'Where dat white 'oman lib by herself in de woods,' he explained, as delicately as he knew how.

'Go on,' Cavin said impatiently. It was worse than he had feared. No matter if the woman wasn't worth killing, she was white, and Pete must have been crazy. He walked toward his horse, and Lucina followed him.

'Den us heard all hell breaking loose inside,' Horace said, suiting his stride to his master's. 'Us run in den,' he went on, 'an' dar was de woman wid a axe in her hand, an' Pete layin' out dead on de flo'.'

Cavin's mind flew out to take in all the possibilities. He knew this fire would be hard to put out. Then a circumstance struck him as strange.

'How'd Pete know' there was a hole in the floor to crawl through?' he demanded. There was more to this than appeared on the surface, he suspected.

'He must-a been watchin' whar she hide her money, under a loose bode.'

'What was he doing hanging around her place, anyway?' Cavin persisted.

'Mebbe dey bofe in wid dat gang o' robbers been stealin' our cotton,' Horace suggested.

Cavin digested the idea in silence, then glanced down at Lucina standing beside him in the dark.

'FitzHugh's got his gun, and Jake ought to be on his way up here soon. I'll send Reeves back.'

'Yes,' she breathed.

'We'll have to get the patrol out, or there'll be a hanging before night,' he told her. 'The riff-raff'll be raiding every nigger cabin in the bottom!'

'I know,' she said, looking straight at him. 'Go on,' she said, 'you'll have to hurry.'

He gave her a long appraising look which seemed to satisfy him. 'I'll be back as quick as I can,' he said, and was in his saddle as he spoke.

That night was the first time, since the agreement on his front gallery between him and Warren Hughes, that he called out only a portion of the Hunters.

'Might as well serve notice on 'em right now,' he decided, 'that the deal's off, and they better watch their own step.'

By sunrise, groups of armed deputies were patrolling the roads. Jeremiah Blake and old Mr. Joseph O'Fallon were among them, but not one of the Hughes gang with whom Cavin had earlier joined forces.

Frank Barclay was riding along with Cavin when they came upon Warren Hughes, square in the middle of the sandy road that edged the Locust Hill fields.

'Ah! Mr. Darcy!' Warren said pleasantly. Folding his arms across his chest, he sat a moment obviously meditating on his next words. Then he moved closer. 'I infer, gentlemen,' he remarked lightly, 'that you are no longer in need of my assistance.'

Cavin checked his horse.

'As you choose,' he answered significantly. 'We're going to have order in this county. If that's your idea, too — ' he suggested, and waited for a reply.

Warren's lids fluttered. 'I'm afraid,' he said regretfully, 'that our wishes begin to diverge.' He sat a moment completely at

ease with an absent smile coming and going on his delicately
cut lips. 'Good morning, gentlemen,' he said, and spurred his
horse, then checked him, so that his front feet made an arc in the
air. 'We shall meet again, no doubt,' he said politely, and was
off.

But not before Cavin felt, rather than saw, him exchange a
sudden, darting glance with Frank. Reaching out, Cavin laid
his hand heavily on his brother-in-law's shoulder, and felt his
muscles stiffen under his fingers. 'You'd better tell me,' he
warned him, 'if you know anything about that gang.'

For a bare second too long, Frank hesitated.

'I'm warning you — now,' Cavin said slowly, not moving.

'Rats!' exclaimed Frank, shaking his shoulder free. 'What's
the matter with you, Cavin? Are you crazy?'

He turned, then, and smiled equably. 'You must be seeing
snakes. Come on home to dinner with me.'

They rode along in silence, until they were opposite the
Little Creek drive.

'Come on in,' Frank urged Cavin, with his hand on his gate
latch. 'Margaret'll enjoy seeing you.' Then he gave Cavin
a straight look.

'Listen,' he said, 'I'd-a had to shoot anybody else that asked
me a thing like that.'

'All right,' said Cavin; 'just put it down to my being a fool.
It's not the first time. Margaret,' he added slowly, 'is Lucina's
sister — in case you've forgotten.'

'Forgotten!' returned Frank, and his thin face darkened.
'Lucina has our two children at your house now, hasn't she?
I am,' he concluded, 'hardly in a position to dispute your
interest in my affairs.'

Suddenly his face lost its guarded, mocking expression.
'She doesn't get any better,' he declared, as his fingers dug

deep into Cavin's arm. 'Do you think there's anything I wouldn't do for her?' he demanded, 'anything on God's earth?'

'We've written to ask Shelby to come out,' Cavin said. 'Did Lucina tell you? His wife is sick, though. I don't know how soon he can start.'

Frank's hand dropped to his side.

'Ah!' he said, 'that will please her.' For a moment they sat without speaking. Then he reached down again to open his gate.

'Coming?' he asked, looking back.

'I hope you've got mustard greens,' Cavin said, swinging the gate to behind him.

For a week or more the excitement in the county was intense; and then gradually it died down as people began to realize that the military courts were no longer in control of affairs. There was even a stretch of two months when Cavin hoped that Warren Hughes had decided to quit the county.

Then, all of a sudden, there was trouble springing up everywhere. Somebody broke into Colonel Brashear's smokehouse one night and walked off with two hundred pounds of bacon. Six of David's mules disappeared in one week, and Alexander Winston's best saddle horse was stolen. Then, to top this series of minor crimes, one of the younger men in Colonel Rutherford's warehouse was shot down on the prairie, robbed of his bags of silver, and left to die in his buggy.

The night after that happened, Cavin sat down and wrote up to the penitentiary at Huntsville asking them to let him know where he could get some good bloodhounds.

Very soon, a dozen dogs with gentle eyes and long, drooping ears and jowls were established in kennels at one side of his front yard.

Lucina protested, but Cavin was firm. 'I've got to have 'em where I can hear 'em at night,' he explained.

The first Saturday afternoon he had the dogs, he started a custom which soon began to take on all the excitement of a weekly horse race. That noon, he and Horace and Jake and the new overseer, Henry Reeves, had decided that the dogs needed a good run to keep them in training. While they were talking together, the dogs were jumping all over Horace, who was stooping low over their feeding pans.

'All right, Horace,' Cavin said, 'they've got your scent. You leave me your shirt and cut off home and climb a tree. In an hour, I'll start 'em after you.'

'Lawd!' cried Horace, hastily backing into a corner and holding up his pink-palmed hand. 'Not me, Mas' Cavin. Dey'll claw me alive when dey ketches me.'

'Did you ever hear of a dog climbing a tree, Horace?' Cavin inquired, laughing at the negro. 'Here, hand me your shirt. Where you reckon I'm going to be, anyhow?'

Then he told the overseer to go back to the quarters and send all the hands up to watch the hunt.

Soon the negroes came hurrying up, laying bets on whether the dogs could actually track Horace down or not. Jake held two dogs on a very long leash, Cavin two, and Henry Reeves two more. The next Saturday, they would try out the other six hounds.

Cavin held Horace's shirt under the dogs' noses and guided their quivering nostrils into the tracks his feet had left in the sandy road. Then, almost before he could throw a leg over Derby, the hounds were sniffing and whining and then racing in confident excitement down the path through the woods and along the river, yelping in long, resounding howls. Cavin thought, as he listened to them, that nothing, except maybe a coyote's wailing cry, could be more mournful than a blood-hound's doleful, resonant barking. Usually they were a gentle, affectionate breed of dogs, but once on the trail they turned into wolves.

Horace, sitting comfortably up in the tall cottonwood that hung over his back fence, heard them, and climbed a branch higher. Then, clutching a limb, he leaned way over to see what was happening below.

There, thank the Lord, was Mas' Cavin riding out of the woods, right along behind the dogs.

'De front one's old Ramrod,' Horace decided, 'an' de one on de nighest side is — lemme see — dat mus' be old Jupe. Yeah,' he speculated, proud of his reasoning, 'I kind-a figured dem was de two bestest houn's in de lot.'

Behind Cavin, he could now see a few of the field hands running hard to be in at the finish of the race. This was every bit as good, they seemed to think, as hunting possums on dark nights, by the light of a yellow, swinging lantern. Horace leaned over the branch and clapped lustily. 'Hi, dar, ole Ramrod!' he cheered in proud acclaim; 'I know'd you could tree me! Rufe,' he called down to a negro below him, 'hand me up dat-air two-bits you bet me.'

By this time the dogs on the end of Cavin's leash had spied Horace and were leaping in the air, in eager, lurching jumps, seemingly anxious to try climbing up the rough bark. Cavin got down and walked over to them, offering them each a chunk of fresh meat which the cowboys had butchered day before.

'There! there!' he said. 'That's a plenty,' and pulled back hard on their leash. His eyes were bright and eager, his cheeks flushed. This was good enough fun for anybody. He was as proud of his hounds as he was of his bird dogs and his greyhounds. He had over two dozen dogs on his place now, he calculated roughly, and it kept a colored boy busy looking after them and the boys' ponies. Old Hector, his lead bird dog, could scent plover where there wasn't any — Hector, with his splotched white sides, his brown, loving eyes, and ears that drooped the length of his strong jaw. Then there was Goliath, his fleet-running lean greyhound, sharp of face and with quivering flanks almost meeting underneath his lank, blue body. Racing across the prairie, with the pack yelping at his thin heels, he was a pretty sight. Yes, Cavin thought, his dogs suited him to a T. Especially his last acquisitions — these bloodhounds.

After this beginning, the negroes almost fought with one another for the privilege of being tracked down on Saturday afternoons, and spent the week devising involved and intricate mazes with which they hoped to trap and puzzle the hounds. Soon all the children, white and black, took to trailing after the chase, and the half-holiday began to get on Lucina's nerves.

'Cavin!' she complained. 'That's an awful lot o' racket to have to listen to every single Saturday.'

'Well,' he returned easily, 'they have a good time, don't they? And' — he broke off, looking at her meaningfully — 'you haven't heard about any stealing on our place, have you?'

'Oh,' she answered; 'now I see.'

'That's it,' he said. 'Besides, didn't they elect me justice of peace last fall? These dogs ought to save me a heap o' work; besides,' he added smiling, 'keeping everybody in a good humor.'

And for some time that was how it worked out. Cavin's dogs had no chance at all to grow fat and lazy, and Lucina had to put up with their weekly yelping.

Chapter 25

More and more, when they wanted to go into Galveston, they were beginning to get on the cars at Berryville, change at Houston, wait overnight, and take the morning train on. Cavin fumed a good deal about doing it because, he said, a man could gallop into town nearly as fast as the wheezing narrow-gauge engine could take him there. In fact, he'd tried it once for a stretch of three miles, and won a bet — and nearly killed Derby doing it. He wouldn't try *that* again. The train had better speed than he had thought, he confessed; and he began to admit that maybe the trip was a little easier on the cars. Anyway, they had decided to bring Shelby back from Galveston that way.

For Shelby's wife was so far recovered that he planned to take Captain Baker's boat at Savannah and to arrive in Galveston the second week in May. Lucina wished he could have put Camp Mountain in his pocket. Sometimes this flat country, this low, black Brazos bottom, oppressed her beyond endurance. She wondered if she would never get over feeling homesick here, where as soon as one danger was over another seemed to spring up almost instantly in its place. She argued with herself, but it was no use. Even yet, after more than ten years, whenever she stopped to smell the wet, heavy coastal air, she longed for the light breezes on Cedar Ledge. Or whenever she waked in the middle of the night to hear a fresh norther shrieking around the house, shaking it till it quivered and turning the chimneys into wailing chambers, she shivered, feeling again the same prickly fright that had overtaken her the first night she ever spent on the prairie.

It was strange, she thought, this love for a place, the way a person's heart had of twining itself around particular rocks and mountains and rivers and pines. It was as though some essence, some curious, charged force passed back and forth between in-animate objects and people. Sometimes, she thought, people who lived long in one place were conscious of the lives of their ancestors taking new shape in them, uniting them to the world around them — the earth spirit, the Indians called that feeling moving in one. What link had she to this prairie, this dank, dripping bottom?

It was not that she was unhappy. No, she told herself, it was something different — more the way a man floating out in space, with no chance ever to touch the earth again, must feel. Texas interested her mind and exhausted her strength, but in it she had never taken root.

She knew, of course, that born Texans, like Judge Dickerson, loved their foggy bottom land the way she loved her mountain top, but the knowledge did not much ease the long ache inside her, the sense of separation that so often afflicted her. People, she thought, ought to live forever in one spot, journeying out from there to see the world, of course, but always returning to where they first drew breath. Cavin seemed to have that idea himself, the way he was always talking about the things Beau would accomplish on the Brazos. She would have to learn to feel about Texas the way he did, she told herself sternly; and once again she would make the effort, and always she would fail.

Ah! it would be good to see Shelby! What would she have done without Margaret to talk to, these years? Poor Margaret, who kept saying every week that she was getting better, when, only to look at her, anybody could tell she was getting worse.

Her two children, Cecilia, the elder, and Tazewell, stayed almost altogether now at Locust Hill, for Margaret felt easier with them in Lucina's charge.

Cavin seemed to take them and all the other children into his heart in one sweeping gesture, being hardly aware, Lucina sometimes thought, of his own varying relationship to them. He seemed to have the same kind of affection for children that he had for puppies and colts and young cotton just pushing up out of the earth; and he watched his children and his crops developing with the same serene confidence that the end was bound to be good.

One day with a droll smile he asked Lucina what Shelby was going to think about this large and vociferous family she had acquired. She laughed, imagining Shelby's surprise if, on their return from Galveston, they were to find FitzHugh's fawn and Felicia's little white pig asleep on the parlor floor. That might very well happen, she knew from experience, for every morning the children washed and scrubbed and brushed their pets, and saw no reason why they should keep them out of the house. Felicia's pig followed her about all day, like a puppy, squealing and grunting whenever he lost her; and once Lucina had come upon the deer asleep on top of FitzHugh's feather bed.

'Shelby is going to be surprised,' Lucina observed, in considerable amusement, for he had always been fond of order, and order was hardly to be had in a family like hers.

They met him in Galveston late one warm afternoon when the breeze was blowing in fresh and cool off the Gulf. Like flecks of white spray, the gulls were rising and falling above

the waves, and the air was full of the apricot light which Lucina
had learned to expect at sunset on the prairie. It seemed to her
a long time, now, since she had stepped off the boat in Galveston.
Ten — no, eleven years, it had been. Shelby would probably
be as much changed as Cavin, who quite certainly had ceased
to be a boy.

Far off, they saw a boat slowing up for the sandbars. That
must be the *Mary Frances*, which was still plying back and forth
between the Southern coastal ports. Had it taken Captain
Baker that long to make shore when she and Cavin were
aboard, Lucina wondered, and thought it had not.

But little by little the boat drew in, and then, at last, they
could make out a figure — no, two figures — leaning out across
the water searching the shoreline. One of those figures must
be Shelby's.

Who the other man was she did not guess until, as the ropes
were being drawn in, he began to wave to them and then, turning, moved toward the gangplank which Cavin was already
ascending. Then she saw the traveller's limping gait, and, as
he took off his hat, the dark, shining hair about his brow. John
— that must be John — with whom Cavin was vigorously
shaking hands. Suddenly she was full of joy, and a tumult of
thoughts arose in her mind. She had a million things she
would enjoy talking over with him.

'Well!' said Shelby, stepping on shore and lifting Lucina off
her feet in a vigorous embrace. 'You seem to have taken good
care of her, Cavin!' John said not a word, but only smiled
at her, as Captain Baker came up to speak to her, with the
generous, affectionate smile she remembered.

They stayed that night down the beach at a hotel surrounded
by oleanders where a negro cook prepared barbecued pom-
panos and red snappers outdoors over an open fire. It was

Shelby's first taste of the fiery sauce the Texans preferred, for Georgians always left out a share of the red pepper which Texans swallowed like water.

'I've learned to like red pepper,' said Lucina, laughing to see her brother choke.

It was a bright, clear night, and the waves lapped at their feet. Lucina sat silent while the men fell to discussing what had happened since they were together in Georgia. John was representing his district now in the legislature and hoped to go on to Washington. What the South needed, Lucina heard him saying, was men who would give their full time to studying its problems. Cedar Ledge was once more in fairly good shape, Shelby told them. Mrs. Connor was well, and still living in the overseer's house.

'I'd like to buy her land,' said Shelby meditatively. 'She has no one to leave it to, now. She'd rather I had it than a stranger.'

Tomorrow, thought Cavin, he would show them what he had been doing in Texas. No use *telling* them anything now.

Lucina, listening, decided that they must invite the Brazos Literary Society to Locust Hill, while Shelby and John were there. It had been months since they had had a meeting anyway; it was full time to revive the custom of assembling regularly at one plantation or another. She sat there, with the hum of the men's voices and the beat of the waves in her ears, hardly realizing that they were not all back on the Georgia island where her family had so often spent their summers.

Next morning they were up early to catch the train for Harrisburg, where they knew they would have to wait several hours for stage passengers from Austin and San Antonio. Arriving there about eleven o'clock, they got thankfully off the hot, clanking cars and entered a carriage driven by an old negro

who, Lucina had once told Cavin, was the living image of
Uncle Ned in the song she so often sang to Beau:

> 'Lay down the shovel and the hoe.
> Hang up the fiddle and the bow;
> For poor old Uncle Ned am gone,
> He's gone where the good niggers go.'

The negro's name though, she knew, was actually Uncle
Randall, and he had belonged to Mr. Jefferson Randall on
Groce's Bayou.

    The old man knew exactly how to treat the occupants of his
rattling old carriage. They wouldn't want to be bothered about
anything, would expect him to know what to do without being
told. They would want to ride up and down the bayou under
the big trees that overhung the road and — he reached over
and patted a parcel by his side — in about an hour he would
draw up somewhere and invite them to step out and rest in
the cool shade, whilst he fixed them a little lunch. He tried to
remember what his old wife, Aunt Big Sally, had done up in
the package by his side. Yes, fried chicken and stuffed eggs
and salt-rising bread would do to offer his passengers, and it
was good fresh buttermilk, too, that sat at his feet in a bottle
dropped in a bucket of cold water. They could see everything
was clean and nice, all wrapped in a dish towel and when they
got out of his carriage they wouldn't ask him 'How much?' but
would say, 'Thank you, Uncle, for a nice ride' and drop a
little silver in his yellow palm.

    Taking off his hat, he bowed deeply, waiting for them to get
in. Mas' Cavin's company would soon see that their driver
had been raised right and knew his business.

    He supposed they'd want to see the old capital of the Republic
of Texas. It wasn't much to look at, for it was about to fall
down; already its wooden porch had caved in, and some of the

posts that supported the gallery roof were missing. Still, everybody always wanted to ride around to the place where Sam
Houston, in buckskin and leggins, surrounded by his dogs, had
received the French ambassador in a silk hat and tail coat.
There was something about that story which seemed to amuse
everybody, more than it had his old master who, he remembered,
had remarked at the time that it was, to say the least, an unbe-
coming way for a President to behave. But then Mas' Jefferson,
the darky reflected proudly, had always been what you'd call
a mighty keerful dresser. Well, he thought, rolling his yellow
old eyeballs backward toward his passengers, he reckoned
they'd want to be getting along. Lifting his cracked reins, he
clucked to his rawboned, gray horse.

'Gid-dap, Jaybird,' he said. 'Us got a ways to go.'

Uncle Randall had come with his master to Texas in 1829,
and had accompanied him, all dressed up in black velvet, to
President Houston's inaugural ball. Many a night Uncle
Randall had sat fanning old President Lamar — another careful
dresser — while Jefferson Randall and the President sat together thinking up ways to raise money and get rid of the
Indians; he had listened to Colonel Ashbel Smith and all the
other white men arguing, 'way back yonder, about whether to
join the New Nited States or not; and he had, finally, hurried
on to the war in Virginia with his master, whom he had left
there with the Lone Star flag spread out on his breast. Lord!
Lord! Here he was, now, back in Texas driving a rusty old
hack, a free nigger they said. There wasn't much to be said
for that state, he thought; but, anyway, he could tell Mas'
Cavin's visitors whatever they wanted to know about this
country around Galveston and Houston.

'Dis-yeah,' he said with a flourish, 'is us's old capitol. Dar's
a new 'un, now, up de ribber a ways.' He hoped they wouldn't

ask him about that one, because even though, due to the war, he was a traveller, he never yet had been way up to Austin.

Cavin let Uncle Randall talk on while they ate the lunch he set out before them. The old darky could tell Shelby and John more than he could about all that had happened in the days William used to be always remembering. Cavin wished, as he often wished, that Philip had stayed in Texas when he first came out in 1832. Really, he reflected, 1855 was too late to have settled on the Brazos. He was comforted only by the thought that the title to his land was written out in Spanish and went back, through William, as far as anybody's.

It was late afternoon before they got off the wheezing, jerking narrow-gauge train at Berryville and watched it draw up on a siding, where it always stayed overnight until time for the return trip next morning. Cavin looked around. Yes, there was Jake; and the carriage lamps were lighted. It would be heavy dark when they drew up at Locust Hill. Lucina was glad she could count on Aunt Emmy's providing a good supper for them — probably a chicken pie, with hard-boiled eggs and cream in it, and some little, tiny butter beans, and maybe lemon custard, or pecan pie. There — her heart rose proudly — there, running around the carriage to meet them, was Beau, his blue eyes shining under his dark long lashes. Shelby would see he was all she had described him to be. The child had an open, friendly way of meeting people, a charming air of confidence that always reminded her of his grandfather, Beauford. Shelby would notice the resemblance at once.

'You're well named,' he told Beau promptly, smiling at him and turning to her. 'Doesn't he remind you of Father, Lucina?' He stooped to look more closely at his nephew. 'He's got the long Lyttleton eye, all right, but the color comes from Cavin's side.'

Cavin laughed. 'Nathaniel's all Darcy. We haven't decided about William, yet.'

'Beau,' said Lucina, touching him on the shoulder. 'This is your Uncle John.'

'Oh!' said Beau, looking straight into John's face. 'How's your mother?' And then, quickly, 'And Samson? I expect he's getting old?' he inquired.

John smiled at Lucina. 'I see this boy's part Georgian, Lucy,' he remarked, putting his hand in his pocket. 'I brought you a book,' he said to Beau. 'I hope you like it.'

'Oh!' said Beau, and, turning the pages, forgot to say 'Thank you,' an omission of which Lucina was about to remind him when John shook his head at her. Beau had started toward the carriage, reading as he went. Already, John saw, the boy was on board the Greeks' hollow black ships, gazing across unharnessed seas.

They went by Little Creek Plantation, on their way home, and left Shelby there with Margaret, who seemed no worse, if anything better. She was cheerful and hopeful, as usual, and not at all surprised to hear that her brother was outside.

'I knew it. I dreamed it last night,' she explained. 'Do you remember our family dream?' she asked Lucina. She looked well, extraordinarily well, and the color flamed in her thin cheeks as she put the question. 'The white ship that sails *in* when someone is coming, and *out* when someone is dying? It was sailing *in* last night,' she went on, expanding her dream, 'and I knew that Shelby was on it.'

'Oh!' Lucina replied, not at all startled by the coincidence. The dream had occurred to too many of her family for it now to surprise her. But their conversation, they could see, made Frank, who was sitting by the bedside, somehow uneasy. After fidgeting a little, he rose abruptly and went out to welcome Shelby.

Margaret smiled. 'Men are funny,' she said to Lucina, who was arranging her sister's hair.

'Aren't they?' agreed Lucina promptly.

They smiled at one another in perfect accord. You had to allow for men's ways of thinking, if you lived with them, their smile said; but there was nothing to prevent a woman from having her own ideas, at the same time. It was comfortable, thought Lucina suddenly, having Margaret married, very comfortable.

Shelby was to stay with Margaret, they had decided. for a time at least; but the next morning, Cavin said, as they left, he and John would pick him up for a ride around all the plantations.

Day in and day out, Cavin and John and Shelby argued about the coming fall elections. They couldn't see, they said, that it made much difference to the South whether a New York Democrat, like Tilden, was elected President in Grant's place or not. What they had to do was to hold the gains they had made in their own states. The poll-tax requirement in the new Texas Constitution, Cavin told Shelby, had eliminated practically all the negro vote; for what colored man on earth was likely to pay his poll-tax nearly a year ahead of time, as the law demanded? And if he did try to vote, all you had to do, wasn't it, was to shift the ballot boxes around? Any darky'd be sure to get his vote in the wrong one; or you could tell him to put some kind of mark on the outside of his slip, and then you could throw it out when it came to the counting. Yes, things were quieting down a lot, all over the South, they agreed, since the white men had learned how to beat the devil around the stump. The Yankees had learned something, too — learned it cost good tax money they wanted for pensions to keep an army below the line. It looked like, if the Southerners used sense, John observed, they could get along, from now on. But it would take sense.

'Plenty of sense,' John repeated, absorbed in his thought. 'Sometime we've got to figure out a way to count the colored vote, without letting them run things. Oh, well!' he said, narrowing his wandering interest, 'that'll have to come later. How does the situation stack up here in Texas, now?' he asked Cavin.

'We're sending Governor Coke up to Washington,' Cavin replied, 'and everybody expects Lieutenant-Governor Hubbard to take his place. He'll hold the state down,' Cavin prophesied and grinned. 'He ought to. He's big as a mountain. He'll have a tough job, though,' he added more seriously, 'with the Populists and the Greenbackers and I do' know who all running up to Austin every time they want a drink o' water.'

'Well,' said Shelby slowly, 'we're getting a lot o' people at home with mighty funny ideas in their heads. You've heard, I suppose,' he inquired, 'about our state-owned railroad? How the manager of it, on a salary of two thousand dollars, accumulated a bank deposit of thirty thousand — all in one year.' Shrugging his shoulders, he remarked in a puzzled voice that there were other Georgians whose main ambition seemed to be to turn their state into New York.

'Oh, yes, Georgia's full of wild ideas, too,' he concluded.

'Yes,' Cavin said, looking up with sudden interest, 'I've been reading in the *Constitution* and the *Courier* a bunch o' letters from somebody named Henry Grady. Who's he, anyway?' he demanded.

'Why, you know him, Lucy,' replied Shelby, turning animatedly to his sister. 'His father was killed at Petersburg — old Colonel William Grady who commanded the Highland Guards. Don't you remember?'

'Well, for pity's sake!' exclaimed Lucina, startled. 'Whatever is the world coming to? If it was anybody else, I'd say he wanted to be postmaster at Atlanta,' she conjectured, 'but Henry Grady — why would he want the job?'

'No,' said John soberly, 'I think he honestly means what he says, Lucina. I've talked to him by the hour. He wants us to build factories and get on good terms with the Republicans and educate all the negroes. I can see there is something in his argument,' he conceded, 'but I can't follow him all the way. Why do we have to imitate the North, like that? Besides, where'd we get the money to build all the factories and railroads he wants? Why,' he said, turning to Cavin, 'it's as clear as day. To raise it, wouldn't we have to sell out to the New York banks, and then where'd we be? The Yankees would be running our country then, just as much as if they were quartered on us in uniform. No,' he asserted vigorously, 'Grady's wrong. We're a farming country; it'd be poor business to start turning ourselves into storekeepers.'

'The idea!' said Lucina spiritedly.

John looked at her with sad eyes. 'Lucina,' he asked her, smiling, gently, 'don't you remember Homer remarks on the fact that men are always willing to squander *other* people's wealth "with insolence and without sparing"? That,' he predicted, 'is bound to be the end of Grady's dream, it seems to me. The North'll be squandering our wealth and,' he added regretfully, '"without sparing." Even the poor darky won't be exempt.' He began to laugh, but without any trace of mirth. 'Just count the hair-straighteners running around all over the South!'

'One thing I see right off,' said Cavin thoughtfully. 'If Grady has his way, the South'll be all cut up with railroads. Old Governor Davis had the same notion, and, if we hadn't-a stopped him he'd-a handed over the whole state o' Texas, kit and boodle, to the International Pacific. Lord!' Cavin snorted, 'it's a disease — this business of wanting to hear wheels turning! I wouldn't let a railroad cross an acre o' my land,' he declared irascibly. 'I'm too close to one now. Sometimes I can hear the damn thing whistling across the prairie at night.'

'You know,' Shelby broke in, 'it looks to me like in this world there's always been *one* war going on and only one — a war between the people who want to live on their own land and do as they please, and the other people who want to live jammed up in cities with somebody *telling* 'em what to do. We thought we were fighting the Yankees,' he said, resting his chin on his palm and staring at Cavin, 'but I'm beginning to think President Davis was right. He saw it, before the war, and made a speech about it in Congress. We weren't fighting only the Yankees,' he repeated. 'We were fighting all the people everywhere who want to run the world just one way and make everybody alive fit into their tight little system, whatever it is.' He rested his round, bronze head against the back of his chair and looked off down the road, sighing heavily. 'Sometimes,' he said, 'I like to remember that there are Spaniards buried in Florida and Georgia clay who once thought *their* system was destined to cover the earth.'

'You're going too far back for me,' said Cavin. 'What I want to know is, can Beau settle down right here on the Brazos and run his life the way he wants to? That's what I've been aiming at, ever since the day I ran off to the army! That's what Nathaniel lit out o' Virginia for, wasn't it?' he asked, squaring around to look at Shelby. 'So he could build himself a place on top of Camp Mountain and live to suit himself. What's the use of being an American, if you can't do that?' he demanded irately, pounding the arm of his chair. 'I'm getting plumb sick and tired of reformers. They've got all sorts of fancy names, but scratch 'em and they're all the same, under the skin. All they ever think of,' he concluded in hot scorn, 'is how to spend some other man's taxes making him do what he don't naturally want to do — you can always count on 'em doing that, cain't you?' he asked John irritably. 'Economy's a word they hate like the devil, and they take to authority like a duck to water. As long's I live,' he declared, 'I'm going to fight 'em, tooth and toenail. We've got 'em on the run now, all over the South, haven't we, John?'

'I don't know,' John answered, less confidently. 'People o' that mind are born in the South, too, you know.'

'Well,' Cavin replied, 'we can keep this county, anyway, clear o' pushers and shovers and ——' He waved his hands with increasing ill temper. 'Train blowers and tell-you-what-to-do-ers — the whole lot of 'em. Lord, what's the matter with Henry Grady?' He threw the question out helplessly.

'He's progressive, Cavin,' said Shelby dryly. 'We'll all be hearing that word a good deal, I expect, from now on.' He was quiet a moment and then added: 'They say there's a hundred new machines patented up at Washington every day. What Grady wants to do is to start 'em all to running at once, down here.'

'Well,' said Lucina suddenly, 'one of 'em's a blessing. Do you remember, Shelby,' she inquired, 'how we used to have to seed raisins by hand? You ought to see the contraption Cavin saw advertised and sent for. Aunt Emmy just turns a handle now, and seeds enough raisins for Christmas in about an hour.'

John smiled at her. 'Lucina,' he asked gently, 'what difference does it make to you how long the women take to seed raisins? What earthly difference?'

She stood up to him stoutly. 'As soon as we have to begin paying our cooks, it will.'

'Time! Time!' cried John clapping his hands softly together. 'That's the whole trouble. People with machines want to divide it into split seconds and charge you for every tick of the clock. I'd as soon be dead as live that way.'

'La! la!' said Cavin. 'A man can make himself dizzy, thinking.'

The week after this conversation Cavin had a note from Colonel Rutherford inviting himself out to the Brazos, 'to eat fresh hen eggs and swap tall stories,' he wrote. He had been in Philadelphia and New York, and had enjoyed himself hugely.

Lucina took advantage of his impending visit to invite the Brazos Literary Society to meet at Locust Hill. She knew how the day would run and laid her plans accordingly. The guests would assemble about noon and would linger on till night playing Authors, putting on charades, and exchanging books, or copies of *Southern Society* and *Godey's Lady's Book* and papers from Atlanta, New Orleans, or Louisville. And Judge White was practically certain to bring along a few old copies of his favorite journal, the *English Quarterly Review*, to pass around. There would be a light lunch to provide at noon and a hearty picnic supper later in the day. Like as not, she thought, smiling to herself, before the occasion was over Cavin would have to mix up some vile concoction to pour down Mr. Archibald Bland's old mule, who always got the colic from eating too much corn at Locust Hill. She might as well remind him to make up a big brown bottle of the stuff and put it up in the buggy-house, all ready for use.

The night before the gathering, Colonel Rutherford arrived,

and sat until late rocking on the front gallery and reporting the financial outlook in the North.

'We can get money up there, all right,' he remarked positively, 'but I'm dead against doing it.' He hitched his chair nearer Cavin's, and continued. 'We've got to pare expenses to the bone in this state. Our revenue's less'n half of what we're spending.' He turned anxiously toward Shelby. 'How do you manage in Georgia, Mr. Lyttleton?'

'The Radicals have gutted *our* treasury, too,' Shelby replied. 'Where is the South going to end up at, borrowing hand over fist to keep up with the rest of the world? Can you tell me that?'

'One thing's clear enough, Shelby,' Cavin asserted. 'It's no kindness to your children to load 'em down with debts. As for railroads — bah!' he exclaimed. 'About all they're good for is to run over your cattle and set your grass on fire. If we go in for 'em in this state,' he said, pursing his mouth and narrowing his eyes, 'I know one thing: We've got to manage them, and not the other way around. All these newfangled do-dads,' he declared with rising indignation, 'are bound to bleed the life out o' you. Shucks!' he maintained, 'I can get along without any of 'em.'

'Yes,' said Shelby slowly, '*you* can, Cavin — as near as anybody — just as long as you can hold on to your plantation. How long do you reckon, though, they're going to let you do that — the people who want to make money out o' selling you — well, say, horse collars? They're not going to like it because you make your own out o' shucks, are they? And,' he concluded dourly, 'you've got to remember they are the ones who won the war!'

Cavin rose, and, as was his custom when he was agitated, began to pace the gallery from one end to the other.

'Well,' he returned, 'they haven't won the war in *this* county. We've won it.' Then he yawned. 'You all sit up, long as you please. I'm going to bed. Excuse me, Colonel?'

'Coming myself,' said the Colonel, rising ponderously. 'Didn't get any sleep at all in New York. I'd hate to have to live in that place.'

Chapter 26

THE next day was clear and warm, as the members of the Literary Society began to arrive.

'Well,' thought Lucina, 'this is one day they won't all be talking about politics.'

For it was an old rule of the Society that, at its meetings, the discussion would be held strictly to topics of a literary nature. There was always some talk of plays, too. Once, before the war, the group had been ambitious enough to put on *The Taming of the Shrew* outdoors, under William's oaks, and they had intended to try staging *Romeo and Juliet*. But since the Surrender, who had had the time to think about such things?

Toward noon, the house was full. Here, Lucina suddenly thought, were all the people who had come to Philip's old house, eleven years before to welcome her to Texas — all, or nearly all. Some of them, though, were gone now, she remembered with a thrust of pain.

She was standing on the gallery with Cavin, smiling at their guests as they arrived. She still wore her black hair drawn behind her ears in a style that accentuated the shape of her head and the cast of her features, but her face could stand such treatment better now, even, than in her girlhood. For her nose which then had seemed a little blunt and her mouth a little wide were now both overshadowed by her eyes, which had deepened to such luminous warmth that a stranger, seeing them and the delicately arched brows above them, noticed no other feature. From time to time, she glanced approvingly at the three men beside her — all so different in appearance yet with something about them all almost exactly identical. Between arrivals, she let her attention dwell on her husband and her brother and John, as a nascent idea about them began to plague her.

There was Shelby, not so tall as either John or Cavin, with eyes a lighter, redder brown than hers and a mass of bronze, not black, hair that he had never been able to smooth down to please him. None of Nathaniel's descendants were likely to be bald, Lucina thought, a sudden smile appearing on her lips at the idea. John's black hair, as straight as an Indian's, was already thinning over his fine temples, though his eyes were as darkly blue as ever and even more remote. He was thin as a sapling, too, with shoulders that stooped a little, and elbows and knees that, when he grew older, would press sharply against his hunting clothes, pushing them out in odd, pointed sacks where his joints bent into the corduroy. Now, Lucina meditated, except for Margaret, her family ran to a more rounded, fuller stature. Cavin, she noticed, was filling out himself, and — strange, this was the first time she had observed the resemblance — growing all the time more like Philip, with his nose settling down into a beak and the lower half of his face taking on the cast of his father's. Of course his coloring was different, and even she admitted that he lacked something of Philip's fine balance and poise; but yet you knew instantly, sometimes when you looked at him, that Philip's spirit was momentarily flitting through his son's body.

All different and yet all alike, these men standing beside her. What is it, though, Lucina asked herself, that makes you know they are all three sprung off one stem? It was an air they all had, she decided, a manner that appeared identically in each of them, in their gestures, in their expression, in their way of moving and answering you. She found the question interesting and she pressed it further.

What lay behind their similar bearing and manner, creating it? Was it not a confidence in themselves, and in their ability to meet whatever they had to meet? Yes, in them all was the same quiet, unconscious assumption of being able to deal with whatever circumstances they might encounter.

'Now take even old Mr. Bland,' Lucina meditated, pursuing her idea. 'You never have the feeling life's really beat him down, but that he's drawn a kind of truce with it — one that satisfies him, all in all. Whether he's wearing his long-tailed old coat or his dirty old fishing outfit, you know he's doing what he wants to, as near as he can, not what somebody else thinks he ought to want to do.'

She pushed her notion further, finding it, as always, a pleasure to let her mind circle clean around any notion that tempted her. To break an idea up into fragments and then watch each fragment expand, was a keen and growing delight to her, as the years passed. That, she thought, with sudden understanding, was why she and Cavin so often looked at things differently. He plumped right into life and tackled it bare-handed, hardly thinking about it at all, while she always stood out on the edge somewhere, watching and mulling over what was happening, as if she were only a spectator, not a participant. Cavin, on the other hand, was always right in everything up to his ears.

'Whatever it is,' her mind ran on, 'that makes you know Cavin and John and Shelby are all of one blood, it's that same thing you see in every race. Maybe that's what makes people a race. Maybe they aren't a race until they naturally think about things so much the same way that their agreement shows in their faces. Take the Germans at the end of the county, or take Chris, or yes, even little Henry. You know, just to look at any of them, that what they're thinking isn't going to affect their expression, and that they're not apt to give up anything they start. Or take the Englishmen at Galveston. They all look the same way — sort of slow, and they sit around kind of carelessly and awkwardly. But that's because they've already decided how they think is the best way to do everything.' She laughed a little. 'They are as confident as Southerners that their way's best.'

'Lucina!' said Cavin, in a low voice, jiggling her elbow. 'Here's David coming!' 'Lucina's wondering about something,' he thought indulgently. Well, if it pleased her, it suited him. Maybe that was how she thought up some of the good suggestions she was always offering him. But she'd better come to, now. He glanced shrewdly at John and smiled. Cut out of the same cloth, he and Lucina. First thing you knew, he'd have to be jiggling John's elbow, too.

David was coming up the steps now, with a young lady on his arm, and, just behind them, the new Mrs. Blake was saying something to Jeremiah, who, since his marriage, had been automatically drawn into the Society. In marrying Jeremiah, Evelina had shown the usual sound judgment which had always characterized her family's dealing, but anybody could look at her and tell that it had been more than that which led her on. She was in love with this fiery-headed, slow-moving man; that was clear enough.

Lucina smiled at them both across David's shoulder, and then at him directly. He was holding his head high and his curiously dissimilar eyes were blended by his excitement into an identical hue. The small woman at his side wore a becoming flowered white lawn dress caught together at her throat with a pale-blue ribbon bow, and her slender, dark face glowed with the same warmth that shone in David's.

Lucina did not have to guess what it was that pleased them both. Only a few days before old Junius, Judge Brashear's body-servant, had dismounted at their front gate, and, instead of going around to the back, had walked importantly up to the front door and twirled the knocker. Matt, who could still see well enough to answer the bell, had flung open the door and confronted old Junius, who was standing there very erect, holding a silver plate on which rested two white vellum cards enclosed in tiny envelopes.

'Wid de Colonel's compliments,' Junius said, grinning, presenting another larger envelope addressed in Colonel Brashear's free, easy hand.

Lucina had received the cards from Matt in some excitement. Who was getting married? she wondered.

'Why,' she said to Matt, opening the first tiny envelope, 'it's Miss Sabra Brashear and — guess who?' She smiled at the old colored man, and pulled out the other card.

'Doctor David!' exclaimed Matt promptly. 'Now, dar! Dat's fine!'

She leaned over, now, therefore and kissed Sabra, while Cavin began to tease David.

'Miss Sabra,' said Cavin, shaking his head pessimistically, 'you got a terrible job on your hands trainin' an old bachelor like David. How on earth you reckon you're goin' to get him in hand?'

'I'll take a few lessons from Lucina,' Sabra parried.

'There! There!' cried David. 'You better give up, Cavin!'

'Lawd-a-mussy!' returned Cavin. 'What chance has a man got anyway? All right, David,' he laughed softly. 'You come around to me for some good advice!'

Cavin was in fine fettle. There was nothing he enjoyed more than having a house full of company, unless it was seeing a field of cotton in full bloom. He passed David and Sabra on with regret. He'd have to talk to them longer, later.

'My brother, Shelby, and Mr. Martin,' Lucina said, turning her attention to her next guests.

'Oh, Evelina, it's nice seeing you and Jeremiah.'

Cavin began to tease them, too.

'Jeremiah,' he said, as sober as a priest, 'I bet you've already forgotten how to swear.'

Lucina heard some commotion at the gate and glanced that way. There just getting down off a restive black horse was a thin, wiry little man with a mass of scraggly chin whiskers. He was accompanied by a servant and a flock of spotted dogs that, at a word of command, crouched down around the horse, whining rebelliously, with their pink noses laid out flat on their shaggy paws. Lucina knew who he was — Colonel Ashbel Smith, who, although he was Connecticut-born, had served as colonel of the distinguished Second Texas Infantry, being cited for gallantry both at Shiloh and Vicksburg. She smiled a little, anticipating the conversation that always took place between him and Cavin regarding the relative merits of their regiments. Once when they were in Houston, they had driven out to Evergreen to visit Colonel Ashbel on his plantation where he lived, a bachelor, alone. Cavin and he, she remembered, had spent the whole evening comparing the number of citations in their respective regiments, and sparring about where on the Brazos there was the most malaria, whether in the Colonel's or in their own county.

Well, Colonel Ashbel Smith was entitled to his opinions and his pleasures. She had been in Texas long enough to know that. For he had served the Republic both as minister to

England and as secretary of state, and the state in its legislature and army. Now everybody was talking about getting him to run again in the coming election.

William and he had enjoyed a long friendship, although their political opinions had not always been identical. And since the Colonel was a physician, with training acquired abroad, like Philip's, the two men had often pooled their recollections and sometimes their knowledge. In Philip's library was a copy of Colonel Ashbel's treatises on yellow fever and cholera. Just now, the Colonel had told Lucina on her recent visit to Evergreen, he was engaged in writing up his reminiscences and his recollections of the Republic. He was getting feeble now, though, and hardly ever left Evergreen any more. Indeed she had not really expected him here today, although Cavin had dropped him a note informing him of the occasion.

'Ah, Colonel,' said Cavin, hurrying down the steps to welcome him, 'I am delighted to see you here, sir.' He grinned wickedly. 'I hope you're prepared to admit that the Fourth Texas —— '

The Colonel shook his small fist lightly under Cavin's nose. 'Bah!' he retorted and stood off facing his host with an accusing glance. 'I'll wager there are a hundred people down with chills in your good-for-nothing county!' Then he smiled warmly and touched Colonel Rutherford on the shoulder. 'Of course I'm here! Do you suppose I was going to let an old man like Wharton Rutherford get the better of me?' he demanded. 'Soon's I heard he could make it, I decided I could.' He laid his thin fingers on Cavin's sleeve. 'I took the cars to Berryville and stopped at Mrs. Symington's last night. She said tell you she'd-a been here, if she could.'

He mounted the steps with a more buoyant tread than one would have expected from a man of his years, and bent over Lucina's soft hand.

'And this is your brother?' he inquired, lifting his fine eyes toward Shelby.

'And Mr. Martin,' added Lucina, 'our other guest.'

'Let me welcome you both to Texas,' said Colonel Ashbel warmly.

The Colonel was the last arrival. It was now time for Jake and Horace to begin passing sandwiches, coffee, wine, and lemonade under Matt's anxious direction. For, though the old man was too near blind to assume such duties himself, he insisted on standing by to remind Jake that Colonel Brashear preferred grape wine to blackberry, that young Mr. Thomas Abernethy always took brandy in his coffee, and that lemonade was the best thing to offer Mr. Archibald Bland and Mr. Tripp Cuttross. Later on, when the picnic dinner was spread out on long tables under the trees, Matt hoped, but hardly dared to believe, that things would go all right.

'Dese-heah young niggers,' he grumbled. 'Lawd God! Whut does dey know?'

When the sandwiches had been around several times, Judge White arose during a lull in the conversation and lightly tapped a column on the gallery with his small cedar gavel.

'Colonel,' he said in his deep voice, turning to Colonel Ashbel Smith, 'I hope you have something you want to say to us today.' He expected the Colonel to respond. Neither Sam Houston nor the Colonel, Judge White reflected, could ever look at a bunch o' Texans gathered together without wanting to suggest ideas for improving the Republic they both loved like a child.

'Only this, ladies and gentlemen,' said Colonel Ashbel, raising his spare figure briskly out of his chair and bowing to his listeners. 'Only this. Charlottesville is a long way from Texas, and — he smiled — Yale, my own college, farther yet.

Besides there are unfortunate reasons well known to us all why a Southerner prefers not to cross the line. Now,' he argued, 'since the Republic, we have had lands set aside for a university in this state. Since 1858 we have even had a board of regents, but,' he asked, 'where is the university? Is it reasonable,' he went on, watching his listeners closely, 'is it reasonable to expect the Baptist denomination to continue to carry the burden of educating Texans? I should like therefore to propose for your thoughtful consideration the establishment of a university to be supported and nurtured out of state funds. A university second to none,' he added, bearing down on his words, and pausing for them to sink in. 'One other suggestion I have, my friends,' he continued, looking earnestly at the faces around him, 'one I do not need to argue here, I think. It is that we endeavor also to provide adequate training in the various trades and household occupations to the colored people in this Republic. I suggest this course,' he said, measuring his words, 'not only for their welfare but ours. I have no doubt,' he concluded, 'that some of you, in your own thinking, have already formulated clearer ideas than my own upon both suggestions.'

He took his seat amid a vigorous clapping of hands, and when the applause had subsided, Judge White got to his feet.

'I am certain, sir, that you will find all of us here in complete agreement with you,' he said, bending his white head, about on a level with the Colonel's, toward the members of the Society. 'Do I reflect your sentiments, ladies and gentlemen?' he inquired. Listening to the repeated applause, he smiled toward the Colonel. 'You see — you'll *have* to go up to Austin again, Colonel,' he declared.

Then holding up his hand for silence, he introduced the next speaker.

'Colonel Rutherford,' said the Judge, 'has been up in New York and Philadelphia. Maybe he'll tell us about his trip.' His gray eyes invited the Colonel, who drew his stout figure reluctantly out of the comfortable rocker he occupied. But he knew the custom: every traveller was expected to report his wanderings to the Society.

'I've had quite a trip,' said Colonel Rutherford. 'I wished for you all.' He stood still a moment, considering what they would most enjoy hearing about. Ah! He must try to describe to them the delight he had had in watching the shambling, pathetic figure of Joseph Jefferson in *Rip Van Winkle*.

The Colonel had a considerable amount of dramatic talent, and, before he knew it, he was acting out the part, even repeating some of the lines from memory.

Straightening his cravat, which he still wore, on dress occasions, wrapped stock-like around his heavy throat, and knotted in a generous bow beneath a low wing collar, he went on.

'I saw young John Drew, too, in Philadelphia,' he told them, 'playing in *Cool as a Cucumber*. He's a handsome boy. Everybody was talking about Miss Ellen Terry's Shakespearian parts in London and Sarah Bernhardt's acting in Paris. The producers are trying to bring them both over here. My bookseller gave me a list of the new books,' he continued. 'I brought a few home — one by Bret Harte, *The Luck of Roaring Camp* and another by Mark Twain called *Tom Sawyer*. The ladies may find them' — he paused, smiling ingratiatingly — 'may find them — er — perhaps a trifle robust. Mrs. Lewes,' he said, using the name the Brazos preferred, 'has a new novel out, *Daniel Deronda*. I brought a copy along for Miss Lucina. Oh, yes,' he said, preparing to sit down, 'I also attended a lecture on the *Descent of Man*. Very atheistical,' he observed. 'All about a new theory put out by an Englishman named Darwin.'

'I've been reading his book,' said Lucina quickly. 'Somebody sent it to Uncle Phil.'

At this point, the Bishop arose, seeming, in a familiar gesture, to settle his head and neck into his shoulders before he began to speak. 'I am preparing a series of sermons on the evolutionary theory,' he remarked, 'to which I invite you all — especially the gentlemen.' He sent a slanting, accusing smile toward the men around him. 'I see no occasion to get excited over Darwin's conclusions,' he continued slowly, his ruminative eyes kindling. 'Many men have reached many conclusions about many things in this world, and the Lord, it seems to me reasonable to suppose, is hardly bound to support any of them.'

Cavin got on his feet. 'Bishop,' he said admiringly, 'you've got mo' plain ordinary horse sense than any o' my cowhands.' His eyes shone blue and sparkling in his brown face as he turned them on the Bishop.

'If I have,' the Bishop countered, 'I need all I've got, Cavin.'

Judge White rose again. 'I know,' he said, 'that it's against the rules to discuss politics at our meetings, but I believe that you would all want me to waive the custom this time in favor of a member of the Georgia legislature, who is our honored guest today.'

Lucina was not surprised that John, as he stood up, seemed a little hesitant, almost timid. She remembered, from the past, that it always took a few minutes for his olive cheeks to flush and his tongue to loosen up.

'Ladies and gentlemen,' he began in his pleasant voice, 'how shall I thank you for your many courtesies and kindnesses to us on our visit to the Brazos? We have never once felt ourselves strangers here in your midst. How could we?' he asked, dwelling on his question and repeating it. 'How could we? To you, Georgia once gave a President; and Georgians have marched with Texans in a cause equally revered by us all.'

Pausing to marshal his thoughts, he threw his shoulders back and thrust his weight forward on his one sound foot. He was wearing a white tucked shirt with a high upstanding collar cut away beneath his clean-shaven chin and a loosely tied, wide cravat. Standing with one hand slid inside his waistcoat, just below its turned-back revers, he faced his hearers, who judged rightly that the introduction to his speech was over.

'My friends,' he began again, speaking slowly and reflectively, 'one question presses particularly hard upon every thoughtful Southerner today. It is this: What *is* our position in this nation? Let us face the truth — the bitter truth. We are a minority, in a government that our fathers framed. As that minority, we have' — he held up a newspaper — 'I will read you what the editor of your Brazos *Signal* so accurately asserts.'

Opening the little journal, he readily found the column.

'We now have,' he quoted, 'the onerous privilege of tax-paying and the dubious distinction of serving as subjects of experimental government under second-class cobblers, fanatic preachers, and bankrupt political theorists. That is our exact position, my friends,' he declared. 'There is no use deceiving ourselves.'

'What, then, is our future?' he asked, bending forward. 'As I see it, we have one hope, and one only. If we have the patience to endure comparative poverty, we *may* succeed in creating anew a world in which we can honestly believe. It is a chance — a bare and meagre chance. I admit it.'

He was silent a long moment, while his pensive face settled into sadder lines.

'I do not know that we shall have the courage to act upon so uncertain a choice. And yet if we do not, we ought to remember that the South — no country — can eat its cake and have it, too, for *all goods have their price*. And the price of imitating the North, whose ways are not our ways, will be nothing less than the gradual surrender of all our convictions. One by one, we shall be called upon to relinquish our peace, our quiet, our independence, even our schools, our courts, and our systems of credit and taxation to those whom we are imitating. For when,' he demanded, leaning intently forward, 'were vassals ever free?'

His voice sank and then rose again, as he faced his audience, confident of his conclusion.

'And the end?' he inquired firmly. 'Who can predict it? Of one thing only am I convinced — that it will be worse than the beginning. For, as the night follows the day, so must decadence tread fast upon the heels of a people weak enough to prefer imitation to creation.'

There was a splatter of applause, which he hushed by throwing up his hand. For a moment he stood silent, with his dark head pushed forward and his whole body poised and motionless.

Then, holding up his hand again for silence, he said in a clear, ringing voice, 'Ladies and gentlemen, I give you the South — the free South, subservient only to God.'

Instantly, as his hand fell, there was an outburst of spirited applause that kept on and on. And when at last it began to die down, it rose again and again, swelling higher than at first. Judge White was wringing John's hand when Cavin stepped up to his guest and clapped him on the shoulder.

'John,' he declared heartily in a voice loud enough for all to hear, 'I wish you'd stay here and run for Governor.'

His remark set his guests to cheering again. Lucina, sitting next to Shelby, was conscious of being proud and happy, as if Beau had somehow grown up overnight, and had suddenly risen to put all her own emotions and thoughts into clear words. In some ways, she still felt closer to John than to any-body. That is, her mind ran along with his, as it did with Beau's, following the same channels by instinct, not by logic. She wished he would marry some nice girl and settle down.

She was old enough, now, to wonder a little at why, long ago, she had just missed loving him, why never once in his life had she felt about him as she still did about Cavin, whenever she caught a glimpse of him galloping down the road on Derby, or heard him calling for her the minute he entered the house. Some spark of fire even yet passed between her and him that never once had come to blaze in her long relationship with John. She felt a deep tenderness when she thought of John, that was all. That had always been all. She smiled at him now, across the crowd that surrounded him, and he smiled back.

After dinner, the ladies sat looking through the stereoscope that usually rested on the parlor table, and the men fell to exchanging items of stray information — how best to train cucumbers against a fence, for instance; or how, if you wanted to keep your roof from rotting over your head, it was a good idea to sprinkle slacked lime on the shingles. How Galligan's Pills worked wonders in turning a fever, how the best cognac was none too good for burning on lump sugar. How depend-able a crop the new Hungarian grass was likely to turn out to be. What kind of barber the new man at Berryville actually was — the one who was advertising himself in the *Signal* as a Parisian hairdresser. Where the fish were running thickest, and where the crab and shrimp and Spanish mackerel were biting best, what were the prospects for fall shooting.

There was so much to discuss that the meeting was quite late breaking up. So late that Cavin went immediately inside to bed. But Lucina sat up talking to Shelby and John about many things: about Mrs. Connor and Cedar Ledge, about Philip and her own life in Texas, and then about Sunny Fields, now, since Mrs. Martin's death, without a mistress.

'Why don't you find John a wife, Shelby?' Lucina asked her brother, and then put the question to John himself.

'It's time you were married,' she urged him affectionately. 'Like Shelby.'

'I'm always telling him that,' Shelby laughed. 'Always, but it doesn't do a mite o' good.'

John looked at them with shrouded eyes.

'I don't want a wife,' he said at last, and, getting up abruptly, left them alone together.

A wrinkle appeared between Lucina's dark eyebrows. 'Shelby?' She hesitated, reluctant either to go on or to omit her question.

'Yes,' her brother replied. 'Life's like that, Lucina.' He patted her hand and smiled at her. 'John's wedded to the state. He's got a long way to go — as far as Calhoun, I think,' he said thoughtfully. Then, for several moments, they sat rocking, looking at the moon through the trees that screened the end of the gallery, where their chairs were drawn up.

'Shelby,' said Lucina at last sighing, 'I hate to have you go back.'

'Why don't you let me take Beau along with me?' he suggested, out of the air. 'I've been thinking about it. He ought to know where he comes from, the boy ought to,' he argued.

'I will!' she cried, deciding on the instant. 'I will, if Cavin'll let him go.'

All at once, she knew she wanted more than anything to have Beau wandering around on Camp Mountain, learning to follow the paths that led around its rocky slope, and to know at what hour the shadowy dusk began to fall over the valley.

Of course, she would let him go; she would be proud and happy to let him go. Then she was suddenly frightened at her decision. 'Take care of him, Shelby,' she pleaded. 'I don't know how I'll ever get along without him.'

'Of course,' he answered. 'Of course!' and looked at her regretfully. 'I hate to leave Margaret. I can't make out her husband.'

'No,' agreed Lucina slowly. 'Nor can anybody else. But he's devoted to her and the children.'

Shelby nodded and sighed again. 'I can see that. Well, I'll stay as long as I can.'

'You're doing her good. At least, you're making her happier.'

'I hate to go, but there's Vivian — I left her at a bad time.' He got up and walked to the edge of the gallery, looking out into the night.

'Lucina,' he said, reflectively, 'life's always pulling you to pieces. Cavin's the only man I know who runs all the time on one track.' Shelby turned to face his sister, who got up and moved over to join him.

'It's not,' he argued, 'that he's hard or thoughtless. He just — what is it?' he asked her, puzzled. 'Well, he just decides what he thinks is most important, and starts doing it, while everybody else is fumbling around. It's a gift,' he declared. 'I wish I had it.'

'There've been times,' Lucina admitted, with a half smile, 'when I've scolded him about what you're praising him for!'

'Well, I wouldn't,' her brother advised her earnestly.

'I don't — not any more,' she remarked. 'How long have you been married, Shelby?' Not waiting for his reply, she touched him affectionately on the cheek. 'La!' she exclaimed, 'you've got a heap to learn yet, my dear.'

'That,' returned Shelby, laughing, 'was exactly what I thought about you, on your wedding day.'

'Well, you were right,' said Lucina suddenly sober, 'entirely right.'

Chapter 27

Cotton-picking was well under way when John and Shelby started home taking Beau with them. If Lucina had not loved the child better than her own peace of mind, she could never have let him go. But she stiffened her resolve and sent him back to Cedar Ledge, where he could trace the names of his grandparents and his great-grandparents on their tombstones, where he could read, on one of those marble slabs, that the Nathaniel for whom his own brother was named was born, not in Georgia, but in Virginia, long before the Revolution.

She liked to think of Beau standing on the Ledge at sunset watching the dark pines move against the sky. He would climb up into the tree over the creek and sit there reading, as she had done, while he listened to the pigeons whirring overhead. Never once did she doubt that he would love the changing light over the valley and Martha's old gray cabin, the way the road twisted around the mountain, and the white house facing the rose-garden. She went to sleep every night with a sick heart, and yet she would not have had it otherwise. To think of Beau's eager blue eyes opening every morning on the smooth leaves outside her window at home gave her a certain exquisite, satisfying joy.

She tried to think why this was so. Why did she feel it so

important for Beau to be in Georgia? She was quite sure that Cavin had consented for the child to go merely because he had sensed the strength of her own desires — sensed, not shared, them. The responsibility for her decision weighed on her, and she tried to analyze the emotion that had prompted her to let Beau accompany Shelby home.

She had done so, she thought, because, more than anything else, she wanted him to feel that his life ran back farther than his own existence — back to Beauford, to Nathaniel, and to Andrew buried beside the dark James, and, yes, far back of them, to their people in England and Scotland. These countries ran in her own blood like a song, though never in her life was she to hear a skylark singing or to watch the cliffs of Dover rising ghost-like out of the running sea.

She wanted Beau to acquire some feeling of the continuity of all the past, some instinct that bound him close and deep to his own ancestors. To the Englishmen who had written back from Jamestown, when they no longer had any food, that at least the water was sweet and the air gentle and soft, beyond measure. To the Virginians who, later on, had dared to venture into North Carolina and out into Kentucky, scorning the Indians, down into Georgia, and then on to Mississippi, Louisiana, and Texas, where the shining Gulf stopped them at last.

If Beau had stayed home with her, where she wanted him to be, he would never have thought of himself thus, as the inheritor of a tradition, as only one link in a long chain. No, Texans seemed to think they all had sprung fresh out of the loins of Jove, with no past back of their own Republic worth thinking about, nothing that tied them to some deeper course than their own particular destiny. She wanted Beau to understand that the Republic — and by now she thought of it naturally — was not something *set apart* from a long tradition, but part and woof of it.

That was it, that was what she wanted Beau to feel — that he *belonged* somewhere in this world, was not just set down blindly in it, to scurry around, like a cat or a dog, fighting for food and place on it. That settled past, that feeling of historical continuity in his own personal destiny, he would acquire in Georgia and bring back with him to Texas, not in words, but in a deeper, more poignant awareness than words could ever express. Thus, he would be doubly close to her, not only as her own child, but, like her, the child of the race from which she also stemmed. Yes, she was glad Beau was in Georgia, even though she missed him, as the darkies said, like a misery — a slow, corroding misery around her heart.

One thing she had admitted to herself that she had never suggested to Cavin. If the child went away, he would have to stay a long time, or he might as well not go. It would take more than a few months for him to learn all she wanted him to learn. After all, she strengthened her purpose, didn't people send children all the way home from India? Not to brothers, either, but to great English schools full of stern masters. She could do as much for her boy, she thought, and, uncertain just how long it would be till she saw Beau again, she steeled her heart to endurance. There were nine other children to be looked after and schooled on Locust Hill Plantation; two of them her own boys, Nathaniel and William, and she wrapped her heart more closely around them.

She was sad and lonely for another reason, too — because Margaret was no longer there in the house across Little Creek. For after Shelby left, she had grown steadily weaker, as though some strength flowing out of him had held up her own waning energies; and then, before he had even landed in Georgia, she had looked up at Frank one night, smiled, pressed his hand, and never stirred again.

The day after her funeral, Frank closed the house and started off for New Orleans, leaving his children with Lucina and Cavin, where they had been for some time already. His dark, despairing face haunted Lucina whenever she thought of him. It seemed to her all that had happened since the night he had invited Margaret out to talk with him on the gallery must be part of a strange, unhappy dream, out of which she would, in time, awake. But there were the two children, Tazewell and Cecilia, to remind her it had not been a dream.

Cavin seemed actually glad to have Frank out of the county, where conditions were now again getting out of hand. The particular occasion that set off the final spark was serious enough, but not more shocking than other events which had preceded it — events like the murder of the cotton factor in his own buggy on the prairie in the spring. The wounding of Mrs. Spurlock, however, suddenly fanned all the smoldering flames into full blaze.

For everybody pitied and loved the delicate woman who held up her head and took in fine sewing to support her charming, but incapable, Horatio's fine tastes. During the fall she had been staying a week at Locust Hill helping get the children's winter clothes in order and was returning home, behind her prized Kentucky mare, when, late one evening, just before dark, she was held up on the open road, shot in the arm, and robbed, not only of the bills Lucina had slipped into her pocket, but of her one valuable possession — the beautiful mare she had raised from a sickly, unpromising colt.

Cavin was at supper when the news reached him. He was just serving himself to a large pie-shaped slab of hot corn bread, and thinking of how good the cold turkey in front of him was going to taste, when he noticed Jake, who was passing the plate of corn bread, stiffen himself and turn his head sharply to listen.

Cavin arrested his own hand in midair and listened too. The bloodhounds at the side of the house were restless, emitting the short, sullen growls that usually announced a stranger's arrival. Taking the plate from Jake, he flung his free hand toward the door.

'Go see who 'tis, Jake,' he said.

Lucina got up and drew the shades in the dining-room down their full length. Ever since somebody, a few weeks before, had aimed at David, as he sat at supper in front of an open window, she had drawn every shade near Cavin. Quietly she pulled them down, now, and resumed her seat. If there was one thing she had learned by this time, it was to do everything quietly, without announcing her purpose. It was likely, if she told Cavin why she drew the shades, he would fling them all up again. So she said nothing, but laid down her knife and fork, listening too. Suddenly she began to wonder how much of her married life she had spent in strained listening.

At the same moment, they heard a stumbling at the back steps, and Cavin sprang to the side door opening out onto the back gallery, with Lucina pressing just behind him.

'It's Jake,' he said, 'and ——' He tried to peer through the darkness, but he had to wait until the two men stood in the lighted doorway before he saw that the darky with Jake was Mrs. Spurlock's driver, Hosea — a little, shivering wisp of a black boy not more than eighteen years old. He was frightened out of his breath, and his blue-white eyeballs rolled against his high black cheekbones.

'What's the matter with 'im, Jake?' Cavin demanded.

'Do' know, suh,' said Jake, supporting the boy, who appeared ready to fall to the ground. No use trying to get anything out of him while he was in this shape, Cavin decided.

'Take him back to the kitchen,' he ordered. 'Give him some coffee and a swallow o' whiskey and see what you can find out.'

Unconcernedly taking his seat again at the table, he began to eat his corn bread. Whatever there was up, he'd need his supper, more so if there was trouble. Lucina, who could not swallow a mouthful, watched him in amazement.

'*What* do you reckon's the matter?' she asked him, somewhat irritated by his calm.

'Do' know, Sweet,' he returned, dipping into his bowl of thick, sweet clabber. 'Butter me another slice o' corn bread, won't you? I may have to cut for it.'

'Cavin,' she asked nervously, taking the glass top off the silver butter-coaster, 'how can you sit there and eat like that?'

'Like what?' he asked, holding out his hand. 'Oh!' he responded and laughed, twitching his light eyebrows, 'I never saw it did anybody any good to go hungry.' Suddenly, he scraped his chair back.

'What is it, Jake? What'd you get out of 'im?'

'It's Mrs. Spurlock, suh.' Jake bent his brown face lower. 'Dey done shot her and tuck her money offen her, an' stole her mare, to boot.'

'Oh!' cried Lucina, standing up and holding on to the table. 'Cavin, we must hurry!'

'Wait!' said Cavin, his eyes turning hard and cold. 'Who shot her? Where is she?'

'Down the Berryville road a piece,' Jake answered. 'Hosea say he got a good look at de man, when his mask slip.'

Cavin looked up sharply, open suspicion in his glance.

'Yas-suh,' Jake continued, catching the look. 'Yas-suh. Dat's right. Hosea say it was dat white man who been runnin' aroun' heah stealin' all de hosses out fum under you. Hosea don't think he meant to do no shootin' dis time, but his gun went off when Mrs. Spurlock got to pullin' on his mask.'

'Pulling — !' Cavin ejaculated.

'Yas-suh,' Jake replied firmly. 'She th'owed a heap o' red pepper in his eyes. Hosea say he wuz sneezin' all time he undoin' de traces, and swearin' to beat de debbil.'

'I judge,' said Cavin, repressing a smile, 'that Hosea lit out when the trouble began?'

'Yas-suh,' said Jake, also without a smile. 'He clumb out de back o' de buggy when de gun got to goin' off, an' hid in de weeds, an' lay dar till de coast was clar; den he help Mrs. Spurlock tie a handkercher aroun' her arm, an' she tell him go run, fine' you quick as he kin. She settin' in her buggy down dar, now.'

'Lucina!' said Cavin, turning, but she was already in her room assembling bandages and liniment. He pursed his lips, considering.

'I'll take the carriage,' he said, after a second. 'You get on Derby and go after Doctor David. Any o' the other men you can turn up, tell them to get here as quick as they can. Wait!' he said, 'you might stop by Horace's, first, and tell him and Doctor David's boy to help you get the word around. And Jake,' he added.

'Yas-suh?' the negro inquired, whirling in his tracks.

'You better hurry.'

'Yas-suh,' said Jake again. 'I already sont Hosea to pull out de kerridge.'

Cavin limped back to the room. He was wearing slippers, having taken his boots off for comfort, and, without them, his shorter leg dragged. Sitting down on the edge of his bed, he pulled them on, now, and reached under his head board for the loaded pistol that always lay there. Then, buckling his cartridge belt around him, he stood up, shaking his thick hair back until it fell into place behind his ears.

'Ready?' he asked.

'Yes,' said Lucina, unsteadily.

'There's nothing to bother about now.'

'It's later I'm worrying about.'

His long jaw tightened.

'You know this can't go on?' he asked her, turning hard, blue eyes on her. 'Who's to stop it, if we don't?'

'I know,' she answered. 'There's nothing you have to tell me. But I wish —' she began, and her voice broke.

'Wish!' The word cut the air. 'Wishing won't tie up men like Warren Hughes!' Suddenly his arm shot out and he lifted her off her feet, in the curve of his elbow, nuzzling his cool cheek against hers.

'Listen, Lucy!' he said gently; 'you don't want Beau to have to tackle this crowd, do you?' Then he set her hurriedly down.

'We'd better bring her back, hadn't we?' he suggested. 'Horatio cain't be much of a nurse.'

She nodded smiling, with tears in her eyes. 'I know just what'll happen. You'll leave Henry Reeves or old Mr. Archibald here with me, and the other men'll leave their overseers home, too; and then you'll all go galloping off, and we'll all wait and wait and wait and not know ——' She sighed tremulously and kissed him, holding his face between her hands. 'Is it ever going to be better!'

'Yes,' he promised her, his eyes focusing on some point far behind her. 'It's going to be better, Lucy, from now on. We're going to put this gang in the penitentiary at Huntsville, where they belong. And thank the good Lord,' he concluded, 'the Freedman's Bureau won't be here to let 'em out!'

His glance fell on her worried face.

'In case you don't know it —' he began, smiling.

She leaned against him a moment.

'I do,' she said, and gathered her courage. 'Of course I do.'

'I'm ready,' she said, then, and took his arm.

By midnight Mrs. Spurlock was resting in the bed upstairs, but until early in the morning men were riding up, dismounting and joining the group already on the gallery, plotting their course. Then, all at once, toward dawn, Lucina heard the clatter of their spurs as they rose, and knew they had settled on a plan. Standing in the doorway, she watched them riding down the drive, and then she turned inside.

She felt as if she no longer had any capacity to react to shock or danger. She was not aware that her eyes were taking in anything around her, and yet, as she entered the hall she noted the exact shade of the paint on the parlor door — a pale, pinkish brown with wavering lines cut into it to simulate a grain the door did not possess. All at once she knew she couldn't endure that deceiving paint on her doors any longer. Jeremiah had put it on that way, and she had not had the heart to shatter his delight in it. Now, she decided, she could say the door was getting shabby and have it repainted the way she wanted it — a clear, rich cream, almost yellow.

She stepped into the room, running her gaze over the walls. There was no use trying to sleep. She might as well invite old Mr. Archibald in and let him start telling her the stories she already knew by heart. Then she looked down at the door swinging in her hand. How long had it been since they built the house? And yet never had any of them remembered when they were in town to buy a lock for this door, which was still held shut by a blue velvet ribbon. For a long time Lucina had been scarcely conscious of the missing knob, but now she was suddenly aware, irritably aware, of the omission. She glanced around the room with a curiously sharpened, intensified vision.

There over the fireplace was the portrait of Letitia's grandfather, old Brewster Charlton, and, on another wall, the miserable charcoal sketch of the twins which, in the old house, had hung on the dining-room walls. Philip's secretary was drawn up nearer the fireplace, and on a round scalloped table sat a lamp with a majolica base — Caroline's lamp, but Lucina did not know that. Close to it was Philip's walnut chair, with the bunch of grapes carved on its high, curved back, and across the room, directly opposite from Philip's secretary, stood Letitia's old square Chickering. Above it was a large photograph, in a round walnut frame, of Philip, and another of Letitia. Lucina wished that she could see old Andrew, in the portrait that had hung in the parlor at Cedar Ledge, looking down on her here in Texas. One thing only in this large square room was hers — the Lyttleton family Bible that Margaret had brought out to the Brazos.

She went over to Philip's secretary and opened it, hardly thinking what she was doing, conscious only of a necessity to keep her mind busy, a necessity which prompted her to count the small panes in the secretary's leaded glass doors. Then she flung open the folding top to the desk and began absently to study its writing surface lined with green felt, Philip's army pistols that Cavin had put up in the compartment set aside for letters, and his writing pen, with its top of mother-of-pearl. There seemed to be some letters there, too. Lucina turned them idly over, and then crammed them hastily back into the pocket from which she had pulled them. They were addressed, in

Philip's squarish, angular hand, to Miss Mary Hartwell, Savannah, Georgia, and stamped with large purple stamps.

The sight of them affected her strangely. Wrought up as she already was, it seemed to her that Philip's and Mary's wan, gray ghosts were standing on either side of her, regretting the loss of their pulsing young flesh. Life seemed to close down around her then, hard and desperate, full of grief and danger. She was cold to the bone and shivering, when she flung the desk shut, and went in desperation to seek old Mr. Archibald's company.

But, first, she went up the stairs and leaned over Nathaniel and William. They were eight and four years old, now, and much more like one another than they were like Beau. She was grateful that he was in Georgia, that these boys were sleeping unconscious of the terror which had so suddenly fallen upon her — not only terror of what might be happening tonight, but terror of life itself, of the way it seemed to sweep over everybody's desires and hopes and loves, carrying them all away — where?

The night wore on and the day broke over the prairie. Aunt Emmy brought her and Mr. Archibald some coffee, and then, later, some breakfast, and yet the drive was empty — the drive down which Lucina stared, unable to pull her tired eyes away, unable to quiet her thoughts.

Then, when it was almost dinner-time, they saw, far down the road, where it turned, a wagon slowly approaching the Locust Hill gate.

Lucina saw it first and turned toward old Mr. Bland, catching her breath. Her eyes were deeply shadowed and her face no longer looked young, but drawn and pallid.

'Miss Lucina,' the old man said gently, for he was fond of her, 'nothing lasts. No joy, no grief, no pain. You always want to remember that. You don't think now it'll help you, but it will.'

His solemn voice fell. Lucina was already running down the drive to meet the wagon just turning inside the big gate, and had no idea how deeply the slow words had sunk into her consciousness.

David pulled up his mules and got down when he saw her, walking to meet her.

'We had a running fight out in the prairie,' he began, without any introduction. His own face, usually so full of color, was white and tired, and his reddish hair fell in unnoticed disorder across his forehead. 'They were headed for Galveston with all the cotton and horses and mules. They thought we'd be plowing after 'em in their usual hideaways in the bottom.'

She could not bring the question she wanted to ask to her lips, but stood paralyzed, as if all her life she had been standing with her hands clasped in front of her and would never again stir out of that position.

'It's over now,' David said. 'They're all in jail, every last man of 'em, except three.'

'Three?' she gasped.

'Yes, poor fellows,' David answered. 'They'd been warned. They knew what they were risking.'

Her lips parted, but still she could not ask what she wanted to know.

David put his strong hands on her shoulders and braced her.

'We lost Alexander Winston and old Mr. O'Fallon,' he told her sadly. She had not seen him look like this, she thought, all at once, since he had sat, helpless, beside Letitia, watching her die.

She raised her dark eyes to his face.

'He's alive,' he said, and tightened his grasp. 'They had

wagons full of cotton to hide behind. We had to ride around, to drive 'em out. I think,' he said gently, 'they were determined to get him before they gave up. He's bad off, Lucina,' he warned her. 'I stopped by home for a mattress.'

She closed her eyes and began to tremble, shivering from head to toe, while the black earth whirled around her.

'A minute,' she begged him. 'Just a minute.' Then, to his amazement, she drew a long breath and stilled her shuddering.

'He's there?' she inquired, looking toward the wagon.

'Yes,' said David, and held her back. 'Wait until I've had a chance —— '

'No,' she said, and, climbing into the wagon, sat down beside Cavin, taking his hands in hers, holding them to her cheeks. 'Go on,' she said quietly; 'I won't be in your way.'

She pointed to his own left arm, bandaged tight.

'Oh, that!' he said. 'I'll get you to help me with it later.' He raised the reins and turned back to look at her. 'Lucina,' he said, 'I'd never have gotten up the courage to marry Sabra, if I hadn't known you.'

'There's a bullet I can't probe for,' David said, as they laid Cavin in his bed. 'We have to wait. That's all we can do.'

'Wait!' Lucina said to herself. Already she had waited a lifetime. Every breath that Cavin drew she counted. 'One more,' she thought triumphantly, 'one more.' All night they watched him, and all next morning, but there was no change. Then Jake came in to say that David was wanted outside. Someone else sick, Lucina supposed.

He came back, though, after a little with a note in his hand which he handed to her. 'They found this letter on Warren Hughes,' he said. 'It's to Cavin.' He glanced at his patient and felt his pulse. 'You'd better come outside to read it, hadn't you?'

She nodded and followed him out into the hall.

Then, opening the folded sheet, she held the undated page in front of her. The writing was clear and fine, each letter accurately formed, like steel-point.

Cavin Darcy, Esq.,
Locust Hill Plantation

My dear Sir:

I trust you will understand the motive that prompts me to beg you, in the event of my probable end, to communicate with my father, Judge Armistead Cawthon at Crestoaks, Virginia, in such terms as your generosity may dictate.

I am, Sir, with assurances of respect, not Warren Hughes but,

Your obedient servant,
ARMISTEAD CAWTHON, Gent. as the saying goes.

'Ah!' said Lucina, studying the cynical, impudent signature. 'How like him! I always thought ——' Hesitating, she looked down again at the note.

'Yes,' David answered. 'We all did. I wish I knew — no,' he added almost at once, 'I'm glad I don't. I'll write his father, Lucina,' David proposed, 'and tell him' — he looked at her confidently — 'and tell him his son helped restore free government in this county and was buried, with appropriate honors, on my plantation. That's all true, or will be true,' David insisted. 'The old Judge needn't know the rest.' He looked down at her questioningly, and his figure sagged a little.

'Lucina, I'm glad Frank Barclay was in New Orleans tonight.'

'I am too,' she admitted, 'but we don't know, David — you must remember that.'

'We do, now,' he replied, speaking reluctantly. 'One o' the men in jail is cussing him up and down for quitting and running off to New Orleans. Judge White's looking into it. I thought you'd want to know.'

'Oh!' she exclaimed. 'His sweet children!'

He started toward the door and then stopped, running his hand across his face as if to wipe out of his mind something he did not want to remember.

'Alec, poor Alec!' he exclaimed, 'and here's Cavin ——' He shook his head. 'There wasn't any way we could have avoided it.' His eyes besought her to believe him. 'We all ran the same chances, Lucina, exactly the same chances.'

'I know that,' Lucina answered quietly. 'Don't you suppose I've been in Texas long enough to know that?' Her eyes were dull and strained, and she kept her lips steady only by the greatest effort.

'David,' she pleaded with him, 'Cavin's got a strong constitution.'

'I'm counting on it,' he answered her, but without assurance. 'Would you mind letting me take that note along?' he asked her, stretching out his hand. 'I'll be answering it, tonight.'

It was New Year's before Cavin was able to go around his places as usual, though not, even then, quite as usual. All his life he would have to move cautiously, lest the ball embedded in his flesh should give him a sudden twinge. But soon he never consciously thought of it, any more than he did of his short leg.

'It had to happen,' he told Lucina while he was recuperating. After a long silence he said again: 'It had to happen. They knew it, and they chose it. Poor Alec!' he said. And then: 'Have you been down to see Mrs. O'Fallon? The county'll have to help her.'

He sighed. 'You know there must-a been some good in a

man who fought as hard as Warren Hughes did against old
E. J. Davis. I kept hoping we wouldn't have to shoot him.'

He looked white and wan lying there among his pillows, and
almost as thin as the boy Lucina had seen sitting on the steps at
Cedar Ledge, the day she came home from Orchard Hill.

'Listen!' Lucina cried, bending over him. 'Is there going
to be any more fighting? Because if there is, I tell you I can't
stand it.' She dropped her head on the bed beside him, and the
whole room seemed to quiver and shake around her. Cavin
smiled at her, his old tantalizing, teasing smile.

'It looks like I cain't myself,' he observed, and tentatively
lifted his thin arm, then let it fall. It was two months after that
before David let him get on his horse.

Christmas passed without Lucina's missing Beau as much as
she had feared she would. He was having a happy time, he wrote,
exploring the mountain and riding old Eagle, who was getting
stiff in the joints. He stayed with Uncle John a lot, but he was
in the legislature now, and Uncle Shelby was soon going to
take him, Beau, down to hear John speak.

'He says,' Beau wrote to his mother in big round letters, 'to
tell you it will be the same speech he made last summer at the
Literary Society Meeting, only he's added some to it. Aunt
Lottie talks to me a lot about when you were little.' Then there
followed some crosses. 'I send you some kisses. Your loving
son, Beauford Cavin Darcy.'

That was like Beau, Lucina thought. He seemed never to
think of himself under the diminutive name he was called, but
always signed himself by his full title, fitting into it easily, as if
by right, with a certain quaint, unconscious dignity that was
his own.

Chapter 28

AFTER the penitentiary doors had swung to behind the gang that had so long ravaged the bottoms, events soon began settling down.

The deal that old Colonel John B. Gordon had made up at Washington in February of the new year with the Republican President Rutherford B. Hayes didn't make any real difference to Texans. For before the new President, in order to assure his own inauguration, had agreed to withdraw Federal troops from all the South, the Texans themselves had regained control of *their* state, banishing Yankees and bandits in the same spontaneous burst of wrathful purpose.

Sometimes, indeed, as things began to quiet down, Lucina wondered if this could be the country she had lived in since her marriage — the country that, until now, had never enjoyed, during her residence in it, more than a few months of peace. In a year's time, life had shifted into a tranquil routine, and for all she could see, the war might almost never have been fought.

Things had different names, now, that was all. Cavin had told the darkies they might just as well start addressing him as Mister instead of Master. And the colored people, no longer called slaves, now worked the land on shares, but their actual position was little, if at all, changed. True, they regularly celebrated their freedom on the nineteenth of June every year;

but so, for that matter, did the planters. For with every cook in the county off picnicking, the best thing a hungry family could do was to pick up and follow along, close enough to the negroes' barbecue pit for their cooks to bring them over a good meal. This soon became the accepted and convenient arrangement.

The nineteenth following the jailing of the Hughes gang, Cavin invited Colonel Rutherford out to see his crops and to enjoy the customary barbecue and baptizing, an invitation which was accepted with alacrity.

Right after breakfast, Aunt Emmy and all the house servants dressed themselves up and started off for the plantation in a wagon.

'Go along with 'em, Jake,' Cavin told his servant, winking at the Colonel. 'The Colonel here's a good driver.'

When the white people got down to the quarters, it was well on toward noon and the festivities had already taken on the fervor that accompanies a camp meeting.

'By George! Colonel,' said Cavin, hunching his back against a tall pecan tree, 'I believe to my soul we have more fun on the nineteenth than the niggers do. Doggone it!' he exclaimed, looking in complete good humor at his guest, 'if you started trying to make sense out o' life, you'd go crazy!' He began to laugh in his full-throated way. 'The Yankees think they won the war, but calling a mule a horse don't make him one, does it? I cain't see,' he argued, 'but what we've got things now to running pretty much the way they did before we all lit into killing each other.' Laying his brown hands behind his head, he gazed across the river toward the long blue line, where, across the widest field, the sky appeared to slope downward to meet delicate cotton stalks heavily weighted with large pink blossoms and spreading, heart-shaped leaves.

'Colonel,' exclaimed Cavin with hearty conviction, 'there's nothing on this earth as pretty as a cotton field! It ought to be pretty,' he added, the enthusiasm suddenly leaving his voice, 'to make up for the price. How much lower is it going, Colonel?'

The Colonel shook his head.

'You got to remember,' he said, 'the Yankees were taking both the bales and the profit, when cotton was up. It was good business — for a while,' he said with grim earnestness. 'For a while,' he repeated thoughtfully.

A shadow dropped over Cavin's face like a cloud. For a moment he whistled softly in the tuneless monotone that always indicated his complete absorption in an idea. 'You know,' he admitted, still looking across the river and speaking in a voice that, for him, was strangely dead and lifeless, 'sometimes I wake up at night and get to thinking about that rail fence at Sharpsburg, with dead men banked up against it, one on top o' the other, like sandbags.' Then his eyes sought the Colonel's. 'All for what?'

The Colonel's round, rubicund face was grave, as he spread his hand like a fan across his chin, meditating his reply.

'God knows,' he said at last, picking up a pillow and thrusting it behind his head. Then he began feeling through his baggy pockets, which he always kept stuffed with cotton samples, and receipts, and smoking material and ordered his servant never to touch. The result was that you could always tell the Colonel a block off by his bulging pockets which emphasized his natural breadth. Now, feeling through them, he produced, with obvious triumph, a cigar and lighted it with reflective care. 'Just listen to the Glory Hallelujah racket the Greenbackers and the Farmers' Alliance are getting Southern people to swallow in this state, nowadays!' he continued, after puffing a while in silence. 'You might think they were all abolitionists, born and bred.'

Taking his cigar out of his mouth, he examined the cotton field in front of him. 'You got a pretty crop, this year,' he added, without a pause, 'a mighty pretty crop.'

'Yes, sir, I have,' Cavin replied, pulling meditatively on his chin. 'I reckon I'll mighty nigh pay you off this fall.'

'You'd save on your interest,' the Colonel agreed amicably, resuming the tenor of their conversation.

'You know, Cavin,' he remarked, dropping his voice, 'we've had a bitter lesson; we won't dare think about anything but holding the poor darky down — not for God knows how long. But some day, our children are going to have to figure out what's best to do with all the niggers we've got down here.' He looked at Cavin darkly. 'God knows what they'll decide. How're we ever going to pay for two systems of everything?' he demanded. 'Two school systems, two waiting rooms, two hospitals, two everything! And all the money going up North!'

Cavin ruminated a while in silence. 'Well,' he said sensibly, 'we've got to have 'em. Maybe Judgment Day'll come along before we have to meet all the bills.' He rose, then, and extended his hand to the Colonel. 'Ought to be 'bout time for the shoutin', I reckon.'

They walked slowly down the path, the stout, almost obese Colonel having some trouble matching his steps to Cavin's long, uneven stride. Lucina was already sitting on a bench, with the children ranged beside her in a quiet, solemn row. Just behind them was the colored church, and in front of them, the deep, yellow river swollen by spring freshets.

'Now, listen,' Lucina was sternly warning the children. 'You have to all be as respectful to Uncle Arthur as you are to the Bishop. You have to remember this is their *religion*, and nobody but poor whites laugh at them.'

The children nodded solemnly, and FitzHugh fell to wondering why grown-ups were always reminding you of things you already knew. He thought suddenly, with a vague, wriggling pleasure, that some day he'd be bringing his own son down here to a baptizing in this river, and he'd know enough not to tell him a lot of things he didn't need to be told. Wrapping his feet around the plank that ran from end to end of the shaky church bench, he leaned forward examining an ant's nest on the ground in front of him. 'They say baby ants are white,' he meditated, looking intently at the hole.

The Colonel and Cavin took their seats by Lucina, and then, almost at once, the church door opened and Uncle Arthur came out in the long-tailed coat Philip had given him when the call to preach first struck him in the corn row. He was followed by a procession of black men and women, all swaying and singing as they advanced toward the muddy river. They were not yet, however, caught up in the kind of ecstatic trance into which they would have to fall before they would step willingly into deep water in front of them.

Uncle Arthur swept his heavy arms in a wide gesture, inviting his flock around him as a hen invites her chicks under her outstretched wings. This was his great day when he strode the earth like a king, with the majesty of the Lord resting upon him. Here under his black hands was the reward of his winter's labors and struggles and prayers, his full crop of sinners brought in good time to repentance and baptism.

His petitions ranged from Abraham and Isaac to Saint John and Saint Paul, and included everybody from the heathen all over the earth to the black and white people gathered here by the river. Raising his powerful voice, he continued to invoke spirits and angels beneath and above the earth. Then his quick old ear gathered, from the sighs and groans and shouts around him, that his people were now sufficiently enraptured to enter the foaming yellow stream, scorning its sullen depths. Therefore he brought his long prayer to a precipitate end, and, ponderous and dignified, stepped out from among his congregation.

He stood there, with his wrinkled black face turned up to the sky, and his long white beard floating in the air, while Horace and Jake drew off his coat and enveloped him in a white robe. That done, he took from them two very long poles to steady himself with, and, advancing with precise, measured strides, entered the cold river, shivering perceptibly as the water crept up over his portly figure. The black people behind him fell again on their knees and began a rhythmic chanting, punctuated by shrill, unexpected shrieks, as, from time to time, one of them came through to salvation.

Then Horace and Jake appeared at the church door supporting between them a shouting woman dressed in white, as they were. Grasping her firmly, they steered her through the brown flood to where Uncle Arthur, assisted by two elders in his church, had taken his stand with the poles pushed down into the muddy river bottom and the water coming well up under his armpits.

Colonel Rutherford had been watching the whole ceremony with the closest interest, and now he leaned over to catch his host's ear.

'Cavin,' he whispered, 'you watch old Uncle Arthur. He's as careful how he walks and how he lays his hands as the Bishop is.'

Cavin started, looked more observingly at the scene before him, and then half-smiled toward the Colonel. 'He's got it all worked out,' he agreed.

Then as Jake and Horace stepped forward to the riverbank, guiding the first dripping candidate to shore, Cavin rose and turned to Lucina.

'I reckon we better be standing over there,' he said and bent a meditative glance on FitzHugh. How old was the boy? Well, old enough, anyway, to be taking on his proper duties.

'Come on, FitzHugh,' he said. 'You better come along, too.'

FitzHugh opened his eyes wide, but got up and followed his brother and sister to the edge of the river, where they began shaking hands with every wet sodden figure climbing tremblingly up on shore.

'Glory be to God, Mas' Cavin!' exclaimed Uncle Arthur, making his way, last of all, to dry land. 'I'se prayin' fur you too.' Conscious of his spiritual obligations, he fixed Cavin with a stern, accusing eye. 'How come I see you drivin' dat 'ar herd o' cows all roun' evy place las' Sunday?' he demanded.

'Keep right on a-praying, Uncle Arthur,' Cavin returned warmly, patting the old man's shoulder. 'You and Miss Lucy're going to squeeze me inside the pearly gates yet.'

The barbecue pit was close by and the white people now made their way to it, sitting down some distance off, perhaps half a field away, under some large pecans where the ground was soft and springy, a rich loam built up of millions of leaves. There Horace and Jake would bring them their dinner, and after that they would go home, leaving the negroes to their pleasures. For, short of a razor scrape or a shooting, Cavin never interfered with them on an occasion like this, though he knew well enough that, come fall, there would be many a colored girl fallen from grace on account of this day's festivities.

'What can you do about it?' he would say to Lucina, who worried a good deal about the matter. 'You can't make 'em all over, can you?' he would ask her seriously. 'The Lord must allow for a po' darky same as we do, Lucy,' he always concluded, reminding her that Judge White had once ruled from the bench that it was a negro's natural, inalienable right to eat watermelons, wherever he found them.

Today, as usual, after they had enjoyed the spicy barbecue, Cavin gathered the reluctant children together and started home, telling Lucina maybe they ought to stop by and see how a new white tenant family was getting along.

'Po' Mrs. Ridley!' he explained to Colonel Rutherford. 'I feel sorry for her with all those chillun. How many's she got, Lucy?' he asked, turning to Lucina who sat in the back seat of the carriage with William and the youngest children grouped about her. Nathaniel was old enough to ride his pony now. How she missed Beau — like a toothache! She was thinking about him, when Cavin spoke to her.

'Oh, I don't know,' answered Lucina, bringing her mind back, with a wrench, to Texas. 'Twelve, no, I believe it's thirteen.'

'Well, we better go by and see if Jay Ridley's feeding 'em,' he remarked, flicking the off horse lightly with his whip. 'No telling if he is or not. He ain't worth killing,' Cavin turned again to the Colonel. 'I wouldn't-a let 'em on the place if I hadn't felt sorry for his wife and chillun, ridin' aroun' in the cold rain in a wagon, the way they were. I had this new house over here by the creek I was planning on letting Chris live in, if he wanted to. That was befo' he died ——'

'Died?' broke in the Colonel. 'Chris Gruber dead? Good honest man,' he observed heartily. 'It's a pity. He had a blind mother, too, didn't he? An' more flowers than you could shake a stick at. Now why don't other tenants take that same kind o' pride in their yards?' he asked hopelessly, knowing there was no answer.

'Yes,' Cavin agreed, 'Chris was a good man. Well,' he resumed his story, 'I gave Jay Ridley some seed for a garden and told him he could move in, an' I reckon I was a fool to do it. Mind if we go by there, Colonel?'

'No, no, indeed. Nothing else to do,' his guest replied.

They drove on down a narrow road used for hauling cotton and corn and turned into a lane. There, at its end, with the creek behind and a stretch of black, rolling ground in front of it, stood a three-room, unpainted house built of boards running, not across like clapboards, but straight up and down, all held together by narrower strips. The house was still the bright, reddish-yellow color of new shingles, not gray and mellow, like wood bark, as it would in time become, and the well-sweep looked raw and new against the dark fig trees grouped around it.

Cavin drew up the carriage and got out, wondering that there seemed to be no one about. But in a minute the yard seemed to be full of ragged, dirty children, barefooted, with uncombed hair and light, staring eyes.

'Where's yo' pappy?' asked Cavin of one of them, who shook his head and retreated hastily behind the wagon shed.

Cavin stepped over to the house, intending to knock on the door, and paused, blinking to see that there were no steps leading up to the porch and that a good many of the planks in the porch itself were missing. He didn't need to ask anybody what had happened.

'Ridley's the kind of man who *would* burn up his steps — and the house over him,' Cavin swore, 'rather than step out in the woods and stoop to pick up a piece o' dead brush! I bet the scoundrel hasn't put a seed in the ground either,' he thought, and, glancing over his shoulder to the garden plot, saw that he was right. The wagon and poor old horse were gone out of the shed. Well, he'd better rap and tell Mrs. Ridley to send her worthless husband up to see him, as quick as ever he got home.

'What's he been feeding 'em all on?' he wondered.

Putting one foot up on the gallery, he drew himself up by a post, wincing a little as his position somehow stirred the muscles around the bullet still in his side. Treading cautiously on the loose boards and with his spurs clicking against his heels, he approached the door and knocked — knocked once, twice, and then again, and received no response.

Hesitating a moment, he took a step and looked inside the window that opened on the porch. This house had glass panes; he had thought Chris would appreciate them.

'Lucina,' he called, 'come here!'

Lucina put William aside, and impelled by the ring in Cavin's voice, hurried up to the porch.

'Here,' said Cavin, holding out his hands and helping her up. 'You better go in. I don't know — she's in bed.' He gestured toward the window. 'I knocked,' he explained.

Lucina frowned and drew back, reluctant to enter.

Cavin tested the door, and it swung open. 'Looks like you'd better,' he insisted. 'Maybe she's sick. I'll stand right outside here.'

Lucina gave him a shuddering glance, but pushed open the door and went in. In a few minutes she was out, wrinkling her short nose in disgust.

'There's a whiskey bottle under her bed,' she said. 'Where do you suppose her husband is?'

'Lawd knows!' said Cavin darkly, 'but he better stay out o' my sight. Now, what'll we do?' he asked Lucina. 'All those children — did you look in the kitchen?'

'There's a skillet o' cold corn bread on the stove,' she replied. 'That's all.'

Cavin whistled softly. 'My Lawd and Maker! I was a fool!' He darted his bright eyes around at Lucina. 'Jay's quit 'em

— that's what it looks like to me. After ruining my house, too — wonder he didn't burn it up!' he exclaimed. 'Well, I've got to think what to do.' He stood meditating, resting his shorter hip.

'I'll take you all home, first,' he decided.

'Well, yes,' she agreed. 'I better go get some clothes for 'em, and you better go get Maria and Jake, or Horace, or somebody to come help me.'

He looked at her questioningly, his mind still on the missing man's whereabouts.

'Why,' she exclaimed impatiently, for the prospect was not very pleasing, 'we've got to feed all these children and put clothes on 'em, haven't we?'

He nodded. 'What's going to become of 'em all, though, after that? I've been standing here trying to figure out what to do with 'em.'

'Well,' she said, moving toward the carriage, 'you and Judge White can worry about that.'

Cavin called one of the older boys to him.

'Listen!' he said, holding the child's arm in his grasp. 'We'll be right back with your supper.' The boy's dull eyes brightened. 'He understands,' thought Cavin, satisfied, dropping his hand. 'Go wash your face,' he told the child severely. 'Wash it two, three times in the creek yonder.' Then reaching out he patted his shoulder. 'Which you ruther have — grits or rice?'

'Lawd, Colonel,' he said, climbing into the carriage, 'there it is — just what we were talking about this morning. If it ain't the poor nigger you have to struggle with, it's the poor, worthless white. There's too many of 'em,' he declared. 'Too many of 'em.'

He drove along in total silence for a while and then, at the bottom of a sloping sand hill said, 'Whoa!'

'Look, Colonel!' he said, pointing with his buggy-whip toward a tombstone looming up in the late afternoon sunshine. It was one of the few stones in the common county burying-ground at the top of the hill, and under it rested Chris's poor bones. To comfort his old mother, Cavin had set it up a month before — a tombstone with Chris's staring photograph in it, covered over with glass.

'Now, where,' asked Cavin curiously, 'do you suppose the old lady got *that* idea?'

'I wonder,' replied the Colonel, 'I wonder.' Then he dropped his short stout hand on Cavin's angular knee.

'You'd think, the way the Alliance crowd talk, that *being* a tenant pulls a man down — but there's Chris and there's Jay Ridley. How're they going to explain them?' he demanded. 'Then,' he sighed, 'take Warren Hughes — plenty o' good blood in him, and look how he turned out.' He gazed at Cavin in irritated disgust. 'Populist reasoning's beyond me!' Then, sinking back against the surrey's leather cushion, he inquired, 'What's Chris's old mother doing? I'll be glad to ——'

'Oh,' said Cavin absently, 'Aunt Elvy and Aunt Emmy and Lucy kind-a look after her. 'Twon't be long, now,' he said. 'I reckon all those po' chillun'll have to go up to Waco to the Baptists' Home,' he decided, relieved to have the matter off his mind.

Then he pointed to a small stream of water flowing out of the base of the sand hill and covered with an opalescent film. 'You know, Lucy,' he suggested, turning around to look at his wife, 'sometimes I think maybe there's oil on this place. Why not?' he demanded. 'Oil's pouring out o' farms in Ohio, the papers say.'

Early that fall, Felicia and Letitia and FitzHugh went off to school at Chapel Hill, where there was a school for girls in connection with Independence Academy. They were not very far away — only about forty miles — and they came back often, or else somebody went down to see them, taking them pound cake and fried chicken, and sometimes a whole roast turkey to share with their classmates. FitzHugh would probably go there for a year or two, and then on up to Charlottesville to study medicine. Cavin hoped his cotton crops would bring him in all the money he saw he was going to need.

Beau, too, went away — back to Georgia after his summer at home. Lucina thought that Beau was going to be a handsome man. She admired the way his dark eyebrows arched above his straight nose, and the way he scrunched his eyes together while he laughed and then opened them wide, looking full at you.

He had learned a great deal from his year away, as Lucina quickly saw, and much as she wanted him at home with her, when Shelby wrote begging her to let the boy return for his winter schooling, she could not bring herself to refuse.

Cavin grumbled and hesitated. Indeed, to Lucina's surprise, he seemed more restive than she at having Beau away. She had the strange feeling, whenever she thought of Beau on Cedar Ledge, that two parts of her, long separated, had somehow now come together and, for the first time, she knew she was content in Texas.

Somewhat against his better judgment, Cavin yielded, and the boy went back to Shelby, where he took lessons from his Uncle John and old Mr. Curtis, who had studied classics and law at Williamsburg before theology began to trouble his mind.

'The thing is,' said Cavin anxiously to Lucina, 'how's Beau ever going to run a place like ours, if he's *all* the time studying books in Georgia? Why,' he declared, 'the child's getting so

he cain't rope a calf.' But he saw how she felt and agreed to
one more year. 'That's all, though,' he said positively. 'I
don't know what's the matter with you, Lucy. You usually
have good judgment.'

She countered weakly, 'They don't have malaria ——'

'Malaria!' grunted Cavin scornfully. 'Malaria! When did
any of our children ever have a chill? Don't they drink their
quinine every morning?' he demanded. 'Children on the
Brazos are as healthy as anywhere.' He glared at Lucina,
really angry, and then relented. 'Well, a year.'

Naturally, with Beau away, he picked up Nathaniel oftener
to ride around his place with him — Nathaniel and William.
But of the two, Nathaniel seemed to have the born gift of cotton-
raising.

'Why,' Cavin often told Lucina, 'the child can tell just by
squeezing the ground whether it's time to plant, and already
he knows every team on the place.'

He began to study the other children, now, to see where and
how they fitted into the running of all his places. There was
plenty of land for them all; that much was certain, especially
now that he had induced Shelby to take over his mother's
place in Georgia and had persuaded Helen, who was growing
feeble, to let him buy Holly Grove, leaving her a life interest
in it — an interest that proved to be very brief, for before the
year was over, she had gone to join William.

This was a venture that his own children's fortunes seemed
to demand, and one that Colonel Rutherford, after some conversation, agreed to help finance.

Leaning back in his swivel chair, the Colonel looked at
Cavin across the tips of his white fingers. 'It'll take you a long
time to pay for Holly Grove, Cavin,' he said, 'even with the
income from Shelby coming in.'

"Twouldn't take so long,' Cavin shot back at him, 'if you'd reduce your interest. What you figuring on charging me this time?' he inquired, with some acerbity. This was an old argument between him and the Colonel.

'Depends on how long you want to use the money, Cavin.' Colonel Rutherford shut his eyes and meditated, and when he opened them there was a bargaining gleam in them. 'I'll make you a proposition,' he countered. 'If you'll pass your word to pay me back' — he paused, looking Cavin up and down and whistling softly — 'oh, say, in five or ten years, I'll charge you about what a Yankee banker would. But,' he insisted, 'if I do, you'll have to pay me interest on the dot, keep your taxes up to the minute, furnish me an abstract to prove your title to all your land, take out life, and flood, and fire, and storm insurance — and let me see, what else? Oh, yes, establish your bond as these children's guardian. That'll be about all, I reckon,' he ended judicially.

'Aw, go on!' said Cavin, rising. 'Charge me what you have to.'

Holly Grove was his now, but he had been managing William's plantation so long now that neither he nor Helen was ever really conscious that the place had changed hands.

He had, he figured, several thousand acres under his control in Texas, and litigation over Letitia's Mississippi property was still going on. He owned, or held for his brothers and sisters, his father's plantation, Povey's, William's, and, as a matter of fact, the Barclay place on Little Creek also. For Frank had sent him one brief note from New Orleans, enclosing in it both his will, in which he left his land to his children, and another paper appointing Cavin his agent to administer the property for them. After that, he had simply dropped out of sight and, in his own mind, Cavin did not much doubt the truth of the accusation openly made by several of Warren Hughes's men who were now up at Huntsville behind bars.

Cavin accepted the new task thus thrust upon him with some misgiving. Yet, what else was there to do? Here were Margaret's children, Cecilia and Tazewell, living under his roof; they had to have some source of income. How were their needs to be met, if he did not do the best he could with Little Creek Plantation? So he plowed and sowed that land also, deciding that James, poor Marie's child, ought to share, to some extent at least, in this arrangement.

It seemed to him that, with all this rich black bottom land at his disposal, each of his children ought to be able to get along well enough in the world. The four girls — Felicia, Letitia, Philippa, and Cecilia — would doubtless marry and their husbands would look after their property. They would have to have an education, of course, but their husbands, or their brothers could be expected to attend to their business. The boys were a harder problem. What were they going to turn out to be?

Now, take Beau. By every indication, Lucy was going to make a bookish fellow out of him. Well, that was all right. Let him go on and be a lawyer; there was certain to be enough business on all these four places to take up a good lawyer's time. Or, if Beau wanted to be a teacher, say up at Charlottesville, that was all right too. In that case, he could get Nathaniel to run his share of Philip's place. William — what could he do? Time would tell, Cavin reflected. William was only a baby yet. His own children disposed of, Cavin began to count off his brothers.

FitzHugh, nobody had ever doubted, was going to be a doctor. Well and good. He and David both would have plenty of business. Just looking after the black people on his own plantations, Cavin estimated, would keep one good doctor busy.

They were always having to be vaccinated, now that you knew how to prevent smallpox; and they were always getting cut up with razors on Saturday nights, or coming down with cholera morbus or slow fever. Besides, it was mighty convenient and comfortable to have one of your own blood doctoring you, when you yourself caught a chill. FitzHugh's future career seemed settled. Philip — the youngest twin, the one so much like his father — had not yet revealed his inclinations, nor had Tazewell Barclay. They were still just boys running around roping calves.

But it was different with James Barclay and the German orphan, whose name had long ago been whittled down to Henry Helm instead of Heinrich Helmholz. Sometimes Cavin thought these little waifs were the smartest boys he had.

James, for instance. That boy could take a pencil and a piece of paper and draw things to make your hair stand on end. The boy had talent, there was no doubt about that. Every time you turned around you saw him sitting on top of the fence drawing something — maybe just old Uncle Matt asleep by the chimney, or a negro behind a plow, or a flock of geese in a flying wedge across the gray, autumn sky. Whatever he drew, you thought you were looking at the thing itself, and then, all of a sudden, you saw that somehow it was *more* than that. Maybe the Bishop, who knew about such things, or the tutor, young Mr. Moseley Allen, who was mighty fond of James, would have something to suggest, Cavin mused.

When it came to Henry, though, he knew exactly what that child was destined for. Just to watch him throwing a rope or dashing out on his pony after Jake, to help head off a steer, made you know right away that the boy was born to handle beeves; and yet, how was he ever to set himself up as a rancher? Of all the children, Henry had absolutely no inheritance.

When it came to Cavin what could be done about Henry's

prospects, he wondered, as people so often do, why he had not thought of it before. He had come in from hunting ducks one evening in late December, when the idea first occurred to him.

That evening the thick, ragged clouds hung low over the wet prairie, and the nipping, frosty wind suggested that it was about time to start making sausages and laying down bacon and hams. All week he and Jake and Nathaniel had been down on the Gulf, pushing their rowboat between reeds, watching the mallards circle and then settle over the still, silvery bay. Toombs Dicker- son had been along, and Tom Abernethy and Goodwin Breck- inridge, too. Nathaniel had bagged a few ducks of his own, and Jake's bag was almost as full as Cavin's.

There'd be plenty of good eating for everybody, Cavin reflected, looking with warm satisfaction at the brown canvas bags tied across his and Jake's saddles. There'd be wild duck rubbed all over with sage and roasted, with an apple and an onion stuck with cloves inside its cavernous body. And there'd be buttery hoecake, brown and floury on top, to go with it; and yams baked till the sugar ran out of them; and coffee laced with caramel and brandy. Cavin's mouth watered at the prospect. There'd been good quail weather, this year, too, he remem- bered, and plenty of beautiful wild turkeys almost too pretty to kill, and venison also, though deer were getting scarce. Cer- tainly the Lord, Cavin told himself for the thousandth time, never intended anybody to go hungry. What you couldn't catch, you could raise, here on the Brazos.

As he tied his horse, he chanced to glance back down the avenue, and the sparse beginnings of his fruit orchard caught his reluctant eye. No, the orchard didn't please him, but in time he would have one that did. Meanwhile, he was enjoying persimmons, and figs, and wild grapes, and dewberries, and sweet red pomegranates, and oranges, and bananas that you could buy for almost nothing at the Galveston wharves. It was as exciting as a poker hand, though, to see if you could make bananas grow in your own front yard. He thought of the two spindling plants that flanked his front steps — plants now as tall as his head and with long, thin, glistening leaves much like those on the magnolia tree by the back steps. If it got any colder, Cavin decided, he'd get up and throw a quilt over the banana plants tonight. They were ornamental enough, Lucina admitted. Well, he'd show her they'd actually grow fruit too. Maybe, if they did well, he'd put in an acre or two of them. He hadn't seen anything yet you couldn't grow on the Brazos, he told himself again. Why not bananas?

Lucina's flower garden showed that. There, the snowdrops and narcissus which he had dug up for her in Georgia on his wedding day were now, in December, pressed against the white fence, thicker than they ever grew on Camp Mountain in April. It'd be about a month before they'd be in bloom, but there were roses now on the bushes — roses with petals slightly blackened along their edges by the norther now blowing. He was able to identify the dark, yellowish-green cedars, with lacy, sticky leaves, and the blue-green shiny cape jasmine bushes. But there, by the gate, those two gray-green, dusty-leaved plants full of long, floating fronds of delicate yellow — what were they? He'd have to ask Lucina. Her flower garden was coming along. Right now, he knew if he got down and walked around in it he would find the garden paths marked off by red bricks set slantwise in the ground and raked neatly in the same crisscross pattern that Beauford had insisted on at Cedar Ledge, and Andrew, before him, in Virginia.

His gaze rested longer and even more proudly on his vegetable garden — a responsibility he shared with Uncle Matt. The old fellow might be nearly blind, Cavin meditated, but he knew how to teach young negroes to raise vegetables. Cavin looked with critical appreciation at the straight brown furrows, and at the evenly laid off squares filled with fresh green turnip tops and with sweet winter lettuce that you had to cover up with crokersacks on frosty nights. He noticed, too, how yellow the lettuce leaves looked curling back against the dark earth, how the heavy reddish beet tops brought out the delicate, frothy green of the carrot rows and the feathery herb borders. A man would have to be blind not to enjoy looking at things grow, Cavin thought, with a comfortable sense of plenty suffusing his content.

Plenty for black and white, for this garden that Matt looked after would supply a lot of families. Things were always growing faster than they could be eaten up, and Uncle Matt was always sowing new seeds. If you could eat carrots at all, Cavin reflected, they had to be no bigger than your little finger, and beets about the size of a pullet egg. As for snap beans, who would touch 'em after they had strings on 'em? They'd have to throw away too much, if the negroes didn't help eat everything all up; throw away vegetables, the way they sometimes had to pour milk out to the pigs—buttermilk, clabber, even good sweet milk, because the negroes wouldn't drink it.

He felt suddenly sorry for all the city people who had to go into stores and buy food, or who lived in a climate where things wouldn't grow except for a few months a year. Why, right here on his own place, in December, was every kind of vegetable and fruit and flesh — gray spotted guineas nearly as good as prairie chicken, great blue turkeys, chickens too numerous to count, young calves, little sucking pigs, geese, and duck. Besides that, there was a smokehouse full of sweet smoked meat, and the Gulf and bayous were swarming with fish and crabs and shrimp for the taking.

He laughed, then. Aunt Emmy would be surprised to find at the bottom of his enormous hunting bag half a dozen huge, blue crabs in a tight can of sea water.

'La! la!' thought Cavin, 'Who could want a better life than this?' He had listened to Englishmen and Northerners talking in Colonel Rutherford's office, and had decided that London and New York must be worse places to live in than Galveston or Houston or San Antonio; and God knows, he always thought, they were bad enough.

He began to unstrap his hunting bag, telling Nathaniel to do the same. Then it was that the idea unexpectedly came to him about Henry's future.

The child was waiting on the gallery for him; and as quick as he stepped on it, Henry dashed up to him and began pulling excitedly on his canvas sleeve.

'Br'er Cavin!' he exclaimed excitedly, using the name all the children indiscriminately employed. 'Br'er Cavin, can I have him to keep?'

'Keep what?' returned Cavin, rubbing his stiff arms, and opening the nose of his brown bag. 'Look in here, you rascal,' he urged Henry. 'You want to go along next time?'

'Reckon Miss Lucy'd ruther you *would* take Henry,' Jake grinned. 'Seem lak she didn't keer much about Nath goin' dis time — or no time.' He sent a glance of superior understanding toward his master. 'Maria don't like it no better, wheneber I fixes to take Josh out shootin'.'

'A boy's *got* to learn to hunt *sometime*,' replied Cavin absently, and stooped to answer Henry's persistent questioning.

'What you talking so much about, boy?' he asked him, rumpling the child's almost white hair. 'You going to have duck for supper,' he assured him.

'My calf!' Henry repeated, careless of his evening fare. 'My spotted calf! Mr. Reeves said he was going to die and then he said I could have him, if I could make him get well. Is he really all mine?' he asked again, tense with suspense. 'He's walking around and eating.' His round, very light blue eyes besought Cavin to answer yes.

'Sure,' said Cavin, doubling up his hands and making a playful pass at the child. 'Come on, young 'un, put up your fists!'

'No-suh,' said Henry, retreating and stubbornly holding his ground. 'Tell me for *sure*, Br'er Cavin,' he implored. 'Is he mine? Can I brand him?' His round face, under his stubby light hair, was puckered and drawn into a kind of tight knot.

Cavin dropped his fists and threw his arm around the boy's shoulder. 'What you so worked up about? Didn't I tell you you could have him?' he assured Henry. 'Sure, you can have him. You can pick out a brand, too.'

Then at that precise moment, he saw a way to make the German orphan boy independent.

'Listen, Henry!' he exclaimed. 'I'll send get you some books somewhere.' He stopped then and looked closely at the child. 'There must be some somewhere — some books about taking care of sick animals.' A light dawned on him then. 'You know that doctor up at San Antonio — the one Mr. Chilton, who raises all the Herefords, was telling about, the one who's studying how cattle get tick fever? Well,' he proposed, 'supposin' I ask him how you can get to be a cow doctor, yourself?'

The boy's expression had relaxed and he was listening with close attention.

'You know,' said Cavin discriminatingly, 'you got a natural hand with cattle.' He kept his eyes on Henry's brightening face and felt his idea growing. 'Right now, if Mr. Allen'll help you,' he hazarded, 'I bet you could learn a lot more'n I got time to study out about sick colts and calves.'

Looking inquiringly at the boy, he announced the conclusion he had arrived at as he spoke. 'I tell you what, Henry, I'll put your brand on every critter you cure, and give you a calf, to boot, every time you save one.'

'I already know what to do when they get cut on barbed wire,' Henry returned, considering the offer, 'and if they get into the sorghum field or break off their hooves; and,' he went on carefully, watching Cavin as he spoke, 'I know now how to cure bots, and scours; and carbolic acid'll stop fly worms, and salt and ashes and sulphur'll help the colic — 'twon't always, though,' he asserted cautiously.

Cavin held out his brown, square hand, keeping his face as sober as Henry's. 'It's a bargain, sir,' he said.

He felt as if he had dropped a load off his mind, and slapped Henry on the back.

'Hurry up, pardner,' he said. 'I want you to get on your pony and carry some ducks over to Colonel Brashear and Doctor David. Mr. Blake, too,' he added. 'Miss Evelina is mighty fond o' roast duck.'

'Jake,' he demanded, 'what was it Mrs. Rideout was telling us, the last time she was up here about cooking duck? What was it, can you remember?'

Jake scratched his round head and screwed up his black, shiny eyes, painfully searching his memory.

'Seem like I heard Maria talkin' sump'n 'bout it. 'Twarn't orange peeling you cook 'em wid?' he inquired dubiously.

Cavin slapped his thigh enthusiastically. 'That's it! Go tell Aunt Emmy to try laying a slice o' pickled orange on each breast. Wait!' he said, holding out a restraining hand. 'Tell her to try fixing just one duck that way, this time. I better see how I like it. And while you're inside,' he added, 'stir us both up a toddy. Lawd!' he shivered, 'it's getting cold.'

Limping a little, he started toward the steps and, going up them, opened his front door.

'Lucy!' he called as he always did, before he was well inside, 'where are you?'

Aunt Elvy answered him, on her way to the kitchen. She was old and bent and shrivelled now, but she held on to life as tenaciously as a nut that refuses to slip out of its dry brown husk. She told everybody she was a hundred, but neither she nor anybody else remembered when she was born. Now she looked at Cavin with her lower lip pushed out — a sure sign of disapproval.

'She got Nathaniel settin' in a tub o' hot water, an' drinkin' lemonade, dat's whar she is,' the old woman told him crossly. 'How come you let dat chile get his feet wet?' she grumbled.

Cavin put back his long head and laughed.

'Wet feet!' he exclaimed. 'How's a hunter going to help wetting his feet?'

Aunt Elvy gave him a withering glance. 'Men ain't got no mo' sense'n a picked jay bird,' she declared. 'An' some of 'em,' she scolded, 'ain't got dat much.'

Chapter 29

IT WAS several years after her thirtieth birthday before Lucina became aware of how quickly each new year was returning. In her first youth, the rhythm in her own veins seemed always to be moving faster than the envelope of time which enclosed her, and, like most people, she was surprised when this sensation vanished. She could never put her finger on the exact day when she was first aware that the seasons were coming and going in amazingly rapid rotation; but all at once she realized that winter had hardly set in before it was summer and then, like magic, it was drizzling January and thick sea fog was floating again across the prairie.

One morning she would look out on bare, brown fields overcast by the subdued light of the lowering sun, and the winter quiet that hung over the fallow land would beat upon her senses like slow, solemn music. It was a time she loved, when blue smoke floated out of every chimney, when all the stirring life of spring and summer lay quiescent and sleeping. For the short Brazos winter suggested neither suffering nor death, but merely a brief solstice when all nature seemed to draw its breath, tranquilly resting. Lucina would sit, then, for hours in her deep wicker chair by her fireplace, reading, feeling in herself the same slowing and slackening of effort that seemed to characterize the outside world.

She read anything she could lay her hands on, those short winter days, not once, but twice, and three times over. After their late supper, when the fire danced against the window-panes, projecting a whole new world outside the glass, she would read aloud while the younger children watched Cavin sketching out in the ashes on the hearth the rough terrain of Chickamauga or the Wilderness.

'There,' he would say, laying his strong, brown finger on a heaped-up ashy slope, 'right there, by that little house, was where we took our stand.' And the black-and-white shepherd that always lay at his feet would catch the harsh note in his master's voice and begin to growl deep in his shaggy throat.

Sometimes Cavin would call Jake in, on a chilly night to lay on more wood, or to stir up a hoecake to bake in front of the fire, the way they did in the army. Or he would take eggs, and, wetting newspapers in the kettle steaming on the hearth, would wrap them in many limp folds of paper and bury them under the ashes, bringing them out at precisely the proper moment.

While they waited for them to bake, Lucina would read aloud the sorrowful tale of Little Nell; and of how poor David went out into the world and lost his Dora; how another David slew Goliath and how Joshua commanded the sun to stand still in the sky; how King Richard defied Saladin; and how once there was a pilgrim sunk deep in the Slough of Despond, and how, after many long trials, he at last caught sight of the Golden City behind walls of amethyst and pearl.

So the six or eight weeks of the mild winter would pass, and Lucina was always startled, as late February came on, to see the fields again full of mules, fat and stubborn from their winter's rest. Trudging along behind the ponderous teams, the negro men who guided the plows seemed almost to have sprung out of the moist, dark earth, so perfectly did their pace suit that of the slow-moving river and the gently swaying moss. All around them the air was honey-sweet; and every sunny slope was covered with blue bonnets and rich red wine-cups, and, after a shower, with delicate white rain lilies, gone almost as soon as they appeared.

Sometimes in the spring Lucina would put on Susanna's velvet habit and her little velvet hat, with its drooping plume, and accompany Cavin around the plantations. One day, to her astonishment, she saw a pile of seashells in a cotton field — shells turned up on the Brazos by deep spring plowing. Standing there dryshod on the solid earth that morning, suddenly she felt herself surrounded by unimaginable waters roaring out of the cavernous past. Never again did she see mules lifting their feet out of the soft, wet soil but that she remembered by what precarious tenure man and beast alike occupy this drifting, shifting earth.

Then, every year when the plowing was over, she would watch the negroes dropping gray, furry cotton seed into the pliant ground. Something in the scene, something in the warmer, ruddier light of April always reminded her, then, of the long sequence of aeons in which men had planted seed in rich soil, receiving it back, in due time, a hundred fold increased. And, as she watched the unhurried figures moving along the furrows, there would fall over her spirit the same deep calm that possessed her on clear winter evenings, when she caught a glimpse of black branches moving across a pale, opaline sky. Planting and growth, she told herself, sun and shadow, wind and rain, cold and warmth, had endured and would endure, regardless of any individual's brief pitiful life; and past, present, and future would always merge in a ritual of seed-time and harvest shared by all mankind. She wondered if men who lived in cities, cut off from the earth and its seasons, must not become,

like fishes in dark caves, blind and directionless, swimming forever in circles toward some dimly remembered light.

Before she could believe it, there would be no more plows
in the rich, sloping fields, but, instead, long lines of choppers
lifting and dropping their strong arms in common rhythm.
Every day she would see them stretched out, lax and indolent,
under the shade at noon, or coming home, at dusk, like Queen
Dido, 'with slow, reluctant step.' Marching across the fields,
with their hoes slung across their drooping shoulders, they
seemed to her to be invested with that primeval dignity which
belongs to every perfect matching of human effort to human
need.

Then it would be early summer, with the cotton plants knee
high, and the negroes shaking Paris green over the great drooping leaves, lest the worms should destroy the crop. Overnight,
sometimes, the fields would burst into bloom; and then, soon,
the delicate blooms would turn a rich, dark pink, and the many-
angled green bolls would begin to form — bolls that in August
would turn brown and fall open, exposing their rich white
wealth.

'Is it cotton-picking time again?' Lucina would ask herself,
then, startled to see that the year had rolled around so fast.

The negroes would pick from sunup to sundown, dragging
their heavy white canvas sacks behind them; or, sometimes,
if the season was very warm, Cavin would let them work on
bright, moonlight nights and sleep through the hot days.
During the season, Lucina always responded to the excitement
that animated the pickers, as, tensely competing for first place,
they raced to get in the crop before rain or storm should defeat
their work. Cavin, too, seemed extraordinarily stimulated
whenever he came in from the plantations, where wagons
heavily loaded with white fluff were backing up, every little

while, to cotton houses already full to overflowing. She did not misinterpret his reaction as greed or cupidity. Long ago she had learned that he took a deep, almost sensuous, pleasure in mastering the earth or any circumstance, irrespective of his gain, and that a successful end did not so much create as intensify his satisfaction in his efforts. Cotton-picking, she could see, was a source of some deep inner gratification to Cavin, a kind of catharsis which he never named even to himself.

Then the noisy gin would begin to turn, and at all hours of the day she would hear its shrill whistle, as the overseer called for more wagons to come up with more cotton to be pressed into bales. The younger children liked to go down to the gin house with Cavin and slide into the soft mountainous masses of white, pretending that they, who had never seen snow, were sliding on icy slopes. Lucina let them go, holding her breath until their safe return, lest they should somehow be suffocated under the fluffy cotton. When, however, she confessed this fear to Cavin, he only laughed.

'You must think they don't have any sense,' he chided her.

So she yielded and they went along, learning to time their slides with accurate precision between every fresh deposit from the grinding gin.

After the cotton was all in, it would be time again for the colored people's revival and for gathering walnuts and pecans, if the frost had burst open their green coverings, and time for making sugar-cane syrup in the huge, iron kettles William and Philip had long ago ordered from New Orleans and hauled over the muddy prairie to the Brazos. Time for hunting up stray cattle and marketing spring calves. Time for picking persimmons and wild grapes, and, then, for making the Christmas cakes and the eggnog, and for sending into town after the fireworks.

Before Lucina knew it, the year would be gone. The older children would be off to school again, and the younger ones at their lessons in the garret, where boxes containing old letters and uniforms and strange money invited them to learn American history out of sources that scholars prize. And then, once more, it would be still, peaceful January, with the cold gray fog again floating inland from the Gulf.

Thus, year after year passed in the same sequential rhythm, and even the younger children were growing up. Why, William, her baby, was nearly ten years old, Lucina told herself in dismay, on the day they celebrated Felicia's and Letitia's twenty-first birthday. And she herself was nearly thirty-five.

She had more physical strength now than she had ever had in her life. It was as if nature were trying to recompense her for the illnesses she had endured during her first years in Texas. Sometimes, if she got tired of swallowing bitter quinine she would have a brief attack of malaria, but not very often, for they were having less and less of that disease, even in the deep bottom.

She did not suspect, however, that there was any connection between that fact and Cavin's hatred of mosquitoes, against which he waged a war every spring, spreading gallons of kerosene over the slough and over the still backwaters of the creek, and sending Jake or Horace out to empty every waste can or bottle. But, whatever the reason, she felt burgeoning within her a certain tough, resistant physical strength that she had never enjoyed in her first youth. It was as if a small and tender shoot had developed into a sapling, after much buffeting by strong winds. At times, she was vividly aware that a different quality of life now rose and fell in her veins. No longer did her blood course through her like a freshet, but, instead, it seemed to move with a steady, even flow like that of a deep river, well grounded inside its high banks.

Whenever she looked at Felicia and Letitia, she wondered if she had once possessed their resiliency and their confident optimism. What she had in place of those qualities was a certain increased capacity for endurance, a willingness to admit that the world was scarcely designed for her own pleasure, and a warmer pity for most people than she had been able to summon in her first youth. She could see that Felicia and Letitia unconsciously placed her in some remote sphere of age, far removed from the exuberance of their own vaunting emotions. Well, she thought, smiling a little, perhaps they were right, and she was not sure she regretted the fact.

They had been out of school two years when the birthday which marked their full maturity came around — two years spent entertaining beaux and visiting friends and practising on the piano and embroidering fine linen, and learning to make themselves dresses to supplement the outfits Cavin was beginning, now that they were young ladies, to let them order from Baltimore or Louisville. They had their own visiting cards, too, now — oblong, narrow cards with scalloped edges and their names written in shaded ink upon them. For some time they had been trying to make up their minds when, not whether, they wanted to get married; and now, with the coming of their twenty-first birthday, they had begun to think more seriously about the matter.

That summer both FitzHugh and Beauford were home from school — FitzHugh from Charlottesville, where, for a year now, he had been living with Justin Hartwell's family studying medicine, and Beau from Georgia, where Cavin had finally consented to his remaining about half of each year. The two boys were strangely alike even for near relatives, alike not in coloring or feature, but in their carriage and manner and points of view. FitzHugh's eyes were steady and gray, where Beau's were

deeply blue and bright, and the hair on FitzHugh's head was
Letitia's, not Lucina's; but in their gaze was the same quality
of luminous concentration which had marked both Beauford's
and Philip's expression, a certain inner certitude to which the
young must usually grope their painful way. All summer
FitzHugh followed David around with a centered interest that
indicated he had chosen his profession well; and all summer
Beauford continued to read the books he had been studying
in Georgia, and to discuss with Judge Dickerson, whenever he
saw him, a lawyer's calling.

In a year or two, Mr. Curtis wrote, he would be ready for
college. Would they send him on to William and Mary, to
General Lee's college at Lexington, or, as he thought probable,
to Charlottesville, where FitzHugh was? In Georgia, of course,
he could go to Athens or Mercer. Cavin thought there was no
use considering any of these places: the boy had better stay
home and study at Independence. There was talk of making
that a great school, combining it with Waco University and
renaming it Baylor. The decision, however, was some time off,
and this fall, anyway, Beau was going back to Georgia.

Both he and FitzHugh looked at Felicia and Letitia with a
certain new respect, now that they were of age and legal owners
of their own land. The fact seemed to invest them with a
certain new dignity that the boys envied.

'Your land's all clear,' Cavin told them, and on the instant
set himself a new goal.

'I'm going to try to turn over every single piece of land free
of debt to every single one of you children — entirely free of
debt,' he told them all, gathering them together. 'You'll have
to help me.'

This was a larger task than he had ever set for himself when
he was busy trying to rid the county of the Freedman's Bureau,
but its difficulty seemed to whet his interest.

'I believe I can do it,' he said to Lucina, thoughtfully narrowing his eyes. 'There's twelve years between the girls and William. Yes,' he said, looking meditatively off down the avenue with his hands thrust deep in his pockets and his lower jaw pushed out, 'that's exactly what I'm going to try to do.'

Then his eye fell on James and it occurred to him that the boy would have nothing, and Tazewell and Cecilia little more, if somebody did not keep on working their land to full capacity.

That, he knew now, Frank Barclay would never return to do; for, the preceding winter, he had lost his life in a shooting scrape in New Orleans, leaving his children orphans. Nobody was surprised at what happened, but the occurrence cast a gloom over the whole county, for, as was repeatedly admitted, nobody could help liking the man. That he was his own worst enemy, everybody agreed, pitying the children, who, by this time, had almost forgotten they had ever had any other home than Locust Hill.

As for James, he had always lived there, ever since the day Cavin had picked him up, set him on his shoulder, and brought him home. Looking at the tall, dark lad now, a possibility for his future occurred to Cavin.

'James,' he declared, 'you're old enough now to begin taking care of the place on Little Creek. That way, if you're a good manager, you might could make enough money to study drawing in New Orleans.'

'Oh!' said James. 'Yes, sir!'

'Well — that's all,' said Cavin, rising. 'You be thinking about it.'

That day — the day Letitia's oldest twins were twenty-one — Cavin began his self-appointed undertaking — an undertaking that was to consume all his strength and energy during the next ten years, as cotton continued steadily to fall.

Fortunately, he did not have to worry about public affairs, for at the onset of his task, Oran Roberts was still governor, and certainly a Confederate officer who had been Chief Justice of Texas and President of the Secession Convention could be trusted to understand that, if the Populists succeeded in splitting the Democratic vote, there was grave danger of the Republicans and the negroes again getting control of the state. And the governors who succeeded him — Ireland and Ross — were also Confederate soldiers who did not have to be persuaded to avoid that eventuality.

Cavin's own uncompromising attitude toward the Populist uprisings was based far more on the necessity for preserving the delicate balance of white supremacy than on a disposition to deny the justice of some of the claims put forward by the dissenters. Instinctively he distrusted the extravagant temper of their expectations, but he was ready to concede that many of the arguments the small farmers pressed were valid. They did need better schools in Texas and better railroad rates — nobody knew that better than he did — and the occupation taxes were certainly excessive. But all these and other benefits would be dust and ashes with Radicals and negroes again in power. Besides, the only thing, apparently, they could think of doing was to saddle unborn children with debt, the way they had set out to do during Reconstruction.

One day when the Democratic Committee was assembled at Austin, under the blue shadows of Mount Bonnell, he asked Governor Roberts what seemed to him the best policy to adopt, in view of the increasing demands of the dissatisfied in the state.

'Pay-as-we-go,' replied the Governor immediately, brushing a meditative hand across his white moustache and beard and turning his deep-set eyes on Cavin. 'That's the only honest policy, any time. This state,' he asserted, 'has been assuming extraneous obligations beyond the capacity of the productive wealth of the country to sustain.' Cavin went home satisfied.

Maybe though, he kept thinking, there's some way of getting schools and improvements without raising taxes sky-high as the Davis régime had done. There was always some way to twist and turn, if a man could just think of it.

Thus began his second long period of preoccupation with a definite goal that he had set himself. Always, during these years, there was a child just coming of age and payments required to clear a particular tract of land. Every penny counted, for even if a planter had all the credit he needed, and much land and labor, yet only gold and silver would serve to lift a mortgage. He began, for the first time in his life, to keep a watchful, jealous eye on his deposits at Galveston.

Lucina, however, laughed at him whenever he complained that the bills coming in from town were getting too heavy, much too heavy. She knew what his resources were, as well as he did. For she helped him keep the books ranged on top his big black safe — a long, gray ledger for each child. She knew exactly how many bales of cotton there were on Colonel Rutherford's wharves, how many beeves in the pasture, how well Jeremiah's trading was panning out.

'You can't dress boys and girls on nothing,' she would remind him cheerfully. 'Besides, I need some clothes myself.'

And she would go into town or write letters to a dressmaker in Louisville, sending measurements, and, before long, she would be wearing a cape or a frock as becoming as any the girls had.

She was combing her hair differently now, in a way the girls had gotten her to adopt after they began to frizz their own bangs over their eyes. Now, instead of parting her black hair and drawing it back, she wore it raised in a soft roll immediately over the centre of her forehead, and then drew it smoothly upward into a high knot held by a comb on the crown of her head. The change in her hair dress altered her appearance a good deal and was, on the whole, becoming to her, although Cavin never thought so. Looking at her, he sometimes had the uneasy feeling that he had acquired a new wife.

Then she began persuading him to go into Galveston and be fitted to a fine suit, and at last he consented, more to please her than himself. After he had it on, he would not even look in the mirror, but it gave Lucina great pleasure to see him so well turned out. He was now getting on toward forty, with a stouter, stockier figure than Philip had ever had, with brighter eyes than his father's and a ruddier skin, but with a strong, long jaw and a fierce nose, much like Philip's and FitzHugh's. Lucina thought him a handsome man as he stood in his vigorous maturity, beside his younger, slimmer brother.

'Nobody on earth would suspect,' she thought, looking hard at him, 'that his hip is broken and that there's a bullet in his side.'

That fall he bought a great quantity of barbed wire and enclosed the prairie land he had not yet fenced in, hiring a surveyor to help him get his lines exactly straight. They were talking about fence cutters working all over the state now, but the contingency did not deter him. If they cut his fences, he supposed he and all the other men in the county would know how to stop it. But most of all that trouble was out in West Texas, a place that seemed to him nearly as strange and remote as Kansas. He was almost as pleased as William and Nathaniel when he discovered how well the new wires would serve to convey tapped-out signals along their shiny length.

That same year, too, he bought three tall steel windmills, one for his well in the back yard at home, and two more for new ones he intended to dig on the prairie, in case his dams should happen to dry up in the summer sun. The first time he watched John McGaughey's mill pumping away on an almost still day, he took out his little notebook and jotted down the name and address that was printed in big, black letters on the windmill's fan; and that very night he sat down and wrote a letter ordering three mills exactly like the one he had seen on Lost Island Ranch pumping up clear, gushing water out of the dry earth.

When he had one up in his own back yard, he raised over the milk house a high tank and ran cold, dripping pipes down from it into the long troughs where the milk was set. Then, finding that venture good, he piped water to his back door.

'Jake'll be getting too lazy to live, I reckon,' he said to Maria, who came over from her cabin to marvel at the ease with which Jake now filled all the pitchers and buckets in the house.

Large expenditures like these, where he could see his money's worth, did not distress Cavin the way the little frippering expenses did.

'Ribbons!' he would read on his bill. 'Ribbons! Umph! What are they for, Lucina? And all these little items?' He would run an accusing finger down a long page. 'One dollar. Three dollars. Five dollars. It all counts up.'

'You like the way the house is looking, don't you?' she would reply, undisturbed. 'And you're proud of your sisters, aren't you?'

From time to time now, Shelby was making payments on Cavin's mother's land and was also sending Lucina something to represent both hers and Margaret's interests on Cedar Ledge. She used her own share of these funds, and more of Cavin's money, to buy new books, new curtains or carpets, and to have the kind of paint and paper she wanted put on her walls.

Gradually the house on Locust Hill began to take on a look of increasing comfort. Now, on wintry nights, she drew heavy, dark red curtains in front of her bedroom windows and watched the firelight falling on a carpeted floor.

The girls, too, had rooms as large and comfortable as her own with beds covered in ruffles, and easy slipper chairs, and silver toilet articles ranged beneath their swinging mirrors, but not the boys. Cavin made them all sleep in two large connecting rooms bare of curtains or carpets, but warmed by big fireplaces and full of books and rocking chairs, and collections ranging from skins to spiders. The older boys occupied one room, the younger the other, and Cavin would not let Lucina fix the dormitories up as she would have liked to do.

'Doodads!' he said scornfully. 'Give 'em to the girls!'

He was impatient if the boys did not get up early, in turn, to see that the negroes did the milking, or to gallop down and help Mr. Reeves get the teams started. Once he even put Beau in the cotton field, over Lucina's anguished protest that he would get brain fever.

'He'd better, if he hasn't got any sense,' Cavin replied, not yielding a jot. Then he went out to look up his son.

'Now, listen,' he told Beau severely, 'I agreed you could draw on me for fifty dollars, not seventy-five. You get right out there and start to picking cotton until you've picked enough to make up the difference. You'll never amount to a row of pins, if you don't learn how hard it is to earn a dollar.'

To Lucina's astonishment, Beau accepted the fact as true and cheerfully picked his cotton. Men and boys! Who could understand them? Lucina asked herself, not for the first time.

All Cavin's energy, however, was not expended on his own affairs; for, even if he was opposed to a general increase in taxation, he was not opposed to citizens pooling their resources in order to get what they wanted.

'It's cheaper to build schoolhouses ourselves than to pay out taxes and have half of 'em sticking to the tax agents' fingers,' he argued, having rather complete acquaintance with the questionable capacity of most men, including himself, to withstand temptation. So, with the white tenants furnishing the labor, the other planters the lumber, and Cavin the land for the building to stand upon, there was soon a new schoolhouse on the creek's bank, and a teacher paid out of a collection that the taxpayers took up among themselves. Then, since it was winter and most of the negroes were idle, anyway, Cavin turned out his mules and scrapers and laid down a good firm roadway to the school which he knew his own children would never attend.

Before Lucina could catch her breath, it was 1884, and Ireland was governor, and Letitia's and Felicia's wedding day was at hand, and FitzHugh was back from Virginia, a full-fledged doctor ready to celebrate his majority.

Whenever she thought of the girls' marrying, Lucina felt suddenly dizzy, as if the heavens were swinging around her. What had become of the time, anyway, since she had first seen the little five-year-old girls? And here it had been three years since they came of age and they were turning twenty-four — a nice age, she thought, to be married, but one some people regarded as perilously near the line where a girl began to be an old maid.

Both she and Cavin, however, had always urged the girls not to be in a hurry to marry, that youth was short enough, anyway. And the twins were always retorting that their elders hadn't followed that advice. Still, it must have made some impression on them, for they had danced and sung and kept a number of young men anxious until all of a sudden, the preceding winter, they had both made their choices — choices that pleased everybody. For Felicia was going to marry Lacey, the younger brother of Goodwin Breckinridge, and live in Berryville, and Letitia, Cox Gordon's cousin, Gordon Middleton, who had recently come out to the Brazos from South Carolina for a visit and would now probably remain there.

One Sunday morning in January the twins came down to breakfast dressed for church. They entered the dining-room diffidently, with their arms around one another, wearing their new winter dresses — dresses made with full pleated skirts and tight basques and with collars topped by narrow blue ruching which brushed their chins. Felicia's dark head was almost exactly on a level with Letitia's light curls, but she lifted it with a more provocative air than was apparent in her sister's more retiring carriage. There was a forthrightness, too, in her smile, and a challenge in her glance that did not appear in Letitia's gentler, more meditative gaze. Felicia, it was plain to see, had a good share of her oldest brother's practical energy, and, in any undertaking with her twin, would be apt to take the lead.

This morning, though, they both smiled a little uncertainly at Cavin, not knowing whether he had yet seen the two young gentlemen whom, the night before, they had promised to marry.

'Br'er Cavin,' Felicia began, and stopped, not knowing how to go on.

'Save your tongues, ladies, save your tongues,' he urged them, brandishing a sharp, gleaming knife above the ham. 'I've been hearing about your charms since crack o' day.'

The girls opened their eyelids wide.

'Yes, sir,' he grumbled. 'They got me out o' bed, your beaux did, on Sunday morning too, to see if I had any objections.' He scowled in mock anger at the girls, and then threw an arm around each of them. 'Listen,' he said laughing; 'I told 'em to

go on home and let you think it over; that you might change
your minds. 'Twouldn't be the first time you have,' he observed sagely. Then, stilling their protest, he added, 'They'll
be back soon enough to see how you feel.'

And here it was summer again, Lucina thought, and Beau
was getting ready to go off to Virginia, not Georgia; and the
girls' wedding dresses were lying spread out upstairs on long
white sheets; and FitzHugh was a grown man, ready now to
take over his own land and practise medicine with David.
Where did the years go?

On Beau's eighteenth birthday it had been settled, almost
without discussion, that he was to go up to Charlottesville and
study, first classics, and then law. For, after all, was not Justin
Hartwell's own daughter living there? Justin, own brother to
both Susanna and Cavin's mother, Mary. Why, yes, that was
the natural place for the boy to go, both David and Lucina
thought, and old Mr. Curtis agreed. David and FitzHugh, now
home for good, spent a good deal of time coaching Beau about
what to expect at Charlottesville, where boys were supposed to
be men, no longer requiring oversight or even much direction.
David often recalled, as he talked to Beau, how little hope he
had had that the scrap of a baby who had grown to be this tall
young man would ever live to breathe, much less to go up to
Virginia and study as he, David, had done — was it possible?
— nearly a quarter of a century ago. He smiled a trifle dourly.
Pretty soon the boy'd be back, a full-grown man, making him,
David, feel like an antediluvian. 'Sabra,' said David meditatively, 'I wouldn't have given a nickel for his chance.'

All this conversation about going off to Virginia bored
Nathaniel, who, at sixteen, had made up his mind what he
wanted to do — and it was not to follow in the footsteps of his

brother, whom he admired, however, with the generous, half-envious affection so often bestowed by younger children upon the ones next above them. Nathaniel was a wiry, slender boy, with small, active feet and hands, who, already it was apparent, was never going to be very tall. But he had fine, square shoulders and a well-turned head covered with yellow hair exactly the color Cavin's had been in his youth. His round hazel eyes looked at you frankly, and his chin was a little heavier than you would expect, if you had glanced, first, at the upper part of his face. Even at sixteen, his character was laid down: here was a sensible boy who knew exactly what he wanted to do. And he did not want to go way off to Virginia or to Georgia, either; for already he watched over the cotton-planting as carefully as Cavin, and rose, before sunup, to see the pickers starting off down the long rows.

Whatever was the matter with Beau, he thought impatiently, wanting to study law and go way off to the mountains? He, Nathaniel, had no such idea; he was going up to that new school at Waco that they were beginning to call Baylor. Then he could get home often to see how the crop was coming along.

As the time approached for his leaving Beau wondered a little, himself, if he really wanted to go so far away. But his hesitation did not last, for, long before he ever laid eyes on the Rotunda, he had learned enough from FitzHugh and David to make him feel that he could walk around it, stooping low in the dark, and make his way across the lawn, between the ranges of columns, with never a single misstep. Then, as the day neared for him to leave, Cavin's own recollections began suddenly coming to life.

'Good thing you're used to mountains, Beau,' his father observed as he stretched his length out in a hammock. 'There's a mighty lot of 'em where you're going. Why, I was at Charlottesville once,' Cavin suddenly remembered, sitting upright again in his excitement. 'Lawd! When had I thought of it? That was — let me see — musta been in June, 1862, right after Seven Pines. We were in camp at a pretty little town in the valley — what was it?' Searching his dormant memory he brought out the name. 'Staunton, it was. There was a girls' school there, Lucina,' he recalled, his eyes twinkling, 'with two enormous iron dogs on each side of the door. I remember 'em yet, with their red tongues hanging out, and all the pretty girls standing on the gallery back of them waving to us as we marched into town. You ought-a go over there, son,' he advised Beauford. 'It's all up-and-down, though, I warn you, that place. The ladies brought us cakes,' he went on dreamily, 'and there was an old brick church, with a graveyard around it.'

'Then — whoopee!' he exclaimed, snapping his firm fingers. 'Like that, it was all over! We were ordered to march double quick across the mountain to Charlottesville. We didn't have much time to look around there, I can tell you, for they loaded us on flatcars to Hanover. After that,' he said, his voice dropping, 'there was Cold Harbor, and Malvern Hill, and then Manassas again.' Pronouncing the names, he looked at Beau with renewed interest. 'Manassas is close to Charlottesville. You'd better go look that place up, too, Beau.' He began to laugh, chuckle after chuckle.

'Did I ever tell you about an old gray mare scaring us all mighty nigh to death, there?'

'The one that came stumbling down the hill, all loaded with water cans, the night before the battle and made you all think the Yankees were right on you?' Beau asked with a quick smile of recollection. 'The one you used to always be singing about?' He began to hum in a slow singsong, 'The old gray mare, she came a-tearing out o' the wilderness, out o' the wilderness ——'

Laughing, he broke off. 'I can say it in my sleep.' Facing his
father again with renewed interest, he inquired, 'That was
where the Texas troops captured an ambulance too, wasn't it,
and when somebody — who was it? — ordered them to turn it
over to the South Carolinians, Hood said they'd have to court-
martial him, first.' Beauford laughed. 'Looks to me like I
ought to feel right at home in Virginia.'

'Of course,' said Lucina. 'Why not? You remember that
picture of your great-great-great grandfather Andrew, hanging
over Uncle Shelby's fireplace? Well, you only have to go down
to Williamsburg to see where he lived, before his son Nathaniel
— the one your own brother's named for — came down into
Georgia. Why!' she exclaimed in sudden recollection, 'the
Travis family home is there, and the Wythe place, too, where
all the Texas Wythes came from, and Povey's home too —
you've heard all about him many times,' she broke off.

'There's Chatham, too, and Danville,' said Cavin reminis-
cently. 'Maybe you'd never been here, Beau, if I hadn't found
friends in those places.' He laughed. 'Looks to me like you'll
be spending most of your time running around Virginia.
Listen!' he warned Beau. 'If you meet any boys named — let's
see.' His mind groped back through the murky, receding past.
'Let's see — Prentice, that's it, and Porter —— ' Frowning, he
turned to Jake. 'Wasn't his name Porter? Yes, that's right.
Porter. Well,' he reminded Beau, 'if you meet any boys named
Prentice or Porter, you be nice to 'em.'

No sooner was Beau settled in his little cell-like quarters off
the range of corridors adjoining the lawn than he knew that
this was exactly where, all his life, he had dreamed of being.
It was as if old Andrew's spirit coursed eagerly through him,
glad to be home again. Never once did Beauford feel himself a
stranger in Virginia. From the very first, he loved the crispness

of the air floating off the Blue Ridge, and the beautiful serene houses set back down their long avenues, the trails leading up the mountain to Mr. Jefferson's old house, the long walk through the falling leaves out past Patrick Henry's birthplace to Shadow Lawn, where the loveliest boxwood in the world, he thought, must be growing. He enjoyed his classes, the library, where he could always find something to read, the curving serpentine wall with the hollyhocks blooming against it, and his friends gathered there from every state in the South. What he had loved in Georgia and Texas, he realized, with more perspicacity than the young usually possess, was what lingered of Virginia in both places. Now, here at Charlottesville, was the very same air he had breathed, somewhat diluted, all his life; and only a mile out in the country, behind a clipped hedge, his own blood kin. Why, a Brazos Texan could move to Virginia and never know he had moved!

That, at least, was his first judgment; but soon he began to suspect that it was premature. In Georgia and in Texas, but especially in Texas, the transplanted Virginia life had assumed a character all its own — a saltier, more vigorous strain had somehow come into it, a strain, he thought once, more akin to the early Virginia he was studying about than to the present, older state. Every summer, when he returned home, this impression deepened in him.

During the years he was away, he always came back to Texas talking as naturally about the Blue Ridge as the Brazos; referring to Thomas Jefferson as easily as to Mirabeau Lamar, but this bilingual capacity never failed to irritate his brother, Nathaniel. He would listen with impatience to Beauford's accounts of his life at Charlottesville, and could never be persuaded that there was any virtue in going that far away from home.

Beau's last year in Virginia was Nathaniel's second at Waco, and that summer the brothers began putting on their starched white suits and going calling together, with William always pleading in vain to be allowed to accompany them, as Josh always did.

For Josh — a tall, slim colored boy with Jake's shining black skin — had now taken to looking after Beauford and Nathaniel as expertly as his father did after Cavin; and Beau's old clothes fitted him quite as well as Cavin's did Jake. Sometimes the three boys would go off for a week's fishing or hunting together; and whenever the white boys got off the train, Josh was certain to be there, waiting to pick up their bags and, as quick as they got home, to press their clothes and polish their spurs and their high-pommelled Mexican saddles, so unlike those Beau had to learn to ride in Virginia. Thus, imperceptibly to them all, Josh's relationship to Beau and Nathaniel shifted from that of playfellow to body servant, but neither he nor they were aware of a change. Nearly always Josh had a black girl he wanted to see on the same plantation where his young masters were bound, and Maria and Lucina used to watch them all start off with nearly equal pride.

The last year Beau was at Charlottesville, he wanted to take Josh back with him, but cotton was low that fall and Cavin frowned on the idea.

'By George!' he demanded. 'Do I have to send Josh off to college too? You boys are about to put me in the poorhouse,' he warned his sons, whom he required to hand in a strictly balanced account of their expenditures. But he glanced approvingly at them as he spoke. They seemed to be profiting all right from the money he was spending on them, and they showed some sense about how and when they drew on him.

Of the two boys, Nathaniel was less careful of his money than

Beauford, a fact which surprised Cavin.   Although Beauford
was watchful of creases, yet he was well satisfied to wear the
same clothes a long time; and he dressed with great restraint,
preferring outfits an older man might well have chosen.
Nathaniel, however, had a flair for braided coats, with patch
pockets to hold his big, gold watch; and he had a supply of
broad, soft neckties, which he knotted in large loose bows
just above his waistcoat. 'You look like a girl in those ties,'
Cavin grumbled, unimpressed. Nathaniel also liked to carry
a cane and to encase his feet in the latest style.   Still, his
father observed, when he came back to the plantation, he shed
these city styles as a duck does water, and speedily got into his
high boots and took hold, keeping the grass out of the crop.

No, Cavin did not regret the money he was spending on his
sons' education. He hoped to goodness, though, that, if they
ever felt like taking a drink too much, they'd get over that
foolishness at college, where their mother would never hear
about it. And so he always counselled them whenever they
started off.

'Aw, shucks!' they always answered.

'Shucks, nothing!' said their father. 'Your mother won't put
up with any foolishness along that line.'

Then he would look at them sternly. 'And don't you let me
hear of your losing much money on poker. You ought to know,
by now, when you've got a good hand.'

'Well, considering our teacher, we ought,' said Beau, and
smiled widely. 'I've found it right handy knowledge, at the
University.'

'Umph!' Cavin replied, and gave him a sharp glance. 'You
know what you've got to spend for foolishness.'

The years Beau was in Virginia were the years railroads were expanding all over Texas. And the people who were demanding them, Cavin often reflected, seemed not to mind what they cost. After the Conservatives came into power and stopped throwing away the public lands, there were still people willing to buy watered bonds and put up with extortionate railroad rates and poor service, all just to have a screeching whistle wake them up at night.

The whole business made Cavin sick and tired. He thought that John, in his speech at the Literary Society, had forecast all that was now happening. Just to know where all the rail money was coming from was enough to make anybody suspicious; and after the competing roads formed a merger called the Texas Traffic Association, he was glad he had plenty of wagons and mules of his own, and corn to feed the animals on.

For since the roads no longer had to meet competition in the state, they had set local freight rates out of all reason, and actually hauled cotton goods from Georgia mills at lower rates than they would carry cloth from one locality to another inside the state. Why, Cavin reflected, it was absurd. On account of the railroad rates, the town of Weatherford had found it cheaper to buy iron pipe in Tennessee than in Rusk, Texas. And, despite their excessive rates, the railroads were all the time cutting down the wages of their brakemen. Who could blame the trainmen for banding together into the Knights of Labor and refusing to work? Hadn't John predicted all this, Cavin thought, rubbing his chin? It was all happening, right under your eyes. Why, Governor Ireland had had to send Rangers up to Fort Worth to keep the strikers from burning up the place.

All this strengthened Cavin's decision never to let a railroad cross his land, and he made no secret of his open hostility to them. Apparently they knew how to bribe their way where they couldn't force it. Weren't they distributing passes to every tax collector, sheriff, and judge in the state? It had gotten so he felt like a poor white paying his way into Galveston from Berryville. He knew well enough he wasn't going to have a yard of track on his land.

One hot July afternoon, he was reiterating this resolve to himself, when he looked down the drive and there, rising and falling in their saddles, with a hippity-hop motion, he saw two strangers approaching. Strangers he knew they were from the way they rode, and he remembered that Beau had told him the Virginians trotted their horses, like that, and bounced in their saddles.

'Fool way to ride,' said Cavin under his breath. 'Jake, you might as well go mix up a drink. They'll be swearing at the heat.'

No Texan would have little enough sense, Cavin thought, to be out in the sun this time of day, when everybody was inside taking a nap. He continued placidly to fan himself with a big yellow palmetto, as he tried to guess who his visitors were.

As soon as he saw them draw up at the gate, and lift their hard, black hats to mop their streaming faces, he knew. Englishmen, and just off the boats, at that. Englishmen who had been in Galveston for even a few weeks always laid aside hats like these in favor of a kind they said were worn in India. Right comfortable, too, they were, those lined, ventilated, shovel-like hats, draped with silk. He had one in the hall closet now that he had picked up in Galveston intending to give it a trial, but he'd never quite gotten up the courage.

Laying down his fan, he advanced down the steps just as Jake appeared at the door with a tray.

'Good evening, gentlemen,' he said, resting his arms on the gate's white crosspiece, and waiting for the riders to explain their business. He hoped they'd hurry. It was hot standing out here in the sun.

The men raised their hats again and consulted a memorandum. They were both slight, hardly more than medium height, with light eyelashes and eyebrows, rosy cheeks, and eyes as brightly blue as Cavin's. He had no idea, except for his wider shoulders and greater height, how much he resembled them in appearance, though not in voice or manner. One was slightly less than middle-aged and evidently as hot as Cavin had expected him to be, but the other was much younger; maybe his son, thought Cavin.

'We are looking for Locust Hill Plantation,' the elder said, in a voice that sounded oddly muffled, if not half swallowed, under his closely clipped, blond moustache.

'This is the place, sir,' said Cavin, briefly and non-committally. He wished again they would get on with what they had to say.

'Colonel Rutherford sent us,' the same speaker explained, and again held a card up to his near-sighted eyes. 'We should like ——'

'Come in,' said Cavin heartily, swinging open the gate. 'Walk right in, sirs. You are welcome. Come in, out of the sun.'

A little precipitately, he urged them toward the cool gallery, where Jake offered them a fan and a silver cup.

The Englishmen blinked rapidly, said nothing, and sank into chairs, accepting the drink in obvious doubt as to its merit. But after the first sip, their faces brightened.

'Very good, sir; quite extraordinarily so,' the elder exclaimed. 'Remarkable what you find in this state.' He sipped a while in silence and then bethought himself of his business. Again he produced his memorandum and studied it, as if he had never seen it before.

'You are Cavin Darcy, Esq.?' he inquired, and passed him his own card. He bent his head toward the younger man. 'We represent ——'

'I see you do,' said Cavin coldly. 'Colonel Rutherford might have spared you your trouble.' He swept a blank eye upon them. 'As long as I'm alive, no railroad will ever cross a foot of my land.'

'Ah, sir!' said the younger man, speaking now for the first time, and with great charm. 'We understand that, I assure you. Colonel Rutherford told us that was your feeling. But he thought you might gratify our wish to see a plantation.' His eyes suddenly lighted up. 'My grandfather,' he explained, 'hoped to the end to see Texas in our Empire; my father supported the Confederacy, in Parliament.'

Cavin arose and offered the young man his hand.

'As long as you will stay, sir, you are welcome,' he exclaimed cordially. Then he bent a somewhat more suspicious glance upon the elder of the two.

'Railroads,' he explained with deliberate care, 'will ruin any man's peace o' mind!'

'No, sir!' returned his older guest, shrewdly seizing the occasion to present his most telling argument. 'You're wrong there. They'll save *yours*. What we're offering, Colonel Rutherford authorized us to say, is more than enough to —— '

'You might as well stop right there, sir,' Cavin replied adamantly. His eyes were hard and china-blue. 'The Colonel says your government is building railroads in Egypt,' he went on, after a moment, never shifting his gaze. 'In my opinion, that's a good place to build 'em — not on my land.'

When he thought his point had hit its mark, his expression altered and he sank again into his large rocker, inviting his guests also to lean back and make themselves comfortable.

'I've always wondered,' he said with a complete change of tone, and an extremely interested manner, 'what kind of shooting you have in England.'

They stayed a week, but the subject of a railroad right-of-way was never once brought up again. Instead, they talked of hunting and fishing and strange countries the Englishmen had visited, particularly Africa where the slaves had come from; and of how the jam pot, with the glass rose on top of it, and the large glass salt cellars, with stars underneath them, were exactly like the jam pot and the cellars on the younger man's own home table.

'Fancy that!' he kept exclaiming. 'Fancy that! Out here in Texas!'

'Take a piece of corn bread, sir,' Cavin urged him. 'You'll learn to like it.'

'If you don't mind,' returned the Englishman, 'I'll take another waffle.' Turning astonished eyes again on the jam pot, he murmured to his companion that nobody could ever have made him believe it, nobody.

When they left, Cavin asked Lucina if she could understand why Englishmen were all the time running all over the earth.

'Looks to me,' he observed, 'that a man's better off in his own country — especially if he's peddling railroads.' He looked sternly at her, as if she were the agent of all the inroads into his privacy that were beginning to press upon him. 'Railroad salesmen and hair-straighteners,' he observed succinctly, 'are cut out o' the same piece o' cloth.' Getting up, he shook his heavy shoulders irately. 'It's a damn shoddy piece, too. I'm going down to the gin house.'

Chapter 30

THE summer that Beauford came home from Virginia for good seemed to Lucina the happiest she had ever spent in Texas. For Beauford and FitzHugh were back now, and both of them were fitting into the places prepared for them as if they had never been away. She felt more grateful than Cavin did for this piece of good fortune, because she knew how many other young men there were, like Frank Barclay and Warren Hughes, who had thrown away their lives. But Cavin had never seemed to feel the least tremor about any of the boys. Whenever she remarked that they were turning out well, he always looked at her in astonishment.

'Why, of course. Why not?' he always demanded.

To signify his coming of age, FitzHugh now had a room to himself directly over the gallery at Locust Hill, and he and David had formed a partnership. Every morning now, the younger man got up and rode down to the little white office where David kept his few instruments, his dusty books, his big safe, his shabby couch, and his comfortable padded rocking-chair. There they would go over the cases they needed to look after that day, and FitzHugh would take the hardest, longest rides.

'Do you reckon they'll trust me, after you?' FitzHugh asked David, feeling strangely less competent than he had at Charlottesville. Out here on the prairie and in the dark bottom, a doctor met up with many things he'd never read about, any place. And Philip's and David's patients obviously expected him, also, to know more than he had ever learned out of any book. Already, FitzHugh saw, they were going to lay open before him wounds deeper than medicine could cure. He hoped he would find a wife as good as Miss Sabra was at holding a chloroform cone tight down over a patient's nose.

He mentioned his doubts to David, who chuckled over them.

'You'll learn. I'm only a piece of a doctor. You've got a sheepskin, boy!'

Thus began a long relationship between the two. David advised FitzHugh to get out Philip's notebooks and case references and study them, learning the family histories of the people he was doctoring; and FitzHugh persuaded David to go down to New Orleans to a medical meeting at Tulane. It was, apparently, from the beginning, a productive partnership.

Beauford, everyone said, the summer he came home and hung out his shingle, was heading toward the county judgeship. That office was at present held by a less able man than Judge White, who, to everyone's surprise, had died on the bench some years back, his head falling quietly forward on his breast, as he had sat hearing a case. The Judge was never sick and the county had grown to think of him as perennial. There seemed nobody to take his place; but now a number of people were drawing Cavin aside to tell him that his son looked smart enough to be a judge himself, before very long.

When Beauford first got home his father offered him a sheaf of papers he had tied together to send down to Judge Dickerson for scrutiny.

'You ought to know enough now to handle these,' said Cavin, a little doubtfully.

'I tell you,' suggested Beau, 'let me carry 'em down to the Judge myself, and go over them with him. There's a lot in Texas law ——'

Cavin surveyed his son approvingly. 'You'll get along, if you know that much. Maybe,' he suggested, eyeing him calculatingly, 'maybe you better go on up to the university they've got started up at Austin, and study some more under old Governor Roberts. Not,' he added, holding up his hand to silence Beauford's protest, 'not that I think you've been wasting your time in Virginia. I've got enough sense to know a lawyer who wants to get very far ought to know how to quote Latin.'

Then he observed him a few moments longer in silence, taking note of his gestures, his appearance, his expression.

'Beauford,' he decided, 'I think you better make some sort of arrangement with me and Nathaniel to look after your land for you. You've got too much on your mind to make a good cotton planter.'

'Why, yes, sir,' replied Beauford promptly, in some surprise. 'I hadn't ever thought about doing anything else.'

'All right,' said Cavin tolerantly, 'you get on with your studying. Takes all kinds o' people to make a world. But listen!' he said, leaning over and squinting up at his son, 'tell me, how in the devil can you stand it, bending over a book when it's planting time? Or when the ducks start flying? Lawd! Lawd!' he exclaimed, getting on his feet, 'Go talk to your mother. She understands your way o' thinking better'n I do.'

As Lucina did. All that summer she took a great deal of pleasure in her conversations with Beauford, who loved his books, not because they afforded him a release that he never thought of desiring from himself or his environment, but because in the best of them he could already see his own experience — any man's experience — clarified and explained. He was not the best lawyer in his class he told Lucina, who did not believe him; but he had enjoyed his legal training, just as he had enjoyed his Latin and his Greek, and for the same reason. In both cases, one was seeing a thing straight and clear, not clouded up. A good lawyer was as careful as Sophocles to weed out every irrelevant detail, and yet to show all that could be involved in a simple happening.

Lucina, listening carefully, saw that his mind reflected both Beauford's and Philip's, and she found the combination good. Then, with a certain startled happiness, she realized that the same questions which strayed in and out of her own thoughts strayed in and out of Beauford's, too — only he never appeared to expect to find any satisfying answers to them, the way she kept on hoping to do.

One day they went down to the old house — vacant now, since Jeremiah was on his own land — and she began telling Beauford about her first years in Texas, when she had lived in this house. They sat for a long time on the steps, looking out over the garden where Letitia's rosebushes still flourished. 'We were sitting right here, Beau,' Lucina said, 'right here where we are now, when we looked up and there was Povey riding down the lane.'

As she talked, it seemed to her strange, beyond belief, that all the heart-break of that old, unhappy time arose in her heart now, not any more like a storm of anguish, but like a sweet, almost forgotten sorrow, mellowed and softened by the years.

'Old Mr. Bland told me it would be so,' she remembered, the very tones of his thin voice returning to her mind, 'but I didn't believe him, then.' No more, she thought in quick certainty, than Beau would believe *her* when the day came that she would want to repeat to *him* Mr. Archibald's words. 'Nothing lasts, Miss Lucy,' he had said. 'No grief, no pain, no joy.'

She rose and, borrowing Beauford's knife, cut a few shining branches off the rosebushes. There were no roses now, in the heat of summer; these branches would have to serve.

'Come!' she said to Beau, and they made their way through the back yard, past the old oatfield, down toward the river, where often, as a child, Beauford had come to help decorate the graves there under the live-oaks. He was standing, now, looking down at the slanting stone with Povey's name upon it.

'One who has suffered much now sleeps at peace, forgetful of what he has suffered,' he said quietly, lifting his head to meet his mother's gaze.

Her memory went out instantly to meet his.

'"His spirit was broken,"' she answered him softly. '"He no longer had any desire to live and behold the light of the sun." Your Uncle John taught me that, Beau, years and years ago,' she informed him, with a slow smile.

'"Gone like a wild bird, like a blowing flame ——"' Beauford repeated the words absently, stooping to push aside the myrtle that covered the rounded earth. 'Maybe you know that, too, Nannie?' His voice flowed on, as if he were talking to himself. '"Gone to the singing and the gold, beyond the End."'

'No,' she said. 'No. Say it again.' Twice she murmured the lines after him.

This child of her flesh she suddenly realized was turning out to be also the child of her spirit; and, at the thought, her eyes blurred over. She supposed, with a flash of insight, that life afforded no joy so tender, so delicate as this.

Glancing up, he drew her arm through his, misinterpreting her emotion. 'It's the way they make you feel — the Greeks,' he said, with a puzzled frown. 'How do they do it?' he went on absently. 'Compared to them, Shakespeare's — well, grandiloquent, involved — ornate. Ah!' he exclaimed, his voice rising eagerly and his glance coming back to her. 'You must read every single book I've brought home, Nannie.' He began to laugh. 'I'm going to try Lucian out on Br'er Cavin — read him how easy it was to scare all the wise, learned Greeks with artificial snakes. That'll tickle him! And Lucretius!' he exclaimed, laughing. 'You know there's a line he wrote that describes Br'er Cavin to the life — "This, if you can or cannot, you *must* do." That,' said Beau positively, 'is Br'er Cavin down to the hilt!'

His mother smiled, agreeing with him. Then she leaned over and kissed his cheek. 'Beauford, darling,' she exclaimed suddenly, 'marry a nice, lovely girl, won't you — one who'll love you as much as I do.'

He lifted his beautifully traced eyebrows in astonished amusement. 'I'm going to start right in looking for her,' he admitted. 'If she'll have me.'

'Have you!' said his mother.

He smiled down at her and continued. 'First, though, I'm going up to Austin. Br'er Cavin,' he chuckled, 'is worried about whether I learned enough in Virginia to support a wife.'

'Yes, I know.' She kissed him again and took his hand between hers. 'I'd like to see you married before I die, though,' she told him.

'Die!' said Beauford, astonished into sharp attention. 'You aren't going to die.' He fixed her with accusing eyes.

Tragedy and death in literature were familiar enough to Beau; but Lucina understood from his startled glance that, as applied to his mother, the words had no meaning. For him, she still personified the source of all life, as everlasting as Cybele, the earth goddess, the mother of men, deathless and eternal. She did not know whether to be glad or sorry that he thought of her so; but she restrained her hand from destroying his faith.

When they were in the carriage, he began to tell her about a group of plays he had seen in Washington the winter before, and then he stopped, gazing at her in quick remorse.

'Why!' he exclaimed, wonderingly, as if the fact were incomprehensible, 'you've spent your whole life here and on Cedar Ledge! There's all the world ——' Flinging his arms wide, he smiled at her. 'The whole world! You wait!' he promised her. 'I'm going to see it all, and you, too. We'll go to Rome and Florence and Athens, and London ——'

'Jerusalem and Ephesus and Philippi and Corinth ——' murmured Lucina.

'Everywhere,' said Beau grandly. 'But,' he added, amused at the thought, 'I bet you we'll never persuade Br'er Cavin to come along.'

On and on he talked, without interruption, never doubting they would do what he planned. Lucina smiled. Beau was like Cavin, too — more so than she had thought.

She let him indulge his fancy, hoping, as he spoke, that his wife would want to see all these places.

The early summer passed, and with it Beauford's birthday, when everybody in the county came to wish him years of happiness and many of them. It seemed to Lucina that there was always a round of birthdays, now, with no time in between them. Only last March, the youngest twins had celebrated their majority, though neither of them had been home at the time. For in March Philip was busy learning the cotton business in Galveston under Colonel Rutherford, and his sister was studying music up at Belton, where the girls' school at Independence Academy had been moved the preceding year. Young Philip was almost never on the plantation, any more. Somebody was going to have to look after his land, as well as

Beau's. Cavin saw that, but without any resentment. They
could well use a member of the family in the selling end of
the cotton business.

Now, right after Beauford's birthday came William's —
sixteen years old, he was now. Lucina always remembered her
last child with a strange yearning tenderness, as if she were
apologizing secretly to him for being so preoccupied with all
the other children that she had scarcely had time or strength
to attend to his development. She resolved, from now on, to
pay more heed to him than to anybody else.

'Not that he feels the need of any attention,' she mused.
'He's the most independent of them all. He's had to be,' she
admitted.

As each child grew up, she seemed to feel a lightening of her
spirit and a release of the anxieties that had so long enfolded
her every waking moment. Gradually she was becoming
conscious of a development and an expansion of her own
personality, as if, until now, her spirit, pushed aside by the
demands of other people, had never had room to grow in her
own body. She revelled in Beauford's society, in the reading
she was doing, in Cavin's satisfaction with the way his undertakings were turning out. And for the first time in her whole
life in Texas, she suddenly realized, one day, that she was no
longer an alien, in a strange land. Somehow she had managed
to take the circumstances surrounding her and make them hers;
to twist and shape them into a pattern which, at last, had begun to enclose her in an outline so familiar that she could
breathe and move without any longer taking conscious thought.
And now that FitzHugh and Beauford were back, she could
rest, certain that the life she had loved on Cedar Ledge would
be perpetuated here on the Brazos, would not cease when she
did — that her life and Susanna's and Martha's and Cecilia's

would not come to some dead end here, in this far outpost of the South.

A woman, she thought one day, brought with her into a new land more than her own life and her own children's; she brought not only the future, toward which men always seemed to strive, but the past, without which any future was shallow and incomplete, lacking in beauty. She recalled handling an old bottle, very small and delicate, that Beauford had cherished — one Andrew had given Nathaniel, and which had come out to Georgia stored in a bureau drawer. Turned up, by chance, in an English field, it had acquired a lovely sheen, a greenish-blue patina, from long burial under earth. 'Some Roman may have dropped it,' said Beauford to his daughter, unaware that his would be the last generation of Americans to refer thus easily, as if by right of kinship, to great Rome on the Tiber. Now, remembering that bottle, Lucina thought that perhaps no present was beautiful until it had been buried a long while under the past — the past that women must remember, if it was going to be remembered, and must teach their sons to carry on into the future, to give it sheen, color, fragrance. That kind of unconscious memory, she saw now, FitzHugh and Beauford had already acquired, as part of their natural inheritance. Through them, it would endure on the Brazos.

All this came into Lucina's mind by slow degrees, bit by bit; and not so much by taking thought as by a kind of intuitive sensitivity which taught her, whenever she looked at the children, that her work had been more than to care for their physical needs. Her task had been, also, to place them in time, to connect them with their origins. And in this task, at least in the case of FitzHugh and Beauford, she had been successful. Looking at them, she felt an odd peace course through her.

It was as though her spirit sighed, and momentarily took its rest, after long battle.

That summer, however, there were hours when she felt moving beneath her passive content, a deep stirring, as if, within her, all her scattered questionings were seeking some new balance, some new ordering. Sometimes she sat on her gallery late at night watching the shadows creep over the locusts, or stood, at sunset, as the yellow glow fell upon the sandy drive, turning it to gold, and wondered why so deep a yearning was in her; why she reached out — always in vain — trying to draw into herself some beauty, some meaning, beyond her touch. If she could stretch her heart, not her mind, only the least bit farther, she often felt, she could understand what it was that sometimes moved so restlessly within her, and at other times was still. Occasionally, for a few quiet moments, life would flow around her soft, like a benison; but soon again an ache that puzzled her would supplant her peace. She knew there was no use trying to hurry toward whatever feelings and impulses were coming to focus within her. When they were ready to take clear shape, they would appear to her. She had no suspicion that, having passed on to her children all she could give them, her own soul was now struggling to second birth, to a new growth, wherein her old age could find quiet anchorage.

Perhaps that was partly what she had been wanting, all these long years when she had thought she was homesick for Georgia — to feel again that sense of strong, bright awareness that so soon fades when experience first begins to crowd in upon the young, dissipating their former sureties. Maybe it took years and years, she meditated, to learn that everyone carries the country of his heart imperishably around with him, safe in his breast, sowing its seed wherever he pauses. Then, in due time, it rises around him, anywhere he chances to be, in fresh, new sweetness; and life again seems to him whole, unified, as it does to the young and the untried.

She began to meditate oftener and oftener on these deepening impressions, as the fall came on.

That September, after Beauford had gone up to Austin, and Nathaniel had returned to Waco, Lucina and Cavin realized this would be the last year they would require a tutor's services. Miss Winnie Lee, they supposed, would stay right on, visiting around and coming back as she wanted to. Next fall, though, Tazewell and Cecilia and William would all be going off somewhere to school, Margaret's children probably to Shelby in Georgia, for a few years. Plainly they no longer needed a tutor.

They had all grown fond of young Mr. Moseley Allen, as they still called him, though he was no longer so young. He had been with them on the plantation now for fourteen years, instead of the ten they had first thought they might require his services. Cavin decided he must have a talk with him and find out what his plans were. Perhaps he could get a position tutoring at Baylor, where students were increasing more rapidly than the staff. In the late fall, however, he began to suspect that his concern was misplaced.

'Bless my soul, Lucina!' he exclaimed, 'Moseley's courting Philippa!'

'Why,' said Lucina, 'I never thought of such a thing in my life!' She was surprised, but obviously not entirely displeased.

'Well,' Cavin predicted, 'you'll see I'm right. If Philippa's got good judgment, she'll accept him.'

'He's fifteen years older ——' Lucina objected.

'What difference does that make?' Cavin began to count up. 'He can't be more than thirty-five, and his father lived to be nearly ninety. As fine a gentleman as anybody ever saw, too. She'd be safe, marrying Moseley.'

By Christmas it was plain that Philippa was as much in love as Moseley, and the engagement was announced when New Year's Day brought the county together for eggnog.

'Lucina,' said Cavin that night, 'before you know it, we'll have to be adopting a houseful of children to keep us company.'

The next summer, however, the house on Locust Hill seemed in no immediate danger of being empty. Philip was back on a month's vacation. In the fall, the Colonel was going to send him to England to transact some business, and he was happy and buoyant at the prospect. Moseley and Philippa had only to drive over from Holly Grove, where they had gone to live after their marriage. And the other children were all home, off and on, throughout the vacation, Beauford now for good, it seemed.

Cavin, therefore, set about building his oldest son a white office out in the yard to balance his own, an office where Beauford could keep his books, receive his clients, even sleep if he felt like it. For there was to be a central double fireplace in the building, and a bedroom.

'You'd better hang out your shingle on the big gate, though, Beau, where everybody'll see it and know you're in business,' Cavin suggested. 'Reckon you know enough now to start out?' he inquired, banteringly.

Beauford smiled. 'That's what I asked Judge Roberts.'

Fishing around in his pocket, Cavin produced a letter, and glanced, with a swift change of expression at his son.

'We'd better go hunt up your mother,' he said soberly. 'She'll want to hear this.' He gave Beau a serious look. 'I don't want to decide it. I want you to do what you feel like.'

'I?' Beau asked. 'Feel like what?' Puzzled, he followed Cavin into the house.

Lucina was sitting by her bedroom window, in the padded wicker rocker where she liked to read. She glanced up as they entered, and smiled, finding it hard to believe that, twenty-two years ago, the tall young man in the doorway was once a frail baby struggling for life, between warm bricks. He was taller than his father, now, but his shoulders were not so broad, his muscles not so well covered.

'Neither were Cavin's, twenty years ago,' Lucina thought, surprised to notice that, beside Beau, Cavin looked a middle-aged man. Never yet had she thought of him as such, but all at once she realized that he was now past forty, a man with graying hair, and lines in his face, a man with a broken hip and a bullet below his shoulder. Yet his complexion was as ruddy as ever, his eyes as clear, his glance as vigorous, and his ears as well shaped against his head. Something in Beau's carriage, however, indicated that the curve of his life was drawn tauter than Cavin's now was, and the arc of his expectation wider.

They did not stop to look at her, but, if they had, they would have seen a woman with a sensitive face, smooth, clear skin, now as pale as in her youth she had yearned to have it, with tender dark eyes and hair still as black as on her wedding morning. She was wearing a white muslin wrapper sprigged with a delicate bouquet, and Maria was brushing her long hair, for it was in the heat of the afternoon.

'Maria,' Lucina had just said to her, when the door opened, 'I'll declare, you don't change a bit. Now, I'm taking on weight, but you don't, not a pound,' she remarked, turning around to estimate her maid's comparative size.

'No'm,' Maria laughed. 'How's I gonna git fat, wid all my chilluns runnin' me down all de time?'

Seeing Lucina's husband and son at the door, she laid down
the brush. 'You rings when you wants me,' she said, and puffed
Lucina's hair lightly about her face. 'Lawd! Miss Lucy!'
she exclaimed, 'you'se prettier'n ary one o' yo' own chillun!'

'That's right, Maria,' said Beau, grinning. 'Prettier'n me,
anyhow.'

'Go on wid you!' Maria returned. 'You'se turned out right
good, allowin' fur how you looked like a picked jay bird at de
beginnin'.' She stood scrutinizing him in absorbed interest.
'Right good, now, ain't he, Miss Lucy?' Closing the door softly,
she went out.

'You have something on your mind. I can tell that much,'
Lucina said, looking at once toward Cavin. Swiftly her
thoughts canvassed the various possibilities, but not the correct
one.

'It's from John,' Cavin remarked, handing her the envelope
in his hand and coming to the point directly, as he usually did.
'He proposes to leave Sunny Fields to Beauford. His mother
is dead. There's no one else. That means' — he paused, while
Lucina scanned the short letter and handed it on to Beau —
'that means, of course, Beau may want to practise law in
Georgia. He'll have to decide.'

Beau's dark head was bent over the page, and Lucina could
see only his profile, with its clear-cut lines, and the corner of
his smiling mouth.

'Why!' he exclaimed, swinging around and raising his eyes
full to his mother's. 'It took Uncle John fifteen years to build
his brick wall up again, after the war. Nannie, you remember
it — you've played all over the place!'

'Yes,' Lucina answered, 'I have, Beau. In the very cave
where John's mother hid the *Odyssey* Uncle John gave you.
Oh, Beau!' cried Lucina. 'That was' — her warm voice broke

— 'that was sweet of your Uncle John!' She looked at Cavin. 'What did you write back?'

'I haven't,' he replied. 'Beauford better do his own writing.' He scrutinized his son carefully. 'What do you think, Beau?'

'Think!' he exclaimed, throwing his head back and laughing the easy, spontaneous laughter of youth. 'I'll write him that I hope Sunny Fields won't come to me for many a year.'

His father looked at him in silence for some minutes. 'You intend to stay on here, then?' he asked, 'and take over your grandfather's place? You're sure that's what you want to do?' He pressed his inquiry and stood waiting.

'Why, yes, Br'er Cavin,' said Beauford, obviously surprised at the inquiry. Then he smiled as if it also somehow amused him. 'By this time, I ought to know the road between Georgia and Texas. Anyway,' he went on, easily, 'Uncle John'll be here for a long time, yet.'

Cavin turned to Lucina, who forestalled the questioning in his eyes.

Not waiting for him to speak, she answered as promptly as if it had not taken her nearly a quarter of a century to decide on her reply.

'Beauford's a Texan,' she said quietly. 'A Brazos Texan. This is where he belongs.'

Beauford smiled at her. 'A Brazos Texan, with the Chattahoochee and the James and the Santee and the Mississippi and nearly every other Southern river running in his blood. That's a Brazos Texan for you. That's what makes him one.'

'Beau,' said Cavin, putting on his newly acquired steel spectacles and looking his son up and down, 'going off to school hasn't damaged your brains as much as I thought it might.'

That evening Cavin and Lucina sat out on the gallery,

rocking, as they usually did before they went in to bed. It was
the twenty-third anniversary of their wedding, but even Lucina
had forgotten it until she chanced to look at the calendar, just
before she came out to join Cavin. The breeze had come up
cool and fresh off the Gulf, and the screech-owl in the chinaberry tree by the chimney had begun his weird murmurings.
Inside the door Lucina could hear Cecilia lighting the candles
attached to Letitia's long mirror — the mirror her mother had
hauled out to the Delta in a creaking wagon, on her honey-
moon. In the dusk outside a vine with large white blossoms was
hanging sweet and thick over the garden fence, and even in
the dim, shadowy light the waxy leaves of the banana plants
gleamed like metal, reflecting every ray of light. Far out on
the prairie, the frogs had begun their nightly croaking and, one
by one, the brilliant stars were coming out.

Cavin raised his feet against a white column — his feet,
which, even inside his heavy boots looked small for a man of
his size. Heaving a long sigh of content, then, he tilted back
his chair. Wherever he shifted his boots, next morning Jake
would be certain to find black streaks to wash off; but it had
never occurred to Cavin, in the nearly twenty-five years he
had sat here at night to notice either the appearance or the
disappearance of the marks. Neither he nor Jake, in all their
lives, had ever imagined an order of existence in which a man
might have, not only to manage his own business, but also
attend to saddling his own horse, polishing his own boots, and
keeping his own columns white. So Cavin moved his feet freely
about, and from time to time reached down to pull Sheba's
long, silky ears. Sheba, his favorite pointer, whose brown and
white head rested against his knee.

Thus taking his ease, he hummed beneath his breath a tune
he had picked up from the cowboys the preceding spring when

for two weeks he had camped with them every night, hunting up strays. There were not many of these now, for the free grass was nearly gone, and in his own pastures he had built long wind-shelters and deep dams and running wells for his white-faced herds. But there were enough wanderers, even yet, to make it pay to lope around the prairies in the spring, looking for stray cows with sawed-off horns, and with the Locust Hill brand on their thin flanks — cows usually followed by bawling calves which, then and there, somebody had to jump down and brand.

Cavin did not suspect the truth: that, even if there had been fewer stray cattle around, he would still have hated not hearing the clattering wagon drawing up before his door every March, with the cook already inside it, and the cowboys, on their prancing paint ponies, gathered around it. Never, except on his own cotton field, did he enjoy life so much as when he mounted Derby's successor — another powerful gray, almost white, named Hero — and felt himself swinging easily out toward the open prairie looking for his cattle. Each one he found was like a nugget picked up from the discard; and the air was sweet and the sun was warm and the world was a good enough place for any man.

So now, sitting on the gallery by Lucina he began to hum a song that had lingered with him ever since his return from the spring drive. At night the cowboys always stretched themselves out on their blankets, and began to sing, unimpressed by the studded heavens. Was not the prairie on which they lay nearly as wide, nearly as endless as the sky? And Cavin sang with them, a man who could throw a rope and brand a steer or cut out fifty beeves as quickly and neatly as any of his cowhands. Lying there on his own blanket, as close to the hard earth as any of his men, he hummed and whistled with them; and, out of kindness, they forbore to tell him his voice was always far off key. As Lucina forbore tonight.

Over and over he was repeating a refrain, repeating it endlessly like a lullaby, first in words, then in a subdued humming
rhythm.

> 'I'm a-going to jail tomorrow,
> A place I've never been before,
> With the cold iron bars around me,
> And the jailor at the door.'

Lucina, rocking, hardly listened. The song was like the
soughing of the wind in the trellis on the sunny end of the
gallery, like the soft movements of the katydids in the grass.
Or like the barely perceptible sound of the servants' voices out
in their own house in the back yard, like the gentle champing
from the stables and the shifting of the turkeys in the chinaberries, before they all settled down to sleep. The subdued
murmurings all ran together into one — this was the way night
sounded, as it fell over Locust Hill Plantation.

She was not listening, because her thoughts were occupied
with a matter in which she knew Cavin would find little interest
or significance. Most things, indeed, he took for granted,
without ever probing into them. She smiled fleetingly in the
dusk. Just so, Cavin would find nothing to marvel at in her
affirmation that Beau was a Texan, a Brazos Texan. She could
hear him, now. 'Why, of course,' he would say, in his pleasant,
deep voice — a voice, for all of its pleasantness, not so mellow
and smooth as Philip's. 'Why, of course,' he would insist,
'the boy's a Texan. What else would he be, Lucy?' But when
she had heard herself admitting the fact, she knew, right then,
that some time soon she would have to puzzle out, to her own
satisfaction, why she had spoken up as she did, almost instantly.
The words had not even been in her mind one minute; and
then, the next, they were hanging in the air, settling a question

she was not aware of ever having come to final grips with, in her own thoughts.

It was strange. When she was first married to Cavin, his way of always thinking of things precisely as he wanted to think of them had seemed to her a serious defect in him — a certain blindness, even a lack of complete honesty with himself. But as the years had gone on, she had learned to recognize it for what it was — the source of his phenomenal energy and determination. If he saw a thing one way, it simply had to be that way, sooner or later, that was all; and, sooner or later, she had learned, so it usually was.

It was also a quality that by now she not only had grown to recognize in him, but even to love, as a part of him. It always aroused in her, though, an affectionate, protective, and tender response which she knew he never even remotely suspected. People did fail — and fail miserably, horribly, sadly — in this incomprehensible world, and for no fault, no weakness of their own, even if, so far in his life, Cavin had refused to admit the fact into his own reckonings. 'Some day,' she thought — and could not bear to think it; 'some day ——' The emotion that plowed through her then was more like pity than fright — pity for a strong, brave man who never in his life had asked it of any human being, or ever, for that matter, supposed he required it.

She recognized the emotions that tore at her whenever she thought of him like this; for it was just the way she used to quiver with fright whenever she got to worrying about all the things that might happen to the children. Some of them did, too, though Cavin had not seemed ever to be aware of the fact. He would find it amusing, she had no doubt, to know she was feeling sad about him, lest something she could not put her finger upon should prove too strong for him, and hurt him unbearably — him who was almost never hurt, and who had no fearful forethoughts, none at all, as far as she had ever seen. Well, she wouldn't tell him; there were lots of other things she had never told him.

But he would not find even that idea so perplexing as her present concern about what motives and impulses, hidden even from herself, had caused her so impulsively to name Beau a Texan — him whom, of her own free will, she had sent away from her back to Georgia. Already she knew why she had been willing to let him go; that she had already thought through. But this was something else. Why, now, was she willing to consent to his returning to the Brazos — nay, more, prompt to encourage him to do so? That would bear thinking about; and she applied her mind steadily to understanding why she had spoken as she did, thus instantly, without hesitation or meditation, committing herself to a decision which she had so long postponed actually facing.

Then it welled up in her, why. It was because so often the heart was quicker than the brain, because she had felt, before she had allowed herself to comprehend, the fact that it was better, far better, for Beau himself to be whole-heartedly attached to the place of his own birth — indeed, to any place — than to hesitate between two loyalties, torn as she so long had been. And then he had solved her unspoken difficulty for her, by refusing, in precisely Cavin's own way, to recognize the dilemma at all, taking the Chattahoochee, the James, and the Brazos all to him in one royal, sweeping embrace. She breathed a great sigh of relief — that was what she had wanted him to do all the time.

A mother who did not put her child's own wholeness, his own happiness before her own — what kind of mother was that? If it was natural and easy for Beau to call himself Texan, he should do so. And — she went on pressing her inquiry — a mother who refused to let her child either go on, or stay back, because his impulses were not her own — what kind of mother was that? No, she warned herself, facing, as was her usual custom, the oncoming years, Beau would be going on, and on, and on, even, if in his body, he stayed here in the bottoms. On and on from her, at any rate; for his life was waxing, hers waning. As the final measure of her love, she consciously laid his freedom from the need to consider any wish of hers whatever on top of all her gifts to him — her crowning gift of devotion that left her soul stripped and shivering. Well, there it was: that was all settled and clear in her mind, that much of her thinking.

She knew, however, there had been some other motive entering into her decision — the decision which, Cavin never so much as suspected, had taken her all her married life to make. What was that other motive? When she understood that, she would be at peace. Ah! she knew what it was now. Like a torrent it swept over her, that knowledge. It was the whole cumulative sense of Cavin's long work here on the Brazos. Was she to prevent his eldest son from entering into it as his natural birthright? All the last twenty years crowded into her mind — all of Cavin's activities passing before her, all his nearly ceaseless effort.

She looked at him with sudden tears in her eyes. She had loved him, she had married him. One thing only had she ever withheld from him, and that, in his generosity, he had never asked her for — his first-born to inherit his labors. Gathering her strength together, and with a final decisive spiritual act of abnegation, she laid Beauford — even Beauford — on the altar of her love for this man to whom, long ago on a Georgia verandah, she had joined her life.

There — it was over. She knew now exactly what her remark had meant — all that it implied. She had given Beauford his complete and utter freedom; and she had given Cavin back his son. What had she left, herself, then? She did not yet know; all that she was certain of was that that renunciation had been right, and that her instinct had led her to it. She had no intimation, however, that, then, in the moment when she made her two decisions, her own spirit had entered into the new life toward which, all summer, it had been dimly groping, moving restlessly within her. Feeble and frail, that spirit hesitated now before a future wherein it must learn, like a newborn child, to stand alone, in an ever-increasing loneliness.

For a woman's life, Lucina saw clearly now, had two parts, one when she must transmit, like stored honey, all that she had to give. Then, unlike the queen bee, she did not die, her work done; but out of the inexhaustible core of her deepest personality, started in again to weave for herself a soul, a being, strong enough to face the rigors of eternity. That is, she did if she was wise. She had another choice; she could wither, turning dustier and duller every year, content to have served her biological function and to die. There was no hesitation in Lucina's lucid mind. Timidly she set her foot on a path that she knew she must tread alone, depending on nobody — nobody at all — no matter where it led.

As yet, however, she did not suspect that this knowledge which she had come upon, like bitter fruit, was the sad possession of many women in this world. She would have to grow older, to know that. To understand fully that the very nature of a woman's work in this world causes it to flee progressively from her, and in the end, to escape her, without leaving so much as a shadow for her to see. For the seed that women sow takes a generation to come to flower; and then it is intangible, not to be counted and handled, as men may measure their labors. This completer understanding she would have to wait for. But now, tonight, she was conscious only of having started, alone and trembling, on a road whose end she could not foresee.

What capacities had she, though, with which to face such a journey? It was a question that her life had never permitted her to put to herself, not once. Now, she would have to discover what her abilities, if she had any, were. There seemed a good many years ahead of her in which to do so.

Glancing over at Cavin, she meditated again, in quiet amusement, that he would no doubt be surprised to hear all that she had been thinking about while they sat there silently together. But it had not taken very long for the ideas to pass in and out her consciousness, even though their range had covered — 'My goodness!' she thought; 'nearly a quarter of a century!'

At that moment, Cavin ceased his humming, and almost automatically Lucina switched her attention back to him. She could have predicted what he was going to say next. Hardly a night had passed since they moved into the house that he had not sighed, stretched himself, and remarked that he wished he had his gates up. Gates at the end of the long drive, like those, he never failed to remind her, Mrs. Martin had up, before the war, at the entrance to Sunny Fields. By now, indeed, those gates had become legendary; and, as his fancy had played over the idea for nearly a quarter of a century, symbolic. His tasks would not be finished until a hammered sword-gate swung clean and true at the end of his white Texas drive, marking off his house as his home, a place removed from any curious gaze or uninvited intrusion.

Cavin shifted his feet lower and clasped his strong hands behind his head.

'We ought to get the gates up this year, Sweet,' he observed, with his sleepy eyes on the avenue between the tall locusts.

But there was no fire in his voice, nothing like the impatience that rose in it when a mule stuck his feet in the mud, laid his ears back, and refused to budge. Or when, on a morning plainly laid down since the very beginning of time for cotton-planting to start, his overseer chanced to oversleep. No, what he was feeling now was something quite different. It was like that reluctance which seizes any artist when he hesitates to lay his last brush strokes on canvas, knowing that the finished picture can never equal its imagined perfection. In the same way, and without ever being aware why he restrained his impatience, Cavin felt there was no hurry about setting up his gates. They would never be so beautiful as the ones he carried in his mind. Subconsciously he sensed the truth.

'You've done everything else you wanted to do,' Lucina comforted him.

'I'll do that, too,' he retorted. 'You wait and see.' He looked at her sitting there so still in the dark and wondered, without worrying in the least about the answer, whether she recalled how he had promised her once that, some day, things would be just like they were before the war. He felt a quiet satisfaction surge over him, at having so nearly redeemed his promise. The ends to which his life had been directed lay out clear and sharp before him. They pleased him, as he turned them over in his mind, handling them as a miser does his treasures. The things he had accomplished he could see, touch, feel; and they gave promise of increasing, as the years went on, not diminishing. His was not the temperament to remember how evanescent are men and nations; and his past caused him to think of the future only with confidence. More and more Lucy would see nothing was changed, not really, by all the booming cannon.

Then his attention was caught by her low voice. She was speaking, though he never was to know it, directly out of the course of her meditations as she had sat there by him, analyzing her own mind.

'You've done three men's work, anyway — even if you *never* get up your gates,' she was saying. 'You've cleared new cotton ground, and drained rattlesnake swamps, and brought in fine cattle and horses on the prairie, and raised all these children, and handed their land over to them clear, and risked your life hunting down thieves ——' She paused for lack of breath, faltering in face of the emotion that had stopped her tongue.

Almost never had she understood this man beside her, a man who always kept his eye set on some other star than the one that gleamed brightest in her eyes, a man who looked at life from one side, and she from the other. Almost never had their spirits even momentarily met, as hers and Beau's so often did, not even as hers and John's had, in the past. Yet never in all her life had some bell ceased to ring deep inside her at his voice, at the sound of his limping steps. Whether she understood him or not, she had loved him from the very first moment she had seen him sitting, with his poor bound-up feet, on the verandah at Cedar Ledge, surveying all their prospects. She had followed him to Texas; and, she smiled faintly in the darkness, while she lived she would keep on following him; and — she smiled again, admitting the truth without displeasure — he would never once suspect that she might have any other wish on earth, never dream that, as final proof of her devotion, she had returned his son to him.

Memories sometimes have a strange baffling way of appearing in the mind not in succession, as is usual, but in swift, panoramic combination. Then past and present seem to merge and time to have no significance. Thus it was that in a brief, bright moment all Lucina's life seemed to rise and pass before her, while Cavin was merely shifting his position.

'You've done all that—' she began again in a steadier voice, 'paid your debts and Uncle Phil's too, raised other people's children like your own, made even your bare prairie ground earn you a good living——'

'Why that's nothing,' said Cavin sleepily. 'What's the matter with you, Lucy? A man would naturally have to do that much. Anybody ought to could make a living off of good land.'

'And,' she went on, disregarding him, 'you've been justice of peace and built roads and schools and served on the school board and been deputy sheriff and everything else. And lots of it was dangerous work, terribly dangerous!'

'Dangerous!' exclaimed Cavin, startled out of his lassitude by her remark. 'How on earth's a man worth his salt going to keep himself safe?' He looked at her in open amazement.

'I don't know,' Lucina answered sorrowfully. 'I wish I did. It's what I've been trying to find out, since the first day we landed in Galveston.'

'What else would I have done?' Cavin asked her, locking his brown, square hands across his breast, entirely unimpressed by her recital of his achievements. 'A man has to do his own job in this world as well as he can, or somebody else'll be doing it for him.' Settling himself back again, he prepared again to fall into the somnolent quiet with which he liked to meet the close of each day.

'But,' she persisted, 'think of the years you put in driving the Yankees out of this state——'

'By George!' he replied enthusiastically, dropping his feet to the floor, and rising to face her. 'You're right about that. Where'd we a-been, if we hadn't driven 'em out? Where'd Beau and the rest of the children have been?' he demanded hotly. 'Where they'd have to kill half the good colored people in this county, that's certain; where they couldn't have moved hand or foot without asking some little two-by-four Federal agent whether they could or not. That's where they'd a-been! Where they'd a-had to spend their lives filling out contracts to suit the Freedman's Bureau,' he asserted, scornfully stressing the last two words, 'and a lot o' their good money paying out bribes.'

He smiled in sudden sharp relief and sat down again, laughing at his own anger. 'Makes me swearing mad yet,' he apologized, 'to think of what went on in this state.'

As he settled himself in his chair, his eyes fell again on the shadowy avenue, thrown now into white relief by the round and rising moon.

'This year,' he murmured, reminded of his gates. 'This year — maybe.' But he pursued the thought no further; for the night dropped around him, the quiet, starry night, and even that familiar dream seemed superfluous, so deep was his content.

Soon, however, he stirred, pressed by a goading thought. 'Whining beggars!' he affirmed with conviction. 'That's what they wanted to make out of us, Lucy. Whining beggars!'

'Time after time,' she sighed, 'I've sat and wondered why!'

'Ah, well!' he said, dropping his head back against his chair and thrusting his recollections from him. 'There's a lot o' life ahead of us, Sweet. There's no use harping on what's done and over with. Thank the Lord,' he exclaimed, fervently, breathing a long sigh. 'All done and over with, now, forever.'

'Forever?' Lucina asked, laying her soft hand on his. 'Forever, Cavin?'

'Why, yes,' he replied, turning to look at her in surprise. 'Of course.   What are you talking about, Lucy?   Of course, it's forever.'

  She sat listening to the dim murmur of the cypresses and the locusts and her thoughts grew still.   'Of course, darling,' she echoed. 'Of course.'

THE END

Author's Note

Neither the characters nor the places described in this novel represent, or are intended to represent, specific persons or places. The author has tried, of course, to supply, out of her recollections, a veridical background to the events and people portrayed, but in the writing of this book all remembered characters and happenings have become so changed and merged as to lose any possible identity outside these pages.

The author has enjoyed checking the stories heard in her youth against the writings of the distinguished Texas historians, Mr. E. C. Barker, Mr. Walter P. Webb, and Mr. Charles W. Ramsdell. She alone is responsible, however, for her use of certain historical events which, as a novelist, she has felt free, in a few instances, to shift slightly both as to time and immediate circumstance.

Grateful acknowledgment is made to Random House, Inc., publishers of The Modern Library, for permission to use brief quotations from their copyright translations of classic authors, to the publishers of *The North American Review* for the extract from *Bentonville* by James Gilmer Wharton, to Longmans, Green & Company for a quotation from their edition of *The Bacchae* of Euripides, and to The Macmillan Company for a quotation from the Butcher and Lang translation of *The Odyssey*.